2

Adam had learned long ago that the quality most essential to surviving the Tower was not luck, nor strength, nor wisdom.

Even experience was not without disadvantage because as complacency dulled one's vigilance, longevity inflated one's sense of permanence. The Tower loathed nothing more than a smug survivor.

No, the true patron of old fools and street urchins was *elasticity*. To survive, one had to be flexible.

Flattery had not softened the sparking men, so Adam abandoned the strategy. It was just as well: The fawning toady was an unpleasant disguise. He needed to light upon a new tactic, and quickly, before he met the soldiers' superiors and the game began in earnest.

The trouble was, Adam had spent recent months suppressing his devious instincts in an effort to conform to the noble ideals his captain espoused. It had not escaped Adam's notice that Senlin's principles came at the expense of his plasticity. Senlin had been half a pirate, half a thief, and half a killer because he was, at his core, unbending. He could change his sails, but not his course; he could swap his suit, but not his heart.

Adam doubted he could afford to pursue such rigid principles here and on his own. Besides, he had come with the intent of burgling heaven.

Praise for

The Books of Babel

"It's rare to find a modern book that feels like a timeless classic. I'm wildly in love with this book."
—Pierce Brown, author of *Red Rising*

"*The Hod King* is a compelling and original novel; the Books of Babel are something you hope to see perhaps once a decade—future classics, which may be remembered long after the series concludes."
—*Los Angeles Times*

"Josiah Bancroft is a magician. His books are that rare alchemy: gracefully written, deliriously imaginative, action-packed, warm, witty, and thought-provoking. I can't wait for more."
—Madeline Miller, *New York Times* bestselling author of *Circe*

"*Senlin Ascends* is one of the best reads I've had in ages. I was dragged in and didn't escape until I'd finished two or three days later."
—Mark Lawrence, author of *Prince of Thorns*

"Deeply compelling.... A classic in the making."
—*B&N Sci-Fi & Fantasy Blog*

"Wonderfully unique and superbly well written. I loved every page."
—Nicholas Eames, author of *Kings of the Wyld*

"Senlin is a man worth rooting for, and his strengthening resolve and character is as marvelous and sprawling as the tower he climbs."
—*Washington Post*

"*Senlin Ascends* crosses the everyday strangeness and lyrical prose of Borges and Gogol with all the action and adventure of high fantasy. I loved it, and grabbed the next one as soon as I turned the last page."

—Django Wexler, author of *The Thousand Names*

"What is remarkable about this novel, quite apart from its rich, allusive prose, is Bancroft's portrayal of Senlin, a good man in a desperate situation, and the way he changes in response to his experiences in his ascent."

—*Guardian*

"Brilliant debut fantasy.... This novel goes off like a firework and suggests even greater things in the author's future."

—*Publishers Weekly* (starred review)

"*Senlin Ascends* is a unique masterpiece. A brilliant debut. Highly recommended!" —Michael R. Fletcher, author of *Beyond Redemption*

"With deceptive simplicity, Bancroft brings this gothic place and its denizens to colorful life. I loved it!" —Adrian Selby, author of *Snakewood*

"An impressive display of imagination and humor." —*SciFiNow*

By Josiah Bancroft

THE BOOKS OF BABEL

Senlin Ascends
Arm of the Sphinx
The Hod King
The Fall of Babel

The Books of Babel
Book IV:
The Fall of Babel

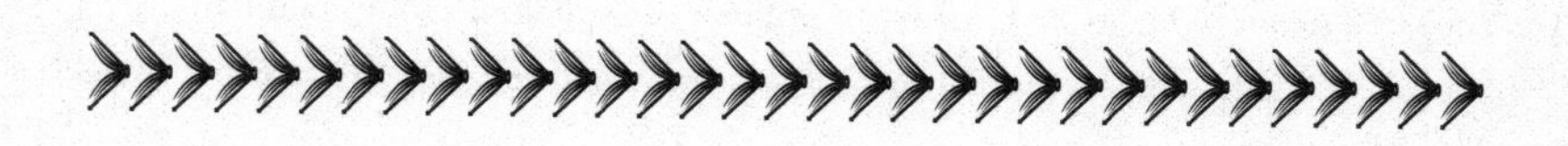

Josiah Bancroft

orbitbooks.net

This book is a work of fiction. Names, characters, places, and incidents are the product of the author's imagination or are used fictitiously. Any resemblance to actual events, locales, or persons, living or dead, is coincidental.

Cover art by Ian Leino
Cover copyright © 2021 by Hachette Book Group, Inc.
Catalog by Josiah Bancroft
Author photograph by Kim Bricker

Orbit
Hachette Book Group
1290 Avenue of the Americas
New York, NY 10104
orbitbooks.net

First Edition: November 2021
Simultaneously published in Great Britain by Orbit

Orbit is an imprint of Hachette Book Group.
The Orbit name and logo are trademarks of Little, Brown Book Group Limited.

Library of Congress Cataloging-in-Publication Data
Names: Bancroft, Josiah, author.
Title: The fall of Babel / Josiah Bancroft.
Description: First edition. | New York, NY : Orbit, 2021. | Series: The books of Babel ; book 4
Identifiers: LCCN 2021005591 | ISBN 9780316518192 (trade paperback) | ISBN 9780316518178
Subjects: GSAFD: Fantasy fiction.
Classification: LCC PS3602.A63518 F35 2021 | DDC 813/.6—dc23
LC record available at https://lccn.loc.gov/2021005591

ISBNs: 9780316518192 (trade paperback), 9780316518185 (ebook)

Printed in the United States of America

LSC-C

Printing 1, 2021

For my untiring pioneering folks,
and
Maddie, my impatient adventurer.

THE DAILY REVERIE—ARTS & THEATER

A Refresher for the Devotees of the Senlin Saga

(In Anticipation of Its Conclusion)

by Oren Robinson

Another theatrical season; another entry in the Books of Babel melodrama!

Per usual, the burden of revitalizing the acts and exeunts of the overpaid playwright's prior works falls to me, dear reader. I, Oren Robinson, cultural critic and man about town (or at least my own townhome), shall hitherto attempt to puff upon the dwindling coals of your enthusiasm for a tale that, like the besotted guest who has begun to drape upon the drapery, departs not a moment too soon! I offer this recapitulation out of the largesse of my heart and my contractional obligation to the editors of the *Daily Reverie*.

In last season's *The Hod King*, Thomas Senlin, having infiltrated our ringdom at the Sphinx's behest, was at last reunited with his betrothed, the incomparable Mermaid née Mrs. Senlin. Thomas took the long-awaited tender moment as occasion to confess his infidelity, though not the identity of his paramour. (If you, dear reader, do not recall the name of Tom's forbidden love, then you will not have read my award-winning essay, "Edith Winters and Why the Headmaster from East Fish Piss Does Not Deserve Her." Shame on you.) Marya, fearing the wrath of her new husband, the nefarious Duke Wilhelm Pell, released Tom from his tattered vows, but elected to keep the existence of their daughter, Olivet, a secret for the safety of all involved. The lapsed headmaster only learned of his unobserved fatherhood shortly before Duke Wilhelm stuck a bucket on his head and banished him to the convoluted service tunnels that knot the Tower walls like chitterlings—pig entrails that share in common with the black trail a certain aroma.

Condemned to the bleak thoroughfares of the hods, Thomas was reunited with two characters from his past: John Tarrou, his tippling friend from the Baths, and his former employer, the humiliated port master Finn Goll. The trio soon found themselves conscripted into Luc Marat's army of zealots. Thomas and company were alarmed to learn of the existence of a mighty excavator, the unroyal Hod King. Poised at the threshold of his roughly carved throne room, the zealot shared with Thomas his intent to unseat the Sphinx from her lofty perch. In a move that seemed to straddle the line between self-preservation and martyrdom, Senlin promised to assist Marat's assault of the Tower's enigmatic and unpopular warden.

The ambitions of Marat and his siege engine are foremost in the mind of the formidable Captain Winters, who has recently knocked the ashes of Pelphia's Port Virtue from the soles of her boots. Before departing our vaunted (if somewhat diminished) ringdom, Captain Winters called upon Duke Wilhelm to offer his unwilling wife succor and safe harbor. Marya readily accepted her offer and, though traveling light, thought to pack at least her offspring, who came as some surprise to her liberator. Before withdrawing, Edith warned the duke off any notion of pursuit, famously punctuating this caution with a gory, ruinous handshake. 'Twas the sort of grip that makes an impression upon both the recipient and the rug!

Aboard the *State of Art*, the Sphinx's now silkless flagship, Voleta began to convalesce from her recent death. Having been shot in the head by the rapacious Prince Francis Le Mesurier, Voleta was only revived by the ministrations of Reddleman, the reborn Wakeman once known as the Red Hand. Reddleman plied Voleta with the Sphinx's medium, an energetic and mysterious brew. Though the consequences of Voleta's resurrection remain to be seen, Iren, the ship's imposing first mate, is greatly relieved to have her charge and friend returned.

The manifest of the *State of Art* grew by three souls. In addition to the aforementioned aeronauts and Byron, the Sphinx's buck of a butler, the gunship now serves as home to Marya, Olivet, and Ann Gaucher, a recently unemployed governess and Iren's new amour.

It has fallen to Captain Winters and her unlikely crew to collect a series of nearly identical paintings that feature a girl clutching a paper boat in the shallows of the Baths. The Tower's elusive architect, the Brick Layer, distributed these artful tokens, one to each of the sixty-four ringdoms, shortly before his disappearance, an event shrouded in mystery. The paintings, collectively entitled *The Brick Layer's Granddaughter*, were destined to one day be reassembled within the panes of the Sphinx's zoetrope, a baroque device that promises to reveal the encoded combination for opening the Bridge of Babel, whatever the devil *that* is. While the precise purpose of the bridge remains unclear, the Sphinx assured Captain Winters that unlocking the bridge was the only way to keep a great reservoir of poorly bottled lightning from igniting a conflagration that would turn the mortar of the Tower into a pestle of a crater. To make matters worse, Captain Winters has been cut off from her master by sabotage. One of Marat's youthful conscripts crippled the central fuse station entombed beneath the streets of Pelphia, an act that apparently sealed the Sphinx inside her home.

But what of Adamos Boreas, beloved mope and devoted sibling to the irritatingly insouciant Voleta? His conspicuous absence from *The Hod King* can only lead one to suppose that the playwright temporarily forgot of his existence, much as one forgets a draft until the weather turns. Unseen since his inclusion in *Arm of the Sphinx*, Adam was left to languish upon the foggy peak of the Tower in the custody of knights who cast lightning as readily as I cast water into my thunder pot. And how, dear reader, did those guards of that crowning fog know Adam's name? Why did they quiz him on the details of his life? What grim snare has our long-suffering older brother bumbled upon?

There's only one way to discover the answers to these questions. Stay at home! Close the curtains. Don't answer the door. I shall attend the evening's premier of *The Fall of Babel* on your behalf, and tomorrow, when you unfold the *Daily Reverie* and thumb through to find me waiting for you, I shall embrace you with revelations startling, strange, and disappointing perhaps, but a finished and decisive end, at the least. Good night, dear reader. Tomorrow shall banish every question, every doubt. Good night and more pleasant dreams!

Your Humble Savant,
Oren Robinson

We painted cavern walls to own the shadows with our palms.
We carved the ground with county lines to legislate our qualms.
We drew on heaven human shapes to stake the cosmic plot.
Man would write upon his soul if pen could reach the spot.

—*Music for Falling Down Stairs* by Jumet

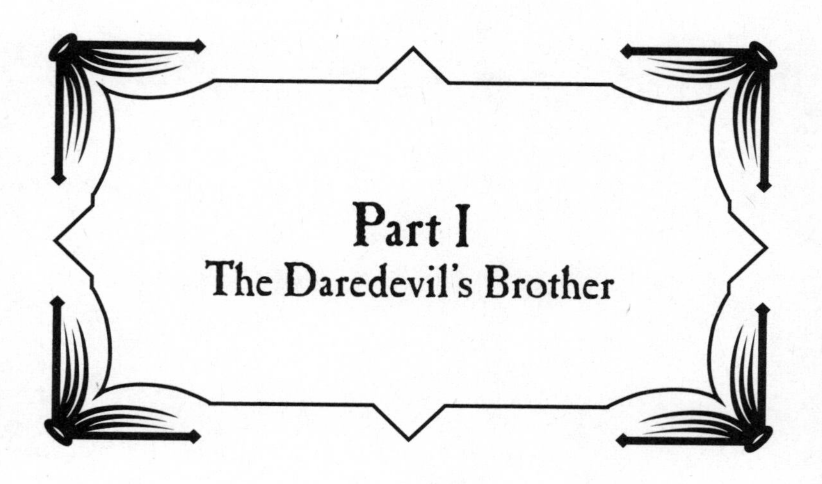

Part I
The Daredevil's Brother

Chapter One

Courage circulates like a melody sung in a round. It is an infinite canon, an infectious and intoxicating performance.

—from the diary of Joram Brahe, captain of the *Natchez King*

The lightning seeded the fog with a fire that churned like a restless embryo.

The rubber-clad soldiers hurled another volley of blue bolts into the mist, staining Adam's vision with jagged fissures of white. Inside the burning cloud, a dozen voices first bellowed, then pitched toward a hopeless animal plea. Their screams concluded at a stroke when the hull of their silkless ship crashed upon the silver plateau that crowned the Tower of Babel.

Furnace coals and gunpowder mingled amid the wreckage. The explosion arrived in waves: first flash, then warmth, and finally wind. Adam heard ejecta kick across the ground and turned his back to the coming spray of splinters, glass, and nails. He was sure he would've been grievously injured had not one of the vulcanized soldiers moved to shield him from the shrapnel.

The ground beneath Adam rang with a solemn note that seemed to peal from the mouth of a mountainous bell. The wind shifted again. Smoke darkened the fog, replacing the sweet, metallic scent of electricity with the stink of sulfur, burnt silk, and death.

A flaming cocked hat tumbled past Adam's foot.

He thought of Senlin. What would he make of all of this? Before Adam could explore the thought further, the soldier who had a moment before sheltered him gave his shoulder an ungentle push. The troop resumed its march into the mist.

The murk had robbed him of a sense of time, but he supposed it had been about two hours since Mister Winters had left his side, two hours since the youthful soldiers had quit bickering, screwed their ghoulish helmets back on, and gone to war with the clouds. They had not spoken to him since, only smirked like fishhooks. Between their tar-black armor and red-copper visors, Adam could not tell one from the next. They shoved him when they wished him to go, bumped him when they wanted him to stop, and fired over his head when something in the fog required it. The sparking men's eyes telescoped and twisted like a chameleon's, often in contrary directions. Though it seemed one eye or another was always on him, huddled like a calf inside their herd.

Adam wasn't sure whether he was a captive or a guest, but since he was unarmed and outnumbered ten to one, he chose to treat them as his generous hosts until they corrected him with a pillory, a prison, or a firing squad.

Whenever there was a calm between clashes, Adam tried to ingratiate himself to his hosts. He complimented them on their weapons, their discipline, their fierce masks and imposing suits. These overtures passed without remark. The sparking men continued to stalk the mist and fire on unseen enemies. Cannons boomed in the scud above them, and rifles cracked. Occasionally, an errant ball pelted near enough for Adam to hear it ricochet, but a second shot never followed the first. The invaders appeared to be firing blindly. The sparking men, meanwhile, aimed the forked prongs of their tethered wands, tracked their quarries, and shot confidently into the wool. They did not appear to ever miss. The mist glowed with burning ships.

They came to a towering sculpture of a kneeling woman, plated in lineated wootz steel. Her hair hung straight as a scarf. Her figure was maternal, her robes modest. She sat rocked back on her heels, eyes lidded, jaw slack, palms raised in worship or perhaps beggary. The extreme angle made her expression difficult to read.

The troop halted beside her knee, and Adam thought perhaps it was to allow him a moment to appreciate the apparent artistry that had gone into fashioning such a thing. He praised the monument's beauty, the whimsical striped steel, and her ambiguous posture, which seemed at once noble and humble. Then the towering woman turned her head, the movement smooth and nearly lifelike. She vomited a ball of lightning into the cluttered air.

The clouds swallowed the crackling missile.

In the distance, an explosion rumbled like thunder.

One of the sparking men raised a finger to his lopsided grin. Adam shut his hanging mouth.

Adam had learned long ago that the quality most essential to surviving the Tower was not luck, nor strength, nor wisdom. Even experience was not without disadvantage because as complacency dulled one's vigilance, longevity inflated one's sense of permanence. The Tower loathed nothing more than a smug survivor.

No, the true patron of old fools and street urchins was *elasticity*. To survive, one had to be flexible.

Flattery had not softened the sparking men, so Adam abandoned the strategy. It was just as well: The fawning toady was an unpleasant disguise. He needed to light upon a new tactic, and quickly, before he met the soldiers' superiors and the game began in earnest.

The trouble was, Adam had spent recent months suppressing his devious instincts in an effort to conform to the noble ideals his captain espoused. It had not escaped Adam's notice that Senlin's principles came at the expense of his plasticity. Senlin had been half a pirate, half a thief, and half a killer because he was, at his core, unbending. He could change his sails, but not his course; he could swap his suit, but not his heart.

Adam doubted he could afford to pursue such rigid principles here and on his own. Besides, he had come with the intent of burgling heaven. Such an undertaking was far from virtuous. He could only hope that the conniving, wiling part of him had not dulled from disuse.

All the flash, fog, and jostling had distracted Adam from something he should've recognized from the start: He was walking into some sort of grift. The fact that the sparking men knew a few details of his life signaled either a cold reading or a confidence game, and he had seen enough of both in his time. New Babel had a robust population of clairvoyants, each of whom claimed to commune with the dead, though all they really did was interrogate the living. Then there were the mind readers, who could open the human psyche as easily as a billfold. You couldn't walk a single block in New Babel without being accosted by a shell game operator who would demonstrate the fairness of his game by feeding winnings to a planted player who invariably took the good luck with him when he left.

The locals of New Babel had learned the obvious lesson: Leave the soothsayers and game runners to the tourists. But Adam had learned a more subtle moral: *Sometimes hucksters make easy marks*.

A compelling ruse took an awful lot of concentration to perform. The more a charlatan thought of another man's wallet, the less he attended his own.

Before he was banned by New Babel's Guild of Cups and Mystics, Adam had slipped the rings from the hands of a dozen palm readers; he had picked the pockets of the pickpockets who wove through the crowds of the telepaths; and he had convinced the shell game operators to hire him as a stooge, only to evaporate with the exemplary loot. Naturally, he had made one or two (or three or four) enemies along the way, but as an employee of Finn Goll, who sponged up most of his ill-gotten gains, Adam had enjoyed the protection of Iren and the port guard.

Which of course would not be the case here. If these rubber golems turned out to be cannibals, no one would rush in to pull him from the pot.

The bleak thought was strangely exhilarating. For the first time in a very long while, he was responsible for no one but himself.

Obviously, the rubber knights were trying to fool him by pretending to be familiar with his past. Adam didn't know why they were doing it or how they had discovered the personal details they knew, but neither mystery mattered. Let them play their game while he played his.

Adam was so taken with his own thoughts that he hardly noticed that the battle had ended until one of the guards halted and twisted his visor free of its collar. It was the same soldier who'd first recognized him and called him by name. The soldier's blond hair and beard were as yellow as pollen. His features were angular, his brow as jutting and sharp as the eaves of a roof. He might've been imposing were it not for his eyes, which gleamed with a sort of doglike eagerness. He said, "You're not a tenor at all. You're a baritone, like me. I'm not surprised, of course. In fact, I knew it. Oh, I can't wait to see the look on Piotr's face when he hears you. This has been a *wonderful* morning. First a conflagration, now a vindication!" He hiked an arm in squeaking triumph.

Adam had no idea how to respond, so he said, "Who were you shooting at? Pirates?"

"No, a navy. Mundy Crete's navy, to be exact. They're a bunch of idiots. You could set your watch by their invasions: first Monday every July. Every year they send more ships, and we make more ashes. I wish we could just convince them to burn their summer fleet while they were still anchored in port and save us both the trouble." He tossed his hair, heavy with sweat, and smiled at Adam, who felt a little towered over. The guard was at least a head taller than him. "But who cares about all that? What's left of them will be swept up and gone before tomorrow. Tell me, what have you been up to, Adamos? Pinching purses? Impersonating tour guides? Getting Voleta out of jams?"

This sudden topical shift, peppered with personal details, was unsettling. Adam dug his hands into his pockets to affect a casual air. He felt reassured by the book he found there. It was the diary of Captain Brahe, which he'd rescued from the derelict *Natchez King* down in the Silk Gardens where the spider-eaters wallowed. It had become something of a talisman for this whole ill-advised adventure, and its presence settled his nerves as readily as the hand of a friend. He responded to the question with a breezy sigh. "Oh, you know. I've been doing this and that, going here and there."

The soldier gave him a sidelong look that contained a certain amount of amusement if not satisfaction. But if this man's curiosity was all that was keeping him alive, Adam wasn't ready to surrender all of his mysteries just yet.

"Well, it's a lucky thing you clawed your way up during my patrol. I admit: I'm something of an admirer of yours. If you'd come by ship, I would've finished you off and never realized it." The sentry cocked his head to one side, his lower lip jutting out from under his mustache. "I wonder if I've killed a lot of famous people."

"You've brought down a great many ships, I suppose?" Adam made the remark as if he were alluding to a pastime and not the fate of many souls.

"Oh, hundreds! I've wrecked pirate ships, colonist scouts, royal envoys, naturalist expeditions, tour boats, racing yachts, and a barge full of orphans." He made a constrained, snuffling sort of sound. It was a laugh that would've been well suited to a formal tea and an absolute liability in a public house. Adam smiled at what he hoped was a joke.

One of the other guards removed her helmet. It was the woman who had previously informed him that Adam *absolutely did not tell jokes*. Based upon her expression, it didn't seem she enjoyed hearing them much either. She said, "And as I recall, Elrin, you've shot a thief or two."

"It's Sergeant Allod to you, Corporal! And Adam is more than a thief!" The soldier's cheeks flushed with exasperation. "He is a phenomenon! He's a bird of paradise. You don't shoot a bird of paradise when it lands in your backyard."

"But a barge full of orphans..." She stuck out her hand and rocked it—an equivocating gesture.

"You know I was joking."

"Perhaps we should amend our oath." She held her hands out, palms up, the same pleading pose of the titanic sculpture who'd spat a ball of lightning. " 'I shall defend our gates and gardens from waste, war, and trespass unless the interloper is particularly famous or interesting or attractive or—' "

"You know what, Runa, if you want to shoot him so badly, go right ahead. Roast his bones!" The blond sergeant pointed at her. "But *you* have to explain to everyone why you shot Adamos Boreas while he was coming along peaceably, *and* you have to tell Mother."

Discovering the two were siblings explained their bickering habit and also why a sergeant would endure such a back and forth from a subordinate. Though if Adam had learned anything in recent years, it was that orders delivered by one sibling to another were seldom welcome or followed.

The woman the sergeant had called Runa rolled her eyes and dropped her arms. "I'm not saying we should shoot him, Elrin."

"Oh! Well, then." Her brother's voice took on a condescending quaver. "I suppose we could take him in and call an accord and share this judgment with our countrymen as is our custom and law." He touched his forehead, mimicking the arrival of a revelation. "Wait a moment! Is that exactly what I was doing? Are you telling me, your superior officer, to do exactly what I was doing?"

"For god's sake, Elrin, don't be such a—"

"Shut up, Corporal. That's an order. God, Runa, you're insufferable.

And do you honestly not want to know what happened to Voleta? Because I certainly do. Here, let's just take a quick poll." Elrin turned to the rest of his troop. "Any of you lot curious to know what happened to the little acrobat? Is Voleta happy? Is she whole? Is she coming up next? Well? What say you?"

A lump gathered in Adam's throat as one by one each of the lizard-headed soldiers raised a rubber hand.

Chapter Two

> Those who claim to be "ready for anything" are over-packed and invariably unprepared for the one obstacle every adventurer must eventually face—*disappointment*.
>
> —from the diary of Joram Brahe, captain of the *Natchez King*

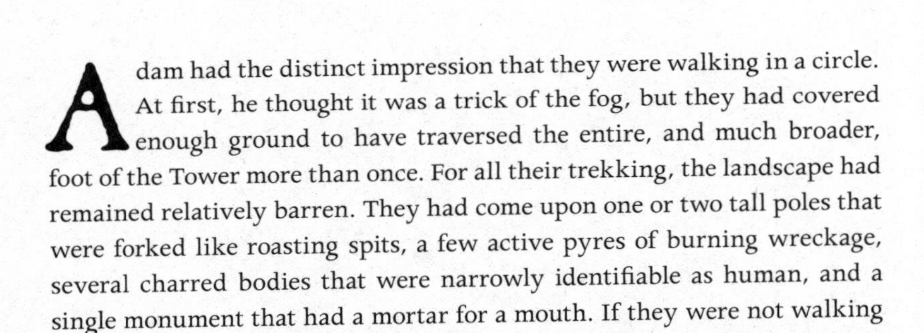

Adam had the distinct impression that they were walking in a circle. At first, he thought it was a trick of the fog, but they had covered enough ground to have traversed the entire, and much broader, foot of the Tower more than once. For all their trekking, the landscape had remained relatively barren. They had come upon one or two tall poles that were forked like roasting spits, a few active pyres of burning wreckage, several charred bodies that were narrowly identifiable as human, and a single monument that had a mortar for a mouth. If they were not walking in a circle, then the Tower's penthouse was lamentably unfurnished.

In his diary, Captain Brahe had alluded to rivers of gold and trees of silver, which Adam supposed might describe the present landscape. Gold plates cut across portions of the steely floor in a manner that might be said to evoke a river or stream to a sufficiently dreamy or nearsighted person. The branching silver aerials were vaguely treelike, and perhaps would appear more so to a native of the Tower who hadn't much experience with forests or lumber or picture books.

But Brahe had also referred to something grander, a larger object, a more splendid structure buried deep inside the mist. The captain of the *Natchez King* admitted to having glimpsed the mysterious feature for scarcely a moment, and then only through a heavy veil of mist, before being driven back by a barrage of lightning. And yet the impression had been an indelible one. Brahe called the anomaly an "ethereal terrarium." While in the Sphinx's home, Adam had looked up both words in the dictionary, and still the description made little sense to him.

But the fact remained: They had to be circling something.

"I can't remember the last time the lumenguard took a prisoner. It was well before my time, I'm sure. You're going to be quite a surprise for Captain Dyre." Elrin nudged Adam in the ribs with a round, squeaking elbow. "I hope you don't mind my calling you a prisoner."

"Oh, please, I'm used to it," Adam said, swatting the air with a dismissive scoff. "I'm something of an authority on jails, prisons, dungeons, that sort of thing. I should write a reference book. Something like, *An Insider's Guide to the Inside*."

"I like that!" Elrin smiled broadly enough to expose a row of large and crooked teeth tucked beneath the lovelier coverlet of his mustache.

Runa squinted at Adam's attempt at humor. Her eyes were pronounced and close set, which, in combination with her upturned nose, made her look a little as if she had just suffered some minor surprise. And yet, for all of that, her expression was alert and probing.

She said, "What was that message for Voleta about the owls and your birthday? Some sort of code?"

Adam contrived a yawn to hide his surprise at her well-aimed guess. "Oh, that. My sister forgot my birthday once. I've never let her live it down. You know how siblings are: always teasing each other."

Elrin's pinched laughter sounded like a man trying to discreetly blow his nose. "That is true!"

"It may be true," Runa said, fixing Adam with a penetrating stare. "But it's not the truth."

The silver-plated plateau seemed unending, the fog inexhaustible. Adam began to suspect Elrin intended to march them around in a circle forever. But then the bank of clouds turned colorful. Green and gold blotches grew larger, clearer, nearer. Something immense loomed before them behind the thinning shroud. The others stopped, but Adam hardly noticed. He felt compelled to huddle closer, drawn by a mounting sense of wonder. At last, he would see with his own eye what so many aeronauts had attempted to conjure with song, rumor, and rum. How many had died while groping after this view? Here at last was an end to the Tower and the limit of humanity's reach.

The city seemed to materialize before him as if called forth by magic.

The bards had not gotten it quite right—not because their similes were overwrought, but because their imaginations had been insufficiently bold, their dreams too pedestrian.

The city's skyline was like a signature: a scrawl of unlike shapes that somehow strung together to form something organic, exquisite, and unique. Each wall, roof, dome, and spire was plated in gold that glittered softly in the thin sunlight. The city seemed to roil like a mirage. Adam could not imagine how many mountains the Brick Layer must've squeezed to milk such riches from the earth.

As arresting as the gilded edifices were, to Adam's surprise, it was the vegetation that stole his breath. At first glance, he mistook the greenery for paint or tapestry, because everything green inside the Tower was dyed. But no, verges of real grass grew between yellow lanes. The fat canopies of fruit trees peeked over rows of golden igloos, the foundations of which were encircled with budding bushes, full as the frill of a dress. Adam felt giddy at the sight of so much blooming life inside a city of treasures.

He was still smiling like a child when he walked face-first into an invisible wall.

The collision brought tears to his eye. He backed away, clutching his nose and hissing.

Elrin laughed like a kitten sneezes—with delicate, nasally puffs. He clapped Adam on the back unhelpfully. "Oh, tears are appropriate. You're the first outsider to set eyes on Nebos in a very long time."

It was a moment before the watery cataracts cleared from Adam's eye. When they did, he saw the oily imprint of his mashed face upon the crystal wall. He made a fist and gave it a speculative knock. It made no sound at all.

"The Brick Layer called it diamond cob. It's eighteen inches thick. Believe me: You'll need a much harder knuckle to make it ring," Elrin said, tugging Adam along. "But come on. No reason to dally now. You are about to enter the prettiest prison you will ever see!"

They skirted the barrier for a short distance before arriving at a steel gatehouse that jutted from the diamond bubble. The walls of the outcropping bulged with an intricate system of plumbing and tanks. Elrin called it a windstile. Through the fog, Adam could just make out two more of the kneeling monuments, with upturned hands and gaping mouths, set out on either side of the gatehouse.

The windstile's hatch was composed of the thickest slab of steel Adam had ever seen. It resembled a dam hung upon a hinge. When it closed behind them, it appeared to do so of its own volition. The door sealed so gently it sounded like a book falling shut.

The inside of the gatehouse was spacious but charmless: an empty metal box containing air and little else. After glimpsing the green-and-golden city through the crystal bubble, the windstile seemed a sort of obscenity, like a tin can in a flower bed. Elrin's troop scarcely began to fill the space, and yet everyone huddled expectantly about the inner door. An older man's face peered through a small porthole in the colossal hatch. His features were distorted by the thick pane of glass, and yet Adam marked the moment that his gaze fell upon him. Surprise widened his eyes just as quickly as displeasure narrowed them again.

Elrin depressed a rubber button under a caged box beside the inner door. "Hullo, Captain Dyre! Look who I found."

Captain Dyre's voice emerged from the box as if carried on the backs of buzzing flies. "Sergeant Allod, what have you done?"

"It's Adamos Boreas, Captain! You know, from the scintillation. He's my prisoner." Elrin looked over his shoulder at Adam and winked.

The captain's magnified lips turned pale as he studied Adam, who did his best to look harmless. "Prepare for cycle," Dyre said at last.

Elrin released the button with a happy sigh. "That's the first hurdle cleared," Elrin said as he bundled his long hair into his helmet and prepared to reseat it.

"Will he be all right?" Runa asked as she held her own visor above her head. "Doesn't he need a suit?"

Elrin scowled. "I don't think so. Half of protocol just exists to give the old dogs something to bark about. He'll be fine." Elrin rolled his eyes upward, searchingly, speculatively. "Well, probably fine." He shrugged and hid his face behind his smirking mask.

Runa looked at Adam with an expression approaching concern. Adam felt almost flattered, then she shook her head as if to dispel a bad idea and seated her helmet back in its collar.

A clang as loud as a railroad switch rattled the chamber. A violent wind sucked at Adam's clothes and hair, causing both to twist and thrash wildly. It felt like the follicles were being pulled one by one from his head. His skin pimpled against the abrupt and heightening cold, a cold that was as sharp as a mountain pass, and soon much sharper. Adam shivered and jammed his hands into his armpits. Just as he began to wonder how long the frozen cyclone could possibly last, the scourging wind quit.

He had never known that silence could be a felt sensation, but the stillness that followed was like a tangible, forceful calm.

Then he realized he could not draw a breath. He was being strangled by empty space. His gaping mouth worked like a fish on a pier. The saliva on his tongue began to sizzle. His lungs felt like clenched fists inside his chest. He swayed on his feet, which felt small and far away. The tears in his cloudy eye began to boil. He cinched it shut. It made no difference.

His legs buckled. Strong arms caught him, though awkwardly—by his forearm, around his waist, cupping his chin.

The air returned, but not as fiercely as it had departed. It washed over his shoulders and flowed down his back.

He gasped and choked upon the returning breath, swinging his arms until he was free of the hands that held him. Feeling caught, suffocated, caged, he pushed through the black rubber bodies and crashed upon the inner door. He pounded upon it, the smack of his fist hardly louder than a pat. He might as well have beaten upon a mountainside.

Chapter Three

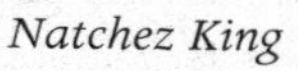

The birds do not dwell upon the miracle of the air, nor do the fish marvel at the currents that carry them. I suspect such is the case for the lords and ladies of the Tower. For them, gold has become the invisible medium of life.

—from the diary of Joram Brahe, captain of the *Natchez King*

Her helmet wrenched free, Runa gathered Adam by the hands. His wrists were bruised by his attack upon the hatch, and her grip felt, for a moment, like further confinement. He tried to twist away from her, but she resisted. She brought her face near his. Her eyes were as blue as a midday moon. Their close proximity stalled his panic. She told him to breathe with her. He breathed. And while his heart rediscovered its former rhythm, the great gate to the treasured city puffed and swung open.

The fecund scent of turned soil, geraniums, and grass flooded the vault. The perfume assisted his revival. The air was much richer and sweeter here. Adam had sucked in so many lungfuls of thin atmosphere aboard the *Stone Cloud* he'd forgotten what the good air that hugged the earth tasted like. He smiled like a drunk. Runa released his hands as abruptly as she'd taken them up.

Elrin yanked the helm from his head, shook out his sweaty locks, and said, "Very dramatic! But we'd expect nothing less of you! And see, Captain, it really is him. It's Adamos Boreas!"

The captain wore a gleaming white jumpsuit that was piped in canary yellow and padded at the shoulder. The soldiers who milled about the gatehouse were similarly attired, though with fewer golden laces. Captain Dyre had a lantern jaw and combed-over hair that was so pale as to be almost indistinguishable from his broad pate. He had the look of a man who enjoyed scowling at babies and crossing his arms at fine art.

"What are you looking at?" the captain asked.

Adam shook his head. "Nothing. I...well, I mean..." He made an expansive gesture. "Also, *everything*." He turned to let a soldier pass, and as he did, his gaze roved up a gold-plated path as it wound between a low flowering hedge, seething with bees, and ran on toward a row of domed houses, each with a trim lawn, a furnished porch, and flower boxes beneath the windows. "This is all very strange," he said, feeling not so much recovered from the trauma of the windstile as distracted from it.

"Yes, it is," Captain Dyre said. The other soldiers in Elrin's troop—Runa among them—filed toward a squat structure, partly veiled by a wall of climbing peas. They stripped off their lightning packs and helmets as they went. The muffled hiss of showers sounded as the soldiers disappeared inside. The captain turned again to face the sergeant. "As I recall, you took an oath, Allod. Perhaps you could remind me of it."

Drawing himself to attention, Elrin held out his palms and said, "I shall defend our gates and gardens from waste, war, and trespass until the Tower quails and the sky fails!"

Dyre spoke with a crisp precision, each syllable sharp as the hammer of a typewriter. "So, it's not your memory that's lacking. It must be your judgment, then, because you appear to have brought a foreigner into Nebos."

Though he kept his chin raised, Elrin's expression was as abashed as a scolded dog. "Yes, sir. I just thought—"

The captain cut him off: "You thought your mother would want to meet him."

Elrin's eyelids fluttered in surprise. "I...I thought we all would, sir."

The captain asked for the details of the encounter, and Elrin described discovering a pair of climbers near the southern border. He summarized the ensuing argument and his decision to let the one-armed woman go and to bring Adam in, describing it as "extraordinary circumstances."

The captain pounced upon the phrase. "Surely, there is no circumstance more extraordinary than our own. We serve the legacy of the Brick Layer inside the crowning city of the Tower of Babel. Or do you really think all of this"—the captain paused to wave his arm from the crystal horizon to the verdant, gilded skyline—"is inferior to a muddy pickpocket?"

"No, sir," Elrin said, his chin dropping at last. Adam wondered how he could possibly burgle a city full of people who considered him a thief.

The captain waved a dawdling butterfly from his face. "Have you let climbers go before?" Elrin insisted that he had not. In fact, he had killed hundreds of climbers over the course of his career. "What a glorious streak to have ruined," the captain said, turning toward a short column that resembled a hitching post, though there were no signs of horses anywhere. Dyre opened an ornate plate in the pillar's capital and turned the key encased within. A run of musical notes, dulcet as a harp, reverberated through the city. It was the gentlest alarm Adam had ever heard, but even so, it made him shiver.

Dyre stepped nearly upon Elrin's toes, and though he was a hand shorter than him, the captain seemed to menace the tall sergeant well enough when he said, "You will explain yourself for the accord. You will go directly to the assembly. You will not seek out your mother first. You will bear your punishment with dignity and will embarrass the institution of the lumenguard no further."

"Yes, sir," Elrin said.

"It's unfortunate that you had to mar what would otherwise have been a triumphant day. You're a keen marksman, Allod, and you've been a fine leader until now, but we'll have to review your rank and future in the guard once this is settled. Until then, the prisoner is under your charge."

The captain called for a set of "bonded bands," and a private quickly returned with a pair of bracelets, each about the width of a shirt cuff. Composed of some black metal, the bands were featureless except for a small depression, no larger than a fingerprint, on one side. Elrin offered his right arm to the private, who opened the cuff like a shackle, then closed it about the sergeant's wrist. When it became apparent that Adam would be the recipient of the second manacle, he presented his arm without protest. He was surprised to find the band was neither cold nor heavy. In fact, it was so inoffensive, Adam wondered what possible sort of restraint it could represent.

Adam hadn't any doubt that if Voleta had been present, she would've mocked the captain and bucked when they came at her with a black manacle. He would've apologized for her, begged them for restraint while scowling at his scolded sister. And he would've developed an ulcer in the doing.

Part of him had expected that being away from her would make it easier for him to be himself. But now he wondered if he knew who he was without her. He was the one who waited, the one who worried, the one always scrabbling to swindle and steal enough to keep her safe, or at least to delay the inevitable disaster. Take away that vigilance, the paranoia and guilt—guilt for having brought her to the Tower in the first place—and what was left? Who was he if not Voleta's brother?

Apparently, he was a notorious thief.

Gloomy, bat-infested New Babel had been laid out with all the flourish and variety of a gridiron. The angles and facades of the buildings were all brutally bland there. Other than the Lightning Nest, which spat sparks and immolated moths, New Babel's distinguishing feature seemed to be its absolute indifference to beauty or human inhabitation.

But in Nebos, everything flowed, curved, and coursed. The paths forked like the branches of a tree, and then converged again like streams to a riverbed. The roads were plated in gold and guttered in silver, and still their brilliance was nearly outshone by the emerald grass that crowded at the edges of everything. Bowl-shaped cottages encircled the city where the glass of the protective crystal dome was lowest. Further on, the avenues widened, and the buildings grew tall. Each was unique. One structure called to mind half of an immense cockleshell laid flat upon the ground. The neighboring tower evoked a beehive, and the next resembled a pair of ribbons, twisting together in a shining ladder of gilt and glass. Behind a stand of mossy live oaks near the apparent center of the city rose a seamless, gilded pyramid. Its perfection was only slightly blunted by the lack of a capstone.

The variety of designs was almost overwhelming, though the visual confusion was somewhat tempered by their material harmony: Everything was composed of precious metal. Adam suspected he could steal a doorknob and live like a lord for a year, or steal an entire door and retire.

He was also struck by just how empty the beautiful city seemed. A scattering of souls occupied the streets, a few faces peered at him from windows, and one or two drivers passed them in the lane, riding upon curious horseless chariots. But there were no crowds and certainly no hods. The denizens of Nebos seemed to rattle about the empty city like pennies in a beggar's cup.

Though they were all dressed handsomely enough. Adam felt conspicuous in his humble shirt and trousers. Insisting there was no time to shower, the sergeant still wore his sealskin armor that scored their march with rattles and squeaks. Elrin rambled on breathlessly about "scents" and their vital importance to their culture, and how the docents, who created these "scents"—Adam wondered if perhaps he meant perfume?—were so highly regarded that they wielded disproportionate influence in an otherwise sortitionist society.

"What do you mean, 'sortitionist'?" Adam asked.

"Every able-bodied Nebosan, sixteen years and older, is required to attend and vote on any decisions that have some bearing on the public: property disputes, disagreements over authorship, petty crimes, that sort of thing. 'Accords.' They're usually very dull." Elrin combed a tangle from his sweaty hair with his fingers. "Though I don't think that'll be the case today. I don't mean to worry you, but you're about to be the subject of a vote that will decide your fate, and there aren't a lot of options on the table. That's why I want to introduce you to my mother first. She'll argue on your behalf. But there isn't much time: Once the bell rings, we have half an hour to assemble before they lock the doors."

Their amble brought them to the base of a building that reminded Adam of a voluptuous pepper mill. Inside the white marble lobby, a massive lagoon-blue rug called to mind an oasis. Cauldron-deep planters burst with spears of forsythia along the walls, nearly obscuring a bank of elevators.

Once inside the lift, Elrin selected the gold-rimmed button for the ninth and uppermost floor. Then, as the car began to ascend, he leaned to the side and spoke to Adam from the corner of his mouth. "Mother can be a bit . . . *abrasive*. But it doesn't mean she doesn't like you. Just don't be rude. And do what she asks. And never talk back. She can slap the teeth out of a tiger's mouth."

Adam could only suppose that anyone who dwelled in the top floor of a golden spire that stood on the peak of the Tower of Babel might be somewhat unaccustomed to disagreement. He would endeavor to be gallant and pliant, or at least to appear so.

Their carriage dinged, and the doors opened upon a second lobby that was smaller than the first and more subdued in its decor. The empty chairs, end tables, lampshades, and carpets were all varying tints of white. It seemed a sort of waiting room, a sterile and numbing environment that fostered anxiety and boredom in equal measures. Adam had been introduced to such torment during his time in the Parlor, when he had been made to wait many, many hours before being dismissed without answer. He recognized this and every waiting room for what they really were—a dam to the public that existed to assert the inhabitant's supremacy.

Five colorful posters hung in frames upon the wall that faced them; their subjects were rendered inscrutable by Adam's distance from them, though their vibrancy was a welcome interruption to the stark environment. A secretary, dressed in a slim gray morning suit, sat at a long colorless desk before an imposing gray door. His hair was dyed an obvious, uniform black, which did not suit his creamy complexion or pellucid eyes. His hands rested upon a large register, bound in white leather, as if it were a sacred book and he were taking an oath. The ledger was the only object on the desk. He did not look up from it.

"The docent has a headache," the secretary announced before Elrin and Adam were halfway across the room.

"She always has a headache when there's an accord," Elrin said to Adam in a hurried sidelong manner. Then he raised himself up on the balls of his feet, bouncing forward like a happy hound come to play. "Hullo, Lamprey! You're looking fit. I'd be so fat if I sat at a desk all day. I'm just here to introduce a visitor to Mother. Look who I—"

"Madam Allod is not accepting visitors at this time. Would you like me to check for the next available appointment?" the sallow youth said in a voice as high as a boatswain's pipe. Adam was a little surprised to realize the secretary was so young. Adam would come to learn that Docent Ida Allod only engaged receptionists who were too young to vote in accords, as she could not have them running off and leaving her door unguarded.

Lamprey opened the ledger with a holy sort of lethargy and began to feel along the rows of names and dates, all drawn in the same small, tilted hand. He took up his pen and said, "Next Wednesday at 3:15 in the afternoon is the soonest that I can—"

"Lamprey, look up! Look who I have with me. Look up, you oily dorbel!" Elrin slapped the desk, making the ledger and Lamprey jump.

The secretary lifted his chin at last. When he saw who stood at Elrin's elbow, he scowled in revulsion. "An outsider?"

"Not just an outsider! This is Adam. *The* Adamos Boreas!" Elrin pointed over the secretary's inky scalp at one of the posters on the wall.

Adam followed Elrin's finger, squinting at the framed subject. All the thoughts that had a moment before been sitting at the fore of his mind like birds on a wire scattered to the winds.

The poster featured a young woman, large in the foreground and haloed by a spotlight. She wore a blue leotard. Her hair was a bramble of dark, unruly curls. Her knees hooked upon the bar of a trapeze; she held her arms out in upside-down flight. In the background, standing in a much smaller puddle of light, stood a young man with olive skin and two amber eyes.

Beneath the scene, a title was drawn in a rolling cursive: *The Daredevil's Brother: The Story of Voleta and Adamos Boreas.*

Adam realized the Nebosans were not enacting some elaborate scam or cold reading. No, their intimate knowledge of his life was much, much worse than a ruse.

It was real.

Chapter Four

Never was a line untangled by heaves and tugs. An unwanted knot requires a flexible stratagem to undo. One must give a little here to make some progress there. So it is with most of life's snarls.

—from the diary of Joram Brahe, captain of the *Natchez King*

dam's anger and horror felt like a hand shoving upon his back, pushing him toward Elrin and an all-out brawl. He wasn't intimidated by the tall lumenguard, a man who was probably accustomed to warring at a distance, a man who did not know how to fight through poor odds, dirty tricks, and pain. But Adam did. He was sure he could knock down ten of the golden-haired soldiers.

Though ten would be hardly sufficient to subdue an army.

Adam made a conscious effort to uncurl his fists and to fill his lungs. He could not box his way out of whatever sort of trap he'd blundered into.

But the effort he made to open his hands and lungs seemed to unlock his throat as well. He was startled by the ramble that spilled from him. "Why in the world would you spy on me? My sister, I understand—she finds the limelight wherever she goes, and the Tower is full of awful men who like to leer at her. But I am Adam: Captain of Nothing, Lord Boreas of Western Nowhere. I am no one! Why would you spy on me?"

Elrin put his hands up. "Adam! Wait, wait! You have it all wrong." He grinned to vent his apparent shock, the appearance of which calmed Adam a little. The big Nebosan had assumed Adam would think the discovery a pleasant surprise. Elrin rushed to reassure him: "My mother isn't a spy. We aren't like that. We are a placid people. I know the lightning is off-putting, but that's just part of the life we inherited. We are not aggressors. We don't meddle in the Tower's affairs. My mother is an artist. That's all." Elrin pointed at the grim door. "But please: She will do a much better job of explaining everything to you. We don't have much time. They are going to vote on your life soon, and I don't want them to choose to end it."

Lamprey mewled and spluttered as Elrin pushed through the door to his mother's office. Adam followed, but silently. Not even Elrin's threat of death could drown the single question that now rang inside his head, the question of *How?* How had the citizens of a bottled city learned of an acrobat in a burlesque house tucked far, far below inside one of the Tower's poorest, nastiest ringdoms? How were the painted likenesses of Voleta and himself so precise? And how in the world would he escape a city where apparently everyone knew his name, his face, and the criminal nature of his past?

He wished Senlin were there. The captain would've produced a theory in an instant, and a plan the instant after that. Adam had to think like the sly headmaster. What would he do? Probably change his hat and declare himself the mayor of Cloud Town.

"*I said*, may I present the docent Ida Allod!" Elrin half shouted into Adam's ear.

His trance snapped, Adam realized he was standing at the edge of a black room. The floors were onyx dark, the furniture ebony, and the curtains bleak as mourning veils. They hung parted over a window that let in the room's only source of light, a yellow spear that staved the air. That beam fell—with great theater—upon a woman wearing a tuxedo the color of dried blood. She sat straddled upon the end of a jet-black fainting couch as if she meant to ride it into battle.

"Elrin, could you call Lamprey in for me?" Her voice was without inflection but so resounding it seemed to shrink the room. Elrin ducked back out the door, leaving Adam twisting in the docent's company. She did not appear to notice him. Elrin returned with Lamprey in tow. The youth held his chest out bravely. He seemed to know what was coming. "Lamprey, your assistance is no longer required. You may go."

The young man bowed and departed without argument.

"Your rudeness has consequence, Elrin," she said.

"Did you hear the chime, Mother? An accord has been called," Elrin said, approaching the couch.

"Don't call me that," she said, and Elrin's stride broke like a man discovering a stone in his boot. "What do you want?"

Elrin turned and waved Adam forward with a pleading grimace. Adam intruded upon the beam of light as Elrin introduced him in a nervous ramble: He had found Adamos Boreas, the famed subject of her work, skulking around the verge. Elrin had recognized him at once, and thought to bring him back to the city because he knew she would want to see him, then Captain Dyre called an accord to decide whether to let him stay or to put him in the furnace, and perhaps she could save him if they hurried.

As he spoke, Ida Allod rose and walked past her son, who tracked her with an eagerness that seemed to steal a decade from his maturity. Docent Allod approached Adam, stopping out of arm's reach. Her corn silk hair was cut short and slicked back. Her face was devoid of blemish, fat, dimple, or wrinkle. She looked to have never laughed or cried in her life. Her hairless brow and prominent eyes made her gaze owl-like and awful.

She surveyed Adam from head to toe, then sniffed at what she saw. "You are not Adamos," she said. "Why are you trying to fool me?"

The absurdity of the situation elicited a short, cynical laugh from Adam. He had been caught many times before trying to pass himself off as one thing or another—a train porter, a tour guide, once even as a youthful lieutenant in the Market guard—but never before had he been accused of posing as himself. "Well, I suppose my mother might not recognize me either," he said, adjusting the strap of his eye patch.

"What is your mother's name?" Allod asked.

Adam had been prepared to present an agreeable, polite facade, but then he'd seen how much she scorned her servile secretary and obsequious son. If Adam had learned anything from Finn Goll, it was that egotists respected other egotists. So, he answered her question with all the arrogance and disdain he could muster. "Usually, I call her *Mother*, but she also answers to *Mum*."

Allod's impassive expression was briefly cracked by a minute scowl. "Adamos is not a comedian. He is a tragic figure."

Adam made a show of surveying her room. "Well, I haven't painted my room black yet, but I suppose I've had my ups and downs."

Allod turned to Elrin. "Deliver this fraud to his fate and leave me to consider my disappointment in a son who cannot even spot a—"

"Her name is Esther," Adam said loudly, making no effort to hide his irritation at having been strong-armed into answering. "Last I saw her, she was living under my uncle's roof in the Depot of Sumer."

Allod, who had turned her back on him a moment before, came around slowly. She slipped a hand in her vest pocket and took out what seemed a jeweler's loupe. She wedged the eyepiece between her cheekbone and brow, the pinch of which was sufficient to hold it firm. Adam resisted the urge to retreat when she took his face in her hands and stared into his eye through the silver-clad lens. The inside of the loupe glittered like a geode. He felt the woman's breath upon his face, warm, thin, and reeking. She released him even as he was about to pull away and plucked the loupe from her eye. "My god, it is you," she said in a softer, almost intimate voice. Though her expression remained impassive, her iron-blue eyes darted with amazement.

"What a relief!" Adam said, smiling wanly.

Ida Allod reached for his temple. Adam resisted the urge to recoil. The docent twisted a ringlet of his hair. "You've changed," she said. "But of course you have. You were so young. You were so—" Through the open window, the chime repeated its arpeggio. The bells seemed to break the spell, and Allod withdrew her hand.

"We have to hurry," she said, already striding for the exit with her arm hooked tightly through Adam's. Elrin bounded after them into the garishly bright lobby. "Captain Dyre would like to see your ashes on his mantel, I'm sure. The man is a fetishist for oaths and honor. But I'm not going to let him have you." Adam struggled to negotiate her hold and the waiting room's chairs as she plowed her way toward the doors of the lift. "Now, I know you hate to trust a stranger. But on this one occasion, I beg you: Trust me. Do not object to the purgatorial stool."

"Do not what to the what?" Adam blurted as the docent reached for the call button.

Elrin cleared his throat. "I'm afraid we're going to have to hang you." The tall sergeant sucked his teeth in sympathy with Adam's alarm. "Oh, but don't worry. It's only for a little while."

Adam sweated softly in the shade of a majestic live oak. The tree's many limbs curled and stretched with sculptural grace. Gray moss bearded its branches and birds nested in its knots. An itch developed beneath the bonded band upon his arm. He decided to ignore it. Before him, the dark leaves of blueberry bushes shone with an apparently inexhaustible dew. Beyond the hedge, unlit streetlamps guarded the blunted pyramid's slope that reached for the apex of the crystal dome. The jib arm of a crane towered above him. Climbing ivy had entirely swallowed the latticed boom and pilothouse. It looked like some sort of prehistoric leviathan rather than the modern marvel that it was. He wondered what had happened to make the natives surrender such an engine to the will of the garden.

At least Adam now knew the answer to one mystery, albeit a minor one. He knew what had happened to the pyramid's capstone: Someone had dropped it in the garden. The eight-foot-tall black pyramid stood plunged into the lawn not far from him. The haphazard tilt of the pyramidion seemed at odds with the tidy fence and bed of tulips that hemmed it. The pyramid was as smooth as polished obsidian, and featureless except for the interruption of a square borehole, which pierced it about two-thirds of the way up from the base. He thought the addition too plain to be ornamental, and so spent some moments wondering after its function. The question provided him with some welcome entertainment. Though it did not last.

Adam was still adjusting to the difficulty of standing upon the seat of a wooden stool that was unevenly poised between the breaching knuckles of tree roots. His hands were bound behind his back. Elrin had done a very good job with the knots, though he had apologized the entire time he had tied them. There was, of course, a moratorium on allowing strangers to participate in the accords held inside the pyramid, and since he could not be allowed to wander about unsupervised through the city while her constituents decided his fate, the purgatorial stool had been summoned.

The cord that encircled Adam's neck laid upon his shoulders comfortably enough. At the moment, the noose was no more imposing than a scarf.

But he was well and truly caught. If the citizens of the golden city voted against him, he doubted there would be much delay with the carrying out of his sentence. If he were lucky, they would hang him rather than roast him, which seemed a much worse way to go. It was odd to be weighing the desirability of deaths, particularly because he didn't want to die at all.

He was overcome by a sudden feeling of intense woe. The anguish was so profound it seemed to suck at his feet, and empty his knees, and turn his spine to melting wax. This could be the end, his last day, his last hour. He wondered if it was a cruelty or a kindness to die in paradise.

The stool teetered, and suddenly, he found himself very much alive and fighting to keep his feet under him, and the stool from toppling. It bucked back and forth between his toes and heels, and the scarf about his neck turned into a garrote.

After an excruciating series of tiptoes and hip thrusts, he managed to settle the stool and plant his feet again.

He had nearly hanged himself while languishing over being hanged. What a worthless end that would've been, though of course it was the only other option he had at the moment to patience. He could hang himself or he could wait for the verdict. It was as simple as that.

Adam's mother had taught him the value of pragmatism, and the lesson had served him well in the Tower. She had taught him that sentimentality was never necessary and often calamitous. It was sentiment that drove people back into burning houses to die while attempting to save an ancestral quilt. It was sentiment that invited in stray dogs that stole food from your table. Sentimentality let a pathetic vagrant spend a rainy night on the kitchen floor, and it was sentiment that slit your throat while you slept.

It had always struck Adam as a little unfair that he had inherited his mother's practicality without the complementary stoicism. When she turned a beggar out on a stormy night, she felt no guilt about it, and she slept through the whimpers of pups in the alley, and she watched, unmoved, as the treasures of her life were destroyed by disaster and accident. Adam knew well enough what had to be done, but he suffered from the agonies of guilt.

He had done his best to feign stoicism all his life, to tell himself and others that he did what he had to do to protect his sister (which was true), and that he did not feel guilty for those deeds (which was not). He carried with him the memory of every person he had robbed, swindled, betrayed, or misled. Senlin was just another in a long line of souls who he felt beholden to.

Many times in the past, he had wondered if perhaps he should not cling so tightly to a life that made him suffer twice: once in the surviving and again in reflection. Why cleave to something that had been so cruel?

And yet, teetering on that purgatorial stool, Adam realized that he had grown quite attached to his life.

He recalled the pact he had made with Voleta, which he'd alluded to in his final coded message to Mister Winters: *Tell the little owl not to forget my birthday.*

It had seemed clever when they'd come up with the plan shortly after arriving at the Tower. They had settled on one day of the year and a specific location where they would meet should they ever be separated. But now the thought of Voleta loitering outside of Owl Gate at the foot of the Tower once a year for the rest of her life, the thought of her celebrating his birthday without knowing that he was dead, long dead, hanged or incinerated—it filled him with sorrow.

His mother had been right: Better not to feel anything at all.

Chapter Five

The crowning ringdom's only known import are the lustful gazes of stupid men. Her primary exports include shrieks and orphans.

—*Everyman's Guide to the Tower of Babel,* IX. XVII

The chime that had called the natives to accord sounded once more, though this time the notes rang in a descending run. A din of overlapping voices followed as the doors of the pyramid opened, releasing the populace from their civic duty. Soon after, Elrin and his sister parted the blueberry bush. Runa was dressed in a curious suit that looked something like a formal set of pajamas, or perhaps a casual tuxedo. Her coat was blue, her blouse white, and her expression black.

Adam did not take it as a good sign.

But then, a grin split Elrin's yellow beard, and he said, "You are a lucky man, Adamos Boreas! It was a narrow vote, but you've been invited to stay in Nebos. On a provisional basis, of course. But isn't that wonderful? Mother tipped the scales in your favor, as I knew she would. You should've seen her! The captain roared like a storm, but she shone like the sun!"

As a very excited Elrin went to loosen the rope that anchored his noose, it dawned upon Adam what Runa's scowling implied. "Did you vote to put me in the oven?" he said, feeling a pang of betrayal. Why save him from the airless windstile only to turn around and vote for his execution?

Runa flinched but before she could answer, Elrin butted in, "It's rude to ask how someone voted. Ballots are anonymous for a reason: to discourage resentment and division. Once the accord is over, we can all pretend to have been in the right, if we want."

As the noose fell slack, Adam said, "Well, I wouldn't want to seem *rude*."

Working to unbind his hands, Runa hurried to speak her mind before her brother could fill the silence. "I didn't vote for your execution. In fact, I voted to manacle myself to you." She stopped her efforts long enough to stick her forearm past Adam's knee. He looked down to see a bonded band peeking out from under her loose sleeve. "I don't know how I'll get anything done with this thing on. I'm in the middle of a piece!"

Elrin sucked a breath through his teeth. "I'm sorry, Roo. I really am. But Mother made a compelling case."

"A case for what?" Adam asked.

"A case for why Runa should be your guide, your warden, and if need be, your executioner," Elrin said, coming around to stand under Adam's nose, where he gripped the seat of the stool to steady it. "I'm just joking about that last part! Well, there's a little truth behind every joke."

His hands now free, Adam climbed down from his purgatory. "What do you mean?"

"Just that if you try to escape or turn out to be a threat to anyone's safety, Runa has the authority...really, the obligation, to shoot you." Elrin tried to stave off the awkwardness of the moment by inspecting the rope as he coiled it. "You are wearing your sidearm, aren't you, Roo?" His sister pulled her blue coat to one side to reveal a small holstered pistol. The weapon was silver-clad and shaped like a roosting sparrow with tapered ends and a bulbous middle. Adam wondered if it were a black-powder piece. Somehow, he doubted anything in Nebos would be so ordinary.

He was relieved that she had not voted for his execution, and he wasn't particularly concerned about the possibility of being shot (at least not at the moment), but he still hadn't gotten an answer as to why she had been chosen to be his custodian rather than Elrin, who seemed the obvious choice. When he put the question to him, Elrin's bright-eyed confidence cracked again. His moods flailed like a telltale in a storm.

"My mother always has an excellent reason for everything she does," Elrin said wretchedly, then brightened at a new thought. "*But* she did say that you might not be a tenor, so she may have to rethink her casting choice. And I suspect I may know who she might have in mind." The tall sergeant rocked on the balls of his feet happily. Adam thought he was grasping for encouragement where there was none: His sentiment had been full of too many *mays* and *mights*.

Runa rolled her eyes at her brother and said, "Docent Allod picked me because she likes to insinuate herself into my affairs, and she knows I'd rather be left alone. The woman is pure spite!"

"Then I suppose I should be flattered that your mother took a break from being spiteful long enough to argue for my life," Adam said, touching his neck where the rope had abraded it.

The remark seemed to embarrass Runa. She had the expression of someone who'd just noticed the muddy footprints that had followed them indoors. Then, as if struck by an idea, she pressed the indentation on her bonded band and jerked her arm back like a woman pulling upon the reins of a horse. At the same instant, Adam felt his own arm pulled toward her, as if towed by an invisible string. Elrin's arm spasmed, too, causing him to drop the stool he had just collected.

Adam grasped his disobedient limb in shock, but Elrin threw back his head and laughed.

"Abusing the bonded bands, eh? Well, Corporal, I'm afraid I'll have to write up a full report about this scandalous mishandling of—" Elrin activated his own band and threw his arm back, shouting "Aha!" as he did. Adam's and Runa's arms lunged in his direction. Adam yelped, and Runa called Elrin several obscenities that only grave enemies or siblings would ever think to employ.

Adam found the sensation of being jerked about by unseen forces physically unpleasant but intellectually enthralling. Apparently, the bands were tethered by some sort of powerful magnetism. He pressed the indentation on his own cuff and hiked up his arm.

To his disappointment, nothing happened. He flailed his limb a little further, though with growing hopelessness.

Elrin and Runa stared at him as if he were mad.

"You have to be wearing a primary bond to summon," Elrin said as if it were something Adam should already know. The cuffs were used by the lumenguard to keep the troops together. Should one man get lost, he could follow the pull of the summoner, and conversely, the summoner could feel about for the direction of the lost man by searching for resistance. The bonded bands were not meant to be jerked about wildly. "But it is good fun!" Elrin said, then gave the two a final yank before declaring the lark at an end.

"Well, since I'm not going to be hanged today, I would like to talk to Docent Allod. To thank her of course, but she also promised an explanation about one or two things," Adam said, affecting a cool he did not necessarily feel.

Runa shook her head. "I'm afraid you'll have to wait a little longer. The accord also decided to schedule a few appointments for you. But don't worry, you'll have your fill of my mother soon enough."

Elrin had to deliver his report to Captain Dyre, but first he assured Adam that they would reunite. The sergeant was looking forward to a quiet moment when Adam could regale him with his recent adventures and Voleta's latest escapades, which surely were incautious and numerous. Then Elrin climbed aboard one of the horseless chariots that was parked on the street outside the garden and drove away.

Runa called the chariots *bandies*. They were the common form of personal transportation in Nebos. Riders stood side by side on a semicircular footboard that was open at the back and sandwiched between two spoked wheels treaded in white rubber. A third wheel, essentially a caster, was affixed to a stabilizing beam that jutted from the rear of the chariot like the tail of a stingray. The bandy was steered by an elegant throttle set within the front panel beneath the crossbar.

Adam stepped aboard one of the bandies and immediately gave the throttle an experimental push. The steel plate beneath him trembled as a mechanical hum rose first in pitch and then in volume.

Runa slapped his hand away from the stick and throttled the engine back. "What are you doing?" she asked.

"I thought I was—"

"If you rev the turbine with the mag-brake on, the whole thing could explode."

Adam cocked his head to one side. "Really? That seems like a design flaw."

Adam watched as Runa depressed a brass stop in the dashboard. "The point is, don't touch my controls."

The bandy was very quick and nimble enough, though Runa seemed determined to test the limits of the chariot's handling. They careened through intersections and tilted through turns. The bandy's stabilizer wagged and bounced behind them. Yet for all the abuse, the bandy's engine made hardly a sound. A standard autowagon banged along like a bucket of nails tumbling down a flight of stairs, all the while belching coal smoke that was ideal for cultivating pneumonia. Runa's bandy, on the other hand, hummed like a gnat and produced a bridal train of white lacy steam.

Adam wondered which of the golden spires they would visit next. But instead, they left the central towers behind and reentered the neighborhoods that ringed the tightly laid city. Rounding a heavily treed park, the lane sloped suddenly downward toward the copper-rimmed entrance of a cave.

When they passed from the milky light of day into the gloom of the underground, Adam felt a brief electric shock. It was not strong enough to hurt, but it made him jump nonetheless, and he looked around for its cause. Runa explained that they had passed through an electric curtain, which was there to discourage insects from exploring the underground.

The steel-ribbed tunnel they now thundered down was lit by blue veins of glass, which frayed and veered like lightning along the ceiling. The tunnel forked and forked again, feeding into a five-point intersection, where the avenues splayed like the fingers of a hand. Already, Adam wasn't sure he could find his way back to the surface without help. Two turns later, he was certain he could not. Their tunnel expanded and shrank and then grew again when they passed what seemed a bandy station, where the riveted walls gave way to opalescent tiles. A long mosaic portrayed a bizarre aquatic scene full of unfamiliar creatures; there were elephantine eels, swarming schools of opalescent prawns, and beds of mammoth shellfish bearded with blue light. A dozen portals interrupted the seascape amid a great confusion of signs, none of which Adam had time to read before the view was shuttered by the resumption of the tunnel. They passed other pearly stations muraled with unfamiliar animals: immense black minks with raptor-like claws, one-horned oxen with bifurcated dewlaps and piercing yellow eyes, red-jacketed bees that swarmed about dripping combs full of pink honey. It wasn't until they passed a station decorated with rearing spider-eaters under nimbus-like webs that Adam began to suspect that the unusual beasts featured in the murals might all call the Tower home.

And yet for all their teeming decorations, every station was perfectly deserted. He asked Runa where all the people were.

Shouting over the wind, she explained, "We call this area the Warren. Most of the machinery down here is dead or dormant or we-don't-know-what. The Brick Layer was a little vague about what all of this was for. I've been told there are a thousand doors, and all of them are locked."

Adam thought of Voleta. He was glad she wasn't there. This was too much mystery and territory for her to resist. She would have gotten lost forever in an afternoon.

"Do you know a lot about the Brick Layer?" Adam asked.

"I remember about half of what we're taught in school. I remember most of the Brick Layer's edicts and bits of the history of the build. But you know how it is; a lot of what you learn in school just sort of falls away after a while," she said, as if these secrets were tedious or inconsequential. Adam had a hundred questions, but this wasn't the time for any of them.

During a particularly long straightaway, one side of the wall was replaced by an immense transparent pipe full of some bubbling, rushing fluid, braided with tendrils of pale blue light. He asked Runa what caused the glowing, but she only shrugged and said it was called "slow water" and that if you drank it, you'd freeze from the inside out.

Just as she finished her explanation, they rounded a bend and surprised a pair of persons standing just off the track. They appeared to be grappling against a massive elbow of the luminous pipe. The young man and woman froze when Runa's bandy appeared, and in that split second, Adam saw that they were not fighting at all. In fact, they were doing quite the opposite.

"Sometimes couples like to come here for a little adventure," Runa said, as she throttled the bandy on. "They think the light is romantic and that being near the slow water has an invigorating effect on the act. Honestly, it's just because the pipes shiver a bit, and they feel nice to press upon."

"Oh. I see," Adam said, blinking away the lingering image of what he'd just seen.

Soon after, they came upon a little cul-de-sac that abutted a most curious facade. An iron door with a frowning arch stood between two round windows that bulged like the eyes of a bullfrog. Their colored glass cast the dead end in a boggy green light. After touring Docent Allod's offices, this seemed as charming as an oubliette.

As he followed her off the back of the parked bandy, Adam asked, "Who is my appointment with, exactly?"

"You're not attached to your clothes, are you?" Runa asked.

"Not physically. I mean, they do come off. Why?"

"I'm sure he'll have something that fits you. He has two of everything." Runa put her weight behind the effort of pulling the hatch open. The door was only half swung when she abruptly pushed it shut again. The door closed with a boom that ran down the throat of the tunnel like a gunshot. Turning only enough for him to see the corner of her eye, she said, "Ossian is particular about his collection, but he's generous and kind, and I like him very much. It would upset him if you took anything. It would upset me, too."

Adam's first instinct was to defend himself, but then he recalled that everyone here knew him as a thief. He bit back his reflexive denials and said, "I'll keep my hands to myself."

She plied the door a second time and led Adam into what seemed an immense pawnshop.

In New Babel, pawnshops were an institution unto themselves, as popular as the Crumb chapels and as profitable as the sporting houses. As repositories of misfortune and vice, the shops were always well stocked, so well in fact that they attracted a tourism all their own. Prospectors came from every ringdom to paw through cases and crates that overflowed with family heirlooms: snuffboxes, hatpins, pocket watches, lockets, wedding bands, and silver baby spoons, all of which had been promised, once upon a time, to a friend, lover, or child.

But the collection before them in the Warren of Nebos was not so mean nor bleak. No, if it was a pawnshop, it was a pawnshop of kings.

A thousand unlit chandeliers hung from the ceiling, dense as bats in an attic. The shelving that consumed the high walls of the chamber bulged with all manner of clothing, bedding, and drape. Dolls and bobbles spilled from cabinets. The floor was a maze of piles. There were walls of books, stacked high as a garden hedge. A ziggurat of unmatched teacups rose on a counter beside pillars of stacked saucers and plates, all of which chimed and chattered softly.

It took Adam a moment to discern the cause of their trembling, but then he realized the shiver was coming up through the floor. The ground shook as if from a passing train.

That, Runa explained, was the work of the furnace, or rather the work of the steam the furnace produced. A scalding vapor coursed through massive pipes beneath the floor. They spread out in every direction from the furnace, running outward to the Tower's surface. Adam found the revelation difficult to believe because there wasn't a hint of smoke or fuel in the air. If there were a furnace nearby, it was quite inconspicuous.

"Wait a moment," Adam said, halting beside a sheaf of cello bows. "Are you telling me that this furnace is responsible for the cloud that wraps the city? Is this where the Collar of Heaven comes from?"

She looked at him a little dubiously and said, "So, it's sabotage, is it?"

Adam flinched with genuine surprise. "What?"

"You could be a little more subtle about it."

"I'm not a saboteur!" Adam said, with a little too much zeal, an excess that he corrected by adding in a lighter tone, "I'm a thief."

Runa gave him a tight, lipless smile. "Ossian is a good judge of character. We'll see what he thinks of you."

As they continued to snake through the warehouse, she explained that in addition to acting as the furnace's attendant, Ossian was entirely responsible for amassing the collection and its organization. "*If* it really is organized," she said quietly, as if it were a secret.

They found the fireman building a wall of music boxes upon a counter that was already crowded with lacquered pillboxes and coin banks.

Ossian wore a green plaid nightcap that fell so low on his brow, his eyes were all but hidden by it. A head shorter than Adam, Ossian had a cherry red nose, gin-inflamed cheeks, and a cactus's white whiskers. Most notable of all was the color of his skin. In contrast to other Nebosans Adam had met, who were all a uniform shade of milk, Ossian's complexion was a rich umber, not unlike Mister Winters's.

Sometimes a hug can be so friendly and warm that it makes an observer feel as if they have been embraced as well. And so it was for Adam as Ossian wrapped his arms around Runa, and the two rocked back and forth in greeting as Ossian murmured something Adam could not hear into her ear, something that made her blush and roll her eyes and sputter out a refutation that he ignored as he released her and faced Adam with a grin of delight.

"You brought company! You never bring company! I hate company!" He tottered when he approached Adam, who at first assumed his stiff gait was owed to age, but then he saw the braces peeking out from under Ossian's shapeless tartan smock. The sole of one shoe was also thicker than the other. "But you look like a nice enough young man."

"He really isn't," Runa said. "In fact, famously not. He's the subject of my mother's latest, greatest spectacle."

"Runa doesn't like scintillations," Ossian told Adam in a confiding way that endeared him to Adam immediately. "But then, I haven't sat through a scint in years. They make me so sleepy. To be fair, though, most things do. Even naps make me drowsy, now. One day I'm going to close my eyes and just go sliding from one nap to the next and the next and the—"

"Don't say that, Ossian. You're going to outlive the Tower."

"I'll drink to that. You'll stay for tea of course."

"We came on official business, I'm afraid. We came to use your furnace."

Ossian's indomitable smile finally broke. "Oh, no. Do you have to? I have room for it, whatever it is. I made a little space this morning. I finally burned something."

"What did you burn?" Runa asked, sounding surprised.

"My breakfast!" Ossian said. Adam laughed, and the fireman smiled at him. "I don't know, Runa. I like him." He patted Adam's shoulder.

Runa said, "Wonderful! Because you're in charge of finding him a new set of clothes. The ones he's wearing have to be destroyed."

Ossian surveyed Adam from collar to pant cuff. "All of it? Even the boots?"

"That was part of the accord, I'm afraid. We agreed he can stay, at least for the time being, but his lice have to go."

"Oh." Ossian examined the hand he had lately used to pat Adam. "Well. You get the lice powder; I'll get the fire tongs."

Chapter Six

A lord once told me that wealth is squandered upon the poor, much as rain is wasted upon puddles. But who wants the rain to fall all in one place? Is that not what cleaves the levee, what drowns the valley, what empties the boneyards only to fill them again? More puddles, I say. Fewer floods.

—from the diary of Joram Brahe, captain of the *Natchez King*

Adam stood naked in a grove of unmatched curtains that pressed upon him like a crowd. He did his best not to dust the drapes as he peppered himself with a shaker of strongly scented pyrethrum powder. He had assured Runa and Ossian both that he was not in the least bit lousy, but Runa had replied that his choices were these: flour himself in lice powder or submit to the incinerator.

Ossian had taken Adam's measurements shortly before taking his clothes and had asked what sort of fashion he preferred. Adam was only dimly aware that there were different styles of men's clothing. He encouraged Ossian to pick as he pleased.

It seemed the right thing to have said, because Adam could still hear Ossian singing tunelessly in a distant corner of his vast storehouse.

"I have to ask: What is all of this stuff?" Adam spoke to Runa between powder-inspired coughs. "Where did it come from? Why is it here?"

"All of this is slated for disposal and has been for years and years. But our fireman, you may have noticed, prefers to starve the furnace." Runa's voice developed an affectionate lilt as she continued. "Ossian sees the care that went into the making of these things. More than that, he imagines the people who once used and loved them—the infants who clutched them in their cradles and the princes who displayed them on their mantelpieces. Of course, all of this comes to us secondhand. We let it fill up our homes for a season or two, then cast it off as junk, as fuel for the fire, though it never gets that far because Ossian adopts it all into his heart."

"Ossian isn't a native, is he? He seems to have the complexion of a southern—"

Runa cut him off with a brusque command, though Adam wasn't sure if it was because she hadn't heard him or didn't wish to. "All right, stick out your head. It had better be snow-white."

Adam parted the drapes just enough to frame his face. She smirked when she saw his powder-caked locks. Satisfied, she presented him with a fine-toothed comb. Before he ducked back behind the drapery, he said, "But how did it all get here, here in Nebos, a city under clouds, under glass, under guard? I've seen what your cannons do to visitors."

He combed his hair as he waited for an answer, raising again the specter of the pyrethrum powder.

It was a moment before Runa replied. "They're gifts." Her voice sounded flattened by some emotion, though whether it was sorrow or shame, he wasn't sure.

Before he had the chance to press her further, Ossian returned with the clothes he had selected for him. The fireman passed the first article through, a pair of cotton pants, saying, "They're not new, but they are clean."

Adam decided to not take a page from Ossian's book and imagine the previous owner of the under garment. There were still a few things in the world—among them false teeth and love letters—that were best left in service of a single master.

He dressed without quite knowing what he was putting on. Inside the clutch of curtains, he could do little more than worm his arms into sleeves and feel about for the trouser legs with his toes. He was happy to see the new boots, though less happy to see the outfit included a vest. When Ossian presented him with what appeared to be some sort of necktie, he pushed the drapes aside and broke from his dusty cocoon.

"Do I really need a tie?" he asked, pinching the band of silk as if it were the tail of a dead rat.

"Well, it's part of the ensemble," Ossian said, pushing his nightcap up on his brow. "A hundred years ago, every lord in Tigrisse wore a tie with a knot as fat as your fist. It was considered handsome, or so I've read. Here, I'll tie it for you."

Seeing no alternative, Adam stooped and presented his throat.

With the knot made, Ossian led him to a wall full of handheld mirrors, the conglomeration of which did not make for a very useful looking glass. Adam regarded himself in pieces and parts. The trimly tailored waist of the black dinner jacket made his broad shoulders look a little apish, and the fat tie all but vanished his neck. But as strange as he looked to himself, Ossian promised Adam that he was perfectly dashing. A man ready for a night on the town.

Ossian gave him a leather valise that he had packed with other clothes. "And if you find anything in there you don't like or something doesn't fit, bring it back. There's plenty more."

"Thank you," Adam said.

"I'm just happy to see it find a use."

"May I see the furnace?" Adam asked. He hadn't been able to stop thinking about what sort of boiler could be at once silent and smokeless, yet sufficiently powerful enough to create a bank of fog that was large enough to hide the head of the Tower, a cloud that had held its shape for a hundred years or more.

Suspecting that his question had caught Ossian off guard, Adam explained, "I was a boilerman for a while. I know what a challenge it can be to keep a furnace happy, but I always found the mechanical aspect of the work interesting."

Ossian's eyes twinkled. "Oh, the Nautilus is no trouble!"

Adam smiled. "That's a lovely name for a boiler. I called mine 'Shep.' It would make sense if you saw it. It was definitely a Shep. But I would love to see your Nautilus."

"I'm afraid we really don't have time," Runa said.

"Of course you do!" Ossian patted the pockets of his smock. Adam half expected him to pull out a watch. Instead, the fireman produced a set of darkly lensed goggles.

Runa leaned nearer when she asked, "Are you sure, Ossian? He could be a saboteur."

Ossian pulled the strap of his goggles over his capped head and let them dangle at his throat. "The only thing that could sabotage the Nautilus is if the Tower fell over and rolled off a cliff, and I'm not sure even that would do it." Ossian laughed and linked arms with Runa, an act that seemed to dispel the last of her hesitation. "Come on. It won't take a moment."

The fireman led them toward the far end of the storeroom. Incredibly, the clutter thickened the farther they went. Runa asked him jokingly if he hadn't finally run out of room. Ossian said, "There's always more room. There are closets inside of closets; drawers inside of drawers!"

After squeezing through a mob of overladen coat trees, they had to crawl on their hands and knees under an elephantine credenza, and then on through a seemingly endless grove of table legs, until at last they broke upon a clearing.

Adam noticed a difference in the atmosphere at once. It wasn't warmth, precisely, but the air seemed to cause a sort of subdermal humming. His very bones shivered and buzzed like a kazoo.

The wall before them was black and lustering. Ossian explained that the sheen came from a layer of diamond cob, which covered several feet of lead. A formidable hatch with a heavy bar lock stood centered in the wall. Above it, in blocky embossed letters, appeared the words THE NAUTILUS.

As a boy, Adam had seen drawings of nautiluses in his schoolbooks. They were ancient sea creatures that looked like a bouquet of tentacles flowing from a snail shell. Their fossilized remains could be found in the walls of the river gullies that scarred the Western Plains. When split in half, the inside of a nautilus shell looked like a ladder coiled and shrinking toward a center.

Ossian set down the gunnysack that contained Adam's doomed clothing and took a moment to seat the goggles over his eyes. The round black lenses, which fit snugly under his wiry brows, made him look a bit like a jumping spider, though a good-humored one. Ossian said, "Don't worry; you don't need these. My eyes are old and unforgiving. If I go in there without them, I'll be blind for a day. Anyway, a bit of advice: When we get in there, look up. It'll give your eye time to adjust."

Adam observed a plaque on the bulky hatch that read WILL NOT OPEN WHILE FLOODED. As he turned the phrase over, Ossian unlocked the entrance. The light that poured forth was as bright as a surgeon's lamp. Adam squinted until he was all but blind and felt around ahead of him until he found Runa's hand. He wasn't sure if she had been reaching for him or if he'd caught her arm swinging in stride, but she did not pull away when he gripped her narrow palm. They walked into the furnace linked and in a file.

Adam's first thought was that the floor was on fire. There was no accompanying heat, nor hint of smoke, but the space was as brilliant as a blast furnace. His companions seemed unperturbed, so he resisted the urge to look into the bed of coals. Instead, he peered up at a dome of ancient lead, which was vented like the head of a saltshaker.

When the glare ebbed a little, he looked down with all the trepidation of a man coming to the end of his plank.

The chamber was circular and large enough to echo. The floor appeared to be a single, seamless disc of diamond cob that ran from wall to wall. The source of the blinding light came from beneath the transparent floor. There, a gyre of blue paling to white swirled about the drain of a maelstrom.

Almost at once, Adam saw in the design a resemblance to the ancient sea creature that was its namesake. What at first seemed a formless whirlpool of light was in fact quite structured. The flow ran through a channel that was separated into cells by locks. Outermost from the center, the stream was bluish, broader, and slow moving. The farther it ran down the spiral, the narrower the channels became and the more the blue light veered to white, growing brighter as it bleached. The gates of the locks were composed of a pearly membrane that writhed and wavered when looked at directly. At the center of this fantastic vortex was a speck of flashing white that he could scarcely glance at before its afterimage stained his vision. Though the Nautilus was silent, it had a turbulent effect upon the air like a static charge waiting for release.

"Mind your feet!" Ossian called. Adam looked down to see he was toeing a gap in the diamond floor. The opening, about the size of a cottage door, lay near the chamber wall where the flow was a pure and placid blue. He suspected it was the same fluid he'd seen bubbling through a crystal pipe on their ride down, what Runa had called "slow water." The stream passed near enough that if one so wished, one could sit on the edge and bathe their feet in its current. Adam shivered at the thought and at the brutal cold that rose from the breach.

He took a step back. "Why is this open?"

"Emergency overflow, I think. It's always been open, and I don't know how I would even go about closing it. Perhaps I could put a board over it, but that seems a little silly," Ossian said, his face lit from below to eerie effect. "Besides, it's easier to get the puddles into the furnace this way."

"Puddles?" Adam asked, even as his eyes adjusted enough to see the red puddles that spotted the floor here and there. In the brash light of the room, the puddles were hardly distinguishable, but even so, Adam thought he recognized the fluid: It was the same stuff that fired Mister Winters's arm. He looked up in time to watch a drip fall from a vent in the ceiling. Somewhere, a pipe had sprung a slow leak.

"This is your furnace?" Adam marveled again at the galactic swirling drain trapped beneath a diamond floor that suddenly seemed insufficient. "Can you walk out over the middle?"

"Well, *you* can. I won't. Makes my brains itch and my britches wet. The Brick Layer called that flashing thing there at center the Allonomia. It's a hungry little beggar. And very, very hot."

"And this stream of slow water chills it?"

"More or less, I think. The Allonomia turns this current into steam, which is vented downward, and then piped out to the surface."

"So, it's just a very hot coal?" Adam asked.

"Well, it's a little stranger than that. Here, watch." Ossian dropped the gunnysack and extracted one of Adam's boots. The fireman made a show of turning the shoe this way and that like a street magician proving the ordinariness of an object. Then he bent over, his braces squealing out a fanfare, and deposited the battered boot into the flowing water.

For a moment, nothing of note happened. The boot bobbed like a cork, meandering down the sapphiric stream as Adam paced along after it, skirting the red puddles as he came to them. But when the heel of the boot breached the membrane into the next cell, it suddenly began to stretch like taffy pulled upon a hook. The deformed heel, now a ribbon, flowed onward, inward, carried by the brisker current. Adam began to jog. The elongated heel touched the next membrane, and there transformed into a thin black skid. In the next cell, it was hardly as thick as a pencil line that whipped about the curve. Then, Adam could not discern when that remnant leapt from one lock to the next as the stretched boot continued its inward spiral, taking on speed at an exponential rate. Soon the bootheel was nothing but a streak of light falling into the blinking crucible at the heart of the storm.

Dizzy from running a lap about the chamber while staring at the floor, Adam returned to the open hatch where Runa and Ossian waited. Leaning over to catch his breath, Adam was shocked to see the top cuff of his boot was still visible in the water of the first cell. Then it passed through the membrane and emerged in the next chamber stretched like dough under a rolling pin.

"What is this? What are the dividers made out of? Where does this water come from? Is it what's stretching everything out like that, or is it the...what did you call it, the *Allonomia*? How is any of this possible?" Adam's voice shook in sympathy with his hands.

Ossian seemed to beam with pride even as he said, "I haven't the vaguest idea. But isn't it wonderful?"

"Who built it?" Adam asked.

"The Brick Layer. One of his last installations, I believe."

"What is it for?"

Ossian shrugged. "For eating boots and making clouds, I suppose." The fireman stared at the funneling light, his black lenses gleaming, his mouth open, his cheeks flushed and raised in an expression of pure wonder. "What is any of this for?" He looked like a child marveling at fireworks.

Whatever its purpose, Adam was certain the Nautilus was never intended to serve as a ringdom's firepit. To call this incredible apparatus, this preternatural phenomenon, a *furnace* was like calling a waterfall a *tap* or a tempest a *broom*.

Then a bleaker thought intruded, and Adam turned to face Runa. Her face shone with the kaleidoscopic glow of the Nautilus. The swimming light had the curious effect of making her expression seem to flicker from friendly to sinister, from approachable to impervious. Or perhaps it was not a trick of the light. All day, she had seemed to vacillate between a desire to help him and the urge to estrange him. Adam had no sense what she thought of him. She was as unreadable as a book in a dream.

"You voted on whether or not to put me in there," Adam said. "Is that where most of your guests end up?"

"We don't have guests," she said, looking away. "Now, come on, we have a supper to spoil."

Chapter Seven

Some of my crew are convinced an old rope will continue to hold purely because it has held for so long. As if a ship was buoyed by precedent. As if the past promised a future.

—from the diary of Joram Brahe, captain of the *Natchez King*

As Runa drove her bandy back through the cold light of the underground avenues, Adam's thoughts lingered on the Nautilus. When he closed his eye, he still saw its ghost. Was it an engine? If so, where were its pistons and gears? If it was a turbine, what did it power? Perhaps it was not a machine at all. Perhaps it was an elaborate churn or mill or still that condensed the slow water. Or perhaps the Nautilus was merely a receptacle, a prison for an exotic, ravening spark.

Adam had come to Nebos for adventure and treasure. And while he still very much wanted the gold, he already felt a little overstuffed with mystery. He wondered if it was too much to hope for a quiet dinner.

Runa said she needed to make a quick stop-off first to feed her hound, Celeste. They lived in a stone turret tucked inside the largest of Nebos's parks. The square tower had three floors, a crenelated parapet, and a discernable tilt. Its red-painted door, leaded windows, and curtains of ivy, which obscured fully half of its facade, were all charming enough, but in a manufactured way. It seemed a decoration posing as a ruin.

Seeing Adam's bemused expression, Runa said, "It's called a folly. An artist built it years before I was born. It's not supposed to be lived in.

There's no plumbing, no electricity. And I had to evict one or two spiders before moving in."

"Is Nebos running short of houses?" he asked.

Runa snorted. "Far from it. There are ten houses for every one of us. *But*"—she pulled a steel hoop that bore a single key from her jacket pocket—"this has something that none of the igloos do." She fit the gap-toothed key into the lock. "Flat walls."

She hesitated, seeming to reconsider, then spoke once more in a much less cavalier tone of voice. "Please, don't touch anything."

Adam took a step back. "Wait a minute. Look, I was part of a crew with a first mate who was wonderful and terrifying and very good at her job, but she absolutely did not want anyone in her cabin. We all understood. We did not take offense. That's just how it was. I'm happy to wait here."

She studied his face for a long moment. She seemed to be searching for a glimmer of treachery in his eye or some sly crimp to his smile. Adam understood her suspicion. He knew better than most that distrust was not always a sign of hostility.

"Wipe your feet," she said at last, and walked inside.

The interior of the folly reflected its shell: It was cozy, rustic, and all a little crooked. There were no dividing walls. A skeletal stair ascended to an open hatch in a ceiling that was close enough to touch. The walls were crowded with canvases, many of them unframed. Adam asked if she was the artist, and Runa said she was. A gray, woolly dog slept upon a well-chewed sofa. The hound, who seemed very old, lifted its head and opened its mouth in a canine smile. Runa went to it at once, nuzzled the beast, and murmured a string of praises. The animal's ropy tail thumped the cushion in pleasure.

Sensing that this was a private ritual that would not be improved by intrusion, Adam occupied himself by looking at the art. The subjects of her still lifes were all of a theme. Each contained a morbid element—a skull, a lifeless bird, or a hare hanging by its hind quarters—and then some contrasting vital object like a bowl of fruit, an arrangement of flowers, or eggs resting upon a doily. The piece that first caught his eye was of a bull's horn cradled about a bunch of grapes that still clung to the vine. The background was inky and yet the varnish made the black seem to glow. It was a luminous dark. "You're very good," Adam said, craning forward to peer at the blending along the edge of one plump grape. "Beautiful."

Her greeting of the hound complete, Runa said, "I could name fifty painters that live within a stone's throw of here who are better."

He felt her draw alongside him. "*Fifty?* Really? Is everyone here a painter?"

"Mmm, no, some are docents, poets, novelists, composers, musicians—"

"But who does all the work?" Adam's voice shook with disbelieving laughter. "Who collects the rubbish? Who washes the clothes and trims the lawns and—"

"There are automatons for all that. There are gyromowers to cut the grass, autobins to collect the trash, arachnocrofters to pick the fruit, and dinnerflies to carry the meals, only the most lavish of which are prepared by humans—chefs who consider themselves artists and food a medium. The only compulsory service is the lumenguard."

"That's not a bad trade." He turned his head but not his eye when he replied. He could not quite pull his gaze away from the veins of a grape leaf. All day, he had struggled to get a sense of his reticent host. But now, seeing the world transcribed by her eye, in all its exquisite detail, its grotesque glory, he suspected some of her character had been caught inside the paint, like an insect trapped in amber.

While she chopped carrots and sausage for Celeste's dinner, Adam shifted his attention to the next canvas on the wall: a snaggle-toothed skull amid a garland of fresh roses. "You own a lot of skulls?"

Runa's voice was suddenly cool and formal when she said, "I'm sure it seems a little morbid, but—"

"I think it's interesting. Placing a dead, hollowed-out thing alongside something living . . . It somehow makes them both look more alive."

Setting the hound's bowl down before it, Runa returned to Adam's side, ostensibly to share in his scrutiny of her work, though Adam suspected she was actually scrutinizing him. "Most people say it reminds them that they need to make out their will or visit a sick aunt."

Adam snorted and turned to face her. "You know what it reminds me of?" He tapped his eye patch. "The rotten and the ripe, all on one plate."

He watched as her focus leapt back and forth between his leather patch and his eye. It was for him, sadly, a familiar view. For some people, the compulsion to gawp at scars, facial asymmetries, and blemishes was irresistible. The Tower was full of people who would pay money to barkers for the pleasure of ogling a boy with deformed hands or a hirsute girl.

But with Runa, the scanning was not furtive or voyeuristic, and it did not leave him feeling freakish or hollow. He felt, instead, as if he were the subject of one of her still lifes.

When she spoke again, she seemed to be standing closer to him, though he was certain she had not moved. "Going by your logic, I suppose the question is, 'Do you need the patch?' Wouldn't the lack of one eye make the other brighter?"

"I...I don't know," he said. She had a wide, wondering expression on her face, as if a butterfly had landed on the tip of her nose.

Something seemed to crack open inside of him, and behind that barrier, which he'd not known was there, he discovered an emptiness that seemed to cry out for exploration, an absence that wanted to be filled. It was like discovering a new floor within a house he'd lived in all his life.

Then Celeste, who a moment before had had her snout buried in her bowl, suddenly howled, coughed, and howled again. Runa rushed to her side to console her, saying, "Hush, girl. Shh. You're all right."

Adam felt soothed by her gentling efforts. It was nice to be inside someone's sanctuary. He'd lived as an interloper for so long. He smiled as the dog calmed.

Then the ground began to leap and shake like a gangplank stretched over an abyss.

The Tower was shaking, and all the world with it.

Adam had grown up in a house that quaked, on a street that quivered, in a town that trembled on unsteady stilts. But in all the years he had lived in the Depot of Sumer above an industrious railyard, he had never grown comfortable with the incessant rumble of locomotives. And there was reason to be uneasy. Sometimes a neighbor's house was swallowed in the night, done in by termites, or dry rot, or the clip of a breakdown crane.

When Adam first arrived at the Tower, he had been struck by its imperviousness. Already centuries old, the Tower still managed to seem new. It appeared to be immune to decay and erosion and collapse. The world would buckle before the Tower did, Adam had felt certain.

It had been a very comforting illusion.

Runa's teacups rattled on their shelves and the canvases clapped upon the stone. Believing the folly was about to collapse, Adam charged at

Runa, startling her to her feet. He scooped up the hound and fled through the door, calling for her to run, run for her life. But the moment his feet touched the grass, he realized there was nowhere to run. The green canopy above swayed and shed leaves. The whole city chimed and rang. Somewhere in the distance, a window popped, glass splashed.

The Tower was falling. Adam hugged the old hound and wished she were his sister. He hoped Voleta was safely aboard a ship. He wished he had not been so oblique with his goodbye. Why had he not asked Mister Winters to tell her he loved her? Had he ever said he did? When he was gone, would she believe he'd considered her a pest and a burden? How had he sacrificed so much of himself and still given so little?

He shut his eye and braced himself for the descent into oblivion.

But then, the trembling faded. The quake seemed to rumble off like thunder into the distance. The slow shower of leaves ticked upon the lawn a moment more before a nervous silence fell.

Adam shouted when Runa put her hand on his shoulder. He whipped about to find her looking both concerned and somewhat amused. "It's all right," she said. "It's all right. They happen all the time. It's just a little shiver. We're perfectly fine. Really." Gently, she took Celeste from him. The old hound licked her face. "You had a little adventure, didn't you? Yes, you did."

"A *shiver*?" Adam said, still stunned. "How long has the Tower been shivering?"

"Oh, years. It happens every once in a while. Of course, we were all terrified the first time. Everyone ran for the parachutes and out the windstiles. We put our toes on the edge. But then the quake was over. Nothing happened. Then a little while later, another quake came, and again we all put on our parachutes, and made for the verge. But again, we didn't fall. So, now we just call it a shiver."

The offhandness with which she treated the quake calmed him a little. Though he could not believe the quakes were as innocuous as she claimed, at least they didn't seem to herald their immediate demise.

"But thank you for rescuing Celeste," Runa said.

"Rescue?" Adam said vaguely, and then in an attempt to recover his poise, went on, "Oh, no, you misunderstood. I was trying to steal her. She seems a very good dog."

"She is! Oh, she is. But you can't have her." Runa snuggled the hound's curls. Celeste, in turn, looked a little drowsy. "Come on, we have our own supper to get to. I hope you like spinning plates."

As Runa carried Celeste back inside her crooked castle, Adam wondered how much harder the golden city could shake and spin before it knocked him off his feet.

Chapter Eight

To scrounge funds for this expedition, I haunted the courts of the middle ringdoms. Taking advantage of the romantic feelings the middle class hold for rogues, I presented myself as an adventuresome rascal embarking upon a noble quest. Their purses burst open for me. I robbed them, and they applauded.

—from the diary of Joram Brahe, captain of the *Natchez King*

una wished to walk, and Adam was grateful for a reprieve from the whiplash the bandy inspired.

Though she had seemed at ease in her own home, Runa's good mood dissipated as they followed the road back toward the heart of Nebos where the blunt-nosed pyramid squatted behind a grove of golden aerials. She said nothing that explained her ill humor. Indeed, she seemed to grow more polite—if distant—the further she slid into misery. Adam found it interesting how she, like he, seemed to turn inward when troubled. While his sister had always dealt with her black moods acrobatically, he preferred to pace back and forth along a shallow depression, though it only served to deepen it.

Now that he knew to look for them, he began to see the automatons of Nebos in action everywhere. Some were discreet: A green copper crab, no larger than a footstool, crept across a lawn, chewing the grass as it went, while a tortoise-shelled slave with a spinning brush under its belly swept the clippings from the street. Other machines were more startling:

A spider, with legs as long as flagpoles, strode over rows of tomato plants, picking fruit with black mandibles.

Had he the time and opportunity, he would've liked nothing more than to study their systems and mechanisms. And yet, in the presence of empty streets, the unhurried industry of those automatons seemed almost skulking. Their gentle hum, which in a more bustling environment would've been undetectable, amid the uncanny silence droned like black flies on a carcass. It was strange to find so much luxury so scarcely possessed.

It came as something of a relief when he saw a small crowd pressing into the dining hall. The venue had a ridged, sloping roof that joined the ground without the imposition of walls. It looked like a scallop shell pressed into yellow sand. The crystal entrance of the banquet hall was fogged by a pattern of handprints arranged in a sort of herringbone. Above the doors, an arching pane of etched glass proclaimed the name of their destination: THE MINGLER.

Adam whispered to Runa that "the Mingler" sounded like some sort of back-alley fiend. Despite her black mood, Runa smirked, and replied that he wasn't exactly wrong about that. "It's a bit like being strangled with small talk," she said.

The main chamber of the dining hall was lit by a stained-glass medallion, which consumed much of the ceiling. Adam recognized its subject at once: He'd seen the design not long ago, emblazoned upon the Sphinx's front door. The men and women who made up the Brick Layer's round seal carried sheaves of wheat, sacks of grain, and cisterns of water, all in a merry ring. Powerful lamps illuminated the green, yellow, orange, and white panels, casting a light like a sunset sifting through a forest.

The floor of the hall was consumed by perhaps a hundred stations that bore a passing resemblance to the sort of writing desk Adam had once sat in at school. But these desks were not made of splinters and ink stains. No, they were silver clad and inlaid with scrolls of gilt. If one overlooked the tabletops that were hooked over the lap, the seats were almost throne-like. Beneath them, copper rails laced the floor of the hall in intricate, orderly loops.

Adam was so dazzled by the environment that it took him a moment to realize nearly all of the stations were already filled with the pale, blond denizens of Nebos. He hoped to find two empty seats near each other, preferring not to sit alone among strangers, but Runa told him there wasn't any reason to bother, then went winding through the staggered thrones in search of a vacancy.

Keenly aware that he was being watched by the room, Adam ducked into the nearest empty seat and folded his hands upon the golden shelf, disturbing an immaculately laid twelve-piece set of platinum cutlery.

His nearest neighbor, a woman twice his age with colorless hair and a turned-up nose, winked at him and, in a conspicuous whisper, said, "You're the thief!"

Adam picked up a lovely, long spoon, the purpose of which he could scarcely imagine, and making no effort to disguise the act, tucked the utensil into his dinner jacket. He patted his breast and said, "No, ma'am."

She smiled broadly, showing a rack of crooked gray teeth. Before she could antagonize him further, a deep gong reverberated through the hall, and the throne beneath Adam began to move.

He was not alone in his transit. All the dining chairs began sliding about like cannonballs on an open deck. The thrones spun as they coursed. It seemed a miracle that none collided, though they often passed within a hairsbreadth of each other. Adam looked for Runa amid the churning faces, but the effort only made him ill. His fellow diners melted into an indistinguishable, nauseating blur.

Then as suddenly as it had begun, the scramble ended, and Adam found himself sitting in an intimate circle with five other diners who might've passed for second if not first cousins.

Adam was beginning to recognize the predominance of certain features beyond the obvious uniformity of blond hair and pale skin. The Nebosans had heavily lidded, narrowly set eyes, ruby-red lips, high cheekbones, and ears that from the front appeared to come to a point. He wondered how long the clan had been isolated.

The similarities of their features, however, did not extend to their taste in clothes. Even to someone like Adam, who had an astigmatic view of fashion, the variety of styles was glaring. The people of Nebos seemed to sport the fads of every age and every ringdom all at once.

The eldest of his dining circle wore a tall, black fur cap, a black cassock, and blue paint on his prominent eyelids. He leaned into Adam with an accusatory squint. "Oh god, it *is* him. Ida is going to be insufferable."

"*Going* to be!" The woman at Adam's side sniffed dryly. She wore a sleeved basque, the bodice of which pinched her so fiercely it drove the blood to her throat and cheeks. She looked positively sunburnt. "Haven't you heard? Ida Allod has reinvented the art form!"

They all laughed, but without any joy. When Adam joined in, the joke abruptly ended.

The hairless young man across from Adam wore a glass mask that encompassed the entirety of his face, which could only pose a great inconvenience for dining. The mask, which bubbled out like a watch crystal, had the effect of making his head look like an egg. He said to Adam, "At least you're not your sister. She would've started a riot."

"Why can't one of my subjects wander into town?" the elder moaned.

"Because they're all dead, Ove!" the egg-headed youth replied. "When was the last time you released a new scintillation? Ten years? Twenty?"

"Mediocrity hurries! Genius dawdles!" Ove barked back. "Shoveling out smutty little reveries fortnightly is not the same thing as building a worthy body of work, Master Frey! We are in the business of reminding our audience of the boundless mystery of the human condition, not their prurient urges."

The youth puckered his lips as if he meant to spit. "If entertaining is a sin, then I am a sinner. Though I can understand why you would think art is all yawn and no quiver." The mask muffled the youth's voice like a head cold.

Ove loaded his lungs for a retort, but Adam interrupted, asking, "Excuse me, are you docents?"

The red-cheeked woman said, "Oh, my dear, darling little whiffet, yes, we all are! We've come to have a look at you and to talk about ourselves. It's a time-honored tradition."

A droning sound rose above the chatter. Something darted through the air overhead. Adam assumed a bird had wandered into the hall. Then he lifted his chin a little more and saw that the air teemed with dozens of translucent dragonflies, each as large as a seagull.

He shouted in surprise when one of them plunged past his nose. The thing's wings beat so rapidly they seemed to smudge the air. The dragonfly had come with cargo. It deposited something upon Adam's tray and, its chore complete, rose and darted off once more.

Adam stared at the tall glass that stood before him and the greenish sphere that filled it.

"It's just lime sorbet, darling. It whets the appetite," the corseted woman said.

"Oh, isn't eating just the most tedious thing?" the bubble-faced youth said to Adam as if he would naturally agree. "There's only one way to be full, but ten thousand ways to hunger!"

"The only thing tedious at this table is you, Frey," the woman said. Then her eye fell to Adam's place setting. "Oh, you don't have a parfait spoon. Here, darling, use mine."

When she presented Adam with the her long-handled spoon, he thanked her, and immediately tucked it into his coat pocket where it clinked against its twin.

Everyone laughed, then laughed again when Adam asked the elder Ove if he might borrow his parfait spoon. In short order, Adam had collected everyone's spoons, and the breast of his coat bulged with the loot.

Adam had never seen people so pleased to be robbed. It seemed an effective icebreaker, too, because the conversation poured forth. He learned more about the nature of scintillations. They were generally brief performances, lasting no more than a half hour, and often much less. Each docent professed a unique style and preferred genre. The corseted woman, whose name was Jelka, said that she was known for presenting her audience with riots and frenzies, a genre called *Pandemoniums*. Ove created vignettes called *Anthronalogies*, which he described as being concerned with "the profundity of human squalor." His most famous work was a scintillation called *The Washer Woman and the Gravy Spot*. Frey, the masked youth, was known for producing what he described as "scintillations of an explicit nature, which explore the artistry inherent to carnal activities," or as Ove put it, Frey was the city's foremost smut peddler. The two remaining docents, who had said next to nothing since the meal had begun, appeared awed by their inclusion in the conversation. They were students of the art form and declared their subgenres to be *dare-me-nots* and *pugilisms*.

"Well, enjoy your irrelevance while you can, young men!" the youthful Frey said without apparent irony. "Nothing ages you so quickly as scrutiny!"

Adam also learned Ida Allod was roundly disliked by her peers. Only a year earlier, she had been a relatively unremarkable docent who specialized in chorus lines. Then she had released *The Daredevil's Brother*. It was a scintillation the likes of which no one had ever seen. Allod had devised a novel technique that allowed her to produce a much longer and more intricate work. What irked the other docents (even more than her success) was her steadfast refusal to share her unique process with them. Of course, docents had tried to pry it from her with threats and compliments, and some had even attempted to observe her at work, but all to no avail.

A dinnerfly returned to retrieve Adam's sorbet, which he had not touched. "But what *is* a scintillation? How are they made?" he asked.

Jelka said, "Well, darling, I think the only satisfactory answer is to see one for yourself. The grande dame is showing her famous *Daredevil* at the Cavaedium this evening. At least you can rest assured that the subject of your first scintillation will be of some interest to you." The sound of the gong filled the hall a second time, and Jelka reached over to pat Adam's hand. "And I don't care what Ida says. I like you better in the flesh."

Before Adam could digest the remark, their thrones parted, turned about, and renewed their sickening reel.

Each course of the meal arrived on the wings of a glass dragonfly and was shared with a fresh batch of strangers, all of them docents, all more or less alike, or so it seemed to Adam, though he was wise enough not to voice the heretical opinion. Each docent was convinced they were a creative phenom, a luminary, an original. Who was he to argue?

Adam continued to brazenly steal cutlery from his fellow diners, and they continued to take the burglary as a joke. Their wealth was apparently so boundless that treasure no longer held any value. Adam carried in his pocket enough platinum to purchase an airship, one much newer than the *Stone Cloud*. He could leave now, collect his friends and his sister, find a shipyard, procure a vessel, and fly so far from the Tower, it would set behind the horizon and never rise again.

But even as the vision played itself out in his head, he knew he was not ready to leave. He wanted to know how he had come to be the subject of a scintillation, who had been spying on him, and why.

It wasn't until the final course that Adam found himself reunited with Ida Allod. The famed docent, still dressed in her sanguine tuxedo, had the air of a regent humbling herself to dine with inferiors. She radiated superiority and condescension. The moment their circle was complete, the four other docents began to cut their eyes at her and whisper to one another. Their loathing seemed to please her.

"I meant to ask you before," Ida said, drawing a napkin from her lap. She daubed the immaculate corners of her lips. "How is Voleta?"

"Oh, she's fine. Still a pest who takes every request as a call for mutiny. Her hair's a bit shorter; she's a bit taller," Adam said, slipping again into the arrogant tone that the docent seemed to respect. "I think you'd still recognize her, though. She has one of those faces."

"I've figured out why I did not recognize you at first. You seemed so unlike yourself."

"Funny," Adam said, and reached across to his neighbor's tray and plucked up an unused butter knife. "I don't feel like anyone else." He dropped the knife into his overloaded pocket.

"You misunderstand," Ida Allod said, folding her napkin in shrinking triangles as she went on. "I'm just accustomed to knowing you as you exist in my scintillation. That version of you is so compelling because it is consistent; it is a distillation of all your tempers, impulses, and desires. It is the soul of you, the true you. This version—the one with cutlery in his pockets and crumbs on his chin—this is the sometimes-you, the shadow-you. The scintillation of you is eternal. I have given you that. It is a gift few ever receive."

Ignoring the blackberry-crowned custard that a dragonfly had just delivered, Adam said, "You're saying that your scint is more me than I am? That makes no sense. Without me, there is no scintillation. It is the echo. I am the voice."

Ida bared her teeth, effecting one of the most unconvincing smiles Adam had ever seen. "This is difficult to explain to someone who has seen so much of the world but absorbed so little of it. But I will try." She drew the jeweler's loupe from her vest pocket and began worrying it as if it were a charm of inspiration. "An analogy. You're familiar with painting as an art form, I assume? I think it's a little primitive, but it has its appeal. My daughter is certainly taken by it." Ida appeared to interpret Adam's insulted scowl as sufficient answer. "Let us consider the model of a great and exalted work of art. Let's say this model is a young woman. She is to herself, of course, a reality. She is conscious, as much as any individual can be, she has hopes and aspirations and a murky sense of the world." Allod counted these virtues upon the fingers of one hand; then tallied the imaginary woman's faults upon the other. "But she also is pliable, malleable. Her self-awareness is blown about by daydreams, hand mirrors, shopwindows, flirtations, disappointments, dances, and biscuits." When she ran out of fingers, she dropped her hands to her tray as if in exhaustion. "She changes constantly—and does so because she is always looking outward. She is a prisoner in a cell trying to picture what the prison looks like. She is a mystery to herself."

Adam heard a rushing sound that he realized after a moment did not signal the arrival of another swarm of crystalline insects. No, the roar was coming from within. His blood was boiling.

Ida appeared entirely unaware of Adam's rising anger as she continued her homily: "But once a master painter peels away her pretension, denudes her, poses and paints her, she at last can glimpse what she truly is. Not some flighty, flittering, farting girl, but an icon. A beacon. A truth." The docent's voice trembled with passion.

Adam trembled with a different sort of emotion.

Allod raised a glistening blackberry to her lips and, just before popping it in, said, "You'll see for yourself soon enough, Adam. Tonight, I will show you your truth."

Chapter Nine

The night is haunted. I cannot sleep for thinking of home—home, where my son still rocks in his cradle; home, where my love's hair is still red as a cardinal. Our garden is green. Spring is unending. I grow old in the company of youthful ghosts.

—from the diary of Joram Brahe, captain of the *Natchez King*

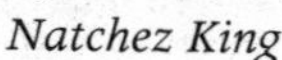

The sky was a deepening purple by the time they left the Mingler. Ida Allod drew in her wake a retinue of a dozen or so persons, most with the bloom of academia still brightening their eyes, and all apparently hoping to distinguish themselves in the presence of greatness. When the luminary passed her daughter and Adam waiting in the street, she paused long enough to say that she expected them to follow close behind. She didn't want them to dawdle, lest they in their languor delay the gratification of her adoring fans. Adam ground his teeth until they squeaked but managed to tilt his head in receipt of the command.

"I know that face. What did she say to you?" Runa asked as her mother strode on.

"Oh, you know. She just called me a shadowy farting girl—something like that."

"That doesn't sound like her at all. She's usually so supportive. She once called my work 'excessively bony' and 'a sad little mewl for help.' "

"Seems fair," Adam said. "I suppose I should be grateful. I owe her my life, don't I?"

Runa looked suddenly miserable. To cheer her up, Adam reached into his pocket and proffered her some of his spoils. "Teaspoon for your thoughts, madam?"

She smiled thinly as she took the spoon and studied it, seemingly to avoid having to look him in the eye when she replied, "You don't owe her a blessed thing."

As soon as the gloom began to blot the gleaming spires with shadows, a whole new battery of lights, red and white, shone forth from the aerials, the rooftops, and the undulant edges of the extravagant skyline. Nebos seemed to have put on her evening jewels.

Adam and Runa followed behind the docent and her fawning disciples as they paraded down the middle of the empty street like revelers after last call. More than once, Ida seemed to concoct some excuse to twist about—to answer a student's question or pay them the compliment of her notice—but each time she turned, she did not fail to mark Adam's presence, a fact that did not go unobserved by him.

"Your mother seems to think I'm going to make a run for it," Adam said to Runa as he waved to the docent, who found his salute unamusing.

"It wouldn't be the first time someone ran away," Runa said. "Most of her friends, my father, me... all of us eventually dashed off when she wasn't looking. Though, to be fair, that was most of the time."

Adam sensed he'd struck a nerve, and not wishing to drive her back to the dark mood she'd so recently escaped, he changed the subject, and asked about the curious glass mask Frey had worn at dinner. The ostentation was not unique to the bald youth. Adam had noticed that several docents wore similar watch crystals pressed nearly to their noses.

"It's so they can look at themselves," Runa said. "They're called overlay masks. The inside is polished so that you can see your reflection superimposed upon the world."

Adam scoffed. What an extravagant sort of narcissism! Walking around with a looking glass strapped to your face had to be the absolute pinnacle of vanity, he thought.

In a city of bejeweled golden towers, the Cavaedium turned out to be remarkable in its modesty. Adam had expected another golden shrine, but instead, he was faced with a wooden structure—the only one in Nebos, according to Runa. The structure was squat, circular, and devoid of windows. A single narrow entrance, framed with bark, stood under a hand-carved sign that read THE CAVAEDIUM: MIND THE LIGHT.

The interior was similarly humble. Adam had prepared himself for a theater, but there was no vestibule, no stage, and no seating. The round walls of the Cavaedium contained only a valley of lush, dark grass. Already much of the ground was occupied by groups and couples who sat upon blankets or lay on the slope in an array of finery and dinner wear. A frosted lens of translucent glass capped the Cavaedium, further dimming the already wan evening light. Here and there, the air blinked with the green nodes of fireflies.

The only feature that interrupted the lawn was a golden mortar in the valley's basin. The barrel of the stout cannon pointed directly upward.

At the periphery of the vale, pressed against the walls, musicians warmed their instruments. A pale conductor with a long, braided queue stood between two individuals who Adam took for singers. The young man and woman perused the pages of their sheet music with stiffened postures and tranquil expressions.

Runa led him to an open spot on the incline, and they sat down in the cool grass. Adam watched Ida Allod descend the hill. She was intercepted again and again by members of the audience who wished to shake her hand or speak a few words. She appeased them with perfunctory phrases and economical gestures. This seemed a part of the performance, too—this gauntlet of admirers, worshipping the entranced artiste as she made her way to the stage.

Once Ida reached the mortar, she began tinkering with the cranks and dials that crowded the gun's carriage.

As irritating as he found the docent's affectation, Adam was quickly pacified by the languid atmosphere of the space. He began to relax. It seemed more natural to recline, so the two of them lay back on their elbows and took in the fashions of the other loungers: a mistletoe circlet, a black cocked hat, a pair of silk turbans, and a quail feather boa. Amid his survey, Adam discovered he was the object of many glances and gawks. He decided not to encourage the voyeurs with his own attention, which seemed better spent on Runa.

Her demeanor had changed again. She seemed neither arch nor withdrawn, neither cagey nor curious, nor any of the other many moods she had shown him over the course of the day. Instead, she wore a tender and disarming expression. She reached toward him. For a moment, he thought she was going to touch his cheek. A draft seemed to blow through the long-shut, unexplored chambers of his heart, pushing open doors, sweeping up the dust.

Then she gently plucked a firefly from his collar.

Runa let the insect crawl around her open palm, the limits of which it explored like a castaway on an island. "My father loved fireflies," she said. "He studied them for years. He once told me that their light produces almost no heat, which means that the chemical reaction that generates the glow is almost perfectly efficient. Nothing wasted. They shine very, very bright, but do not burn." The firefly opened its wings and flew away.

"The way you talk about him, I... I assume he has passed on?"

She looked down when she replied, seeming to answer a question he had not asked. "I'm sorry, Adam. I hope you'll forgive me."

Before he could voice his confusion, the mouth of the mortar began to glow, and the orchestra pounced upon a five-note melody that was as trite as a doorbell. The ceiling shone like an alabaster lamp.

Standing by the base of the beaming cannon, posed with one hand in her pocket and one clasping the air, Ida Allod spoke with her usual resounding, uninflected authority. "Welcome, friends. Welcome to this evening's performance. This is a once-in-a-lifetime event for me, for you, for all of us. Because for the first time, I will share my vision with the object of my inspiration. For the first time, artifice and artifact will join in communion." She had laced her fingers together—a symbol of unity—then swept an open hand in Adam's direction as if she would hold him in her palm. "Tonight, at last, a masterpiece gazes upon itself."

The audience clapped. Allod nodded at the air so sharply she seemed to peck at their applause. She produced from her jacket pocket a small, gilded cannonball. She said, "I give you *The Daredevil's Brother*!"

Allod raised the sphere to the mouth of the mortar. It made a muffled whump when it fell into place.

The ceiling began to waver and peak like milk rippling in a pail as light fanned out from the bore of the mortar. A lonely flute struck up a lullaby as a vague ochre-colored oval emerged from the pool of white above. The oval became an indistinct face that seemed to float freely. The visage drew closer, grew larger. It seemed a young woman, though her features were all but colorless. Then, slowly, red came to her lips, her eyes darkened, and her cheeks blushed pink. Her black hair was pulled back, though a strand hung loosely, and dangled toward the watchers on the lawn. Adam had the queasy sensation that there was a giant outside, bending over the building and peering in at them. Then a pair of fat hands and fatter arms swung up from either side of the image and reached for the face. They were unmistakably the arms of an infant, which, though impossible, had to be the source of their perspective. They were peering through newborn eyes.

Though her features were still a blur, the woman was familiar to him. As Adam tried to think how he might know her, a third arm, also an infant's, swung into view from the periphery. It reached for the strand of hair. A second child lay alongside the first.

Then the arms and face flashed away, and the scene vanished, erased by two bands of color, vivid as a flag: the shocking blue of an afternoon sky and the drossy gold of buffel grass. The cellists in the Cavaedium began to bow a minor key, evoking the chugging rhythm of a locomotive. Someone blew upon a wooden train whistle. The sound lifted every hair on Adam's head. The ceiling filled with a vision of billowing steam and sleeting coal dust as the cellist's staccato slowed, then fell still.

A voice from the verge of the Cavaedium called: "My name is Adamos Boreas, and this is my story."

Adam lifted his head from the lawn long enough to see who had spoken: It was the young man he'd mistaken for a singer. Then the swimming colors above reclaimed Adam's attention.

There, the turmoil of clouds resolved upon the plate glass of a shopwindow. The general store's display contained pitch-sealed kegs labeled *corn*, *rice*, and *flour*. A bright red tin drum stood on its edge, propped against a zinc washboard. The toy seemed out of place among the sacks of sugar, pyramids of soap cakes, and jars of pickled eggs.

Even as Adam suffered the nausea of dawning revelation, the focus changed from the contents of the shopwindow to the two persons reflected in the glass.

And there he stood: a beardless youth beside his sister, who was grinning like an imp. Her black curls had been blown into knots by the rail cars passing beneath the boardwalk. She wore the cornflower-blue dress their mother had sewn for her. The waist hung crooked, the shoulder was patched, and the hem of the skirt was unraveling. Voleta had always been hard on her clothes.

She looked so young.

Voleta held up two small coins. In the reflection, Adam's younger self frowned at her. She stuck out her tongue.

He still remembered the day. It was his birthday and his mother had sent them to the store with two pennies to buy licorice whips for dessert. But instead they had—

The woman at the verge spoke when Voleta's mouth moved, giving a foreign voice to her familiar image, "I'm going to buy it for you. But you have to promise to share."

The man acting as Adam's voice said along with his young reflection, "Don't be stupid. We don't have enough money. We're getting the licorice and going home."

"No, we're not! I'm going to turn these two pennies into a tin drum. I have an idea for a dare, a new one, and Harry said he'd put up a shekel to see it. Come on!" Voleta's reflection turned, and she ran from the frame of the shopwindow. The view followed after her, and then the Depot of Sumer—the city upon stilts, and killer of fathers—filled the ceiling of the Cavaedium. Once more, he beheld the depot's gray clapboard buildings, the steaming troughs and warped boardwalks, the islands joined by rope and plank bridges that swung and bucked in the gust of passing trains, all slowly baking to brittleness under an unblinking sun.

The vision bounced as he ran after her.

Violins sang as the actor giving voice to young Adam said, "That's my sister, Voleta. She is a brat, a daredevil, and my responsibility. I fear it is my fate to one day watch her fall. Will today be the day I witness her extinction? It is my birthday. Thirteen years ago, I came into this parched world, already thirsty."

Voleta stamped across a rope bridge, skipping slats and ignoring the rope handrails. She slipped under the arm of a bonneted woman who was blocking her way. Young Adam's hands flew out to steady the unsettled pedestrian. "Our home is an island of wood and rails in the grass sea of western Ur. And today, Voleta is going to gamble her life to win me a drum upon which I shall learn to beat the rhythm of my manhood." A timpani began to play a slow, booming heartbeat. "Because if I am to protect her, I will have to become what I am not: elusive, decisive, and unburdened by the morality of men. I must become her net. But will I have the strength to catch her when she falls?"

The thoughts were wrong, the words were not his, but the vision... It was not a trick. It was not a play or recreation. It was the past, just as it had happened, just as he had beheld it.

Inside the Cavaedium, Adam stood on unsteady legs. The incline very nearly tipped him forward. The grass glowed with the bounced light of the scintillation. Cocking his head back again, he saw Voleta look over her shoulder down at him, watching him shiver through a hole in time. Then she cut the corner between a boardwalk and a bridge and leapt over the open air. The violins in the room swelled with the thrill of her transit.

Adam shouted, his voice crag with emotion, "What is this?"

Someone in the grass shushed him. From the well of the valley, Ida Allod pressed a finger to her lips. Adam staggered down the hill through the unhappy audience toward the docent. He had never felt so detached from himself. They were not his hands that gripped Ida by her bloodred jacket, not his arms that shook her, not his voice, though it seemed to come from his throat, that roared: "That's me! That's my life!"

"Yes, it is," Ida replied with infuriating poise. Adam tried to jolt the calm from her. Forks and knives fell from the pockets of his dinner coat, stabbing the tender ground. The music died, though the cannon light continued to blaze mutely upward behind the grappling pair. Men from the audience stood and gathered. They seemed about to pry Adam from Allod, but the docent waved them away. "No, no! Let him! Let him rage. Adam has never had an opportunity for catharsis. This, *this* is the Adam I know."

Adam felt his heart beating inside his fists. "How are you doing this?"

Ida Allod replied as if it were a simple thing: "I took these visions from the eye the Tower took from you."

Chapter Ten

It is bad manners to inquire into an airman's past and imprudent to divulge your own. We must behave as if each of us emerged fully formed, not from a womb, but from a sculptor's block.

—from the diary of Joram Brahe, captain of the *Natchez King*

As his life flashed on behind him, Adam broke from the Cavaedium in search of air, though he found only more of the same rich, humid, unstirring atmosphere. He felt like he was drowning in cream.

He wrenched the tie from his throat and threw it into the immaculate gutter. He needed wind, and since there was none, he had no choice but to make his own. He began to run.

He wished for the lamp of the moon and a sky bountiful with stars, but not a single celestial body pierced the fog overhead. The city lights bounced against the dome, drawing a mockery of the cosmos. He ran through the empty streets of paradise as if pursued by hounds.

For the moment, he didn't care how the cruel trick was technically done. He did not believe in magic, but even if that proved to be the cause, he was neither curious nor impressed. No, he wanted to know how his eye had found its way from the squalor of the lower ringdoms to the roof of the world. Was this the fated destination of every eye that was plucked out in the Parlor? Were the Nebosans behind the barbaric practice of blinding unlucky tourists and desperate rogues?

He had gone into the Cavaedium hoping for a chance to prick Allod's ego, and had emerged wishing to destroy everything he saw. He wanted fire, the most unforgiving pyre ever to burn. He wanted the golden city to melt and pour down the Tower like candle wax.

He ran until his legs were rubber, ran until the road gave out. He stood in a bed of daisies with his forehead pressed against the diamond wall, his hands spread flat, fogging the glass. He panted and surprised himself with a sob. Beneath the abrasion of his anger lurked a deeper wound—something like shame, but more helpless. He felt like he was standing naked in a public square. Who knew what the rest of his scintillation revealed? No wonder the Nebosans treated him with such casual familiarity. They had seen his life laid bare, had scrutinized and weighed it. They were all experts in the subject of himself. *Adam is a thief. Adam doesn't tell jokes. Adam has never experienced catharsis. This, this is the Adam I know!*

He did not hear the bandy until it stopped in the street. Adam pushed himself off the barrier and began stalking away through the flowers. He didn't wish to be seen, didn't wish to be cursed by anyone's pity or insulted by their superior opinions on his life.

Runa called after him, "Wait, Adam! You don't have to run from me. I'm not here to catch you. I don't want to take you back."

He swung about to face her, and the fury in his heart leapt to his face. It pulled back his lips; it bared his teeth. "Why didn't you tell me? You steal eyes and use them for light shows? You lie on lawns, and have clockwork slaves do all the work, and then argue about who's the bigger genius. You are a city of ghouls—perverse, unfeeling fiends who have for some reason decided to turn my life into an amusement and put words in my mouth. This is sick!"

Runa raised her hands, reaching for his shoulders, but he turned away, and her arms withered back to her sides.

He wasn't finished: "And you, painting away in your toy castle, do you have any idea how much we suffer down there? How much I've suffered? My sister? Is her imprisonment by a groping sex slaver part of the show? What a fun little scene that must be! Is there an encore where you get to see the moment my eye is pulled from my head? I bet that gets a real round of applause." She tried to speak, but he raved on. "You know what the funny thing is? If you asked any one of those poor wretches down in the Market or the Basement or New Babel what they think happens up here in the clouds, not a single one would guess that you're up here watching them like Peeping Toms as they suffer for your pleasure!"

Runa's mouth was as round as her eyes. She waited as if to be sure he was finished, then said, "I agree. You're right. It is disgusting. We are a horrid tribe. If I could walk away from—"

He gripped the hair at his temples and shouted, "You should've told me!"

"I should have. I didn't know how. I'm sorry."

"You've watched it before. *Adam doesn't make jokes*. That's what you told me the first time you saw me. Well, I suppose not the first time. I thought you didn't like scints."

"I don't. I hate them. I think they're exploitive and dishonest and mean. But everyone was so in awe of this revolutionary masterpiece, and my mother was so insufferable about it, I finally broke down and watched it just so I could tell her how horrible it was. And I did. I called it pretentious, jarring, hackneyed. I told her that you weren't a likable subject at all, that you didn't deserve the sympathy or attention or the affection of the ladies moaning on and on about how handsome you were—"

"Oh, thank you very much," Adam said, throwing up his hands.

"I wanted to make her angry! I succeeded. And this is my punishment. You are my flail. She told the accord I should be your warden because I wasn't charmed by her scintillation and would not be impressed by your fame. I could be relied upon to be vigilant, unwavering in my duty, to shoot you if I had to. But really, she did it just to turn my nose in her success, to put me at the center of the endless, insatiable vortex of her ego."

"Well, I'm sorry this has been so unpleasant for you."

"Adam, please. Please. I know you are the victim here. But I need to say something. Please, just..." She patted the air as if she were searching for something in the dark, then gathered her hands into a wringing ball. "What I told my mother after watching your life, after it had been cooked down to three hours and passed through the filter of her insanity, it was not the truth. Because when I looked past the sappy music and the dumb monologues my mother wrote to dramatize your misery, what I saw in you was someone who was not like us. Someone who was willing to sacrifice themselves for love, someone who was *capable* of love. You carved yourself to bits for the sake of your sister. You were fearless and resilient and, though a thief, more honorable than anyone here. And I—"

Upon hearing the word *honorable,* Adam balked. Shaking his head, he said, "You don't know me!"

Runa looked drawn and thin and fragile when she said, "No, I don't. Which makes it all the more absurd that I... I have all these tangled-up feelings for you. I know I don't have any right to them, but I can't change how I feel."

Adam turned and stared back at the trampled white flowers. He didn't know what to say. What would've been a welcome revelation an hour ago now kindled no joy. There was a resounding sort of emptiness inside him. He saw again the giant's oval face that had looked down on him in the Cavaedium and the reaching infant arms. He knew her now. It was his mother, and the arms were his own.

He sighed, coming around again as he pulled a shining hodgepodge of forks and knives from his pocket. "You know, there was a time when this would've been enough to buy my sister's freedom. This would've carried us home, or somewhere else. Somewhere better. This would've seeded a new life."

"It still can. I know the windstile guard on duty, Catherine Evreux. We're childhood friends. She'll open the gates for you if I ask. You could leave now. If you climbed up, I'm sure you can climb down again."

Adam frowned as he played the scenario through. He wondered if he would be able to climb down by hand; it seemed a harrowing prospect, though in truth, even if he could snap his fingers and be back at the dinner table with Voleta and his friends, he knew he would not. Not yet.

"I'm not finished with this place. There's too much left I need to do," he said, returning his loot to his pocket.

Runa seemed surprised. "But there's *nothing* to do here. That's why we're all mad."

"I want to correct the record. If I'm going to be known, I want it to at least be the truth. I'm going to rewrite your mother's scintillation."

"I don't think she'll let you do that."

"I think she will."

"Where do you want to start?"

"I want to know how the scintillations work."

Runa nodded, hands on her hips. "We'll have to start from the beginning. First the history. Then a demonstration. Eventually, you'll have to meet the Conservator, but let's not get ahead of ourselves." Already, she was walking back to her chariot, not looking to see if he followed. She seemed grateful for a distraction after her unrequited declaration.

She was smiling by the time he joined her on the bandy. "I need to stop by my place to pick up a few things. Then, I suppose it's time that you picked out a house."

Adam had never once in his life felt like the king of anything. And yet, when Runa pushed open the door to his very own home, Adam felt for a moment as lordly as a cock on a roof.

She assured him that all the igloo-like homes were, more or less, the same. They boasted a small garden, a patch of lawn, and a winding path to the door without a lock. The homes were divided like a walnut into two hemispheres. On one side was a common area and a kitchen; on the other, a large bedroom with an adjoining bath. Some of the domiciles were a little larger to accommodate families, but many were built for one or an intimate two.

What most distinguished the homes was how they were furnished. Some were overstuffed with tapestries, gewgaws, lamps, and sofas. Others were like shrines to austerity, containing nothing but a mattress on the floor and the luxury of a single chair. The home Runa had recommended to him was uncrowded but comfortably arrayed with simple but sturdy pieces.

Adam followed after her as she explained the esoteric secrets of his domestic slaves. Here was a vent that blew warm or cool air at the turn of a dial. Here was a shower that spat water of any temperature from nearly every direction at once. It was like a storm caught in a closet, she said. In the kitchen, an electric oven warmed without the assistance of fire and an icebox cooled without ice. Food could be summoned via a switchboard on the kitchen wall, which contained rows and rows of buttons, each bearing a label: butter, tea, apple, meat, bread, and so on. Runa pressed the switch for *pudding*, and said that before the hour was up, a dinnerfly would deposit the dessert on his doorstep. They unpacked the valise Ossian had given him and hung his jacket that rattled with cutlery inside a wardrobe that slid open at a touch with a gasp of compressed air.

Their tour complete, Runa turned her attention to the wooden crate she had retrieved from her garden folly. She pulled back the thin tarp of canvas that covered it, revealing a dozen or so small, gilded spheres and a larger leather-wrapped cylinder. Adam recognized the balls at once. They resembled the munition Ida Allod had loaded into the mortar inside the Cavaedium. They were cannonballs that turned memory into light.

Picking one up, he said, "Are you *sure* you don't like scintillations?"

"Those aren't scints. They are espials. I know that doesn't make sense yet, but bear with me. Here, sit down. I'm going to make tea, and you're going to learn a little history."

"What sort of history?" Adam asked, pulling out a chair from his kitchen table.

"The sort that ends with a clan of simple folk presiding over jars full of eyeballs inside an empty paradise."

Nearly two hundred years ago, the Tower stood complete but crownless. The pinnacle was a windswept bald pate occupied by pipits, swallows, and an unassuming, beardless hermit. The Brick Layer slept in a bentwood yurt and subsisted—so the stories went—on the fruit of a single potted fig tree. He sat on the lonely verge of heaven for years, building in his mind a vision of a capital unlike any other, a utopia that would epitomize human imagination, ingenuity, and beauty. The Brick Layer meditated and fasted under the stars until the city of Nebos rose from the pools of moonlight, frost, and guano like a desert mirage.

His plans made, the Brick Layer spent nearly a decade scouring the nation of Ur for workers who possessed the talent and the temperament the labor would require. He found his people in the mountain crags of Arriga: a clan of miners who had dwelled within the lightless fissures for nearly a millennium. They were an adaptive race who filled their lungs with strangled air, shrugged off rockslides, bathed in blizzards, and mined the earth with the diligence of ants. Despite the great wealth of gold and silver they had amassed, the Arrigans were virtually unknown to the world. They prized isolation over imported comforts and discretion over fame.

The Brick Layer transplanted nearly two hundred smiths and their families to the top of the Tower where he revealed to them the shining city bottled inside his head. The task of extracting that ideal would take nearly three generations to complete. Children were born, grew tall, fell in love, married, produced children of their own, and eventually died inside the Brick Layer's unfinished dream. The Arrigans bore the cold, the wind, and a meager diet of desiccated fruit and salted meat without complaint. And after the diamond dome was poured, they did not balk when the Brick Layer asked them to study botany, agriculture, and irrigation. The same clan that had once pulled riches from the jaws of mountains now teased green shoots from imported soil.

When the last tree was planted, the Brick Layer charged his pale-skinned farmers with a third task. They would become spark-smiths, engineers, and machinists; they would lay an electrical circulatory system, assemble automatons, and build the bolt cannons that would safeguard the city.

When the spire lights flared to life for the first time and the city buzzed with clockwork slaves, the Brick Layer offered his faithful flock a choice: They could return to the frozen clefts of their forefathers, or if they wished, they could remain and become the stewards of Nebos. In addition to maintaining the automatons, they would defend the city from the hordes who'd come to press upon the glass like a glutton upon a bakery window.

The vote was quick and unanimous.

The culture of the lapsed mountain tribes—once defined by rockslide, yak wool, and grit—was quickly expunged by their new purpose and an environment that asked little of them but gave much in return. Their former austerity wasted in the span of a generation, and what grew in its place was an entitled sort of indolence, a holy boredom. They basked in the honeyed glow of the spires their fathers had built, napped in the dewy gardens that no winter ever stripped, and hurled ruination at all comers.

The Tower was finished at last. It was, the Nebosans agreed, a very good life.

"Which brings us to this," Runa said, lifting the leather-shrouded cylinder from the wooden crate. She set the parcel among their empty teacups, then peeled the cover away.

A valve wheel dominated one side of the unpolished copper drum. Its handle, painted a lurid red, seemed to cry out for a twist.

But Adam knew all too well what happened when you turned a blinder's screw.

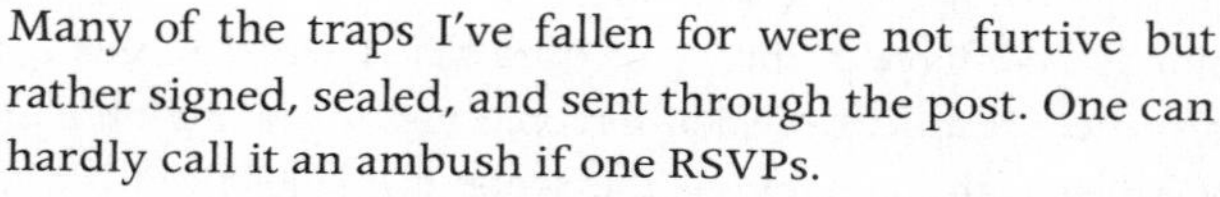

Chapter Eleven

Many of the traps I've fallen for were not furtive but rather signed, sealed, and sent through the post. One can hardly call it an ambush if one RSVPs.

—from the diary of Joram Brahe, captain of the *Natchez King*

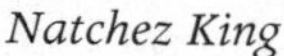

Adam's chair clattered to its back as he leapt to his feet. He seemed to fall backward through time, landing in a tangle of white sheets and strong arms. Four nurses pinned him to a rattling hospital bed. He arched his back till he thought it would break and screamed in the foreign tongue of animal terror. Then, as it would again and again in haunted dreams for years to come, the blinder descended over his head, and the world was split in half forever.

Adam leaned heavily upon the kitchen table. The cylinder was missing the valve wheel that activated the terrible mechanism inside. He would later learn that valve's rather grisly name. It was called a skull key.

His voice quavered when he said, "Why do you have a blinder?"

Apparently stunned by his outburst, Runa replied faintly, "We call them reliquaries."

"I don't care if you call them raspberries! What they do is blind people!" Adam shouted.

Her eyebrows leapt with the abrupt realization. "Oh. Oh my god. I'm so sorry. I don't know what I was thinking. They're just so commonplace, I forgot that... I'll put it away." Her hands trembled as she rewrapped the grim instrument.

Adam took a deep breath. "I haven't seen one of those since—" His voice faltered, and he cleared his throat. "I just want to know why. Why do those things exist?"

Runa tucked the loathsome parcel back into the crate. "Because the Brick Layer was overly cautious, perhaps neurotic. More than anything, he feared forgetfulness. He hated the thought of an engineer or a gardener dying and taking all their expertise with them."

"Don't you have books?" he asked.

"Absolutely. We have a library of libraries. There are racks and racks of manuals; there is an entire shelf devoted just to the maintenance of the dinnerfly," Runa said, conveying the scope of material with a stretch of her arms. "But the Brick Layer understood that he had delivered us all to a point of such advancement that the written word just wasn't an efficient means for conveying everything we needed to know. He was afraid that if the wrong person died, or a catastrophe wiped out half of us, the survivors would be doomed. That's why he created the reliquaries, so anyone could look through the eyes of a machinist, or a spark-smith, or a horticulturalist—could watch and rewatch as they welded a seam, or patched a wire, or grafted a branch to a trunk, until they could mimic what they saw. We were supposed to only take the eyes of the recently dead, and only if they agreed to—"

"I wasn't dead! I was very much *not* dead. I don't understand why anyone would even want my eye. I was an eighteen-year-old expert in nothing!" Adam said, his rage surging again.

"I know, I know," Runa said, attempting to calm him with a quieter tone. She reached for his shoulder, then thought better of it and dropped her arm. "My point is, the Brick Layer had good intentions, but was shortsighted and overly ambitious. Though he had assembled all the espials we would ever need to keep the city well-lit and the air fresh and the gardens growing, he wanted more: He wanted a collection of human genius. He..." She held up a finger as if to shush herself. "You know what, he can explain it better than I can."

Runa retrieved from a shelf an object that Adam had mistaken for an ugly vase at first, though on second look, he saw it resembled the mortar from the Cavaedium, though in much smaller proportions. Blowing the dust from its barrel, she declared it a "projector," an appliance common to every house in Nebos.

"This first espial is of the Brick Layer giving one of his more well-known speeches. We all had to watch it in school. The observer who donated his eye was a man named Bihto Calmmi, a popular singer at the time, who thought this a deserving contribution to the record."

"Why do you have it?"

"I was trying to draw the Brick Layer's skull," Runa said as she dropped the golden ball into the mouth of the machine. She picked up the projector and, looking up, began lugging it about the room. Adam realized she was searching for a blank spot in the ceiling. Finding an open space between fixtures in the dome of white plaster, she sat the projector on the floor. "Turns out, it's harder to peel off a person's skin just by looking at them than you'd think."

"I don't think I've ever thought about peeling—What are you doing?"

She dragged a heavy, woolly rug across the room. "The floor's hard." He watched as she positioned the thick rug near the projector and sat down upon it. "How are you at reading lips?"

"I can tell when someone's called me a name in a noisy pub. That's about it."

She patted the open spot beside her. "All right, I'll narrate for you." As Adam lowered himself onto the shaggy rug, she flipped a switch on the projector. They lay back together and watched the beam of light splash upon the ceiling, then resolve into a tidy circle of green and gold.

Adam discovered that he could appreciate the marvel a little more now that he was not the subject of it; the ability to peer back through time through the eyes of another was nothing short of miraculous, though it took him a moment to ignore the peripherals of the viewer's own face. The side of the observer's nose and the hairy ledge of his eyebrow were both visible, though out of focus. Quickly, they became as invisible as the frame of a painting. The observer stood at the front of a crowd, a fact that was revealed by a sweeping glance. Some sat upon the grass. Children picked blueberries from a hedge, collecting the fruit in the bowls of their untucked shirts. In the background Adam saw the uncapped pyramid rising above the trees.

The Brick Layer stood on a crate at the head of the crowd. He was perhaps sixty years old, deeply tan, and even with the boost of a box, still quite short. The white hair on his head was closely shaved and thick as a brush. He had prominent ears, cheeks that were carved by laugh lines, and a warm, alluring gaze. A necklace with a barrel charm bumped upon his breastbone that showed beneath a half-laced shirt.

"Huh," Adam said, feeling mild surprise that the vaunted figure looked like a farmer come in from the fields for lunch.

Though truth be told, Adam could've fit everything he knew about the Brick Layer into a single sentence: *The Brick Layer built the Tower.* Of course, on reflection, there was no way that could be true. Adam just presumed that appellation of "the Brick Layer" was more a title than an individual. By all accounts, it had taken many, many centuries to raise the Tower. The foreman who began the work and the one who finished it were surely not the same person.

The Brick Layer's mouth began to move, and Runa gave voice to his words. "Friends, it is tempting to think our work is finished. We have accomplished so much. We have raised a finger to the heavens. We have planted a garden among the clouds. We have breathed life into machines that will ease our days and serve our children. And yet this is not the end. No, this is a commencement. It is the beginning of the Tower's ripening. And we must not neglect its fruit."

The Brick Layer paused, his eyes scanning back and forth. Veiny hands blocked the view for a moment as the observer applauded.

His speech resumed in Runa's voice: "I propose a new undertaking. I propose we assemble all that is remarkable, meaningful, or beautiful in the Tower and conserve it for posterity. To do this, we must be humble. We must ask our brothers and sisters below what they believe should be preserved. Let them submit their beloved composers, bakers, inventors, sculptors, poets, winemakers, weavers, and on and on... I cannot imagine what genius they will send us, because I do not know what we lack. We will seed the Tower with reliquaries, and ask them to entrust us—the city of hods—with the espials of their idols."

As the light of the projector faded, Adam rolled onto his elbow and said, "That doesn't make sense. The Brick Layer wanted to keep everyone out of Nebos but also absorb all the brilliance from the Tower? And how is this a 'city of hods'?"

A musical jingle, light as a cat bell, rang the air. Runa stood and fetched a small tray from the stoop. She returned holding a bowl of lavender custard and two spoons. "There's disagreement about that. Some people claim the Brick Layer said 'the city of gods,' not the 'city of hods,' which is moronic because we are obviously not gods, no matter what my mother thinks, and also ridiculous because the Brick Layer wouldn't have gone to all the trouble of building paradise just to give the custodians somewhere to live. We like to forget it, but we are a clan that has more in common with roofers than royalty."

"Well, why didn't the Brick Layer correct them?" Adam asked, taking the offered spoon, though he hadn't any appetite. "How did you go from collecting genius to trafficking in eyeballs?"

Runa said the answer to those questions would require a few more espials, a little recitation, and a bottle of red clover wine, which she procured from a cabinet and poured into crystal flutes. As she sipped her pink nectar, Runa began the answer that would take her half the night to finish.

The reliquaries were distributed to the ringdoms with the Brick Layer's compliments and an invitation for the people of the Tower to submit the eyes of their luminaries. To secure the transmission of these sacred, irreplaceable artifacts, the Brick Layer converted a small shaft, once used for ferrying blueprints, into a dumbwaiter. The small car could be called and dispatched by any ringdom, though only for a single purpose—to deliver reliquaries to the care of the guardians of Nebos.

The terminus of the dumbwaiter, set snugly against the diamond dome, resembled a springhouse with river-stone walls and a moss-covered roof. What might've been unassuming in a more pastoral setting stood out like a wart in the paradise of gold and glass. The Brick Layer called the structure the "Cupel of Babel," an implement familiar to smiths. A cupel was a vessel used to separate gold from lead. So would the springhouse filter the precious from the commonplace.

In the years after its unveiling, the Cupel was considered one of the city's most august military posts. It was an honor to receive the preserved visions of the Tower's prodigies. The first reliquary to arrive drew a crowd. The reliquaries were extracted from the dumbwaiter with perfect reverence and, in the early days before the practice grew tedious, with a little fanfare blown upon a trumpet. At the end of each day, the lumenguard who welcomed those immortal treasures loaded them onto a ceremonial bandy, garlanded with ivy and white roses, and drove them past children waving from parks down to the underground and the vault of the Delectus, where the noble Conservator resided.

Decades passed. The Brick Layer died unexpectedly, and it was like a great ship had shed its rudder. After generations of purpose, direction, and expansion, the Tower seemed an aimless thing. Some thought it a natural progression: Once a volcano builds itself up from the ocean floor and establishes an island in the sea, what is there left for it to do but to cool and subside and turn green with the crust of life?

Still, with the Brick Layer gone, the ringdoms began to first neglect, then forget the purpose of the dumbwaiter. Some ringdoms sent word that they were withdrawing from the ghoulish bargain for reasons of good taste and a lack of volunteers. Other ringdoms bricked over their dumbwaiter doors without notice or explanation.

Then there was the problem of the Parlor, which sent reliquary after reliquary, day after day. The lumenguard doubted that a single lowly ringdom could churn out so much genius with such regularity. It was a suspicion that the Conservator would ultimately confirm when he announced that the eyes were apparently being removed from unwilling and living persons. The bureaucrats of the Parlor appeared to be laboring under the misapprehension that the reliquaries were part of an obligation to the Tower, similar to the maintenance of the fires. Failure to submit reliquaries, the Parlor's management informed the Nebosans, would result in their own eviction, which was perhaps the first time in history that a tenant forced a payment upon a landlord.

Of course, the Nebosans denounced the barbarous practice at once, and tried to correct the confusion regarding the imaginary duty, but no number of sternly worded letters or grim-faced ambassadors could convince the managers of the Parlor that there was no need to collect the eyes of the innocent.

The roses on the ceremonial chariot dried, crumbled, and were not replaced.

Being posted at the Cupel of Babel lost its charm, partly because the loathsome effort seemed pointless, and partly because the reliquaries that the Conservator rejected had to be cleaned out by hand, a process that bore an unlikable resemblance to cracking an egg. The detached eye contained within the ocular vault was suspended in a red glowing medium that smelled like a hog wallow. The vaults were opened over a glass urn that caught their contents with a sickening *plop*. The urn gradually filled over the course of weeks and months, until it could hold no more. Then the foul-smelling vessel, brimming with eyeballs, was capped, sacked, and buried in a park in the dead of night.

The glut of tragic reliquaries inspired first a crisis of conscience, then a cynical malaise, and eventually a creative revolution when a band of enterprising young artists began to intercept the unwanted ocular vaults and review their contents themselves. Rather than search for subject matter that was instructive or profound, as was the Conservator's charge, they rummaged through the lives of strangers for entertainment and voyeuristic pleasure, for instances they found *scintillating*.

Since the raw espials could only be viewed in real time, many aspiring docents spent days, weeks, even months watching another's life flicker in reverse while they searched for a single scene that was sufficiently arresting, enticing, or arousing. Unlike the Conservator, the docents lacked the technology to edit the visions they curated. Scintillations were, as a result, only a few minutes in length because while pleasures in life are brief, the tedium between joys is long.

The Cavaedium, which had been built for public education, soon evolved into a playhouse and a hub of entertainment. Musical scores were composed for and performed with scintillations. Scripts were written with the guidance of lipreading, which had become an almost ubiquitous talent. Voice actors were a natural innovation. The art form evolved rapidly. Though the greatest leap forward would not come until the arrival of a certain daredevilish girl and her ever-vigilant brother passed under the nose of one Ida Allod.

Adam shut his eye and rubbed it with one knuckle. It felt as dry and brittle as rice paper. They'd watched hours of espials as Runa exposed and explained the sordid history of scintillations. He felt no less repulsed by the so-called art form, but at least he understood how such an abhorrent practice could emerge from noble aspirations.

He still had many questions—not least of all, what had happened to the Brick Layer—but the hour was already very late, and Runa had begun to talk with her eyes closed and her cheek sunk into the shag of the rug. She seemed to have one foot in the valley of dreams when she murmured, "No one knows how she did it, my mother, how she edited your life. She has to be an enigma. Always a riddle. No one could possibly understand how deep she runs. She is a mys..."

When Adam was certain Runa was asleep, he rose and crept to the front door. Runa had assured him there was no need for locks, and yet he felt better once he'd wedged the back of a kitchen chair under the doorknob. He slunk to the bedroom, feeling like a burglar in his own house, and pulled his dinner jacket from the wardrobe. Wishing to avoid a clamor, he emptied its pockets onto the bed's plump duvet. Once his fortune was arrayed there, pretty as a diadem, the impulse to hide the loot seized him. Searching the room for a suitable spot, he discovered a plate in the wall held in place by four screws, which he removed with a butter knife. The cavity behind the panel was draped with wires that were wrapped in a variety of colorful thread. Beneath this rainbow, he buried his treasure inside a pillowcase.

It wasn't until he had begun to replace the screws with the knife that the absurdity of what he was doing struck him. The screws were made of gold. The plate was gold, too, as was the front door, and its hinges, and the roof above him. He could be rich beyond reason, beyond sense, beyond use. Suddenly, he wasn't sure whether his little sack of treasure was too little or too much. Would it impress his sister and the captain?

All his life, Adam longed for someone's approval. His mother, his Parlor superiors, even Finn Goll, whose occasional praises warmed him like a father's embrace.

But now that he was surrounded by people who esteemed him, he felt no less hollow, no less incomplete. And it occurred to him that the only approval he'd never courted, and certainly never won, was his own.

When he asked the question: "What do *I* think of me?" The answer was like an expanding pit, a sinkhole that had been thinly covered by the opinions of others. He found that he thought rather little of himself. What was there to admire? His intermittent loyalty? His unwanted mothering? His penchant for glumness? His greed?

Flopping onto the pillowy duvet, Adam stared at the cracked plaster of the ceiling and the gold glimmering beneath. He wondered why the Brick Layer had been so frivolous with his fortune. Why had he called it a city of hods? Runa had said that the great foreman died unexpectedly. Perhaps the Brick Layer had died before his work was finished. Perhaps the Nebosans had mistaken a respite in activity for the end of growth. Perhaps the Tower was not yet complete. Not every stone had found its place.

Perhaps the same was true of him.

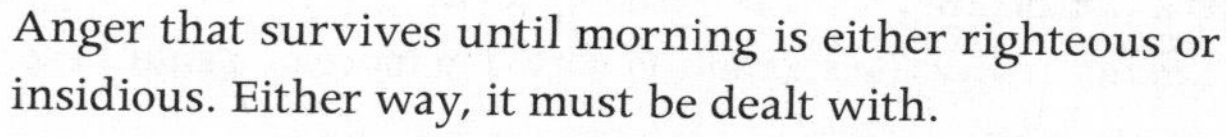

Chapter Twelve

Anger that survives until morning is either righteous or insidious. Either way, it must be dealt with.

—from the diary of Joram Brahe, captain of the *Natchez King*

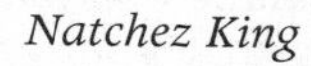

The hammering of a fist was accompanied by a throaty shout made insensible by the drumming. Adam sprang from bed and charged into the kitchen just in time to collide with Runa. Both of them gave a startled squawk, which only quickened the pounding.

When Adam pulled the chair aside, he had to leap back to keep from being swatted by the door as it flew open. Elrin's height required him to duck under the lintel, which only made his entrance seem more bullish. He had Adam by the shirtfront almost at once. When Adam attempted to return Elrin's hold, his efforts were foiled by the snugness of the sergeant's leathery uniform, so he had to make do with gripping a fistful of beard.

Then Elrin appeared to hear Runa's calls for him to stop. He looked at his sister with an expression of astonished relief, though it quickly curdled into anger. He dropped Adam and began backing Runa across the kitchen, ranting as he went: "Mother said to let you go last night, and I did, but when I went to your folly this morning, Celeste was sleeping in your bed, and you were nowhere to be found. I gave the bonded band a tug"—he raised his arm, pointing to the black cuff—"and when you didn't pull back, I thought, my god, he's killed her. She's dead! Buried! The worms have her! But, no! Instead, here you are, caught in the act—"

"What act?" Runa said, interrupting both her brother and her retreat.

"You know what act!"

"What? No! No, I was just asleep."

"Look, it's not my business if you want to muddy your sheets with an outsider, but you can't just disappear like that. If you'd been strangled, Mother would've killed me." He brandished a finger at her nose.

"Mother would've yawned," Runa said, and activated her own bonded band to jerk her brother's hand from her face.

"And I'm not really the strangling sort. I'm more of a smotherer," Adam said.

Elrin huffed with ironic laughter. "Well, I wouldn't have put anything past you after your performance last night. You were incensed! Raving! You're lucky Mother is so unflappable."

"Of course I was mad! Your mother revealed that she's been building her celebrity on the back of my childhood, and then acted as if it were a great honor," Adam said. He began buttoning up his shirt cuffs, his jaw sawing upon his anger as he did. "Speaking of your mother, I'd like to see her. I want her to show me the rest of this fairy tale that you all think is my life's story. Just because you can read lips doesn't mean you can read minds or interpret motives or—"

"Oh, I'm afraid not." Elrin crossed his arms, smiling at some private joke. His blue eyes shone when he said, "Your day is already booked, recruit."

"What?" Adam said, his confidence softening.

"Every able-bodied Nebosan must answer the call. So. Welcome to the lumenguard, Private Boreas. Time to go. We need to stop by the barracks and slap some armor on you. You can't go on patrol in a rumpled tuxedo."

"What's the duty?" Runa asked, her mouth drawn tight with concern.

"Oh, it's everyone's favorite." Elrin clapped Adam on the shoulder and shook him. "We're going to the Fundament!"

The tiled barracks echoed with a symphony of squeaks, the splatter of showers, the high conversations of those at the beginning of their shift, and the exhausted mumbles of those returning from patrol.

The long underwear Adam was given to wear beneath the armor was made of flocked wool: a material that proved ideal for wicking up sweat, which was just as well because he was already dripping. The unbreathing rubber suit smelled like something that had been pulled from a drain.

Though Elrin insisted it was the smallest they had, Adam's armor was still several sizes too large. It bagged at the knees, and when he let his arms drop, his fingers fell out of the attached gloves, which then swung like udders until he waved his arms over his head and wriggled his fingers back into place. These spontaneous gestures of exaltation struck the other soldiers in the changing room as the epitome of hilarity. Elrin said it was not his fault that the lumenguard's armory did not stock children's sizes. Whatever friendliness had existed between them the day before had obviously spoiled overnight. Adam suspected Elrin was more infuriated by discovering his sister asleep under the same roof as a "muddy foreigner" than he let on.

They called it a barrack, but Adam found the facilities more luxurious than anything in the Baths. The benches were made of some sort of ceramic that was warm to the touch. Every locker was as stately as a grandfather clock and fashioned from an exotic metal called aluminum. The only thing that spoiled the environment was the stale reek of bodies and the incessant chirping of rubber.

Adam discovered that if he made and held a fist, he could keep his gloves in place, though of course, that meant he struggled to pull on his boots and fold his clothes and shelve them in his locker. Drawing his sidearm, he suspected, would be nearly impossible, though that was no loss. At first, Adam had been excited to learn that every draftee, by law, had to be armed. The big lightning throwers, the ones that could bring down an airship and which required a backpack to power, were called "ionastras." Elrin said that they weren't necessary for their patrol, which would carry them under the dome rather than outside of it. For narrower quarters, a more discreet weapon was required. A small arm he referred to as a "dianastra."

Elrin unholstered his sidearm to show off the svelte weapon. The dianastra had no hammer, no frizzen, no pan. The muzzle was no larger than a peppercorn. The barrel tapered at both ends, and the grip was set nearer the center than the back. It looked a little like a silvery yam on a stick, though an elegant yam and a handsome stick. Intrigued, Adam held out his hand to receive his sidearm.

But Elrin holstered it again and retrieved from his locker a much different pistol. It seemed a parody of the one he had just shown Adam. It was made of duller tin and dented in several spots. Elrin pointed the barrel at his own temple and, pinching his eyes shut, squeezed the trigger. Adam jumped when a snapping spark leapt from the muzzle, traveled about an inch through the air and died with a pop.

Elrin held the pistol over the bar of his forearm as if it were making a ceremonial presentation. Adam took the toy with a glum expression and fired a second spark into the air.

"You'll be assigned a dianastra at the end of your probation. In the meantime, keep your sidearm close, Private. Our mission relies upon it!" Elrin said with a decorous snuffle of laughter. "Now for the rest! The lumenguard visor is one of the most remarkable pieces of technology in our arsenal." Elrin took a helmet from a long shelf of smirking heads. "It allows you to peer through fog and dark and across great distances. It can track the movement of two objects at once... well, you won't be able to do that last part with only one eye, though honestly, it's probably just as well because it takes a lot of practice and even more vomit. Let's make sure the respirating vents are open since we won't be going outside..." Elrin peered into the helmet, located a dial near the neck and turned it. The smirk broke into a semi-grin, one that contained a barred vent rather than teeth. The result was somehow more unnerving.

Adam did not want to give Elrin the satisfaction of seeing him flinch a second time in as many minutes, and yet it took all his determination to lower the visor over his head. The claustrophobic dark that followed was distressingly familiar though mercifully brief. A beam of green light struck his eye, then quickly resolved into a vision of Elrin's left nostril. Adam had to reach out his hand to convince himself that Elrin was not standing at his toes. Elrin laughed at the errant swipe, but soon explained that Adam could broaden his view by widening his eye, while squinting would focus on objects that lay farther off.

It took Adam a moment to acclimate to the mechanism, but once he did, he found the ability to telescope his view of the world enthralling. It was like the first time he'd been given a magnifying glass as a child. He'd spent the remainder of that afternoon peering at monstrous flies on the windowsill and the faces on stamps, drawn finely as fingerprints.

He continued to experiment with the telescopic function as he rode through the city aboard a bandy at Elrin's side. He trained his eye on the needle point of a spire, then on the petals of a flower, then on melons in a garden, until he understood why Elrin had mentioned vomit. He quit the game to stop the lurching of his stomach.

Adam had been told the visors would relay his voice to the ears of every man and woman in the troop, and yet no one answered when he asked what the Fundament was, and why it required patrolling. He tested the depths of the silence that ensued with a few hellos until Elrin's voice, bracketed by a burst of static, funneled into his ear. "There's no reason to jabber at us, Private. You'll see for yourself soon enough."

The sergeant steered the bandy down into the Warren. His prior foray into the tunnels hardly made them less mysterious or more comprehensible now. The usually chatty Elrin was silent as he focused on leading the train of six bandies through the tangled intersections and animal-themed stations of the blue-lit underground. A small wheeled cart had been hitched to the tail of each bandy. This addition required special attention around tighter corners. They passed through a section, brightened by crystal ducts that carried the effervescing slow water, and soon after, they crossed a gloomy intersection where the thrum of the Nautilus cut through his armor, making his bones purr against his muscles. And still the way before them sloped downward and the empty wagons chattered like teeth and the troop held their silence like a talisman against the onset of confusion, claustrophobia, and dread.

When Adam could stand the silence no longer, he asked a new question, one that was simple and contained. He could only hope that Elrin would not call it jabbering. "How did the Brick Layer die?"

The finger-drum of the bandy's treads filled the silence. After a moment, Adam assumed that would be his answer, but then Elrin surprised him by saying, "He was the victim of a construction site accident. A capstone was being transported by crane to the base of the pyramid when some of the lines snapped. Poor devil was crushed under his last brick."

Even as he grappled with the idea that the Brick Layer had been stamped beneath the heel of the pyramid's capital, Adam discovered that the silence had been more fragile than he'd thought as other members of the troop began to pipe up with their own answers. A private with a phlegmy voice said, "My father told me it was sabotage. The Brick Layer slept with someone's wife, and he got what was coming to him."

"Obviously, it was suicide," another higher voice said. "How else do you explain the fact that he was standing underneath the stone as it was being moved? You don't survive the raising of sixty-four ringdoms by being so careless. The man just couldn't stand the thought of retireme—"

A third, more dulcet voice began speaking before the last had finished: "No, he was killed saving a child who'd wandered under the path of the stone. It was just a horrible accident, and the Brick Layer died doing what he always did: looking after us."

Adam was surprised to find there was so much disagreement over the basic facts of what could only be considered one of the most important deaths in human history. Surely there had to have been eyewitnesses? Adam had learned, where there were eyes, there was the possibility of a permanent, indisputable record.

Before further theories could be aired or he could inquire after the existence of an espial of the death, Sergeant Allod silenced them all, his tone sharp and humorless. Adam was surprised the same man who'd been as happy as a hound while shooting down airships was in such a poor temper now. There seemed to be something about their present assignment that set his teeth on edge.

Then the tunnel, which had been coursing along at a gentle grade, sloped sharply down, curving as it did. Elrin did not apply the brakes. If anything, he seemed to lay on more speed, the force of which pushed Adam to the bandy's sideboard. Adam clung to the rail and tried to keep from following his top-heavy head overboard. What seemed a curve quickly turned into a tightening coil. The wagon leapt behind them. The bandy banged over the seams between floor plates. Adam wondered if Elrin hadn't lost control, but when he looked, the sergeant's posture showed no sign of distress. In fact, he seemed calmer now than he had before.

Adam had known stevedores who played with loaded guns, men who stuck their hands into boxes of scorpions just to snatch at pennies, men who dropped knives between their naked toes, a game that grew progressively easier as the playing field gradually cleared. These violent gambles were meant to lance the boil of a cancer that grew too deep to eradicate—depression, anxiety, numbness. Adam wondered if Elrin was one of those whose torment was soothed by needless risk. The thought stirred a tinge of pity in him.

The corkscrew road broke upon a circular bay that was just large enough to accommodate the circling of six bandies and their wagons. Centered in the room stood a small, rectangular stage enclosed on three sides by a thin rail. The rest of the chamber was nearly devoid of fixture or ornament, though as Adam climbed down from the chariot, he marked a pattern of scarring on the floor, a ghostly grid of some sort of adhesive or mortar. The room had been tiled once. Looking up, he saw bare wires jutting from conduits in the ceiling, evidence of former light fixtures, perhaps. The Fundament appeared to have born the start, but not the conclusion, of some ambitious renovation.

"Private Boreas," Sergeant Allod said, laying a heavy hand on Adam's shoulder. "I know you hate to pass up an opportunity for heroics, but I'd like you to stay close, keep your mouth shut, and try not to get in anyone's way. Is that understood? Good."

Adam followed, squeaking and stumbling and cursing under his breath. He caught up with the sergeant as he collected an old oil lamp from where it hung on the stage's rail. The glass and brass antique looked slight and fragile in his gloved hand. Set into the wall behind him were two panels: one gridded with a pad of numbers, the other marred by a half-dozen axe blows that obscured its original design.

Raising the shade on the lantern, Elrin said, "All right, Private, it's time to do your part."

Adam cocked his head in confusion as his visor filled with snickers and laughter, which flash-boiled Adam's temper, though he managed to keep his rage from spilling out of his mouth.

Elrin spoke over the laughter as he held the lamp out to Adam. "Your sidearm."

Understanding at last, Adam drew his battered pistol, set the muzzle near the gleaming wick, and fired a spark. His vision flared white with the lighting of the lamp.

"Good work, Private!" Elrin returned the lamp to the rail, then approached the panel in the wall. He pecked at the keypad with his pinky finger. The floor quivered beneath them as a weighty gear engaged. A vertical seam appeared in the wall and began to expand amid the groan of machinery. At first, Adam thought he was being crowded from behind, nudged forward by his fellow guards, but he soon realized the opening door was pulling at him. He grabbed the wheel of a bandy as his boots squeaked upon the floor, inching toward the widening dark.

The draw of the vacuum slowly subsided as the gap continued to grow. By the time a punctuating clang marked the end of the cycle, nearly a quarter of the bay stood exposed to the open air, or rather, to a violent storm.

The wind coursed in a single direction. It coiled upward, howling like a train through a tunnel.

"Come take a look, Boreas. It's quite a sight," the sergeant said.

Releasing the chariot wheel, Adam forced himself to approach the threshold. He had assumed that the presence of wind meant the chamber opened to the world outside, but he realized at once that they were still within the confines of the Tower. The bay appeared to hang like a stalactite inside a great, unlit cavity. The inner walls of the Tower were set some two hundred feet away. The stone cavern, which appeared to be roughly circular, was ringed by a battery of titanic vents. He couldn't tell whether they were inhaling or exhaling the storm.

The wind carried with it an array of domestic debris: Pages, dresses, curtains, and canvases enlivened the currents that streaked past Adam's nose. It was difficult to see through the frenzy, though he thought he glimpsed something directly across from them—a shimmer in the gloom, an interruption in the mammoth blocks that composed the Tower's internal wall.

"It's like looking up a tornado's skirt, isn't it?" Elrin said. Adam thought it a needlessly crass comparison, but he could not deny the resemblance the bottled storm bore to the twisters that carved the plains of Sumer like the black talons of an irate god.

"What are we doing here?" Adam asked. In answer, Elrin clucked his tongue and reminded him that he wasn't allowed any more questions. They had work to do. They had to launch the windscow.

As Adam was shooed from the entryway, he observed a lumenguard crouched before an open panel set inside the central stage's riser. They appeared to make several small adjustments to the battery of controls secreted there. Once they had closed the cover and backed away, a light began to emanate from beneath the stage. This luminous skirt grew brighter as the stage began to float. Adam could not guess what mechanism or magic buoyed the hovering barge, but it seemed to float upon a film of wavering air. Before he could study the miracle further, the thing Elrin had called a "windscow" slid forward past the boundary of the bay and out into the storm.

"Private Shaw, the signal, if you please," Elrin said, and in response, one of the lumenguard toed the edge of the chamber, drew his dianastra from its holster, and fired a seething bolt into the air. It bounced between objects in the whirl of trash, igniting them and drawing a scotch of flame over the abyss.

Though it had no pilot, the windscow's course did not seem in doubt. It traversed the chasm in pursuit of the twinkle Adam had glimpsed on the far shore. He trained his telescopic lens on that apparent goal, and through the static of flying objects he saw a lamp, sister to the one fixed to the front of the scow, hanging upon a pole at the mouth of a tunnel. Figures began to converge upon the cave's edge, their shaved heads catching the lamplight. They could only be hods. There appeared to be dozens of them. No, hundreds.

It was a moment more before Adam realize he was looking at the end of the black trail.

Through the telescopic eye of his visor, Adam watched a procession of hods lay their burdens upon the docked windscow. What began as a scattering upon the open bed of the floating sled quickly accumulated into a pile, then a heap, then a hill. He watched the arrival of unpaired dining room chairs, framed works of art, rolled carpets, musical instruments, and open crates as they were surrendered by one wretch after another, each at the end of a march that may have taken months, years, even a lifetime to complete.

Runa had called them "gifts," but Adam saw quite clearly what they were—offerings, desperate offerings from a maligned tribe thrown upon the floating altar of the sparking gods who sat atop the Tower as if it all were just a plinth built to hold and display their wealth. No wonder Runa had been ashamed. Adam pictured Ossian's overflowing storeroom, filled to the ceiling with unwanted sacrifices destined to be fed into the Nautilus's gulping void.

The windscow, now burdened to its rails with domestic goods, pushed off from the mouth of the cave, steered by the same automated pilot that had guided it out. And suddenly Adam understood how the blizzard of dreck was fed. As it sailed along at a walking pace, the barge was robbed of its lighter cargo. Handkerchiefs, parasols, slippers, and stationery blew from the mound like cinders from a fire. All told, the windscow would shed nearly a fifth of its freight over the course of its return, losses that appeared to concern no one.

To Adam's surprise, five of the lumenguard took up a defensive posture with their dianastras drawn and trained upon the windscow as it slid back into the bay. Even before it had settled to the ground again, the five lumenguards who had not drawn their weapons rushed to the sides of the scow and began to unload the disheveled heap onto the bandy-drawn wagons. For a moment, Adam wondered why half of the guards were menacing a heap of household goods, but then the natural cause occurred to him. Under his breath, he said, "Stowaways."

He was surprised when Elrin responded to the whispered comment, saying, "They're usually too clever to risk it, but every once in a while, we have to deal with a hod hiding in a sack or cowering under a table."

"Deal with? You mean you shoot them?"

"Not always. But honestly, when we do, they generally seem grateful. The Old Vein is not a charming place."

Adam was about to point out that the Nebosans were an inbred tribe squatting upon a nearly empty paradise that would surely benefit from an infusion of new life and blood. But before he could express the outlandish thought, one of the guards standing upon the windscow said, "I found something, Sergeant."

There was a general commotion as the guards with weapons drawn moved forward, and those without fell back. The object of the furor appeared to be a large crate full of apples that were packed in straw. The fruit seemed to Adam a miraculous product to have emerged from such a desperate place, but the box held something more remarkable still. Nestled amid the hay lay a swaddled bundle.

Adam pressed in to see the round cheeks and staring eyes of the infant who seemed, for a moment, too amazed by the appearance of such strange figures to cry. Then the dam of wonder burst, and the babe began to bawl.

Chapter Thirteen

I hope to be rich one day, but not miserably so. I once rubbed elbows with a gold-drenched lord. He had a staff of dozens, a harem of admirers, and a seat at every table. Yet I have never met a more paranoid, anxious, and isolated wretch. The only medicine for gout is moderation; the only cure for excess is charity.

—from the diary of Joram Brahe, captain of the *Natchez King*

Adam's entire experience with infants was confined to a single afternoon years earlier when he had been dispatched to Finn Goll's house to pick up a parcel. He had walked into a bedlam of children, one of whom had apparently gotten ahold of the package he'd been asked to retrieve, and was now running about the house with it while his siblings chased him.

Before Adam could join in the pursuit, Finn Goll's wife, Abigail, intervened. Holding her youngest child half over her shoulder, she said, "You'll never outrun Liam. You have to ambush him." She presented the infant to Adam, saying, "Here, take Nathaniel. I'll get your package."

Adam would've preferred that she offer him an unwilling porcupine.

"How do I . . ." he began weakly, leaving it to her to intuit the rest.

"One hand under the bum, one behind the neck. His head's still a little droopy, so keep him on your chest. That's fine. Now, don't stand there like a post. Bounce a bit. That's it. He likes you. I'll be right back."

And that was how Adam found himself holding his first baby. It was a squirming, dribbling little person that watched him with round, unfocused eyes like a fish laid out at market. The experience was at once terrifying and strangely exhilarating.

The discovery of the infant aboard the windscow inspired something closer to panic. Everyone began speaking at once, and it was some moments before Elrin could shout them all down. When he did, he decreed that the windscow would be emptied on the double and the infant returned to the Old Vein.

Elrin said that returning the apples would effectively reward bad behavior, and that could establish a precedent. The lumenguard couldn't very well start giving away presents every time a hod sent them a baby in a box.

All this was hashed out over the inconsolable cries of the infant, which had grown so intense that the poor thing had begun to choke.

While the rest of the troop hustled to empty the windscow, Adam undressed. He knew the child would never calm so long as it was surrounded by grinning monsters. Unscrewing his visor, he was momentarily disoriented by how dark the bay was. The only illumination came from the undercarriage of the windscow, which shone with the Sphinx's familiar ruddy light, and the signal lamp that swung in the breeze and threw long, switching shadows. He undid the heavy latches on his chest and shrugged his shoulders free of the swampy suit. The cold wind struck his sweat-soaked long underwear, drawing steam from the fabric even as it turned icy against his skin. He was pulling off his boots when Elrin at last noticed what he was doing.

It seemed to Adam that Elrin only twisted off his own helmet to make sure Adam could see his expression of bewildered disgust. "What are you doing out of your armor, Private?"

"I'm taking the baby."

"No, you're not."

"I'm taking it home. I have room," Adam said, rising to his feet.

"You really are a glutton for applause, aren't you?" Elrin crossed his arms into a squealing knot and bounced on the balls of his feet.

"This has nothing to do with praise. You don't throw orphans back, not if you have a conscience."

"Let's examine your perfectly noble idea for a moment, shall we? If you took the baby home, assuming you didn't drop it on its head along the way, it would be subject to an accord. I'm sure my mother won't argue on the runt's behalf."

Adam stuck out his chin and tried to appear taller, but without his boots on, he had fallen below the sergeant's shoulders. "I'd argue for it," he said.

"Who cares? Best case scenario, they decide to bestow upon you the privilege of delivering it to the Nautilus. And, how do you even know it's an orphan? Really? Its parents might be standing just over there, relieved to have passed along the burden of an unwanted mouth. If it stays, how many more do you suppose will follow? I imagine it wouldn't be long before whole scows overflowing with infants and toddlers and children and adolescents and young men in baby bonnets started flooding in. What then?"

"We raise them. We give them homes. We have the room."

"No, *we* have the room. You have a tentative arrangement. And yet, you think you're going to convince the populace to let our city be overrun with starving, unruly, unloved children? What happens when they grow older and, embittered by their miserable existence, turn upon those who once gave them refuge? You really think we're going to vote for our own eradication?"

"You have no conscience against this?" Adam asked, his hands balled, his feet spread.

"You keep using that word. But we did not summon them. We did not starve them. We did not ask them to burden themselves with children."

"No one asked for you to be born, either, but we're all making do," Adam said.

Elrin snorted. "I ask you, where is *their* conscience? All we have done is tell them no."

"How can you say that when you're standing on their heads! You decorate your houses with their suffering. You squeeze their stolen eyes for entertainment. You take their food! You depend upon them to endure and not rebel, though they have the numbers to. They could pull the Tower down like a clapboard house. Even if only out of self-preservation, you should take this child. Stop behaving as if all that you have is some sort of birthright. The city of gods! That's what you think you all are, isn't it? Gods! Ha! You aren't even a man!"

Elrin drew his dianastra. "The baby goes back, Adam."

Looking about, Adam realized that the other guards had finished unloading the windscow and were now encircling him. More pistols were drawn. The coursing wind outside howled over the infant. The lamp's shadows swiped at Adam like a scythe. He swallowed hard and said, "Then I'll take it back. I'm not going to let a baby roll around on a bare deck."

"Fine," Elrin said, holstering his sidearm with an alacrity that expressed just how small a threat he considered Adam.

By the time Adam plucked the swaddled infant from its bed of straw and fruit, it had grown hoarse from screaming. Spittle shone on its flushed cheeks. Its eyes were bleary, its lids swollen from grief. It did not quiet at once, but as he clutched it to his chest, he recalled Abigail's advice: *Don't stand there like a post. Bounce a bit*. He did, and the child's sobs soon turned into deep, shuddering sighs.

Stepping aboard the windscow, Adam tried to appear unfazed by the fact that he had volunteered to ride upon a floating slab of metal through a pelting storm all to reach what could only be the most loathsome port in all of Ur. And once there, what greeting could he expect from a desperate horde who had begun to cast their children at the feet of indifferent gods?

Kneeling before the control panel in the vessel's hull, Elrin said, "After the windscow docks, you'll have five minutes before it returns. If you miss your boat, I hope you like walking. It's a long way down." His modifications made, the sergeant slapped the cover shut.

The gory light that wreathed the ship grew brighter as it rose a step higher in the air. Adam wished he could grip the rail of the thin barrier, but he could not bring himself to take a hand off his precious cargo. The barge slid forward. The darkness yawned.

It was like stepping into a flock of panicked birds. Silks and rags, wicker and paper slapped at his face and snagged on his limbs before being violently torn away. The spine of a book struck his thigh as sharply as a whip. He winced but resisted the urge to reach for the aching spot. Tucking his chin over the infant's head, he shielded it as best he could with his hands and arms. He had to concentrate to keep from squeezing too tightly. He murmured small encouragements for the benefit of them both, though the wind stole them the moment they left his mouth.

He peered over the rail down at the seething black, which seemed to swarm with monstrous moths. If there was an end to the darkness, he could not see it.

Through a slitted eye, he marked their agonizing progress to the farther shore. There, the pallid light of the signal lamp still shone, illuminating the round mouth of a cave that was rimmed by a weathered frieze. Decades of scouring winds had flattened the figures, yet the scene was still recognizable and strangely familiar. Clean-headed hods gathered in a ring, much as they did upon the Brick Layer's seal, only here they appeared to be lounging. Some of the eroded figures reclined, others stroked guitars, or raised goblets, or loafed in each other's laps.

Even as Adam pondered whether the idyllic pageant was cruelly ironic or merely misplaced, he saw that a crowd had gathered at the cave's entrance. It occurred to him that they might be conscripts in Luc Marat's babbling army. It was strange that such an obvious possibility had been so slow to dawn upon him. He was becoming as reckless as his sister.

Faces emerged through the flying rags of the storm.

Adam expected to be met by a wretched congress of hunger-carved cheeks, and toothless jaws, and eyes like sinkholes. He had seen enough desperation to know what it did to a man's posture, his breath, and his speech, and so he thought himself well prepared.

And yet, he was unprepared to be met with a sea of children.

Hundreds of small, round faces peered at him with wide, unblinking eyes. The older children held infants. The toddlers held the hands of the few adults in their midst, all of whom seemed well into their dotage.

The children parted before his scow, touching its rails, petting its hull with the reverent curiosity of the very young. The moment he passed into the lee of the cave, the wind abated, exposing Adam's senses to a new assault. The black trail smelled like a dead man's socks. His stomach rose but stopped short of a full revolt.

The barge settled upon warty cobblestones, snuffing out the red light it had sailed upon.

The children's clothes were old, but mended; their hair was thin, but combed and parted. Their bodies were lean, but not emaciated, and though they stood in a great mass, there was a sense of order to their presence. A few babies fussed or whimpered, and still, Adam had never imagined that so many children could be so quiet.

Beyond the amber glow of the two signal lamps, Adam could see the passage broaden. The chamber beyond glowed an eerie blue, not unlike the twilight of the porcelmores in the Silk Gardens. When he stepped down, the children recoiled. They seemed both awed and disbelieving. And why wouldn't they be? A god had deigned to cross the abyss at last and had chosen to come in his pajamas.

When no one spoke, Adam realized the burden of a beginning had fallen to him. Which was a shame because he'd had no practice speaking to a crowd. He wished Senlin were there. But, since there was nothing else to do, he filled his lungs and bellowed, "Hello!" His voice cracked mid-word as if someone had goosed him from behind. Some of the children snickered.

He cleared his throat and tried again at a more moderate volume. "Hello, from... over there. We received your many, many fine gifts. They were all very nice. Thank you. Um, but, we, uh, noticed that you... forgot a baby. These things happen. I'm always putting my spanners down and forgetting where I left them. So. Do any of you know where its mother might be?"

The man who stepped forward had been standing near the front of the crowd, though Adam had hardly noticed him because he was no taller than a ten-year-old. His skin was dark, his beard august, and his hair similarly white, but longer and braided into plump locks. He used what appeared to be the haft of an axe for a cane and was dressed in a sarong that was so heavily patched, its base fabric was indiscernible. His strained voice quavered when he spoke, and yet he projected more authority than the visiting god had. "His mother isn't here, but the child was given to me to mind. I'm the one that sent him."

To his surprise, Adam discovered he was not ready to relinquish the infant, despite Elrin's clock, ticking inside his head, and the fact that he had no real alternative. Yet, he loathed the thought of returning an infant to someone who had cast him aside. "Why did you do it?"

"Desperation," the elder said.

The infant in Adam's arms began to babble, and it reached up to feel his cheek. The contact struck his temper like a percussion cap. The words came more quickly than he could consider or censor. "I've been desperate before. I've done desperate things, but I've never left a baby in a crate!" Even as the accusation flew out of him, he knew his anger was misdirected. The person he really wished to throttle stood smirking on the shore behind him.

The elder tapped his stick and tilted his head, as he took all of Adam in. "You're not what I was expecting. Your arm—it's branded. You're missing an eye. You've been through the Parlor. You've got mud on you."

The flame of Adam's anger guttered. Suddenly, the child seemed a weight that, even after he'd let go, he'd never be able to put down. He said, "I do. The city above us is not my home. I'm an . . . unwanted guest."

The elder looked down at a girl with bobbed hair who pulled at his robe. She offered him a braid of hay she had split and twisted to resemble a thistle. He thanked her and tucked the straw flower behind his ear. "Yet, you are here representing them?"

"No, I'm only here because I didn't want to let an infant roll around on a deck in a storm. I can't speak for anyone."

"What a pity." The elder looked back at his gray-haired men and women interspersed among the children. The glance seemed to conclude an argument. Heads dropped. Some turned and shuffled back down the passage, each drawing along with them a clutch of children who followed without command.

Adam sensed the interview had come to a close, but he had one thing more to say. "Don't send any more. They will either ship them right back over, or they'll kill them."

The elder raised an arm and let it drop, a gesture of supreme frustration. "What are we to do? We are caught between a precipice and a long, slow decline. The black trail is dying. The fountains are failing. They are overused and under-kept. The mushroom beds have turned to dust. The Brick Layer's gifts have rotted. We eat beetles and bats and worse."

"And yet, you send them apples," Adam said, swaying to quiet the stirring child in his arms.

"We send them offerings in the hopes that they won't think we're stealing from them. We keep the bruised and half-rotten things for ourselves." He lifted his chin, pride shining from beneath age-hooded eyes. "And why shouldn't we? I won't starve my children to feed a bottomless god."

The old hod's exasperation was contagious, and Adam couldn't keep it from his voice when he replied, "Why are there so many here? Surely there are better places for them? Where are their parents?"

"What stupid questions!" The elder's bark surprised the young girl at his hip who shrank away with a whimper. He leaned over, stroked her head, and hushed her with a flurry of half-audible apologies. When he spoke to Adam again, his voice was more constrained, though his anger was still evident. "I thought you were one of us. Perhaps you do not understand how orphanages work, young man. How often do you see them on a corner of the city square, or nestled in the shadow of the mayor's house? Orphanages grow where the mold does, where the mice nest, where the children won't prick the consciences of people who might have their morning walk spoiled by the sight of something so unpleasant."

Adam began to reply, but the hod spoke over him. "Do I really need to tell you how brutal the black trail is? Can you truly not imagine how these poor dears were parted from their mothers and fathers? Have you never encountered disease, starvation, murder, separation, chimney cats, or worst of all—cruel necessity? As meager as provisions are, we feed them. As perilous as this place is, we are safer here than among the gatehouses and zealot camps. We have all taken a vow to raise them as best we can for as long as we can."

"I'm sorry," Adam said, feeling a shudder of shame rattle through him. "I didn't mean to—"

"Didn't mean to what? Judge us from the kangaroo court of your good luck? These children haven't been blessed, like you, with being an unwanted guest of heaven. They were cursed instead with being an unwanted burden upon hell!"

"I don't think that this is right or fair or—"

"Who cares what you think?" The old hod gently turned the bob-haired girl around and sent her toward the arms of an older boy, who stooped to receive her. When the old hod turned again, Adam wondered if he hadn't removed the girl so he would spare her the sight of him cracking a stranger on the head with his axe handle. But the elder only stacked his hands on the butt of his cane. "You're too young to remember, but hoddery was an honorable vocation once. We were the Tower's porters, her flowing blood. The work was hard, yes, but not inhuman. Of course, that was long ago, before the ringdoms built their skyports, and we became inessential. Before they abandoned our plumbing and siphoned off our water. Before they started flushing their convicts into the walls. That's what they've been doing for generations. They filled our home with criminals and rabble-rousers and debtors. Then they put us all in shackles and locked the doors. They told us that if we did not wish to be here, we could pay back our impossible debts, which double every year, or we could crawl our way down, cross the desert on our knees, and summit the mountains on our bellies!"

Adam winced at how familiar the suggestion was. Finn Goll had needled him with the same false offer of freedom: *If you don't like it here, why don't you just go home?*

The old man went on. "The ringdoms changed the agreement. Now, there will be war, and the children will bear the brunt of it, as they always do. We are caught. We are locked in and locked out. I sent the child to test whether there was any mercy left in those who have decided to accept the burden of our gifts, but not our lives. The fact that you are here is all the answer we need."

Adam approached the old man. The children behind him shrank back. Adam eased the infant from his chest, bundled up the swaddles that had fallen loose, and handed the child over. The elder took him with one arm, and set him upon his shoulder, where the babe seemed to fit as snugly as a dovetail joint.

In the span of five minutes, Adam had felt brave, angry, and ashamed of himself. Now, he felt only an obligation. He'd gone to bed the night before secreting his little hoard of gold. It seemed a low and petty thing standing in the presence of such need. He said, "Don't send them any more food. They won't miss it; and it wouldn't sway them either way."

"Even if we keep it, we cannot linger here much longer. Some of us believe there may still be time for an exodus. We could descend upon the Market before we starve or the zealots begin fighting in earnest. I think even if we survived the descent, we would overwhelm the bazaar. We would be like locusts, and they would greet us as such. It would take a city to absorb five thousand children, not a shantytown."

"Then I'll give you a city. You won't have to stay here long," Adam said, his mind churning upon the problem, even as the skirt of the windscow began to glow, and the stage rose. He took three steps back, and swung under the rail, rattling the signal lamp as he did. His face was a wash of shadows when he turned and said in a voice that sounded much surer now, "Give me a week. Two at most. I'll figure it out."

"Figure what out?" the elder called after Adam, even as the wind began to rise about his ears.

He had to shout to keep the storm from swallowing his words: "How to build a bridge!"

Chapter Fourteen

Men who brag about how they would've risen to the occasion amid some unattended crisis are pigeon-livered liars. There is nothing more flattering to one's ego, nor more insulting to a survivor, than armchair courage and the valor of the parlor.

—from the diary of Joram Brahe,
captain of the *Natchez King*

dam considered himself a most unlikely revolutionary.

He was a conformist at heart. Whether he was shuffling papers in the sham offices of the Parlor or bedeviling tourists in the Market for the enrichment of Finn Goll, he had always believed that if he were sufficiently dependable in his service and flexible with his own values, one day his efforts would be rewarded. For years, Adam had reassured himself that his preference for compliance was not indicative of a weak character. No, he only wished to fit in so that he could better protect his sister.

Though his protection had always been illusionary.

Deep down Adam knew that if Rodion had decided to sell Voleta off to some noble predator in the dead of night, he wouldn't have been able to stop him. And hadn't it been Adam's vow of conformity that had led to his betrayal of Senlin? Voleta had been freed *despite* his efforts, not because of them.

In the days that followed his exposure to the black trail, Adam would occasionally allow himself to entertain a fantasy in which he devised and delivered a public speech so rousing that it thawed the native hearts and convinced the Nebosans to throw their doors open to the children of the hods. But he knew no such magic words existed. He believed the only hopeful solution was to force the Nebosans to face the needy throng themselves, not from a distance or from behind a visor, but in the flesh and in great numbers. Much as his own conscience had been pricked by the sight of so much need, he hoped the Nebosans would rediscover their humanity when confronted with the foundational suffering their paradise rested upon.

To Adam's surprise, his brief adoption of an infant hod became the cause of much celebration in Nebos, though the details of the episode were heavily revised. The baby boy was transmuted into a girl who bore a striking resemblance to Voleta in complexion and eye color. In this version of events, Sergeant Elrin Allod had panicked, had ordered his guard to break their oath for the second time in as many days and bring another outsider into Nebos. But Private Adamos Boreas had pointed out the obvious truth: Somewhere a mother was missing her child, and he was determined to reunite them. Adam had braved the storm, crossed the yawning chasm sheltering the infant from the lashing flotsam, and returned the babe to the arms of her very own mother, who had of course not abandoned her child. No, she had innocently tucked the wee one into a makeshift crib only to have an overeager hod whisk the crate away.

Adam could only guess who had authored and spread this doctored version of events. It seemed to suit the local presumption that the hods came willingly, happily, and bearing gifts from their heart. Still, he made no effort to correct the lies. He could not argue for the truth without revealing his revulsion or his budding plot, so he let the locals have their fantasy.

When Runa appeared on his doorstep that first evening after his patrol, finding his face nicked by the edges of ten thousand flying pages, Adam was elusive about his impressions and evasive when she pressed him for details. He said only that the Old Vein was an unfortunate necessity like sewers or cemeteries or gallows. She seemed shocked by his shrugging apathy, but he made no effort to improve himself in her eyes. As much as he would've liked to trust her then, as much as he wished to believe she would sympathize with the plight of the hods and the necessity of some radical solution, he could not risk including her in his plans.

Though there was not much to divulge on that front. At least not yet.

His initial inquiries were done subtly and under the guise of an outsider attempting to learn more about his new home. He found that he had to make no effort to seek out a native to converse with as his domicile quickly became something of a local attraction. All he had to do was open his front door, poke out his head, and see who was loitering on his lawn. On many occasions, he didn't even have to go that far, as faces would appear in his kitchen window, wide-eyed and peering like children around a fishbowl. He would greet them and answer their questions. Always, they wished to know about Voleta and her amusing, daring exploits. He would recite a venturesome anecdote about lead soldiers, drove spiders, or menacing warships as his audience listened and munched peas from his trellis. Then he would pose a question of his own. He'd ask how did one go about borrowing books from the Libris Library? Did maps of the city and the Warren exist? If so, where could they be obtained? How many windscows were there? What fueled them and for how long?

Not all of his questions were answered—some for lack of knowledge, others, a lack of interest. In fact, the most common form of payment he received for his stories was not answers but silverware. Word of his pocketed cutlery had spread. Often, oglers would arrive on his lawn or at his windowsill with a knife, fork, or spoon in hand. He accepted their gifts and let them pile up on his counter, making no effort to add to the treasure cached inside his bedroom wall.

From this fragmented inquisition of his visitors, he learned that the lumenguard patrolled the Fundament every other day, which left him with a rather small window of time to move thousands of children and their minders. Though he had told the old hod he would build a bridge, the only practical solution was to employ the existent ferry. Unfortunately, while there were indeed other scows in the city, there appeared to be no way to get them to the Fundament. He'd have to make do with one. Adam estimated a round trip, including onloading and offloading of wiggly children, would take approximately half an hour. The windscow had to be refueled once every five circuits, a process that required the replacement of a battery of vials, similar to the ones that fired Mister Winters's arm, but larger. Refueling by experienced persons could be done in half an hour, a time which he doubled in his own calculations. The number of passengers that the scow could carry was trickier to estimate. He paced off the deck's dimensions in his living room and, using books to represent passengers, moved his riders about until he was confident he could transport twenty-four souls per trip.

If he ran the scow through the day and night and allowed for some buffer of time around the commencement of the patrols, he felt reasonably certain he could move 1,750 hods, barring any setbacks, of which there would surely be some.

The old hod had put their number at five thousand.

There was no way around it. He'd need to build a bridge. Or find two more windscows. And quickly, before the orphans were compelled by desperation and hunger into a dangerous retreat down the black trail, into the pitiless market, and beyond into the desert.

The infeasibility, the absurdity of what he had promised the old hod settled upon him on the fifth night. He could dream of bridges and save none of them, or pilot the scow he had, and save a third. But which third? And who would choose?

Adam wanted nothing more than to close his curtains, turn off his lights, and sit on the floor eating buckets of pudding. In short, he longed for a nice wallow.

But his despair had terrible timing. He had already agreed to accompany Docent Ida Allod to another screening of *The Daredevil's Brother.* Though he could hardly think of a more loathsome activity, he knew that his celebrity and the docent's endorsement came with a measure of power and influence, and he suspected he would need both in the coming days. The orphans' lives might depend on his good standing. So, he had agreed to a second showing, and this time, he had promised to keep his seat.

He stood in the lashing shower until his fingers puckered, then explored the bathroom cabinets, finding a straight edge and strop, a brush and hair tonic, all apparently new. He thought of the poor hod who had crawled up through the bowels of the Tower just so a stranger could shave his cheeks and tame his hair. Somehow, the prettier he made himself, the uglier Adam felt.

Docent Ida Allod told him she would pick him up in her bandy. She arrived at his doorstep at the appointed hour of seven dressed in a jade-green tailcoat. The matching trousers were cut so short their cuffs dangled above her ankles. Her feet were bare, her toes long and pale. It was, however, the nearly unbuttoned white shirt beneath the coat that seemed most pronounced. Her breastbone protruded like the knuckles of a fist. Her silvery jeweler's loupe bounced upon those bones at the end of a chain.

Adam did not know where to look. He would've been less surprised if she had shown up wearing a false mustache.

Adam had not seen Runa since he'd lied to her about what had happened on the black trail. She had collected her crate of espials, muttered something about feeding Celeste, and left without looking him in the eyes. The rug still lay where she had slept upon it.

He'd not seen Elrin either, though one of the visitors at his window had told him the sergeant had been demoted on the grounds of his violations of his oath and posted full time at the Cupel. Elrin was now collecting and sorting eyeballs with the most junior conscripts. It was, so the rumor went, a punishment Elrin's mother had made no effort to shield him from.

The same mother who stood before Adam now in a neckline that reached for her navel.

"Let me have a look at you," Ida said. She brushed off his shoulders, tugged at his lapels, and smoothed his shirtfront in a manner that made his stomach churn. His nausea was not helped by the appearance of a bonded band on her thin wrist.

"Is that bound to my cuff?"

"Just looking after my investments. There. Quite handsome," she said at a volume much lower than her usual boom. Somehow, the intimacy of her tone was even more domineering. "You oiled your hair. It looks nice like that. You should do that more often."

"All right," he said, and shuffled forward, expecting her to unblock the door. She did not.

"That's not very polite, Adamos. I know your mother wasn't the most polished woman, but surely, she taught you that it's only civil to repay a compliment. So, tell me: How do I look?"

Having no experience in complimenting women, especially one more than twice his age, Adam didn't know what to say. He stammered out a few unrelated adjectives before recalling what his father had said to his mother once when he was feeling unusually affectionate.

Adam said, "You're as pretty as a cat's eye."

The phrase appeared to puzzle Ida at first. Her inexpressive mouth crimped subtly downward, and Adam held his breath. But then she seemed to decide she was pleased. She paid him the largest smile he'd ever seen her wear, which was still no wider than a thumbnail. "Very good," she said, and turned toward the street at last.

When they arrived at the timber-framed Cavaedium, Adam was surprised by the size of the crowd filling the street outside the theater. Everyone was overdressed, and none of a set. The mob had the air of a masquerade. Before he could disembark from the bandy, a man in a white suit with a matching bowler offered him a silver gravy boat. Adam accepted the token awkwardly. He began to thank the man but could not finish before the bonneted woman behind him reached over his shoulder to force a gold ladle into his hand.

A cheer broke out. They shouted, "Ta-da, Adam! Ta-da, Adam!" A phrase he would later learn was meant to commemorate all the bows he had to take.

Soon, his hands were overloaded with so much silverware, he began to leave a trail behind him.

Adam wanted none of it, of course: not the gifts, nor the cheers, nor the attention. But he needed their goodwill, condescension and all.

When he and Ida passed through the theater's portal, her arm hooked tightly through his, the atmosphere abruptly changed. The boisterous voices fell away. The slope before them was nearly covered over with blankets and bodies, but rather than the lively preshow conversation he'd been greeted with upon his first visit, there hung in the air a composed, conspicuous sort of quiet. He was no longer the object of glances but of stares.

Ida directed him to a wicker basket near the entrance where he could deposit his presents. It seemed to have been provided just for that purpose, as was the tar-black quilt spread out and stocked with a bottle of rose-hip wine and a pair of crystal goblets.

The arrangement surprised Adam, as did the realization that Ida Allod had turned the duty of loading the ocular vault into the projector over to a new dark-haired secretary. When Adam asked if she planned to introduce the scintillation, she just sat down on the quilt and patted the open spot beside her. He tried not to look as if he were squatting on a cactus as he sat down, though that was precisely how he felt.

The docent proffered one of the chalices. Adam took it by the stem. She wrapped her hand over his to steady the cup as she filled it. "You never said thank you."

"Well, you haven't finished pouring yet." He tried to ignore how she stroked the notch between his knuckles with the tip of one finger.

"Not for the wine. No, for securing your medical exemption from service in the lumenguard, of course. Or did you think Captain Dyre had simply forgotten about you? Silly boy. You're fortunate to have someone so thoughtful looking after you." Releasing his hand, she wiped the wetted lip of the bottle with her thumb, which she then drew down the side of her tongue.

Adam suppressed a shudder. "But I'm perfectly healthy."

"Healthy, no doubt." She surprised him by reaching out and stroking his cheek beneath his absent eye. "But not quite perfect."

Despite the fact that both he and the orphaned children benefited from his release from military duty, Adam felt compelled to argue for his undiminished ability to serve. Yet even as he opened his mouth to speak, the docent shushed him and pointed to the valley below.

Once more, the golden cannon fired its light, the dish in the ceiling glowed like a frost-covered skylight as the cellos and violins raised their voices. Three infant arms swam about his mother's face, which emerged again through a keyhole in time.

Having survived the shock of his first exposure to *The Daredevil's Brother,* Adam was able to absorb the scene in the shopwindow more fully. It was strange to see how young he had been. He had felt so mature. And yet, despite the familiarity of the scene, the details seemed wrong. For one thing, the Depot of Sumer was much dirtier and ramshackle than he remembered, and he had not remembered it fondly. Every surface was coated in either black soot or red dust. White steam billowed up from the train yard below. The city looked like an unwell calico cat.

Adam found many of the moments of his life that Allod had spliced together similarly strange. His birthday dinner in review seemed so staid, so unremarkable, though at the time it had felt like the greatest celebration of his life. And Voleta! How he had watched her like a hawk! How quickly he pounced whenever he thought she was walking too fast, or straying too far, or speaking to the wrong sort of person, or the right sort of person in the wrong way. The actor who gave voice to Adam's supposed thoughts (thoughts penned by Docent Allod) narrated a series of small scenes that were meant to exemplify Voleta's recklessness, proof that she was a lamb in need of a shepherd. But Adam saw something different. It seemed she was not running toward something else so much as she was running away from him.

He hardly blamed her.

Then Adam-the-actor referred to Voleta offhandedly as his twin. And Adam turned on the quilt to speak to Ida, only to find her staring at him.

He said, "We're not twins. I'm older by ten months."

"You don't still believe that, do you? No, that's just what your mother started telling you after you both turned four. She told you that Voleta was going to need someone to look after her, and that you had to be the older brother. She moved your birthday back two months, then started telling Voleta she was a year younger."

"What? No, she did not!" He had always been the older brother. He was the deliberating sibling, the voice of reason, the steadfast elder. "That can't be right," Adam said with softening conviction.

"I can show you the moment your mother tells you if you like. But later. Right now, I don't want you to miss anything."

In the circle of light above them, his face appeared in the window of a passenger railway car. Outside, out of focus, the piebald banners of a bazaar crawled by.

He knew the day at once. It was the day that they had pulled into Babel Central Station in the shadow of the Tower.

And yet, the expression his younger self wore was not at all what he remembered it to be. He had once told Senlin that the boy in him had evaporated over the course of their two-day passage to the Tower, and yet now he saw how gilded that memory was. His eyes were wide, his complexion ashen, his cheeks wet. Suddenly he recalled how he had insisted his sister hold his hand the entire journey, even while they slept, slumped in their seats. The scintillation's narrator described this deathly grip as being for Voleta's benefit. His tears were for her! But Adam knew the truth.

He wondered how differently they would have treated each other if they had known they were twins. Would he have admitted that he was afraid? Would he have been quicker to confess his mistakes? Could he have told her that when she ran from him, he felt not only frightened for her, but also abandoned?

The more he turned the question over in his mind, the more he knew Ida was telling the truth, at least in this one regard. He remembered his confusion over his birthday when he was young. He had believed that, while he was certainly a year older, he and his sister had coincidentally been born on the same day because he dimly recalled sharing a birthday with her. He assumed his mother had changed his date so they wouldn't fight over presents or puddings...

The third infant arm that had reached for his mother's face at the beginning of the scintillation—it had belonged to Voleta.

He was sure he could not endure any more revelations, but fortunately for him, once they arrived at the Tower, the scintillation increasingly became the story of two strangers. Entire episodes, which had been essential to his evolution from a nervous youth into a cynical young man, were skipped over, including the months he'd spent working as a clerk in the Parlor. The scintillation rushed forward to the point where Voleta began working as an acrobat in Rodion's cabaret. This version of events downplayed the horror of the situation, making it seem as if Voleta were clamoring for the spotlight. More absurdly, Ida Allod had managed to splice from Adam's vision a picture of Rodion that was nearly sympathetic. In Ida's scintillation, Rodion was Voleta's long-suffering employer who was always having to chase her out of the stage ropes, or extract her from a cupboard, or chastise her for spitting at customers. When she tore her leotard while attempting to climb out a transom window, Rodion appeared to take her escape as some sort of impish prank rather than a desperate attempt to get away from him. In this historical sham, Voleta was happy and hungry for fame, and Rodion bore the brunt of her ambitions.

When the scintillation did not focus on Voleta, it followed Adam as he picked pockets, stole luggage, and slipped rings from fingers. But according to the narration Ida had written, her version of Adam gave these ill-gotten gains to Rodion as bribes to keep his sister on stage longer, to improve her schedule, to remove another dancer who was soaking up too much of the applause. Ida painted Voleta as a mercurial talent, and Adam was her ambitious manager.

It was so far from the truth, Adam knew that even if he wished to, there would be no way to correct the record from this assemblage of events. The scintillation's finale, if one could call it that, was of Voleta swinging on a trapeze over a packed house in the Steam Pipe as he watched from the footwell of the stage. Jets of sparkling wine sprang up around her, the geysers coming from the stands as men shook bottles in attempts to strike her with their affection. The real him had been worried her trapeze would grow so slick that she would lose her grip and fall. But the faux-Adam's parting words were more blithe.

The actor said, "And so may she swing—higher and higher—forever. May she break through the ceiling, burst from the Tower, and soar past the last cloud into the triumphant blue sky!"

When the applause began, Adam automatically lent his own hands to the effort. He fixed a smile on his face for Ida's benefit, who continued to watch him without expression.

As soon as the ovation receded enough to allow it, she asked him what he thought of her scint. He knew her well enough to know that her ego would require many compliments, which had to be thoughtful or at least passingly sincere, and preferably open-ended, leaving her room to expound upon her accomplishment. Because there remained not a person alive who could compliment Ida Allod half as well as herself.

And yet, even as Adam lavished her with praise, privately he thought just how trite the scintillation was. The plot was meandering and episodic, the transitions were jarring, and the philosophical ruminations were transparent and dull. She hadn't imagination enough to conjure motives for anyone that did not reflect her own. This lack of empathy stripped her work of nuance. Her message was parabolic; her characterizations, inhuman.

When she suggested that they adjourn to her offices so that they could review the scintillation scene by scene once more from the start, Adam had already run out of nice things to say. And still, she wanted him to expound upon his enthrallment, preferably somewhere that others were not vying for her attention, preferably, somewhere private.

Adam was quick to say that as much as he would've liked to spend the rest of the night talking about her superlative creation, he was unaccustomed to scintillations and the strain they put upon one's eyes. He said he felt as if his head might pop and asked if they couldn't reschedule. She stroked his cheek and said, "I don't enjoy being around people who are unwell."

In a show of her boundless charity, Ida Allod offered him and his headache a ride home. Adam demurred, insisting the walk might do him good.

Without a thought for his offering basket full of cutlery, he departed the Cavaedium with his collar up and his hands buried in his pockets. He skirted the pooling of the streetlamps in a manner that felt natural. It was as if he'd spent the past two hours back in New Babel, inhabiting the mentality of a grifter—a trustworthy appearance wrapped about a paranoid lack.

That recognition gave him the evening's second revelation. He had, in his plotting to save the hods, fallen into old ways of thinking. Had he learned nothing from Senlin? Faith was not auxiliary to survival. Change could not be won alone. He had tried to escape on his own for years and failed. What on earth made him think he could sneak thousands of orphans into an unassailable city by himself?

He needed help. Which meant he had to put his faith in someone.

Runa came to the door of her garden folly with a paintbrush clenched in her teeth. Not appearing especially pleased to see him, she pivoted about and stalked back to her easel, where it stood before a rib bone on a velvet pillow. She began mixing paint with a palette knife as if she were scaling a fish.

Adam sat on the tatty couch, or the corner that the sleeping hound had left open to him, and leaned forward on his knees. "I had a strange evening with your mother."

"Did you?" Her scraping seemed to grow more vigorous. She changed the subject without segue. "I was right about painting with this thing on," she said, pausing to rap the butt of her knife against the black band on her wrist. The bonded band clinked dully. "It's like trying to run with an open parachute."

Adam carried on with his confession, though she did not seem particularly interested in hearing it. "She had on a bonded band. Apparently, it wasn't enough that her son and daughter have me on a leash. No, she has to have one, too. And she was wearing a..." He made vague gestures over his chest before dropping his hands. "I've worn more clothes in the bath."

Runa paused her work long enough to roll her eyes. "She started making her secretaries dye their hair shortly after she began working on your scintillation."

"I...I don't...Well, that's about the most nauseating thing I've ever heard," Adam said, and Runa snorted. "You were right, by the way. That scintillation she's so proud of, it isn't very good. I'm in it, and even I thought it was rubbish. Still, it's chilling to think of her spying on my entire life. She knows everything about me...*everything*."

"She doesn't, though. Not really. It was an absolutely disgusting invasion of privacy, of course, but the fact is, she didn't have time to watch every hour of your life. I think that's why her scint focuses on your birthdays, especially early on. She figured out when you were born, then used your birthday as a sort of touchstone for your development." Runa loaded her brush with paint, then drummed her canvas with vigorous strokes. "Her retelling of your life is so bad precisely because she couldn't figure you out or understand what was important to you. It's like she read a dozen random pages from a book, then went on to waste all our time telling us what the story meant. No, Ida only knows *everything* about herself."

"That is some consolation, actually. But I didn't come here to talk about Docent Allod. She handles that well enough on her own. No, I came because I need your help with something."

"Is it the shower or the stove? I told you, you should've taken notes," Runa said brusquely.

He leaned back and gave Celeste's side a tentative stroke. The dozing hound did not object, so he continued. "Are you any good at building things?"

"What sort of things?"

He blew out a long breath. "Oh, I don't know. A bridge, for example."

"A bridge? What, like bringing people together, resolving feuds, that sort of thing? You've met my family."

"No, like a *bridge* bridge. Something that goes from one side to another, crossing over water or some sort of... gulf. Probably about one hundred and fifty feet long or so."

Runa put down her palette and stepped from behind the easel. "You said you didn't care. You said that all cities have their sewers, their gallows. You sounded as bad as Elrin."

Adam rolled his head. "Of course I care! You can't face that and not care. You can't embrace an orphaned infant and then shrug your shoulders." He picked at a loose thread in the armrest, scrutinizing it as if it were a point of great fascination. "I cared. I just didn't trust you."

She scoffed. "But now you do? What's changed?"

He did not look up as he answered. "Your mother made it seem as if my sister and I were in New Babel by choice, that Voleta performed because she wished to, and that I stole because I was ambitious. The truth is we were imprisoned. We were fed, sheltered, and there was a sense of order, but we were prisoners. But it was all very... *consistent*. And the shameful truth is, I liked the consistency. I defended it, miserable as it was, because I was afraid. I was afraid it could be worse. I was afraid I could lose what little I had." He looked up, quitting his idle work on the protruding threads. "From the outside, it looked as if I liked the way things were. From the outside, it looked as if, deep down, I preferred our prison."

She perched on the sofa's edge near Celeste's head, and scratched the hound behind her ears where the fur was thin. "What are you saying?"

"I think you hate how things are here. You know that it's wrong to have empty houses and abundant food while people suffer and starve at your doorstep. Ossian is your only real friend. I asked one of my window snoopers where he came from, and she told me Ossian was sent up in the Cupel car as an infant. And she told me about the accord where they agreed to keep him, but only after they sent back down the charred remains of a stillborn as a receipt. That was your grandparents' version of mercy. They put the child to work in the furnace room and sent his parents bones to make sure no one else ever tried to send a baby up. How noble! But you're not like them. You can imagine a better sort of ordinary. A fairer status quo."

"You want me to help you bring the hods into Nebos? If the lumenguard don't kill us, the hods surely will."

"They're children. Do you realize that? Thousands of children being looked after by a handful of elders. We're not cracking the doors for an armed horde. We're emptying an orphanage."

"We'd be leading lambs to the slaughter."

"They didn't kill Ossian. I don't think they'll kill five thousand children."

"They'll send them back."

"Then we'll burn the bridge."

"You're going to force Nebos to choose between adoption and mass murder?"

"We'll just have to convince your fellow Nebosans that they need the hods. I was reading through the city's census yesterday. I was looking for an engineer, and by the way, you don't have many of them left. Two hundred and eleven composers. Three engineers. You said that there are around six thousand souls living in Nebos, and you were right. But did you know that the population has shrunk by nearly five percent in the past twenty years? Did you know the average age is rising, and the number of young is shrinking? Nebos needs new blood and lots of it."

"You've obviously been thinking about this a lot. But you're overlooking something."

"What's that?" Adam asked, twisting the bonded band that clung to his wrist to give the skin beneath it a little air.

"You don't need a bridge. You already have a ferry," she said. Adam explained his worry that he would not be able to move all the children in the time between a single shift, and how he was certain that once discovered, their effort would be formally concluded. The Nebosans had accepted Ossian, after all, but locked the door behind him, as it were.

"But you don't need to do it all in one day. You just bring them in and hide them in the Warren until they're all over."

"But is there space enough for thousands?"

"Well, remember what Ossian said. There are closets inside of closets. Drawers inside of drawers. There's always more room in the Warren."

Chapter Fifteen

To lead is to come last. A chef only eats when the dishes are done, and a captain goes down with the ship.

—from the diary of Joram Brahe, captain of the *Natchez King*

The next morning, Adam and Runa were aboard her bandy and tearing down the street before the dinnerflies had begun to deliver the morning milk. Since it was the lumenguard's non-patrol day for the Fundament, the two freshly minted conspirators hoped to reach the Warren before anyone was awake to notice them. Adam thought if he were caught visiting the underground so soon after his encounter with the hods, it might raise suspicion.

The eastern gate to the Warren had just come into sight when Runa applied the brakes so sharply, Adam nearly flew over the dashboard into the street. His surprised annoyance quickly turned to alarm when he realized why she had stopped. Captain Dyre stood in white pajamas before an easel, all but blocking the inclined entrance to the subterranean part of the city. He wore a pair of magnifying glasses on the tip of his nose. They seemed the sort of thing a watchmaker might employ. He held a brush that appeared to bear a single paint-tipped hair.

Adam would come to learn that Captain Dyre enjoyed painting miniatures of the city in the wee hours before his shift began. Once a year, he would display his stamp-sized landscapes in a gallery show where his twelve or so minuscule pieces were spread across fifty feet of wall space. All agreed, the event was the invention of tedium, but everyone with any sense still attended to pay their compliments.

The large-jawed captain removed his magnifying spectacles, blinked bloodshot eyes, and said, "Good morning," in a way that seemed to suggest it had been such until recently. Runa and Adam returned the greeting in a chorus. "Going to the Warren, I see. Why?"

"We're going to visit Ossian, sir," Runa said.

"Ossian won't be awake for hours," he said, swishing the brush back and forth in a little pot of turpentine. "If I try to get paint from him before ten, I just waste my morning pounding on his door." Adam had not known a man could look so imposing in his nightclothes. "Where are you going, Corporal?"

Runa opened her mouth, but all that emerged was an insensible, pitchy warble.

"To press upon the pipes, sir!" Adam blurted.

"What did you say?" Captain Dyre said.

"I'm told the slow water stimulates the senses, and enhances the sensation of—"

"All right, all right, young man. That's enough." The captain looked at Runa, his brow wrinkling all the way to his scalp. "Corporal, on your application for emergency leave, under *Occasion* I believe you wrote, 'Attending to the care of a loved one.'"

"I did, sir. And technically, I am."

"You're going to make your mother furious."

"Yes, sir. I mean, no, sir," Runa said, her throat flushing crimson.

"It's not a criticism. On you go." The captain made enough room for Runa to steer the bandy past. Neither of them dared to look back as they coasted silently down the slope toward the mouth of the tunnel.

It was only after they were through the static curtain and around the second curve that they succumbed to a fit of nervous laughter.

Runa adopted an uncharacteristically moderate pace. Rather than squeal around the corners, she slowed to point out landmarks: an overlit station entrance, a sudden dip and rise in the passage, and a grate in the floor that made the wheels sing, all of which she assembled into a mnemonic for easier recollection. Adam slowly began to build upon the vague map in his head. The effort took all of his concentration, and so he was spared the discomfort of reviewing his decision to out them as lovers to the captain. Though whenever they passed a stretch of crystalline pipe, bubbling with the bluish slow water, Adam felt a warmth bloom in his stomach.

By the time they reached the Fundament, Adam was reasonably optimistic that he could find his way down again, though reversing their course was another matter.

Since they wouldn't have the lumenguard's visors to attune their eyes to the darkness, Runa had had the foresight to bring an electric lantern. It looked a little like a soap bubble caught in a gold teacup, and though it was far smaller than most oil lamps, its cast was sufficient to fill the entire scarred bay with a warm white light.

Runa, who was familiar with the controls that programmed the scow's passage, knelt before the panel. Adam watched over her shoulder as she powered it on, adjusted the time of its return, and checked its plotted course.

"And you're sure it's better just to surprise Ossian with two dozen orphans?" he asked.

She closed the panel and swung aboard the barge. "I'm sure he'll want to help us, but he can be timid. I think he'd be more likely to balk at an abstract request than a doorway full of ready guests."

Adam reentered the pattern he'd watched Elrin peck into the control by the bay doors, and said, "I just hope he wasn't exaggerating about the depth of his closets."

Runa's teacup lamp thrashed upon its hook on the scow's rail. Its light flashed like lightning as it was eclipsed by cushions and curtains and unspooling scrolls.

The transit through the storm was just as much a flail as it had been the first time, and yet it seemed to Adam a little less forbidding since he had Runa to cling to. With backs turned to the onslaught and foreheads buried in the notches of each other's shoulders, they weathered the maelstrom in a cocoon of their own making. Previously, the passage had seemed interminable to Adam, and yet this trip passed in the span of a heartbeat. When the wind abruptly fell away, they unclenched their eyes and loosened their embrace, though not all at once. They parted like dancers savoring the end of a waltz.

They turned to find themselves the focus of scores of unblinking eyes. Children filled the passage. Toddlers straddled the necks of older children. The most dexterous had climbed the rough tunnel walls high enough to see over the crowd.

Adam was sure there were more now than there had been before, and they seemed even more in awe, though perhaps that was owed to the power of Runa's electric lantern. Adam wondered if it did not embody the brightest light some of them had ever seen.

He had not given any thought to his appearance. He'd donned the same formal trousers and dress shirt he'd worn the day before, and Runa was wearing a flouncy, paint-stained smock over black tights. They did not look like saviors or revolutionaries or even, truly, adults.

From the rail of the settling windscow, Adam stared into the sea of faces, hoping to see a familiar one. "Hello! A few days ago, I spoke to one of you. He was an older man. I didn't get his name."

The crowd shifted a little, parting subtly like short grass being pushed about by a mouse. The elder hod emerged at the fore, still leaning upon his axe haft and holding an infant on one shoulder, where it drowsed upon a bed of his soft, ashen locks. "You don't know it because you didn't ask. My name is Faruq."

"I'm Adam, and this is Runa," he said as he swung under the rail.

"Could you turn your sun down a bit? I'm half-blind as it is," Faruq said.

Runa dimmed the cast of the lantern with a twist of the glass bubble.

The old hod sighed and stretched his jaw to clear his eyes. "That's better. Thank you."

"There seem to be more of you."

"Well, word of a boy in pajamas promising bridges is something of a novelty around here. A lot of the children were cross they didn't get to see you last time. Speaking of bridges, how is yours coming along?"

"There's been a slight change of plan," Adam said, and explained their new intention of taking the children in batches aboard the windscow, hiding them in the underground, and presenting them to the natives of Nebos as one body when they were all safely over.

Faruq listened with his head slightly turned as if to train his better ear upon him. He nodded at first, but soon began to frown. That unhappy crack had become a crag by the time Adam finished. "That would also be quite a clever way to cull an unwanted crowd, don't you think? Bring us over in loads, dispose of us, then come back for more."

"I don't understand," Runa said. "Surely, if we wanted you to suffer, we would just leave you here."

"Young lady, all of us here have made the acquaintance of certain persons that enjoy torturing the weak."

"What do you suggest, then?"

"I go with you. You show me where you intend to take us, how you intend to feed and house us. If I do not return, then my friends will have their answer, and the world will only be out one old hod."

"I want to go," said a girl who, though obviously young, was nearly a head taller than Faruq.

"No, Penny, you have to—"

"I want to come, too." This from a boy who had been clinging to the wall, but now leapt nimbly down, or nearly so. He toppled onto his knees, but sprang up again, slapping them clean. "If Penny goes, I get to go."

"But Penny isn't going; she's staying h—" Faruq began, but his voice was soon drowned out by a competitive din of demands and sobs.

With so many children involved, it might've taken an hour for the argument to run its course had Runa not intervened by turning her lantern up to full burn. The blaring light snuffed the squabble as the mob squinted and gasped. Runa dimmed the lamp again and spoke in a voice that had shades of her mother's authority. "We understand Mr. Faruq's hesitation. He obviously cares for you all very much, but this is the truth: We don't have time to waste. Every minute we delay raises the chances of our discovery or of one of you being left behind. There are people above us who are afraid of you. That's a fact that you'll have to get used to. There are people who think you are wild and unruly and unworthy. I do not think that, but we must change their minds!"

Adam expected them to jeer or blow raspberries at her, but the children absorbed her words with furrowed brows and pursed mouths.

He looked back at her with a marveling smile. Later, he would ask her why she had thought to address a throng of children in that way. Runa would explain that her whole childhood, her mother had spoken to her as if she were stupid, as if she couldn't possibly understand anything. And while, in truth, she *didn't* understand the substance of much of what her mother said, Runa always knew when she was being patronized. She hated that feeling so intensely, she became finely attuned to the nuances of condescension. She could tell the moment someone began to talk down to her, and she would turn as hostile as a bagged rat. She assumed all children were more or less the same. So, while Runa didn't expect them to understand everything she was saying, at least they would know she was not belittling them.

Adam climbed up onto the mid-rail of the scow so he could see farther into the crowd.

He shouted, "We will take twenty-one volunteers along with Mr. Faruq on an exploratory mission. It may be dangerous. It will be frightening. So, we need only your bravest. If you believe you are a stout-hearted soul, raise your hand. I will pick twenty-one of you."

"And anyone who argues will have to clean up after my dog!" Runa added, raising a finger high in the air. "And I warn you: She's an old dog with a very messy behind!"

A burst of laughter filled the passage, and then echoed again as her joke was repeated to those farther back.

"You have children?" Faruq asked her as Adam began to select his volunteers from the crowd.

Runa grimaced at the thought. "God, no. Just an awful mother."

They lashed the youngest to the rails of the scow and tucked them up in blankets to shield them from the storm. Faruq, who had passed his infant charge to another minder before boarding, began the passage squatting on his heels with his arms wrapped about the heads of two children. Adam thought he looked like a hen sheltering her chicks.

Brave as they were, the children still shrieked in terror when the scow broke upon the slanting wind and household hail. The lid of a wicker basket, spinning like a discus, struck a boy in the arm. More shocked than injured, his knees wobbled, and Adam gripped him by the shoulders to shore him up. This seemed to work well enough until he tilted his head abruptly down and retched upon Adam's shoes. This inspired a sympathetic response from another child, then a third. They passed through a flock of stiff playing cards, sharp as frozen rain. Someone began to cry. Adam wondered if it wasn't him.

Their short voyage continued in a similar vein. There were glancing blows, violent regurgitations, one unclaimed puddle, and contagious weeping. Adam began to compile a list of wished-for modifications he would make to the vessel: a tarpaulin to cover the top and sides, a padded rug to give bare feet something to grip other than polished steel, and a chamber pot, at the very least.

When they arrived in the derelict and unlit bay, Adam sensed his passengers' relief at exiting the storm, and their nearly simultaneous disappointment with their destination. Faruq expressed it best when he said, "Well, this looks a bit familiar."

With the children unloaded, Adam and Runa cleaned up the mess as best they could, using the protective blankets as mops, before submitting the soiled laundry to the tumbling wind. Adam could only hope they would not see those linens again.

There was no way to take all of them by bandy. Even if they'd had a second chariot and a pair of carts, it wouldn't have been enough. Walking the road to the furnace would've taken a hearty soul an hour at least, and a pack of traumatized children likely twice that. Fortunately, Runa had previously ferreted out a shortcut on an occasion when she had wished to go directly from patrolling the Fundament to visiting Ossian. They still had to walk up the narrow, spiraling incline, which only tortured the stomachs of the qualmish explorers, but once they crested upon the broader, more level road, Runa led them over the curb into a snaking corridor that could only be traversed in a single file. The alley might've seemed sinister in gloomier lighting, but a series of cheery electric sconces lit the way and the silvery walls were etched with an underwater scene. A vast school of mackerel streamed along one wall, coursed over the ceiling, and continued down the other side. The children giggled as they stroked images of eels, turtles, and whales. They asked Adam to name the creatures, and he did, or at least the ones he recalled from his studies.

After wending through several similarly adorned passages, they broke upon a broad hall that included the first instance of carpeting Adam had seen in the Warren. Blue and green paisleys floated upon a purple soup. The hall curved away from them in either direction. Resting on the floor and leaning upon the wainscot were hundreds of framed paintings of all sizes, subjects, and styles. It seemed a sort of deconstructed gallery. But the artwork did not appeal to the children half as much as the rug, which they reveled in. They shuffled their feet through the soft nap and leapt from paisley to paisley. A bank of large gold-faced elevators stood across from them. They appeared to have been designed for freight or large crowds. At first, the children couldn't imagine why they all had to leave the wonderful carpet behind and cram into a small room with a bare floor, and then stand there while the doors shut and the room began to hum to itself. For the benefit of the children, Faruq seemed to be doing his best to appear unfazed by the curious closet. He said, "I suppose this will be our sleeping quarters? Should we make a pile?"

Before Runa could explain, the doors opened upon an entirely different area, where white tile gleamed from the floor to ceiling. A mosaic relaying a rocky scene of jade-shelled bull snails and mice with white ears and pom-poms at the ends of their long tails splayed above half a dozen arched entryways. As the children oohed and aahed, Faruq said, "Yes, of course. A magic box. I see."

As agog as Faruq and the children were at the wonders of the Warren, it was perhaps Ossian who received the greatest shock of the day.

It took the efforts of all three adults to stop the children from pressing upon the round, bulging windows on either side of the entrance to the furnace room. The children peered through the warped green glass and marveled at the knickknacks and treasures held within. When they were corralled at last, Runa beat upon the iron slab with the flat of her hand. She told Adam that she never knocked. Usually, she would just try the door, and if it was locked, she assumed Ossian was sleeping and went away. If it was unlocked, she let herself in because she knew Ossian resented being forced to surrender his work organizing buttons or bundling handkerchiefs just to play doorman. In Nebos, Ossian was something of a notorious curmudgeon, but that was only among the idiots who tormented him with impatient rapping.

Fearing that the children would all scatter the moment they were inside Ossian's voluminous storehouse, Adam said to Faruq, "Is there any hope of keeping them together once we're inside?"

"Oh, yes, of course," Faruq said, and turned to face his charges. His chest rumbled as he cleared his throat and said, "I smell a chimney cat!" The children looked at one another, their faces sobering. Then Faruq undertook the direst singsong Adam had ever heard, one that the children joined in reciting halfway through. "We all stay calm; we all stay close. I shut my mouth and open my nose."

The children began turning their heads and sniffing the air like a pack of hounds that had lost the scent. Faruq winked at Adam and said, "That'll buy us a few minutes."

The next moment, the door flew open amid a squeaking fanfare of

Ossian's leg braces. The furnaceman performed a pantomime that began with a toothy, bulldoggish scowl, that rose into an apple-cheeked grin when he saw Runa, then curdled with confusion, then worry, then horror as he marked first the children, then their number, and finally their condition.

"Hods," he croaked.

"Friends," Runa said. "May we come in?"

Numbly, Ossian stood aside, and Faruq and his twenty-one charges walked into the furnace room, sniffing the air.

Ossian watched the children as they stood in a clump, shoulder to shoulder, staring out over his domestic horde. "Do they have a cold?" he asked.

"Never mind that," Runa said, laying a hand upon his low shoulder. "We need your help."

Adam had worried that Ossian would balk at the plot, that he, being driven by fear, self-loathing, or misplaced loyalty, would out them to the authorities, and end their rescue before it began. Despite Runa's assurance that Ossian's timidity did not make him heartless, Adam had privately estimated the odds of Ossian refusing to assist them to be approximately two to one.

And yet, Adam had neglected to consider the fact that Ossian was an orphan himself, and faced with the opportunity to help other orphans escape a life of scrabbling misery, he did not hesitate. He said he had room enough in his two pockets for the twenty-one children. When Runa said there would be more, he said he had many more pockets. When she said there could be five thousand in all, Ossian had boggled like a new father surprised by triplets, but he quickly said they would find room for every last one.

But the orphans would have to be tucked away elsewhere. Ossian's warehouse was probably the only destination in the Warren, other than the Delectus and the Fundament, that reliably drew visitors from the golden city. The lumenguard delivered the offerings of the black trail every other day, not to mention the callers who came in search of whatnots, knickknacks, and new rugs for their floors. No, if they wanted to hide five thousand children, they'd have more luck in the habitation halls of the lower levels. Ossian had been frequenting those corridors for years—it was where he stored most of the artwork that came into his possession—and he'd never once seen a Nebosan there. That was likely because that while the halls, which ran in concentric circles joined by occasional alleys, contained hundreds if not thousands of doors, all of them were locked. But the corridors alone could hold thousands.

When Faruq raised the question of water and necessities, Ossian explained that the habitation halls accessed each of the twelve bandy stations, all of which contained a fountain and a drainage culvert. As for food, Ossian had a surplus of jarred, canned, dried, and pickled victuals sufficient to feed five thousand for a year. It seemed only fitting that the orphans of the black trail would be fed by the offerings their parents had carried.

As the adults discussed provisions and schedules, the children's fear of chimney cats dwindled, and they began to explore the bounties of the warehouse. The youngest girl reappeared wearing a bowl on her head. Standing nearly under Ossian's chin, she threw her head back, holding her china helmet in place with both hands. She showed a gap-toothed smile when she asked if she could keep it. Ossian said she could of course, but Faruq intervened saying, "You realize, if you give one of them a bowl, all of them will want one."

Ossian said, "Then they'll all have one. I have more bowls than the sky has stars. And how much soup can one man eat?"

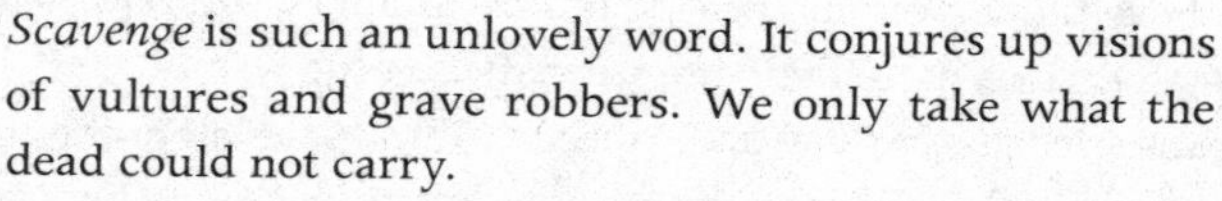

Chapter Sixteen

Scavenge is such an unlovely word. It conjures up visions of vultures and grave robbers. We only take what the dead could not carry.

—from the diary of Joram Brahe, captain of the *Natchez King*

When Adam confessed to Captain Dyre that he was embroiled in a libidinous tryst with Runa Allod, daughter of the esteemed docent, he was unprepared for the resulting furor.

But the moment he and Runa emerged from the Warren a full twelve hours after their descent—red-faced, windswept, and exhausted—they were greeted by a cocktail party being held in their honor and in the middle of the road. Before Adam could object, a flute of sparkling cider was pushed into his hand, and he was thrown into a gauntlet of men who baptized him with back slaps, handshakes, and cries of *well done!* A grinning man with the pronounced gums of a horse said, "Don't you look the worse for wear! My god, your clothes are soaked through—Ta-da, Adam, indeed!"

Adam bore these commendations with as much good humor as he could, though he found the whole practice of congratulating young men on their romantic engagements loathsome. Love wasn't a sport, and the adored was not some woodland game. In Adam's experience, the men who bayed the loudest about such things were often unloved and bitterly so.

Then the throng parted, and Adam found himself standing nearly on the bare toes of Runa's mother. Her face looked like a piece of wax fruit—overpolished and unreal. She was dressed in the sort of suit men were generally buried in. In the absence of a discernable expression, Adam still felt, and quite distinctly, her radiating anger.

Ida Allod said, "How is your headache?"

"Much better, thank you," Adam said, baring his teeth in a defensive smile.

Ida's throat tightened, showing the rootlike system of her veins. "I wouldn't have taken you for the sort of boy to hurry through a courtship. I thought Adam was more deliberate and discerning."

"We're as surprised as you are, Mother," Runa said, stepping to Adam's side and wrapping her hand around his. Adam looked at her, and there passed between them an understanding: They could denounce their love and raise questions about their activities in the Warren, or they could embrace the story, and with it, an excuse to go underground as much as they pleased in the days and weeks to come.

"How did this happen?" Ida asked in a tone one might use to ask after a stain on a rug.

Though he had never crossed a stage, Adam had learned long ago how to affect the sort of emotionalism that garnered a stranger's trust, a constable's pity, and sometimes the giving of small loans. He said, "I think I began to fall in love with your daughter when she rushed to my side in the windstile. I thought I was dying and then—" Adam turned to face Runa. "I'd never seen such eyes before. It was like staring into a kaleidoscope."

He seemed to have struck the right note as far as the revelers were concerned. They clasped their hands and sighed. Docent Allod, meanwhile, looked as if she had swallowed a chicken bone. As the adoring noises faded, she said in her most domineering timbre: "Well, you make a compelling couple. It is nice to see you settling in, Adam. I was right to champion your cause. I'm glad my daughter can be the benefactor of my discerning eye."

Before Runa could form a suitably scathing reply, a call rose from the crowd, the word repeated with all the conviction of votaries and the insistence of rioters: *Kiss! Kiss! Kiss!*

This was beyond Adam's experience as an actor, and yet, what began as a stiff formality—a tilting of heads and a joining of lips—quickly softened into something tender and lingering.

* * *

Thus commenced their very public romance. Their evenings were spent idling in the parks, or promenading down the streets, or as often as not, attending some gallery opening, symposium, or party, where their presence more or less certified the popularity of an occasion. Where Adam and Runa went, so followed the eyes of Nebos.

The couple cut ribbons on gallery openings, sat on the front row of musical debuts, and lounged on the Cavaedium lawn whenever a new scintillation was released. Adam and Runa maintained a perfect performance of love, acting as if they were unaware of their gawking entourage. It was an act the citizenry seemed to relish, with the exception of the jilted Docent Allod.

While their evenings were spent canoodling for the public's pleasure, their days were reserved for the Warren.

Under the guise of lustful retreats, they oversaw the importation of hundreds of children each day. The minders and older youths proved invaluable to the process. It was they who outfitted the windscow with tarps and rugs and pans for unexpected accidents, and they who stripped these amenities away before the lumenguard's patrol. Initially, Adam and Runa had planned to run the scow through the night, but it was soon evident that such a schedule was overly ambitious. It led to congestion in the carpeted halls where the hods made their beds, the interruption of sleep, and a general exhaustion, which was particularly problematic with the very young. Rather than a rushed exodus, they elected to pursue a deliberate, sustained extraction.

On the second day after their operation commenced, Ossian raised the question of what they would do if word spread that the crowning city was accepting refugees. What if an armed band of hods appeared and commandeered the scow? That would surely attract that attention of the lumenguard, who would undoubtedly drive the interlopers back, but then what? It seemed natural to expect increased security around the Fundament. Fortunately, Faruq had a ready solution in mind, one that he had used in the past when his orphan camp had felt pressured by gangs of desperate hods who came hoping to loot their meager stores. Faruq would have the children put rags over their mouths and draw sores on their limbs with red clay. Then he would lay them in rows and ask them to indulge in whatever moans and wails they wished. The threat of plague was sufficient to dissuade even ravenous men.

The question of how to contain the children proved perhaps the trickiest of all. For years, the orphans had been caught between a cyclone and a barren trail. And while they had found a thousand small entertainments in the racing of beetles, the braiding of threads, and the grinding of stones into pendants and figurines, they had still been starved for the opportunity to galivant and explore. The passageways of the Warren called to them like the distant music of a circus.

To entertain and distract them, Ossian decided it was time they all had a bath, a delousing, a haircut, new clothes, new shoes, and a lesson or two in basic manners. The effort required fifty tubs, one hundred pails, two hundred bars of soap, many thousands of towels, and every last shaker of pyrethrum powder in his pantry. Wash stations were set up in a section of the Silk Garden Bandy Station that featured a mural full of bucking spider-eaters. Curtains were raised and bath mats laid. Ossian then delivered eighteen pairs of scissors, three times as many hairbrushes, and a sack full of assorted hairpins, combs, clips, and barrettes.

As vast as Ossian's wardrobe was, the majority of his holdings were tailored for adults. To correct this, he recruited older boys and girls to hem skirts, shorten strides, and trim waistbands. Small shoes were similarly in limited supply, and so Ossian taught them how to make simple sandals out of rolls of cork, glue, and leather thongs. He taught them to say how-do-you-do, to bow and curtsey, to chew with their mouths closed, and to not pick their noses in the middle of a conversation.

Increasingly, Runa and Adam's role in the effort was inessential. Once Runa showed Ossian and Faruq how to program the windscow and change its power cells and the location of the storehouse where more cells could be procured, there was nothing that could not be done without them. Which was just as well because it was growing more and more difficult for them to enter the Warren without attracting a crowd of admirers. Before the first week was out, Adam and Runa elected to suspend their morning trips underground entirely, and by the time the second week had drawn to a close, the slow invasion of the city's cellar had taken on an almost commonplace quality in their minds, an impression that allowed them to pretend that perhaps the eventual revelation of the orphans would not induce an existential crisis or provoke the city's choler. No, the children would emerge like a crop from the ground, and the garden would make room as it always had.

It was a pretty if implausible illusion.

Finding themselves abruptly without anything to do, Runa had announced that she would like to paint Adam if he would be willing to sit for her. It had been days since she'd had a chance to pick up a brush, and both found the prospect of a little time outside of the public eye enticing.

She posed him on her couch and began to sketch upon a new canvas while Adam cast his eye about her castle. Taking in the varnished bones that filled her walls, he thought how much her home resembled a gleaming catacomb. The more he looked, the more he liked it. It was then that he at last felt comfortable approaching a subject that had always seemed so tender with Runa. He said, "Tell me about your father."

The scratching of her pencil slowed, but did not cease. She seemed to find it easier to talk while otherwise occupied. "Dad was the absolute opposite of Mother. He was an entomologist. While everyone else was composing dirges and writing odes, he was looking after our insects."

Doing his best to remain still, he asked, "Honestly, I don't understand why you have pests at all. You live in a bubble. Why let the moths and wasps in?"

Her voice sounded wistful when she answered. "Dad always said that we were the pests—always trampling the grass and picking the flowers. He would've sooner swatted a man than a fly." She paused to scrub at an errant line with a rag that was as colorful as an opal. "Insects are pollinators and decomposers. Without them, the plants wouldn't bear fruit, last year's crops wouldn't rot properly, and the soil would suffer. We'd starve to death in a world without insects. Of course, we try to keep certain things—like lice—out, but my father knew just how dependent we are upon all those so-called pests."

Adam thought of the hods that filled the Tower walls, how they carried life up from the ground, how they kept the Tower green and growing. "What happened to your father?"

"He just died one night. Drifted off in his sleep. No one knew why. I was eleven. My mother had left him a few years earlier." Runa held her pencil out at arm's length and closed one eye. "I think she married him just to torture him, honestly. But Dad was never any good at suffering. She would needle him, call him names, flirt with other men, not come home for days, and he would shrug and say, 'Well, that's just your mother.' Then he'd go back to work.

"I never forgave her. I had to live with her after he was gone. I stayed in my room as much as I could. Dad knew what he did was important, so he often wore an overlay mask so he could narrate his work. I would fall asleep with his face glowing like a ghost on the wall. He'd count caterpillar eggs and identify aphids and chart the life cycle of a bee, and I would read his lips until I knew every word by heart."

"An espial?" Adam asked.

"Yes. It's almost two and a half hours long from start to end."

"Are you in it?"

"No. No, all of it is of him working with insects: counting, tracking, hunting for blights. My favorite part is when he introduces a new queen to a colony of bees. I wish my hands were as steady as his." She set aside her pencil and approached him on the couch. "Even when I was grown, I would play it every night for company while I ate dinner, or read a book, or sketched."

"Where is the espial now?"

"Hold on. I want to re-pose you a bit." She combed his hair with her fingers and smoothed his shirt collar. His hand rested on the sofa's arm, and she took it in hers. Though the small gesture was a fixture of their public performance, it felt quite different in private. Adam's heart seemed to float to the surface of his chest. She said, "I had to stop watching it. I was obsessed. I know he wouldn't have liked that. So, about two years ago, I returned his espial to the Delectus. I haven't watched it since."

Adam stroked one of her knuckles with his thumb. The small movement seemed to spark like flint upon steel. "If it wouldn't upset you, I'd like to watch it with you."

"I'd like that," she said, leaning into him, pressing one hand upon his shoulder. Her hair was like a muslin curtain pulled over a sunny window. She lifted his chin with her fingertips.

A tremble passed through him, into her, down through the Tower, and on into the earth.

Chapter Seventeen

Any airman who has ever killed another in battle has learned the unhappy truth: Ships sink; ghosts float.

—from the diary of Joram Brahe, captain of the *Natchez King*

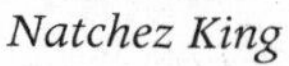

Later, in a pleasurable daze, Adam and Runa rode through the night-emptied streets. The gold spires appeared dull, their jeweled lights waxen. Dinnerflies and picnic-pelicans passed overhead, vague as wraiths. An unsettled dew shrouded the city, veiling the trees, blanketing the lawns, and muffling the flowing melodies of the tumbling brooks.

Adam felt strange. He could not describe the sensation except to say it reminded him of the wall beside his bed in his childhood home. His room, small and squeezed into a back corner of the house, had served many purposes over the course of its history, which had begun long before he was born. The room had been a nursery, a pantry, a laundry room, a kennel, a privy, and a bedroom for dozens of other children. Each time the room was reinvented, a new layer of wallpaper or paint had been added, until, by the time Adam's bed was pressed up against it, the wall was as spongy as a croissant. When he could not sleep, he'd lie in the gloom and pick at a seam in the marigold paper that his mother had put up. He worked his way back through time with the edge of his thumbnail, exposing the long and varied record of colors and patterns, until one day he struck lumber that was rough, pale, and still redolent of sap.

That was how he felt—like an uncovered piece of green wood in a very old room.

They had agreed that Runa's garden folly had shrunk unexpectedly. They needed to escape, to put some distance between themselves—it, and what they had done. It was Adam's suggestion that they visit the Delectus where Runa's father's espial was housed, and Runa had agreed that it would be a welcome change to go somewhere that was in service of neither the orphans nor her mother.

Runa steered her bandy down dim alleys, into cul-de-sacs, and off the road, through garden cut-throughs and desire paths, until she was certain they were not being followed. Visiting the Delectus required a return to the Warren, though a corner of it that was well removed from the Nautilus, Ossian's storehouse, and the halls where the children slept. If they were tracked, at least it wouldn't put the orphans at risk.

As they at last turned onto the incline that would deliver them to the Warren, Adam asked, "The Delectus, it's like a library for espials. Is that right?"

Runa said, "Yes, sort of. Though a library where membership is mandatory. Every man, woman, and child in Nebos has an account there. We're signed up as soon as we can open our eyes. I suppose you'll have to register, too."

"And the Conservator is the librarian?"

"Except less helpful. He's pretty . . . *eccentric*. And it doesn't help that he's getting along in years. Try not to set him off if you can help it."

"What sets him off?" Adam asked.

Runa blew a long breath. "Devil if I know."

The entrance to the Delectus was an airy courtyard held inside a bubble of brushed steel. Water cascaded from the tiers of a central fountain, the plash of which reverberated like surf. An alabaster globe crowned the fount. That sphere beamed like a cataractous sun. Its light snagged upon etched points in the domed ceiling, making it seem to glimmer with stars.

The edifice of the Delectus broke upon the courtyard like the shadow of a gibbous moon. It was a windowless, bowing wall of ashen block that appeared to have been laid without the assistance of mortar. The ornate carriage porch that fronted the Delectus gave it an officious air, calling to mind a royal bank or provincial courthouse.

Runa steered the bandy through the porch's archway and under the flat roof that was held aloft by nine stout pillars. Broader at the plinth and narrower at the capital, each column had been carved into models of the Tower of Babel. Though it wasn't until they'd passed the fourth replica that Adam realized each was subtly different. In their grand dimensions, the pillars were models of the Tower, but in detail, they were unique. Adam wondered if these represented discarded designs, or if they were aspirational. Though he could hardly imagine the nation of Ur supporting (or indeed *surviving*) a second Tower, much less eight more.

Runa powered her bandy down, and as they stepped from the footboard, she said, "Oh, um, don't call them *scints* or *scintillations*. The Conservator hates those words. His preferred term is *espial*. He's particular about that. He's particular about lots of things."

Sensing her nervousness, Adam gave an encouraging smile. "I'll try to be charming."

The suggestion inspired a single note of laughter from Runa. She took his hand, kissed his cheek, and pulled him toward the entrance.

The entryway was tall, austere, and unencumbered by a door. The Delectus seemed to invite all who approached. The interior looked nothing like a library. Adam imagined that if a king kept his crown jewels in a gilded grain silo it might look like this. The walls were filled, from marble floor to vaulted dome, with cubbies, forming a honeycomb of cells that numbered in the many thousands. The air swarmed with glass-bodied scarabs that flew on gilded wings. Each was as large as a garden tortoise, and all were lit from within by a crimson light.

Standing there, poised upon the cusp of this mesmerizing spectacle, Adam felt the all too familiar tug of his bonded band. He looked and saw Runa had felt it also.

"She *must* be joking," Runa groaned. "It's three in the morning!"

"Maybe it's Elrin."

"What's the difference? She's probably just trying to torment us, ruin our sleep."

"Well, I hardly felt a thing," he said.

She smiled. "You know what: Me neither."

The floor of the silo was unfurnished except for a central, ominous podium that was as black as basalt and shaped like a molar pulled from a giant's head. As unfriendly as that dead tooth seemed, Adam liked the look of the person standing behind it even less.

The Conservator gave the general impression of an inhumanly tall, unhealthily thin man. His head seemed far too narrow for the shoulders it sat upon. The Conservator wore a dusty dinner jacket that might've accommodated four or five grown men, an age-yellowed dress shirt, and a pink bowtie that had likely once been red. His skin was a mottled verdigris, that unique shade of green common to old copper pipes. His mouth was as wide and thick-lipped as a grouper, and set in a similar frown. The top half of his head was eyeless and polished, and it took Adam a moment to recognize it for what it was—a blinder.

The fact that the Conservator was an automaton with a blinder for a brain surprised Adam only slightly less than what came out of his mouth. The Conservator shouted, "Nautilus! Nautilus! The unfinished birth. Bitumen, sand, gypsum." The Conservator reached for something in the air, something only he could see. He grasped it and moved it to his desktop. It was as if he were picking invisible cherries. "Nautilus! Nautilus! The unfinished birth." His voice was like a street organ that was being cranked too slowly. It was an unsettling, haunting sound. Behind him, Adam saw cartloads of blinders stacked in precarious heaps, and more scattered across the floor.

Runa whispered in Adam's ear, "Like I said, he's eccentric."

"But not insane?" Adam asked.

"Dotty at worst," she said.

The Conservator abruptly swept his arm across his desktop, clearing away whatever invisible things he'd collected there, and shouted, "Discard!" He bent his tent-pole arms, gripped the sides of his blinder skull, and removed the top half of his head as if it were a hat. Everything above the midpoint of what might charitably be described as a nose was now missing except for a single periscopic eye. The eye twisted, stretched, and retracted like the ocular stem of a crab.

The Conservator threw the blinder over his shoulder. It bounced and tumbled, raising a dreadful racket as it careened across the marble floor.

Runa stepped forward, towing Adam along with her, and said, "Good evening, Conservator. How are you?"

The automaton settled his stovepipe arms upon the lectern and leaned forward as if to see them better. "Runa Ilmr Allod, you have six outstanding circulates. None are overdue. Your account is in good order. Privileges: Common." The Conservator's eye, black as the bowl of a pipe, twisted around to Adam next. His immense fish mouth opened and shut, once, twice, then spoke at last. "Adamos Déantóir Boreas."

Startled, Adam murmured, "You know who I am?"

The Conservator spoke over him: "You have no outstanding circulates. Your account is in good order. Privileges: Special."

Summoning his strongest voice, the one he used to speak over the wind aboard the *Stone Cloud*, Adam asked, "How do you know my name?"

A scarab began to circle the Conservator's head, which swiveled fully around, tracking it, before returning to face Adam. "You are a contributor to the Delectus." His words were chugging and distinct like the knocking of a cold engine.

"Oh," Runa said, drawing the vowel out as she squinted at a revelation. She rubbed the side of her face and said, "A few months ago after a viewing, one of my mother's assistants was trying to be helpful. He returned your ocular vault to the Delectus. But since Docent Allod had pulled your reliquary from the pile at the Cupel, it had never been registered. When she found out what her assistant had done, she was furious. She fired him, of course, and hired a new boy, who she sent to reclaim her masterpiece right away. She complained for *weeks* after about how the Conservator had ruined her work. Apparently, he'd re-edited your life down to a few minutes of you putting together something... a boiler valve, I think. She had to remake *The Daredevil's Brother* from scratch."

Adam didn't know which was more insulting: that his life had been turned into a fictitious seedy adventure, or that the only thing of value he'd ever done was to rebuild a safety relief valve.

"What did he mean about 'special' privileges?" Adam asked.

Runa shrugged and shook her head. "I have no idea. I've never heard of anyone having anything but common, restricted, or revoked privileges." She raised a finger as she listed each option, but her fingers quickly curled in again. "Except... Sometimes I'll ask to see something that's not in circulation, and he'll deny the request by saying 'special privileges required.'"

"What isn't in circulation?"

"All sorts of things. Like, if you ask for an espial that explains how to unlock the doors in the Warren or how to brew slow water or—"

"Or how the Brick Layer died?" Adam interrupted, ducking as a scarab swooped a little too near his head.

Runa eyes widened. "Yes, exactly like that."

"What do I say?" Adam asked, and Runa suggested how he might phrase the request. Adam cleared his throat and raised his chin, which did nothing to make the automaton's pulpit seem any less daunting. "Conservator, I would like to view an espial of the Brick Layer's death. Could you please suggest a record?"

The Conservator's halved head began to twist about, screwing into his shoulders with quickening speed. His jaw had passed beneath his collar, followed shortly by his unfinished nose. Then all they could see was the twirling periscope of his eye. Adam began to fret that he'd somehow managed to break the antique, had sent it shrinking into its shell like a turtle.

Then the Conservator's head popped up to its original height, and he said, "Jan Ulrich. Cross-reference: hydraulics; hoists; crane operation; crane maintenance; the Brick Layer's death. Not in circulation. Privileges: Special."

The automaton raised one pike-long arm in a languid gesture. A single scarab parted from his swarming fellows, whose wings chimed like distant school bells. It flew to a hexagonal cell in the silo wall. It was too far up for Adam to see precisely how the beetle extracted the contents from the shelf, but as it began its descent, he could see quite clearly what it now clutched in its legs.

Crystal wings ablur, the scarab sank toward the Conservator, aligning the bottom of the blinder with the shelf of the Conservator's unfinished head. The automaton reached up, took the cargo in hand, and pulled the reliquary down. His periscopic eye blinked as it disappeared inside.

The Conservator head wrenched this way and that like a stubborn cork, then stopped abruptly and said, "A transcript is available. Shall I narrate?"

Adam looked to Runa, who gave an encouraging shrug. He said, "Yes, please."

A white circle, some three feet in diameter, appeared in the front of the inky lectern. It was as if a lamp had been lit behind a frosty porthole. Adam and Runa huddled a little nearer, and as they did, found each other's hands without looking away.

First shapes, then colors pushed through the whitewash as the keyhole in time opened.

The Brick Layer's face appeared, all but filling the field of view. Adam recognized him at once: ears protruding like the handles of a sugar bowl; face furrowed as if groomed by a rake. But gone from his expression was the warmth and surety Adam had seen before. The Brick Layer was angry. A flush swathed his brow. No, not a flush—a welt. He'd recently suffered a blow to the head. The resplendent hillside that cradled him made his skin seem all the paler. The scene expanded as their observer leaned away and stepped back.

The Brick Layer lay lashed to the lawn by his arms, legs, neck, and waist. One man held his right arm down while another hammered the final restraining spike into the soil. The view swung about several times, and Adam saw six men—all ashen with fear and gripping clubs and hammers. They stood in a circle about the founder. The park seemed otherwise empty. It was early morning. The indigo fog outside the diamond bell was just beginning to tint toward pink.

The Brick Layer's mouth moved, and the Conservator spoke for him in a voice that sounded like an unwell doorbell. "The hods are not your enemy! They are your fathers, your mothers, your children! Do not fear them, do not shun them, do not send them away! The sun will not rise if we don't finish what we began. Do not leave this birth unfinished!"

One of the men leaned down to stuff a rag into the Brick Layer's mouth. He was a snub-nosed youth bearing a mustache as insubstantial as a child's eyebrow. When he straightened again, he addressed another in the circle, a balding, squarish man with a browbeaten look on his face. "What are you waiting for, Owen? Don't lose your spine now. You know what happens if we let him go. This is our home. Our grandfathers left everything, gave every ounce of treasure they had to build this place. It is ours!" The young man gestured at the bound man with an expression of pure animus. "And he told us to protect it from marauders and thieves and saboteurs! What is the black trail but a spring of criminals? All this would be trampled. Your children would be collared, your wife would be tied to another man's bed, and you would be thrown into the Nautilus like slag. What is the Brick Layer if not a saboteur?"

The view rocked again toward the Brick Layer. The diminutive architect bucked against his restraints, making the barrel-like pendant that hung from his neck bounce upon his chest. Adam's breath caught in his throat.

Their view swung upward again, and there high in the air dangled a perfect square of black. The pyramid's capstone hung from the crane's long arm. Owen left their morbid circle and, climbing up the engine's treads, passed through the open door of the pilothouse.

"No," Runa murmured.

The hoist breaks released. The pyramidion plummeted.

A blue flash, brief as a meteor, lit the ground just before the grim capstone crashed down, throwing out clods of grass and soil. Then the view was obscured by trembling fingers as Jan buried his face in his hands.

"What was that?" Adam asked, pointing at the screen where he'd seen the short burst of light. "Conservator, can we see that final moment again? Just before the stone hits. Could you replay that—and slowly, please?"

In a display of what Runa would later call unusual compliance, the Conservator showed them the final seconds once more, stretching the frantic moment into an almost tranquil tableau.

The blue light lingered. It seemed to come from the Brick Layer. Not his clothes, but his exposed skin. Then something seemed to happen, something impossible, but before Adam could be sure, the black stone fell like the final curtain of a play.

"What was that?" Runa stood with arms crossed, one hand over her mouth.

"Please, once again, Conservator," Adam said. "And when I say stop, would you please hold the image for a moment? Thank you."

The dreadful plummet of the stone replayed, and the second the flash of light flickered out, Adam called for a halt.

The two of them gaped at the frozen image—still as a painting, bright as a mirror. The Brick Layer's clothes, necklace, and boots hung in the air. The rope that bound him now clung to nothing. The Brick Layer had vanished.

A commotion of bootheels behind them brought their heads around.

Docent Allod strode alongside three lumenguards dressed in their white-and-yellow uniforms, though without their visors. They came with their sparking wands drawn, battery packs bouncing on their backs, a grimacing Elrin at the lead. Adam recognized the two behind him as having come from his former squad. One was a young man called Dunn who had been unfairly aged by hair loss; the other was a young woman named Hallux with hair shaved to her crown and gold rings crowding the verge of either ear. Adam had observed both of them demonstrate an affinity for their lapsed sergeant beyond the requirements of his rank.

Runa took two steps toward intercepting her mother, and then everyone was frozen by the Conservator, who spoke in a voice that roared like a pipe organ. "Ida Blaire Allod, you have one outstanding circulate. Your account is not in order. Your privileges are revoked!"

Ida made a vague gesture, the sort of automatic rebuff a wealthy man practices upon a beggar, and said, "Conservator, we don't have time for a scolding. I'm afraid this young man poses an imminent threat to the sanctity of Neb—"

"You have no authority to use it!" the Conservator thundered on. The school of gilded beetles grew suddenly agitated and began to swoop lower. The Conservator grasped something from under his podium, something that rasped upon the ground. "Your privileges have been revoked!"

"There's no need to go into that now," Ida said with cracking confidence, then almost in the same breath, she beckoned to Adam and her daughter in a considerably more urgent tone. "Come here this instant. Come here!" She began backing toward the entrance as she spoke.

"Your account is not in order!" the Conservator boomed. The lanky giant stepped from behind his pulpit. He dragged along with him a sword that was as long as a church pew.

The Conservator lifted the claymore as his scarabs flocked about the brass bullet that crowned his head. "Ida Blaire Allod, return the Brick Layer's Eye!"

Chapter Eighteen

Retreat is an ancient art. Generals have studied it; conscripts practiced it. Nearly fifty years of survival has taught me that often the best time to run away is shortly before you arrive.

—from the diary of Joram Brahe, captain of the *Natchez King*

Hurry! He can't leave the Delectus! Run!" Ida cried, though no one appeared to need the direction. Elrin's two former privates, who stood nearest the exit, were already out the door. Only Elrin refused to retreat. He wore a plastered smile of frightened exhilaration as he dashed toward his sister.

Adam felt as if someone had glued his shoes to the floor. His thoughts were still fixed on the Brick Layer—his body embellished by blue light one moment and entirely vanished the next. Even as his mind balked at the impossibility of what they'd been shown, Adam became aware that the Conservator's leg had entered his periphery. The automaton wore the tattered remnant of trousers that had been chewed by the angles of his joints into something closer to knee pants. His bare feet were like those of a monstrous bird; he stood upon talons that curled like scimitars.

But Adam was not afraid. He had special privileges. He was a contributor. He was safe.

Then Elrin shouted at them to duck.

They stooped just ahead of the Conserva[illegible]d, which raised a breeze as it passed over them and bit into the edge of the lectern, leaving a great notch in the black stone.

They straightened again, Runa gasping in shock, as she twisted toward the looming automaton. "Conservator! It's me, Runa Ilmr Allod! My account is in good—"

"Nautilus! Nautilus! The unfinished birth!" the Conservator moaned, drawing his blade back again like a reaper cocks his scythe.

"Run!" Adam said.

Fleeing as quickly as they could in leather shoes on polished marble, they slipped and held each other up in a mad scramble back toward Elrin even as he raised his sparking wand. Runa shouted at him not to shoot, but the bolt was already out and flashing over their heads.

Glancing back, Adam saw the lightning strike a stream of scarabs that had coursed into its path. A dozen of the buzzing porters burst into fiery shards.

Runa shouted, "Don't hurt him! Think of what we'll lose! Think of Father!"

Elrin seemed shocked that she was so displeased with his rescue. But there was no time to argue. The Conservator lurched after them, his strides deliberate and resounding as a siege engine knocking upon a city's gates. Ida Allod, dressed in a tightly tailored red suit, waved them on from just outside the entryway. She wore an expression that was the most transparent Adam had ever seen cross her face. She was afraid.

Adam was the last one out. He wished there were a door that he could slam behind him, but once again, Ida assured them, the Conservator was incapable of leaving his domain.

Two more bandies in addition to their own waited in the carriage porch.

"What was all that about the Brick Layer's Eye, Mother?" Runa asked.

"Oh, you heard him! He was raving! He's gone completely mad," the docent said, slicking down the pale blond hairs that had come unglued from her scalp.

Runa shook her head in stubborn, short strokes. "No, no, no. He is temperamental, but you set him off. What did you—"

The lumenguard behind Ida, the young woman named Hallux, gave a warning shout and raised the wand of her ionastra. Adam turned in time to see the Conservator stooped in the doorway of the Delectus.

"Nautilus! Nautilus!" he said, dragging his sword behind him as he emerged.

"He can't—" Ida began, and the rest was drowned out by a crack of lightning.

The bolt from Hallux's ionastra struck the Conservator squarely in the chest. The violent spark frayed into tendrils that wrapped about his ribs and snaked up his neck. His ancient clothes erupted into flames. Runa screamed, even as Adam pulled her farther from the immolating giant.

Hallux stood motionless, stunned by the dramatic result of her discharge. The automaton lurched and reeled within the fire that engulfed him. They waited for his collapse.

The sword burst from the confusion of flames like a javelin. It lanced Hallux at her core and passed through her pack as it carried her backward. The sword's point pierced one of the carved pillars, staving her to an effigy of the Tower. She hung there, chin on her chest, eyes open but unlit. Elrin shouted her name as he ran to her side, took up her hand. Beneath her, the Sphinx's glowing battery fluid mingled with her spilling life in a growing puddle.

The Conservator shook off the vestiges of his burnt clothes. Naked, he looked like a titanic anchor that had sprouted arms and legs. Adam saw at once it was a hopeless fight. Their only chance was to take to their heels. And yet Elrin's remaining disciple, the pink-scalped Dunn, had not been dissuaded by the failure of his compatriot. From behind the shelter of one of the bandies, he leveled his wand and plied the automaton with more lightning. As the bolts scattered harmlessly across his pocked and mottled skin, the engine stepped toward the soldier.

Free of his clothes, the keeper of reliquaries seemed quicker now. With one hand, he swatted the bandy away; with the other, he grasped Dunn by his head, lifted him, and whipped him back and forth twice before his body came free and flew in a gory pinwheel into the wall of the Delectus.

The bandy, which had been tipped onto its side by the Conservator's swat, clipped Ida's leg in its tumble. Thrown onto her hands and knees, the astonished docent began an uneven, halting crawl. When the Conservator had attacked Dunn, Adam and Runa had taken shelter behind the remaining bandy. They waited to see if the Conservator would turn on them or pursue Runa's mother, who slunk along in the opposite direction. It seemed to Adam that Ida was moving blindly, addled by either her injury or the traumatic scene. She could've taken cover behind a pillar, but no, she continued to skulk along the middle of the carriage porch floor.

The Conservator's periscope eye twisted at them, then to Ida. Adam held his breath. The engine's hips turned in the docent's direction with a heavy groan.

Elrin slid in beside them, his face pale as paper, his hands slick with Hallux's blood. He peeked about the chariot's sideboard, and said, "Oh my god, it's going to kill Mum."

"Elrin, can the two of you right the other bandy?" Adam asked.

"I think so." Elrin appeared shocked by the brutal deaths of his compatriots. Adam wondered if it was the first time he had witnessed such violence so intimately. "What are you going to do?"

"I'm going to try to save her. Get the bandy ready. We're going to need a ride." Then, before Runa could argue, Adam hurdled the cart's sidewall, and started the engine.

As soon as Runa and her brother were clear, Adam throttled the chariot into reverse. He had gleaned a lot about the bandy's controls from observing Runa, and still it came as a relief when he did not immediately drive the chariot into the wall. The Conservator stood between him and the docent, and the ambling engine hadn't been considerate enough to leave enough room for him to squeeze by. Adam saw no option but to circle around the colonnade and come to Ida from the far side. He could only hope there was enough time for the detour.

Steering the three-wheeled bandy in reverse proved more difficult than he expected. The chariot rocked and bounced unsteadily as he overcorrected his steering first one way, then the other. Still, he managed to keep from tipping over. When he cleared the porch entrance, he opened the throttle to full and began to tear along the outside of the line of columns.

Adam was confused when he passed Runa and Elrin hiding behind a column, but then he glimpsed the Conservator through the pillars nearby and realized the automaton had changed course. It wasn't until he rounded the far end of the porch that Adam saw what had waylaid the Conservator. He had paused to retrieve his sword. The great sword's central vein shone red where blood ran down the fuller like the gutter of an abattoir. Unsheathing the blade from the soldier's pinned corpse, the automaton turned again toward the scrabbling docent.

Adam parked the bandy between the docent and the approaching titan, who continued to repeat his obscure mantra about unfinished births and bitumen as he swatted the air with his claymore. Adam pulled a brass stop on the dashboard, applying the mag-brake, and then reopened the throttle to full. He searched his pockets until he found a teaspoon, one of many unwanted gifts, and jammed its handle into the lever's base, locking the control in place. The ascending wail of the turbine prickled his skin. He had not forgotten Runa's first lesson about bandies. He bounded from the footboard without any sense of how long he had before the chariot exploded.

When Adam reached Ida's side, he found the docent still pulling herself along, her effort hampered by her impulse to hold her wounded leg with one hand. She muttered in a quaking voice, "Take it, take it," over and over again. Adam shouted at her, asking if she could stand, asking her to lean on him, but she was insensible to his questions.

He looked up. The Conservator was two steps away from the whining bandy. Adam grabbed the docent by the collar, flipped her onto her back, and began dragging her toward the last column, hoping that they would cross behind it before the fireball came.

The Conservator seemed almost curious when he reached the quivering cart. He bent and probed it with the tip of one finger, ringing the handrail dully, and causing the bandy to rock on its struts.

Still hauling the docent along, Adam turned his face and closed his eye in anticipation.

But the explosion did not come.

Tiring of the diversion, the Conservator knocked the bandy onto its side as casually as a dog tips a footstool. The chariot lay upon one wheel, where it continued its plaintive, breathless wail. The Conservator stepped past the toppled carriage and settled the flat of his sword upon his shoulder like a bindle. It took him two strides to catch up with Adam and his ungainly baggage.

The docent's eyes gleamed bright; her cheeks were flush from the strangling effect of being towed by the collar. Adam willed his hand to let go, to leave to her fate a woman who had done nothing but exploit and abuse him and his sister. But he found he could not abandon her without also forsaking his conscience.

"The unfinished birth," the Conservator said, his musical bellows sounding almost elegiac. Adam wondered if the machine's fury hadn't crested.

Then the Conservator said, "Ida Blaire Allod, I hereby cancel your account." He raised his sword high over his head, and Adam saw it was not mercy that had soothed the Conservator's temper. It was triumph.

The mag-brake failed with a pop, and the hub that pressed upon the ground began to spin, whipping the whole carriage about as it did. The stabilizing tail of the bandy careened around, striking the Conservator on the edge of one shin. The blow was enough to make the copper giant lurch. When the tail came back around for a second pass, it succeeded in sweeping the leg entirely. The automaton dropped his sword as he fell to one knee. The gyring bandy began to leap and bounce from wheel edge to handrail to bull nose to hub, hurled about by the wild swat of its stabilizing beam. The Conservator, catching the blows of the chariot's spasms, held up an arm to defend itself. The crash of metal was as deafening as a derailing train.

Adam did not wait to see how the fracas would end. To revive the docent, Adam clanged his bonded band against hers, an act that he knew made the bones buzz uncomfortably. The abrasive sound and sensation had the intended effect. Her eyes focused upon him. He hoisted the docent to her feet and, with her arm held around his neck, began a three-legged run.

It was a relief to see they hadn't far to go. Elrin and Runa had righted the remaining bandy and brought it about to the edge of the porch. Runa helped pull her limping mother up. There wasn't enough room for Adam to put his heels down, but he toed the edge of the footboard, and clung to either side of the guardrails with a grip that could've cracked stone.

The overloaded bandy did not exactly speed away. And all were relieved when it reached the exit tunnel and did not stall upon that incline.

Adam's last vision of the Conservator was of him pulling a wheel off the chariot and hurling it between the pillars at the alabaster sun that crowned the fountain. The lamp burst with a flash of fire and shattered glass. Darkness seemed to reach up the tunnel after them like a grasping hand.

Chapter Nineteen

Trust no man with a secret unless its preservation will enrich himself as well. The soul of discretion is not integrity but stock.

—from the diary of Joram Brahe, captain of the *Natchez King*

"You said it would explode!" Adam shouted at the wall of backs at the fore of the racing bandy.

Elrin, who was steering, dominated much of the cockpit, pinning his mother and sister to either handrail with the breadth of his shoulders. Runa craned her neck so Adam could see her puzzlement. "What are you talking about?" Adam reminded her of the occasion when he had first stepped aboard her bandy. Runa gritted her teeth, though they failed to cage the uneasy laugh that followed. "I was joking! Of course they don't explode if you leave the brakes on. Can you imagine? I just didn't want you fiddling with my controls."

Adam opened his mouth to reply before he knew what he would say. He wasn't sure whether he felt tickled or traumatized to learn his moment of bravery had been fueled by ignorance and pardoned by good luck. And he'd felt so clever a moment before.

The rumble of the bandy's wheels, the coursing air, and their awkward proximity to one another made conversation all but impossible. Adam overheard Runa ask her mother at a shout if she were badly injured. The docent replied at a similar volume that her leg was only bruised. Then silence took them all.

The quiet allowed Adam a moment to reflect upon the recent revelations. He now knew that a gang of Nebosans had not wished to open their city to the hods, and had colluded to murder the Brick Layer so that they could interpret his vision without his help. What Adam didn't know was why the Conservator had gone to such lengths to conceal the crime. He supposed the answer had something to do with the Brick Layer's vanishing trick. Had the Brick Layer been some sort of magician? Where had he gone, and why had he not come back?

Though he had not yet had a moment to share the revelation with Runa, Adam had discovered something else: He was virtually certain he knew how Docent Allod had edited *The Daredevil's Brother*. She had used the "Brick Layer's Eye." The eye was not a literal organ, but an eyepiece. When Adam saw the Brick Layer lashed to the ground, he had gotten a much better look at the pendant that hung from his neck. What he had previously mistaken for a large thimble was in fact a silver loupe—the same loupe that now hung about Ida's neck. She had somehow excavated it from under the black pyramidion. The Conservator's outburst had only confirmed Adam's suspicion. The eyepiece that she loved to fidget with, the lens that swirled like a liquid pearl, could search through and stitch together moments torn from time.

Adam found all of this very interesting, but it did not explain why Ida Allod had come to the Delectus in the middle of the night, nor why she had dragged her son and two of his lackeys along with her. And what had she said before the Conservator cut her off? That Adam *posed an imminent threat to the sanctity of Nebos.*

The answer struck Adam with all the pleasure of an electric shock. Allod could only be referring to the orphans. His and Runa's plan to bring the hods to Nebos had been exposed.

From his tenuous position clinging to the back of the bandy, Adam regarded the docent, squeezed to the rail by the bulk of her son. She watched him from the corner of her eye. Her expression did not waver when he caught her staring. She continued to observe him with an indolent sort of vigilance as if he were a spider on the ceiling and she were still deciding whether to get a broom.

"Where are we going?" he asked.

She did not reply.

* * *

Adam expected Elrin would deliver them either to Captain Dyre's doorstep or to one of the gatehouses where the night guard kept watch over the windstiles. Or perhaps Docent Allod, ever the dramatist, would want to confront them with their crime directly, in which case they would be bound for the bandy station where thousands of young hods slept in new clothes and dreamed of green gardens.

Adam was surprised to discover their final destination was the furnace room.

As Elrin parked the bandy before the frog-eyed windows of Ossian's home, Runa asked what they were doing there at such an ungodly hour. Ossian would be asleep.

"He's waiting for us," Elrin said, skirting Runa's gaze by busying himself with powering down the bandy. Obviously in no mood for mysteries, Runa pelted her brother with questions, demanding a real answer, putting herself in his path, and pushing on his chest when he tried to step around her.

It was her mother who responded at last: "I always knew you enjoyed being disagreeable. You're a contrarian, which is such an easy thing to be." Ida paced away from the bandy, thin arms folded, hands almost on her shoulders. The pose reminded Adam of a corpse laid in a casket. He suspected the docent just wanted to hear her own heels aggrandized by the echo of the Warren. "But underneath all that agitation, you are remarkably ordinary. You never could come to grips with your artistic mediocrity." She pivoted on her heel, pinched the loupe between her fingers and began rubbing it like a charm. "Even so, I did not think you were this wicked."

"I don't know what you're talking about," Runa said, but with little conviction.

"The night shift at the Cupel is an awful post," Elrin said in an exhausted growl. "It's dark. It smells. You can't think. There's no one to talk to. You just have to sit there on a stool with an urn full of eyes at your knees. I actually look forward to the drive to the Delectus. It's lonely and boring, but at least there's a wind in your face to keep you awake. When I delivered the new arrivals this evening, the Conservator asked me to take a load of battered reliquaries to the furnace. I almost dumped them off at the side of the road, but no, I thought, *Be a good soldier. Earn your way back.*"

"What are you talking about?" Runa asked.

"When I saw Ossian piling his cart with tins and jars in the middle of the night, I knew he was up to something. I followed him to Silk Garden Station. They scattered like roaches when they saw me. I couldn't count them all. There were dozens . . . *hundreds*." Elrin looked at his sister at last. His eyes were as red as raw meat. "Why did you do it, Roo?"

"How could I not?" she fired back, the heat returning to her voice. "We had the same father. You heard the same lessons. He taught us how much we depend upon the bee, the moth, the beetle, the ant. He told us what madness it was to believe that we could be superior to something we cannot live without. He knew this was always meant to be the city of the hods. He knew that was what the Brick Layer wanted and what we could not allow. But our father, wise as he was, was also a timid man. Browbeaten. Defeated." Runa dipped her head toward her mother but seemed incapable of raising her eyes to look at her. "I was, too. But not anymore."

While brother and sister argued in the green-lit cul-de-sac, Adam let the shadows obscure his shuffling advance. If he could just get behind the tall guard, he could make a grab for the ionastra's wand. Adam knew he'd have no chance of wresting the cumbersome pack from Elrin's shoulders, but if he could just get a hand on the lightning caster, perhaps he could—

"All right, Adam. That's enough," Ida said, pointing a gleaming pistol at him. "Back away, please."

Seeing the tapered barrel of the dianastra, Runa cried, "Mother!"

"Don't call me that!" Ida snapped without shifting her hawkish glare from Adam. "I have tried to protect you from the beginning. I came to your defense in that first accord. I explained away your outburst in the Cavaedium. I excused your thievery as a charming quirk. I rewrote the story of your disastrous patrol to make you appear heroic. I have done my best to save you from yourself, but you are a relentless masochist." Her tongue whipped so quickly it raised a froth in the corners of her mouth. She swallowed and continued at a more measured pace. "We are here because it's not too late for you. You have one final choice to make."

Adam crossed his arms. "You want to be rid of the orphan children, is that it? Well, too bad. This is their home. The Brick Layer built it for them, not you. You are nothing but a clan of night watchmen who started sleeping in the master's bed. That doesn't make it yours. It's their right to be here. And you couldn't send them back if you wanted to. If they were discovered, they had orders to scuttle the windscow. I'm sure that barge is sunk by now." This was an absolute lie of course, but Adam delivered it with such contempt he was nearly convinced of it himself. "There are too many of them for you to sweep under the carpet. You'll have to hold an accord, let the people decide."

"All right," Ida said, visibly bored by Adam's impassioned speech. "If you're finished..." She twitched the barrel of the dianastra toward the entrance of Ossian's storehouse.

Adam had come to know the storeroom well enough to perceive Ossian's enigmatic style of organization. More importantly, Adam could tell when that order had been upset. He saw the signs of a struggle in the clothes that had been half-pulled from their hangers, in the dented tepee of rolled-up rugs, and in the cleared spot on the counter amid the teacup pyramids.

The fireman lay on the floor behind that glass cabinet. At first, Adam feared Ossian had been killed, but then he saw him move.

Docent Allod went behind the counter, her sparking pistol pointed downward. She made a noise of amusement that sounded eerily like a startled dove. Bending, she retrieved something from the ground, then stood again, holding a pepperbox pistol. Ossian gave a groan of frustration.

"Was this what you were worming after? Were you going to kill me? I'd never kill you," the docent said, then fired a spark into Ossian's back.

Runa screamed and lunged toward her mother, but her brother hauled her back by the wrist. She wheeled about and slapped him, recoiled to strike again, but he flung her to the floor. When he drew the sparking wand from his pack, his expression had gone as flat as a coin.

"Stop being so dramatic!" Ida said. "I didn't use a full charge. He'll be fine. My god, do you really think I'd murder my tailor?"

"Why are you such a toad?" Runa asked, looking up at her brother through the hair that had fallen over her eyes.

Ida intercepted the insult, assuming it, like everything else, was meant for her. "I am the most civil person you will ever met," she said, slipping back around the counter. "You're just ungrateful. As was our poor friend here." She examined his four-barreled pistol before tucking it in the pocket of her bloodred jacket. "There was a much more pleasant option available to him. Now, where did he put my hat. Ah!"

She plucked a pink hatbox from the bottom of an open wardrobe, the bar of which was crowded with wedding gowns and veils. "I think I'd like to talk somewhere where the lighting is a bit more dramatic."

Carrying the hatbox by the cross of the white ribbon that sealed it, Ida nodded at her son. Elrin hauled Runa to her feet, keeping his lightning caster leveled at Adam as he did. He shoved his sister forward so that he could menace them both with his weapon as they walked.

What before had been a slow and picking passage through Ossian's overstuffed storeroom was made easier by the recent dispatching of towels, clothes, blankets, basins, and washboards. The way was neither straight nor wide, but a path to the Nautilus stood clear.

Adam's thoughts raced ahead. Obviously, Ida meant to threaten him with a ride down the slow water rapids, and though Runa would probably be spared the same fate, Adam was not sure how far Ida might take things. His best hope was to wait until they were just inside the Nautilus, when everyone would be momentarily blinded by the radiant light. Then, Adam would throw himself at Elrin and trust the docent would not shoot at her own son.

But his plot was soon dashed outside the leaden shell of the Nautilus when Elrin reminded his mother to put on her spectacles. Ida extracted a pair of goggles, the lenses of which were as big as tea biscuits and black as a boot. They made her head look like an empty skull. Elrin donned a similar set. He did not offer anyone else a pair. He commanded his sister to open the Nautilus door and said that Adam would be the first through.

Entering the Nautilus was like walking into blindness. The air seemed more agitated than before. It ground against Adam's skin like sand under wet clothes. He gasped as he shuffled forward, stumbling on the lip of the hatchway. He squinted at the chambers of slow water under his feet, the galactical whorl of blue and white, his gaze drifting along the drain toward the hungry light of the Allonomia. The speck strobed and seethed like a crumb fallen from the sun. Adam's nerves fizzed with an unending shiver.

Through the glare, puddles began to appear underfoot. There seemed to be more of them this time, too many to avoid in places. The toes of his boots glowed with the Sphinx's curious serum. He glanced up at the vents in the ceiling that resembled oversized showerheads. They dripped with ruby light.

Vainly, Adam hoped that Elrin or Ida would slip and stumble into the opening in the diamond floor, saving him the trouble of having to dream up an escape. But they were not hampered by the glare of the room, and predictably, the portal to the icy flow was their intended destination.

"I promised I would offer you a choice," Ida said.

"And I already told you, the hods aren't going back."

"Oh, I don't care about that. I'm sure Captain Dyre can handle a few brats. We've been arguing about canceling the Fundament patrol for years. The votes grow narrower every accord. It's not like we *need* their gifts, which grow stingier and more wretched by the day." The docent drew a ring in the air with her pistol, the flourish signaling a change in subject. "No, I'm offering you a different choice, a more important one."

Though their figures had not fully emerged from the blinding white, Adam could now see more than teary blurs and indistinguishable halos. He saw the docent turn her hatbox over to her son. Once she settled the bead of her sparking pistol on Adam again, Elrin holstered his sparking wand and began undoing the ribbon that held the parcel. Ida told her daughter to stand next to Adam so she could keep an eye on them both. The docent chided Runa for always taking his hand like some sort of needy child. The scolding did not discourage Runa's grip.

"I'm afraid my earlier criticism of your behavior may have glossed over some of your finer moments," Ida said to Adam. "Though ill-advised, your visit to the black trail was certainly good theater. And you came out looking valiant enough after a little revision."

"Not all of us were so lucky. The edits left me looking like a stooge," Elrin said with a pout as he continued tugging at the knot. "Bring a larval hod into the city? As if I ever would!"

"And you've been rewarded for tarnishing your reputation," the docent said.

"Adam should've been a baritone from the start. Everyone said so!"

"You did all of this for a part?" Adam made no effort to conceal his disdain.

"I did all of this for a career!" Elrin shot back.

Ida pinched the top button of her shirt, twisting it in a dreamy fashion. "I am so glad, Adam, that you got to see some of my better qualities, too. I wish you had not allowed yourself to be seduced by my daughter. I know the people liked your tryst well enough, and I'm sure I can weave a nice little romance from all your ogling and pawing. People do love a good doomed affair. Still, it would've been nice to have finished what we started." The pink tip of her tongue flashed between her teeth. "Oh well. Even the greatest play must come to an end."

The knot undone, Elrin drew from the box a shining brass reliquary, a spangling new blinder.

"My other eye. Of course."

Ida's nostrils flared in disgust. "Oh, don't act like you saw this coming! You were too distracted by your heroics and your hand-holding and your needless, childish running away. I do not chase! I am pursued."

"Docent, if you really want to surprise me, don't do this. Show a little decency."

Ida put a hand to her chest and sighed. "You don't need to be afraid, Adam. I won't abandon you to the dark." Her voice took a lilt of tenderness that made Adam's heart rise into his throat. "You will live with me. You'll want for nothing. I shall bathe you and shave you and dress you myself. You will be fed from my table and warmed in my bed. And you will not talk of the hods, nor mention your feeble attempts to free them. No, we'll say they slunk over here on their own; there was no conspiracy. Because no one wants to watch the adventures of a traitor. So, you will be good, you will be quiet, and you will do what you're told."

Runa's grasp of Adam's hand turned hard as a fist. Uncomfortable as the strangling was, he found her anger reassuring. "You said I had a choice?"

"Yes. You can willingly contribute to the greatest creative endeavor ever undertaken—the sequel to *The Daredevil's Brother*—and live the rest of your life in luxury and obedience. Or we can take the eye and let the Nautilus have the rest of you. I cannot allow you to tarnish my work with your lack of . . . good sense."

"And Runa? What are you going to do to her?" Adam asked.

"That is up to her. If she behaves herself, nothing. If she requires correction, then I'll provide it."

Adam was accustomed to being backed into a corner. For most, the corner, the dead end, the edge of the precipice were all illogical, thoughtless places that were devoid of deliberation or hope. But Adam had done some of his best thinking with his back to a wall.

"All right," he said. "I'll do it." Runa began to argue at once. Turning to face her, he took her other hand in his, and as soon as she drew a breath, he said, "I've been nothing but a hindrance to your work since I got here. Now, you can paint again without the encumbrance of having to entertain some muddy rogue." He squeezed her hands when he said *hindrance* and *encumbrance* and hoped she understood his meaning. "And when my sequel comes out, you can complain about how trite it all is, how predictable. But at least you'll see how I've looked at you. You'll see how beautiful you are, how gifted, how patient, how full of love."

"Oh, that's quite enough of that," Ida said the instant Adam's and Runa's lips touched. "It's all very moving, but none of this is usable. I said, stop that! Both of you. Hands at your side. My god, Runa, you looked like you were trying to feed him an eel. Is that really how you kiss? Revolting."

Under her mother's instruction, Runa walked a dozen paces away from Adam even as Elrin advanced upon him with the reliquary raised. Elrin told Adam to face away, not because the procedure required it, but because it seemed he did not wish to look into the eye he was about to rob.

Ida kept her dianastra trained on Adam's chest, but her attention was necessarily divided between him and her daughter. Runa stood with her hands low and clasped together, a submissive posture that seemed to please her mother enough for her quick glances at her to grow less frequent.

"Be sure you have it lined up before you push it down," Ida told her son. "I don't want any unnecessary scars. That's it. There it is. Good. Now, slowly..."

Adam felt the bottom collar of the blinder press upon his hair like an unwanted crown.

Runa activated the bonded band and threw up her arm so violently her feet left the ground. The docent gave a startled yelp as her own arm flailed over her head in sympathy, carrying the pistol with it. The dianastra slipped from her grasp, bounced off the wall, and skittered some distance across the floor.

Adam's arm flew up, too, carried by the invisible strength of the bonded band. He added his own force to the effort. He drove the cuff into Elrin's knuckles, cracking several open and breaking his hold on the reliquary. The heavy visor clipped Adam's shoulder before clattering to the floor at their feet.

Elrin reared back, reaching for the sparking wand as he retreated. Crouching, Adam gripped the blinder by its valve and swung it in an uppercut that started on the ground.

If he had caught Elrin on the jaw, as he'd hoped, the blinder would've shattered bone. But Elrin got his arm up in time to steal the bite from the blow, though not without consequence. Elrin shouted in pain. He dropped his weapon to free his fist, which he drove at Adam's head. The blow landed squarely on Adam's ear, knocking him off his feet.

Adam landed awkwardly, still clinging to the blinder, which seemed more an anchor now than a weapon. He pushed himself into an unsteady kneel, hoping to take aim at Elrin's legs, but the toe of a boot found Adam's chin first. It lifted him off his knees only to drop him on his back. Adam's head bounced upon the diamond floor. Darkness bloomed, its petals spreading across his vision. Through the murk and pain, Adam saw the blinder spin away from him on its side and carom off the chamber wall.

He rolled his head the other way. It hardly felt attached to his shoulders. He saw Runa scrambling for her mother's dianastra. She appeared to slip on a puddle and fell into an ambling four-limbed lope. Even so, she was quick, spurred by desperation. She had nearly reached the pistol when her mother drew the pepperbox from her pocket and fired at her daughter.

The chamber rang, first with the crack of gunpowder, then with the singing track of the bullet as it skipped upon the floor, rang the dome, plinked against a ceiling grate, and finally rattled into silence.

At the sound of the shot, Runa abandoned her pursuit of her mother's sparking pistol and threw herself into a defensive ball, cradling her head between her arms.

"Stop it, Roo!" Elrin shouted. He stepped over Adam, who lay in a sprawled daze, pawing at an ear that had grown wet with blood.

As if through a party wall, Adam heard Elrin make coaxing noises as he advanced upon his sister. Elrin went cautiously, as if testing the boards of an old bridge. He appeared to understand that his sister might be provoked into doing something rash. Elrin's back was to Adam, and for the moment, the broad-shouldered guard blocked the docent's line of sight.

Knowing he would not get a better chance, Adam willed himself to his feet. The crystalline floor warped and swam beneath him as he rose onto elastic, unready legs. His jaw was a sponge of agony. But there was no time to recover. He fixed his eye on his goal and threw himself into a staggering trot.

He must've veered into the docent's view because she shouted a warning to her son, who had just begun to turn when Adam hurled himself at the lightning caster. He wrenched it free of its holster but hadn't time to turn the tip of it toward Elrin before the brute laid his hands on the barrel.

The tether tightened and leapt as they grappled over the rod. Elrin jerked the wand to his chest, yanking Adam along with it. Attempting to headbutt Adam on the nose, Elrin drove his forehead down, but not before Adam threw his head to one side. With the big man's face buried in his shoulder, Adam clamped his teeth upon the top of Elrin's ear. Yelping, Elrin rocked the barrel to one side, catching Adam under the chin and finishing the bite.

Pulling back, Elrin's face, what was not obscured by black lenses, was disfigured by an expression of absolute horror.

Adam spat out the warm cartilage and was about to knee Elrin in an unfriendly place when the big man spun around, in an attempt to dislodge Adam's hold on the barrel. Adam's grip held firm, and though his footing was less certain, the real crisis was that Elrin's turn had exposed Adam's back to Ida's sightline, a fact which appeared to alarm Elrin almost as much as it did Adam. The docent swung her aim from her daughter to the wrestling pair. Adam made himself as mobile a target as possible, dodging and feinting as he continued to heave at the sparking wand. Elrin shouted over Adam's head, "Don't shoot, Mother! Don't shoot! For the love of—"

The docent fired. Adam felt the air scatter above him and felt the bullet thump against something close by. He looked up to see a chunk from Elrin's pack was missing. A spray of gauzy insulation jutted from the gash. Elrin continued to shout at his mother, but Adam found the words unintelligible. The second gunshot had filled Adam's ears with an overwhelming whine. While Elrin continued to waste his breath, Adam took advantage of his distraction. He twisted the wand as he jerked it to one side. Elrin's grip slipped, and for an instant Adam thought he had wrested the weapon free. Then Elrin's fingers slid over the throttle-like lever that was the ionastra's trigger.

A fizzing bolt of electricity leapt from the barrel like a startled bird. Even as Adam felt a flicker of relief that the weapon had fired away from Runa, the spark struck a sizable puddle of the Sphinx's medium, which touched off the strangest reaction Adam had ever seen.

It looked a little like a shock wave, but one that expanded at a walking pace. This film of the slow bloom swam with every color, all swirling together like the surface of a soap bubble. It grew in much the same fashion, gobbling up other nearby puddles, which burst into spectral spheres that vanished as they melded with the central mass. This lurching expansion only halted when it came to a gap in the ponded medium, and there the cheerful bubble popped.

He'd only been to the seashore once, but Adam had never forgotten the sensation of being hit by an unseen ocean wave. It had caught him on the back and thrown him through a tumbler of sand, darkness, and panic that had lasted just long enough for Adam to be certain he had died.

The explosion caught him in much the same way.

As he hurtled through the air, arms and legs thrown out like the wings of a whirligig, Adam marked the surreal moment when his shoes flew from his feet.

The explosion came with no warmth, no fire, only violent force. He had no sense of how far he traveled before he slammed upon the floor. He was lucky enough to land on his back rather than his head, though he did not feel particularly grateful for the cascade of pain that traveled up his spine. He slid a short distance before coming to a stop in the crook where the dome met the floor.

He lay there panting for a moment, and when he felt reasonably sure that he had not broken his back, Adam rolled over, sat up, and surveyed the chamber. Runa was lying propped on her elbows with her hair in her face. She looked as dazed as he felt, but she was alive.

In a staggering limp, Adam went to her side. He asked her if she was all right, a question he had to shout into her ear. She nodded, but distractedly, and continued to squint at her brother, who appeared to have fallen into a full genuflect.

Runa scrambled to her feet, using Adam's shoulder to push herself up. She charged at her brother with stumbling urgency. Adam followed a few steps behind. Even as he ran, something in the floor caught his eye, a ribbon of crimson flowing through the chambers of the Nautilus's shell.

From his knees, Elrin gripped his mother's hands. He seemed to be pulling as hard he could, and yet the effort only kept her arms, shoulders, and head above the surface of the slow water. Her legs were caught already, devoured to the knee by the rollers of the next chamber. A crystallizing frost crawled up her neck even as Elrin fought to keep it in the air. Though her mouth moved, and her eyes fluttered, Adam saw at once she was beyond saving.

Runa must've seen the truth, too, because she was already on her brother's back, roaring into his ear and pulling on his arms, entreating him to let go. Indifferent to her prying, her pleas, her oaths, Elrin stared into his mother's terrified eyes as the ice reached them and they paled like breath upon a mirror.

Knowing Elrin was never going to let go, knowing he would allow himself to be dragged to his death by a corpse, pulled down one last time by a woman who'd berated him his entire life, Adam took a running start.

He tackled Elrin from the side and knocked him from his deathly hold. The three of them rolled away in a tumbling pile. The moment they stopped, Adam sat up with his hands shielding his face, expecting a fight. Instead, he saw Elrin moving in a scurrying crawl, recovering the distance to the hatch.

Elrin dove into the slow water, reaching after his mother's sunken hands.

Though he could not hear it, Adam felt Runa's screaming through his skin. He held her, and she fought him but did not battle long. They huddled about her grief, heads together, arms ringed around each other. Neither wanted to see the unraveling of her mother and brother as they threaded through the Nautilus.

They might've clung to each other there on the floor for much longer, but then the light that filled the room suddenly dimmed. It was as if the umbra of an eclipse had passed over them. The ever-active air took on an almost tacky quality, as if these new shadows were beginning to stick to them. Then Adam saw the blinking spark of the Allonomia had been replaced by a pinprick of infinite black.

He blinked, and it vanished, or rather the flashing crumb of sunlight returned, and with it, an earthquake.

The chamber shook so violently that the puddles of medium broke and leapt. A fresh shower of red fell from the grates above, spattering their shoulders and pecking the crystal expanse. Adam and Runa could only let the floor beat them and rattle their bones. They clung to each other while the Tower of Babel rocked like a dead tooth.

After a brief eternity, the titanic spasm softened to a dwindling shiver. They clambered to their feet and were halfway to the hatch when Adam spotted the broken chain of a necklace tangled on the floor. A little farther on, he saw its pendant.

Without breaking stride, Adam bent and scooped up the Brick Layer's Eye.

Chapter Twenty

I have done it. I have scrabbled into heaven . . . All the Tower under the Collar now seems little better than a poorhouse.

—from the diary of Joram Brahe, captain of the *Natchez King*

It was a lovely morning. The sort of morning that calls for a second cup of tea, a second pass through the almanac or post. The sort of morning that seems to teach birds a new verse to their songs and feels at once warm and cool, eternal and fleeting. Butterflies flitted about the base of the pyramid's black capstone. They perched on the blooming lavender, wings pressed together like praying hands.

Adam stood on the purgatorial stool with a rope around his neck and his hands bound behind his back. He was feeling philosophical. From the high throne of retrospective wisdom, he could distinguish error from the inevitable. He had long suspected that he was destined for the plank, the noose, the firing squad. Such was the fate of thieves.

But he had never dreamed he would be executed for a noble cause.

It had been six days since he and Runa had emerged from the Warren, their clothes ripped and dripping with the Sphinx's medium. They were greeted by a crowd of their admirers, who had gathered expecting to see a romantically rumpled pair of lovers, not two bloody and bruised ghouls who smelled as if they'd slept in a vulture's nest. Adam and Runa retreated to her garden folly as quickly as they could.

Before leaving the underground, they had revived Ossian. The fireman was groggy, bruised, and unhappy, but he made no complaints after seeing their distress. Runa told him what had happened in phrases broken by anguish, deafness, and pain. Ossian embraced her, spoke to her out of Adam's ringing earshot, and then told them both at a shout what they'd been too stunned to realize. All these deaths would bring the Warren under scrutiny. Someone had to warn Faruq.

When Adam and Runa bandied to Silk Garden Station, they found Faruq sitting on a stool, brushing the tangles out of a young girl's hair with quick practiced strokes. They warned him of the likelihood of increased activity and the need for them to make do with what they had for a time. Faruq assured them that they could survive for a few days, perhaps a week, but that the last of the nearly five thousand children had just arrived. The exodus was complete.

The old hod asked Adam when they could expect to be introduced to the gardens he'd planted in the children's imaginations. Adam begged for a little more time. He still had to prepare the natives for the orphans' appearance.

In truth, Adam had no idea what he was going to do or say to soften the hearts of the locals, but he didn't wish to worry Faruq, who already had plenty to fret about. Though they had imported the discipline and structure they'd established on the black trail, Faruq and his clan of caregivers were discovering their new circumstances came with fresh challenges. There were dirty bowls, lost shoes, broken lamps, and stains spreading everywhere like a pox. Each moment came in with a crisis and went out with a patch. The lambs were growing restless; the shepherds, exhausted. They could not delay forever.

After escaping their admirers and returning to her garden folly, Runa went upstairs to bathe and change. The Sphinx's medium had lost its luster, and as it dimmed to a gray muck, it had taken on a putrid smell. Downstairs, Adam stripped, then searched for somewhere to hide his reeking clothes, eventually concluding they could not stay indoors. He threw the pile out a window and into the hedge. He washed himself from the kitchen sink. After he'd scrubbed himself pink and made quite a puddle on the floor, it occurred to him that he had nothing here to wear. Then he saw Runa's smock hanging upon a peg. It was strangely liberating to be dressed in nothing but a loose cape. He felt as free as the clapper of a bell. When Runa returned and saw his bare knees sticking out from the bottom of her color-stained smock, she laughed, then just as quickly looked ashamed of herself.

Adam didn't know what to say to console her. How did one go about mourning the loss of an abusive mother? The passing of Runa's brother seemed to tighten a knot that had tangled over a lifetime. Adam had no doubt that Elrin's fatal choice—which seemed the piteous act of a bullied boy—would be a slow-to-heal wound that Runa would have to tend for many years. But Ida's death appeared to leave Runa with something much worse than a wound. It left her with one side of an argument that could never be answered and a grievance that could not be heard.

Though Adam knew better than to tell Runa what he imagined she might be feeling. Instead, he made her tea, asked if she would like to talk, and did not argue when she said she just wished to sit with Celeste for a while. The old hound proved the perfect comforter. Nuzzled together on the sofa, the pair soon fell asleep.

While they napped, Adam sat at her table with pencil and paper, trying to compose a few lines that would summon forth the communal conscience of the gilded city. He couldn't very well lead a mob of children up from the Warren, take a bow, and shout, "Ta-da!"

He was still fussing over his *hithertos* and *wherefores* an hour later when Captain Dyre knocked on the folly door, making Celeste bark and Runa leap.

The captain had not come alone. An armed squad flanked him, all with visors on, perhaps to make the confrontation of one of their own a little less awkward. Dyre had the look of a man who'd been called in on his day off. The breast of his uniform was only half-buttoned, and the long threads of white hair that usually blanketed his bald head now hung over one ear.

Adam imagined he did not present a very polished figure either. He had one swollen red ear, a bruise covering half his jaw, and he was standing barefoot and barelegged in a painter's smock.

At first, it wasn't clear how the captain's line of questioning had led him to Runa's door. Dyre began by telling them of his desire to know why two of his privates had been called out of the barracks in the dead of night by Elrin Allod and why the disgraced sergeant had deserted his post. The captain naturally assumed it had something to do with Elrin's mother, but he had already called upon Docent Allod, only to find her out of the office. The docent's current assistant informed the captain that she had left home late in the evening and not returned. Where was she? When Adam feigned ignorance, the captain reminded him that he and Runa shared a bonded band with the docent and her son.

"They're broken," Adam said.

"That seems unlikely. But if it's really the case that the bands aren't functioning, we'll just have to search the Warren from top to bottom."

"My mother is dead," Runa said, stepping past Adam. "My brother, too. The bands won't lead you to them because they're both in the furnace. They attacked Ossian. He's bruised, but alive. Then they tried to take Adam's eye. My mother wanted to make a sequel."

The captain scowled. "You're claiming self-defense, then?"

"It was more of an accident. There was a shiver. It knocked my mother into the slow water. Elrin leapt in after her."

"And my troops, Private Hallux and Private Dunn, they can confirm this?"

"No, unfortunately, they can't," Runa admitted.

"But we know where they are; we can take you to them," Adam hurried to add. Much as he dreaded the prospect of returning to the gory scene, they couldn't afford to let the lumenguard search the Warren.

"Then let's be on our way." The captain turned, his unsettled hair flailing like a whip.

"Could we first stop by my house for a pair of trousers and shoes?" Adam asked.

In hindsight, given the captain's own unready appearance, Adam shouldn't have been surprised when his request was denied.

The shattered remains of the orb that had once lit the fountain outside the Delectus crunched under their wheels as they approached the hall of records. Adam was relieved to see that the Conservator was not waiting for them in the courtyard.

The captain and his men were forced to inspect the carnage of the carriage porch by the light of their chariots' headlamps. It was immediately evident that his two privates had not been killed by Adam, nor indeed by any man. The captain asked for and accepted Adam's version of events, which was true, right down to the cause of the Conservator's rage and the tool behind Ida Allod's creative genius. Adam only omitted the fact that he presently carried the Brick Layer's Eye in the pocket of his smock. He feared the captain would confiscate the instrument, and Adam still had need of it.

After giving some of his soldiers the unenviable chore of gathering the remains of their compatriots, the captain announced his intention to question the Conservator himself. He had to know whether the aging automaton's derangement was temporary or permanent. Adam explained his special standing as a contributor to the collection and volunteered to initiate contact with the automaton. Runa was not at all enthusiastic about the idea, but he insisted, and in the end, the captain agreed. Adam would go in first, and if he was not mauled, the others would follow.

It was not courage that carried Adam over the ashes of the Conservator's clothes, not bravery that led him along the snaking gouge the claymore had carved into the floor. It was not valor but optimism that propelled him. Adam had decided to believe that the Conservator was not an indiscriminate murderer, not malfunctioning, not acting without cause. The automaton's disturbed muttering was warranted. Whatever was happening to the Nautilus was getting worse, and while the Nebosans were content to shrug at the shivers that were growing in frequency and severity, the Conservator was understandably alarmed. Indeed, Adam could only hope that he had not delivered thousands of orphans to the orlops of a burning ship. The Conservator's reaction to Ida's possession of the Brick Layer's Eye had been unquestionably extreme, but so had Ida's abuse of a tool that could peer through time and into the private lives of anyone. Adam chose to believe that the Conservator still served the Brick Layer's vision, a vision that favored the hods and sought to preserve the shining city rather than the lordly squatters.

Adam found the Conservator behind his bleak pulpit, plucking unreal cherries from the air and murmuring to his flock of golden scarabs. Noticing Adam, the Conservator reiterated his good standing with a nonchalance that Adam found heartening. He swallowed the fearful lump in his throat that his optimism had failed to entirely dissolve and announced that he had come to return the Brick Layer's Eye. When Adam pulled the loupe from his pocket, he half expected to hear the rasp of the Conservator's claymore as he dragged it from behind his post.

Instead, one of the scarabs dove at his open palm and snatched the eyepiece away. The beetle carried the instrument back to its master's desk. The Conservator accepted the loupe, which the great pipes of his fingers seemed to miniaturize. He said, "The unfinished birth," opened the hatch of his mouth and, to Adam's surprise, popped the loupe inside.

Captain Dyre's voice rang from the doorway, asking for a confirmation of safe passage. Knowing he was out of time, Adam requested the retrieval of an espial, and as the Conservator dispatched one of his minions to fetch the requested vault, Adam called the others forward.

Dyre entered with some officious bluster about his authority to interrogate and, if need be, depose the automaton, though his words were quickly drowned out by the Conservator's recitation of each person's full name and the status of their borrowing privileges. The captain was standing at Adam's side at the foot of the Conservator's desk before he could be heard again. He said, "The lumenguard's oath to defend Nebos does not excuse native appliances who threaten the sanctity or safety of our people. You will be held accountable for the murders of—"

The captain was interrupted by the arrival of a reliquary. The brass cylinder settled upon the waiting shelf of the automaton's bisected head. The dial in his desk began to glow, even as Dyre complained, "Conservator, I have not requested a retrieval. I am explaining your duty to—"

"Excuse me, Captain," Adam said. "I think he wants to show us something."

The Brick Layer's face pressed to the fore of the milky glass. Curious, the men in Dyre's squad huddled nearer. The scene expanded, revealing the bound body of the Tower's architect. The captain swore under his breath.

The Conservator gave his street organ voice to the Brick Layer's words: "The hods are not your enemy. They are your fathers, your mothers, your children! Do not fear them, do not shun them, do not send them away! The sun will not rise if we don't finish what we began. Do not leave this birth unfinished!"

Once word got out that the Conservator was screening an espial that featured the attempted murder of the Brick Layer and his abrupt disappearance, everyone in Nebos wanted to see it for themselves. Even the reclusive poets were teased from their hermitages by the prospect of an answer to the long-standing question of the Brick Layer's fate.

They came to the Delectus in droves. The lumenguard were forced to set up barricades and organize a queue. Viewers had to be admitted in groups because the Conservator's espial portal was only so large, and his insistence that every visitor's lending status be announced in excruciating detail was insufferable when practiced upon a mob. But the automaton's willingness to replay the espial, to slow the moment of the Brick Layer's flashing disappearance, was tireless. So long as Adamos Boreas was in the vicinity to exercise his privileges, the Conservator was willing to play the Brick Layer's final moments on a loop.

When the hour grew late, a cot was brought for Adam to sleep upon. When he thought he might be driven mad by the Conservator's jangling voice, cotton wadding was provided for his ears.

The espial had a marked effect on the mood of the natives. By the evening of the second day, many had begun to rally in the parks, making speeches and holding public debates. The birthright of the hods became a point of extreme contention, and the natives of Nebos began to fall into several camps. There were those who claimed that the hods who the Brick Layer had meant to welcome into the fold were long dead, and while they may have been noble laborers once, the criminals and lunatics that clogged the Old Vein now certainly were not. The wrong had been done and could not be undone. Others complained that it was hardly fair that they be held responsible for the sins of their fathers. Even if the hods had once been promised the gardens, that was before the highland clans had expanded to fill them. There was no room to accommodate all the wretches of the world.

Not all were so unsympathetic. Some saw the hypocrisy of pretending to live at the will of the Brick Layer only to ignore his dying edict, and they perceived in their neighbors' selfishness echoes of the murderous gang that had attempted to crush the Tower's father. These Nebosans believed in both a manifest need and their duty to address it.

There followed proposals for the formation of an immigration office that could undertake a trial program of admittance, a process that could be observed, studied, and refined over the course of several years. The incoming hods could be socialized and integrated in small numbers over the course of a generation or two.

It wasn't until the third day after the revelation of the Brick Layer's near death that the crowds in the Delectus at last emptied and Adam was able to return aboveground. There, he found Runa standing before the inky pyramidion, delivering an impassioned speech to a rather sizable crowd.

Though Adam would never have insulted her with the thought, there was something in her delivery that reminded him of the docent. Her voice rang with a similar dominance; it allured with a similar authority.

But she was not as domineering as her mother. When there were counterpoints or rebuttals, she listened to them and replied. When someone in the gathering pointed out that defending Nebos also required that it be sustained, and overcrowding would threaten the enduring health of the gardens, Runa gave a rebuttal that would be repeated many times in the coming days. She said, "My friends, the Tower is trembling. We can hide in our salons, in our picnics and painting, but it only grows worse. Something *must* be done. The Old Vein is expiring. We can cower behind oaths and excuses, but it does not change the fact that many are suffering and dying. Perhaps we are not responsible for the crimes of our fathers, but make no mistake, we are *beneficiaries* of those crimes, which makes us answerable to its victims. The Brick Layer's will is not in doubt. Our devotion is.

"I have listened to you murmuring about who the Brick Layer really was, *what* he really was. 'What sort of man vanishes like that?' you ask. A magician? A devil? A god? But I say you are asking the wrong question. The question you should be asking is: If he can disappear, can he not reappear? And if he does, *when* he does, what will he think of us? What will he think of you—hiding in his cloud, hiding behind his lightning, hiding in his gardens while his children starve? You think that opening our city to the hods will be our end, but I say it may be the only thing that can save us. Do not forget your oath! The Tower is quailing, my friends. We cannot wait until it falls to act."

Though some jeered, many of those gathered about her rock applauded her cause. She raised a hand as if to catch the cheer, then brought it down again, clapping it over her mouth. She had the look of someone who'd just swallowed a fly. The ovation turned into a roar of terror and panic.

Adam turned to see Faruq, leaning upon his axe haft at the front of a file of children that was, to its end, five thousand strong.

Adam stretched his neck inside the slackened noose.

He could just see Runa out of the corner of his eye. She stood upon her stool with a roving gaze; she seemed to be taking in familiar haunts from a novel height.

The live oak that would be their gallows cast a silvery lace across the lawn. Bees bustled through the clover. The ivy-strangled jib of the abandoned crane loomed over the pyramidion, which shone like a jar of molasses. In the distance, Adam heard the murmuration of public argument.

Faruq and his flock had been ushered back to the underground, and while the lumenguard held those tunnel entrances, the natives had answered the call of an accord that would decide the fate of the intruders and those who'd conspired to smuggle them into Nebos.

"It was a very good speech," Adam said.

Runa blew at a bee who had begun to inspect her nose. "I thought so."

"Could've used a few more hithertos and henceforths."

"I'm saving those for our last words. I'm really hoping to drag that out."

"Feeling morbid?"

"I can't imagine why," Runa said, then cocked her head so she could observe him out of the corner of her eye. "You don't seem worried. Why aren't you worried?"

"Maybe I'm just getting used to this view. Or maybe...I came here to make my fortune, or steal it. I felt worthless and thought that jangling pockets might help me to feel differently about myself. So, I gathered a little gold, put it all in a pile, and waited for the trumpets to sound. But I still felt the same way, like a worthless imposter, a bad forgery of a person. And I kept on feeling that way about myself until I discovered that I felt something for you, which grew into sympathy for the hods, and then for my sister, too, who'd always just been a source of guilt and resentment. And that's when I started to feel a little kindness toward myself. Now, I'm standing here on a stool with my head in a noose, and I...I have never been happier."

Runa's initial marveling at the intimacy of this confession was muted, it seemed, by the reminder of how close they stood to their end. "And here I thought I was the morbid one."

Adam gave a small, tranquil shrug. "What about you? Any regrets? Do you wish you'd put a spark in me when you had the chance?"

"At the moment, I regret drinking so much tea this morning." Runa sniffed at her own joke, though her levity did not last. She sobered and said, "I regret not listening to Ossian. When I drove you down to get deloused, he took one look at my face and whispered in my ear how happy he was to finally see I'd found someone. He knew before I did. I wasted so much time fretting and pretending and—"

"I think we can be accused of a lot of things, but wasting time isn't one of them. We went from perfect strangers to conspiring lovers inside a month. That's quite a clip."

"But we hurried through the best part, I think."

"We shall go slower henceforth."

Her voice quavered with amazement. "You *really* aren't worried, are you?"

Adam smiled. "I've never felt more hopeful in all my life."

From the Belly of the Beast

1

We have spent our lives scrabbling up the mountainside without the promise of a mountaintop.

—from the sermons of Luc Marat
(translated from hoddish)

~~speck in her harkening eye. Gasping once~~,
I ~~could not deflate my corporeal start,~~
~~the gorge of blood. No matter of months,~~
~~nor years have yet to unblush my full-flushed heart~~.

Thomas Senlin felt like a trussed-up Sunday roast burning in the oven.

Tucked deep inside the lowest deck of the cavernous Hod King, Senlin sat strapped to a rumbling seat. His bare feet pumped a treadle that looked to have been salvaged from a sewing machine. His hands gripped a pair of throttles, each stiff as a fence post. The peppery smoke of burning paper stung his eyes and crowded his lungs. His chest was bare, his waist wrapped in a sweat-soaked sarong that was always riding up when it wasn't falling down.

The heat was feverish, volcanic, unbearable. It radiated from the inner bulkhead and poured from the air vents above. When he was allowed to rest—a relative rarity—Senlin would lay his shaved head on the slightly cooler outer hull. That quilt of welded scrap made for an unforgiving pillow. But while his skull ground between the ribs of a sewer grate and the lid of a soup pot, Senlin would close his smoke-scratched eyes and dream of the seaside—of cool waters and cleansing winds.

Though it was of little consolation, he was far from alone in his misery. Ahead of him, fifteen hods were likewise lashed to iron chairs, each cozy as a pew. Sixteen more stations stood at his back. They were like rowers in the galley of a ship, but rather than pull an oar, each operated one of the Hod King's numerous legs, a role that earned them the title of "stepper."

Marat had been in a confiding mood the morning he'd cut Senlin's hair in the windy mouth of a hole that stood in testament of the Hod King's terrifying might. But the zealot had not been as frank about what a challenge it had been to carve that short burrow. Yes, the Hod King was an absolute miracle of engineering, a creation that rivaled even the ingenuity of the Sphinx. Yes, the excavator's trident could nose through stone like a snake through grass. But the vessel was hampered by the complexity of its operation and an overreliance on manpower. Even at a dallying pace, the crab-legged locomotive was nearly impossible to steer. Of course, if they hoped to summit the Tower, to engage the ringdoms and outmaneuver their navies, the Hod King would have to do much more than dawdle. It would have to climb, scurry, pivot, and ram.

And so, the unending exercises were begun.

The Hod King had sixty-four legs, thirty-two to a side, all of which had to rise and fall, grip and release, step inward and push outward in perfect harmony with one another. If even a single stepper fell out of sync with the rest, that error would ripple and magnify until the siege engine staggered, stumbled, and fell. The Hod King had dropped to its belly on many occasions in the days since their training had begun, and yet rather than raise a callus, the violent repetition had merely buried a bruise.

The throne room, where the Hod King was built, had been as snug as a stable before their practice runs enlarged it. The first time Senlin experienced the deployment of the trident-drill, his head was nearly rattled from his neck. The rapid, jarring sensation reminded him of riding a bicycle down a cobblestone street. When the Hod King wasn't digging out its den, the steppers practiced making the brute turn on its axis, pull itself up the throne room walls, or reverse down the borehole without tripping and adding new bruises to the old.

The fact that the Hod King walked like a drunkard on stilts was a source of comfort to Senlin. After all, there was no need to hobble a lame warhorse. And yet every day, the ungainly thing seemed to march a little quicker, turn a little more sharply, belly flop a little less. Senlin observed these small improvements with mounting unease.

Marat's Ingeniare, the cadre of scholars who had designed and overseen the construction of the mighty engine, were distinguished from the rest of the crew by the addition of a simple green coif. The humble cap was not an ostentation but rather a signal that they should be given the right of way in the narrow corridors. The Ingeniare, armed with grease guns and spanners, could regularly be found tinkering with the hydraulics hidden under floor plates or fine-tuning the daisy wheel valves that budded from the plumbing in the low ceiling. Senlin found it interesting that the Ingeniare appeared to prefer the common tongue, a fact that made their voices seem to rise above the babbling of the other steppers. Senlin supposed the linguistic preference was owed to how technical their conversations were. Hadn't Tarrou said that hoddish lacked a certain breadth of vocabulary? Perhaps there wasn't yet a word for *regulator, piston,* or *condenser.*

Whatever the reason, Senlin found himself regularly eavesdropping on the Ingeniare, which was how he learned of their frustration that they had not been given the chance to contrive a more sensible mechanism for steering the Hod King. Relying upon the coordination of sixty-four distractible, fatigable, and fallible souls was far from ideal. An alternate system had been developed, but it would take months to build, install, and test. According to the green-capped geniuses, Marat had been unequivocal in his rejection of the redesign. His evening homilies echoed his belief that the Sphinx was vulnerable and the upper ringdoms were distracted. And so, despite the Ingeniare's protestations, Marat decreed that the Hod King's sixty-four independent legs, fired by sixty-four independent minds, would be melded into a single congruous entity in the span of a fortnight.

The success of the effort depended largely upon detecting the weak links in the mortal circuit. Steppers who lacked sufficient rhythm or stamina were identified by the Ingeniare and roughly removed. As much as Senlin wished to escape the steamy torment of his station, he was quite determined to keep it. He could hardly imagine a more effective spot for a saboteur. So, he made a point of distinguishing himself as a capable, reliable stepper.

Naturally, Senlin would've preferred to pass the responsibility of slaying an iron-bellied leviathan on to someone else: someone more skilled and courageous; someone less devoted to a wife and indebted to a daughter. But opportunity, like misfortune, could not be ceded. He could either take advantage of his luck and bring the Hod King down or step aside and let the tyrant ascend.

He had no illusion about the dangers that lay ahead. If he was outed before he could wreck the siege engine, Marat would have him killed. If his sabotage was successful, he would likely perish with the crew. Either way, Marya would never hear of his sacrifice or know how heavily the loss of her and Olivet weighed upon his conscience. In her eyes, he would die as he had once been: a naive and feckless academic who thought only of himself.

Fair enough, he thought. One act of sacrifice could not forgive a lifetime of selfishness.

*   *   *

When it came to the coordination of the steppers, the Ingeniare took their inspiration from the drummers of the ancient galley ships. But rather than booming timpani, they elected to use a series of chimes. The person in charge of the ruckus was called the Master of Bells. She stood at the fore of the galley, behind an array of bronze bowls with a rubber mallet in hand. The note of each bell signaled a particular action. An A directed steppers to throttle their leg forward, and B directed them to throttle it back. A G prompted an inward step; an F an outward step, and so on, with certain directions being reversed by the steppers on the starboard side. Naturally, if every stepper raised their leg at once, the engine would collapse. And so, a delay had been built into the system. When the first stepper received the Master of Bells' cue and applied the right pedal or throttle, that action rang a sympathetic chime on the back of his seat, which alerted the next stepper to repeat the order, which then in turn signaled the stepper behind him.

In theory, it was an elegant system. In practice, it was a jangling nightmare. The resulting din was so deafening as to be disorienting. It was like having one's head stuck inside a piano while a maniac banged upon the keyboard. Only after many hours of blinding headaches was Senlin at last able to train his ear to the chimes of the man stationed immediately before him, a feat that required him to stare fixedly at the bells as one might watch the mouth of another when conversing in a noisy room.

Presumably, the Master of Bells took her direction from the pilot on the bridge, a place Senlin had heard referenced but not seen. In fact, other than his designated station against the roughly welded bulkhead, Senlin had observed very little of the Hod King's three decks, though he had gleaned some sense of their contents and function from his evening conversations with John Tarrou and Finn Goll.

In addition to offering access to the castles, the uppermost deck housed the mess hall and crew cabins, both of which stood unused since the engine was still in its berth. The middeck contained the bridge at the fore and the engine room at the aft, where boiler fans roared like an endlessly crashing wave. Finn Goll had noted that the engine room scarcely occupied a quarter of the ship's length, and it seemed incredible to imagine that the wheelhouse consumed the rest. Something else occupied the heart of the Hod King, though what it was, they could hardly guess.

Senlin would've liked to explore, but steppers were not allowed to roam about. Wherever he glimpsed a beckoning door, he'd also find one of Marat's personal guards gripping a truncheon and looking bored. Not wishing to provide them with entertainment, Senlin was always quick to go on his way.

Though on one occasion he had come upon a ladder up to middeck that was momentarily unattended. When he peered up at the open portal, he was surprised to hear the deep thrum of a turbine. It seemed to suggest the presence of a boiler room, auxiliary to the one Finn Goll toiled to feed. Senlin wondered if the Hod King was like an earthworm—possessed of more than a single heart.

The mystery of the middeck was only heightened by the noises Senlin heard emanating from the ceiling during the brief moments of respite between maneuvers. There were heavy footsteps, bursts of muted laughter, and a roaming rhythmic pecking like fingernails drumming on a windowpane. The sound was enough to make the hairs on his neck stand straight.

John Tarrou had been assigned to the aftercastle, which boasted six forty-pound guns and the Hod King's largest mortar, known as the "Quibbler." An absolute cauldron of a cannon, the Quibbler fired five-hundred-pound balls of solid granite. Four men and a winch were needed to load the gun, which, owing to the extreme scarcity of missiles, had never been fired. The ship's full complement of five-hundred-pound balls numbered only three.

Still, the smaller guns were given regular exercise that allowed Tarrou a chance to learn the duties of a cannoneer. The first lesson John learned was to stuff his ears with cotton wadding, this after his inaugural loading drill had left his ears ringing like a tuning fork. He described his gun nest to Senlin as being a crowded, frantic, and violent place. Tarrou had no love for black powder. "Occasionally, I had to resort to the stuff in the mines back home. The experience taught me two things," John said to Senlin over their dinner rations one evening. "First, black powder is fickle. And second, it is absolutely unforgiving."

Yet as dangerous as John's station was, the castle was open to the air. After days of roasting in the galley, Senlin thought he might prefer an explosive death so long as it was preceded by a gentle breeze.

As a young man, Senlin had never been at all tantalized by the prospect of a military career. It wasn't just the possibility of a brutish, early death that put him off. No, it was the drudging, inflexible schedule that had seemed so disagreeable. A soldier's existence was like that of a bead on an abacus: a thing slapped back and forth on the same path for hours and years until it finally broke. Of course, Senlin did not find all schedules equally abhorrent. In fact, he had reveled in the consistency of his school days in Isaugh, though the routine had always been sweetened by indolent evenings, a luxury that was markedly absent in Marat's zealot camp.

The floor of the throne room was as charmless as a rock quarry and, when the Hod King was dormant, as crowded as a bazaar. There were cesspits for necessities and rags for bedding, and neither privacy nor the familiar bounds of decency to direct the use of either. Amid this human muddle, Senlin found himself essentially living the life of a conscript. He was awoken by the blast of a tuneless bugle at an hour so early it scarcely qualified as morning. Bellying up to a long slab of stone that sufficed as a table, Senlin's day began with a lukewarm bowl of mealworms that had been milled into a hateful porridge. This, while tens of thousands of bats streamed overhead, returning from their nocturnal hunt. If one was so unfortunate as to have guano season their breakfast, one could not expect a replacement until the following morning.

Next came calisthenics, a battery of physical abuses that were led by a young and vital hod who did not seem to appreciate the contentiousness of middle-aged backs. This was followed by a short devotional session, during which time books were methodically redacted either with lamp black or walnut ink. The more devout hods obliterated their books with the verve of a child scribbling on a slate. Senlin, however, could hardly resist the impulse to read the lines he was forced to destroy. As almanacs, biographies, histories, novellas, poems, and encyclopedias vanished at a stroke, he tried to emblazon them upon the palimpsest of his memory, as if one day he might be able to resurrect them all. It was a pleasing illusion.

After their morning desecration, the steppers were allowed the extravagance of a "dry shower," which was like a bath, except for the absence of a tub, water, or soap. The process involved standing near the edge of the borehole where the wind whipped about. There, the hods, men and women both, stripped off their sarongs, faced the mortifying light of dawn, and scrubbed themselves with handfuls of sand. Senlin would not call the resulting state *clean* exactly, but it was at least a different sort of dirty, and the fresh air was nice.

And on more than one occasion while dust-bathing like a bird, Senlin had seen hods arrive, by grapple and by rope, via the ledge of the borehole. They came towing sacks that clinked and chimed like a bar cart. It struck him as unusual because most of the camp's supplies came through Mola Ambit via the treacherous vents or the black trail. Whatever was arriving on the backs of daredevil rappelers was delivered directly to the siege engine and the enigmatic middeck.

So it went. Morning turned to noon inside the iron leviathan. Lunch, which was consumed at one's station, consisted of bat jerky and a cooked yam served still in its skin—the yam, not the bat. When many hours later Senlin and the other steppers finally emerged from the Hod King, they were greeted by the gloom of dusk and a dinner that was not unlike their lunch. What was left of the evening was spent ruining books while Marat sermonized from the comfort of the Hod King's wheelhouse. Marat's disembodied voice boomed over them from a trumpet that curled from the engine's fierce jaw. Evening orations were delivered in hoddish, and so, much of the content was wasted upon Senlin, though Finn Goll did his best to interpret the sermons for him.

On the fifth evening since their initiation into the zealot life, Senlin listened as Finn Goll lent his gentler voice to Marat's wild barking: "We bend this metal to our will. We fuel it with our hope. We breathe our breath into its lifeless bellows. It rises and walks, not as a machine, but as an assemblage of our humanity. This vessel throbs with the blood of a hod. The Hod King is you; it is I; it is every man, woman, and child gagging inside the grave of the black trail. Here is our fist!" At this, the drill began to turn above the heads of the congregation. "We shall plunge it into the Tower and pull out the black clockwork at the heart of this wicked gin."

Were it not such an insidious feat, Senlin might have been amused by the transparent effort to metamorphose a machine into a human being. But what choice did Marat have? He'd already cast the Tower as an indifferent and insatiable engine. Its cruelty was a function of its technological advancement; the two could not be divorced. Marat destroyed knowledge and romanticized primitivism, yet the Hod King was a machine—a very advanced one at that—and functionally, the steppers were cogs. It was his metaphor made manifest! But all Marat had to do to dispel this apparent contradiction was to call the thing by another name. It was not a machine, but an "assemblage of our humanity." This flagrant hypocrisy, this evidentiary dissonance, was tyranny parading under the flags of freedom.

Practically, the only liberty the camp enjoyed came in the short minutes after they spread out their tattered bedrolls and before exhaustion delivered them to unpleasant dreams. Though the newcomers were denied this momentary reprieve. Marat had appointed Finn to be Senlin's tutor; the minutes before bed were meant to be spent expanding his hoddish vocabulary and familiarizing him with the eccentricities of its syntax. But the main of their lessons were frittered by Finn, who could not help but revel in the former headmaster's slow progress and clumsy pronunciation. After that evening's particularly unproductive lesson, Finn asked Tom to stick out his tongue for inspection. Finn declared the organ too long and thin. No wonder Tom couldn't roll his *r*'s; he had a tongue like a garden slug!

Senlin bore the teasing because he suspected it was the only bit of fun Finn had all day. The once well-heeled port master had been humbled to the role of furnace stoker. Stationed in the Hod King's boiler room, Finn and a crew of two other firemen spent their shifts alternately feeding blacked-out books into the furnace and bailing the ashes out.

"Why not wood or coal?" Finn Goll complained as he balled an old onion sack into a makeshift pillow. "Books make terrible fuel. The glue smokes, the leather stinks. They burn quick and cold. It's like trying to cook a turkey on the head of a match."

"Coal is hard to get," Senlin replied, plucking a tick from his cheek. He crushed the fiend between his fingernails. "But we have plenty of books. Besides, I'm sure he thinks it's poetic."

"A poet is just a tramp with a thesaurus," Finn said.

"It sounds like the sermons are starting to wear off on you, Hodder Finn." John clucked his tongue and shimmied his shoulders, as if snuggling into a mattress rather than a thinly veiled stone. "Poetry is the soul of man!"

"And squeals are the soul of a pig!" Finn said.

"I didn't know you were a swine priest. Please sing me a hymn!"

Senlin frowned as the two men continued to bicker. They quarreled like songbirds. The constant noise made it easy to say nothing of substance, to continue to skirt a subject they had spent days avoiding. Senlin would like to think they were merely being prudent, making certain that they would not be overheard and exposed. But the truth was increasingly apparent: They were afraid. They were like the unwell man who delays a visit to the doctor, not because he believes his dawdling will cure him, but because denial is a desperate imitation of hope.

And yet, they could delay no longer.

Senlin interrupted the arguing pair abruptly, though his voice was hushed: "We have to destroy it."

Finn Goll made a sound like a suppressed cough—a choke of surprise. "Easily said! They watch us like dogs in a kitchen. We're prisoners in a walking citadel that's stuffed to the ramparts with goons and fanatics. But, oh well! *The thing must come down,* he says. You're mad!"

"You sound like Adam." Senlin smiled at the memory. "He said escape was impossible, suicidal. It was insanity to think we could take on an entire port, without resources or reinforcements. Yet, here I am. Here you are."

Finn growled softly. "You've made your point. I suppose you have a plan?"

"All the practice walking up walls—you have to suppose it's for a reason. Marat seems the sort who will want to take his monster for a walk. Show it off. Scare the crowds. He's too keen on spectacles and inciting terror to just dig along like a mole. No, he'll want to be seen."

John gave a revelatory grunt. "You think he'll crawl up the face of the Tower. That certainly wouldn't leave much room for mistakes. I mean, one misstep and—" He sucked a breath through his teeth.

"I've been stumbling all my life. It's about time all that practice paid off," Tom said.

"We don't survive this plot of yours, do we?" John said.

Finn snorted. "I'm disappointed, Headmaster. Outliving the odds was always one of your better qualities."

John's fingernails rasped upon his stubbled cheek. "A classless headmaster, a poor crook, and a thirsty drunk. What a sorry lot of martyrs we shall make."

"Why waste good men when middling ones will do?" Goll said darkly.

Senlin spoke with the measured calm of a man who had made up his mind. "I don't want to die. But that monstrosity . . . well, it is like a termite on a life raft. We cannot let it go. Perhaps our children won't have their fathers, but at least they'll have their lives."

The three men digested Senlin's grim proposal in silence, until Goll spoke at last, his voice thickened by emotion. "It's quite a steal, when you think about it. I would've died a hundred times for my kids. Just the once seems a bargain."

~~the value of a fig. Often, seller and buyer will not so much agree upon the final price, as submit to the fateful number as if it were the culmination of a love affair. In the end, neither party wishes to see the other ever again. Often nothing is exchanged and certainly little is learned.~~

Six days after his training as a stepper had begun, Senlin was familiar enough with the rippling sensation of pending disaster that he was able to brace himself before the vessel careened first to starboard and then to port and finally down in an unchecked collapse. The sound was as jarring as an avalanche of pots pouring from a cupboard.

No sooner had that cacophony faded than the Master of Bells shouted a hoddish curse loud enough to make it echo. The steppers groaned, released their throttles, and began massaging their aching ears, palms, and posteriors.

A diminutive woman named Lely—who everyone, from cook to cannoneer, feared—stepped out from behind the bank of bells. The Master of Bells made the floor plates of the aisle ring with the *tock-tock-tock* of her bare heels. Her march ended in front of a pale, potbellied stepper several stations ahead of Senlin. The hod appeared to be attempting to hide in his own armpit. She grasped him by the ear and pulled him into the aisle where she took to berating him in the common tongue.

"Tone-deaf, rhythmless oaf! You said you were a musician!"

"Madam, I *am* a musician. Please, let go of my ear!"

Rather than surrender the lobe, Lely towed him along by it, moving the hod this way and that until the man was fairly forced to dance. "Tell me, what instrument did you play? The hambone? The nose whistle? Or did you just learn to hoot on an empty gin bottle?"

"Madam, I am a master of the noble concertina. I have played in the highest courts of—"

"Shut up! What note is this?" Lely let go of his ear so she could reach past him and pull the nearest lever. The resulting chime reverberated in the now conspicuous silence of the rowing deck.

The potbellied man licked his thick lips and squinted in deliberation. "It's in the broad and auspicious, one might say *august*, family of, uh . . . G."

"It's a D, you fraud!"

"Surely, the two are second cousins, madam, and certainly kindred enough to harmoniiiii—" The stepper's voice rose to a shrieking pitch as she resumed her grip upon his reddened ear.

"I never want to see you on my deck again, Mr. Marblemay, or whatever your name is. You will report for bat harvesting duty, and if you fail in that charge, I will hollow out your skull and see what note it makes when I blow on it!"

The humiliated stepper hurried from the deck with one hand cupped over his ear.

Senlin's brief amusement at the Master of Bells' vicious wit was cut short by the realization that she was staring directly at him. Physically, she was not an imposing person. She was shorter than average, in the autumn of her years, with one hand curled into a claw by arthritis. But her wrinkle-ringed eyes were black as tarpaper and her sun-white brows seemed almost to glow. She had the kind of stare that could stop a dog from barking, or a child from crying, or a man from smirking.

Again, her heels drummed upon the grates and steel plates of the deck as she strode at him. Senlin wondered how on earth he was going to save the Tower, his wife, and his child without any ears.

Now standing before him, Lely crossed her arms, adopting an almost studious expression. "You're the bad captain," she said in a voice as dulcet as a cowbell.

Senlin swallowed, feeling suddenly hemmed in. "I am."

"Perfectly rehabilitated, I suppose?"

Senlin found holding her gaze as comfortable as resting his hand on a hot stove, yet he persisted. "No. Not really. Not yet. Though I am trying."

She turned her head and spat dryly. "Modest! I never trust a modest man. Half of them are being coy about their usefulness, and the rest are *actually* useless."

"I suppose that's true," Senlin said, realizing that Lely seemed to be picking a fight. If he lost his station, then he would lose his chance at sabotage. He screwed up his courage and his mouth, saying, "I'm a good hod and a good stepper, and I deserve to be in this seat."

Rather than seem impressed, Lely picked something from the corner of her eye, examined it, then flicked it at the floor. "You saved Sodiq, did you?"

"I did," Senlin said, squaring his shoulders to hide his surprise at the turn in conversation. In a rainy alley in Pelphia, he'd once stopped two brutes from harassing a frail-looking hod, who then turned about and killed them both. So had Senlin's acquaintance with Sodiq been made. "I like to think he saved me in return."

She spat dryly again, though this time without turning her head. "Modest!"

"You seem to have confused sincerity with modesty, Hodder Lely. The truth brags well enough without my help."

"I don't much like braggarts either. Bah! Doesn't matter." She hiked her chin at him. "Hodder Luc wants to see you. Come on. I'll show you to the wheelhouse."

As Tom followed Lely down the aisle, it occurred to him that this was not a positive development. He'd not seen so much as Marat's shadow since the man had shaved his head. Even before that interview had ended, Senlin had sensed the zealot's waning interest in him. The second his hair was in the wind, Senlin and his friends were ushered from the zealot's presence by his hulking guards. But Senlin had thought Marat's indifference a good thing. Never had scrutiny made sabotage any easier.

Now, Senlin's imagination leapt to the conclusion that Marat had merely wished to lull him into complacency. The zealot had been spying on him the entire time. Someone had overheard his seditious conversation with Finn and John the night before. Their true intention had been revealed! All was lost!

Once they'd passed behind the battery of bells, Lely waved a bull-chested guard away from a hatch. When the guard tried to open the door for her, Lely slapped his arm hard enough to leave a welt. She pulled the door open without the aid of her arthritic hand. Senlin followed her into a short corridor that ended upon a steel ladder. The light that spilled from the open hatch above frosted the rungs.

"Up you go, what's-your-name," Lely said.

"It's Tom."

"I wasn't asking." Lely gave him a shove on the small of his back and slammed the door behind him.

Scaling the ladder, Senlin felt the weight of his dread settle upon his shoulders like a yoke. It seemed to pull at him, to drag him toward the exit. He could try to run.

But, no—if this were to be his end, he would not go out gibbering and begging. He would confront his death as if it were an unruly class: with calm temper and resolute posture.

The ugly seams, sallow light, and cramped aisles of the stepper's galley made one feel like a clog in a drain. The bridge was in every way the antithesis of the lower deck. Here, the light was as bright as a welder's spark. The burnished steel floors, broken into two tiers by a curling handrail, lustered like a looking glass. The ceiling was high, the air sweet. A crew of twelve sat in three rows; their stations faced a bulkhead that was crowded with a score of dials and gauges, some small as a pocket watch, others imposing as a grandfather clock.

The crew's individual posts were fitted with a battery of controls—throttles and chokes, all orderly as a tacklebox and colorful as lures. Branching over each panel were an array of bugle-mouthed pipes that Senlin came to learn could carry the voice of each post to a particular destination aboard the vessel: the gun deck, the furnace, the Master of Bells, or any of the engine's dozen vital organs. Jutting from these racks of plumbing, stretched the long barrel of an eyepiece. Again and again, the heads of the crew dipped to these scopes, before craning back and speaking into one pipe or another. Voices returned, sounding as if they had traveled through a rainspout. The bridge was a noisy, lively place.

It did not pass Senlin's notice that here Hodder Luc was hailed as *sir* or *captain*. These hods had been inducted to an echelon where the zealot was less a distant familiar and more an intimate authority. Much as Senlin had over the course of his adventures, Marat appeared to have learned the utility of professional duplicity.

A high-backed chair sat at the rear of the wheelhouse, cushioned with red tufted velvet. Luc Marat stared back at Senlin from his throne; the corners of his mouth rose in what seemed a mortician's anodyne smile.

A brassy cone flowered above either of the throne's arms. If the pipes at the officer's stations suggested bugles, then Marat's communication horns were like tubas. The armrest to his right included a simple hand crank that, when plied, lowered a periscope from the ceiling. At the moment of his arrival, Luc was in the process of cranking the telescopic barrel back up into its nest. The captain's chair appeared to come with ears, eyes, and a mouth.

Marat leaned toward the cone on his left, harkening to the bubbling of dim and overlapping voices, eavesdropping on the traffic of commands that ran to and from his bridge. Then he turned his mouth to the trumpet on his right and began to speak in hoddish. Even through the Hod King's skin, Senlin heard those words bounce about the cavern. He recognized the hoddish for *study*, Marat's ironic term for blacking out the words of a book.

His brief speech at an end, one of Marat's crew rolled his rickety wheelchair around. The immense guard who'd been scowling at Senlin since he'd scrambled up from the floor shifted the zealot from his throne to his wicker-backed chair. The guard tucked a blanket, sparse and frayed as an old fishing net, over his master's gilded legs with maternal tenderness.

The tatty lap cover had always struck Senlin as conspicuously humble: gold shone through the many tears. Or did Marat expect him to believe that his clockwork legs were prone to chills?

"Ah, I see Lely found you! Wonderful." Marat eased his chair forward, expanding the display of his china-white teeth. "She tells me you've distinguished yourself among your peers. Lely is not liberal with her praise. I'm fairly sure she thinks I'm only a passable prophet." Marat laughed, though no one joined him. "How do you like being a stepper?"

Again, Senlin was caught off guard by Marat's congeniality. He began to splutter like water from a hand pump. Realizing that his floundering might suggest a guilty conscience, Senlin covered his confusion by looking past Marat at the glittering gauges with an expression of wonder. "It's magnificent! Absolutely incredible."

Marat's cheeks dimpled with pride. "I forget how affecting it is to see for the first time. The Sphinx is not the Tower's only genius. Come, come, take a look through one of our eyes."

With what he hoped was the appropriate amount of agog, Senlin bent over the lens at the only vacant station. Though he'd been feigning amazement a moment before, Senlin did not have to contrive the gasp that came. It was like looking through the many-windowed eye of a dragonfly. He not only saw the circle of blue sky at the mouth of the borehole, but also the walls of the throne room on either side, and the floor beneath them, and nearly half the ceiling as well. The view made him feel both giddy and ill. When he pulled away, it was with both eyes squeezed shut.

Marat laughed. "It's called a pentascope. One of Mr. Gedge's more devilish innovations. It had a similar effect on me at first, but you get used to it. Here, allow me to introduce my crew. This is my pilot, Funada, and her second, Sonam. My engineer, Titus, and his second, Llewelyn..."

As the battery of introductions continued, Senlin quickly lost track of anyone's name, though he did absorb that there were six stations in all: tactician, navigator, pilot, engineer, communications, and munitions. Each post was staffed by a primary and a second, all of whom seemed agreeable enough, if not distinct. Senlin had suffered a similar feeling at parties long ago, upon being introduced to a room full of strangers all at once, one after another. Rather than making those partygoers seem more familiar to him, the experience had merely turned them into a hazy jumble and a confusion of appellations.

What did stand out to him was the fact that the men and women attending the grand controls of this marvel of engineering did so in sarongs. While the half-nakedness of the steppers in the galley had seemed appropriate to their wretched station, the bare backs and threadbare wraps seemed a funny incongruency here, like a locomotive pilot in a loincloth or a symphony of nudists.

The introductions finished, Marat wheeled past his mountainous sentry, coming to a halt in front of a sealed hatch, one of several at the rear of the bridge. "Of course, I didn't call you up here just to enjoy the view and meet my crew. Come, Hodder Tom. There's something we should discuss." Even as Senlin made to follow, Marat's tall sentry stepped in front of him. His puckered mouth shifted from side to side. He looked like he was trying to dislodge something from between his teeth, a comical effect that was spoiled by a flat and murderous light in his eyes. He gripped the long hilt of a blade at his belt that reminded Senlin of an exaggerated meat cleaver, a one-sided knife that was boxy and blunt but much longer than anything a butcher would ever wield.

"Stay here, Hanif," Marat said, to his guard's apparent surprise. "It'll be fine."

Grudgingly, Hanif unblocked Senlin's path.

"Would you mind?" Marat gestured at the wheel lock. Senlin put his hands to the screw, opened the hatch, and held it while Marat maneuvered his squeaking chair through. The zealot asked him to seal the hatch behind them, and Senlin obeyed.

It only took Senlin a moment to realize where they were. This was

Marat's private chambers. If one overlooked the polished steel of the bulkhead and ceiling, the cabin bore some resemblance to Senlin's quarters aboard the *Stone Cloud*. There was a made bed and a small desk, its cubbies stuffed with envelopes and papers. Centered in the room was a table without any chairs. A foot locker, a bedside nook, and a wardrobe finished out the room's furnishing, all of which appeared to be bolted to the deck. Senlin was surprised to see books in a barred shelf inside Marat's nightstand, and more volumes lining the desktop behind a glass door. Their spines were dark and waxy from the passage of time and many hands. A large book lay open on the table, its pages pristine and unmarred.

"You read?" Senlin said.

"I do, of course. 'What is a poison to the simple may be a liquor to the wise.' Are you familiar with Jumet? Such a flawed man possessed by such occasional brilliance. His verse can amuse and infuriate, both at once. He was like a sage jester or a mad king." Marat laughed almost wistfully, and without looking, he shut the book, revealing what the cover had concealed: a letter opener, eight inches long, with a point like a needle and a hilt like a sword. Marat didn't seem to notice the blade or Senlin's awareness of it. "Perhaps you think my being a reader makes me a hypocrite?"

Senlin forced his gaze away from the letter opener just as Marat wheeled back around. "No," Senlin said, his voice pinched and foreign sounding in his ears.

"Why not?"

Realizing that Marat was looking for a particular answer, Senlin tried to imagine what the aspiring tyrant would most like to hear. "I... I suppose books are like a surgeon's scalpel. The same blade that can kill when wielded by a fool can save lives in the right hands."

Though Marat did not turn around, something about the posture of his shoulders seemed to suggest a response. Approval, perhaps. Or suspicion. He said nothing as he continued to his desk where he commenced a methodical inspection of his drawers.

Senlin felt the presence of the blade on the table as if it were a coiled viper. Marat's bare neck stretched above the back of his chair, appearing as vulnerable as if it rested upon a block. Senlin felt the weight of his own life lighten and his sense of mortality grow abstract. The beast in him whispered, *Don't think. Kill him*. His hands quaked at his sides.

But then, before the primitive impulse could entirely possesses him, Senlin recognized the moment for what it could only be: a test.

No, not a test: a trap.

"If you're looking for your letter opener, it's here," Senlin said and surprised himself with how calm he sounded.

Marat swiveled about, eliciting a shriek from his chair. His handsome cheeks balled to make room for the grin. "So it is." He plied the wheels, inching a little nearer to Senlin, who suddenly found his gaze drawn to the golden toes that peeked out from beneath the drab afghan. "And you didn't think to use it?"

"I haven't anything that needs to be opened."

"You have me. I am but organs in an envelope that many, many men would like to see slit open."

Senlin's chin rose in indignation. "I'd sooner spill my own blood."

"Really?" The zealot picked up the letter opener, thin as a blade of grass, and presented the gold wire grip to Senlin. "Show me." His grin shriveled.

Senlin had never put much thought into the question of how he would carve his body should he find himself in a position where such a thing was necessary. But as he took the knife, he swiftly tallied his unlikable options. His hand? Perhaps, but a slice across the palm seemed a little ordinary; it evoked adolescent blood oaths and deals done between men who were suspicious of notaries. Hardly an impressive display, and the resulting wound would ruin his grip for weeks. The neck, then? An absurdity! To slice at his own throat was certainly theatrical but also very dangerous. A man who was killed by his own charade could hardly be considered an actor.

Realizing that any further vacillation would spoil the gesture, Senlin decided to slice at his chest near the sternum, to cross his heart, as it were, or at least draw a bar over it.

Senlin would've preferred to be quick about it, but he was unprepared for just how difficult it was to convince his hand to continue doing something that every fiber in his being revolted against. His instincts howled at him to stop. His resolve roared at him to carry on.

What might've been merely painful at a reasonable speed became excruciating in deliberation. Purpling from the effort, Senlin finished the laceration with an agonized gasp. His fingers went weak. He dropped the letter opener. It clattered to the plated deck, throwing a wing of blood across the hem of Marat's blanket. Trembling, Senlin felt the encroaching effervescence of unconsciousness. He swayed on his feet.

"You're bleeding," Marat said as if it were a shock. His brow wrinkled with artificial concern. His seat creaked, raising a new, deeper note that called to mind a tree limb twisting in the wind. The shabby throw slid from the golden shields of his knees as Marat rose from his chair. He stood half a head taller than Tom, whose lightheadedness seemed to have turned to hallucination.

Then Marat gripped him by the shoulders and said, "Sit on the bed. Let's have a look at that scratch."

~~men who are incapable of attracting a mate naturally. Avoid black, too; it suggests severity and independence. Blues, greens, and yellows are generally appealing to the stunted tastes of the hunchbacked gnomes who slink dow~~n ~~from their filth-crusted birdcages and ignoble bloodlines. Be prepared to~~

Rather than focus on the uncomfortable intimacy of Luc Marat's effort to dress his wound while he sat perched on the foot of his bed, arms raised above his head to make room for the winding and winding of gauze, Senlin forced himself to think about something else. Anything else.

Had Marat regained the use of his legs recently? Had he only feigned the inability? The zealot must've gotten his hands on some of the Sphinx's medium. Senlin recalled Byron bemoaning the fate of the Sphinx's brick nymphs. They had become a target for the makers of Crumb. Perhaps Marat had milked the same dwindling resources for his own use. But why hide his mobility from his followers? Was it too great a hypocrisy for even the silver-tongued zealot to justify? Or did he just prefer to project a certain weakness, a vulnerability that might set his enemies at ease while inspiring the empathy of his followers? Most importantly of all, why was Marat revealing this fact to him—a recent convert, a killer of hods, and a lapsed spy for the Sphinx?

Marat tucked the tail of the white bandage into the wrap he'd made and patted Senlin on the ribs. "There. Make sure you change this every day. We don't want it to fester." Marat looked Senlin in the face, and what he saw there made him laugh. "You have questions!"

Senlin tried to soften his expression of bewilderment. He lowered his arms and tested the tightness of the bandage with a few breaths, each of which made him wince in discomfort. "Is it permissible to have questions?"

"I'd take you for an imbecile if you didn't." Marat stooped, picked up the letter opener, and began to polish off the blood with a strip of gauze.

"Why are you letting me see all of this? The wheelhouse. Your cabin. Your books. Your..." Senlin waved at Marat's golden stalks. "I'm just a hod."

"Oh, we both know you're more than that. And don't be so humble around Hodder Lely, or you'll never hear the end of it." Marat returned to his desk, the deck rumbling beneath his feet. His gait was fluid, if not exactly human. Something about his posture called to mind a man pedaling in the high seat of a penny-farthing.

When Marat opened a cabinet in the desktop to stow the dagger, Senlin saw the grip of a pistol lurking there. The firearm almost certainly would've been introduced to him sooner if he'd attempted to rush Marat when he'd had his back turned. It *had* been a trap. "You were an agent of the Sphinx, Tom. And while he views every person he recruits as a mere instrument of his will, he does not choose dull or useless tools."

"I have my talents, I suppose."

"You do. And you have been inside the Sphinx's house. Very recently. I have not walked the halls of that clockwork castle in more than a decade. My memory has grown... faint, I'm afraid."

Senlin's stomach tightened as he suddenly understood the direction the conversation was taking. "It is a rambling place."

Marat watched Senlin very closely when he asked, "But perhaps you would recall the way to the zoetrope theater and the Bridge of Babel?"

"Through the Bottomless Library, you mean?" Senlin finally thought it safe to stand, though he did so slowly and with unfeigned pain.

"No, no, that's hopeless. Even with the cat on your side, which he never is, that path would take far, far too long. Not to mention the traps. No, I'm talking about the elevator. Could you find it again?"

Unwanted came the memory of a soft chime, and the doors of an elevator parting, and his friends crowding in. Edith had wet hair and a searching, hopeful smile. His heart had felt as airy as a soap bubble, and just as fragile. "Yes," he said.

"Are you sure?"

Senlin shut his eyes. "I can see a series of gouges on the wall that Ferdinand made and a peculiar rug with paisleys like a peacock plume and the painting across the way and... yes, I'm sure."

"Excellent," Marat said, and was about to say more when a rap on the hatch to the wheelhouse brought his attention around. He picked up his blanket, sat down in the chair, and called for them to enter. Hanif appeared holding a gunnysack by its cinched neck. Senlin recognized it as resembling the parcels that arrived on the shoulders of sunburnt grapplers.

The sentry frowned at the blood on the floor and the darkening gauze around Senlin's chest. "Ah! A new harvest!" Marat said happily. "Could you take that for me, Hodder Tom? Gently, now. That's precious cargo." Senlin did as he was told. The lumpy sack jangled like a coin purse, though it was not as heavy. "Don't worry about this mess, Hanif. Just a little accident."

Senlin attempted to look innocent or at least harmless, though it might've been a more calming show if the sack that he held against his stomach had not begun to wriggle. He yelped in surprise, which made Marat laugh and Hanif scowl a little harder. It took a moment for the leader of the zealots to shoo his guard off, and once he had, he rose once more and said, "All right, bring that with us." He picked up a hoop full of keys from his desktop. "It's time you met the rest of my crew."

Sandwiched between the noisome orlop where steppers labored and bells ruled, and the gun deck where cannon fire rattled the cotton-plugged skulls of cannoneers, was the mysterious middeck: the source of faint laughter, the source of the *tap-tap-tap* of fingernails on a window in the night.

The narrow chamber beyond Marat's quarters lay behind a hatch like a bank vault. A series of white-hearted electric bulbs dotted the ceiling. Silver-faced lockers filled two of the walls. Not expecting to be shown any of the room's secrets, Senlin was surprised when Marat fitted a key into one of the cubby doors, turned it, and opened the locker for Senlin's appraisal.

A copy of *The Brick Layer's Granddaughter* caught the light. The edge of each brushstroke was as fine as an eyelash.

Senlin marveled, not at the beauty of the piece with which he was quite familiar, but at the number of unopened doors that surrounded it. "How many?"

"Enough. Or nearly so," Marat said, shutting and securing the door. "You saw only one of my repositories in the Golden Zoo. There were others. I have assembled them all here."

"You're going to open the bridge."

"Yes, we are."

Beyond the vault was a spacious room with half a dozen hatches on either side. The ceiling was low and the lighting dim, though somehow still unflattering. The floor was clean swept, and a strong scent of antiseptic nearly eclipsed the lingering reek of humanity. Unlike Marat's cabin, the steel surfaces here were unadorned and unsoftened by the trappings of domesticity.

What Marat introduced as the "wardroom" was dominated by a table that might've been better suited to the boardroom of a central bank. It was circular with a great void in the center, a design Senlin had once read was used to suggest equality, to foster unity and generally keep the peace among attending parties. After all, if a table had no apparent head, the seat of power could not be fought over. The twelve chairbacks were all of one height, each with armrests, shoulder straps, and a base that was riveted to the floor. The table's thick slab was composed of lustering copper. Its top was lightly etched with a grand circuit of lines and nodes, a pattern that seemed neither repeating nor random.

Notably, the table's circle was incomplete. A gap opened upon the center where coiling ovals, like something a pendulum might draw, scored the floor and caught the scant light.

At present, both table and wardroom stood empty. Marat strode through the break in the table, making no effort to temper the tolling of his golden heels. Something told Senlin he should not follow him. He suspected the egalitarianism that a round table might infer elsewhere was here meant to act as a magnifying lens, focusing both attention and deference upon the zealot.

Coarse laughter blatted from the cracked hatch of an adjoining cabin. Marat forked two fingers to his mouth and piped a shrill whistle. The rabbling noise stopped at once, and a head that was nearly enveloped by a great cloud of black hair poked out into the wardroom.

"Hello, boss!" the head said.

"Don't call me *boss*, Cael. Come on out."

Though the man's voluminous mane—which ringed his face from brow to chin—was impressive in its own right, it was his titanic arms that most distinguished him. His shoulders were as swollen and round as the helmets of deep-sea divers. His fists, each as large as a picnic ham, hung past his knees. His legs were short, stout and, since the man was dressed only in white undershirt and felt shorts, obviously human. His iron arms, though, could only have been the work of the Sphinx.

"Sorry, Hotterlook." The man mispronounced Marat's preferred title, seemed to realize it, and to stave off a further rebuke, he raised his gearbox hand to show the cards he clutched between piston-fat fingers. "Delyth's teaching me to play whist. I just beat her. Now she's sore."

"Never mind that, Cael. I want you all to meet someone. Could you please summon the rest of the crew?"

Cael turned and shouted into the cabin behind him at a volume that could not possibly be necessary. "Boss says line up!"

The next person out, who Marat introduced as Thornton, was an older man who appeared to have spent recent decades consuming primarily a diet of hard drink. His face bloomed red and blue with the flowers of his vice; his eyes were as pink and hooded as a hound's. His nose and chin collapsed about an apparent paucity of teeth, and his lips had been stained a muddy sort of ochre by the bulge of chewing tobacco that swelled his lower lip like a tumor. What hair he had lay in gray oily laces across his spotted pate.

The general impression that his face gave was of a man loitering about an open grave, and yet it did not match the rest of him. A silver banded neck braced his sorry head, and all of his long limbs seemed to move in lithe, powerful strokes. Thornton didn't wear a stitch of clothing, but he possessed no organs that needed concealing. He was a sexless golem of mercury-bright metal that banded him from his toes, out to his fingertips, and up to the brink of his white-stubbled chin.

When he spoke, Thornton's voice was as grating as a raven. "Keep calling him *boss*, Cael, and he'll shave you bald as an egg!"

Next to emerge was Mr. Gedge, an avuncular-looking fellow with carefully combed sandy hair, chipmunk cheeks, and a rosebud mouth. He wore wire-rimmed spectacles, a starched collar, and black braces. He looked for all the world like the sort of man who would not complain if you cut in front of him in a queue. He was perfectly ordinary except for his ears, which were larger, almost mouselike, and crafted from a pinkish gold.

When Gedge saw Senlin, he docked his gaze in the safe harbor of a corner and mumbled, "Pleasure to meet you."

Had the procession ended there, Senlin might've thought the crew agreeable enough. His experience with Edith had taught him empathy and respect for those who had suffered both a catastrophic injury and the uneasy gifts of the Sphinx. Obviously, these men had fallen from grace. They had thrown their lot in with a villain. But even so, they were not monsters to be shivered at.

Senlin was about to offer himself some private congratulations on his high-mindedness.

Then she crawled into the wardroom.

And there it was: the source of the sound of fingernails on a window. She ticked across the steel deck on eight javelin-pointed feet and forty-eight undulating knees. She was a chimera. Below the waist, she was a mechanical spider; above it, she was a woman wrapped from forehead to hip in strips of tea-colored cloth. Thin, blue-black hair hung about her face like a veil. Her arms and fingers moved slowly, dreamily, like a cobweb in a draft. She seemed a body preserved for burial. The impression that she belonged in a mausoleum was only compounded by the fact that the entirety of her upper body was held inside a crystal bell jar.

At first Senlin saw no gaps in the wrapping for her eyes, mouth, or nose, rendering her featureless, ageless, inscrutable. But then she turned her head to look at him directly, and he beheld pinhole pupils staring out from under the gauze. Her mouth raised the fabric just enough to show the pearlescent shine of small white teeth.

Senlin could not suppress the shudder that ran through him.

She tapped the floor in a stuttering broken manner. Marat snickered.

"This is Delyth. And she just called you 'rude,'" he said, even as Delyth continued to tap the floor. Senlin realized that this was how she communicated; her voice was either stifled by the dome or her wounds. The manner of her expression called to mind the system of knocks that he and Edith had invented. Senlin disliked the association.

Marat continued to translate: "She says you aren't much to look at either."

"Well, I sincerely apologize," Senlin said, attempting to maintain a friendly expression as he held her arachnid gaze. "I startle easily. It's a nervous condition. A congenital weakness, if you like. An em—" Delyth resumed her tapping, ending Senlin's ramble.

"You are forgiven," Marat declared. "*But* you must pay her a visit in her web tonight."

This inspired guffaws from all except Senlin. Even Delyth's shoulders shook under their swaddling while one back foot rang the deck with the rhythm of her laughter.

Senlin felt somewhat undone by the jarring tone of the scene. Delyth's eerie appearance aside, the crassness and Marat's chumminess with his crew seemed out of place and out of character. Though perhaps the zealot who rumbled his nightly sermons through an alphorn was the act, and this standing, laughing, at-ease manifestation was closer to the true character of the man.

Or perhaps neither were the real Marat. Perhaps he was like a wound-up scroll, made up of layers upon layers. And yet if one were to cut into a scroll in search of its crux, rather than a heart, they would discover a void.

Senlin was reminded of Duke Wilhelm's duplicity. He seemed to have accrued his power by embodying several personalities and showcasing them to his various audiences. Senlin had tried to appear unassuming, in the hope that by showing the duke his neck, he could win his trust. But Senlin had the distinct impression that if he were to pursue the same act here, he would be trampled. This was not a place for Boskops. This was no time to be modest.

"What do you say, Hodder Tom? Care to be drained in the lady's web?" Marat said as the chuckling dwindled.

Senlin had spent enough time in pirate coves and men's clubs to know his line, crude as it was. He delivered it with a smirk. "Well, I should warn the lady: I have a stinger, too."

Marat introduced Senlin as their operative, their man from the inside, the one who would pilot them to their moment of triumph. Soon, they would pull the Sphinx from his burrow, unmask him, spit in his face, pluck the fingers from his hands, the toes from his feet, and the ears from his swollen head. They would strap his corpse to the front of the last wall-walker, then parade that gory figurehead up and down the Tower until the flies devoured him, atom by atom, and his bones were scattered across the Skirts.

This gruesome rehearsal of their coming revenge seemed a familiar pageant to them all. Senlin did his best to cheer when they cheered, to embody their ire with equal heat.

When their fury was at last exhausted, the crew returned to their game of whist. Marat surprised Senlin once again by showing him to what would be his private berth. It was little more than a deep closet with a bunk, room to turn around, and a shelf for personal effects, which of course he did not have.

Yet compared to his scab-spotted bedroll, it seemed a suite in the Bon Royal.

"You'll eat with the crew. They'll need to trust you if they're going to follow you into the Sphinx's maze. They are a tight-knit lot and naturally suspicious of outsiders."

"As they should be. I realize I have not suffered the same torments at the hands of the Sphinx as they have, but she did rob me of my wife and child. And I do mean to pay her back."

Marat's mouth puckered to one side. "You think the Sphinx is a woman?"

Senlin squawked a nervous laugh. "No, of course not! I just like to think of him as being nothing more than a shriveled woman hiding behind a looking glass."

Marat smiled back. "That is a pleasing thought. He's not an immortal snake; he's just an old hag, a hag who's been awful quiet since I cut off his lights. I wonder if he isn't already dead. I certainly hope not. I'd feel cheated if he were allowed to die in peace."

Senlin was about to reply when the floor pitched beneath him. The siege engine was up and walking again. "I should return to my post," he said.

"In the stepping galley? You've already been replaced, Tom."

Senlin could scarcely keep the distress from lifting his voice. "But why? Even Hodder Lely thought that I had proved myself a worthy—"

Marat waved the argument away. "I have thousands of hods, any of whom could be steppers, but I only have one Tom."

Senlin saw his plot spoiled at a stroke. He could not trip the beast from a closet in its belly. He knew, too, that he could not argue the point further without rousing the zealot's suspicion. Who would choose the rowing galley over a clean, well-lit berth?

Still, Senlin could not banish his disappointment quickly enough, and Marat laughed at his miserable expression. "Oh, don't look so forlorn! I still have work for you to do. Come, I'll show you."

A long passageway stretched out from the wardroom. Many of the hatches they passed mumbled and thrummed. Even as Senlin wondered about the unseen machines chuffing away behind those doors, Marat announced that those chambers and their contents were off limits to all but Mr. Gedge. Marat called the mouse-eared gentleman his brightest engineer, the Ingeniare in chief. "He's as brilliant as the Sphinx, I think, but timid to a fault." Marat brushed a hatch as he passed it. Like a farmer runs a hand over the heads of his fruiting grain, the gesture seemed one of ownership and pride. "At least, he's shy until you challenge his work or touch his machines. Then you'll see there's a bit of badger in that mouse."

When they arrived at the final compartment, Marat liberated a single key from his ring and presented it to Senlin with a grave injunction not to lose it.

Inside the compartment, a naked bulb swayed on a cord with the pitch of the marching siege engine. The bulb illuminated a mushroom of a stool and a bare steel sink, the plumbing of which curled into the bulkhead. Fixed to the hull over the sink, which lacked a tap, was an instrument that resembled a thermometer. The floor was littered with what Senlin initially mistook for the shells of some exotic nut.

"Sorry. It looks like the last fellow left you a mess," Marat said before directing Senlin to set the sack down on the stool and to look inside. Relieved to at last be putting down his jangling, wriggling burden, Senlin had an uncanny premonition of what he would find even as he uncinched the neck. And there they were: flapping broken wings, twitching the stumps of absent legs, heads twisting in search of an exit they would never reach. A score of the Sphinx's moths and butterflies churned inside the sack in a restless mass.

Marat drew out a thorax at random. "They're really not that difficult to find once you know what to look for." Around the rim of the sink lay an array of picks, files, and tweezers. Marat chose an instrument reminiscent of an oyster knife. With it, he popped open the moth's outer shell and began carving away the exquisite sprockets. Coils, cogs, and fine plates flew out in a spray and landed on the floor among the other remnants.

After a moment, Marat uncovered the heart of the tiny machine: A pill-sized glass vial filled with the Sphinx's luminous medium.

Marat broke the capsule over the sink and watched the five, six, seven drops fall into the drain.

"It's not exciting work, but it does require a trustworthy soul. The last hod I gave the work to turned out be a Crumb addict. He sopped some of the medium with his robe, then tried to boil it down over the cooking fires."

Senlin's mouth suddenly felt very dry. "What did you do when you caught him?"

"I didn't catch him. We found his body. He poisoned himself. It's not a kind habit; the Blood of Time was not meant to be drunk. You never tried Crumb, did you?"

"Certainly not," Senlin said, feigning a convincing degree of revulsion, then quickly moved the conversation forward. "This collection is for you and the crew? For your legs?"

The deck beneath them sloped suddenly. The impact was sufficient to send them both staggering while the hanging bulb danced above their heads. The entire hull rang and quivered, though neither of them were particularly alarmed. They had felt the Hod King careen into a wall often enough to recognize the sensation.

"I should go." The cramped nature of the closet required the zealot to undertake an awkward series of small, mincing steps to turn himself about. It occurred to Senlin that the Wakeman's golden legs, while ideal for crushing foes, could not cross in the manner required to perform a quick about-face. Such were the small inconveniences of great power.

Having freed himself to the corridor, Marat spoke over his shoulder as he strode away: "This is important work, Tom. We'll need every drop, I think. Do your best. I'll see you at dinner."

As Senlin sat cracking open the Sphinx's insects and pouring thimbles of radiant blood into the open drain, an unhelpful thought occurred to him. It was possible that somewhere inside this sack of ginning spies, there was a recording of Marya. Perhaps one of the Sphinx's butterflies had watched as she stole a moment away from the duke to lean upon a balcony rail and listen to the gossiping parrots and breathe in the fumes of the stars. Or perhaps one had observed as she pushed a pram through the clogged lanes of Pelphia, stopping now and then to adjust the blanket that warmed a sleeping Olivet. Perhaps a moth had caught a musical phrase from her piano, or the sound of her laughter, rising over the voices in a room like a banner flying over a battlefield.

It was possible, at that very moment, some sliver of her was hoarded inside the very shell he held in his hands.

But even as the urge to attempt to activate the recording swelled within him, he recognized the madness of the impulse. It was as unlikely that he would catch a glimpse of her inside one of these little spies as it had been that he would find her handwriting tucked amid the tatters of the Lost and Found. He knew for certain that if he had allowed himself to linger a moment longer at the foot of the Tower, he would still be there now, praying to that shrine of hopelessness.

If he had stayed there, he never would've learned he had a daughter.

Olivet.

What had he missed already? Her first cry, of course. Her first nurse. Her first coo. The first time she cracked her eyelids at the world and saw the strange thing that we call light pour in. All moments that were lost to him forever. And what would he miss in the days to come? Her first smile. Her first laugh. Her first unsteady struggle to sit up. The first time she, while clinging to her mother's fingers, would dare to take a step. And then another. And another. Each a stride closer to the person she would become and a pace further from him. He would be little more than a story her mother sometimes told her between a nursery rhyme and a tender good night.

The weight of what he had already lost filled him with such a sense of despair, it overran his other senses: He tasted the acid of it, smelled the rot of it, heard the wheezing rattle of it, like a kettle preparing to scream.

And if spoiled hope were all he had, he might not have survived the day. He'd already started to carve out his heart. Why not finish what he had begun?

But there was something inside of him superior to hope, something more resilient to the lashings of regret and dejection. He had *purpose*.

No setback or quirk of fate would stop him from bringing the Hod King to heel. Because in the end, it didn't matter how Marya remembered him to their daughter or explained his catastrophic pride or her own inexplicable love for a man unfit for affection; he only wished that she and Olivet would live on as long as the sea, till the bright and rolling waves of their days erased the shoals of their troubled past.

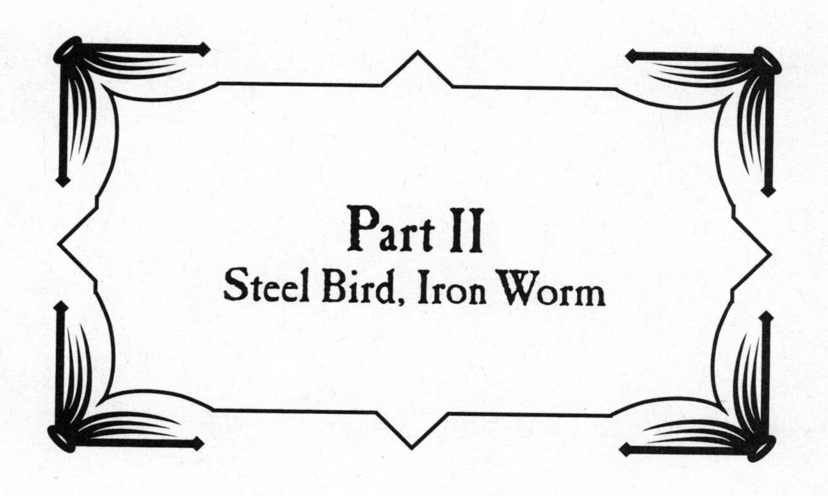

Part II
Steel Bird, Iron Worm

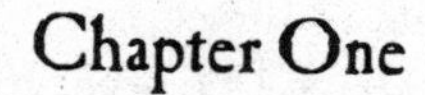

Chapter One

Choose your traveling companions wisely. The Tower has a way of turning quibbles into feuds and a morning spat into an evening divorce.

—*Everyman's Guide to the Tower of Babel*, III. IV

Byron knew that a home was an ephemeral thing. Home was a feeling engorged with memory, a sense of history enlarged by fondness and family and familiar things. Home was a ritual that harmonized with the melody of a day. It was a healer of all the humiliations and failures that must be borne in public but can only be mended in private. A home was the nest of the soul, a refuge more sacred than any chapel or mausoleum.

But what *made* a home was far less sentimental. It was drudgery, pure and simple, that made a home.

When he wasn't catching moths in the Communications Closet, Byron was scouring crockery or scrubbing the deck or changing the linens or polishing the fixtures. It was monotonous work, the sort of lulling exercise that inspired humming, daydreams, and an endless parade of worry.

And there was no shortage of things to fret about. It had occurred to him that one didn't need a gun deck to bring down an airship. He could think of a hundred other ways to hobble a vessel—even one as formidable as the *State of Art*. An undercooked roast could poison the crew. A clog in the wrong drain could flood the ship's delicate instruments. The captain could trip on a bump in a rug and crack open her head. These dreadful fantasies bedeviled him while he peeled carrots and folded nappies. He felt as if he was just barely managing to hold everything together, and if someone were to hand him a potted plant or a goldfish to take care of, he suspected the whole tenuous effort would just collapse, and the ship would fall from the sky.

It didn't help matters that morale was bad. Byron sensed among the crew a subtle recoiling, a quiet retreat. He'd observed Iren duck into a cabin to avoid passing Voleta in the corridor. The two, who'd once been inseparable, now seemed to drive each other from a room. They were like opposing magnets, pushing each other about the ship.

Since her miraculous revival, Voleta was admittedly different. Though the Sphinx's medium had emancipated her from death, part of her still seemed locked away. She was often lost in thought, often muttering to herself. She spent hours and hours idling upon the sofa in the conservatory while Squit scrambled up and down the bookshelves and over the bare strings of the harpsichord, unnoticed by her master. There was something disconcerting about an indolent Voleta. The fact that she had picked up some of Reddleman's dreamy aloofness was particularly troubling. Byron could understand Iren's discomfort, but he also worried that Voleta might fill the vacuum Iren left with Reddleman's company.

It didn't help that the captain was distracted. Edith was always either on the bridge or in her quarters, and she rushed back and forth between the two as if fearing an ambush. Byron suspected she was avoiding Marya and her child, which was reasonable, given her awkward past with Marya's husband. As for the former Mermaid, she was a castaway on the island of new motherhood and entirely consumed by the rituals of feeding, bathing, changing, and nuzzling a three-month-old child. It was work that had previously been shared among several nurses and maids. Though Marya appeared both capable of doing all the labor herself and proud of that fact, she was not so prideful as to refuse Ann's help.

Byron was so grateful for Ann, not least of all because she seemed untouched by the disquiet that had settled over the crew. She was more than happy to hurl herself at the unhappy infant with the sort of professional brio Byron felt when he whipped egg whites or ironed doilies. Byron had quickly learned that if Ann was holding the infant, it meant the babe was either in a bad mood or sleeping, and both were conditions he didn't wish to interrupt. Though he would never say it out loud, the newborn made him uneasy.

Reddleman had always been a furtive fellow, but even he had begun to behave more strangely. Several times, Byron had come across him emerging from unusual hidey-holes. He had caught the pilot popping out of a crawlspace in the observatory, and emerging from the orlop, and creeping from the engine room where Ferdinand's iron husk stood propped against the wall. Byron had reported each instance to the captain. And she had told him to let her worry about Reddleman. As if anyone could hold a monopoly on anxiety.

When Byron confronted Reddleman to question his lurking, the pilot had said that he was only exploring, suspecting the ship had more secrets to surrender.

But there could be no doubt about it: The crew was falling apart. It seemed to Byron a dangerous time for division. They were faced with hostile ringdoms, an aspiring tyrant, the threat of revolution, and the Sphinx's troubling silence. They could scarcely afford to be avoiding each other in the hallways.

The solution was obvious. They needed to institute a formal teatime, a daily occasion that all had to attend. When Byron suggested the notion to Edith, she said that she was all for it. She would gladly hold the bridge while they all took tea. "After all, a crew needs a little unsupervised time to complain, cavort, and plot their mutinies. It's good for morale."

His long ears stiffening with dismay, Byron said, "Forgive me for saying so, Captain, but that is without a doubt the stupidest thing you've ever said. We don't need more complaints, more cavorting, or a *mutiny*, for heaven's sake. We need camaraderie and rapport and a chance to expel whatever has gotten stuck in our bellows before we all pop!" Byron's reply grew more impassioned as it went until his eyes were as large as walnuts, and his remaining antler switched the air like the arm of a metronome.

Edith scowled, appearing to weigh whether she wished to reprimand him for calling her stupid. She said, "You seem to feel strongly about this."

"I was more or less alone for a very long time, and then, all of a sudden, I wasn't alone anymore. Now, I feel that intimacy slipping away again, and I want it to stop."

She laid a hand on his arm. "Then we'll stop it."

"You have to come to tea, too," Byron said.

"Someone has to watch the bridge."

"Then we'll rotate every day, and I'll take a cup up to whoever's on duty."

"Will there be singing?"

"Certainly not. This is tea, not a cabaret," Byron said, tugging upon the points of his vest, though in the end, it was more of a floor show than he would've liked.

Byron hated tea. He hated its bitter taste and the tannic dryness it inspired in the mouth. He hated the smell of it, an aroma like soured wood pulp, and he hated the stains it left in his cups and on his tablecloths.

Yet he drank it because he absolutely adored teatime. He loved the little sandwiches and their excessive variety, loved the sugar cubes and their precious tongs. He loved the jewels of jelly and the crowns of toast. He loved it all so much, in fact, he was flabbergasted when the crew arrived for tea wearing expressions better suited to a public flogging. They moped to their assigned places at the table, dragged out their chairs with a maximum of squeals and clatter, and plopped into their seats like toads.

Iren sat with one elbow planted on her empty plate and her chin propped on her hand. Ann marched up and down the aisles between dining tables, trying to quiet Olivet, who was hiccupping the same woeful sob over and over again. Marya looked like a ghost in need of a nap. She had been listening to her daughter's efforts to shout herself hoarse since sometime before dawn. Voleta muttered to herself, a habit that seemed to be growing more pronounced. Her gaze scanned back and forth as if she were reading the empty air over the table. She wrung her hands in her lap, another new tic, and made little exhalations, which might've been aborted gasps or half-finished laughs. Squit slept on her shoulder with her tail pulled over her head as if to drown out her master's mumbling.

At the head of the table, Edith frowned, her brows knitted with concern. She seemed surprised by Voleta's paroxysms, which her duties had allowed her to overlook. When the captain caught Byron staring at her, she put on a brave, encouraging smile. "The egg salad is very good."

"Paprika," Byron murmured, answering a question that had not been asked. He shook his head to clear the settling fog of self-pity and said with more authority, "Elbows off the table, Iren. Try the potted trout. I think you'll like it. Not too fishy. Miss Boreas, young lady, Miss... *Voleta*!" Byron said sharply, and Voleta at last turned to regard him. A queer, blissful smile curled the corners of her mouth. "I put the sugar plums out for you. You may have two if you like."

"I'm not hungry," Voleta began faintly, then went on more assertively, "Did you know Adam and I were twins? My mother lied to us. I wonder why she did that. Her sake? His sake? My sake?"

"How do you know that?" Edith asked.

Voleta shifted her handwashing from her lap onto her empty saucer. "I remember being born. I was first out, Adam second. Never could keep up with me," she said, finishing with another small gasp, this one more clearly a brief attempt at laughter.

Her fist dwarfing the ornate butter knife, Iren slapped the mashed trout onto a piece of toast as if she meant to punish it. Ann brought the now merely whining infant around to stand behind Iren so she could set a hand on her shoulder. The contact seemed to cool the amazon's frustration, though Ann couldn't spare the hand for long.

"Your brother would probably tell you to eat a sandwich before you blow away," Byron said, trying for a chipper tone that came out almost snide. "Please, eat something," he finished more generously.

"I can't," Voleta said with a languid shrug. "When I try, I just get sick."

"Well, just a sip of tea then. It'll settle your stomach," Byron said, and as if in demonstration, took a sip of his wretched brew. "Mmm. Delicious." He took up the teapot and reached across the table in a fashion that was not quite mannerly, and poured Voleta some tea.

She tilted the cup toward herself, inspecting the bronzy water as if it were castor oil. Then she steeled herself and drank it down and returned the cup to the saucer without a clink.

Byron beamed. "There! That's a good start. Now, why don't you try one of the sugar pl—"

Voleta managed to get a hand up before she vomited. Though she shielded the table from the worst of it, her lap was not so lucky.

Iren rocked her chair onto its back when she stood, then knocked over several more on her way across the dining room and through the hatch. Ann jogged one way then the other as she thought to run after Iren, then recalled she was still holding Olivet. She passed the half-pacified infant to a dazed and apologizing Marya, and then seemed to realize just how much distress Voleta was in. She and Byron rushed to the young woman's side. Suddenly, Voleta needed to be propped up. She shivered, her lips turning a pale blue. She seemed to be fighting off the arrival of sleep. With her eyes half-shut, she whispered, "I can't feel my arms," then slumped against

Byron, who caught her against his chest. Squit leapt onto his snout, ran up between his eyes, and climbed up the branches of his surviving antler.

"I have the kit," Ann said, drawing from her apron pocket a small leather case. She unzipped it, revealing a syringe and four glowing vials of the Sphinx's medium. As she began to load the syringe with the swirling red serum, she asked, "How many do we give her? One? Two? When was her last shot?"

"I don't know. I thought we were weaning her off it. I might've forgotten. I was so busy with... What do you think, Captain? How many doses?" Bryon asked. He looked up from Voleta's colorless ear just in time to see Edith bound into the corridor.

Chapter Two

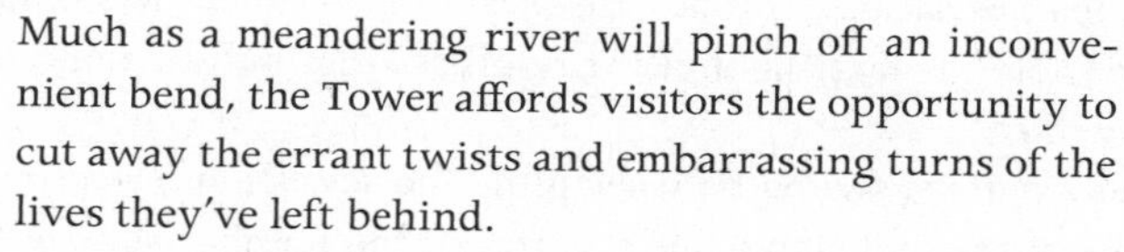

Much as a meandering river will pinch off an inconvenient bend, the Tower affords visitors the opportunity to cut away the errant twists and embarrassing turns of the lives they've left behind.

—*Everyman's Guide to the Tower of Babel*, II. XX

Edith charged through the observatory, past the ornately carved woodland scenes that embossed the walls; then through the conservatory, where the harpsichord's strings rang faintly with the thrum of the ship. She hoped to catch sight of Iren, but the amazon was still quick, especially when she was upset. Edith suspected she knew who the object of her ire was.

The hatch to the bridge stood open. A mighty crash of glass greeted her as she leapt into the spangling light cast by the ship's enigmatic controls. The banks of gemstone lights seemed to strobe with alarm, though Edith recognized the particular pattern as an indication that the autopilot was engaged. Which was a good thing because the ship's flesh-and-blood pilot had just been hurled into the weapons cabinet.

Iren pulled Reddleman back through the jagged remnants of the gun case by his shirtfront. A stand of rifles fell out after him. Iren shifted her grip to the pilot's throat. He had a wild, bewildered look in his eyes as he pawed at the amazon's forearms. His supernatural strength seemed to have abandoned him. His cheeks began to purple as Iren growled, "Where did she go? Who did you bring back? Who is she?"

Edith touched Iren's elbow with the tip of an iron finger and said, "He can't answer you if you kill him. Let him go. Now, please."

When Iren dropped the pilot, his feet were unready to catch him, and he fell into an awkward heap. He rolled onto his back, his arms out, chest heaving. He coughed until Edith thought he would retch. She had watched him walk about with a sword stuck through his chest, seen him shrug off a gunshot as if it were a poke. Now he laid trembling and gagging at her feet. "What's the matter with you?" she asked.

"You forgot my lunch, Captain," he said, running his dry tongue over cracked lips. He sat up, dropped his jacket off his shoulders, and turned a little to show the faint light of the red fuses that bulged along his spine under his shirt.

Edith's emotions swung between guilt and revulsion. Sometimes when she looked at the Red Hand, she saw the all too familiar state of her own affairs: an incredible might tempered by the indignity of dependence.

"Tea threw me off schedule. I'll get your vials." Edith moved to the captain's chair, pressed a panel door under the armrest that opened to reveal a bank of shining batteries.

"Oh, no hard feelings, Captain. I know how easy it is to slip out of a routine. What do they say? It takes two weeks to make a habit and two days to break it? Well, I'm sure we—"

"What did you do to her?" Iren asked again, squatting before the pilot. She put a knuckle under his chin and raised his weakened head. "Voleta died and someone else woke up. Who is she?"

Reddleman held up a wavering hand, a plea for patience. He swallowed and said, "When the Sphinx brought me back, the process took months. He put me in an isolation tank and reintroduced the medium at a drip. He reeled me in slowly, kept me weak, kept me in a sort of twilight state. He gave me time to find my thoughts before giving me back my strength."

"You're saying you lost your mind?" Iren said.

Reddleman smiled, showing teeth round as fingernails under colorless lips. "Did you ever finish reading a book, put it down, then realize some hours later that you were still inside it, still inhabiting that world, still entertaining those characters?" Reddleman asked. When Iren hesitated, Edith answered that she was familiar with the feeling. "It's like that when you first come back. But you're not just caught inside one book. You're lost in every book, every volume ever written."

"You felt like a library?" Iren said.

Reddleman huffed a breathless laugh. "I didn't feel like anything. The medium, it opens a little buttonhole in time that you can push your mind through. I pushed all the way back to the start of things, when the stars were just lumps in an infinite, fiery porridge. I lingered there for an age, an epoch, an eternity. *Infinite. Eternal.* My god, our grandest words are still so small."

"Small words are fine. Just tell me what's happened to her."

"Time is very, very large, much larger than any mind can hold. The deeper I remembered, the longer I lingered, the more my own memories began to scatter and fade. I promise you, Voleta is still Voleta, but she is drifting away from her former life. It's not easy to find your way back, and even harder to stay once you have."

Edith knelt and brushed shards of glass from the pilot's shoulders. She raised the back of his shirt to reveal the steel vertebrae that erupted from his scar-puckered skin. "How do we help her?" she asked as she removed the first depleted vial.

"I'm not sure. In my enthusiasm for reviving the young lady, I believe I administered an overdose, and her system has adjusted accordingly. Too much or too little of the medium can have a similarly disorienting effect. Withdrawal and overindulgence are two sides of the same coin, medically speaking."

Edith twisted a fresh vial into its cradle and clamped down the steel cage that protected it. It was molded to resemble the knuckle of backbone, one of the Sphinx's little flourishes. He always tried to make inscrutable things seem more familiar, though the result was often more queasy than calming. "What if we make an isolation tank for her, like the one the Sphinx put you in? Create a controlled environment. Administer smaller doses more regularly. Could we wean her off the medium?"

"I don't like the sound of that at all," Voleta said from the hatchway. Her skin was pink, and her eyes shone like rubies held up to a candle. Whatever palsy had gripped her before was gone. She seemed to float upon the tips of her toes. "I'm not sleeping in a bubble. Maybe that worked for Reddleman, but I need diversion; I need something to do."

Iren stood, her haggard cheeks tightened by the stress of her jaw, her low brow hiding her eyes. She said, "Do you remember me? Do you know who I am?"

"Of course. You're my dear friend who's been jumping behind doors to avoid me. I remember you, but I'm not so sure you remember me."

"You're different."

"As are you. We're changing, Iren. You have Ann. I have . . . memories. I think it's perfectly all right to be frightened. Sometimes the fear of change is just an expression of love for the life you had. That's nothing to be ashamed of. I like who we were. And I like who you are, and I suspect I'll like who you will be, too."

"Does this mean you're back?" Iren asked.

"I don't know, but I'm finding it easier to concentrate at the moment. It's like I drank a cup of strong tea. Very strong tea."

Ann's head poked in from the passageway. "Voleta. There you are! It's nice to see you looking . . ." Ann recoiled a little when Voleta turned her head enough to show her beaming eyes. ". . . less pale."

"How much did you give her?" Edith asked.

"Four ampules."

Edith looked up from her installation of Reddleman's final vial. She was unable to blunt the look of alarm on her face, or keep the note of shock out of her voice when she said, "Four?"

The former au pair hadn't much height to work with, but still she managed to make herself seem a little taller as she stepped onto the bridge. "The first two shots did nothing at all. The third made her convulse. But the fourth, well, that one seemed to wake her up. And please don't scold me, Captain. I did my best. I'm not a doctor or the Phoenix or—"

"*Sphinx*," Byron said from behind her. "You mean to say, you're not the Sphinx."

"No, I certainly am not. But unless Mr. Sphinx is hiding in a broom closet, I'll have to do," Ann said.

"We're not making do with you, Ann. We're all very grateful for your help," Edith said, clipping the last cage shut on Reddleman's spine. "And it's entirely my fault we didn't decide on some sort of protocol."

Voleta said, "Oh, I think four is just dandy. Four in the future. Four forever. I like four." She looked at her hands, at her fingernails glowing like the embers of a banked fire. Edith watched the young woman marvel at herself and wondered if she liked this version of her better or worse than the semi-lucid mumbler. "I feel so . . . clear."

"Yes! The lucidity is quite intoxicating," Reddleman said with a sigh that made the hairs of Edith's arm prickle. The nodes along his spine flared as he drew a deep breath. She dropped his shirt to spare herself the sight of his resurging power. "But," the pilot continued, "the effect does diminish with abuse. The more you take, the more you need. It's like you're standing on a mesa that's growing higher and higher, swelling from the earth, but shrinking at the peak. One day, you'll find yourself standing on a point so far from the earth, you'll see nothing but the tops of clouds and the bottom of the universe."

That seemed to sober Voleta a little. She tilted her head and jutted her lower lip before asking. "Can I stop it? Can I wring it out of my veins?"

"Oh, no. We are now embryos animated by the Blood of Time. If the medium runs dry, or we drown ourselves in it, there won't be a third birth for us, I'm afraid."

"Excuse me, Captain," Ann said. "But what is that?"

She pointed at one of the magnovisor's many screens and the curious vessel framed therein. To call it an airship would be generous. It was more of an assemblage held together by wire, twine, and will. Rather than a hull or gondola, the main of the vessel was composed of a bicycle frame that had been robbed of its wheels. A youth in knickerbockers with a scarf wound about his head rode the rickety mount beneath a patched balloon that was shaped like an acorn, complete with cap and stem. Papery fins on either side of his mount twisted in harmony with a set of handlebars, the fore of which was crowded with horns and bells. The youth pedaled feverishly, a wild effort that was grudgingly rewarded by the lazy churning of a large propeller behind him. He had the strained posture of a cyclist struggling uphill into a headwind.

"The airman's friend," Iren said.

Edith huffed derisively. "More like the buzzard's gazette."

"I think he means to intercept us. Should I open fire?" Reddleman asked.

Edith swatted the air. "No. He's just a paperboy. Let him come."

"Could be a ruse," Iren said. "The hod who blew himself up in Pelphia was just a boy."

"Well, I could deploy the snuffler," Reddleman said. When Edith asked what a snuffler was, the pilot explained his recent discovery, another gem mined from the *State of Art*'s voluminous manuals. Both of the ship's hatches were equipped with a sensor that could detect the presence of black powder. If the newspaper hawker was armed with either pistol or explosive, the snuffler would sniff it out.

Through her periscope, Edith watched as the paperboy gradually overtook her ship. When at last he was in range, he cast out a small grappling hook, which caught the rail that fenced the hatch. Pulling himself in, he tied his ship off and leapt onto the silvery hull, gripping the strap of a canvas sack that bulged with rolled-up newspapers.

Edith addressed him through the plumbing of a communication horn that flowered from the stalk of her periscope. "What are you doing on my ship?"

The youth startled at the sound of her voice, his head whipping about in search of its origin. Failing to find it, he replied to the empty air. "Ahoy! *The Acorn* is an airman's friend, and an airman's friend is *The Acorn*. Care for a copy, ma'am?"

"What makes you think I want that old rag?"

"Well, because you're in it, ma'am."

Edith turned her head from the mouth of the trumpet to expel a spasm of profanity. Then, returning to the hawker's ear, she said, "All right. Prepare to be . . . snuffled."

Reddleman ticked up a ruby-studded switch with the side of one knuckle. Edith watched as a plate above deck slid open, and the snuffler emerged like a snake charmed from a basket.

Though, in point of fact, it more closely resembled the proboscis of an elephant, albeit one made entirely of brass. The animated trunk probed the hawker's smock, scarf, breeches, and gunnysack, blowing and sucking air with the rapidity of a bloodhound. The youth vacillated between shouts of protest and tickled laughter. The moment the search concluded, the snuffler spooled back into its hole.

Reddleman announced a clear result. The newspaper hawker was unarmed. Still, Edith ordered everyone on their guard before signaling her pilot to release the locks and open the hatch. At the touch of a dial, the handwheel spun, and the hatch rose.

The paperboy clambered down the imbedded ladder, sack bouncing on his back. Skipping the final rungs, he landed with a bang of his bootheels. He loosened his scarf, exposing rosy cheeks and a round, hairless chin. He looked no older than a decade, though already he had mastered the dispassionate expression of a bailiff. Clearing his sinuses, he pursed his cherubic lips and turned his head.

"If you spit on my floor, I will mop it up with your head," Byron said.

Seeming to see Byron for the first time, the hawker swallowed his missile, and with it, some of his swagger. Edith watched his expression turn fearful as he surveyed them: a stag-headed footman, a giantess with a scar-carved face, a young lady with shorn hair and steaming eyes, a potbellied man with an unnerving smile, and a woman with a derrick for an arm.

Edith rose from her captain's throne and crossed the bridge to stand before him. "Are you just an enterprising young man, or did someone send you?"

"It was a bet, ma'am."

"Was it, now? What's the payout?"

"Three shekels six pence, ma'am."

"Not bad." She presented him with her iron palm. "Do you still print cosmograms?"

"Yes, ma'am. Papers are two pennies apiece, ma'am."

Edith looked around at her crew, who undertook the timeworn pantomime of patting empty pockets. At last, Byron heaved a sigh and stepped forward, wriggling two fingers into his waistcoat pocket. Muttering about how there appeared to be something of the bandit still left in all of them, he pressed two coins into the hawker's trembling hand. "You shouldn't gamble. It's a nasty habit."

The boy all but flung the scrolled-up paper at Edith. He was up the ladder, through the hatch, and on his mount before she could unfurl the first page of the gazette.

Edith had been introduced to *The Acorn* during her tenure as Billy Lee's first mate. The paper, a sixty-year-old institution, catered to an audience of naval recruits, bargemen, wharfies, airdales, skippers, pirates, and daydreaming young boys and girls who were clever enough to get their hands on a copy of the often lurid, always enthralling publication.

The editor, Samuel Kilgore, was well known for weaving stories grand as a sail from a single thread of truth. In addition to the thrilling tales of calamity, orgy, and adventure, he was a gossip, an agitator, and a connoisseur of conspiracies. And still, *everyone* read *The Acorn*, not least of all because it contained lists of open jobs, bounties and warrants, port closures, and a weather forecast that everyone agreed was slightly less reliable than the paper's astrological cosmograms.

"So, what does it say?" Iren asked.

Edith didn't have to scan very far down the front page to find the answer, which she read aloud. " 'Steel Galleon Spurns Gravity and Burns

Port. Thousands Immolated at Hands of Famed Inventor and Outed Occultist the Sphinx.' "

"Is that it?" Iren asked.

"That's just the title. It goes on . . . and *on*."

"*Thousands?* Was it really thousands?" Ann asked.

"No," Edith said faintly, the main of her focus still absorbed by reading.

"Well, go on. Let's have it," Byron said.

Prefacing her recitation with a great sigh, Edith began to read the article aloud. " 'The *State of Art*, which flies under the Brick Layer's banner, is crewed by monsters and abominations composed of flesh and metal. Some sources have reported the crew drinks engine oil and subsists on a diet of bolts and screws. Others have it on good authority that the Sphinx's disciples are practicing anthropophagi and will suffer the occasional morsel of veal only because it resembles their preferred supper of . . .' "

"Of what?" Iren asked.

Edith cleared her throat. "Human infant."

"They are delicious," Voleta murmured.

Edith read on: " 'After razing Port Virtue, terrorizing King Leonid in his home, and maiming an unnamed noble, the *State of Art* now skulks the heavens like an indecisive comet. Where shall she strike next? By all accounts, her tour is driven by a desire to extort. Kings and principalities would be wise to gather their jewels and coins, for soon enough they shall be called upon to add their gold to the dragon's hoard.

" 'And a mythical beast he must be! The Sphinx, by shedding the silks of his flagship, has at last revealed the true nature of his genius. He is not an engineer; he is a sorcerer—a conjurer of infernal fires that cheat gravity and mock the wind. He is an occultist surgeon who grafts engine to organ, an enchanter who befuddles us with beer and darkling mirrors. Have you ever asked yourself why the Sphinx prefers his wards inebriated and flummoxed? One only has to ask the question to know the ready answer. And remember: *The Acorn* is an airman's friend, and an airman's friend is *The Acorn*.' "

A pall fell over them as they reflected upon their unanticipated infamy. In every port, on every ship, at that very moment countless readers were looking up from the latest edition of *The Acorn* and squinting out at the silvery splinter lodged in the palm of the sky: a ship full of monstrous cannibals in service of a wicked magus.

After a moment, Edith cleared her throat and asked her pilot what the ship's maximum altitude was. He rattled off the number from memory: fifty-four thousand feet. It was an astonishing number, and only achievable because the ship was airtight and carried a considerable freight of oxygen. Even the long-distance barges rarely cruised at half that height, at which point the air was nearly too thin to breathe and the winds were bitter cold. She asked him to ascend to thirty-two thousand feet, well out of the reach of even the most ambitious privateer, at which point he was to activate the autopilot and join them in the dining room.

"What's happening in the dining room?" Reddleman asked.

"We're going to finish our tea," Edith said.

Chapter Three

The Tower is not without its seasons of unrest, but so it is wherever humanity gathers. Dynasties rise and fall; oligarchs sweep up fortunes for revolutionaries to scatter. The wild swings of history have a way of sawing a society in half. Visitors are advised to be adaptable; when possible ride the saw, not the log.

—*Everyman's Guide to the Tower of Babel*, II. IX

The crew had not been poisoned by a lack of camaraderie, as Byron believed. No, what they suffered from was a dearth of information and a surfeit of uncertainty. They were being battered by obscure and violent forces they did not understand. Edith had given orders; they had followed them, suffering grave injury—both physical and psychological—without knowing, except in the vaguest of terms, what was at stake.

It was an untenable position that Edith herself had maintained under the auspice of protecting her friends from what the Sphinx had called *the curse*. How egotistical! And how convenient! Was it not easier for her to be shielded from their mortal dread, to not have to answer their probing questions or account for choices she herself felt unsure of? The Sphinx could not really believe that he and she were the *only* ones strong and sage enough to bear the burden of a difficult truth? Surely the accumulation of knowledge was not without power? And who knew that better than the Sphinx? He traded in mystery, influence, and subterfuge. But Edith would not. She decided to tell her crew what she knew and hope they would forgive her.

While Olivet slept in her gimbaled cradle and the *State of Art* hung beyond the reach of man, they gathered again around Byron's table and took up their cooling tea.

Edith began her briefing by describing the lightning sea, that reservoir which contained millions of gallons of the Sphinx's medium. The reserve, while built to absorb the lightning the Tower produced, had grown unstable. It was creeping toward a tipping point that would result in the abrupt release of all the energy it had banked. The resulting explosion would level the Tower, blacken the skies, and leave the landscape forever changed.

The Sphinx believed the only way to prevent his boiling reservoir from turning the Tower into a crater was secreted behind a locked door in his home, a door that had been sealed by the Brick Layer himself. The key to this chamber, and their salvation, was encoded across sixty-four paintings of a little girl holding a paper boat. The Sphinx, perhaps at the request of the Brick Layer, had distributed these paintings throughout the Tower many, many years prior in an effort to decentralize power and foster collaboration between the ringdoms. Or so he claimed. It was an aspiration the Sphinx had apparently come to regret, because he had spent recent years recalling the loaned-out art. He'd already recovered all but twenty-eight of the paintings. Byron had provided Edith with a list of the ringdoms he believed to be in possession of the outstanding copies. Of course, not every ringdom on the list would still have their piece of the key, because Luc Marat had already pilfered six, though that number might prove to be higher depending on the zealot's industriousness and the ringdoms' neglect.

In one of their final moments together, the Sphinx had informed Edith that the code could still be read without having all of the paintings present. The Brick Layer had built in a duplicate system of transmission to accommodate the possibility of lost, destroyed, or withheld paintings. This redundancy allowed for the absence of as many as eight panels. Their charge, then, was to collect the remaining paintings before Luc Marat got his hands on them.

Further complicating this awful knot was the possible existence of an immense siege engine that was capable of chewing through the Tower like a mole. Edith extracted from a large envelope a short stack of glossy-faced papers. She split the stack of photographs in half and passed some to her left, the rest to her right. The curious technology responsible for the creation of these frozen images was quickly eclipsed by what they contained: the blueprints of the Hod King.

"Well, that's a big boy," Iren said, pointing to a spiny castle at the aft of the colossal burrowing engine and the cannon that fairly filled it. "What's this word?" she asked Ann.

Ann peered over her arm. "Sound it out, dear. You can do it."

Iren murmured under her breath, then said, "The Quibbler?"

"Very good."

"What's a Quibbler?" Voleta asked.

"Apparently it's an almighty mortar that hurls five-hundred-pound boulders. That *can't* be right." Iren squinted over the top of the photograph at Edith. "They haven't really built this thing, have they?"

"I don't know," Edith admitted, cracking a scone over her plate to give her hands something to do. "It could just be an aspiration, a pipe dream, but Marat's resourcefulness has surprised us in the past."

"Who is this Mr. Marat again?" Ann asked.

"A zealot who's gathered himself an army. He's posing as a liberator of the hods, but really, he's just an aspiring tyrant. He wants to be king of the castle. Depose the Sphinx, take his place. He used to be one of his Wakemen, like me."

Marya took the next photograph Ann passed to her. "What I don't understand is why Mr. Sphinx would gather a sea of electricity in the first place. I mean, it sounds as if he built this bomb on purpose."

"Always on purpose. Everything on purpose," Byron said in a singsong to himself as he refilled Ann's forgotten cup. He stretched the ribbon of tea, raising the pot with a little flourish. Only then did he seem to realize everyone was looking at him in silence. "Oh, don't gawk at me. I just mean to say, the Sphinx doesn't do *anything* on accident, I just thought the attic reservoir was like a pantry, a stockpile in case of an emergency. I didn't know it *was* the emergency."

"If it's all just sitting in a great big tub, can't he pull out the plug?" Ann asked.

"Apparently not," Edith said around a mouthful of her scone, which had turned to cement in her mouth. She pushed the plate away.

"Maybe that's what's behind the locked door: a great big plunger," Voleta said.

"Maybe," Edith said.

"Do we know where Mr. Marat is keeping his stolen paintings?" Ann asked.

"We know where they were, but it seems very unlikely they're still there. We made something of a mess of the place."

"I set off a bomb," Voleta said a little smugly. The memory of the plume of flame seemed to sparkle in her eyes.

"Of course you did." Ann flipped one of the photographs around, a detail of the great chewing prong at the fore of the Hod King. "Do you think he's keeping the paintings aboard this monstrous thing, assuming it's real?"

Edith rocked her head from side to side. "Perhaps. Either way, we'll have to bring it down."

"And how will you do that?"

"I don't know. I've been studying these pictures, but I haven't found any obvious chink in the armor, at least not yet."

"But if you destroy it, won't you damage the paintings, too?"

"That's certainly a possibility. But, it's also possible that Marat chews so many holes with his drilling machine that he compromises the integrity of the Tower. Whether he intends to or not, he could bring the whole thing down."

"Is that better than exploding?" Ann asked.

"Marginally. Millions would still die. My hope is that we'll be able to incapacitate the engine, board it, dispatch any survivors, and search for the paintings."

Reddleman's eyes rolled up and to one side as he did a sum in his head. "These numbers put her operational crew at one hundred and eleven, with room to transport nearly as many troops... let me see... I'd say we can expect upward of two hundred souls aboard? That's about thirty for each of us, presuming of course everyone is comfortable swinging a sword."

The pilot smiled at Ann, who swallowed and said, "Presuming."

Edith surveyed her crew, their tucked-in chins and pinched brows. They all looked rather defeated, which was understandable given that she'd just revealed a pair of pending and entangled apocalypses and their role in averting them. She stood up to gather their attention. "I realize it is a grim errand that I've asked you to join me in. But I can offer you this consolation: We are a *formidable* adversary. We own the sky. We have the advantage of intelligence, insight into our enemy, that they cannot claim to have about us. It may seem hopeless, but I assure you, it is not. If we trust in each other, trust in ourselves, we will win the day."

"Captain, is there any hope of reinforcements?" Marya asked with a glimmer of hope.

Edith sat down, her chair squeaking as she scooted it back in. "I'm afraid we are the reinforcements."

Chapter Four

Never was a rough road smoothed by looking backward;
never was a great height shrunk by looking down.
—*Everyman's Guide to the Tower of Babel*, I. XVI

From a distance, the *State of Art* shone like a crack in a windowpane. Up and down the length of the Tower, lookouts gawked and watchmen rubbed their eyes. She had to be a mirage, a trick of the light. Much as wingless birds did not fly, silkless airships did not float.

Yet the *State of Art* did exactly that.

She seemed to sail upon the light of a sunset she carried in her bilge. Though clad in steel from stem to stern, she flew as deftly as a dragonfly and more swiftly than a hawk. When the Sphinx's flagship had still dangled from a fragile bag of gas, the generals of the great houses had admired her in a condescending sort of way. *What a pretty little sloop! How shiny! How sleek!* They had a passing interest in the Sphinx's return, though it seemed a curtain call for a play that had ended long ago. The Sphinx was a vestigial myth from a former era, and his tin ship was a lonesome antique.

But all that smugness evaporated the moment the *State of Art* dropped her sails and transformed into a flying axe-head. She shrugged off Pelphia's cannonballs like a man brushes rain from his shoulders and fired her own guns with such ruthless rapidity, she made a whole ringdom kneel in the course of an evening.

She was a fleet of one, a navy in herself.

The question then became how could something that should not float be brought down? Finding no answer to this question, some of the Tower's greatest navies withdrew to the encircling mountains. Others docked their fleet in the shipyards for refurbishment. All were adamant that none of these actions qualified as a retreat. When called to explain these maneuvers by their native journalists, the admirals of the mightiest ringdoms claimed these exercises and repairs had been scheduled months ago and had nothing to do with the revelation that the Sphinx had an unsinkable ship. After all, the Sphinx was the Tower's peaceful benefactor. Surely he would not go to war with his own children.

Surely.

Edith was perfectly aware of the impression her ship made, and she used it to her advantage. She hadn't time to rattle sabers with every captain looking to add a stripe to his shoulder. She was in a hurry. A bomb smoldered in the head of the Tower. The Sphinx was unresponsive and perhaps trapped in his own impenetrable home. Tom was lost to the black trail, a deathly grotto from which few returned, and somewhere unseen, an armor-plated siege engine gnawed the Tower like a weevil chews a stalk.

As much as she would've liked to address all of these crises at once, Edith hadn't the resources or knowledge to do so. Searching for Senlin on the black trail would be like hunting for a shadow in the dark. Locating the Hod King would be no easier. She could only wait for Marat's excavator to emerge and trust that the headmaster was wily enough to keep himself alive. For the moment, defusing the lightning sea had to take precedence over all else.

Over a week had passed since the *State of Art* had pushed off from Pelphia. They'd spent the interim returning the ship's interior to a livable state, repairing the damage caused by General Eigengrau's raid, and convalescing when occasion allowed, which was seldom. Amid these restorative efforts, they had found time to call upon three ringdoms: Algez, Morick, and Euphydia. Concerningly, all had failed to deliver their copy of *The Brick Layer's Granddaughter.*

When the Algezian monarch, Wilhelmina Cassira, was told by her abashed treasurer that their painting had been replaced by a fake so egregious he was ashamed to present it, the queen had not believed him. She berated him for presuming he was any sort of art critic and demanded that he produce the painting at once. He did, and all seated at the bonewood table before an untouched feast saw why the treasurer had wished to keep it out of sight. The painting was wrong in every regard. The water was wine-colored, the little girl mannish, and her hair so thinly applied, it rendered her entire head translucent. One of the ladies at the table laughed before she could plug her mouth with her napkin. Edith might've laughed too had she not been so disappointed.

It was a feeling that mounted the next day when they arrived in Port Fortuity in the tenth ringdom of Oyodin. Byron had warned Edith that the Oyodins were a clique of unabashed nudists. But not only did the Oyodins eschew clothing, they also shunned lathe, plaster, brick, doors, and curtains. Every building in Oyodin, from bank vault to bathhouse, was built of glass. This had not been done to titillate, but rather to enforce transparency in all affairs, both public and private. Before Oyodin became the City of Windows, it had suffered from a political gridlock that had slowly slid from clannishness to the brink of civil war. The rival leaders eventually undertook peace talks, but were compelled by mutual suspicion to meet in the altogether. There would be no pockets for knives, no sleeves for cudgels, no boots for pistols. Just skin, long talk, and eventually an armistice.

The resulting Glass Revolution took more than a generation to unfold. Over time, the old city of Oyodin was dismantled. The bricks and wood were sold off so that great sheets of glass could be bought. At first, only public institutions were turned into hothouses, then soon the businesses who wished to convey the honesty of their wares took up the fragile mantle, and soon, the residences followed as the desire for privacy was regarded with increasing suspicion. The result of these efforts, according to the Oyodins, was very little crime, less corruption, and a general harmony among all parties. They were not as quick to claim the curious prudishness that the Glass Revolution also inspired. An explosion of social mores took hold as everyone fretted about whether their formerly private practices would become public shames. There were folkways for every act, from how one engaged the toilet, to how one undertook the reproductive effort, and all prescribed in minute detail. Rather than freeing everyone to behave as themselves, the Glass Revolution had obligated one and all to behave more or less alike.

The fact that Oyodin had become the Tower's foremost bookmakers resulted in a great and near constant stream of tourists. Those who wished to enter the ringdom were required to disrobe, a fact that discouraged most visitors from exploring the City of Windows. The ringdom's industry was necessarily moved out to its ports, where guests were allowed to keep their britches, at least until they lost them at the roulette table.

The four ports of Oyodin became, in the span of a generation, the Tower's foremost casinos. In addition to airship duels, pigeon races, and falconry competitions, odds were given on all manner of subject, from when the next rain would come to the valley to how long the southern train would be delayed. Table games were also available and in high demand. The thinking went, a nude dealer at a glass table was more trustworthy than any clothed card handler could ever be. And yet, the game runners never failed to make a profit. The Oyodins were a wealthy tribe.

When the *State of Art* turned toward Port Fortuity, the air about the harbor was so crowded with the silks of airships, they seemed to merge into a single billowy crown of cauliflower. After days of watching the navies scatter before them, Edith was surprised by how little the traffic thinned at their approach. Reddleman docked the *State of Art* in the shadow of a cruise ship's balloon in a slip that would've been inaccessible to any vessel with an envelope.

Port Fortuity was an overbuilt and underthought structure that continued to sprawl outward, upward, and around the Tower as new games of chance were invented and demand for tables grew. The port bulged from the face of the ancient pillar like burl from a tree, and it exhibited as much asymmetry. One platform loomed over the next; ladders crossed in the air; roulette wheels were squeezed into the hollows under staircases, causing tables and chairs to be trimmed at the leg and gamblers to crawl in on their knees. Railings were scarce. Banisters rarer still. The highest islands were only accessible by ladders and bridges made of frayed rope and weathered treads. This great confusion of tiers and cantilevers was only interrupted by a central mall where an immense betting board was affixed to the Tower's face over and all around the ringdom's entrance. The door to Oyodin was as unremarkable as a mousehole. The betting board, meanwhile, was composed of plates of immaculate black slate and divided by a grid of beaming gold leaf. The board enumerated the odds for hundreds of open bets, figures that had to be updated constantly by men with pots of chalk paint who dangled on swings raised and lowered by pullies affixed to the crest of the black expanse that rose nearly six stories high. The numbers they painted were as large as a fist, and still the board of Port Fortuity was so vast it could only be read from a distance and by spyglass.

The crowds of Port Fortuity were as noisy as a pig farm and nearly as rank. The human stink was so heavy, not even the trade winds could shunt it away. The ringdom's complete lack of accommodations led gamblers to squat at tables for days, and a shortage of plumbing necessitated the renting of buckets and the overapplication of cologne. The traditional dish of Oyodin was a sort of pickled paste that was extruded into boiling fish oil, deep fried, and served with garlic sauce. Some thought it tasted delicious, but all agreed it smelled absolutely foul.

The visiting mob was as colorful as a vale of wildflowers, though their mood was rarely so bucolic. The major exports of Oyodin were debt, disinheritance, and ulcers. The ringdom retained no formal navy, but their ports were defended by a troop of capable hired men. In Port Fortuity's early days, those payday soldiers were outfitted in gold shakos, lavender coats, and black jackboots. But that attire made the innocent uneasy and the unscrupulous elusive. Soon, the rented guards of Oyodin traded their uniforms in for plainclothes that allowed them to melt into the throng. The only thing that distinguished them was a gold star pinned under their lapel. At any given moment, as much as one-tenth of the port's population was composed of overpaid legionnaires. Violence was rare and short-lived.

The moment the *State of Art* slid into its berth alongside the potbellied *Divine Empress*, a team of porters in pea-green uniforms trooped down the cruise ship's gangway, pushing a train of dining carts. Quickly deducing their destination, Edith intercepted the nervous dinner caravan on the pier. The headwaiter, a sleepy-eyed man with oiled hair, told her the feast came from Captain Lismer's personal pantry and with his compliments. Edith assured him that the crew and guests of the *Divine Empress* were quite safe. But she could not accept the generous gifts lest it seem that their protection had been bought. "It's about the precedent, you understand," she said.

"I'll pass your generous regrets on to the captain," the headwaiter said; then, with a glance over his shoulder, he drew from the pocket of his coat a glass canteen. Something clear sloshed about inside. "It's cherry brandy. My wife makes a batch every year. It reminds me of home; it's one of my favorite things. I'd like you to have it. I just want you to realize not everyone is sorry to see the Sphinx's return. Some of us—*many* of us—feel safer with you on patrol."

"I do love a good brandy," Edith said, accepting the flask. As she turned the bottle about, she was reminded of her father's annual pressing of wild pears, which were as small as a walnut and nearly as hard. But the liquor was as sweet as snapped peas and fragrant as a flowering field. "Please tell your wife I said thank you." Edith tugged at the brim of her weathered tricorne, slipping the glass canteen into the pocket of her greatcoat.

Observing the train of dining carts snake back through the raucous crowd that filled the pier, Edith felt a familiar presence behind her.

"Are you sure?" Iren said as Edith turned her head. Her first mate filled the hatchway. A horn-pommeled pistol hung from her belt. Her dark trousers, green jacket, and white blouse showed evidence of Ann's intervention. Iren looked somehow bigger in a well-tailored uniform.

"Sure about what?" Edith asked.

"About leaving Reddleman behind. You really trust him around a baby?"

"He knows to stay on the bridge, and Byron will keep an eye on him."

"What's Byron going to do if old Red decides he wants to poke around inside someone's skull?"

"He's not like that, you know," Voleta said from her perch atop a fat bollard at the pier's edge.

Edith squinted in surprise. "How did you get out here?"

"Jumped down." Voleta pointed up at the *State of Art*'s top deck.

"That's thirty-five feet, at least. You're lucky you didn't break your knees," Edith said.

"I feel fine," Voleta said, and balanced on the ball of one foot to prove it. Edith thought she seemed a little more like her former self, if one overlooked the fact that her head leaked red light. Edith had asked her to wear one of the ship's uniforms, and with Byron's aid she had complied, in letter if not in spirit. Her shirt was untucked, her epaulets unbuttoned, and the collar of her green coat was cocked up on one side. A small dagger in a lacquer sheath hung from her belt. "And you really don't need to worry, Iren. Reddleman won't bother the baby."

"He carves up songbirds and falls on swords for fun," Iren said.

"He's just a little odd."

"He's a monster."

"That's enough," Edith interjected before the two could quip their way into a full-blown spat. She hadn't wanted to bring Voleta ashore, but the only way to keep the young woman from capering off on her own was to invite her along. Edith had considered bringing Reddleman instead of Iren, but suspected the pair would require too much of her attention, and she needed to have her wits about her. Despite their recent show of strength against the guns of Pelphia, it seemed likely that some ringdoms might still risk their own destruction if presented with the chance to take the *State of Art*. She could not afford to be distracted.

Byron had objected to Voleta's going for an entirely different reason. He was apprehensive that the natives' state of undress might corrupt the young woman. But Edith reminded Byron that Voleta had witnessed strangulations, stabbings, shootings, and worse. She had killed several airmen with her own hands. The sight of a few nudists would not be the thing that stole her innocence.

In the end, it was Iren who seemed the most bothered by the display of flesh. The amazon wore an openmouthed grimace when they were approached by the ringdom's minister, a man named Truffaut. His graying beard clung to his jaw and neck like a mane, leaving his face bare. The hair on his head was of a similar length and teased out with wax to make him look even more leonine, which seemed a curious choice, because he was a rather unimposing fellow. He carried a board with a spring clip clamped upon a curling mass of pages, wore leather sandals that slapped his heel when he walked, and was as naked as a newborn and just as athletic.

Though he came without guards or entourage, Edith was aware of the men who lurked in his wake. Amid the pressing crowd of men and women of every nation and station, Edith marked the men who resisted the competing tide of arriving and departing speculators. They watched her furtively enough, but she saw the glint of gold among the cockles of their coats, marking them as deputies of Oyodin's rented constabulary.

"Welcome, welcome, welcome, emissaries of the Sphinx!" Truffaut said, clutching his clipboard to his chest. "I see you turned down Captain Lismer's wine. I assume you were holding out for a better pour? What can I get you to drink? Or perhaps you'd rather go to the tables straightaway? There's dominos on the fourth tier, Oops on the third, dice and flats on the second, wheels and pegs on—"

"No, thank you," Edith said, staring fixedly into the man's wide and friendly eyes. "We've come on a different sort of errand."

"The Sphinx's mark. So, he *is* calling them in. Interesting." Breaking his embrace of his clipboard, Truffaut began riffling through the warped pages. "You know you broke one of our longest open bets: What year and month the Sphinx's flagship would return. We had only one wager for this July at, let me see here, one thousand and twenty-two to one. I lost a fortune."

"Oh no," Iren said.

Truffaut began scrambling through his papers again. "Wait a minute, wait... let me see." As he flipped each sheet over, Edith saw they were barred with columns and rows full of minute handwriting. Truffaut plucked a pencil from his mane and wetted its point on his tongue. "You are Mrs. Iren?"

"Mister."

"Of course. And can you confirm, Mister Iren, that you killed General Eigengrau?"

"Why do you need to know that?" Edith asked, though she was more curious *how* they knew such a thing.

"There was an open bet on how he would die. As options we had, let me see... Ah yes: killed in battle, killed by old age, by mutiny, execution, duel, accident, pox, gout—"

"It was gout," Iren said.

"You didn't stamp on his head while he was retreating from the battlefield?"

"Maybe a little. The gout did most of the work."

"Right. Well, you saved me quite a tidy sum. Obviously we can't take wagers on someone being murdered. That would be as good as a bounty."

"Obviously," Edith said with a pro forma smile. "Now, about my painting."

"Yes, of course. Follow me, please."

If Truffaut was aware of the stares he garnered as he broke through the crowd, he didn't show it. A pair of ladies in ankle-length skirts and straw bonnets tittered at him when he bade them good morning. A bald man with a flat nose and few teeth looked twice, then smirked to himself. A young dandy in a butter-colored coat barred the minister's way with his cane just so he could regale him with a joke about how even small bait can land a big fish. He had not quite finished the jest when he was grasped under either arm by two men who materialized from the painted throng and dragged away.

There were, apparently, limits to the minister's good humor.

Soon their party was free of the mobbed pier, and they broke upon the spotty shade of the casino floor, which was carpeted in equal parts red dust and old rugs. A forest of pylons and ladders propped up a sprawling archipelago of platforms above. Strings of electric lights swooped between food carts where vendors sold chestnuts, dumplings, and lamb. Stained-glass lanterns marked the roulette tables, of which there were dozens. The clatter of those spinning wheels was frenzied; their turning, mesmerizing. Elsewhere, marbles drained through transparent mazes and coins rattled into slots. Cheers chased groans. Laughter overlapped bitter cursing. The distant patter of heels from the plank islands above sounded like rain on a roof.

They broke again into daylight, a clearing between game floors and the system of islands on stilts. The floor there was so crowded it could only be traversed via a nose-to-nose waltz with a parade of unwilling partners. That dance was made more difficult by the fact that many in the crowd were staring through binoculars and monoculars at the titanic betting board, rendering them more or less oblivious to the passage of others. While some had brought their own spyglass, observation decks broke the mob at regular intervals. Each deck contained a bank of telescopes fixed to swiveling posts. For a penny, one could rent a few minutes at an eyepiece to read the board. The board, which was even more monolithic up close, was presently swarmed by nudes on swings who were in the process of scrubbing old odds from the slate and painting in new.

"We have bad timing, I'm afraid," Minister Truffaut said. They were nearly in the middle of the sea of people now, and fairly pinned to the side of an observational deck. "The post must've come in. We're catching up with the news. I hope you're not in a hurry."

"We are, actually," Edith said, defying the pressure of a woman who was attempting to cut in front of her. Edith had to resist the urge to flick her away with her engine.

"Let me see what I can do." The minister put two fingers in his mouth and piped out a piercing note. At first, nothing seemed to happen, but then a small bell began to ring in the distance. As it drew nearer, Edith realized it was coming from ankle level, and so she was looking down when a white-faced capuchin monkey crawled over a man's spats and sat down at the minister's feet. A tiny backpack hung from its shoulders, and a little jingle bell dangled from a ribbon about its neck.

Truffaut tore a scrap of paper from the bottom of a blank sheet and dashed off a few lines. He addressed the monkey as he scribbled. "I want you to take this to the gatehouse." He repeated the desired destination twice more, and the small monkey's eyes shone as it bobbed its head in understanding. Truffaut tucked the folded scrap into its pack, scratched the animal behind one ear, and the capuchin vanished again into the forest of hems and cuffs.

"I'll have the painting brought out. It'll be quicker," the minister said.

Though *quicker,* Edith soon discovered, was a relative term.

The crack of hammers and the panting of handsaws drifted down from somewhere among the floating platforms, all tenuous as spinning plates. "You're still building?"

The minister nodded. "We are. Law of the Tower says every ringdom owns the air around their gates, and the legal definition of a gate encompasses the reach of any port. We are entirely within our rights to build. And build we shall."

"But obviously you can't keep it up forever."

"We are a flowering branch on a mighty trunk. Tell me, have you ever heard of the sequoia? They are immense trees. They grow to truly staggering heights and survive for thousands of years. There are sequoias alive today that are older than the Tower itself. Imagine that! Yet even the mighty sequoia eventually falls. When they do, sometimes a hearty limb, instead of withering, will continue to grow. A new tree may sprout from the body of a toppled giant." The minister beamed at an indistinct point above Edith's head. He seemed to ogle a vision of his port rising from the rubble of the Tower.

Edith thought him mad. She looked around at the cobbled-together and propped-up decks, the flimsy stairs and leaning posts. A little rot, a little bad weather, and the whole thing might fall off like an overfed leech.

The sun warmed their shoulders as it rose. The colorful silks of ships came and went. The wind died, then freshened, carrying in from the foothills the smell of cypress. She breathed the green perfume in, and thought of her father's pastures, the rolling emerald hills she'd once ruled like a cork lords a sea.

Then the minister spoke again, ruining her reverie. "You know, the assistant to the treasurer of Pelphia was here yesterday. Poor fellow lost half his pension in a game of Oops, but he was chock-full of interesting news. He shared with me the fact that Leonid had been sitting on an empty nest. Apparently, he'd lost the Sphinx's painting, and not even realized it. How embarrassing! But then, sometimes it's easier to rob a bank than steal a park bench."

"I'm sorry, what?"

"Some men are so intent on hiding their fortune, they lose sight of it themselves. That's why the vaults of our banks and museums are all transparent. Our treasures are out in the open; they are as public as a park bench. Which makes every man, woman, and child a lookout and a guard by default. Our copy of the Sphinx's painting is in a glass chamber, inside a window box, sandwiched between two sheets of protective crystal, framed in lucent quartz. It is watched over every hour of every day by a hundred thousand eyes."

"I think you may've needed one or two more," Voleta said from the observational platform. She had spent the entirety of their delay borrowing pennies from Iren so she could look through one of the anchored telescopes. Now, she pulled back from the eyepiece and pointed at the board, and more specifically, at a figure scrambling up the rope of one of the dangling swings.

Edith squinted. "What is that?"

"That is a hod," Voleta said, returning her attention to the eyepiece. "And guess what he has strapped to his back?"

"You've got to be kidding," Edith said.

Voleta began to hop on one foot so she could pull the boot from the other. "I'm afraid not, Captain. The rascal has our painting." She attacked her other heel until she was down to her socks. "But don't worry, I'll get him!" Before Edith could argue, Voleta jumped onto the platform's handrail and leapt out onto the unsuspecting crowd. She landed on a tall man's shoulders with her arms thrown out and her hips whipping in search of balance. Her perch staggered beneath her, cursing with surprise. She hopped onto the next pair of shoulders even as he reached for her ankles. She bounded for the betting board upon the stepping-stones of strangers. They roared with displeasure, and Voleta laughed like a goat.

Chapter Five

Though Oyodin's architectural transparency has ushered in an era of relative peace, the war on smudges is unending. Be advised: While fingerprints are considered innocuous, the imprint of a posterior on the glass wall of a home or business is taken as a slight. Visitors should mind where they lean.

—*Everyman's Guide to the Tower of Babel*, VII. IV

arya laid her pale fingers on the harpsichord's black keys, forming one of her favorite chords: A dominant seventh with a flattened sixth on the thirteenth note. Her hand trembled and dropped into her lap, leaving the chord unstruck.

She shivered. Pelphia had been such a warm place, but the steel ship held the chill of the altitude as efficiently as a springhouse. She'd come without a coat, though Byron had found her one: a green ensign's jacket with gold piping down the arms. She had taken to wearing it as a shrug, but now she moved her arms into its sleeves. The silk lining was as soft as a lamb's ear. She stood and approached the great round mirror that hung between a pair of well-stocked bookshelves. She did the jacket up to hide her cream-colored morning dress. She thought it might make her look more like a crewman. Instead, she looked like an usher in a poorly tailored coat.

A half hour earlier, Olivet had fallen asleep on Ann, effectively pinning her to Marya's bed. Marya had offered to relieve the diminutive governess, but Ann had only smiled contentedly and gestured at the straps that hung from the bolted-down bed frame. Byron had shown them how to do and undo the fasteners when he'd first escorted them to their cabins. He'd explained the straps were there to protect sleeping guests from being bucked out of bed by an unexpected turn. Ann looked as if she might doze off, and since her hands were occupied with the baby, Marya did the straps up for her, managing the buckles as quietly as she could.

When she left, Ann was blinking slowly, languidly, like a friendly cat.

The ship had seemed empty. She had wandered the corridors, peering into the cabins and alcoves. Byron, the stag-headed steward, had secluded himself inside the Communications Closet. Marya had listened at the door and heard the murmur of overlapping voices, tinny and frail but full of bluster. She pictured little men shouting into thimble-sized megaphones. Not that she believed in little men.

Though until recently she hadn't believed in talking stags either.

She'd gone to the instrument out of habit, but the moment she sat down at the harpsichord, the distant echoes of applause rang in her ears. She felt the terrible isolation of the stage and the duke lurking behind the proscenium. Often, he would hold Olivet while she performed, an implicit threat that made her quake whenever she slipped a note or rushed the tempo.

Having lost the desire to play, Marya began to roam the ship again, circling nearer and nearer to forbidden territory. While he had gone out of his way to make her feel welcome, Byron had on several occasions adjured her to stay off the bridge and to steer clear of the pilot. Reddleman was, the stag had confided, an unstable fellow.

"Is he dangerous? Should I be afraid?" Marya had asked.

Byron had rushed to reassure her. "No, no, not at all. You and Olivet are safer here than anywhere in the Tower, I'm quite sure of that. Think of Reddleman as a kitchen cleaver: perfectly harmless and entirely necessary, but not something you want to trifle with."

Though cloistered on the bridge, Reddleman's voice was a near constant presence in their lives. The ship was fitted with plumbing that piped voices from room to room, broadcasting from little trumpets set in ceiling corners. At Ann's suggestion, the pilot had adopted the practice of announcing the ship's maneuvers before they were undertaken. He'd say, "Ahoy, steep climb ahead," and Marya would put Olivet in her gimbaled crib and brace herself against the bulkhead. When Reddleman said,

"Ahoy, preparing to fire cannons," Marya would put her hands over Olivet's ears and squint because she could not also plug her own. No matter what followed his announcements, Reddleman's voice was reliably light and serene. Marya quickly began to associate his tenor with the ship, a humanization that she found comforting. He'd say, "Ahoy," and she'd murmur "Ahoy" right back.

The door to the bridge stood open. She held her breath and listened to the low pulse of the unfathomable machinery. She was not afraid; rather she felt the buzz of nerves that often preceded a performance.

The bridge shone with colorful lights, bright and dense as a flowering azalea. The walls above the banks of beaming jewels were flush with gilded frames that boxed colorless landscapes. Stepping over the threshold, she saw that the pictures moved. A flock of gray birds swept across one canvas, leapt to the next, then reappeared inside a third. One frame showed an unfamiliar port. Thousands of souls poured down a pier. She'd not seen the Tower from this vantage since her honeymoon with the duke. She'd spent most of the voyage locked away in a small berth while her unwanted husband slept in the yacht's stateroom. Her pregnancy had made her loathsome to him, which was no small mercy. To entertain himself, the duke had brought a favorite maid. He spent the week doing his best to render her loathsome as well.

Marya shuddered at the memory.

"Ahoy," Reddleman said from his station. He sat with his dress shirt unbuttoned and the ball of his gut swelling against his undershirt.

"Ahoy." Marya's steps were still timid, though her gaze bolted about the room bravely enough.

"I've been told to tell you that you're not supposed to be here." The familiarity of his voice made her smile.

"Well, consider your duty done then." Standing near the center of the bridge, Marya turned in a circle, taking in the full mural of golden frames, the glassless weapons cabinet, and the captain's chair, which looked more like a throne to her. "Absolutely incredible. These pictures show the world outside, do they not?"

"They do." Reddleman stood, and she noticed he wasn't wearing any shoes or socks. The jacket of his uniform hung on the back of his seat. His flat feet slapped the steel floor as he approached her. His smile seemed almost imbecilic, though perhaps that was only because she was unaccustomed to seeing such an open expression on the face of a grown man. She was a little taller, though she didn't feel it when they stood toe to toe. "They said you would be afraid of me."

"Afraid? You threw my husb... threw the *duke* through a window. If anything, I'm fond of you."

"That's right! That was you. The days sort of run together, don't they?"

"I suppose they do."

"You like to play the piano!" Reddleman snapped his fingers, apparently proud he had remembered.

"I did." The pilot gave her a quizzical look. "Music used to be an escape. I'd play and not think about myself or my day or all the little worries that come in with the moths at night. I hardly even gave a thought to the songs or my hands or the piano or any of it. The music just came and went. My friends would sing, stamp their feet, dance. We'd stay up too late and feel it in the morning and smile through it all."

"That sounds nice." The pink rims of Reddleman's eyes beamed a little brighter. "The most rewarding work is the labor of forgotten hands and mindful fingers."

"Exactly. But then my piano moved from the pub to the opera house and everything changed. I started thinking about my technique, my posture, whether I had the ability to play with any real *affettuoso*. My fans raved over my worst blunders; my critics jeered my best efforts. The thing I had once gone to the piano for—the escape, the community—became my public function. I was the people's piano, a thing to be banged on and knocked out of tune. That's what I think about now when I sit down at the keys."

"You should try something different, then."

"Like what?"

"Well, have you ever considered piloting an airship? It's quite entertaining."

"Have I ever considered stealing onto an airship, stoking the furnace with an old ball gown, and fending off the sleepy crew with a stolen steak knife? Have I dreamed of finding a mountain current that runs like a rail all the way home, dreamed of flying into the sunrise with Olivet in my arms?" Marya muffled an unhappy laugh. "Once or twice."

"Then I'd say you're nearly ready. Have you ever driven a train?"

"No."

"Pedaled a bike?"

"I rode on a girl's handlebars once. We crashed and I broke my wrist."

"Oh. Well, I imagine flying a ship is not unlike playing the piano, then. You have to be nimble and quick and timing is essential because if you make a mistake, you might fall out of the sky."

Marya laughed. "Yes, *just* like playing a piano."

Iren snatched the binoculars out of the hands of a woman with a fur stole draped about her neck. Iren wasn't sure who looked more startled: the lady or the dead fox. The field glasses were silver, rimmed with nacre, and attached by a strap, a fact the amazon only discovered after the lady crashed into her side when Iren raised the binoculars to her eyes. From the corner of her mouth, she offered one of the apologetic phrases Ann had taught her at the dinner table: "Pardon my reach."

Through the lenses, Iren saw the hod. He was a bare-chested young man in a leather breechcloth with a crystal box strapped to his back. Though he looked half-starved, he hauled himself up the line of one of the swings well enough. He smudged the chalk as he climbed and occasionally swung from one line to the next, making the painters on their swings scream in fright.

"Where's he going?" Iren asked.

"I don't know," the minister said. "Our ringdom walls are made of marble block, with hardly a seam between them. It's virtually unclimbable."

"So, either he's a rat climbing a ship's mast, or he's got a plan." Dropping the binoculars and their owner, Iren watched Voleta hopscotch onto another pair of shoulders. She felt a mixture of anxiety, anger, and love, a complex knot of emotions that she expressed to Edith with a theatrical yawn. "You want me to go after her?"

"Do it. I'll get the ship. He may not have come alone."

"I don't know how this could have happened," Minister Truffaut said, hugging his papers to his chest.

Iren made a wedge of her hands and peeled away the crowd with a swing of her arms. Ignoring the indignant complaints that followed, she stepped into the void, drew her hands in again, and repeated the breaststroke.

The betting board had become a flurry of activity. The painters had all been either lowered to the ground or hauled up to the decking above the board, an apparatus that reminded Iren of the fly loft above the Steam

Pipe's stage. Rather than accommodate lights and drapes, the fly loft here bore a complex system of pulleys and counterweights that raised and lowered the swings. The ropes that still dangled were now being climbed by a half dozen men. All appeared to be in pursuit of the fleeing hod. Members of Oyodin's plainclothes constabulary, Iren assumed. None of them were as quick as the hod, who also benefited from a head start.

She swam on through the human mire, setting her eyes on Voleta's retreating figure—her fluttering jacket and outstretched arms. She wasn't sure if Voleta had inherited Reddleman's immunity to swords or his taste for blood and sadistic experiment, but she saw quite clearly that death had not cured the young woman's death wish. Iren feared all she could do was plod along too slowly, come along too late, and gawk from afar.

Though if she had not been staring, she might've missed the instant the mob reached up and dragged Voleta down.

Voleta felt as if her entire consciousness had been put into a pencil sharpener and shaved to a brittle point. Time lost its tempo; the seconds stuttered and lagged. Her heart beat like a clock winding down. She felt serene and unhurried as she surveyed the churning mass for her next steppingstone. The way forward seemed so obvious it all but glowed. Her leaps felt weightless. She was a bee buzzing from one blossom to the next; she was an ember running along the steam plume of a freight train; she was a snowflake tumbling inside an avalanche. She felt as if at any moment she might leap into the air and never come down.

Then strong hands grabbed her legs and she fell. The floor rushed at her, quick as a gasp. She bounced upon the planks, cracked her lips upon her teeth, and tasted a swell of salt.

Hands gripped her wrists, pressed them to her back, and yanked her to her feet. Three men and a woman loomed about her. The woman, who wore a brown riding coat and boots buttoned to her knees, pulled her lapel out, revealing the gold star pinned there. "We're going to have to detain you, miss."

"Why? Aren't we on the same side?"

"You just assaulted at least thirty people."

"And you want me to make it thirty-four?" Voleta said.

The rented deputies laughed at her quip and kept right on laughing until they noticed the steam that rose from her eyes. The woman reached for her breast pocket. Voleta removed her hands from the grip of the man behind her as easily as if she were tearing through wet paper and then hurled herself at the woman.

Voleta had only meant to knock the deputy off balance so she could skirt past her and escape. Instead, when Voleta's shoulder caught the woman in the stomach, the deputy just gave way. The collision carried her from her feet, folded her nearly in half, and threw her into the crowd as if she'd been struck by a charging bull. The effect was so violent, Voleta and the remaining men were momentarily frozen by shock. The man to her left thawed before she did. He raised a lead-plugged cosh over his head and swung at Voleta's ear with all his might.

What should've killed her only turned her head. When she pointed her chin back at him, her attacker looked like he had been surprised by the signal light of an oncoming train. She slapped him across the face. Three teeth sprayed from his mouth as he dropped to the deck. The man on her right attempted to tug a nightstick from his belt but the side handle had snagged on his coat's lining. While he struggled to untangle the weapon, Voleta felt a sudden warm pressure in her back as if someone had poked her. She reached for the spot and her hand found the hilt of a knife pinning her jacket to her kidney. She swung her heel back, catching the man who'd stabbed her. He flew into the air, mad as a jack, and landed near the feet of the last deputy, who'd managed at last to free his stick.

He looked at his fallen associates, appearing to calculate the odds of his faring any better. His computation didn't take long. He slipped his nightstick back into its loop, then turned to join the rest of the crowd that fled from the girl with a knife in her back and red, boiling eyes.

Soon after Voleta fell out of sight, Iren felt a ripple of uncertainty pass through the mob. Then all at once, the wall of backs became a sea of rushing faces as the crowd turned and began to flee. There seemed to be some sort of commotion near the base of the board, though she couldn't tell if Voleta's fall merely coincided with, or was the cause of, the panic. Iren leaned into the stampede, raising an arm to break the flow.

The man who flew up over the heads of the horde appeared to be trying to fly away. His arms flapped as he rose, then flailed when he reached the peak of his trajectory. He dropped back again with all the grace of a shot bird.

When the masses thinned at last, Iren found Voleta standing over two unconscious men and staring at the bloody knife in her hand. A woman lay sprawled not far off.

"Who got stabbed?" Iren asked.

"Don't know," Voleta said, smiling as if to chase away her daze. She dropped the knife into the pocket of her jacket.

A shout from above brought their heads up. One of the swing lines seemed to have snapped with two men still clinging to it. They plummeted thirty, forty feet, landing one on top of the other at the base of the betting board with a great crack of bone and wood. The hod had reached the fly loft and was now running down the length of the rig, cutting the remaining ropes even as the deputies that clung to them attempted to slide down ahead of the plunge. The hod's presence in the loft pushed the painters who'd been trapped there out to the far end and the only egress—an affixed iron ladder that they soon clogged with their panicked descent.

"Looks like the rat's run out of mast. What's he going to do now? Sprout wings or..." Iren looked down to find Voleta gone and, in the spot where she had stood, a pair of hastily peeled-off socks.

Scattered about the base of the board was a great tangle of cord, dramatic explosions of white paint, and broken bodies—some breathing, others not. Voleta grasped one of the last remaining lines even as a deputy leapt clear of it. He looked at her as if she were mad, then ran. Pulling herself onto the rope, she set her bare feet on the board and began to run upward with dreamlike ease.

Dimly, she heard Iren call to her from below, but already she was nearly halfway to the top. The grid of gold leaf seemed to cling to her like a net. She felt perfectly secure, perfectly at ease, so much so that she was not concerned to see the hod's bare head peer down at her over the lip of the loft, or his arm saw back and forth, or her rope begin to fray. His eyes grew rounder, larger, as he seemed to realize she was too quick. She would get to him before he could cut her cord.

And she very nearly did.

The moment the hod's knife finished hacking through Voleta's rope, Iren was beneath her, arms out, ready to catch her, and head turned because she could not bear to watch her fall.

The crowd that had retreated behind her shrieked, then gasped. A ripple of laughter made Iren unsquint her eyes and lift her chin.

Voleta dangled from one hand that clung to the hilt of a dagger driven deep into the slate. She hung some fifteen feet from the crest of the loft. There was no sign of the hod.

Iren began a grim-faced march to the ladder at the edge of the great board. She passed several natives along the way, their bare skin scuffed and speckled with chalk paint. They wore taut, traumatized expressions and did not have to be asked to give her the right of way. At the foot of the ladder, she looked up and groaned. Three painters were still making their way down. One appeared to have been frozen by fear, and the other two were coaxing him on with the heels of their feet.

As Iren gripped the first rung, she wondered what polite expression Ann would recommend for the occasion of climbing over a naked man. *Pardon me. Excuse me. No, no, please don't get up.*

Voleta felt an unfamiliar feeling hanging from one hand, fifty feet over the deck. She felt sheepish. It occurred to her that removing a sense of physical consequence, pain, and fear did not pair overly well with her entrenched recklessness, and that perhaps clarity was not the same thing as accuracy. One could feel clearheaded and still be deceived. It seemed a lesson deserving of further consideration at a later time.

For the moment, she had a hod to catch.

She unsheathed her own knife and added its bite to the one already buried in the board, which still had her blood on it. Once she felt sure it would hold, she rocked the first blade loose, raised it above her head and drove it again. It was not the quickest ascent. And with every hole she drove into the board, the chorus of jeers and boos from the betting floor grew more pronounced. When she at last had a hand on the crest of the board, she turned to face the unhappy crowd and deliver unto them an obscene salute.

The floor of the loft was composed of lumber, but the rest of the structure that supported the numerous pulleys was made of iron piping as thick as her arm. She looked either way down the long, narrow deck. It appeared deserted. Still, a curious, repetitive crunching sound convinced her she was not alone. The sheer amount of tackle and scaffolding made it impossible to see through to the sky. She found a crossbar, gripped a hanging chain, and poked her head through the scaffold to survey the top of the fly loft.

The hod straddled two girders in front of a round hole in the Tower's facade. The hole's rough edge and small size suggested it had been excavated by hand. The repetitive sound Voleta had heard arose from the hod's efforts at making the stolen painting in its crystal cabinet fit through the opening. Already the protective panes were cracked, the frame chipped.

"Hey, don't do that," she said.

The hod's head whipped about, and she saw just how young he was, no older than her, she supposed. His dark eyes were large and bright with fear. Even as she began to climb through to the top of the loft, he swung the glass frame at the stone as if he were christening a ship with a bottle of wine. The frame burst open, throwing out shards that splashed Voleta on the cheek and neck. Surprised more than hurt, she ducked down again into the scaffolding. The now freed stretched canvas clattered down through the rigging. Through the thatch of ropes and stringers, she could see the painting had been caught by the notch of a crossbeam not far from her. It had landed, painted side facing her. The girl in a white dress standing in the water seemed aloof, blissfully unaware of all the trouble she was causing. Voleta reached through the tangle for her. Snaking through a small gap in the cluttered scaffold, she wriggled forward until her fingers brushed its edge and the little girl rocked nearer, then away, nearer, then away, taunting her.

The blade of the knife passed through the back of Voleta's outstretched hand, grating against one of her bones as the tip burst from her palm. She recoiled the hand. The pain was not as distant as it had been before. In fact, if anything, this new wound made the one in her back ache. As she pulled the knife out, the hod reached down through the scaffold and grasped the painting.

Voleta hauled herself back atop the scaffold, the short climb more difficult with one blood-slicked hand. She arrived just in time to see the hod's bare feet disappear into the hole.

"Oh, no you don't!" She traversed the batten, a round pipe no thicker than her wrist, as if it were a balance beam, and lunged for the hole. She saw the soles of his feet vanishing into an abyssal dark. She could not see how far the shaft extended, nor what waited at its end. Pushing her head into the hole, she listened to his shuffling retreat. Elbows scraping the limits of the bore, she began to crawl after him.

A hand grasped her ankle and dragged her from the tunnel, back to the open air. Voleta found herself hanging upside down before a familiar scowl.

"Hello, Iren," Voleta said, hiding her bloody hand in her armpit. The amazon stood panting with feet splayed between ledgers in the scaffold.

"Tell me you weren't about to crawl into a strange hole."

"Well, that's the only way to get to know a hole. Every hole's a stranger until you—"

A low grumble broke from the mouth of the bore—the sound like a snoring dragon, a belching volcano, a farting hellmouth. Voleta and Iren stared at the inky dark as if it might leap out at them.

"On second thought, it does seem a rather rude hole."

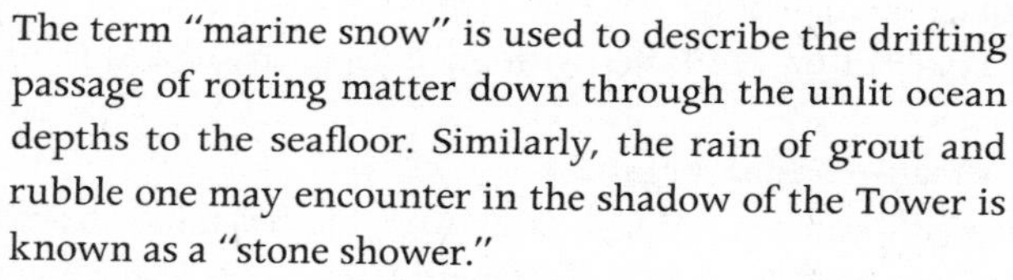

Chapter Six

The term "marine snow" is used to describe the drifting passage of rotting matter down through the unlit ocean depths to the seafloor. Similarly, the rain of grout and rubble one may encounter in the shadow of the Tower is known as a "stone shower."

—*Everyman's Guide to the Tower of Babel*, VI. III

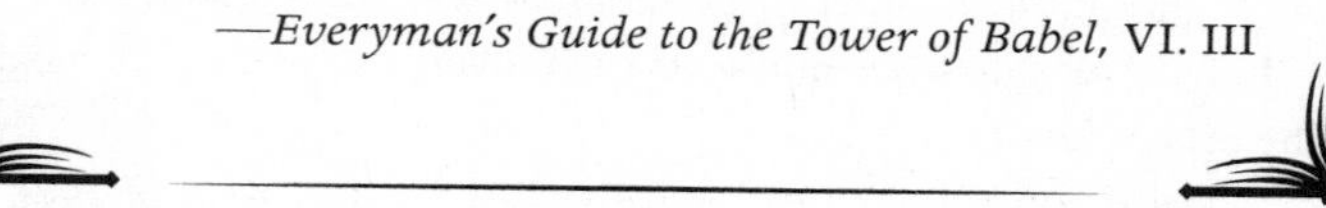

Edith stood on the pier before the *State of Art* with her hands on her hips and her tongue dug in her cheek. She watched her ship roll from side to side as if rocked by invisible waves. The open hatch swung up and down past the pier, passing tantalizingly close before rising ten feet in the air or diving down past the lip. The port's gangway was nowhere to be seen. She could only assume it had fallen into the breach. She considered leaping over the gulf when the hatch passed by, then thought better of it because if she fell to her death, she'd never have the chance to throttle Reddleman.

The ship's gyrations had attracted a crowd. Men and women whooped and laughed at Edith's back. Again, she raised her arms over her head and waved at her ship, hoping to draw her pilot's attention.

The ship ceased its spasms at last. Edith picked up a loose board and laid it over the gap. "Someone's not getting their dinner tonight," she said as she marched across the bridge. Some of the crowd looked brazen enough to try to follow her. So she pulled the plank into the vestibule, cringing at the dirty streak it left on Byron's carpet, and sealed the hatch.

Edith heard the raised voices, including little Olivet's plaintive wail, while she was still mounting the stairs. She was surprised to discover a full bridge. Ann was swaying with Olivet on her shoulder and a trail of white vomit spilled down her back. Byron was engaged in a breathless scolding that prominently featured the words *irresponsible, reckless,* and *ardent nitwit,* phrases that were punctuated with the chopping of one hand into the other. Reddleman was trying to get a word in. Marya had her fingers pressed to her cheek, pulling her eyelids, crowding her lips. It seemed an expression of extreme chagrin.

Edith knocked on the lintel with an iron knuckle, and the room fell silent.

"Reddleman—" Edith began.

"Excuse me, Captain," Marya said, dropping her hands from her face. "This is all my fault. I asked to be taught a few things, and I got carried away. I had no idea how pronounced the movements were. It's hard to tell from the pilot's seat how—"

"You were at the helm?" Edith cut in. "I see. Pilot, we are going to discuss this in detail later. The rest of you, there could be some quick turns ahead. Best strap yourself in."

As Marya, Ann, and Byron fled the bridge, Edith summoned the periscope. A gilded stalactite descended from the ceiling. She pulled the handles down and pressed her face into the mask of the viewer. After a brief survey of the landscape, she spotted Voleta in the rigging at the top of the betting board. Edith observed her confront the hod and saw the spangling crystal spray when he broke the painting's frame.

"Voleta's on top of the betting board. How close can you get to her?" Edith asked.

Reddleman inspected the glittering frames of his magnovisors. "Close enough to tweak her nose, I think."

"Do it," Edith said, lifting the periscope's handles. "I'm going to the hatch to catch her. And if anyone else is sitting in your seat when I get back, I'll stuff you into a cannon and fire you at the sun."

Edith had to admit, as unreliable as Reddleman could be, he was an excellent pilot. He brought the open hatch level with the fly loft, and near enough for her gangplank to bridge the gap. She was surprised to discover Iren had joined Voleta on the rig, and disappointed to see no sign of the hod.

"What's that noise?" Edith asked as she helped Iren aboard. "Sounds like rocks in a meat grinder."

"No idea. Just started a minute ago," Iren said.

Voleta crossed the plank with one arm held out for balance and her other hand buried in her coat pocket. "Sorry, Captain. The hod got away. He crawled into a rat hole."

Unbuckling her pistol belt, Iren shook her head. "That was no rat hole. Whoever dug it knew what they were doing. The hod popped out where no one would see him coming."

Voleta scoffed. "Well, everybody certainly saw him going."

"We startled him. I'm sure he had a subtler retreat in mind," Edith said.

A sound like rain made them turn to look through the open hatch. A sleety mix of grit and pebbles coursed past. Stones bounced through the fly loft, ringing the scaffold like wind chimes. The gravel grew into rocks, big as plums. A cornice piece struck the gangplank. Timber turned to splinters. A cascade of dust followed and something larger still rang the hull hard enough to make them all leap. Iren threw her shoulder against the hatch, sealing off the sandstorm.

Reddleman's voice was as calm as ever as it emerged from the horn that curled from the ceiling of the alcove. "Ahoy! Everyone brace your—"

He did not finish before the avalanche struck the *State of Art*, and the ship rolled like a baking pin.

Edith, Iren, and Voleta flew across the vestibule, landing upon the starboard hull in a mass. Edith's face was pressed to the porthole by the weight of Iren's leg. She glimpsed the betting floor of Port Fortuity beneath them, the long shadow of her ship, and the great torrent of rubble that fell all about. Meteoric boulders opened great holes in the port decking, snuffing out the light of a dozen lives at a stroke. Then the view wheeled on, as did gravity. They tumbled onto the ceiling in a knot of limbs and bowled on, falling onto the hatch. The wheel lock caught Edith on the back of the head. She ignored the shock of pain, focusing instead on keeping her iron arm bent and raised away from the others. She didn't wish to bludgeon her friends. By the time they dropped back to the floor, Edith felt like she'd fallen down a flight of stairs.

She pulled herself up by the lip of the wainscoting, looking over her shoulder to see how her friends had fared. Both seemed dazed, but relatively unharmed. She felt the ship move beneath her but was too disoriented to distinguish the direction of their flight.

"What the devil was that?" Iren asked, drawing herself up onto one knee.

"I don't know. Voleta, check on the baby. Make sure everyone's all right. Iren, you're with me."

Edith's unsteady, hunched-over march down the passageway was impeded by fallen paintings and the ejecta of open cabins that had spilled lamps, bedding, and books into the hall. The stairs were relatively clear, but on the main deck, a chandelier had popped near the bridge hatch. Crystal pendants lay all about like the petals of a blown-out rosebush.

She found her pilot standing in the middle of the bridge stroking his belly as if it were a cat in his lap and staring dreamily at the wall. "I'm sorry for the evasive maneuver, Captain. We were about to be buried. I think we're safely out of range now," he said.

"Range of what?" The toe of Edith's boot caught on the threshold, and she stumbled forward. Her brain seemed to throb behind her eyes. All the lights on the bridge had grown thorns and barbs. She'd taken more of a blow than she'd realized. Still, she straightened and turned her attention to the magnovisor. The portside frames showed the Tower, some two thousand yards removed. Port Fortuity seemed almost serene from that distance. The dozens of ships moored there were moving away in every direction, and all at once. The parting of balloons seemed unhurried, but the simultaneousness of their departure suggested panic.

She recognized the ship that flew toward them. It was the *Divine Empress,* whose captain had plied her with a feast that she'd sent away. The ship listed suddenly to one side, falling toward a long gash that appeared in its envelope. The tear quickly grew into a maw as the outrush of gas tattered the fabric. The cruise ship dropped, rolling as it fell past the bottom of the viewing frame. Edith reached for the pocket of her greatcoat, found the glass flask miraculously intact. The headwaiter's face flashed to mind. She thought of his wife pressing cherries for a husband who would never come home again.

Then the silks of another ship flowered into shreds, and the massacre began in earnest.

Amid the confusion of dust, the smoke of fires, and the bursting bouquet of envelopes, it was difficult to see the cause of the panic or who had fired upon who. Through the confusion, Edith saw a strange shadow on the Tower, a roughly circular spot approximately fifty feet wide set above the turmoil of the casino floor. No, not a shadow: a hole. Two more ships had their silks torn from them, and through the gap that their ruin created, their assassin finally came into view.

The sight of the Hod King scrabbling across the Tower's ancient entablatures seemed as obscene as a tick crawling across a handsome face. Though Edith had seen its bones laid bare in schematic, seen its dimensions enumerated, its cannons cataloged, none of the drawings nor her study of them lessened the shock of seeing the siege engine in the flesh. It was immense, its legs as numerous and coordinated as a centipede. They rose in a wave and drove into the masonry with methodical certainty. The Hod King curled over the port, swinging the gigantic trident that jutted from its bow at the closest islands of wood. That fearsome spear cut through beam and plank as if they were stem and leaf. The western tier of Port Fortuity collapsed in a hastening cascade as one level fell upon the next. Though Edith could not hear them, the screams of the doomed seemed to ring inside her throbbing head.

"Stations," she said to snap them all from their gawking. "Reddleman, make us thin as you can on approach. Bring us within five hundred yards and hold. Iren, cant the port and starboard guns toward the bow. We'll not show it our broadside if we can avoid it."

"Aye, sir." At her gunner's post, Iren pressed her face to the rubber gasket of her scope.

Edith followed Reddleman to his post and leaned upon the control bank as he took his seat before the gold-tipped yoke. "We're going to wag our tail, pilot. When we're in position, angle her to port, wait till Iren gets off a shot, then swing to starboard, quick as you can, for a second volley. Iren, focus fire on its forecastle. Let's see if we can't crack open its skull."

Three more of the scattering airships were struck down by the Hod King's artillery even as the *State of Art* came about and began to plow into the wind.

Cupping her hand about the communication horn that Reddleman regularly used for announcements, Edith spoke to the rest of her crew: "Find something to hold on to. There's going to be a fight. Cannons will fire in ten, nine, eight..."

In the magnovisor frame above her, a flash of light and a black plume of smoke rose from the Hod King's aftercastle. Edith watched the missile arc toward them. The fact that she saw the projectile at all could only mean it was immense.

"The Quibbler," Iren murmured.

"Climb!" Edith shouted, reaching for the yoke even as Reddleman pulled upon it. The ship lurched beneath them, piling weight upon their shoulders. For a split second, the Quibbler's volley seemed to rise to meet them, then fell from view as the shot passed under their hull.

Edith thought of the poor people in the Market who'd catch that grim meteor even as she said, "It must take a moment to load a five-hundred-pound ball. Change of plan, Iren. Target the aftercastle. We have to take out that mortar." Ordering Reddleman to resume the maneuver, Edith moved to her captain's chair. Perched on the edge and leaning forward, she waited till the Hod King swung into the view. The air around the port was now clear of traffic. The excavating engine had begun to move away from the devastated port, crawling westward and upward. "Fire!" Edith barked.

The deck trembled from the force of the salvo. The thirty-two portside cannons and dozen forward guns fired as one. The cannonballs flew in a crowded flock, striking the Hod King's mottled carapace from midpoint to stern. Edith felt a swell of hope as the titanic machine appeared to list to one side and scramble to keep its footing on the sheer cliff of marble. But then the Hod King's back flared with the firing of dozens of mortars, and the barrage swarmed at them.

The clamor of balls upon the hull gouged her ears. The force of the attack pitched the ship to starboard. All the indicators and light bulbs flickered, and the ship fell and bucked up again like a horse trying to throw them. The brief darkness between flares was as deep as death and seemed almost as long. When the flow of current stabilized, Edith realized two of her magnovisor frames had gone white. Those cataracts to her view were unwelcome, but she still had enough eyes left to see the Hod King trundling onward, upward. Their first strike hadn't hobbled it; in fact, their guns hardly seemed to have scratched its iron back. "Track it, pilot. Angle to starboard and fire."

Again, the *State of Art*'s guns bellowed, and the shell of the Hod King seethed with the raised chaff of rust and shrapnel. A scant third of the siege engine's guns returned fire a moment later, confirming what Edith suspected. Marat's gunners could not keep pace with the Sphinx's tin cannoneers. Reddleman yawed to port, and Iren fired another salvo. The Hod King had angled toward a jutting shelf that served as the base for a titanic sculpture. The chimera that rested upon that plinth resembled a leopard with a dozen spotted tails fanned out behind it. The excavator's trident began to churn as it approached the niche beneath the monument.

"They're going to dig. Don't let up, Iren! Give them everything we have."

The engine's drill pressed into the scrollwork that decorated the monument's ledge. Dust billowed out, melding with cannon smoke, and the lingering haze from the burning port. Soon, Edith could only dimly see the aft of the burrowing engine. Iren continued to fire into the murk, her volleys dimpling the fog. The Hod King fired indiscriminately back at them, its wild shots flying wide. A boulder-sized ball sailed over the *State of Art*'s prow, a parting gift from the Quibbler.

"Save the powder. Cease fire," Edith said when she realized the incessant grating rumble that had shivered the air since the Hod King's emergence had receded. The cloud of pulverized stone thinned, pulled clear by the wind. The hole beneath the many-tailed monument came into view. The new pore in the face of the Tower did not go very deep. The excavator left a cave-in in its wake. There would be no pursuit.

The leopard on its ledge seemed to nod its noble head. Then its shelf broke, and the titanic cat tipped forward and tumbled from the Tower.

For a score of souls who scoured the Lost and Found for the pinned notes of misplaced loves, their search came to a violent end that ushered in merciful, untiring, oblivious peace.

From the Belly of the Beast

2

We plow the fields of history with pens and pots of candle black, for the fruits of tomorrow cannot grow until the stubble of the past is tilled under.

—from the sermons of Luc Marat
(translated from hoddish)

~~What are the seeds of bitterness? Here is the acerbic woman who must be understood before she can be understanding; here is the hardened man who must be loved before he can be loving; here is the malingering soul who must be praised before they can praise. We deny that which we wish to be~~

Blood rained in the wheelhouse of the Hod King.

The vertical tilt of the bridge made it seem as if the world had fallen onto its back. What had been the forward hull now was the ceiling. The black needles behind crystal dials gyred like black flies, spinning with growing abandon as the war engine roared toward the limits of its power. Everything creaked and shuddered. Senlin gritted his teeth to keep them from chattering.

Not far above him, the arms of the decapitated navigator swung from either side of his chairback. A steel floor plate had come loose and passed through his neck like the blade of a guillotine, before ricocheting off the barrel of Marat's periscope and lodging in the bulkhead beyond. The hull still tolled from the hail of cannonballs that had knocked the panel free. The volley had arrived in a burst, stinging all at once like an angry swarm. The Hod King's thick shell had not been pierced, but the concerted force of the impact had nearly buckled its knees. The lights had guttered out, and when they had returned, the officer's head was rattling about the aft of the bridge like a die in a cup.

Strapped to his golden throne, Marat wiped the spatter of blood from his face, transforming dark spots into a red mask. "Who's firing on us?"

"An airship, Hodder Luc," the tactician replied.

Marat reached back to grasp the deformed periscope, straining until his muscles surfaced, though he failed to pull it back. The zealot bellowed into the elephant ear of his communication horn, "Fire on her threads!"

Retreating from the eyepiece of her pentascope, the munitions officer answered over her shoulder: "It doesn't have any threads."

"Are you sure?"

"Just steel on sky," she said, her eyes shining with fear.

"Seventy-eight percent traction. We're losing footing. If we fall under fifty percent, we're finished," the engineer said, clenching the sides of his console, as if his grip could shore up the ship's.

The junior navigator, seeming to realize he had been unceremoniously promoted by the death of his superior, shouted, "Insertion point two hundred and twenty feet."

"Full speed!" Marat stamped the heel of his hand on the arm of his throne and barked again into his brass trumpet: "Reload the Quibbler! Fire at will! Fire!"

Near Marat's golden feet, Senlin lay braced upon the guardrail, arms hooked through the spindles, the gauze on his chest blooming afresh with the dead man's blood. Another barrage of cannonballs swatted the hull and shook him like grit through a sifter. The guardrail sawed at him, making his veins and nerves pop against his bones. The engineer shouted "Fifty-six percent traction!" as another plate leapt from the floor and flew past Senlin's ear and over Marat's ducked head.

Senlin felt the onset of terror—a perverse burst of euphoria that muffled his thoughts, dulled the pain, and pushed the present away. He saw Marya's face, not pinched and posed as it had been on the Merry Loop, or vague and idealized as it had been in Ogier's painting, but as it had appeared when her smile had shone down on him from the limb of an apple tree. He smelled the salt of the sea and the sweetness of the clover. He wished more than anything that the world was one year younger and he a hundred years wiser.

Then Marat called him back to the misery. "Tom! I need your eyes! Get up there! Tell me what you see."

While the hull bucked and the gun deck gave its thunderous retort, Senlin stood upon the guardrail and reached for the pillar of the dead man's chair. By the tips of his fingers, he pulled himself onto the cabinet and scrambled around until he straddled the control bank. Senlin did his best not to look at the headless trunk still strapped to the seat before him as he peered into the eyepiece of the pentascope.

The world outside came into view, fragmented as a stained-glass window and churning like a kaleidoscope. He saw the expanse of the Tower's facade and a crowded port teeming with panicked souls. Above them, the sharp snout of a monumental leopard jutted like a bowsprit.

The rest was sky, much of it crowded with the fleeing envelopes of startled ships.

And there, looming before the Hod King's carapace, was the *State of Art*. She looked much as she had in the Sphinx's hangar, except for the notable lack of rigging. The silvery flagship had lost her silks but somehow not her capacity for flight.

In the days before the Hod King finally burrowed from its throne room, Marat's lookouts had reported spotting the Sphinx's cruiser prowling the sky over the Market, apparently without the assistance of envelopes. Rather than believe them, Marat had asked the mouse-eared Mr. Gedge to explain the illusion. Gedge suggested that perhaps the Sphinx had invented transparent silk or had installed propellers that carried the ship along like a sycamore seed.

But Senlin saw at once that the ship was not held aloft by invisible sacks of gas or churning screws. The *State of Art* rode upon a slip of red light that glowed like the vent of a forge.

A moment before, he had been so sure that he alone could stop Marat's colossus, but the Sphinx had put Edith in command of a miracle, an impossibility, a marvel even superior to the Hod King. He felt a burst of pride as he watched the long and lustrous warship swing to port, aim her cannons, and fire all guns at a stroke. Even as the hull about him caterwauled and the lights blinked and he was nearly bucked into the ceiling, Senlin delighted to think how well the Sphinx had chosen her captain.

"What do you see, Tom?" Marat cried.

Pressing his face again to the lens to hide the smile that pulled at the corners of his mouth, Senlin replied, "A wingless bird in flight."

Senlin wondered if anyone had ever been more disappointed to have come so close to death only to survive.

The *State of Art* very nearly knocked the Hod King off its feet. The engineer announced the ship's traction at the fateful fiftieth percentile the same moment the engine's horn staved the Tower, and the iron worm chewed its way to safety.

Through the pentascope, Senlin watched the views turn black as their excavation hooded them. For an instant, Edith's ship was as bright as a bone cameo inside a locket of unblemished turquoise. She was the light at the end of a tunnel.

Then the waste rock of their burrowing eclipsed the sky, and she was gone.

Originally, Marat had planned for the Hod King to surmount the Tower in full view, not only for the terror such a promenade would inspire, but for the time and energy it would conserve. The excavator could burrow for only half an hour before the ship's batteries needed to recharge, a process that required firing the furnace and blowing exhaust for four hours. A public ascent would've allowed them to recharge while they climbed; a dig, meanwhile, would have to be undertaken in stages lest they smother themselves. What might've been a quick jaunt had suddenly become a voyage of many days.

The delay enraged the zealot. While hods from the scullery mopped up his gory wheelhouse, Marat stalked between the anchored tables in the officer's wardroom, his knees hissing steam. "You said it would be impervious to cannons, Gedge. That blasted yacht nearly kicked me off the Tower!"

"The hull is intact. Not a single ball got through," Gedge said, an angry flush rising to his round cheeks. Though retiring in most regards, the unassuming genius was not shy about defending his work. "Typically, there's some variation in the arrival of cannon fire. The force is spread out, diluted by time. The *State of Art* obviously employed some new technology—guns fired by wire or—"

"No more theorizing, Gedge. Face it: A drizzle of lead nearly brought your titan down."

"A raincoat keeps the rain off, Luc. It doesn't mean you can jump in the lake!"

Marat prepared to snap back a reply when one of his feet abruptly slipped out from under him. He stumbled and nearly fell. When he recovered, he bent over to retrieve the cause of the mishap. "And what have I told you about leaving bolts lying around?"

"It must've rolled off the table. But if you'd just wear the leather pads I provided, you wouldn't have this—"

"Why on earth would I wear slippers when I can walk around on treads of gold?"

"It's your choice, of course," Gedge said.

"And where is that blasted towel I asked for?" Marat shouted. Senlin hurried to his adjoining cabin and quickly returned with a towel. Marat snatched it from him and, scrubbing the blood from his face, thundered on: "This was to be my ascension, my heavenward strut! Instead, we have to dig along like a mole because of your lack of foresight!" The zealot's fury seemed to cow the other Wakemen. Cael, Thornton, and Delyth stood with ducked heads and small pouts like children in the company of quarreling parents.

"But how could we prepare for something that should not exist? A ship that flies without silks and fires its cannons at a stroke! Perhaps you should ask Sodiq to account for the buckling. He designed the knee joints, after all, not me!"

"And the floor tiles flying around my wheelhouse like swords? I'm down a navigator and my periscope is ruined!" Marat slapped the soiled towel to Senlin's chest.

"The tiles were Foulke's responsibility. I wanted more rivets. And I will oversee the repairs to your pentascope myself. Rest assured—"

"Rather convenient, isn't it, that neither Foulke nor Sodiq are here to defend their work? I suppose you are the *Ingeniare*"—Marat flourished his hands with ironic grandeur—"when it comes to taking credit. But you're all condottieri when there's blame to be had!"

The flush reached Gedge's thin hairline and began to darken his scalp. His anger was choking him blue. When he spoke, his voice quavered with failing restraint. "We asked for more time. You said no. We followed your orders. This is the result."

Marat came to a halt, his heels clanking like a rifle bolt. "Careful, Gedge."

Recovering a measure of his meekness, Gedge swept the spectacles from his nose and began polishing the lenses with a handkerchief. "This is not a calamity. It is an inconvenience. We can pump in air from the black trail. Yes, it will be stale, but it will do. I can chart the course around the plumbing. If we have to surface again, we'll do it at night. We won't give that flying hammer another chance to strike."

Marat's handsome face slackened, taking on a deathlike drabness. "I want that ship, Gedge. I want it for my fleet."

When Gedge reseated his spectacles on his thimble of a nose, he seemed completely recomposed. "The red light that she floats upon—that can only be the work of the medium. Which means, eventually, she will have to return to the Sphinx's home to refuel, where you shall be waiting to receive her. Have no fear, Hodder Luc: She shall come to you on her hands and knees."

~~The human race will go marching into that conclusive dark, singing our ballads and telling our stories and embellishing our walls with loafing nudes because that is who we really are: creatures who've only begun to believe in the scarce beauty of ourselves, and just in time for the point to be moot.~~

In the days before the Hod King's ignominious debut over Oyodin's crowded doorstep, Senlin had once again felt himself rocked by the mollifying cradle of routine. Though the company he kept was coarse and his labor monotonous, the hours were swift, their assignments unsurprising, and unlike in the crowded, moiling zealot camp he'd lately escaped, here he was once again allowed one of the Tower's rarest luxuries: solitude. Though not as liberating as a blank page nor absorbing as a book, his draining sink, secluded at the rear of the middeck, was an adequate altar for the exaltation of thought. While he could not squeeze his way free through the engine's sealed hatches, he could escape—if only briefly—through the windows in his mind.

Time was divvied into cycles of excavating and recharging. The Hod King's progress was tentative, its course maundering as Marat sought to test his crew and the limits of his craft. Before digging commenced, the pilot would announce the grade of ascent over the communication horn, a garbling plumbing that produced a barely intelligible result, albeit one that rang loudly throughout the ship. If the slope was shallow enough, Marat would have his crew continue their duties, which in Mr. Gedge's case involved whatever lay behind the locked doors inside the Hod King's second heart, and in the case of Delyth, Cael, and Thornton meant the endless shuffling and fanning of cards, an activity to which Thornton added the liberal application of spirits.

As a lad, Senlin had been fascinated by sailors, particularly those who'd spent weeks and months at sea. They seemed to him a different species of person, and indeed, his occasional interactions with the recently returned mariners who skulked the coastal avenues only seemed to confirm their alien nature. There was something different about their broad stance, about how their gaze searched for the horizon, about how they passed him on a boardwalk, their bodies turned flat as a flounder. Sometimes they staggered or swayed while standing still; sometimes they leaned into a breeze as if it were a gale.

Before Senlin had developed the inveterate shyness that would define his adolescence, and indeed the rest of his life, he had taken every opportunity to quiz the merchants and fishers he met. He'd been snapped at by more than one short-tempered seaman who said in one way or another that the ocean was just a prison that rocked from side to side. But gentler old salts had answered that they were only temporarily land-drunk. Their sense of balance was still attuned to the cantering waves and charging winds. The land, to them, felt inactive and strange. It was like being born, they said. Yesterday, they had bounced within the womb of the sea. Today had dropped them on flat, unready feet.

While captaining the *Stone Cloud*, Senlin had felt aligned with the more romantic assessment of what it was like to be underway. But when the angle of the Hod King's ascent required that he and the other lapsed Wakemen strap themselves to the steel-backed chairs in the wardroom, he felt more sympathetic with the grouchy seadogs who had called their vessels jails. When the Hod King juddered and lurched up an uncresting wave, there was little to do but endure it.

He had not seen John Tarrou or Finn Goll since the afternoon Marat had called him up to the wheelhouse. It was quite possible they did not realize that his plot had been spoiled. They might take his sudden absence as evidence that he had been killed or left behind in the zealot camp. Senlin knew he had to find some way of communicating with them. They had a sabotage to plan, after all.

The thought of his friends sleeping in the cramped racks of the berthing compartment and eating rat jerky made Senlin feel a little ashamed. Even the wheelhouse crew were subjected to the same stark accommodations as the steppers, gunners, cooks, and stokers. Meanwhile, his bunk was soft, his showers hot, and his bandages fresh. He was fed cuts of identifiable meat and a variety of vegetables. Dinners with the lapsed Wakemen were raucous affairs, often dominated by Thornton's two loves outside of the bottle: bawdy songs and lascivious innuendos. Cael often laughed himself mute over juvenile puns while Delyth tapped out her own amusing additions with the rapidity of a stenographer.

Though still a recovering prude, Senlin was not unversed in the coarser veins of humor. The cracks bayed by the red-faced patrons of Isaugh's boisterous public house, the Blue Tattoo, were not so different from those he had overheard in his own schoolyard, furtively recited by students to an audience who often failed to grasp the anatomy of these comedic bits, but who were keen to conceal their ignorance with laughter.

Typically, Senlin pretended not to hear such waggery. If a bully at the pub challenged his deafness, Senlin acted as if he were unfamiliar with the pertinent vernacular or euphemism. If the bully insisted on educating him, Senlin fabricated an urgent appointment and fled.

Still, repetition gouges the memory. Between the tavern comics and his schoolyard jesters, Senlin had internalized a veritable trove of lewd anecdotes. He could recite tales of outhouse knotholes, fishing-net pants, and farts in laps with the best of them.

Senlin's jocular efforts seemed to entertain Marat's Wakemen well enough. To be in on the joke was to be in with the crew. They reveled in his ribaldry, and he laughed with relief rather than delight.

After these crass dinners, Marat would invite Senlin to his cabin to listen to him opine on everything from history to science to poetry. Marat still bore the swagger of a captain on a maiden voyage. His vessel was impregnable and unchallenged, and his conquest all but assured. These impromptu salons gave Luc an opportunity to flaunt his education, which was broad enough, though it seemed a stagnant surface. It didn't take long for Senlin to identify Marat as one of those smug intellectuals who talked too much, listened but little, and amended their opinions never.

During one such palaver, while searching for an excuse for reuniting with his coconspirators, Senlin had remarked that he was sorry to have given up his lessons in hoddish. He wondered if it might not be possible, perhaps even prudent, for him to occasionally call upon his former tutor, Hodder Finn.

The question seemed to surprise Marat. "You would rather spend your off hours in the bunkhouse than here?" He waved a graceful hand over the table between them, as if to bless the books, the wine, and the wedge of cheese they were enjoying. "Is my company so tedious?"

Senlin rushed to reassure the zealot. "No, not at all! This is beyond delightful; it's a privilege. I just would like to be able to follow along with your sermons," Senlin said, referring to the homilies the zealot gave twice a day from his wheelhouse throne.

"Hoddish is for hods, Tom," Marat said as he sawed at the rind of cheese with a fork-nosed knife.

The bald-facedness of the admission was a little astonishing. It was difficult for Senlin to reconcile this casual dismissal with the zealot's foamy orations in which he lionized the hods and vilified the great houses of the Tower for claiming superiority over the servant class.

Marat twirled his wrist as if to lasso a thought from the air. "Hoddish is a means of management, a way to cloister the culture. If you wish to control a populace, you must first isolate it. A king *hopes* his subjects won't listen to his enemies; an emperor *ensures* that they won't. If you take away communication, you can install yourself as the only font of truth. Disobedience begins with discourse."

As Senlin made the expected grunts of amazement, agreement, and appreciation, privately he made note of their deepening intimacy. Marat had taken him into his confidence, most likely not out of a superfluity of trust but because the zealot believed Senlin to be without option. Marat's only apparent intellectual rival among his crew was Gedge, and he was alternately too meek and too combative to sit and chat about synecdoche and simile. Marat saw Tom as being just smart enough to appreciate his genius, just eloquent enough to offer fitting praise. Senlin had become the zealot's confidant, booster, and lickspittle.

So be it, Senlin thought.

Marat continued: "We speak the common tongue on the bridge and in here because it is better suited to the nuances of our needs. Formulating a basic vocabulary from whole cloth is simple enough, but once you add in the sciences and the jargon of mathematics and engineering . . . well, it becomes burdensome. You can learn hoddish later, if you like. I can't imagine it'll give you much trouble. Besides, I enjoy our evening talks." Marat's lips took on a petulant pucker as he raised his goblet to them. "Of course, if you'd rather spend time with your former fellows in their bunks . . ."

"Do you really think I long for the company of an old alcoholic who charmed me into self-destruction? Do I miss the swindler who conscripted me into his criminal enterprise? Hardly!" Senlin tapped the book that lay open between them to redirect the zealot's attention. "Now, what were you saying about our friend Jumet's clumsy efforts at iambic heptameter?"

To refresh their memory, Marat again read the suspect lines of verse from the weathered volume. He held the book at arm's length and shut his left eye and recited with the exaggerated timbre of a thespian. It seemed curious that the zealot needed but eschewed spectacles while he did not require but desired the assistance of a wheelchair. Senlin could only suppose the first choice arose out of vanity; the second, a love of deception.

As Marat's pontification on the topic of Tower poets resumed, Senlin's thoughts churned upon the problem of communicating with his friends. He would need to conjure a more furtive communication to keep from exciting the zealot's suspicion.

The solution came to him even as Marat tipped back his glass and failed to refill it, which signaled the conclusion of their dialogue.

"I have a confession that I'm somewhat embarrassed to make," Senlin said.

"Oh? Do tell." Luc smiled. Like all strong men, Marat delighted in the insecurities of others. He took another man's failure as his own accomplishment.

Senlin cleared his throat. "Before we disembarked, I developed something of a fondness for the practice of redacting books. And my cabin, though full of many luxuries, is rather deficient in its supply of strikable materials."

Marat huffed a small laugh. "You know, I developed the habit as a young man. Of course, I didn't black out my books back to front then. No, that was an innovation I developed for the hods to discourage incidental revelations. Anyway, I picked up the habit as a young man. I used to erase the lines of my primers as I read them. I wanted to devour the words, absorb them into myself, and leave nothing behind. If there's no record, there can be no correction. It drove my tutors absolutely mad. I'm sure that was part of the appeal."

Senlin chuckled at the irony. "It was always the bright students who kept me on my toes."

"And the dim students who kept you employed!"

Senlin grinned to hide his disagreement. "I suppose so! And yet, to my own surprise, I've discovered that there's something meditative in the act of redacting a book. Maybe it's just the scratch of the nib or the gleam of the ink—it helps me fall sleep. I don't suppose you have an unwanted volume lying around?"

Marat picked up the book of verse from the table between them, Jumet's *Music for Falling Down Stairs*. "I believe we are agreed: This is not his finest work. All that supernal grandstanding, the moral dithering, and the unsure allusions—it suggests an exhausted imagination and a talent in decline, does it not? Here, take it. May its destruction bring you pleasant dreams!"

Senlin expressed his gratitude as he rose, excused himself, and shut the door upon the malingering zealot.

Alone in the dustless steel vault surrounded by drawers that contained the Brick Layer's democratic key, Senlin examined the small volume in his hand. The red cloth binding had faded to a shade of orange clay. Loose threads bearded its headcap. Most of the gold leaf had been rubbed from its title. Someone had loved this book. Someone had read its hinges weak and its fore edge dark.

He carried it to the wardroom and borrowed a pen and pot of ink from Mr. Gedge. While the Hod King hummed through its charging cycle, Tom perched upon the edge of his bunk. He opened the book, apologized to its author, and attacked it with his nib.

~~A solemn arbitrator counts out the paces while paramours, reporters, and undertakers look on. Clad in white gloves, the two men then turn as if dancing the galop. When the gutshot comes, they both bow at the waist, (one for the last time). Such is the convention of the modern duel. Though~~

Would you mind if I burned this myself?" Senlin asked Marat the following day.

The zealot sat slouched to one side of his captain's chair on the bridge, his head cocked as if attuned to the distant sound of music, this despite the fact that the only noise Senlin could detect was the low and regular woof of the turbines and the murmuring of the crew.

"Why?" Marat said darkly, his mood apparently ill-suited to such an idle request. Or perhaps he only wished to remind Senlin that their evening candors did not entitle him to public favoritism.

Senlin discerned the subtle cocking of ears. The crew wished to eavesdrop upon his answer. "Well, it's just that I've never burned a book before. I've enjoyed them. I've taught them, shelved them, defaced them. But I've never thrown one into the flames."

"How full is your tank, Hodder Tom?" Marat said, referencing the thermometer-like gauge above Senlin's drain that reported his progress toward filling an unseen well with the drips and dribbles of the Sphinx's spies.

"Eighty-nine percent filled."

"Well, I suppose you may spare a few minutes to satisfy your curiosity. Hanif will take you. I don't want you getting lost along the way."

The gargantuan guard scowled like a child who felt unfairly punished.

"Wonderful. Thank you," Senlin said with a bow that he corrected into a nod that ended with a twitch. He felt unsure of how to express deference to a man who posed sporadically as a brother, a captain, a colleague, and a king. The zealot didn't seem to have noticed Senlin's awkward obeisance. Hanif marshaled him to the open hatch like a broom gathering dust to a pan.

"Oh, and, Tom..." Marat swivelled his bare head around so he could fix Senlin with an unblinking gaze. "Don't dally."

Though it had been mere days since he'd left the lower deck, Senlin found the procession through the stepper's galley uncomfortable. While his recent peers still wiped the sludge of sweat and soot from their brow, he paraded past them in a pristine sarong. His chest was wrapped in a white bandage that carried with it the scent of soap. They eyed him as the dogs of a kennel would sneer at a newly adopted mutt.

Just days prior, he'd enjoyed an unexpected kinship with these men and women. They'd rolled their eyes in unison when Lely, the Master of Bells, had criticized their performance. They'd shared a curse when the engine had stumbled. They'd all been bruised by the same unforgiving iron. Once, when Senlin had fallen into an exhausted stupor, one of Marat's burly sentries had attempted to steal the yam he clutched to his chest. But his neighboring rowers had intervened. They snapped and barked at the guard until Tom had roused and reasserted his hold on his sweet potato.

But now as he walked the gauntlet of their wretched stations, the steppers glowered at him with undisguised disgust.

It was strange to discover that the zealot's vision of egalitarianism encompassed such a naked hierarchy. At the top was Luc Marat; under him were his recruited Wakemen, then the Ingeniare, the bridge officers, the cannoneers, the stokers, and the general support crew, which included the cooks, scullers, and custodians; and beneath them all were the steppers—those unenviable treads upon which all else rode.

In the eyes of the steppers, Senlin had leapt from the basement to the penthouse in a single, unlikely bound. He suspected that had his imposing chaperone not been there, he would've been assailed by more than pointed stares.

While they still camped on the floor of the throne room, Goll had once likened his station aboard the Hod King to a closet inside a burning house. Senlin saw now it was an apt characterization. Like the stepper's galley, the walls of the furnace room were a pastiche of scrap and pilfered metal, but here, a thick coat of soot gave the bulkhead a bleak uniformity. All was black except for the orange blaze and the dove-winged pages of the books that flew into it. A half dozen mine carts sat on a track that ran to the tender where fuel was shelved. These carts, heaped with tomes, further crowded the modest space. The roaring oven coughed fresh cinders onto the already woolly skin of the two firemen. The smaller of the pair shoveled books into the flames, while his reedy-limbed compatriot worked the long bar of the bellows.

Though the room was heavily ventilated, the lingering smoke still made Senlin sneeze several times. His whooping brought the head of the shovelman around. He leaned his instrument on the edge of a cart and approached.

When Finn Goll smiled, his teeth shone like a crescent moon. Senlin saw at once it was not a friendly expression, but rather a grimace of anger.

"A clean bandage, a scrubbed face, and a recent shave, I see. Here I was, thinking you had died, and it turns out you'd just gone to heaven!" Finn Goll raked his teeth over his blackened lip and spat upon the floor.

Hanif pushed forward, his hand on the hilt of his cleaver. Senlin managed to coax him back, but only just. "Come, Hodder Finn! I'm sure your heart is too full of revolution to have any room for envy!"

"I have a big heart, Headmaster. There's room for both."

"Ha-ha," Senlin said weakly, feeling suddenly uncertain that Goll's faith in him endured. "I've come to burn a book."

Even as Senlin presented the small, russet-colored volume to the furious Finn Goll, Hanif reached over his shoulder and seized it. Senlin feigned confusion as Marat's enforcer opened the edition and roughly riffled through its pages. He squinted at the margins and shook it by the spine to see what would fall out.

When nothing did, Hanif grunted and tossed the book at Finn Goll.

Senlin disguised his relief with a small laugh, and, hoping to discreetly communicate the importance of the object to Finn, said, "It's dreadful stuff, really—just one long public gutter with a few pennies sprinkled among the turds."

Hanif said, "Enough talk. Burn the book."

Giving them both the practiced scowl of an overworked drudge, Hodder Finn approached the mouth of the furnace that roared gruffly with each pump of the bellow. When he rounded the foremost cart and shouldered his shovel, his elbow grazed the mound of books. The contact was enough to touch off a small avalanche, forcing him to stop and slap the hill back into shape.

The upset averted, Finn waggled the doomed book for Hanif to see before flinging it into the fire.

Swallowing hard, Senlin said, "Thank you for your assistance, Hodder Finn."

Goll showed him his back and the delta of sweat that carved the soot. "Oh, save your pennies for the turds."

There had been a time when Tarrou had called the former lord of port a theatrical ham and a bad liar, suggesting he would be an irredeemable liability in a competitive game of charades. But Finn had proved him wrong on all counts when they all first met the zealot, and their fates had been pinned to Finn's performance. While standing at the lip of a great precipice, Goll had renounced his former enterprise with such compelling ardor that not only was Marat swayed, but Senlin was nearly fooled as well.

Though it hardly should've come as a surprise that Finn was an accomplished liar. One did not build a criminal empire that encompassed a skyport, a theater, and several bordellos without possessing some aptitude for duplicity.

Even so, Senlin had nearly missed Goll's sleight of hand. When Finn contrived to bounce against the cart of books, he had slid Senlin's thin volume of verse into the stack, and extracted another book that bore a passing resemblance, one at least sufficient to fool Hanif during its brief display.

The ruse suggested Finn had understood the importance of the book. Senlin could only hope he'd find the furtive message that Hanif had missed.

When Senlin had directed Goll to look to the gutters, he meant the gutters of the book—its inner margins. It was not the most common of terms, but Finn was sufficiently well read. The clue would strike a chord. Or so Senlin hoped.

He had enacted upon the book of verse an imperfect redaction. When he blacked out the lines of poems and titles, he touched but did not entirely obscure the beginnings and endings of certain lines. Those spared letters, when assembled, communicated a message. It was necessarily clumsy, misspelled, and terse, facets that grated upon his old sensibilities as a headmaster. But this was a time for efficiency, not pedantry.

If Finn and John were able to uncover his system of address, they would find the following message:

pLot fAileD
nU PlAn

finN will sAbOtag furnAcE wile tunNelinG
no cHance of rEPair
sMoke and SMotHer uS Out
I wIll be OUr EYes on briDgE
on My maRk oVR weElhous horN
sIgnl wOrd Is MArya
wE sory lot Of martYrs

The best Senlin could hope for was a surreptitious response, some small sign that they had received his proposal and agreed to it. It seemed a flimsy wish. And if no confirmation came, he would have no choice but to trust that they would act when he seized Marat's trumpet and shouted Marya's name at the end of his life.

~~punishment articulates what the lords and ladies fear the most, namely an uprising. Corruption, genocide, and institutionalized acts of barbarism are~~ s~~eldom chastised, and if they are, it is as a lapse in etiquette. Such crimes against the race are characterized as miscalculations made in good faith by~~

During the steepest ascents, Senlin and Marat's Wakemen were forced to strap themselves into the dinner chairs in the wardroom. Delyth, whose carriage could not be accommodated by any seat, hooked a pair of spidery legs over the anchored table to keep herself from sliding to the aft of the ship.

The slant of the deck made the playing of cards or throwing of dice impossible. Thornton often tried to start a singalong, but Delyth could not join in, Gedge would not join in, and all agreed the tone-deaf Cael should not add his voice to the effort.

They were left with little choice but to converse.

Senlin spent their rumbling climbs trying to learn a little more about Marat's assembled crew. While not all were so forthcoming with their own past, each seemed eager to comment upon the history of their peers. Senlin did note a universal disinterest in discussing the origins of the injuries that had inspired the Sphinx's gifts. It was a choice he could understand. His own wounds, while merely psychological, were nothing he wished to air.

The anvil-handed Cael, whose iron shoulders were as formidable as his woolly head, described his past life in blunt, unembellished terms. Senlin found him a likable fellow, not because he was "simple" (a condescension Tom had always abhorred), but because Cael was self-effacing and good-humored. He bore the interruptions of his peers with a broad smile and laughed at himself even when he'd not been the one to make the joke.

Cael had been assigned by the Sphinx to Norwid, the fiftieth ringdom. Norwid, or the Shipyard, as it was more commonly known, was where the Tower's greatest airships were designed, built, outfitted, launched, repaired, and eventually dismantled. The Shipyard was unique in its structure, with the majority of the ringdom being open to the air. It resembled a pavilion, though the gaps between its vast pillars were large enough to accommodate the passage of ships. The floor of the ringdom was largely consumed by scaffolding, cranes, and ship cradles, with relatively few permanent structures between them. Most of the shipwrights lived in tents or yurts or slept in the orlops of unfinished boats. Many of the designers preferred to lie upon the bare rock when they dreamed of designs for sleek lines and lavish cabins. The shipbuilders of Norwid believed that comfort spoiled genius much as warmth spoiled milk.

It was a rustic existence. Beards and braids were common; baths, less so. The ringdom's only politics came in the form of bidding for contracts. No one cared about one's pedigree, flag, or cause. Formal marriage was uncommon, but long partnerships between mutually obliged souls abounded. It was an environment that Cael had believed himself well suited to.

But it had not taken him long to discover that he embodied the one cardinal sin of shipbuilders: clumsiness. They called him the Mule, not because he was stubborn, but because his hands were as nimble as hooves. He had tried his best to be useful. He towed ships through the yard by himself. He raised beams and plied the blacksmiths' bellows. But every effort was undercut by innocent blunder. He'd drag one ship into another, damaging both. His shoulder would brush a carved detail, turning hours of intricate work into splinters. He'd overpump the bellows and blow out their lungs, resulting in delayed jobs and missed deadlines. Eventually, the Norwidians shunned him entirely, saying the best protection the Sphinx could offer them was protection from his Mule.

Marat had found Cael toting luggage in the port of Dugaray—homeless, friendless, and without prospect. Declaring him the most squandered talent he had ever come across, Marat had adopted Cael on the spot, giving him what he had wanted most: appreciation, community, and purpose.

In addition to the catastrophic physical injuries that had resulted in the Sphinx's intervention, all of Marat's Wakemen shared in common the rejection of their assigned ringdoms. Mr. Gedge had been shunned by the denizens of Asteria, a tribe of solicitors and notaries who, prizing confidentiality, distrusted a man who could hear through walls. The gin-soaked Thornton had proved too coarse a person for the bourgeois of

Simbersae, who preferred to export their proclivities to the burlesque parlors and Crumb chapels of New Babel rather than parade them in the public square and puke them in the alleys. Delyth had been neglected when the Silk Gardens were abandoned, forgotten like an old coat left behind at a party. Marat had given them all what they lacked most: dignity and agency, or at least the illusion of such.

They were devoted strays who would never turn upon their master.

Though it was soon apparent that Mr. Gedge considered himself to be Marat's equal, at least intellectually. The mouse-eared tinkerer lacked Marat's facility and confidence with people, but in the unfeeling realm of engineering, Gedge was the zealot's only peer.

At first, Senlin found it nearly impossible to engage Gedge in a conversation. The ham-fisted Cael and the inveterate drunk Thornton were both eager to include Senlin in their vulgar nattering. Even the inky-eyed lady under glass made sociable overtures, though Delyth seemed to delight in making Senlin squirm. Since he was insensible to the language of her tapping, she would occasionally draw figures on the wall of her glass bell, using her finger as a stylus and her saliva for ink. Her pictograms were always rude and often shocking, but Senlin quickly discerned the point of her game was to scandalize him, and so rather than let her win, he either laughed, rolled his eyes, or paid her bawdy glyphs back in kind, to her great amusement.

But Gedge was so withdrawn he seemed at once aloof and shy. While he thought himself superior to the others, he was also intimidated by them. Perhaps as a result, he did not respond to Senlin's questions, not even when they were trained upon the topic of his crowning achievement, the Hod King, or any of its many parts. Senlin tried complimenting the inventor's ingenuity, but Gedge could not be flattered, either because he did not hold Senlin in sufficient esteem for his opinion to carry any weight or because he was so awkward as to interpret praise as an overture of intimacy, a thing he patently did not want.

Only after many evenings filled with aborted conversation did Senlin at last deduce there was one sort of social bait that Gedge could never refuse: He could not let a statement stand uncorrected if he believed it to be in error.

Senlin made the discovery accidentally. Late one night when they were all being kept awake by the recharging of the batteries and the knock of the pumps pulling foul air in from the black trail, he casually remarked that the Tower, as a whole, seemed an unrivaled mill of human misery.

The comment made no impression upon Thornton, who was frothing drunk, nor Cael, who was attempting yet again to shuffle a deck of cards, an activity that took all of his concentration. Delyth, who was shielded from the grating stink of the new air, had already turned in for the night. And so, Senlin was surprised when Gedge energetically corrected him.

"Our suffering is just a byproduct! More of a lubricant, really. It certainly isn't the Tower's reason for being. It was not built to mill our misery."

Hoping to distinguish himself as someone who understood the Tower's intricacies at least somewhat, Senlin conceded the point. "I suppose it's primarily a giant dynamo."

An hour earlier, when the game of whist had begun to devolve into squabbles and chatter, Gedge had abandoned his hand, plucked from his vest pocket a small pad and attacked it with a pencil, scratching as if it were an itch. Even as he hurried to correct Senlin now, he did not look up from his scrawling when he said, "Not primarily: *secondarily*."

Senlin recognized the response for what it was: the brush-off of an intellectual who believed himself superior. Senlin had experienced a similar scorn for naivete at university, of all places, where many of the aging lecturers grew more astounded and disgusted every year with the unchanged ignorance of each new class. Those teachers seemed to take the fact that their repeated lessons had failed to trickle down into the minds of the unenrolled as an intolerable slight.

"Well, what is it then?" Senlin asked tartly.

Gedge's scribbling paused, if only briefly. "It is a zoo." A finger darted up to rejoin the bridge of his spectacles with the bridge of his nose, and he resumed his jotting.

Senlin did his best to manage his irritation. "Ah, yes! The human menagerie."

Mr. Gedge was compelled at last to stop. He tucked his pencil stub behind his copious ear, and paid Senlin his full and sour attention. "No, a literal zoo. Although, it might be more accurate to call it a farm. A farm would include flora *and* fauna."

"So, you think the Brick Layer built the Tower to be a farm for, what exactly, exotic life?"

"Not just exotic: nonexistent, at least outside of the Tower. Let me ask you, where do you think all these bizarre creatures came from?"

Senlin felt genuinely caught by the question. He had accepted the presence of the curious animals of the Tower to be simply native to it. But of course, the Brick Layer's work was not older than the land it occupied. In the same period of time, the nation of Ur had not summoned up flocks of spider-eaters or groves of ghostly trees.

Senlin shook his head. "I don't know . . . animal husbandry, I suppose?"

Mr. Gedge unsheathed his pencil from his ear so he could gnaw upon its base. It was a quirk that only made him seem more mouselike. "I thought you had some background in the sciences. Do you really think the chimney cat was *bred*? From what? A weasel and a bear? Let me ask you, do you think a heifer gave birth to the bull snail? How would that even work?"

Senlin's composure finally broke. "All right! Where did they come from then? Where did the Brick Layer get them? Tell me, if you're so smart."

Mr. Gedge seemed a little satisfied by Senlin's lapse in decorum. His expression portrayed the superior calm of a victor. "I do not know. But I do know *why* they are here."

"You do?"

"Of course. To make the Sphinx's medium. Have you never heard the Sphinx recite part of his recipe? It's all chimney cat dander, spider-eater bile, elephant eel slime, and on and on. There are more than two hundred ingredients, as the Sphinx will so proudly tell you, and they all come from the Tower's unique livestock and crops. Why?"

"To store energy?"

"The medium stores more than energy. We know from the properties of White Chrom that it is also a hallucinogenic, though I think it's more accurate to say it skews a person's sense of self and time. And it's a preservative as well; it keeps people like Thornton and Delyth alive. I suspect it might be even more. I think it might . . ." He drifted from the conversation as deeper thoughts tightened his expression.

"It might what?" Senlin asked at last.

Gedge seemed annoyed by the interruption of his musing. "Never mind. You won't understand." He buttoned his lip, folded his arms, and told Cael again not to shuffle the cards flat but to pressure them into a curve, to raise them into a bridge.

Try as he might, Senlin could not get Gedge to resume their

conversation, and it wasn't long before the engineer and his compatriots turned in for what little remained of the night.

Senlin was about to retire himself when he heard the shackle-like clank of Marat's heels as they echoed from the vault of zoetrope panels.

"Ah, you're still awake." Marat nodded at the sprawl of playing cards Senlin was presently trying to tamp back into a deck. "I see Cael has been practicing his shuffle."

"He has indeed. I find his determination inspiring. Thornton thinks he's just trying to mark the cards with all his checked corners and torn edges." Senlin struggled to fit the abused cards back into their sleeve.

Marat stopped at the focal of the crescent slab, laid his fists upon his golden hips, and seemed to survey the empty wardroom as if it were crowded with admirers. At first, Senlin thought he was merely a captain taking pride at the sight of his ship. (It was a sensation Senlin frankly missed.) But at a second glance, it seemed as if Marat's eye ran along the noble oxbow table that had lately endured spritzes of tobacco spit and the abuse of Cael's knuckles. The zealot ran his hand along the gleaming edge of the copper tabletop as if he were admiring the plane of a board. "It's good to see you're getting along with the crew."

What began as a chuckle quickly turned into a guffaw born out of exhaustion. "Oh, I think Gedge would disagree with you there."

"I've seen Gedge argue with a slide ruler. He's never wrong. At worst, he's unconventionally correct." Senlin laughed again, and genuinely, thinking of how much he'd once shared in common with Mr. Gedge. His giddiness made Marat smile. "Been trying to keep up with Thornton? I wouldn't advise it. He's thirsty as a desert and just as dead."

Senlin sobered a bit at that and scrubbed his mouth with his hand. "I wish I could blame the bottle. I'm merely intoxicated with fatigue." It was only then that he noticed the books under Marat's arm.

"These are for you," Marat said, presenting the five books in a stack over the barrier of the tabletop. "I couldn't very well have you continue to use my private library as your scratch pad, so I asked the furnace room to send up a few books...for your pleasant dreams. I want you well rested, Tom. We have quite an adventure ahead of us." The zealot smiled, blissfully unaware that the following day would see his bridge sheeted in blood and all his designs nearly spoiled by the guns of the Sphinx's flagship.

Senlin took the books with a sputter of gratitude. "Thank you, Hodder... Captain... Sir."

Marat leaned in, his shapely eyebrows rounding like a pair of rainbows. "Call me Luc when we're alone. We're friends after all. At least we are until we're not. Then it won't matter what you call me." He winked in a way that felt more like a jab.

Once again reminded of his intimate, but quite precarious part in the zealot's play, Senlin conjured a delirious smile and, raising his gift, said, "Thank you, Luc, for the lullaby."

In his bunk, Senlin scoured the volumes for sign of a hidden message. He recognized the desperation of the impulse. Just because the books had been called up from the stoker did not mean they had come from Finn Goll, or if they had, it did not guarantee that he'd prepared some coded communication. Yet, Senlin had grown accustomed to snatching at the chimeras of hope.

A thorough inspection of the pages of each book revealed nothing. The texts were clean, the margins free of scrawl or annotation. The spines and fore edges were similarly clear, bearing not even a remainder mark. He looked for clues in the subjects of the books. There were three dull technical works that shared no apparent theme, a large-type biography with more white space than words, and a flagrant imitation of the *Everyman's Guide* called *All Fellow's Tower Companion*.

He spent an hour jumbling together the words of the titles in search of some cipher but found only nonsensical phrases and tenuous allusions. He then turned to the writers—a diverse group that included a corporate author as well as an anonymous one—wondering if the letters of their names might be rearranged into some intelligible sentiment. He frittered nearly an hour on the effort before concluding such a cryptogram would've been too time-consuming to make and its deciphering all but impossible.

Exhausted and increasingly convinced that there was no code to crack, Senlin lay upon his bunk on his side and stared at the books, stacked smallest to largest, and set as intimately as a spouse's face on an adjoining pillow.

Marya.

He suffered a pang of loneliness so severe it resembled the squeeze of claustrophobia. He could feel the layers of barriers that stood between them: the Tower, the Pelphian court, the black trail, the Hod King...It was an onion of impediments that were separately nearly impervious, and assembled impassible. Strange to think that he himself, lodged in the heart of that hateful bulb, had proved to be the greatest obstacle of all.

The further he traveled from their reunion, the more it seemed an even grander blunder than their separation in the Market. How was it possible for a man to experience so much but learn so little? What could he do now but speak her name one last time into the horn of oblivion and leave the world as credulous as he'd come into it?

His eyes nearly crossed with the summoning of sleep, Senlin's gaze swept down the stacked titles once more.

Mending Silks: Stitches & Glues by Anon.
Actuaries for Merchants & Pirates by The Boskop Insurance Institute
Risqué Bisque! (Memoirs of a Chef) by Malthe Boleslaw
Yallopp's Introduction to Tannery by Sir Piero Yallop
All Fellow's Tower Companion by Kenville, Maminot, Dewey, et al.

Senlin sat up with a start, his heart galloping into his throat.

There it was, Finn Goll's sign. The humbled lord of port had received, deciphered, and agreed to Senlin's plan. The first letters of the titles made that clear, repeating the signal word he had proposed: *Marya*.

Chapter Seven

Anyone who has ever peered into a telescope and spied the unexplored sprawl bottled therein knows that wonder only ceases when examination ends.

—*Everyman's Guide to the Tower of Babel*, VII. XII

Edith hesitated outside of Marya's cabin. She fussed with her collar to buy a little time. She felt much as she had when, at the age of fourteen, she was caught with a stolen sugar loaf by her father. He'd discovered the sweet brick after asking her to empty the pockets of her winter coat on a day too warm to require it. Her preliminary punishment had been to return the contraband, without his intervention or help, to Goretti's General Store. It would be up to Mr. Goretti to decide whether or not to involve the magistrate in the matter. At the time, Edith had argued her father was being unnecessarily cruel. She had not taken the sugar loaf for herself, but to share with her father's horses.

"Do the horses need sugar?" her father had asked.

"No, but they like it," she'd said.

"More importantly, they like you for feeding it to them. And what will you do when the loaf is gone? Steal another or disappoint your friends in the stable? Stolen affection is a bitter investment, Edith. It is a cream that always sours."

Blinking the memory of her father away, Edith at last rapped upon Marya's door. When she received a whispered invitation, Edith cracked the hatch and popped her head in as if she did not mean to stay. "Just wanted to apologize for . . . the rough passage. Are you both all right?"

Marya put a finger to her lips, smiled, then spoke in a sonorous whisper. "We're fine. Well, we both screamed a bit when the room went topsy-turvy. Thank mercy for gimbaled cribs! Olivet had quite a ride. All the excitement wore her out. Look, fast asleep." She tilted the swaddle toward the door to show the captain the infant's expression, one of puckered concentration. It seemed a very earnest nap.

"Good. All right," Edith said in a still quieter voice. She smiled, tight as a garrote, and began to retreat. Marya raised a finger, a small request for patience.

Tucking Olivet into the self-leveling crib, Marya followed the captain out the door, which she narrowed to a crack behind her. In the corridor, Marya asked at a more conversational volume, "I wanted to say again how sorry I am for... commandeering your vessel. I feel perfectly ashamed of myself. I'd like to say it was out of character, but I've been feeling so out of sorts. I'm not entirely sure what my character is anymore. I hope I didn't start all that commotion."

Edith chuckled dryly. "No, you didn't cause any of that. And I'm not at all cross with you. You're not the one I left in charge."

"Please, don't be too hard on your pilot. He seems a decent fellow... or at least, an interesting one. But, I'm curious, what did happen? Who was doing all that shooting?"

"Oh, nothing. No one. We were just playing a little game of cat and mouse."

"Must've been a rather large mouse! Assuming we were the cat, of course." When Edith smiled pleasantly but did not expand upon her answer, Marya's finely drawn brows gathered in concern. "You don't trust me?"

"I don't want to burden you. Some worries leave a stain. No reason to spread the misery around."

"Oh, I see. You're trying to protect me. I hope you're not doing that for Tom's sake. We were always honest with each other, even when the truth was... uncomfortable."

Edith pulled her tricorne from her head. The hair beneath was pressed flat and itching. She attacked it with her fingernails, found the lump on the back of her head, and hissed in pain. "The Hod King came up for air. That's what all the excitement was about. We couldn't bring her down. Honestly, I doubt we even nicked its shell. Now, it's burrowing again. We've lost it. It feels like I let a snake loose in a nursery." She stopped kneading her scalp and looked down at the hat in her iron hand. Her upper lip curled with a flash of grief and frustration. "I should've focused our fire on the edifice, attacked its footing rather than its armor. I should've—"

Marya broke in. "Forgive me, Captain, but I don't think there's any shame in doing your best. Of course, in hindsight, it's easy to see a better course, a wiser choice. When I look back, I see a thousand small missteps that altogether brought me here. I try not to dwell on my mistakes because it doesn't change them; it only changes me. I cannot live inside those awful moments, those naive blunders and prideful errors. It would drive me mad if I did."

"Quite so," Edith said.

"Why didn't you want to tell me any of this?"

"I don't want you to be like me: ruthless, pitiless, bloody-minded. I'm standing here complaining that I failed to slay dozens, perhaps hundreds of hods, many of whom could be, like the rest of us, caught in someone else's plot, innocent but for circumstance. Still. I wish they were all dead."

"We all have a touch of cruelty in us, Captain. If I had your arm, I would've crushed more than my husband's hand."

Since the start of their conversation, Edith's head had felt like a jack-in-the-box. The more they conversed, the faster the crank was turned, the madder the music became, until the coiled-up confession finally sprang from her mouth: "I kissed Tom."

Marya looked down. "I know."

Edith had the startled look of someone who'd just shut her finger in a drawer. "How?"

"Well, he told me, or rather, he told me he had kissed someone. I couldn't imagine it was a stranger—that wouldn't be like him at all—so it had to be someone he knew and trusted. It obviously wasn't Iren or Voleta. Which only seemed to leave you."

Edith had let her gaze rove as they talked because it was easier to suffer her shame while examining the carpet, but now she locked eyes with Marya. "It was a mistake. We were delirious, frightened. Not that that is any excuse. I'm very sorry for what I did."

"*You* don't have anything to apologize for. I can't say it didn't break my heart, but the Tower took everything else; I don't know why I thought it would leave me that."

"There aren't any lingering feelings. There was barely anything between us when it happened. And it's certainly done with now. Whether you want it or not, my apology stands. The Tower isn't responsible for my erring. My failings are my own," Edith said, leaving unspoken that sometimes she felt her failings were all she had.

"Thank you." Marya set her hand on Edith's arm.

"We have to reassess your safety here. I thought that the *State of Art* was invulnerable, but obviously that's not the case. We need to find you and Olivet a safe harbor."

"No, absolutely not. Please, you promised to help me look for Tom. I know no one else will. Besides, where would we go? I don't want to go home with a child and without a husband, and I can't believe there's any place in the Tower where the duke can't find us. Please, don't put us out. I know we're a heavy burden, but I also know that you're very strong."

Edith bowed her head, fearing if she opened her mouth, her whole heart would rush out.

From inside her cabin, Olivet made a mewling sound. Marya thanked Edith again and excused herself to check on her stirring child.

Edith went straight to her quarters, where she discovered her table, chairs, and most of her possessions had all been flung to one end of the cabin by the ship's barrel roll. Incredibly, the rug, which was affixed to the floor, still glistened with tiny shards of glass. Byron had managed to scour away Haste's spilled blood and the black oil of her cracked engine, which had seemed a minor miracle at the time, but the evidence of the shattered cabinets was more stubborn. Even after repeated passages with a broom, a brush, a fine-toothed comb, those grim stars continued to shine forth. If rolling the ship could not shake them loose, she doubted anything would.

Unlocking her bedside table with the key she kept in her vest, Edith removed the wingless thorax of a brass moth, the record of Senlin's last words to her spoken in a moment of abandon when he'd believed Marya had rejected him. It was lingering evidence of her sinful hope, hope that she had not been ruined for love by bloodshed, sacrifice, and duty. She had fancied herself free of her husband, and Tom free of his wife. It had been a greedy, unkind dream.

And yet, she had listened to the recording so often, she could still hear Tom's voice emanate from the inactive recorder in her hand: *I can hardly say how much I love your company, your character, your... But I'll waste no more words. These are sentiments that are better shown than said. I hope to see you soon, and I hope to give you what I could not give her: a man deserving of your affection.*

Edith closed the fingers of her engine about the delicate tube.

She tightened her grip to let the dream go.

Ann had learned long ago to overlook a certain amount of eccentricity. Many of her former employers had had their share of quirks and unusual appetites. The marquis, who liked to sniff ether until he was a mountainous lump sprawled on the divan, was not the strangest of the lot. She'd worked in a manor that regularly hosted mock horse races where the steeds were played by husbands, and the jockeys by wives, though horse and rider were rarely wedded to each other. She had answered to a duchess who had swapped her privy and plumbing for a tray of sand that she kept in the corner. Ann's first position had been at the estate of a reclusive earl, an ancient and still aspiring maker of toys, who had inherited an unwanted orphan from a distant cousin. While Ann raised the child, the earl spent his days creating an array of novelties that all shared in common a single function: self-destruction. He built tin monkeys that climbed to the tops of curtains, then hurled themselves off, and plaster ballerinas that spun like tops and shattered when they fell, and a wax cannoneer who'd stick his head into the bore of a cannon that could be fired to rend him limb from limb.

And on every occasion, in every home, Ann had accepted these curiosities as things that she did not need to understand to tolerate. People were mysterious, and mysteries were generally uninteresting to her. In fact, if someone had asked her just a week prior what she thought of the mythical Sphinx, she would've said, "I suppose I think of him about as often as he thinks of me."

So, it was with natural ease that she accepted the oddities of her present circumstances. The ship's custodian was a stag with one antler, the airship was a silver rail without silks, and the young miss required regular injections of a fiery fluid that was keeping her alive while slowly killing her.

"Now, Mr. Reddleman said we can't reduce the dose, so that leaves us at four, I believe," Ann said, thumping the glass barrel of the syringe with a fingernail. She sat on a plush bench beside a drowsy Voleta in the observatory, which had quickly become Ann's favorite spot on the ship because it was airy, open, and empty in a way that Pelphia never was. The walls were consumed by a mural of intricate detail. Most of the murals she'd ever seen were painted, but this one had been carved into massive panels of dark wood. It featured an enchanting forest scene full of deer, knotty trees, and bird-filled canopies. Ann liked to stroke the noses of the rabbits and squirrels when no one was looking. The room's chandelier was slightly unusual. It had no center but hung like a glass halo over the dance floor, where its shape was mirrored by an inlay of concentric circles set in an intricate whorl. But perhaps the most curious thing about the observatory was the conspicuous lack of a view.

When Voleta did not answer, Ann administered the first injection, humming an old lullaby as she did.

"I'll need five, I think," Voleta said dazedly. Though she sat slumped against the wall with her arm out to receive her injections, her other hand was jammed in her jacket pocket. The young woman now extracted the limb to reveal a hand coated in prune-colored blood. The wound in her palm continued to ooze. Ann gasped. "I sprung a leak," Voleta said.

Ann was quick to recover. "Well. In my experience, children—"

"Not a child."

"No, but *children* hide wounds when they think they've done something wrong. Do you think you've done something wrong?"

Voleta huffed a small laughed. "I scared myself a little." Her head hung over her hand, a posture that looked half-pious, half-tipsy. The gouge glowed faintly like the wick of a freshly snuffed candle. "For a minute, I forgot I could die. No. I didn't care that I could die. It's a strange feeling to be ambivalent about your own existence."

Ann clucked her tongue. "We all forget we're mortal now and then. We have to, to keep from going mad. But I never forget the people I love, and that keeps me from taking myself for granted. I don't want to leave them too soon. I'm sure you don't want to leave us either."

Guiding the needle with a steady hand, Ann administered the injections. When she suggested once more that they stop at the fourth dose, Voleta again presented Ann with the hole in her hand, the blood flow slow as sap. She said it would never close if they stopped at four. If they stopped at four, the medium would all leak out, and they'd have to start again and with a greater dose. When Ann asked how she could possibly know such a thing, Voleta cited Mr. Reddleman, the pilot, who'd said that past infusions would maintain the system, but not repair it. For that, more was required. Ann, feeling she didn't have sufficient experience as a nurse or apothecarist, consented at last.

She administered the fifth injection, cringing as if she were loading a mousetrap.

Voleta's veins began to flush under her skin as the medium circulated through them. The wound shone brighter until it seemed almost aflame. The gash began to close as if sutured by a spark. When the light faded from Voleta's palm, Ann wiped away the coagulated blood with a square of gauze, revealing a scar that was as thin as thread and as white as cotton.

"Incredible," Ann murmured. "That's quite a pretty stitch."

Voleta observed her hand, smiling softly, guilelessly, as one might admire an engagement ring.

Reddleman shuffled into the observatory cradling an enormous open book in both arms. Ann recognized it as one of the ship's manuals he was so fond of reading. He turned in a dazed circle, his gaze passing over the seated women, though he did not appear to see them. He said, "Chiffchaff, chiffchaff, chiffchaff," like a steam engine slowing to a station.

Ann asked, "What's a chiffchaff, Mr. Reddleman?"

He probed the wall with a speculative finger. "A bird. Greenish-brown, small, common, named after its song."

"What are you doing off the bridge, pilot?" the captain asked from the entryway. Ann had not observed her arrival.

"I'm looking for a chiffchaff," he said vaguely, continuing his examination of the mural.

"Hoping for another vivisection?" the captain asked with folded arms.

"No, I thought it might be helpful to have access to a map. Might help us have a better sense of where our adversary will pop up next." He squinted at a bird nestled in the carved scene. "Master Chiffchaff, I presume? No, no, you're just a redstart, aren't you?"

"A map in the observatory? Seems unlikely," Edith said, pausing to scowl at Voleta's bloody hand.

"In the ship's schematic this is labeled as the chart house. Ah, Master Chiffchaff! There you are!" Reddleman pressed upon the raised body of what seemed a rather unremarkable warbler on a crowded bough. The dark wood sank beneath his finger with a click, and the room began to change amid a soft gnashing of gears.

The circles centered upon the floor began to grow like a hoop skirt pulled up from the ground. One circlet drew up the next, the narrowest ring crowning the rest. It took Ann a moment to recognize what was forming before them: It was a model of the Tower. Little scales and plates of silver fell between the wire rings, forming a surprisingly detailed facade that included the jutting of ports and the flourishes of monuments. The skin was not opaque, but perforated like a screen, allowing one to dimly see the whirling machinery inside. As the model rose toward the haloed chandelier, the character of the light changed, beaming more strongly from one side as it softened upon the other. This light, they would come to learn, mirrored the progress of the sun in the sky.

Carried by fascination, Ann left Voleta's side to pace around the model. Even in miniature, the Tower was fully three times her height. She found Port Virtue, Pelphia's most august port, still intact and set at the height of her knee. She had always found Pelphia to be something of an overwhelming metropolis. Despite having spent her entire life there, she would still on occasion become turned around while cutting through its maze of alleys. But suddenly, it seemed small and quaint. She felt a pang of sympathy for Marya, whose husband was lost not in any one ringdom, but among all of them. He was rattling about inside a mountain of mazes.

Something passed by Ann's thigh, snagging lightly on her skirt. She stooped and marveled at what she saw: a miniature of the *State of Art*, no bigger than a child's barrette. It floated along on a wire that jutted from a seam in the model. She brought the detail to the captain's attention. Edith bent to inspect her shrunken ship, then went to the communication horn at the entrance of the chamber and hailed the bridge. "Mister Iren, climb five hundred feet." The order given, Ann felt the weight of their ascent in her stomach and observed as the arm that carried the model ship clicked into a vertical track, turning upward.

"Incredible," Edith said, touching the thorny bow of the tiny *State of Art*. "I think you're right, pilot. This will help our search." She squatted onto her haunches, counted the rings up from the bottom, then pointed at a relatively unassuming port. "It's been built up since, but I believe that's Port Fortuity. Which means the Hod King erupted here, crawled up and over, and submerged again here." She pointed at an embossed plate of silver that resembled a cat with many tails.

Revived by her dose, Voleta came up behind Edith and stood rubbing dried gore from her hands. "But how does knowing where it's been tell us where it's going next?"

"I don't know, but the better we can track it, the more likely we are to see a pattern. Assuming there is one. At this point, I think they're still collecting the paintings. That narrows down the list of possible targets."

Reddleman lifted his nose from the manual. "Or they could just be sowing terror, chaos. They attacked Port Fortuity without provocation."

Edith nodded in a roundabout fashion that was not exactly an agreement. "There's no way to know. Not yet."

"Cuckoo," Reddleman said.

"Pardon?"

"We should look for a common cuckoo. Slender body. Long tail. Looks a bit like a falcon if you squint. I believe it'll unlock a control panel for our map."

Together, they all spent some minutes groping about the wall and pressing upon the birds that protruded from the scrollwork. In the end, it was Ann who found the cuckoo and the switch. It sank into the wall with a satisfying *click*.

A panel opened nearby, exposing a sunken shelf of gilded dials and banks of tumbling numbers, some of which rolled along as quick as the second hand of a clock. Ann glimpsed name plates engraved with letters as fancy and flourished as a royal invitation.

Reddleman approached the station in a state of palpable excitement, propping the fat manual on his forearm. Murmuring to himself, he stroked several of the toggles before voicing a delighted chuckle. "A tele-vibrissa!"

"A what?" Ann said.

"It's like an electric whisker. It catches and records the emission of all the Sphinx's beacons." When it was obvious his answer had not ended the confusion, Reddleman continued, "Many of the Sphinx's instruments emit a signal that can be tracked, at least so long as the transmitter's power isn't depleted and the engine is undamaged. The tele-vibrissa shows the Sphinx where everything is. I thought the only one in existence was in his workshop, but here's a second one. Incredible! Let's see what we can see!" He consulted his manual, identified several switches, and clicked each up with a little flourish of his wrist.

Pin-sized points of light swarmed up from the base of the Tower like embers up a flue. Yellow sparks coursed through the rods and sprockets. It took half a minute for the lights to populate the model, but they seemed to all be moving with purpose and to a predetermined spot. One even began to shine from the top of the miniature *State of Art*. Ann looked closer, and saw the light was carried in the abdomen of a small black insect.

"Mechanical spiders? Incredible. There must be thousands of them," she said.

"Each represents and corresponds to one of the Sphinx's butterflies—his eyes and ears in the Tower." Reddleman toggled through the switches again, and the yellow specks of light blinked out. Ann watched the now unlit spider leave the model ship and crawl back over the arm that held it. A new wave of lights rose from the floor. The second set shone like pale green stars and were far fewer in number. When they settled in place, the pilot said, "These are all the remaining brick nymphs. And these..." He paused to conjure a third wave that was even smaller than the last. These glowed a vibrant shade of crimson. "These are the remaining Wakemen."

Edith perked up at this. "Wait, if we figure out which of these points is Marat, could we use this to track him?"

"I suspect that's precisely the reason Marat allowed his legs to run down. If he continued to use his engine, the Sphinx could find him."

Edith sighed at extinguishment of her hope. Again, a spider had crawled onto the model of their ship. Observing that tiny ruby-bodied arachnid, Edith asked her pilot, "Is that you or me?"

"You, I believe," Reddleman said. "Unlike you and the other Wakemen, I do not have an engine."

"So, the Sphinx is tracking me but not you?" Edith choked on a disparaging laugh. "What a vote of confidence."

"Have no fear! I'm still quite firmly in his orbit. He had to use a different beacon on me, a less permanent one that has to be replaced every few weeks. He called it a guest ingress. Apparently, he used to give them to visitors to make sure no one got lost in his home." Reddleman consulted his manual, then peered at the cursive-scrawled plates. "Here we are." The red nodes all blinked out, and after a moment, a single diamond-white light shone from the bulb of an inky spider perched upon the model of their ship. "There's me. I suppose that makes me the Sphinx's last guest," Reddleman said, patting his belly.

"Reddleman, what did this guest ingress look like when the Sphinx gave it to you? It didn't look like a little black pill that turned into a spider by any chance, did it?" Voleta asked.

"It did, indeed!"

"The Sphinx fed one to Senlin, too."

"Captain," Ann said, pointing into the model. She lifted up a silvery scale, revealing the machinery, dense and tangled as the interior branches of a shrub. Perched upon a buried rod clung a second white-bodied beacon.

Edith gazed at the pin of light, suffering a commiserate prick of hope. "Is that really you, Tom? Still on the trail? I hope not, for your sake."

"Would you like to see how he got there, Captain? The tele-vibrissa has a chronograph that records the place of things. We can turn it back and see where he's been since Pelphia."

"Yes, do that."

Reddleman moved his hand to a new section of the panel where a dial like the tumbler of a safe stood beneath the flipping gold plates of a clock. He turned the dial, and the flipping stopped then began to reverse, the minute and hour plates soon blurred by their speed. Edith observed the white-bustled spider (which seemed to represent Senlin's location) rove about the model, climbing first to the east, then the west, and then suddenly downward. The promising candle popped out from the plate stamped with a nine-tailed leopard and crawled along the Tower's face to the port of Oyodin where it disappeared again into the recesses of the model.

Edith straightened like a bolt.

"Uh-oh," Voleta said. "Does that mean what I think it means?"

But Edith couldn't answer. Her throat had closed up like a stitch.

"What is it?" Ann asked.

Still staring at her frozen captain, Voleta replied, "It means he's gotten himself penned up in Marat's war machine."

In the doorway, Marya gave a small sound of marvelment. She swayed to appease Olivet while gaping up at the immense model that now possessed the observatory. "Who's been penned up? What are you talking about? Why are you looking at me like that, Captain?"

Chapter Eight

A lock tempts a pick. A chain invites a file. But a dung pile courts only beetles and flies. Sometimes the best way to protect your belongings is to shroud them in something foul.

—*Everyman's Guide to the Tower of Babel*, I. III

Byron was surprised to find Edith rooting around in the china cabinet in his galley. The narrow space did not suit her engine, and Bryon winced when her elbow rattled his mixing bowls. He asked what she was doing, and she muttered that she needed a drink and was hunting for a cup because all of the ones in her cabin had been smashed when the ship rolled.

"And that's why you shouldn't keep dishes in your quarters, Captain. That, and we don't want ants."

"How in the world would ants get on an airship?"

"How indeed! I've never been to the moon myself, but I'm quite certain there are ants there. Now. You're not drinking spirits out of a teacup. Excuse me." He reached to the cabinets over the sink, undid the belt that secured the tumblers inside their rack, and presented her with the glass as if it were a rose. "There we are."

Edith tugged the flask from her coat pocket and pulled the cork out with her teeth.

Byron's long ears drooped. "What is that?"

"A dead man's brandy," she said, pouring four fingers of the vaporous stuff into the tumbler. Just a whiff of it made Byron's eyes water.

"Where did you get that? Who gave it to you? Are you sure they were a friend?" he posed the questions in quick succession, resisting the urge to reach out and grasp her wrist.

With the glass tipped to her mouth and the liquor nearly on her lips, Edith paused. "He looked friendly enough."

"So did Georgine," Byron said.

Edith lowered the glass, her expression darkening, then poured the tumbler's contents into the sink.

"What was that?" Iren asked, leaning in from the dining room.

"My faith in humanity." Edith fed the rest of the bottle's contents to the drain. "What is it?"

"We passed Port Nidus last hour. That's the Cistern's port. Aren't they on your list? They have a line of signal flags hung out. They look pretty weathered. I'm still learning the flag alphabet, but I think it spells 'unsafe passage.' That, or 'unsafe massage,' which doesn't sound so bad, really. I have a few knots in my back that could use an unsafe massage. I could give them a meat tenderizer and just let them go to work."

Iren's glibness seemed to chafe Edith's temper. She barked, "Please, Iren! I'm trying to think. I just need a moment to think!" She stamped the empty flask on the counter so sharply it split in half. Iren's scowl made it difficult to say whether she was hurt or perturbed. Byron imagined it was a bit of both.

"Would you excuse us for a minute, Iren?" Byron said in a more diplomatic tone.

Once the amazon had withdrawn, Byron suggested that perhaps a nice cup of tea would be a better pairing to her current temperament than spirits. He put on the kettle and waited for Edith to explain herself, which she eventually did, beginning with the discovery of the tele-vibrissa, and concluding with the revelation that Senlin appeared to be aboard the Hod King.

The tea steeped, Byron poured a cupful and handed it to Edith where she leaned upon the cold steel counter staring down at the toes of her boots. "Does Marya know?" he asked.

"She does."

"And how did she take the news?"

"How did she take the news that I did my best to kill her husband this morning? Well enough, I suppose. She seems to believe that I'll find some way to get him off alive." Edith blew on her tea, and Byron resisted the urge to correct her poor manners. "It's funny, I was just saying to her how willing I was to kill a hundred strangers to bring the Hod King down. I felt a lot more bloodthirsty when I didn't know anyone aboard."

"But he's not *anyone*, is he?"

"No." Edith stared into the steam of her cup as if it were the wool of dreams. "I feel like the whole village is burning, and I don't know which fire to put out first. I never thought I'd say this, but I wish I could speak to the Sphinx. He'd know how to deal with that iron worm, know how to get Tom out of its belly."

"The Sphinx is not omniscient or infallible, Captain. Don't tell him I said so, but when he withdrew from the public sphere all those years ago, it was exhaustion—not stratagem—that drove him indoors. Oh, he said he wished to give society a chance to catch up with his technology, but the truth was he was spent—tired of making concessions, tired of public failures, tired of seeing his efforts undermined, perverted, and destroyed. It wore him down. He chose you, not because you won't agonize over decisions, but because your deliberation won't keep you from action. The Sphinx chose you, not because you won't make mistakes, but because you will own them and overcome them when you do. You are not just his arm anymore. Surely you must realize what you are by now."

"What am I?"

"His understudy," Byron said, and watched as the implication of what he'd said rippled across her face, raising peaks upon her brow and carving valleys around a frown. Quickly, the wave of emotion passed, and her expression turned placid. When she looked at him again, he couldn't quite tell what she was thinking, which seemed appropriate enough.

"I have work to do," she said, setting aside her half-finished cup of tea.

"Aye, sir. One of us has to launder a mountain of diapers and the other has to apologize to a well-meaning mountain. I don't suppose you'd care to swap?"

Edith snorted. "No, and it's not even close."

The ricocheting ring of repeated blows guided Edith to the gun deck. There, Iren swung a sledgehammer against the cascabel of a cannon. The gun had been struck by one of the Hod King's balls, and the impact had jammed the barrel into the bumper at the end of the cannon's recoil track, locking the two together. Iren's effort to separate them had already blunted the cannon's ornate knob; what had been a sharp-nosed wolf now seemed more of a hog.

Iren grunted with each resounding stroke, her neck flushed with swollen veins, her jaw clenched like a steam shovel's bucket. Edith saw her first mate would not relent until either the hammer haft or the cannon gave way.

Lucky for them both, the gun finally broke free of the bumper. When it again slid forward on its track, the warped floor plate behind the cratered bumper popped up. The two women bent to inspect it, and as their heads drew together, Edith could feel the heat radiating from Iren's arm and shoulder. Her sweat spattered upon the floor as she peeled the plate back. Beneath the cover stood a row of delicate hydraulic cylinders, all mangled and sheered like the broken bones of a hand. Iren probed the mess with one finger and cursed between her teeth. "I miss Adam. He was better with the fiddly work. He liked it. Was good at it. It's a bad time to be down a crewman."

"It is. And I regret letting him go." Edith pinched her mouth and shook her head. "I also regret snapping at you, Iren. I'm sorry."

Iren's gaze flickered up briefly, and she shrugged. "Finn was the same way. A short temper usually meant hard choices."

"I don't want to be like Finn Goll."

"You're not. Not in the ways that matter."

"Is that another copy of *The Acorn*?" Edith asked, nodding at the folded newspaper lying on the floor beside a tray of tools.

"It is," Iren said.

"The boy came back?"

"Different kid; same bet."

"You'd think our diet would've frightened them off."

"I don't know. Children like creepy things; they like to be scared a little. Didn't you ever play in the sewers when you were a kid?"

"Not a lot of sewers in the pasturelands. But I did enjoy exploring the odd abandoned manor or collapsing barn, though I didn't think they were haunted by cannibals."

"There were gar sharks and clogworms in the sewers. The fright was part of the fun."

"I think we had very different ideas of what constituted fun. Anyway, what does old Editor Kilgore have to say about us now?" Edith stood and stretched her back.

"I don't know. Ann's been reading it with me, helping out with the big words. So far, we've only gotten through my cosmogram. I'm a Cygnus. I'm supposed to be on the lookout for a tall, handsome stranger whose name starts with G. I knew a Gus once. Smelled like dog piss."

"Mmm. Here, may I see it?" Edith took the paper and was disappointed, but unsurprised, to find another headline about them. She read it aloud for Iren's benefit. "SPHINX DEMANDS SACRIFICE OF SIXTY-FOUR VIRGINS; HIS SILVER FLAGSHIP PROWLS THE TOWER TO COLLECT THE UNSPOILED SPOILS." She refolded the paper and slapped it into Iren's open hand. "Well, that's enough of that."

"What, you're not going to read your cosmogram?"

"We were born in the same month. I'm afraid we'll just have to fight over Gus."

"That's a plague flag," Edith said, pointing to the sparrow-tailed black burgee. The bleak marker punctuated a long line of sun-drained flags that did in fact spell out *unsafe passage*.

"Oh," Iren said, laying a heavy palm on the pommel of her sidearm. "Never mind the massage then." She was wearing her chain again, but over her shoulder like a bandolier, a style that of course Ann had suggested. Edith found Ann's fashionable ministrations a little amusing and very endearing.

Edith surveyed the desolate expanse of Port Nidus. The sun had silvered and curled the neglected wood. Rusty nails protruded from the decking like worms in a rainstorm. Other than the string of flags warning visitors off, the small pier and four berths were unadorned. There were no cranes, no guardhouses, no sledges or crates—just a flock of oil-black starlings prattling on the pollards. An opportunistic hackberry grew from an ancient pile of guano. A green copper gong hung from the dominant bough of the stunted tree. A single strap of leather held it, the other having rotted away.

"We sure about this, Captain?" Voleta asked, her voice tight and quick, her eyes keen and shining from her recent dose. She adjusted the strap on her shoulder that supported a fat clear tube, an airtight case for protecting the canvas, should they be lucky enough to recover it. Byron had told them the case was made of something called diamond cob, which was tougher than steel but half as heavy. "It looks like nobody's home."

Edith turned and looked back into the open hatch of her ship, hovering over the pier. The sun had rolled behind the mountains. Already, the apple-colored sky was beginning to rot. She had wanted to wait until morning. Perhaps they could afford the delay. Tom's beacon had slowed its ascent. The Hod King dallied in the walls. There were three ringdoms between the Cistern and Oyodin, and though Edith knew the paintings from those ringdoms were already safely in the Sphinx's care, the fact might have eluded Marat. His investigation of those ringdoms might take him hours, days, perhaps even weeks to undertake. She had considered continuing to shadow the Hod King, to wait for it to come up for air again. But then what? Squander more black powder and cannonballs on its impenetrable shell? And how many times would Marat have to find her waiting for him before he began to suspect he was being tracked? If he deduced the source of the beacon, her advantage would be lost and Tom along with it.

Edith was tired of being caught flat-footed. She could not let another painting slip away. She had to get out in front of the zealot. Let him catch up for a change.

Looking up to where she knew Reddleman would be watching from the bridge, she raised her engine and waved. The hatch closed, and the ship retreated to a safe distance, gliding upon a shimmering slick of light.

The mallet to ring the gong was missing, so Edith rapped it with an iron knuckle. The noisy splash startled the birds, who leapt to the wind en masse. The flock rolled and stretched and balled again like dough kneaded upon a purpling sky.

The ringdom gate was quite ornate and hinted at a grander history. The alabaster arch had been carved to resemble titanic eels with long snouts and ragged teeth, their bodies twisted together into a monolithic braid. A diadem of conch shells and scallops crowned the lintel. It was beautiful, if tarnished by the presence of an old tarpaulin pinned across the yawning entrance.

A figure parted the shredded canvas. In the waning light, he was at first only a shape, but what a wretched profile it was. He leaned bodily upon the staff of an awkward spear. Its leaf-shaped blade, large as a halberd, was made of some opalescent material Edith did not recognize. His back was severely hunched. Black waders consumed his legs and bunched about a sunken stomach. A scarf, tattered as a cobweb, hid the bottom half of his face, while a formless fisherman's cap obscured his brows. He looked like a shipwreck posing as a man.

"Port's closed! The Cistern is under quarantine. We are riddled with plague. Leave now, or remain with us forever," he said, his voice quavering on the wind.

Iren raised the lapel of her coat and held it over her mouth.

Marching forward, Edith said, "I am Captain Winters, Arm of the Sphinx."

"Our air is unbreathable, our food full of worms. We rot upon the bones of our children, and cry out for the mercy of death. Leave while you still can."

Edith stopped just out of reach of the man's spear. He leaned upon it heavily enough. Still, she couldn't be sure he was incapable of swinging it. "I'm sorry to hear that. Especially since I come with bad news. You're in danger. All of you."

Edith was near enough to see the man's eyes narrow. He seemed only then to notice the silvery hull of a silkless ship floating beyond his port. "What do the dead have to fear?"

"A man is coming to rob you, a very dangerous man driving a deadly engine. Have you heard of Luc Marat or the Hod King?" Edith took his silence as answer. "He wants the Sphinx's marker, the painting of a girl with the paper boat. Are you familiar with it? Do you have it still?"

His hump rolled with the passage of a shrug. "Perhaps."

"If you give it to me, I will do my best to draw the danger away," Edith said, having no idea how she could do such a thing. She watched the beggar's gaze shift, and from the corner of her eye, Edith saw Voleta walk past her, nearer the door, with her chin up. She appeared to be sniffing the air.

"Do you smell that?" Voleta said in an airy voice.

"It is the stink of putrefying flesh, sloughing from the bones of our—"

"No, this is something sweet and rich and—"

"Leave now! Go before the rats awake and begin their evening feast!" the hunchback said, his voice suddenly an octave brighter. He turned on his heel.

"Wait a minute!" Iren shouted, and when the wretch and Edith turned, they found she had leveled the barrel of her pistol at the man. "I worked with porters long enough to know a faker when I see one. That man's not sick. He's perfectly healthy. The question is: Why is he bluffing?"

The sight of the gun seemed to freeze the man. Edith approached him, pinched the bottom of the ratty kerchief that concealed his mouth, and pulled it down. His face was as oval as a locket and just as lovely. His skin was a striking shade of sienna, his eyes a golden hazel. "Seems the plague's been kind to you," she said.

"Did the Sphinx really send you?" A hopeful, almost pleading light possessed his eyes.

"Look at us. Look at our ship. Who else could've sent us?"

"We've been fooled before."

"Who would want to fool you?"

"Chefs, cooks, gluttons, gourmands, culinary journalists." He sneered like a farmer listing common pests.

Appearing to decide the man was no threat, Iren holstered her sidearm. "Well, you don't have to worry about me. I couldn't cook a cup of tea."

"We made pancakes!" Voleta said, surprising everyone with the effusive announcement. She pointed at Iren with an openmouthed smile. "Lumpy, leathery, inedible pancakes. I'd forgotten. They were awful! It was like chewing a shoe. An old shoe with a foot still in it!"

Edith interjected before Voleta could continue. "We've only come for the painting. Nothing more."

He stopped leaning on his staff, and Edith saw he was actually quite tall. What had seemed a hump was in fact a piled-up leathery cape that shook out to hang from his shoulders. He tapped the butt of his spear upon the deck. "Welcome, emissaries of the Sphinx." He swept off his bucket hat, showing a head full of long, dark, lustrous hair. "My name is Tane. I hope you don't mind a little damp."

Chapter Nine

Much as opportunity may turn the placid grasshopper into a locust swarm, panic may convert an idle crowd into a rampaging horde.

—*Everyman's Guide to the Tower of Babel,* I. II

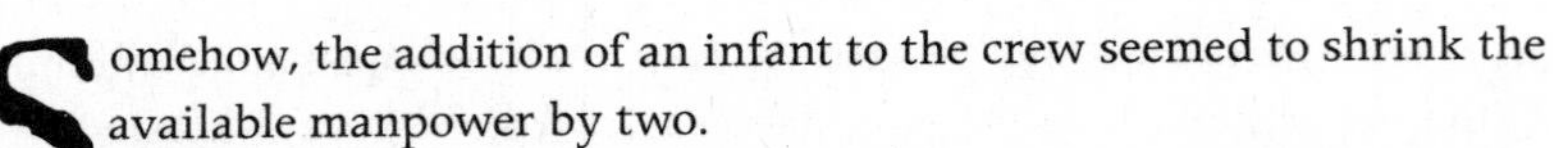

Somehow, the addition of an infant to the crew seemed to shrink the available manpower by two.

How *plus one* could equal *minus two* had been something of a mystery to Byron. Surely only a single soul was required to take care of an infant at any given moment. And yet, everyone seemed to be constantly running back and forth on some essential errand in service of the pink-faced, colicky despot. Or if they were not so engaged, then they were lying sprawled on a divan, driven to unconsciousness by bone-deep exhaustion.

Byron had read that a fawn born in the morning could walk by the evening. Shark pups were birthed swimming, snapping, and eager to feed. But the human race came into the world with all the physical prowess of a custard and all the independence of a pimple.

How one small human could make such an overwhelming volume of chaos was at first baffling. Though Byron realized soon enough that the infant, while occupying the entire attention of one person (and often a second who was needed to take care of the first), was simultaneously creating a mess befitting a small army. A fine silt of talcum powder had settled over nearly everything. The ghostly stains of spit-ups still haunted the rugs, shams, and drapes of each cabin and stateroom. The dishes in the sink seemed to spring up like mushrooms overnight. Laundry, while a priority, was always in a state of utter crisis as it seemed that the infant was determined to leave her mark on every fiber available. And something essential was always missing: the tin of safety pins, a bonnet, a burp cloth, or the tub of rash cream—of which they had precisely one. These necessities were all constantly popping in and out of existence, either snatched away by gremlins or accidentally hidden by the absentminded insomniacs in charge of keeping one wriggling, roaring human spawn from expiring.

Yet, Byron was loath to complain. As onerous as the work was, his role in it was not all-consuming. Marya, on the other hand, was still nursing. She was the one who the tyrant summoned half a dozen times a day and as often in the night. To her credit, she bore the runt's requirements with a drowsy sort of delight. Of course, she had her moments of consternation—she was not impervious to the tedium; her turn at the ship's wheel was evidence of that—but in general she seemed merely relieved to have her daughter to herself. She nursed it, burped it, bounced it, and spoke to it in that secret language shared by mothers and their bantlings.

Ann, who had reared the broods of several families, was the cavalry. She could change a diaper in the time it took Byron to snap open a napkin. Ann seemed as dexterous with one hand bound to the joyless bundle as he was with two free hands. For the most part, he played a supportive role, which meant much galloping about, but very little direct contact with the tiny boarder. As was his preference.

He had managed to get through more than a week without having to change the infant's diaper, a feat that required he busy himself with other unlikable chores and occasionally hide in the Communications Closet.

He knew it was a streak that could not last forever.

His run of good luck came to an end while he was taking the long way from the nursery to the galley to enjoy a moment's respite. Ironically, the gun deck was often the quietest spot on the ship, though he had avoided it for many days because he did not wish to see the gouges in the floor or the damaged cannoneer who stood bent at the waist as if bowing to mark the death of the greatest nuisance and the gentlest soul that had ever lived.

Ferdinand.

Though they had committed his body to a pyre and had packed his shell into the engine room, Byron felt his presence still.

Then he looked up to see Ann charging at him with the infant held out before her like a figurehead.

"Can you change her, please? Marya's asleep at last, poor dear, and I need to go downstairs for a moment."

Byron resisted the urge to back away but did not accept the proffered bundle, which seemed to be staring blearily at some point over his head. He smiled bravely. "Whatever it is, I'll fetch it for you. What do you need?"

"A lavatory, Byron. Now, stick out your hands, please. *Please*. There we are. Support her head. That's it. Very good. Now, remember what we talked about: Wipe front to back, two dashes of powder, and keep a finger under the pin. I believe in you!" Ann said, and left him at a trot.

The moment she was gone, the infant began to cry. It was a feeble sort of sound that couldn't even strike up a compelling echo in the open length of the gun deck. Though what it lacked in volume, it made up for with breathless persistence. He carried the bawling thing to the changing station on the main deck, which was in actuality just a table in the dining room that had been covered in several quilts and stocked with a supply of cloth diapers.

When he laid the swaddled babe down and unwrapped it, the infant began to thrash its legs and arms as if it would run away. He knew for a fact that if it fell on the floor, he would have no choice but to walk down to the main hatch, open it, and see himself out, because that would be the gentlest death he could hope for.

Byron marshaled the imp to the middle of the table and unwrapped its diaper.

"Oh. Oh, no, no, no. It's everywhere. Oh, god. Don't put your hand down there! No, no, no. Don't!" Byron said as he began mopping up the mess with a damp cloth. His efforts made his head shake, and again the infant squinted over his ear. Realizing that it was fascinated by his antler, he began ticking his head back and forth to distract it while he worked. He rehearsed the phrase, "Front to back, dash-dash, finger under the pin," in a singsong voice, which it seemed to like, so he repeated the refrain. By the time he had a new diaper pinned in place, the infant wore a toothless, openmouthed smile.

"Oh, look! It can be happy. You are a jolly little thing, aren't you? Yes, you are. We all like a dry bum. Unless you're a frog. You're not a frog, are you? You do look a *bit* like a frog. Ribbit. Ribb—"

"Her name's Olivet, Byron." Ann stood in the hatchway. She was flush from running, probably whipped along by the worry that he would botch the procedure. As she caught her breath, she said, "She's a baby now, but she's going to get bigger. They always do. And when she does, I will make sure she does not call you an *it*, or a *thing*, or a *frog*, for heaven's sakes. She will call you Uncle Byron. And you will call her Olivet or Little Miss or Niece, if you like."

"Of course," Byron said, suffering a flurry of shame. "She tried to get away. I stopped her."

"It's like that for a long time." Ann took Olivet, and Byron pretended not to notice her subtle inspection of his work. "Then one day, they finally do escape, and you don't feel free. You just feel left behind."

The ringdom's entry shaft was as slick as a sluice, and no more charming. The air felt as heavy as a wet mop. Accustomed as Edith was to the arid winds of the basin and the parched environment of the *State of Art*, it was strange to suddenly find perspiration clinging to her brow and draining down her back. But Voleta had been right: the air was perfumed with something sweet and cool as a limestone spring. And there was some other note she could not quite place, something organic and lush that was not quite grassy, not quite soil-like.

More remarkable was Tane's curious lantern. It resembled a fishbowl with a wire handle. The open glass globe sloshed and swirled with little specks of colorless light that shone bright enough to illuminate the tunnel. When Edith asked what was in the bowl, Tane only replied, "Life."

Byron's vague recollection of the Cistern was that it functioned as a sort of filtration station for the Tower's supply of drinking water. As such, Edith expected to find a space crowded with boiling vats because heating was the only means of decontaminating water that she knew. She expected clamorous pumps and noisome furnaces, but what greeted them at the end of the tunnel was much more pacific.

They stood upon the shore of an otherworldly lagoon. The tranquil expanse of black water was broken here and there by great swathes of light. These radiant bands braided together and fretted apart and curled about the islands of an atoll that was populated by clutches of modest huts. The spine of the Tower rose from the heart of the starry loch where a narrow coast held a handful of larger structures and more of the gray, unglamorous shacks. But what the structures lacked in glory, the water and shore more than made up for. The ground crunched and rolled beneath their boots. When Edith looked down, she found herself standing on an amalgam of crushed mollusk shells and freshwater pearls.

She stooped to pick one up and rolled the gleaming ball between her forefinger and thumb. It had a silvery-blue tint to it like a lake reflecting a summer sky. "Beautiful. Is this why you hide behind plague flags?"

"No, not at all. Our blue pearls are so numerous as to be worthless. Several generations ago, we did export them for profit, but we flooded the market until they were only good for costume jewelry." He bent over the water and gently decanted the contents of his lantern. The splash of living light boiled out from the poured stream, gathered again, then streaked away to join a broader stripe. "That's the real treasure," Tane said, pointing at the glowing stream coursing through the black. "They're schools of tiny crustaceans called egersis krill, though the chefs of the Tower prefer to call them ambrosia because they taste so mild and sweet." He straightened, shaking the last drops of water from the lantern before hanging it on a crook staked into the shell beach. "Our forefathers fished them nearly to extinction. They made quite a bit of money and were famous for a time. They didn't realize the egersis krill were essential to the purification process."

"Those little things clean the water?" Iren asked.

Tane waded a few feet out into the dark where a tied-up gondola swayed on the rippling current. He took the boat by the stern and pulled it nearer to shore. "The oysters do most of the scrubbing, but the krill help keep the plankton in check. When the krill were overfished, the plankton bloomed. The water turned green and uninhabitable. The fish and eels died in droves; the oyster beds began to fail. My father was a boy when that happened. He said the smell was so rank it sank into your bones and never left." He held the long, slender boat broadside to the shore. Voleta ignored his offered hand and leapt onto the bench in the prow, making the boat buck until he gentled it. Iren ignored his hand as well, gripping his shoulder as she stepped unsteadily into the shallow bottom. Her chains rattled as she quickly took a seat and gripped the gunwales until the old wood creaked.

Edith hesitated, recalling her last experience with unfamiliar water in the Silk Gardens. "Is it deep?"

"Fifty or sixty feet, depending on the Tower's tide."

"I'm not exactly buoyant," Edith said, raising her engine.

"I've never in my life tipped a ferry, Captain. I promise, you're perfectly safe."

He had begun to withdraw his hand when Edith grasped it and boarded the gondola. Tane stood in the aft with the oar she'd mistaken for a spear. She realized the curious material that composed the oar's blade was the polished and honed shell of a mollusk. "How big do your oysters get?" she asked as he pushed them from the shore.

"The ones at the bottom are as big as you or I. The oldest of them breathe thick blue water that gathers in pools. It's frigid stuff, but lovely to look at."

He rowed them past several islands of shining pearl and dull shell. None was much larger than the shack they supported. Tane waved to the inhabitants as they passed. When they asked who the strangers were, he quickly assured them that they were friends, emissaries of the Sphinx. The news was apparently welcome and sufficient. After so many chilly receptions, Edith was pleasantly surprised to find the Sphinx was still esteemed in one of the Tower's ringdoms. Though it didn't seem a very populous place.

When she shared the observation with Tane, he said, "You're right. We don't even number three thousand in all, which seems just about right to us. We live off the Cistern's bounty, and we don't want to overtax it again. It took so much to bring these waters back from the brink."

Something cut through the swimming ribbon of light that streamed along near the boat's portside. Iren shouted, pointing at the long, spiny fin that snaked toward the boat. Her alarm rocked the gondola from side to side. Tane bent his knees and pumped his legs to counteract her motion, saying as he did, "It's all right! It's all right! It's just an elephant eel!" He kept the gondola from tipping with surprising grace, and the spasm of fear that had gripped the back of Edith's neck at Iren's sudden flailing softened as quickly as it had come.

The black streak that lurked just beneath the surface sliced left, then right, then arched about and dove away.

Iren's embarrassment quickly filled the stillness it left behind. "It was coming right at us!" she barked over her shoulder.

"I assure you: it was not. Elephant eels eat oysters and fish only, never people. They're completely harmless if you leave them alone."

Iren crossed her arms and said nothing more, but when they reached the shore that gathered about the Tower's spine, she was the first off, high-stepping through the placid surf, her chains bouncing upon her chest. She paced back and forth on the beach, her heels chewing friable shells even as Voleta chased after her, asking her what was wrong and trying not to laugh. "I don't like eels!" Iren blurted at last. "Snakes, eels, anything that's long and slithery, don't like them! What? I'm allowed to not like things. You don't like baths!"

"No one likes baths," Voleta said.

"Madam—" Tane began.

"Mister Iren!"

"Mister Iren, the eels are strictly water-bound. You're out of their element and quite safe."

Iren quit pacing but continued to scowl at Voleta, who puckered her mouth to stifle a smile.

The shoreline was littered with gondolas that were heaped with thick nets and tied up to oars that had been driven into the ground. The sloping beach was thirty or forty feet deep and had been left undeveloped to accommodate the tides. The higher ground that ringed the Tower's backbone was built up like a small town. There was a schoolhouse, a meeting house, a cantina, and a general store that Tane admitted had hardly any stock. There were no roads to speak of and no vehicles at all. The pathways were a dusty white from where the shells had been trampled to grit. The pearls stood out like cobblestones, some large as a fist. Edith could not imagine they were as worthless as their guide claimed, though he tramped over them carelessly enough. The buildings were made of oyster-shell cement, their roofs thatched with dried seaweed that seemed to be the source of the loamy fragrance she had detected before. The faces of the houses were lit by hanging fishbowls full of churning krill. "We change them out every morning, of course," Tane said. Edith found the village charming, though obviously impoverished.

Tane did not attempt to draw out the tour, but even so, they attracted in their passage a growing number of curious islanders. By the time they reached the spine, there were nearly a hundred people straggling along behind them, their eyes round, their whispering pronounced. The Tower's central column looked oddly squat, owing to how low the ceiling was. Most of the ringdom lay beneath the water's surface.

Tane solicited his neighbor's patience before speaking again to Edith and her crew. As he did, he drew their attention to a round plate in the ground that resembled an oversized sewer cover. He stepped on a discreet toe switch, and the plate began to rise, revealing a copper cylinder the size of a coat closet. "Captain, this elevator goes to the observatory, which is where we keep the Sphinx's painting. You just—"

"The observatory is underwater?" Voleta asked.

"It is."

"Will we get wet?" she asked with what seemed a worrying amount of enthusiasm to Edith.

"Only if you wish to. The observatory has a dry dock that's open to the water. But I warn you, it's not a quick dive down. I've done it once or twice myself. How are you at holding your breath?"

"We'll take the elevator," Edith interjected even as Voleta gasped to answer.

"Actually, Captain, I know you're in a hurry, but if you wouldn't mind saying a few words to my friends, I know they would greatly appreciate hearing from the Sphinx's ambassador. One of the necessary side effects of our reclusion is that we don't have a lot of visitors or hear much news from the rest of the Tower. You don't have to make a speech, but could you answer some questions, perhaps? I'm sure Mister Iren and your . . . cabin boy?"

"Close enough," Voleta said.

"I'm sure they can retrieve the painting on their own. The observatory isn't large, and the painting is prominently displayed. They won't have any trouble finding it. You could stay and indulge our curiosity. We could have you all back on your ship before the moon's up. What do you say?"

Edith looked into his honey-colored eyes, searching for some sign of duplicity. The sound of cherry brandy splashing into a drain rang in her ears. She wondered where the line between self-defensive prudence and self-destructive cynicism lay.

She turned to Iren. "You think the two of you can handle it on your own?"

"Long as there aren't any eels."

Tane pressed a nacre-plated button in the face of the elevator, and the cylinder broke open like a clamshell. "Mister Iren, if you find an elephant eel in the observatory, I'll let you feed me to him."

Iren raised her finger to his face. "I'll hold you to that."

Tane suggested that they reconvene at the shoreline where there was more room to gather, and so Edith found herself standing with her back to the lagoon, facing a crowd of several hundred, a number that continued to swell as she spoke. The questions from the denizens of the Cistern were banal enough at first. They wished to know the news of the Tower, to hear who was at war, which regents had died, and the state of several construction projects that had famously stalled or been abandoned. These she answered as she could, but soon, the questions turned to the Sphinx. Why had he abandoned them? Had they displeased him? Why had he not sent aid when they were suffering? Why had he not replaced their Wakeman when she had deserted them? Had he truly returned, and could he protect their port well enough for them to reopen it, and return to some modest, sustainable trade? They couldn't eat eel and seaweed and oysters forever! As the questions piled on, Edith crossed her arms and fell silent.

Tane seemed almost surprised by his neighbors' fervor. He did his best to marshal their inquiries, to impose some order, to remind them of the respect that was owed such an honored guest. But the more he held up his hands and pleaded for civility, the more insistent the crowd became. They did not strike Edith as angry so much as desperate. Their line of questioning was reasonable, but she had no answers. It seemed obviously unfair that they did such a vital service to the Tower without recognition, protection, or the basic luxuries of bread or something other than eel skin to wear.

When Tane turned to her in exasperation and to shout over the crowd, "I'm sorry for this!" she was quick to reply:

"No, I understand. These are legitimate grievances."

"I didn't realize our nerves were quite so raw."

"It's all right. I wish I could give them—give *you* a better answer, but the fact is..." She stopped, cocking her head to one side. The complaints from the crowd seemed to have grown louder, lower, more resonant, but when she looked to them again, she saw there were very few moving mouths. Most of the faces reflected her own expression of bewilderment. Something pecked at her shoulder. Automatically, she brushed it away, just as another stone landed on the back of her hand. She looked up. The ceiling, though close enough, was but dimly visible in the krill's starlight, and yet it seemed to be trembling. The water pocked as if from a passing shower. The streams of crustaceans frayed into an agitated cloud.

Edith shouted with all her might, though it sounded a conversational volume amid the growing roar, "Run, run for your lives!" It was advice she quickly followed herself, dashing down the waterline as the shower of pebbles turned into a cascade of falling rock.

The great whirling horn of the Hod King broke through the crown of the ringdom, exposing the full shriek of its rasping teeth.

Chapter Ten

A half-hearted apology is as good as a half-struck match.
—*Everyman's Guide to the Tower of Babel,* III. I

The elevator ride down to the observatory was uncomfortably close but mercifully short. The doors opened with a gasp upon a hallway like something from a hotel. The change in environment was jarring. The floor was carpeted, the walls decorated with rows of ebony picture frames. The first encased a watercolor of a woman in a short dress sipping sunshine from a wine glass. She sat bare-kneed in the cradle of a crescent moon under a boldly drawn herald that said AMBROSIA KRILL. It was an advertisement. And yet, as Voleta stared into it, she felt the pressure of memory rising within her, the vision of the same model, but living, and not sitting on the moon, but on an unglamorous couch in a smoky studio. Her neck was thicker, her legs not so lithe, and the glass she held wasn't full of light, but liquor, which the painter filled and refilled, adjuring her to *drink up, drink up!* The artist wore a rainbow-blotched smock and his hair in a knot. They would celebrate the commission in the loft, he said. But no, she said, that's not part of the bargain, as he tipped the bottle too much and the spirits overflowed onto her hand and ran down her—

Iren shook Voleta's shoulder, and the memory plunged away from her again.

"What are you doing?" Iren asked.

"Sorry," Voleta murmured, smiling when her friend frowned.

There were other pictures like the first, though Voleta was careful to only glance at them. All were of smoky-eyed, slinky beauties sipping brilliance from a dish, or a slipper, or the hands of an angel. The framed bills were illuminated by warm electric bulbs that held their subjects like spotlights. But the passage of time had frilled the edges of the posters and robbed the dye of its brilliance. The air was thick and stale. The musty smell reminded Voleta of her mother's hope chest where she kept her wedding dress, their baby clothes, and other things too precious to throw away and too painful to leave in view. She had to stop herself from sinking too far into that memory.

Fortunately for her, what lay in the chamber beyond eclipsed the sad history of the hall. They found themselves staring at the bottom of an alien sea.

The depths were lit by serpentine bands of glowing krill. They swooped down from the surface, swept over the jagged hills of shells, through emerald forests of kelp, shepherded by schools of small eels that nipped at the stragglers and tightened the ribbons of light. Larger, slow-moving eels glided over the ponds of shining blue that gathered in the valleys between bubbling oyster beds.

The aquatic scene was trapped behind a great curvature of glass. The immense window stretched between two walls and arched overhead. The observatory was as large as a lady's parlor, its furnishing not dissimilar, though rather than facing a fireplace and mantel, the high-backed upholstered chairs, divans, and settees were turned toward the window that bulged into the water. It was a split-level room, with raised narrow galleries on either side that were railed off, but accessible by a short run of stairs. The floor was tiled in the oily greens, blues, and violets of mother of pearl. Centered in the room, where one might expect to find a rug, was a static pool of open water.

It was a moment before Voleta could stop gawking at the underwater circus long enough to locate the Sphinx's painting. It hung on the wall in the gallery on the right, tucked between a painting of a balloon race and another depicting a ballroom full of dancers.

"There she is," Voleta said, slipping the strap of the diamond tube from her shoulder.

Iren eyed the portal in the floor unhappily. She seemed to expect an eel to jump out at any moment. "Get it. I'm ready to go."

As Voleta mounted the stairs, she said over her shoulder, "You know, I wish you liked me again. Sometimes you seem sorry that you woke me up."

Iren snorted. "You think I'm sorry you're alive?"

"You think I'm a stranger," Voleta said, taking the frame from the wall.

"No, I don't. You're still Voleta. You're just... I don't know... *more so.*"

"I don't feel any more so. I just feel forgetful. I lose my place, I fall out of the moment, and everything gets blotted out by shadows, voices, memories, not all of which are mine." She set the painting facedown on the carpet and began prizing out the staples that held the canvas to the stretcher with the tip of her knife.

"I'm not sorry you survived. I'm sorry you died. I was almost—" Iren's voice seemed to snag in her throat. Voleta watched her through the balusters, though Iren continued to stare into the mirror of unmoving water. "I was almost in time. *But*... I got duped. The Amazon of New Babel, the Chain Maiden, Goll's Hammer—locked in a coat closet. That's why you died. I wasn't clever enough."

Voleta stopped plucking staples, stood, and leaned over the railing, knife dangling from her hand. "Iren, come on. Look at me. You're far cleverer than I am. You see right through people. You saw right through Francis. I've never met a better judge of character in my life. Nor a more kind and faithful friend." She looked down at the blade she had pulled from her back not long ago. "I got a taste of my own medicine recently. Didn't like it. I scared myself—the way I charged after that hod. I knew what I was doing, and I couldn't stop. I would've wriggled into that hole and been chewed up by that beastly machine if you hadn't caught me. Again. As you always do. Make no mistake: I died because the prince killed me. I survived because you saved me."

Iren stood with her arms hanging at her sides. "You're not sorry I did, are you?"

"Not at all! I'm glad to be alive. I just have to stop thinking with my feet. And this time I mean it. I'm not going to listen to my toes anymore!"

Iren laughed. "Your toes are idiots."

"Oh, I love you, too, Chain Maiden."

"Don't."

"I'm sorry, I'm sorry. *Mister* Chain Maiden."

The Hod King's colossal trident carved into the reservoir, whipping the water into froth. The blunt, roach-like head of the engine followed, as its foremost legs emerged from the borehole, spikes crunching deep into the beach. Edith expected the rest of the engine to follow, but with only eight of its many legs piercing the shore, its advance stalled. The whirring drill slowed and fell still. The excavator looked like some great beast come to the watering hole to drink.

Out of the base of the engine's head, a wide panel opened like a mouth, setting its lip upon the shore. A curious trio descended the gangplank. The first was a statuesque masculine figure, bright as quicksilver, naked but sexless. Staked upon that perfect neck was an old man's head. The second in line was a squat hulk of a man with shoulders like potbelly stoves, and iron arms that all but dragged upon the ground. The last of the three was a wrapped-up woman—or rather half of one—caught under a bell jar. She rode upon a carriage of spidery legs. Edith recognized their ilk at once: They were Wakemen. Apparently, Georgine was not the only one to be lured away by Marat's promises.

The spider-legged woman marched straight ahead into the surf, her pick-like feet ticking over the uneven ground with fluid grace. The water rose up the sides of her jar until all that could be seen was a sliver of her dome. It stirred a little eddy as it vanished into the black.

Edith had been caught up in the fleeing crowd, which she now swam against, her eye set on the two Wakemen standing guard at the hatchway. They seemed rather nonchalant for an invading party. The silver-plated statue drank from a stone jug raised on the crook of his elbow. His gorilla-armed compatriot squatted to inspect the pearls that littered the beach. As soon as she was free of the throng, Edith drew her sidearm and fired at the tall Wakeman's head.

The jug at his lips exploded, drenching his face with drink. He staggered backward, blinded by the stinging spirits. He rubbed the backs of his hands on his red swollen eyes, cursing loudly, even as his calf caught on the ship's gangplank, and he toppled onto it with a tremendous clang.

The crouched brute looked up with a start and saw her running at him with her pistol breached open and a new cartridge clenched between her teeth. He sprang forward with surprising speed and barreled at her with his hands stretched out in front of his face like a man deflecting spiderwebs in the woods. Each of his palms was as broad as a skillet. Edith loaded the second shot and closed the pistol with a flick of her wrist. Still charging, and with only a few strides left between them, she tilted the barrel downward and fired at his legs.

The shot grazed the outside of his thigh. He reached for the wound with one hand even as he swung for her head with the other. Edith threw her shoulders back, falling into a slide. She skated past on her knees beneath the swinging boom of his arm.

The miss threw him off balance and she saw him crash to the beach. His shoulder plowed through shells, raising a white dust that powdered his face and thicket of dark hair.

Seeing that the statuesque Wakeman was still lying on his back on the ramp, Edith put her iron hand down and pushed herself back to her feet before her slide had ended. If she could get behind them and board the Hod King, perhaps she could take the crew by surprise. She knew she had at least one ally aboard. She and Tom would fight their way, shoulder to shoulder, from the stem to stern and back again.

She reached the silver-limbed drunk just as he was sitting up and blinking through thick tears. She boxed at his head with her engine. His chapped mouth rounded with surprise as his vision seemed to return at last. His arm flashed up, sweeping her blow aside. Flipping her sidearm, she grasped it by the thick barrel and swung the brass ball of the pommel at his temple. He caught the pistol with his other hand, twisted it from her grip, and dashed it on the gangway, snapping it at the hinge.

His speed was disorienting, especially given the rank vapor of his breath and the far-off look in his cloudy eyes. Spit dribbled from one corner of his mouth down a poorly shaved chin. From his gray jowls up, he looked like a man who was about to be thrown out of the last bar in town. But from his neck down, he was a swift and graceful god.

"Wouldn't you be a pretty thing," he said, the words clumsy and mangled.

She knocked her head upon his nose in answer. He hissed like a cat and swatted her off of him, hurtling her from the gangway. Shells bit into the heel of her hand as she caught herself awkwardly. Rising to her feet as fast as she could, she registered the *crunch-crunch-crunch* of approaching boots and turned her head just in time to see the gorilla-armed brute lower the cauldron of one shoulder at her. He rammed her engine, rattling every bone in her body. She tumbled from her feet, landed flat on her back, and rolled, finally coming to a stop with her cheek raked by the jagged shore. She couldn't quite make her eyes settle on anything. Her gaze kept drifting to the side, falling among the pearls lapped by dark water.

Blood streamed from the nose of the silver-bodied Wakeman. "She broke my nose, Cael. You believe that?" The two were standing side by side now.

"What are you going to do, Thornton?" Cael asked.

He spat a crimson gobbet. "Well, if it's broken bones she wants to trade, that's a tit I can tat."

Iren's breath fogged the glass of the observatory bubble. She wiped the glaze away with her cuff and set her cheek to the window once more. She was trying to get a look at the wall behind them. It rose up sharply toward the beach above, a cliff face of compacted shells and barnacles, flocked here and there with seaweed. She thought she had seen something glistening and spindly crawling down the oyster butte, but she hadn't gotten a proper glimpse before it had descended out of view.

The Sphinx's painting, now free of its wooden frame, hung over the railing as if it were laundry drying on a line. Voleta wrenched at one end of the crystal case, grunting from the effort. Iren glanced at her, saw that her eyes were bright and steaming. "What are you doing?" she asked.

"I can't get it open!"

"Did you try the other end?"

Voleta turned it around and unscrewed the crystal cap with ease. She guffawed in her old silly way. It was a sound Iren had not heard in a while, a sound she'd not known she missed. She pressed a smiling cheek to the cold glass again.

"What are you looking at?" Voleta asked.

An irksome tapping, like a ringed finger clicking upon a glass, reverberated through the observation deck. It seemed to traverse the ceiling, moving toward the window. Quietly, Iren unhooked her chain and lifted it from her shoulder. When she saw the underside of a spidery shape appear on the glass arch above her, she thought perhaps she was looking at some sort of monstrous black crab. Then the thing lost its footing, as the points of its legs first slipped, then flailed down the sloped pane. When the thing tumbled past Iren, she saw a woman dressed in rags was riding on its back. She appeared to be trapped under a crystal cover. Then she and the long-legged crab she rode upon dropped from view.

Voleta stood with her mouth agape, frozen in the act of rolling up the painting.

"I'm about ready to go," Iren said, shifting the hook of her chain to one hand and its eyelet to the other.

Her trance snapped, Voleta scrolled the canvas with greater haste. She slid the painting in the tube and was just screwing the cap on when a bubble broke the surface of the water at the chamber's heart. Rather than burst, the bubble grew larger. The spiked points of eight legs gripped the brass lip of the dock, lifting the jarred woman into view. Thready black hair floated about her wrapped shoulders as if lifted by a draft. Water rained from her undercarriage, and Iren realized the mummified woman was not riding the arachnid: She was a chimera of a corpse and clockwork spider.

The chimera turned, surveying them and the room. Her eyes, black as ink spots, lighted upon the gap in the artwork on the wall, and then on Voleta, and the crystal cylinder she clutched to her chest.

A thickly framed settee stood between Iren and the chimera. Iren put her boot to the front of the couch and kicked with all her might. The settee slid across the floor directly at the intruder, who seemed to raise her foremost legs in surrender. Then the wretch caught the sofa with her spearlike toes, stopping it dead. Between the gauze strips wrapped over her mouth a set of milk teeth emerged. The fiend smiled. She swept the couch aside, sending it crashing into a pair of club chairs.

Iren hurled her hook at the chimera's face, determined to shatter her fragile shell. But the heavy claw of her chain thumped upon the crystal bell like a bird striking a window and fell to the ground. The wretch charged at her with horrible speed. Iren dropped her chain and reached for her sidearm as she backed toward the observational lens. The chilly glass touched her back the same moment the chimera reached her with front legs cocked back like scythes.

The first strike was as quick as the flick of a scorpion's tail. The spear point of the leg pierced Iren's shoulder and retracted before she could level her weapon. As soon as the first leg recoiled, the other one bit, pocking her collarbone. Iren's hand spasmed from the pain, and she dropped her sidearm. She hammered her fist upon the exposed joint of one leg, even as the fiend's other limb pecked at her ribs. It felt as if she were being tickled with a pickaxe. Iren pinned the leg to her side with her elbow, an effort that brought her face nearer to the crystalline case.

The wretch put her hand to the glass, a bizarrely tender gesture that

Iren answered by ramming her forehead against it, once, twice, and again until she left a ruddy flower on the jar.

Leaning nearer, the half-bodied terror opened her mouth. A swollen, purple tongue pushed past her infantile teeth. She licked the glass over the bloom of Iren's blood.

Chapter Eleven

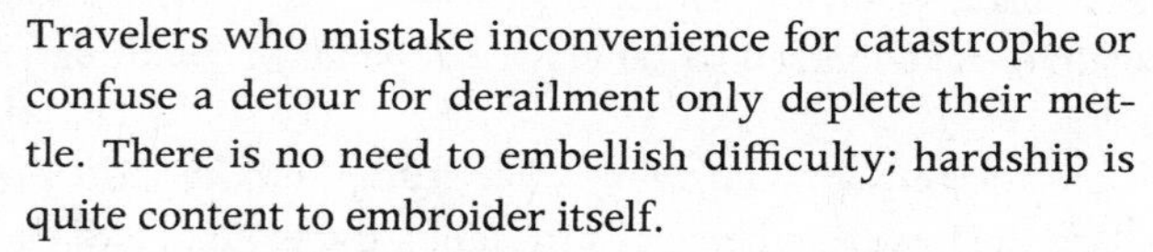

Travelers who mistake inconvenience for catastrophe or confuse a detour for derailment only deplete their mettle. There is no need to embellish difficulty; hardship is quite content to embroider itself.

—*Everyman's Guide to the Tower of Babel*, II. V

Swinging the case like a diamond club, Voleta bashed the bell jar with all her might. The chimera toppled over and slid away on her side, her legs limp and clattering as the pipes of a fallen wind chime. Seeing the warty, dark machinery of the thing's underside exposed, Voleta scooped up Iren's pistol and fired both shells into the matrix of rods and hoses. A spurt of familiar ruby fluid leapt from one of the holes. The fiend's legs hooked inward, imitating the death curl of a spider. Voleta dropped the pistol and wrapped both hands around the barrel of the crystalline case. Byron had assured her it could not be broken, though she meant now to try. Voleta felt the streams in her veins turn to rapids as she raised the rod high overhead and brought it crashing down.

She struck only ground, shattering a section of tile. At the last second, the wretch had pushed herself aside. Voleta turned to see a pair of gruesome mandibles had unfolded from the chimera's base. One was tipped with a three-toed claw. The other tapered into a stiletto-like blade. The fiend used both to first prop herself up, then return to her feet. She lurched from side to side, dazedly. Pressing a hand to either side of her jar, she hung her head, her face obscured by the mourning veil of her hair.

Voleta straightened and glanced, just for a second, at Iren. Her friend was still standing, though in a wavering, unsteady way. When Voleta's eyes flicked back, the wretch's claw was spearing for her face. Voleta caught the arm just in time, leaving the long black talons to scratch the air before her nose. Voleta raised her club to break the appendage at its joint.

The diamond case clattered at her feet. Voleta looked down. What she saw confused her. Someone had dropped a hand on the floor.

It appeared that someone had been her.

She leapt back when the chimera slashed at her with her blade and slashed again to cover herself so her clawed appendage could snatch up the painting in its case.

Voleta did not retreat. She jammed her stump into her coat pocket, as much to hide the loss from herself as to stanch the wound, and caught the free end of the cylinder even as the chimera attempted to jerk it away. It quickly became a tug of war between two equal grips, though Voleta's pull was a little stronger. Which was fortunate for her because she had to haul the case this way and that to fend off the fiend's attacks with her stiletto that reached and swung on an accordion hinge. Again and again, the devil slashed at Voleta's remaining wrist, only to have her knife crack and rasp upon the diamond barrel.

Voleta wondered which of them would weaken first: her with a seeping arm or she with a leaking carriage.

The cadaver's unblinking tar-black eyes seemed to suck at Voleta's sight. The pressure of unfamiliar memories crowded to the fore of her mind. She inhaled the loamy scent of earth and the pheromone stench of spider-eaters. The thorny trunks of porcelmores erupted from the observatory floor. Cobwebs blew across the ceiling like smoke, and glowing moss devoured the tile underfoot as the Silk Gardens bloomed all around her. Voleta knew the encroaching environment wasn't real, and yet either the illusion somehow invigorated the chimera, or its projection drained Voleta's strength. The wretch began to pierce her defenses, slashing her on the shoulder, on the cheek, on the back of her remaining hand.

It seemed Voleta had her answer as to who would falter first.

An anguished wail shot through the ghostly forest, erasing it at a stroke. Inside her bell jar, the fiend's mouth gaped, mimicking the shriek of rending metal. At her back, Iren hunched over one of the spidery legs that she held leveraged upon her thigh like a blacksmith shoeing a horse. She gave one last heave, and the leg sheared from the carriage with a gout of hydraulic fluid. The wretch staggered and dipped, her unsteadiness fueled by Iren's repeated ringing of her bell with her severed leg.

Voleta twisted the tube, unscrewing the cap the chimera still narrowly clung to. When the case came free, Voleta swung the diamond bat at the mandible that had robbed her of her hand. The first blow crimped the accordion hinge against the carriage's lip; the second broke it free.

The Sphinx's medium splashing under her, the fiend bowled into a row of chairs, upturning them, and nearly falling over herself, though she managed to wobble onward. Voleta saw at once she meant to escape back the way she'd come. Iren, hands streaked with her own blood, pursued the fiend, lashing it along with its own limb. Voleta had no doubt Iren would follow the devil into the water if she didn't intervene.

"Let her go!" Voleta shouted as the amazon vaulted a couch to get in another blow. "Let her go, Iren! I need you!"

Iren slowed a step as her quarry scurried faster. The villain plunged into the waiting pool and was gone.

Iren let the leg clatter to the floor.

Voleta breathed in shallow, quick puffs. She felt spent and disoriented. For a reason she could neither fathom nor examine at the moment, all of her attention had funneled upon the diamond case in her hand. The painting had slid a little from it. She tamped it back down with a bloody wrist, and began looking about for the cap. But the cap was nowhere to be found. The wretch had taken it with her. Byron would have a fit. The case was one of a kind. Irreplaceable. She wiped cold sweat from her upper lip. Her teeth chattered as she turned in a little circle, searching the floor, yet knowing it was lost.

Iren caught her up in her arms and clutched her to her chest. Voleta looked down at her hand where it lay palm up, fingers curled. It seemed at once perfectly familiar and utterly strange. She murmured, "I lost the cap. I can't find it anywhere."

Iren shushed her and said, "The Sphinx asks too much of us. He asks much too much."

Edith was not feeling particularly hopeful. She was laid out on her ear. The world had taken on a blurry quality. All the colors were bleeding through their lines. The two Wakemen were shuffling toward her and enjoying an unhurried discussion of what they would do to her, and whether they should leave anything for Hodder Luc to interrogate. Edith knew there were a hundred more armed men waiting in the Hod King's holds and perhaps more Wakemen as well. Marat could only have dispatched so few because he did not perceive a threat.

Edith hated to think he might've been right on that count.

The tall one called Thornton packed a wad of chewing tobacco in his front lip, licking up some of the blood from his broken nose in the process. If she only got one more swing in, she decided she would use it on him. *Wouldn't that be a pretty thing?*

Then Thornton jogged forward, propelled by something that had struck him in the back, then clattered noisily to the beach. He turned to look and was struck by a second projectile. Edith lifted her head a little and saw the bleary vision of Tane leading two dozen men and women. They were hurling their oars like spears.

The long-armed Cael raised his hand to shield his face. "You want her or them?" he asked.

"I'll take her," Thornton said, dragging the back of his silvery hand over his mouth as Cael turned to face the natives, who Edith could only pity. Thornton looked down at her, his jaw working to milk the poison from the plug of tobacco. He spat. "You're the bint who broke out of the Golden Zoo, aren't you?"

"It's Captain Bint to you." Her words slurred together.

"You mowed down a lot of good, decent people that day."

"They tried to pillage my ship."

"We're all vultures here, dearie. There aren't any doves in the Tower. You can't—"

Edith swept a leg at Thornton's ankles. Though his stance was unyielding, his footing was less so. The shells and pearls rolled under him like ball bearings, and he toppled to one side. Though she did not get him on his back again. He threw out an arm to stop his fall, braced himself upon one knee, and kicked back at her. She caught his foot in the palm of her engine and wrenched it to one side, prompting a brief, unmistakable shriek of shearing metal. Thornton withdrew his leg, and they faced each other on all fours.

"I'd like to shove that smirk right down your throat, but I'm betting ol' Hodder Luc would like to have a word with you."

"Well, call him out. We'll have a chat."

"He's more of a come-unto-me sort of man."

"My boss is the same way," Edith said.

"Same cloth, you and me." He bobbed his head at her, a feint to test her reaction.

She scrabbled back a foot or two. Her vision was clearing, but her head still felt stuffed with wool. "Two peas in a pod," she said.

"Let's be friends."

"Let's."

Thornton pounced, and she pitched to one side, rolling farther up the strand until she knocked against a beached skiff. She came to her feet the same moment Thornton found his, though he stood awkwardly, unevenly. The foot she'd attacked folded outward at the ankle like a boot pulled halfway on. He had to hop and hobble to keep his balance, his heels splashing in the shallow surf.

"Well, this has been fun, but it's almost happy hour. Let's pour a drink. You can sit on my lap," Thornton said, adopting a boxer's pose with fists before his face.

Edith reached into the skiff beside her and grasped a mass of netting piled there. Twisting at the hip, she hurled the net at the statuesque Wakeman. Though inelegantly thrown, the web still opened in the air, its edges drawn out by leaden weights. The net struck Thornton squarely, wrapping him from throat to knee. Sewn to withstand the thrashing of an elephant eel, the net resisted his first attempt to rend it. Edith did not give him a second chance. She drove the butt of an oar into his chest. He tottered and reeled, attempting to negotiate an injured foot, loose shells, and the tangling of a net. It was too much. He fell, clapping the surf with the broadside of his back. The water was shallow but still deep enough to cover his face. Edith leapt on him, straddling his chest, pinning the net to his arms, her iron hand on his throat, her other on his forehead. His legs thrashed; his body bucked beneath her. Through the inches of water, she saw the red orbs of his eyes, the shattered veins and terror-blown pupils. She did not look away.

Then in the midst of that moment of grotesque violence, she imagined Senlin standing at some porthole in the Hod King, observing as she dispassionately drowned a man. Seeing how ruthless she had become, would he feel relief at having escaped her? Perhaps he, in his high-minded way, would try to make some excuse for her: She was not wicked, just tainted by the Tower! Would he still think that if he knew she meant to crack the Hod King's shell, even if it killed all aboard—everyone, including him?

They would not fight this war back-to-back. The truth was, if he could not be saved, he must not be spared. She would charge through his ashes and march over his bones to save the world for lesser souls.

Under the force of her hands, the man's spasms grew weak. The surface bubbled with his last breaths. Through that boiling water, she thought she saw Tom's face emerge—his kind eyes, noble nose, and oversharpened cheeks. His lips parted as if he would speak. His eyes lost focus as he gazed through her to some more distant shore.

No, not through her: *over* her shoulder.

A hand like a bear trap wrapped about the forearm of her engine. Cael lifted her as if she were an empty sack. She dangled from his fist, her legs churning in the open air. The moment she was off him, Thornton popped up, quick as a spring. He choked, sputtered, and heaved for breath.

"You all right?" Cael asked him.

Rising unsteadily on his unsocketed foot, Thornton wagged one hand—an impatient, beckoning gesture. "Here. Give her to me. Give her."

Cael held Edith out to his compatriot. Grasping her by the shoulder and thigh, the silvery souse raised her over his head like a dumbbell. Edith only had time enough to call for him to wait before he threw her out past the shelf of the beach and into the starry deep.

Iren knew a state of shock when she saw it. She sat Voleta down on a couch and began ripping a throw blanket into long strips. While Voleta rambled on about a missing cap and how irked Byron would be, Iren retrieved her severed hand, cradling it as gently as a chick fallen out of its nest. Already, it was cold but still pliant. The seeping blood was dark as wine, thick as pitch. Laying Voleta's arm on a cushion, she aligned the lost hand with its origin as best she could, then began lashing the two together with the bandages she'd torn. Iren wrapped it like a boxer's hand, binding it from forearm to finger. Voleta murmured something about the little girl and a paper boat and the orphans of the Tower.

Iren rummaged through the young woman's coat, once a traveling trove stuffed with treats for Squit and all the curious treasures Voleta found on her adventures: rifle shells, smooth stones, scraps of paper, and nests of string. It was strange to find all her pockets empty except for the leather kit of vials Byron had packed for her. The stag had insisted she not leave the ship without a three-day supply of medium, remarking, "The Tower is full of dead ends and detours. Better to travel a little heavy than too light."

How right he was.

When Voleta saw the kit, her distraction fractured. She tried to straighten herself in her seat. "We're onto six, now, eh? Four to five to six in one day. At this rate I'll be drinking pints of the stuff for breakfast."

"Shut up," Iren said, drawing medium from a vial. "I'm operating."

"Yes, doctor."

Iren knew she could not be as gentle as Ann nor as deft as the Red Hand at finding a vein, but even so, with every halting and clumsy jab, Voleta grew more animated, her face less pale. When the sixth injection found her arm, the bound fingers of her recently severed hand began to twitch.

Though it was the result she'd hoped for, the sight still made Iren leap. "My god," she said under her breath. She wasn't sure what the miraculous medium made her feel more: gratitude or dread.

"You're bleeding." A newly revived Voleta touched the shoulder of Iren's coat. Blood wetted the green wool.

"Just a few pricks. Nothing urgent. Think you can walk?"

"I could walk up a wall," Voleta said, drawing a deep breath through her nose.

"You do that. I'm taking the elevator." Iren slapped her knees and grunted as she rose to her feet.

The inky pool in the floor before them suddenly began to boil. Voleta and Iren angled their stance in anticipation of the chimera's return. They expected a spidery leg to hook the portal's rim but were more surprised to see the familiar set of iron fingers.

Edith's head broke the water with a gasp. She coughed and gagged, her human hand scratching at the tile as she tried to pull herself out. Iren and Voleta ran to her side, each grabbing an arm and hauling her onto the observatory floor. Edith pushed herself up on all fours, vomiting water at their feet.

Seeing a small eel wriggling tail-up in her captain's shirt collar, Iren bravely plucked it out and threw it back into the drink. When Edith raised her arm to be helped up, they raised her. Her coat was gone, her boots as well. Between coughs, she said, "Marat is here. He's here."

"That explains a thing or two, doesn't it, Iren? I think we met one of his friends," Voleta said, returning to the couch. Grasping the diamond tube, she waved it like a flag at the finish line of a race. "But look, Captain: We won this round!"

"Hurrah," Edith said, and retched again upon the floor.

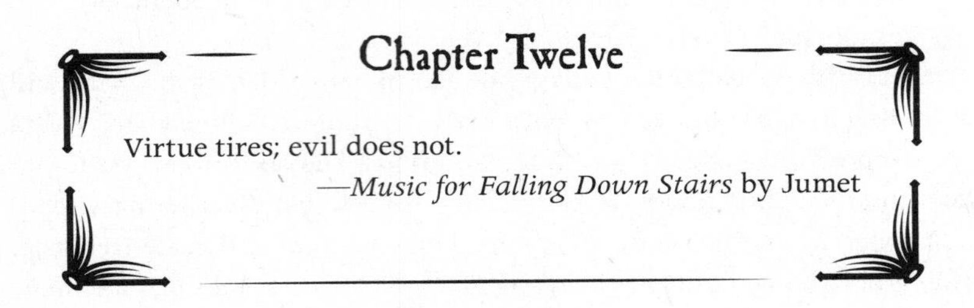

Chapter Twelve

Virtue tires; evil does not.

—*Music for Falling Down Stairs* by Jumet

Byron was beginning to believe himself rather inured to crisis. After all, he had, in the span of a few days, survived a boarding party, the death of a friend, and the near constant implorations of an infant. But when the captain reappeared on Port Nidus under the light of the moon with a mob of strangers and informed him that they would be taking on thirty-five boarders, Byron felt unready.

His first thought was how anyone could possibly expect him to entertain so many on such short notice—no notice at all, in fact. How could he offer sleeping arrangements to thirty-five with only sixteen open beds? Did Edith expect him to saw the beds in half or stack the guests up? Did he even have forty uncracked plates left in his sideboard? The ship's collection of official china, which had been produced by the peerless Mersey Brothers, had suffered many losses over the years. Byron supposed he could serve a main course on a salad plate, but then, what would he serve the salad on? Perhaps he could just hurl the tomatoes, radishes, and lettuce on the floor and let them graze at their leisure like pigs in a sty!

But when he got a closer look at the parade of men and women, he saw with a shudder their pitiful condition. Their faces were masked with blood, their gazes uninhabited by sense or light or hope.

This was not a gala; it was *triage*.

Byron had no choice but to make bedfellows of the casualties. When he informed Reddleman and Voleta they would have to surrender their rooms, neither protested. Since Reddleman had only a small duffel he'd never unpacked, his evacuation took scarcely a moment. Voleta's bed was in good order because she never slept in it, but she had made her mark on the floor of her cabin. As Byron helped Edith carry a woman with a crushed arm through the doorway of her cabin, Voleta kicked her laundry under the bed.

Byron was not unfamiliar with terrible injuries. After all, the persons the Sphinx recruited into her force of Wakemen always arrived maimed and broken. But he had never seen so many wounded all at once, and he found the abundance of misery overwhelming. The two main causes of trauma appeared to be falling masonry and extreme battery. The worst of the arrivals looked to have been struck by a train.

The ringdom natives helped carry the wounded aboard, though the effort was not without confusion as the corridor, meant to accommodate dozens, suddenly filled with scores of persons carrying ramshackle litters made out of eel skins and oars. Shouting over the chaos, Edith told Byron that they had encountered the Hod King and three Wakemen Marat had turned to his cause. The Hod King had vacated the ringdom, returning the way it'd come, but not before killing nearly a dozen and leaving many more wounded behind. The worst of those Edith had taken responsibility for. Her intention was to split the casualties between three ringdoms: Jinst, Harrakesh, and Valadi. All had better-equipped medical facilities than the Cistern. She only needed Byron to keep the wounded alive (or at least comfortable) until she could convince the ports to accept the refugees.

"But they have the plague, don't they?" Byron asked, discreetly cupping a hand over his snout.

"A ruse. I'll explain later. In the meantime: all hands on deck."

Voleta appeared to recently have been injected with a large quantity of medium, this despite the fact that Ann had administered her last round of shots shortly before she'd left the ship. Though Byron hadn't time to hear the story behind the unscheduled dose, he imagined it had something to do with Voleta's wrapped-up hand. Regardless of its cause or eventual consequence, for the moment he was grateful for her vitality. Her eyes steamed as she charged from cabin to cabin changing out bedpans, delivering fresh water, administering refreshment to those who could take it, and applying compresses to those who could not.

Marya declared herself Lord of the Laundry. While Olivet slept in a bassinet in the corner, Marya marshaled gory sheets, rags, and towels into the automated washing basin, then into the heated drum of the drier, and finally out onto the folding table. Before long, Marya would appear with a basket full of clean laundry on her hip and Olivet on her shoulder. Byron would express his gratitude even as he presented her with a bindle full of freshly bloodied things.

Unsurprisingly, Ann was also an invaluable help, though Iren first had to convince her that while she appeared to have recently played pincushion to a pitchfork, her injuries were not the direst aboard. Iren could look after them herself, which she did, and then took the ship's helm since she was in no shape to help with the wounded.

Ann was remarkably un-squeamish. She did not shy from the worst wounds, nor flee when her careful ministrations were greeted with howls of pain. Perhaps more impressive was her indomitable warmth and calm. She called everyone *dear* and was quick to reassure, comfort, and console. Much later, when Byron asked her how she managed to remain so serene while faced with jutting bones and flowing arteries, Ann explained, "I saw my first birth when I was sixteen. I was assisting Midwife Ina Day, an absolute pillar of a woman who shepherded thousands of souls into the world in her time. When she asked me to come forward with the pan, I took one look at what was happening and dropped like a stone. She left me lying on the floor. When I woke up to the ongoing ordeal of a young woman's first birth, Midwife Ina Day said to me, 'You're in the way. If you can't be useful, be elsewhere.' It's a lesson that stuck with me."

But in the end, it was the pilot who surprised Byron most. When Byron found Reddleman preparing to skewer a blue-lipped man through the ribs with a small silvery pipe, he had shouted at him in horror, calling him a ghoul. Then, before Byron could decide whether to physically intervene or not, Reddleman pierced the man's chest. Air spurted from the pipe, and the moribund man's breath deepened as color crept back to his cheeks.

"His lung had collapsed," Reddleman explained.

"How did you know that?"

"I was a doctor before I drowned," he said as if neither point were a remarkable revelation. Naturally, Byron had a number of questions, but this wasn't the time.

"Can you help them, then?" Byron asked.

"Some of them, somewhat. I was a country doctor, not a surgeon, but I can set a bone and sew a stich." Reddleman wiped his hands on a clean towel. "Still, I've seen enough to know some of these people are not going to survive. We should focus on the ones who have a fighting chance, I think."

"How can I tell which is which?"

"I'll tie a rag to the bedpost over those who are past hope. The ship has a stock of ether. We should use it."

"Agreed," Byron said, and bit his tongue to keep from adding, *There'll be a rag tied to all our bedposts before this is over.*

The hours smoothed into a single unending moment, vast and incomprehensible. Byron wondered, how long had he been awake? How many kettles had he filled and brought to a boil? How many wounds had he washed, wrapped, unwrapped, and washed again? When the morning arrived, Byron did not mark it. When they docked at Port Fraxinus in the ringdom of Jinst, he did not notice. He would have been blithe to Edith's departure, too, had she not stopped him amid one of her jogs to the galley.

She commended the work he was doing and asked if he was all right. He gave the perfunctory answers of a person toiling without reflection: *Thank you* and *Yes, I am*. She said she was leaving to meet the magistrate of Jinst to request sanctuary for a portion of the injured. He told her that the woman with the crushed arm had died. This exchange of facts elicited no emotion from either of them. They parted like strangers disembarking from a train.

And Byron did not notice that it was five hours before Edith returned from her meeting with Magistrate Hadriana Mann. When Edith found Byron assembling a mountain of dry toast in the galley, her mood was palpably foul. Byron soon learned that, in exchange for medical aid, the magistrate had demanded protection from the Hod King, and not the mere promise of occasional intervention. No, the magistrate wanted the *State of Art* to stay tied up at the dock like a guard dog until either the other ringdoms managed to tree the fox or the Hod King lighted upon its final destination, which could be anywhere it wished so long as it wasn't the ringdom of Jinst.

Additionally, Magistrate Mann was concerned about the expense of the requested assistance, and so she wished to know how the Sphinx proposed to compensate her. When Edith said she could not lash herself to the magistrate's port nor pay the woman enough to buy a conscience, Magistrate Mann began to make a myriad of excuses for why they couldn't possibly accept responsibility for so many injured: Their physicians were managing an outbreak of flu; there was a shortage of gauze; and one of the ringdom's most celebrated events—the annual rabbit steeplechase—was just days away.

At last, Edith had interrupted the magistrate's dithering by saying, "Madam, you seem to be operating under the misapprehension that this is a negotiation. It is not. Either you take these men and women and do your utmost to heal them, or the Sphinx will remove all his protection from your ringdom, including protection from me."

Edith instructed Byron to pick the twelve most grievously injured, though Byron did not. Instead, he selected from those who Reddleman had not flagged as hopeless. One such case was named Tane, a handsome and generally pleasant fellow who appeared to hold a position of authority among his clan. He also had a fractured collarbone and six broken ribs. When the question of his departure was raised, Tane politely but firmly refused. Tane assured Edith he would be the last one off. She consented to the demand, directing Byron to take his bedmate instead, a man with half his head wrapped in a cocked and bloody turban.

While Byron worked to re-dress this man's wound in preparation for his departure, Tane begged Edith for another moment of her time. He said, "I am worried, Captain, that in your effort to save us, you will jeopardize the sanctity of the Cistern. If the other ringdoms discover we do not have the plague, we will lose our only defense."

"I told the magistrate you are members of my crew, injured in battle. She doesn't know where you're from."

"But what of our clothes? As soon as they see our eel skins and—"

"We will dress them in sheets."

"But what if one of us confesses our true identity in a state of delirium or despair? Captain, I do not wish to be difficult or melodramatic, but I need to be certain you understand what's at stake here. The last time the Cistern was overharvested, the resulting stagnation had a dire and lasting effect. A virulent fever, one never seen before, spread through the black trail. A quarter of a generation perished in a year. The loss of labor ushered in a decade of famine. The wealthy freighted in food and water while the alleys of their ringdoms turned into morgues. The same or worse could happen again. If the gluttons of the Tower use the Cistern as their Sunday carvery many will suffer; many will die."

"If they come, I will fend them off."

"Captain, how can you guard us when you can't even—"

"Mr. Tane, I have made all the assurances I can make. If it's a guarantee you're after, I can only promise that as long as I'm alive, you will be under my protection. But I need *you* to understand something: If I fail in this coming contest, there will be no oasis left for you to attend. If the Tower falls, it will be without caveat. We will all perish. So, please, say your goodbyes. We must move on."

Voleta lay on her back on the conservatory floor. Squit nibbled and tugged at one of her shirt buttons, scratching at the horn disc as if it were a nut. Voleta hardly noticed. She was too busy listening to the harpsichord. Someone was trying to play several songs on it at once, which was strange, because everyone had already gone to bed.

As soon as the last casualty was delivered to the care of the ringdom of Valadi, the crew had found they could haggle with their exhaustion no longer. Captain Winters had fallen asleep with the door to her quarters hanging open. She lay fully clothed and facedown on her bed like a starfish. Voleta had heard Iren snoring through her door, having recently surrendered the helm to Reddleman after a thirty-six-hour shift. Voleta had watched Ann sneak into that noisy stateroom after mouthing a voiceless good night. Marya's door was closed, the frosted glass unlit, the infant silent. Voleta had found Byron lying beside a mound of clean laundry like a farm boy napping against a haystack. She'd turned off the light before retreating.

And then for some reason she couldn't quite recall, Voleta had laid down on the conservatory floor. Then the music started to play three songs at once: a ballad on top of a dirge with a polka bouncing through the middle. The racket had given her a migraine, but she found the more she concentrated on the music, the more distant the pain became. She rolled her head to the side to look at the instrument. Beneath the bench, the feet of three ghosts shuffled and tapped the parquet. They looked to be separated by layers of velum; one pair of shoes was foggier than the next. She had the impression that the dimmest set of feet was the most distant from her in time, but before she could consider what such a thing might mean, the conservatory filled with more specters, some in fancy dress, some in military uniform, some in half-assembled evening wear. An old man in striped pajamas and a sleeping cap stepped in her stomach as if she were a puddle. Everything inside her, everything that was her, splashed and rippled about his slipper though he did not appear to notice as he shuffled onward to a cut-crystal decanter ensconced in the bookcase. He was one of a hundred ghosts milling about the chamber, all of varying degrees of translucence.

Then she saw a hazy Sphinx walking among the crowd. The Sphinx had feet, a discernable waist and bust, though her robes were black as ever. Her mask still looked like a spoon, but a much smaller one, a comparative teaspoon, one that still concealed her face. The Sphinx appeared to be speaking to a dignitary in a white suit and rose-colored turban. Voleta couldn't hear what they were saying over the cacophonous harpsichord, but the longer she stared, the more it seemed the Sphinx was looking back at her. The Sphinx raised a hand to pause the conversation. Turning her shoulders toward Voleta, the Sphinx parted the gala of ghosts, passing through the older, dimmer specters. Voleta expected the Sphinx to trudge through her as others had, but the Sphinx stopped at her side, looking down. She bent over Voleta, the reflection in her mirror showing nothing but the warped thatch of the parquet floor.

It struck Voleta as strange to stare into a mirror and not see herself. But stranger still when she did appear. Voleta's face flashed like lightning in the bowl of the Sphinx's mask. The Sphinx reached for her with inky fingers.

The smack on her cheek was sharp enough to bring Voleta upright.

Reddleman sat on his heels beside her. "How far back did you go?"

"A long way, I think. I saw the Sphinx. She had legs."

"Hmm. I believe you're dying. Your squirrel seems to think so, too. May I have your arm, please?"

"Why?" Voleta said, even as she offered up the heavy, distant limb. He rolled up her shirtsleeve in tidy little folds.

Opening the duffel bag at his heels, the pilot extracted a bronze cuff, ringed with six cylinders full of ember-bright medium. He cracked it open like a clamshell, showing a halo of needle tips secreted within. He positioned the open shackle on her left arm just above her wrist.

"What is that?" she asked, though she recognized it dimly as having once adorned his arm.

"A measure of autonomy. This will pinch a little." He closed the cuff, and the needles plunged into her skin, not dumbly, but with a snaking intent. They bit in search of her veins. Voleta gritted her teeth, feeling much more present, if a little pained. But the torment was short-lived. Even when she flexed her arm, she could scarcely feel the presence of the needles.

Reddleman turned her arm and the band to show her the row of winged pegs and series of minute indicators that adorned one side. These, he reviewed with her. At full capacity, the cuff held twelve doses that could be administered at a plunge or a drip. An alarm would sound once a minute when her reserves had dwindled to a single dose. The cuff could be removed after disengaging the lock, though the reapplication process would be just as unpleasant as it had been the first time.

As he explained the workings of the cuff, Voleta felt the arrival of the medium in her veins. Her head began to clear. When it did, she felt a little flutter of indignance. "Ann forgot my dose. I could've died!"

"Well, did you remind her?" Reddleman asked. Voleta admitted she had not. "Oh. Well, did you remind her to eat a meal, or drink a glass of water, or go to bed? Of course not. You need to learn to rely on yourself."

"I suppose you're right," she said, examining the cuff more closely. Squit dashed down her arm and inspected it with sniffing suspicion. Its presence would take some getting used to. "Ann says you were a doctor."

"I was. A reasonably good one at that, but not very important or clever, certainly not clever enough to do any interesting work. I had a practice in the eastern dells in a little hamlet called Cudbright. Not a remarkable place, but pleasant. Perhaps tediously so. In search of entertainment, I became a pteridologist. That's what a fern enthusiast is called. The glades were full of ferns, all sorts of varieties. Fascinating plants. They live through two generations, haploid and diploid—two radically different states, one green and rooted, the other minuscule and airborne. They reproduce asexually."

"Asexually?" Voleta echoed, crimping her brow.

"Yes, it means they don't need a partner to reproduce or thrive. They're independent, self-contained."

"I like the sound of that."

"Perhaps you have a bit of fern in you. They're what originally brought me to the Tower. I'd read there were species of ferns growing in the Baths that did not exist in the wild: the blue royal ferns, the cornucopia ferns, all sorts of fascinating specimens. I was very excited. I had been there three days when I fell asleep and drowned in a tub surrounded by hundreds of other bathers. No one noticed."

"That's tragic."

"Not really. I was a small man with a dull life who met a boring end. I don't think about my own past much, but when I do, it's like recalling a biography I read a long time ago and did not particularly enjoy. So, never mind it. Tell me more about this Sphinx with legs. Could you tell if she was a man or a woman?"

"A woman, of course. You've seen the Sphinx without her mask on, haven't you?"

"Yes, but I was curious as to which Sphinx you saw."

"There's more than one?"

"I once saw a fleeting vision of a man in a mirror mask. It made me realize the obvious: Our Sphinx is not the original. There must have been dozens of other generations of Sphinxes, stretching all the way back to the laying of the foundations of the Tower itself. The Sphinx is a title, a role, a costume, rather than a person. Which raises an interesting question."

"Who will replace her. You think it should be you?"

"Perhaps. But then, I'm not the one she took under her wing, not the one she showed her face to scant hours after introductions were made."

"No. No, don't be silly. It can't be me. It could never be me." Voleta spoke with softening certainty as she again saw the younger Sphinx lean down and peer at her through the thinning veil of time.

From the Belly of the Beast

3

We have risen from the chimneys of history—we the soot of empire, we the cinders of suffering. Yet the kings of the Tower would blame us for this great conflagration. They say we are the smoke that lit this fire; we are the ashes that set the world alight.

—from the sermons of Luc Marat
(translated from hoddish)

~~A king surrounded by toadies may feel secure, but so does the goose of the feast feel well fed by the butcher. Fawning should be punished the same as treason—with swift, unflinching execution—for it strikes at the sovereign's eyes. Flattery blinds a man gradually, but forever. Granting all~~

Senlin stood with bare heels braced on either side of the draining closet's doorframe. Accommodating the deck's steep incline took a toll on the muscles of his back and stomach, making athletic what otherwise would've been quiescent work. Mercifully, the Hod King was stationary for the moment and silent but for the tick of cooling plumbing.

It had been something of a rough ride since the firefight with the *State of Art* that morning.

So perched, he cracked the brass thorax of a moth and scraped out a layer of springs with a hooked pick, revealing the lambent capsule hidden within. Filling Marat's tank with such dribbles was a little like attempting to make a quiche from the eggs of a hummingbird. Hopefully, Marat would be satisfied with his efforts. Once again, Senlin felt the need to ingratiate himself to the zealot.

The Hod King's inglorious debut had left Marat at the mercy of his own rage. No one was spared the strew of his bile. After he'd finished admonishing Mr. Gedge for his failures as an engineer, Marat had turned his ire upon Senlin, claiming that his attendance on the bridge had been the cause of a nearly catastrophic distraction. Though it was not clear to Senlin who he had distracted or how, he knew better than to defend himself. He understood that accusations made in wrath drew from the proof of emotions rather than the substance of facts, and as such were incontestable. When Marat announced that Senlin was forever barred from the bridge, all Tom could do was duck his head in acceptance.

But his unanticipated exclusion from the wheelhouse posed quite a problem for Senlin. While anyone aboard could easily discern when the excavator was engaged—the rumble and racket was enough to make one's teeth chatter—it was impossible to know the duration of any given dig. Some burrows were quite long as the engine carved through the massive outer walls of the Tower; other excavations were brief as the Hod King leapt from one passage of the black trail to another. If Senlin and his conspirators wished to entomb the beast, they would need to detonate the bomb when the engine was well and truly buried, and for that, access to the bridge was needed.

As Senlin's fingers shucked the shell from the Sphinx's spies, his mind wandered in search of a solution. And thus was he preoccupied when the Hod King abruptly began to rock and saw beneath him. The mammoth drill roared once more like surf upon a cliff face. They were on the move again.

A commotion in the wardroom brought Senlin's head around. Marat's Wakemen were arguing, not casually as they often did, but urgently. Something had happened.

Gripping door sills and hatch wheels for balance, Senlin made his way up the corridor toward the crashing chaos of the wardroom.

He arrived in time to see Delyth ram her crystal bell against the steel bulkhead, back up, the points of her toes squealing like knives on glass, then repeat the battery again. Fluids, dark and lurid, splashed from her undercarriage and jetted from the ragged stub of an absent leg.

Arms raised as if to gentle a bucking horse, Mr. Gedge danced along the path of her self-destruction. Inside her bubble, Delyth shook her head so violently it lifted her hair into a cyclone. Cael sobbed, facedown on the table, the hills of his shoulders rising and falling about the dark copse of his hair, while Thornton, his nose a bloody ruin, raised a stone jug on the cradle of his elbow and drank as if he meant to drown.

In one hand, Mr. Gedge held a small, bulbous canister, like a light bulb blown from purple glass. When Delyth paused between collisions, Gedge leapt to the lip of her carriage and screwed the bulb into an imperceptible socket. The canister drained into her environment, and her bell filled with a lavender fog. She began to stagger and sway. Gedge barked the dejected Cael out of his seat, directing him to catch Delyth even as her knees buckled and curled. Arms encircling her glass dome, Cael gathered her up before she could crash to the floor.

"Take her to my workroom, Cael. And be gentle! My god, she's leaking like a sieve. Whoever did this to her should be flogged. What monsters!"

As Cael labored under his awkward load, and Gedge flagged him toward a forbidden hatch in the corridor, Thornton pulled his mouth away from his jug long enough to say, "Don't worry, I tucked one in. Tucked her in with an anchor."

But the genius of the Hod King was not impressed. "Oh, don't crow to me about your petty revenge! Perhaps if your brains weren't so pickled, Delyth would still have all her limbs!" Gedge slammed the door of the workshop behind him.

"This body doesn't need a brain!" Thornton yelled, snorting wetly at his uncertain joke. He rolled his raw eyes toward Senlin. "My head's just along for the ride." Thornton turned the jug up once more as blood ran down his chin and over the dancing lump in his throat.

"What happened?"

Thornton stumbled against the round table as he made his way toward the door of his cabin. "They blindsided us. Supposed to be a sleepy little burg. A couple thousand natives, no standing army, no artillery. Just galoshes and shells. *In and out,* Luc said. *Quick and easy.*" Senlin followed the silver-limbed Wakeman as he limped on one crooked ankle to his cabin. Inside, Thornton stamped his jug down on his footlocker before rolling into his bunk. The springs complained and cratered under his great weight. He reached under his pillow and extracted a worn pouch of tobacco. "Let me tell you, 'quick and easy' kicks like a mule."

"You were intercepted?"

Thornton filled his lower lip with a plug of tobacco. "One of the Sphinx's dogs caught us napping. She broke my nose." He turned his head and spat blood onto the floor.

Senlin felt the pinhole abyss inside him begin to grow. "Were there others?"

"Delyth ran into a couple more. A little girl and a big old maid. They twisted her leg off. And here, we all thought she was invincible. Ha."

"You said you put one to bed with an anchor?"

Thornton shut his eyes, folding his immaculate hands upon the sculpture of his chest. "The one who broke my nose—I threw her into the lake. She had an arm like an anchor. Sank like one, too." The bottomless pit inside of Senlin yawned. Voice deadened by the approach of sleep, Thornton said, "Oh, but that look on her face. Never seen someone so surprised to die. My head's just along for the ride, but I'm glad it was there to see that."

Thornton's skull fell deeper into his pillow. His jaw fell open, and he began to snore.

Senlin suddenly felt the chill of the Silk Garden well that he and Edith had once nearly drowned in. They had clung to one another, inspired by the intimacy of mortality, an embrace that had made the boundless dark seem a little lighter.

But then he pictured Thornton hurling her into some bleak depth: her eyes wide and staring as she sank. Senlin watched her flail at the water's receding surface even as the void swelled beneath her, about her, within her.

Senlin reached for the stone jug. His finger gouged the eye of the handle. The drunkard's head would open under the weight; his unwanted brains would leap from his ears like roe squeezed from a sturgeon. If Senlin hurried, he might still catch up with Edith, might find her amid her descent, might again lighten the darkness by sharing it.

"My wine's better."

His murderous trance broken, Senlin turned to find Marat leaning upon the cabin hatchway.

All at once, Senlin knew Edith would've scoffed and rolled her eyes at him and his brutish gallantry. Because he wasn't being noble; he was being selfish. Her death did not absolve him of his own obligations. He couldn't save anyone if he were dead, no matter how chivalrous his epitaph. Embarrassed, he withdrew his hand from the jug.

One of the zealot's arms rested upon the top of his head. It seemed an aggressively casual pose. The other hand, Marat held in reserve behind his back.

"You look upset," the zealot said mildly.

Senlin shook his head as if in sorrow and not to give himself a moment to fabricate an excuse. "Delyth. Her leg. Is she going to be all right?"

Marat raised one shoulder and let it drop in choreographed nonchalance. Still, his gaze was sharp and probing. "Probably. If she can be saved, Gedge will save her. Or perhaps, we'll all lose someone today. You lost an old crewmate, I hear."

Knowing his response would be scrutinized, Senlin put his hands on his hips, reflecting Marat's indifference. "Oh? Who's that?"

"I believe you called her . . . Lizabeth?"

Senlin pretended to ponder the name. "You mean Edith? Dark hair? Iron arm? Her?"

"Yes, her. I thought you were close. You certainly seemed so while you were bedded in my Golden Zoo."

Senlin grimaced. "You do know she stole my commission? Snatched it right out from under me. I should've been the captain of the *State of Art*, but she... well, she went behind my back. Told the Sphinx I was unreliable, a poor leader. I thought we were friends at the time."

"And now?" Marat seemed to shift his grip on whatever he held behind his back.

"Well, now I realize the thing about ambition is that it only seats a party of one. If ambition could be shared, our race would be in a much better spot!" Tom's grin dwindled when he saw that Marat disliked the implication. The zealot seemed to not appreciate the notion that a better world was even conceivable outside his intervention. Senlin hurried on. "But there is something communal about revenge, isn't there? Even if you and I were to compete for who loathed the Sphinx more, both of us would win if he were to suffer and die."

Marat squinted at him thoughtfully and shifted air back and forth between his cheeks like a seesawing scale. Senlin could only hope his performance had been convincing.

After a moment, Marat brought his hand around from behind his back. Senlin could hardly keep from flinching. A capped fountain pen rested in the zealot's palm; the fat silver barrel was embellished with gold bands, one of which, Senlin discovered, was etched with an inscription: TO COMMEMORATE THE PROMOTION OF COLONEL EDMUND H. PAPPERMAN FROM HIS LOVING SISTER, CORDELIA W. P.

"Sometimes my snoops, in their eagerness to root out the Sphinx's spies, bring home innocent trinkets. I thought you might like a better implement for your nightly routine."

Even as he examined the pen, Senlin looked downcast.

"That's not exactly the thanks I was expecting, Tom."

Senlin screwed up his face until it was as wrinkled as a cabbage leaf; it was an expression of supreme misery. "You must think me a simpleton."

Marat crossed his arms. "I don't think you're simple, Tom. I wouldn't confide in you if I did."

"Then why keep me cracking shells over a sink all day? You know I have experience with ships. I'm clever, a quick learner. I distinguished myself among the steppers in a matter of days. And I know you have a vacancy in the wheelhouse."

"Oh, I see! You're sniffing after a promotion. Here I was, worried that you'd be sentimental about your friend being drowned in a pond, when you're really just hoping for a leg up."

Senlin looked briefly abashed, and yet persisted. "Can you blame me? History is cresting! A king is ascending to the throne of nations, and I'm off sitting in a corner like a dunce!"

"You want a front row seat, is that it?"

"I do."

"How are you with navigations?"

"I know the physical principles, and I can learn the instruments. I fabricated a clinometer out of scrap wood and used it to traverse miles of black trail vents. I have no shortage of experience working under pressure. Please, Luc. The reservoir is ninety-two percent full. Surely that's enough. And if it's not, I could crack more moths in the off hours."

Marat seemed to be warming to the idea, though he was not yet entirely convinced. "How do you feel about trampling hods?"

"I beg your pardon?"

"One of the results of being driven from the public route is that we now have no choice but to breach and sometimes travel along the black trail. There have been and will continue to be casualties, I'm afraid."

"What of all the hods who will perish if you allowed yourself to be dissuaded from your goal? When a fire approaches a farm, does the farmer not burn a portion of his crops to create a barrier and save the rest? So it must be with us. The dead we make today will thwart a much greater loss tomorrow."

The lift of Marat's brows signaled that he'd struck upon the correct answer. He sucked his teeth and said, "I tell you what, Tom, on a provisional basis, I'll make you my second navigator. But I caution you, while we're out there in front of the crew I won't address you with this sort of familiarity. No jokes. No discussion. Just quick obedience."

"Aye, sir."

Marat clapped him on the shoulder. "Good. Well, enjoy your scrawling. Morning shift starts at seven." Even as Luc's retreating heels knelled through the wardroom, Senlin began to second-guess himself. What had seemed clever in the moment, on reflection felt unwise. Without question, he had oversold his aptitude for the art of navigation and its related instrumentation. If his incompetence was revealed, he might find himself reprimanded, demoted, or worse—much worse.

He'd always had a knack for solving one problem with two more.

Even as Senlin reflected upon this, Thornton began to gurgle and sputter in his bunk. He appeared to be choking. Seeing the brown froth gathering in the corner of his mouth, Senlin turned the drunk onto his side, an effort that took all of his strength. Wearing a grimace of determination, he dug the wad of tobacco from the back of Thornton's throat.

Senlin flicked the dark clog to the floor before wiping his fingers on the bedsheets. He enjoyed a brief sense of ebullience at his moral superiority at having saved such a dismal specimen of the race before recalling both the bargain he'd just struck and his ongoing plot. He would trample innocent hods if it brought him nearer his goal of sabotaging the Hod King, a deed that would result in the death of everyone aboard.

He was quick to rationalize the necessity of these unfortunate casualties, but it did not escape his notice that every justification he mounted was eerily similar to the ones that Marat used to excuse his own barbarism.

Senlin marveled at how litigious his conscience had grown, and always in defense of such a bloodthirsty client.

Back in his berth, Senlin lay with the heels of his palms pressed to his eyes.

He could not believe Edith was gone. She was still so immediate in his memory, so near the fore of his thoughts. Perhaps there had been a mistake. Thornton was an unreliable witness if ever there was one. Marat might've confirmed the lie only to measure Senlin's response. Edith had made a career out of defying the odds; it seemed somehow profane that she would've survived so much only to be killed by an old tosspot.

Senlin felt like the man who, upon finding his purse missing, continued to pat his empty pockets. As if disbelief had ever redeemed a loss.

His thoughts fled to happier times, back to the endless, sometimes idle days aboard the *Stone Cloud* when they'd enjoyed good company, sufficient humor, and awkward sleeping arrangements. How skilled they had become at pretending to be deaf! Edith did not hear him bah at his books or snore through the thin door of her chart house, and Senlin did not hear her mutter to herself, both in and out of dreams. It was a polite deafness they sometimes broke when neither could sleep. Then, they would lie in their beds and talk through the wall while the wind played the drafty hull like a flute.

Rarely did their conversation turn to their own histories. Talk of the past seemed to taunt fate, so they reviewed the thousand ailments of their old ship: the rotting rigging, the leaking reservoir, the termites in the bilge...

But then, one odd evening, they had found themselves in a rare mood. It was he who had broken with tradition first and confessed that he missed the scent of the sea. Edith had asked if he missed the smell of his old classroom, too.

Senlin laughed, and said, "Children of a certain age are whiffy, especially when you pile them together in a single room on a warm September afternoon. Of course, you can't tell a child that they stink. You have to act as if you're not smelling what you're smelling, though it is indeed being smelled."

He listened to Edith laugh and toss over in her bed. When she spoke again, her voice was closer to their clapboard chaperone. "I don't know. I've always preferred animal scents to the reek of a lady's parlor. Who was it that decided geraniums smelled nice? They don't. At all. They smell like the fifth day of a wake; like something long dead doused in loud perfume. I'd rather stand over a pig wallow any day."

"Then you've come to the right place!"

Edith's chuckle turned into a sigh. "Do you think you'll ever teach again?"

Stacking his arms under his head, Senlin said, "What would I teach? A Survey of Basic Confusion? An Introduction to Utter Chaos? I'd have to come up with an entirely new curriculum, one full of open-ended questions and inexplicable mysteries. I'd baffle my poor students with ambiguities and contradictions. I'd have to give them tests without knowing the answers."

"The world is confusing. What's wrong with telling them the truth?"

"I wouldn't want to turn their hair white. Besides, cynics don't belong in the classroom. Teaching requires a certain amount of idealism. But what about you? Could you go from swinging a sword back to farming?"

"Maybe. Farming is basically fortune-telling. You have to keep one foot in the future. You live by the almanac. You study the market forecasts to decide what to plant. You hope for the best; you plan for the worst. When you go to bed, your head is full of moldy seeds, overcropping, and long winters. Honestly, it's hard to imagine returning to a life with such a far-off horizon while we're out here..."

"Living at the mercy of the wind?" Senlin suggested.

"I was going to say, eating pigeons for breakfast, lunch, and dinner."

Senlin grinned at the bare boards of the ceiling. "Ah. So, this is the malnutrition talking?"

She yawned and her voice took on a drowsy sort of honesty. "Maybe I've just gotten used to the short view, living day to day. The prospect of obsessing about the future so much seems, I don't know, *naive*. No doubt, the Tower has skewed my sense of prudence." She yawned again. "All I know is, I'm grateful for today, and I accept that there may not be an encore."

"All those adventure books I used to read—you know what they all got wrong? The nature of survival. The heroes who survived their ordeals always came out the other end unchanged. Maybe they walked away with a nice little scar on their cheek or a fitting shock of gray hair. But essentially, in all the ways that matter, they emerged the same as they were before." He clucked his tongue and rolled his head upon his pillow. "That's not how it is though, is it? Survival makes you a stranger to yourself."

"Then we can be strangers together."

Tom raised a hand to his headboard and rapped out their signal phrase—hard, soft, hard—a simple tattoo that had come to mean *good night* and *I am glad you are close by* and *please, don't leave* and a hundred other things they'd not yet found the words or courage to say.

~~all evidence are as objects of taste, like the untested fruit of the wilderness; and as it was with those pioneering humans who first sampled the novel fruit of the desert, so shall great men discover that some fictions will poison~~ h~~im and some will give him succor. If a fiction is honest, if it is vetted by~~

Senlin woke slumped over the draining sink with the sulfurous reek of medium clogging his nose.

His cheek ached from the unforgiving steel; one of his legs felt stuffed full of prickling straw. He had no idea what the hour was, but judging from the distant drone of the turbines and the quiet of the wardroom behind him, he supposed it was quite late. His second shift in the wheelhouse would begin soon. Groaning at the thought, he stood and was nearly felled by his numb limb.

His first day as a navigator on the bridge of the Hod King had not gone especially well. Actually, it had been a disaster; the sort of mortification that somehow reinvigorates forgotten embarrassments. In particular, Senlin found his thoughts returning to a family reunion he had attended as a young boy. The affair had seemed to unnerve many of the children there. It was a queasy feeling, after all, to be introduced to a great-aunt who bore a striking resemblance to your father. But Senlin found the experience supremely traumatic. To his eye and ear, the crowded lawn had seemed a battlefield: salutations rang out like bullets; conversations rattled like swords; and laughter whistled and burst like shells from an artillery line.

Utterly terrorized, young Tom had attempted to melt into a holly bush, but he was only partially successful because holly is prickly and Cousin Bertie, the reunion's host, noticed his distress.

The elder cousin, a kindly fellow with a chin-strap beard, tried to cheer Tom up with lemonade and sponge cake. When that failed, Bertie suggested the two of them abscond to his workshop. Delighted, Senlin declared that he *loved* tools and had a toolbox of his own at home, neglecting to mention that his collection of tools began with a tack hammer and ended with a pair of jewelry pliers. He and Cousin Bertie crept along the hedge like a pair of spies to the slate-roofed carriage house that was the elder cousin's refuge and haunt. The old garage was stuffed to the rafters with all manner of awls, saws, rasps, and rulers hung over racks of ball peens, hand drills, and chisels. The air was sweet with mineral oil and sawdust. Senlin was enthralled.

But then, turning to a project on his workbench, Cousin Bertie had asked the young toolbox-owner to pass him the square riffler. Bertie made the request as casually if he were asking for the salt at the dinner table. Suddenly, all the beaming tools began to sneer at young Tom, identifying him as a fraud and an imbecile. When Bertie repeated his request, Senlin fled and hid under the porch with the pill bugs and granddaddy long legs until the sun went down and he heard his grandmother calling his name.

Senlin's experience of the Hod King's wheelhouse that morning had felt like a return to Bertie's workshop. At first, the gauges at his station had all seemed to wink at him, and the toggles held up their little arms in friendly salute. And why not? He was a quick learner, after all, and well-educated, including a little experience with navigation. Surely he could manage a few flicks and switches!

But the moment they were underway and the orders began to flow, the smiling dials all developed a squint and the toggles thumbed their noses at him, the imposter! The fool! When a helmsman asked for his bearings, Senlin first froze, then stuttered out a tangle of numbers and corrections: "Sixty-five... um, fifty-six. Just the second one. I mean, one fifty-six...I mean, a *single instance* of fifty-six." It was impossible to concentrate while the world rattled and the drill roared. He had to be instructed again and again as to the location of each instrument and the means for deciphering the wild pitch of their needles. Sometimes, searching for his bearings, he would press his eye to the lens of the pentascope, and see, of course, nothing. There was no horizon, no scenery. Just an endless dark.

By the time the pilot requested a countdown to the next waypoint, Senlin was so flustered he said, "Fourteen yards, thirteen, twelveteen, eleventeen..." It seemed a minor miracle that he had not gone on to say ten-teen.

On and on the humiliation went. If he'd not been strapped to a chair and suspended at a dangerous angle in a room full of steel edges, he might've attempted to flee. As it was, he could only endure.

And to his credit, over the course of his shift, he had modestly improved. He recalled, at least, how to count, and began to remember the unique importance of each unmarked dial.

Still, the moment it was over, and the Hod King was resting half-erupted outside a newly deserted black trail gatehouse, Tom retired to his sink, ostensibly to crack a fresh peck of bugs, but actually to remove himself from Marat's scrutiny. And upon that unforgiving stool, he had remained hidden through the inscrutable devotional, through dinner, and through his usual evening salon with the zealot in his private quarters. Tom cracked the Sphinx's spies one after another, as if a few drips more might redeem him. He worked until, quite without his permission or notice, he fell asleep.

Limping now on a dead foot down the bare corridor toward the airier wardroom, Senlin wondered which would win the battle of the bunk: his soporific exhaustion or his revitalizing embarrassment. Then he saw that the door to Mr. Gedge's workshop was standing open, and both weariness and shame were displaced by curiosity. A warm and spectral light like the dwindling of a campfire seeped into the darkened hall. When Senlin slowed, he heard muted speech, and he recognized the vocal cadence at once: someone was reading a book aloud.

Half-expecting to be met with shouts, gunshots, or worse, Senlin peered about the edge of the forbidden doorway.

A monstrous knight in dull black armor loomed just inside the door. He was eight feet tall and nearly half as wide at the shoulder, with thin willowy legs and the feet of a bird, each with three long tapering toes. His visor had a comb like a desert bird and the beak of a raptor.

Senlin was so terror-stricken by the vision of the knight that he did not notice the reading had ceased until the former reader, his voice now distinct, addressed him. "Is someone there?" Luc Marat asked.

"It's just me, Tom. I was on my way to bed and heard a voice." Senlin continued to stare at the raven-faced knight and his wicked poleaxe as he listened to the familiar clank of Marat's approaching footsteps.

Leaning into view, Marat smiled at Senlin's transfixion. "Ah, I see you've met Mr. Grudge," Marat said, waving at the suit of armor. Its breastplate was as round as a potbellied stove, and its arms were like pistons: narrow where they met the shoulder and drumlike above the gauntlets, one of which held a halberd bearing an axe-head that was as wild and thorny as the egg sac of a skate.

"Mr. Grudge?"

"That's what I call him, anyway. Gedge doesn't like it." Marat knocked upon the suit's cuirass with the spine of a book. The metal rang as dully as an empty oil drum. "He means to wear this when he kills the Sphinx."

"This is Gedge's suit of armor? Really? It seems a bit . . ." Senlin searched for the most politic term, though Marat was quick to provide him with options.

"Grandiose? Perhaps he went a bit overboard, but since the Sphinx didn't give him a breastplate or a weapon, Gedge felt compelled to make his own. I'm not sure if he's mentioned it before, but our Mr. Gedge is quite a clever fellow."

Senlin pushed a laugh through his nose. "He has mentioned it, in fact. Well, good night Luc, and good night to you, Mr. Grudge." Senlin bowed to the looming suit of armor.

"Wait a moment. You really don't want to see what's behind the hatch? Gedge is asleep, you know. Come on, Tom. I know you want a peek." Marat held a finger to his lips to signal discretion and led without waiting to see if Senlin would follow. Naturally, he did.

Gedge's workshop was as stretched and narrow as a galley kitchen, and as in a galley, Gedge had made judicious use of his space. A long workbench consumed the inner wall and was occupied by unfathomable instruments, actuators, and half-assembled devices, including Thornton's injured foot, which Gedge had lately replaced. Purring cabinets held up branching aerials that flew ribbons of domesticated lightning. The red and yellow eyes of diodes shone from beneath the bench, accompanied by the boggish sounds of pumps and the hiss of hydraulics. Across the narrow aisle, the inner wall was filled with storage shelves that overflowed with wires, pipes, and scrap. The conspicuous clutter reminded Senlin of the Sphinx's desk, though he wasn't sure whether the disarray was an homage or just a common trait of genius.

At the far end of the workroom stood a strange dynamo that scraped the ceiling and touched either wall. Despite this crowding, its sculptural beauty was unobscured. In shape, it reminded Senlin of a titanic sewing machine. An elaborately spoked wheel abutted a horizontal arm, sinuous as a swan's neck, which bent over two glass-sleeved pistons, each grooved like a honey wand. Polished tanks stood in a line beneath the arm, and it was down the front of the foremost reservoir that Senlin spied a long steel-cased pipette, split by a crimson light.

"The medium," he said at a hush. "Wait. Wait, *this* is what I've been filling, isn't it?" This is where the dribbles from all those cracked bugs has drained to." Senlin waited for Marat to answer, but the zealot only smirked and shrugged his leonine shoulders. He did so enjoy playing coy, Senlin thought. "What is it?"

Still at a whisper, Marat answered, "I call it a lifeboat. But Mr. Grudge calls it the Ardennes."

"Incredible," Senlin murmured, as a gentle movement behind Marat drew his eye. Snugged there between the voluptuous turbine and the end of the shelves, Delyth's wrapped arms drifted like a bather in crystalline waters. Senlin caught the gasp before it escaped. Familiarity had scarcely made her appearance less startling. He had not seen her since she had raged against the wardroom wall and Gedge had filled her bubble with an anesthetizing fog.

Marat raised the book he carried once again, and now Senlin could read the cover. "Turns out the *Everyman's Guide* is good for more than kindling; it's a useful sedative as well. She just nodded off."

Senlin studied her carriage. Gedge had replaced the limb that Iren had ripped off, though it did not match the other black legs. The pale steel stood out from the rest like a crescent moon in the night sky. The sight of her brought the skirmish at the Cistern and the loss of Edith to the front of his mind on a wave of guilt and sorrow.

Senlin could not keep the grimace from his face and, knowing that Marat had observed it, quickly said, "Will she be all right?"

Marat looked at her with an expression softer than Senlin was accustomed to seeing him wear. "Gedge wants to keep her sedated, keep pumping her bell full of gas... but it's just as easy to read her to sleep."

"You care for her."

"I care for all my crew," Marat said with a demure smirk. "But yes, Delyth is unique. To comprehend her, you must first understand the culture of the drove spider, which is not so dissimilar from ants, I think. They are a colony, a unity: a body of many but a mind of one. She had been stranded on the Silk Reef for *decades*. The further the ringdom descended into neglect, the more the flora flourished, and the drove spiders multiplied, and the spider-eaters grew fat." Marat stroked the glass over Delyth's bandaged brow. "Once upon a time, she was as much an attraction as the Golden Zoo: a marvel of engineering and survival.

"But the years of isolation eroded her sense of self. She followed the drove because they alerted her to the presence of spider-eaters, and eventually she went from being their shadow to their adherent—a party to the clan. That's when I found her. She was wild and skittish. It took time to convince her that I was not her enemy and could never be because the drove were also a part of me, much as the hods are, much as all the life in this dying biome are extensions of my soul. For every arm the Sphinx has, I have eight legs!"

Perceiving his cue to heap a little praise, Senlin said, "How true! But how did you discover she enjoys being read to?"

"Well, I'd heard that jockeys read to their steeds, and farmers to their prize bulls. A commanding voice in the ear of a simple mind is old magic, Tom. And if she is anesthetized, she can't be easily awoken. I need to keep her sharp and nearby."

Even as Senlin felt a flurry of sympathy for Delyth's appalling fate, he again gaped at the province of Marat's ego. What Senlin had initially mistaken as genuine affection for another person was in fact just another expression of Marat's megalomania. What Marat admired in Delyth most was not her resilience or her character but her utility to him.

"May I ask you something?" Senlin asked, and Marat tilted his head ever so slightly, the nod of a regent who could move armies with a shrug and wring necks with a wink. "Why the wheelchair? Why pretend to be lame? Your legs are evidence of your triumph over hardship. They are unique, formidable, handsome, yet you sit in a modest chair and hide them under a ratty afghan."

Marat clasped his hands behind his back. "Do you know why the Sphinx closed up shop?"

"No, I don't."

"During the last gala he ever held in his home, there was a lapse in security and a revelation that changed the way the Tower thought of him. It was only afterward that the Sphinx became a bugbear, a devourer of children, an immortal snake in the hearts and minds of the ringdoms."

"What happened at the party?"

"There was an assassination attempt. One of the attending lords had smuggled in a little pistol. He shot the Sphinx, several times, in the middle of a waltz."

"How do you know this?"

"Byron told me. I used to be able to get him to tell me anything. Well, almost anything."

"But obviously the Sphinx survived his injuries?"

"Worse, he was completely unharmed. The three bullets seemed to pass right through him. One hit the piano, another struck a potted plant, and the last pierced an unlucky trumpeter who survived his wounds, though the Sphinx's reputation did not. Before that, everyone could pretend that the Sphinx was only an eccentric who liked to wear long dark robes and looking-glass masks. Though strange, he still threw excellent parties, poured strong drinks, and told good jokes."

"The Sphinx told jokes?"

"Oh certainly. He's an accomplished socialite—well, he *was* until three bullets passed through him and exposed him as a ghoul. What actually happened, I'm quite sure, was that the bullets struck the Sphinx's armor and ricocheted about the room, but that's not what the people there believed. They believed the Sphinx was a monstrous ghost wearing a cowl. No gifts, jokes, or jigs could make him human again. Now, perhaps you look at me and see only a cripple..."

Discerning the pause, Senlin hurried to fill it: "I do not!"

Marat smiled. "...but my followers see me as a hod, someone who is not so unlike them. There's a reason that the Sphinx's Wakemen are, over and over, ostracized and rejected by the people they protect. They, like the Sphinx, are *too* strange, too... unapproachable." Senlin found it telling that in Marat's eyes, the Sphinx's error had not been one of policy, but rather performance. The zealot went on: "If I walked around on golden stalks that could stamp a man into jelly, I'd be as reviled as the Sphinx. The hods would not follow me, fight for me, die for me. No, it is essential that the cretins be allowed to see a bit of themselves in me."

Covering his surprise at the zealot's explicit abuse of his own followers, Senlin smiled and said, "You flatter them."

"Just so. And this act won't go on forever. No, this is just... what would the academics call it... my *exposition*. It's a little tedious, I grant you, but necessary. To take the throne, you can't begin by posing as a king. You must first introduce yourself as a servant: *Oh, the throne is not mine, but ours,* etcetera, etcetera. It's why I keep my Wakemen secluded from the rest of the camp and crew. If they knew our true strength, they would fear us. They would break and run—as they should. It's too soon for such terror to be useful. First, the masses must be coddled and made beholden, then given no alternative, and at last, when their fear is as potent as awe, they will have forgotten any illusion that they were ever my equal. Have no doubt, Tom, I will *stand* at my coronation, and all the Tower shall kneel."

As Senlin listened to Marat again expose the lavishness of his vanity, it dawned upon him how simple the world was in the eyes of a zealot. Everyone was either an implement or an idiot, a rung or an impediment, and the Tower was but a toy he had promised himself. His was not a complex philosophy, but rather an august sort of childishness. Civility, wisdom, and empathy required growth, sacrifice, a willingness to change, but evil never grew up. Evil was as callow and foolish at the end of itself as it was at the start.

Senlin could tell Marat was tiring of their conversation. Having lanced the boil of his swollen ego, the zealot seemed both anesthetized by relief and repulsed by his own honesty. He was, Senlin thought, like a patron of a brothel who flies from ecstasy to the exits at a sprint.

Still, Senlin could not resist one last question: "The person who shot the Sphinx, do you know why they did it?"

Marat sneered, apparently surprised that Senlin would find such a trivial detail interesting, especially after listening to such a lucid vision of victory. "Him? Let's see... I believe Byron said there was a certain lord who was displeased with the Sphinx for repossessing a gift. The Sphinx was always so fussy about how his machines were deployed. If he found out that you were using his street sweeper to pull cannons or his sewer augers to auger your enemies, well, he took it as a personal affront. The Sphinx believed that more elegant tools would somehow elevate our race. In his naivete, he envisioned a hammer that would only hammer nails, never fingers, never skulls. His idealism exposed him to disappointment, and that's why his reign ultimately failed." Marat's eyes cut toward the door. "But enough talk. Tomorrow's an important day. Vital, in fact. I know you'll do better at your post. I believe in you, Tom, and that belief is a currency unto itself. I don't like to see my investments squandered."

"I understand. I will do better. Much better."

"Of course you shall. Now, off to bed. Tomorrow, the raid upon heaven begins!"

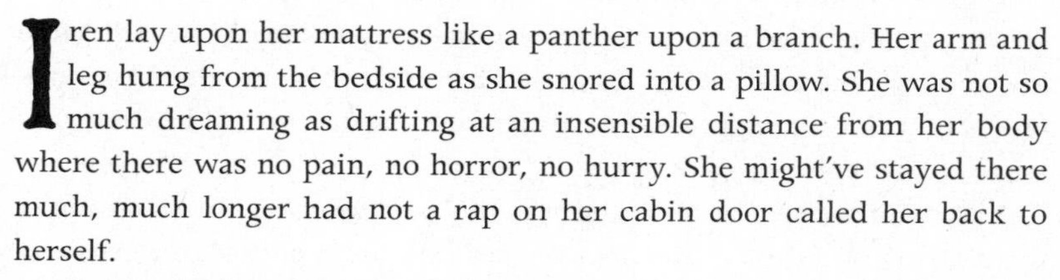

Chapter Thirteen

Do not waste the limited resource of your patience on those who think misery a competition. Spendthrifts of self-pity are always miserly the moment empathy is due.

—*Everyman's Guide to the Tower of Babel*, VI. V

Iren lay upon her mattress like a panther upon a branch. Her arm and leg hung from the bedside as she snored into a pillow. She was not so much dreaming as drifting at an insensible distance from her body where there was no pain, no horror, no hurry. She might've stayed there much, much longer had not a rap on her cabin door called her back to herself.

The deep ache of her puncture wounds returned at once. She moaned when she rolled onto her ribs. Through one squinting eye, she saw the stag standing in her hatchway. His jacket was buttoned, his collar pressed, his cravat plump as a mum. He appeared fully and irritatingly composed. If she'd had something heavy at hand, she might've thrown it at him.

"Captain wants us to assemble in the observatory. Or the chart house, or whatever we're calling it at the moment."

Iren patted about the bedclothes, her senses returning. "Where's Ann?"

"I assumed she was here. But perhaps she got an early start. It is noon, after all. Would you gather her, please? I still have to rouse the captain."

Iren sat up, discovering a new point of agony along the way. Through clenched teeth she said, "I thought she called the meeting."

"Well, she's about to." The long beam of Byron's mouth curled into a hard, humorless smile.

Iren raised a pillow to throw at him, but the stag was already gone.

Iren stepped into the hall, still grappling with the buttons of her shirt. She hated buttons, at least the tiny pearly discs that Ann was so fond of. They slipped through her thick fingers when she pinched them and resisted the buttonholes like a dog would a bath. If Ann ever left her, Iren would have to rip her clothes off and go back to wearing flour sacks.

She looked up from her fiddling effort when her boots tangled on a length of bloody gauze. Though it now seemed like the distant past, when they'd first boarded the *State of Art* it had been as tidy as a hotel lobby. Now it looked like a field hospital. Blood darkened the walls and rugs and spattered the frosted glass of the stateroom doors. Bandages lay in piles among tufts of cotton wadding and chair legs broken to make splints. The cabins were worse: gory, ransacked, and haunted by the misery they'd witnessed. Beside one red-spattered bed, a broken necklace lay on the floors, its pearls spilled, its shells crushed.

Iren was nearly to the stairs when she heard something: a small, strangled sound that was enlarged by the quiet. She followed the noise to a broom closet and pressed her ear to the narrow door. It sounded like someone was trying to suppress a cough and failing to over and over again. "Ann, is that you?"

The noise stopped at once and was replaced by the sound of sniffing, the clearing of a throat. The door opened, and Ann presented a crooked, fragile smile that seemed pinned on. Her cheeks were wet, her eyes red.

"Do you want to come out?" Iren asked.

Ann's chin sank as she said, "Midwife Ina Day said, 'If you can't be useful, be elsewhere.' And so, I'm here, because I can't be useful right now." The last word out, her brave face broke. She caught the sob in the cup of her hand.

"Then I'll come in." Iren ducked her head and pressed into the closet. The buckets at their feet clanged and the handles of mops fell in protest as Iren consumed what little room was left in the cuddy. With Ann fairly pinned against her, Iren reached out and pulled the door closed. A small electric bulb lit their faces like a candle. Iren said, "We can be elsewhere together."

Ann wet the front of Iren's half-done shirt while Iren stroked her head, her pinned-up hair, the back of her thin neck, and murmured the ancient incantation of comfort: *There, there. Shh. It's all right.*

When at last Ann could speak, she said, "I woke up early. I meant to get a jump on the cleaning. But then I saw it all again, and it was . . . too much. I came to the closet for a brush and pail and couldn't quite bring myself to leave again."

"You don't have to hide."

"Everyone here is so strong. I've always thought myself a stoic, but that was when I was only faced with brats and brutes and miserly wages, but this is . . ." She squeezed her hand into the pocket of her apron and pulled out a small folded piece of paper that had blood on one corner. "A man asked me to take down his last words to his family. He kept saying, 'Tell them I love them, how much they mean to me, but say it better than that, *say it better*.' But of course, I can't think of how to possibly say it any better than that, because in the end, there's nothing eloquent about death. There aren't words sufficient to express the final squeals of the heart, except 'I love you.' "

"I love you, too, Ann. I don't want you to think the rest of us aren't touched by all this violence and suffering and stupidity. I get angry. Very angry. Captain drinks. Voleta runs away. Byron dresses up and pretends nothing has happened, nothing is wrong. He sits us down and pours us tea. And if you need to cry, there's no shame in it. It doesn't make you weak. You've carried me for days. That takes a lot of strength. I know I can be a burden."

"Oh, no, no. You're light as a feather. I could carry you forever."

They embraced among the dustpans and detergents. The ship hummed to them as their bodies grew warm.

Ann broke the hug and leaned back as much as she could to survey the great expanse of Iren's chest. "Are you sure you didn't come looking for me just because you couldn't do up your shirt? Look at this, you're one button off all the way up—well, as far as you got, anyway." As the fingers of one hand undid Iren's crooked work, unbuttoning each at a snap, Ann's other hand cupped Iren's round jaw. "Well, I suppose we'll just have to start again from the top and work our way down."

Edith had been almost amused to discover that Byron had arranged five chairs in a semicircle on the observatory floor. There was something quaint about it, as if they had been gathered to play a game of charades. In the seat beside her, Marya nursed Olivet under the tent of a swaddling cloth.

At her elbow, Voleta perched upon the edge of her seat and leaned upon the Sphinx's painting, still scrolled inside its diamond tube, as if it were a cane. Voleta stared fixedly at the grand model of the Tower before them. The mountainous map ticked and whirred like a clockmaker's shop. Byron paced in its shadow, his bootheels clicking the parquet with mechanical regularity. He usually made such an effort to affect a human gait, having studied all the minutiae of movement that distinguished the loping grace of a man. Now, he marched back and forth like a windup doll.

Edith sat with her engine on her knees, greasing the joints of her arm with a small oilcan. The oiler gave a little cluck each time she pumped its base. She found the sound reassuring. And she could use some reassurance, having recently been awoken by Byron, who announced that he and Reddleman had something they needed to show her. She did not expect happy news, and yet her head was still befogged by too little sleep and too many hours on her feet to predict the misfortune he would unveil.

"So good of you to join us," Byron said as Iren and Ann entered with flushed cheeks. They looked like tardy students hurrying to class.

"Just doing a bit of mopping up," Ann said lightly, before appearing to reassess the mood of the room. She took her seat quickly and folded her hands in her lap.

Reddleman stood by the tele-vibrissa's controls, set inside the ornate woodland scene that bordered the room. He turned down the halo of light, and the beacon that marked the model *State of Art*'s proximity to the Tower shone brighter.

"So, we'll begin." Byron halted his march and clasped his hands behind his back. "Soon after you embarked upon the Cistern, the Hod King began to move, and quickly." Byron signaled Reddleman to replay the span of time via the chronograph. The little scales that faced the model of the Tower fluttered to the side to show the track of the light within. "See, here's when it entered the Tower again at the base of the ringdom of Jinst. It moved up and along through the wall, around here, then onto the shelf between ringdoms, and out toward the Tower's spine where it intercepted you."

Edith noticed that the engine's path did not proceed at a steady incline, but wove this way and that, twisting like the bore of a termite. It was a moment more before the more concerning implication dawned on her.

"He didn't stop along the way," she said. The oilcan cluck-clucked again under her thumb, though its comfort was quickly fading. She had tried to get out ahead of the Hod King only to be cut off again. She had counted on it progressing at a more deliberate speed.

"So, we can only assume Marat knew the Sphinx had already recalled the paintings from Jinst, Harrakesh, and Valadi." Byron pointed at each ringdom as he named it.

"His spies have been busy." Edith wasn't particularly surprised. Marat's infiltration of Pelphia had been remarkably well-orchestrated, as had his more recent campaign of terrorizing the shipyards and navies of the Tower with suicidal saboteurs. The leaders of the three ringdoms she'd lately convinced to take in her injured refugees had each expressed alarm at these erratic, unprovoked acts of violence. Two of the ringdoms had taken the extreme steps of purging their cities of hods. People who'd worked as launderers, scullery maids, custodians, and dockers for years without trouble found themselves suddenly expelled from their modest lives, their honest efforts to pay down their debts. They'd been rounded up and turned out onto the already overcrowded black trail. Which of course had been Marat's aim: to spread suspicion, foment unrest, all to the ends of making more zealots.

"He's been more than busy, I'm afraid," Byron said, signaling Reddleman. "This is the Hod King's course over the past forty-eight hours." The white spark again drew near the Tower surface and there continued its winding climb. When it curved out of sight, they all stood and followed its circuit. Byron rattled off the names of the ringdoms as the *Hod King* surmounted them. When it rose above Ann's head, he said, "Tuwin: twentieth ringdom." When it tunneled past Edith's crown, he said, "Rasanadra: twenty-third ringdom." When it crested Iren's gray mane, he said, "Japhet: twenty-sixth ringdom."

And still the Hod King's corkscrewing ascent did not slow. Edith was forced to retreat a few paces to keep sight of it as it crested the Tower's midpoint and moved into the upper ringdoms. The higher it climbed, the lower her heart sank in her chest.

Edith rifled through her pockets and drew out a much-handled square of paper. She unfolded it, read again what she already knew, and let her hand drop.

"Well. That's it, then," she said.

"What is?" Marya asked.

"After the Cistern, he hasn't stopped at any of the places on my list of possible holdouts. That can only mean he already has the paintings. As long as he didn't have more than eight, we had a chance. But now..."

Edith had expected the game of cat and mouse to go on for weeks, perhaps months. Suddenly she found herself running short of opportunity. She'd thought there'd be time for the Sphinx to recover and reopen his doors, time enough for them to snatch up a sufficient number of the paintings to unlock the bridge and tame the boiling sea.

"How many does he have?" Iren asked.

Edith shook her head to collect herself. "By my count? Eighteen of the remaining twenty-eight, at least. Or he could have them all."

"Not all," Voleta piped up, raising the diamond tube that contained the Cistern's copy of *The Brick Layer's Granddaughter.*

"It's not enough, I'm afraid."

"But it's a start," Voleta protested.

Byron intervened before Edith could reply. "I don't think you understand, Miss Voleta. Marat doesn't need us to unlock the bridge. We need *him.*"

"What are you saying? We should make friends? Oh, hullo, Luc! Hullo, spider lady! Forgive me if I don't shake your hand!"

"Captain, there's something else I'd like you to see," Reddleman said, interrupting Voleta's blustering ire. "The Hod King has not moved since this morning. It's been sitting right there for four hours."

Edith squinted at the spot. "Why?"

"Because he built an earth mover, but the Tower is not the Earth. Observe," the pilot said, and toggled a switch that made the model bloom with veins of light, dense as capillaries in some places, sparser in others. "The green lines are sewers; the yellow are freshwater plumbing; the white are gas lines; the blue, electrical conduits. Most are made out of lead or iron, though there's probably some steel in there as well. I don't think his machine can chew through them. That, or he's afraid of being gassed, or shocked, or drowned in sewage. That's why their progress is so erratic. That's why they had to surface at Oyodin. They weren't attacking us; they were circumventing a roadblock. And see, they're stuck again. They'll have to surface to get around this cluster of gas pipes."

"Well, why haven't they?"

"Fear of us, most likely," Reddleman said, crossing his arms and tucking in his chin. "We may've done more damage than we thought when the Hod King was out in the open. Or perhaps Marat knows that his siege engine is only as stout as its footing. He's worried we'll knock his legs out from under him. Which we probably could."

"No! We can't do that," Byron said in alarm. "If that monstrosity falls from that height with that much black powder aboard..." He pounded a gloved fist into the cup of his hand. "The crater would be enormous. The paintings would be lost, and the Tower with them."

"True, but we fired on him once, so he thinks we might again," Reddleman said. "I suspect he's waiting for the cover of darkness. He'll slip out when the moon's behind the Tower. That's what I would do."

"I assume we all see where this is leading, don't we?" Byron said, searching each of their faces. "He's marching on the Sphinx, encroaching upon my home. After he kills my master, Luc Marat will have an army of hods and a battalion of engines at his disposal. He will sit upon a reserve of energy sufficient to power his conquests for decades. The Tower will become like a club held over the head of mankind. All will bow to it and its master."

"Is he really so wicked?" Ann asked.

"I recall the arguments between the Sphinx and Wakeman Luc Marat quite well. They were frequent, heated, and toward the end, antagonistic. Luc was bright and could be very charming, or perhaps it would be more accurate to call him pleasantly duplicitous. But it was clear to me, if not always to the Sphinx, that he never accepted my master's philosophy. He particularly disagreed with the Sphinx's habit of sharing technology and resources with the inhabitants of the Tower. Luc saw the Sphinx as giving away what could be sold. If the ringdoms wanted electricity, plumbing, access to the air, or the protection of the Wakemen, they should pay for it with both money and deference. He accused the Sphinx of shirking his responsibilities. The Sphinx should be a benevolent king, Luc believed, not a recluse living among the clouds.

"But there was nothing benevolent about Luc's vision for ruling the Tower. He saw no difference between the bull snails and chimney cats the Brick Layer bred, the engines the Sphinx built, and the hods who filled the walls: All were insensible instruments to be used. Luc called the Tower an empty throne, a seat which someone would one day take. The only way to protect it, he said, was to claim it. When the Sphinx would not, they had a parting of ways. It didn't take Luc long to figure out how to disable the Sphinx's ability to track him. For years and years after, we didn't know where he was or what he was doing. I hoped he had died, but the Sphinx always thought he was too ambitious for that."

"So, if I understand what you're saying: We have to choose between a despot and letting this 'lightning sea' explode?" Ann said.

"Hardly seems like a choice," Iren said. "Kings can be overthrown, but dead is dead."

"We don't have to bend the knee quite yet," Reddleman said. "Since we know where he's going, we can also guess how he means to get there. The thing about the Sphinx's home is that not only is it quite secure, it is surrounded by a snarl of pipes and cables. Assuming that he would be foiled by the same external defenses that we are, he'll have to dig his way in. Let me see—" Reddleman began to hunt through a bank of toggles, pointing to each as he mused to himself, "Is it you? No. You? No. Ah! Yes, it's you." He flipped the switch and the model before them began to shrink as the hoops of the lower ringdoms collapsed, bringing the pinnacle of the monolith down to chest level. The roof of the Tower was dominated by an opaque dome that gave very little sense of what lay inside it. It was surrounded by open level ground like the brim of a bowler hat. This expanse shone with many threads of blue light, indicating a complex circuit of electric cabling. Though it was only a model, seeing what lay hidden behind the eternal bank of clouds filled Edith with awe. She thought of the sparking men Adam had surrendered to. It was strange to think of them all living under a tortoise shell.

"What is that?" Ann asked.

"That is Nebos," Byron said. "The jewel of the Tower, the Brick Layer's pride, the garden of heaven. Or so I've heard. I've not had the pleasure of visiting it myself."

"That's where Adam is," Voleta said, her voice faint with affection and, it seemed to Edith, perhaps a little guilt as well.

"Let me try one more thing," Reddleman said, and after a few adjustments, gaps opened between the hoops of the model, allowing them to see more clearly inside. Reddleman joined their circle as they peered into the maze of light and metal. Even stretched out, the Sphinx's home was inscrutable, a fact that Edith suspected was entirely purposeful. The Sphinx would not wish to bare all his secrets to the monarchs and generals who had sailed on his flagship. But details of the ringdom directly beneath the Sphinx's home were more distinct. By following the gas lines, she could deduce the presence of roads. Vertical threads of blue suggested the presence of buildings and city blocks. At the center of it all was the Tower's ubiquitous spine.

"The ringdom of Cilicia, vineyard of the clouds," Byron said.

Reddleman pressed a finger into the twinkling assemblage. "I think this is where Marat will pierce the Sphinx's shell. See, all around the spine there is a layer of insulating and supportive rock that's maybe a hundred, a hundred and twenty feet thick. It'll be a tight squeeze for him. If he pierces the lightning stack, he'll sorely regret it... albeit briefly. The point is, the Hod King will have to pass through the open cavity of the ringdom, scrabble up the spine, and bore a hole in the ceiling. If we attack it there, we wouldn't have to worry about it falling off the Tower. We'd have to worry about everything else: the guns, the Quibbler, the spider lady, et cetera, but not gravity."

"A last stand," Iren said.

"I was thinking more of a trap," Reddleman said.

"What sort of a trap?" Edith asked.

"I don't know. Maybe we could smoke them out, or gas them, something that would kill the crew but leave the paintings unharmed."

"I suppose we've given up on Tom, then?" Marya said, fussing with Olivet's swaddle. It seemed to Edith a pretense to avoid looking them in the eye. Marya was not ready to hear the unwanted truth, any more than Edith was ready to speak it. But the continued existence of the Tower could not pivot upon the survival of one person, no matter how beloved.

Voleta hurried to fill the awkward silence that threatened. "Senlin's more clever than anyone ever gives him credit for. I'm sure he isn't just sitting on his hands. He'll have a hundred ideas for sabotage and escape! There'll be devices! Disguises! Once he had us all dress up like swooning ladies, and—"

"I'm sorry, is that really our plan? Hope that he saves himself?" Marya's volume crept upward. Olivet fussed in her lap.

Voleta's propped up cheerfulness collapsed. "I didn't mean it like that."

Marya pinched the bridge of her nose. "No, forgive me. I... I know you're being hopeful. And I appreciate it. I just... can we please talk about some alternatives to gassing him?"

"Indeed, we shall," Edith said. "How much time do he have to lay our trap, whatever it is?"

"Assuming he continues to tread lightly, I'd say we have three days." Reddleman showed them the various dead ends the Hod King would encounter and explained why Marat would likely avoid lengthy circumnavigations across the face of the Tower in favor of brief exposures. He would weave in and out like a needle. "Of course, there's no way to be sure. We'll have to keep a close eye on him."

Their assembly at an end, they began to disperse. When Voleta passed her seat, Marya took her hand and squeezed it, apologizing again for snapping at her. Voleta murmured that it was all right, but the dreamy, hazy look had returned to her gaze. Her attention, her presence had drifted down another historical rabbit hole. Her ambivalence appeared to do nothing to alleviate Marya's guilt. Still, she managed to compose herself at Edith's approach.

"I'm tired of feeling helpless, Captain. What can I do? Please don't say laundry."

"I'd like you to resume your piloting lessons with Mr. Reddleman. I'm afraid I'm going to need him and Iren both for our upcoming adventure."

"Aye, sir. I can do that. And I know Voleta's right. Tom is clever. Perhaps all we need to do is give him an opening, a chance. Just leave the door cracked, as it were. I'm so grateful to you for not giving up on him."

Edith formed her mouth into a smile because it was the kindest way to endorse the lie.

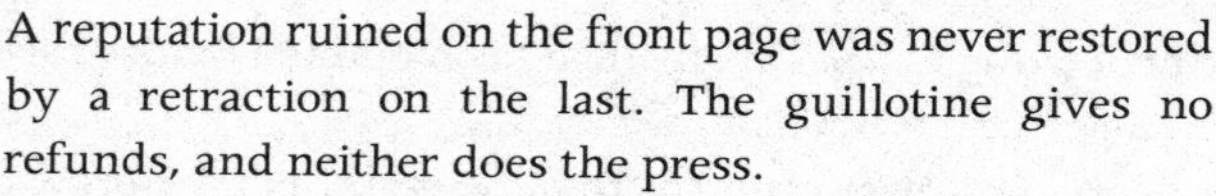

Chapter Fourteen

A reputation ruined on the front page was never restored by a retraction on the last. The guillotine gives no refunds, and neither does the press.

—*Everyman's Guide to the Tower of Babel*, XII. I

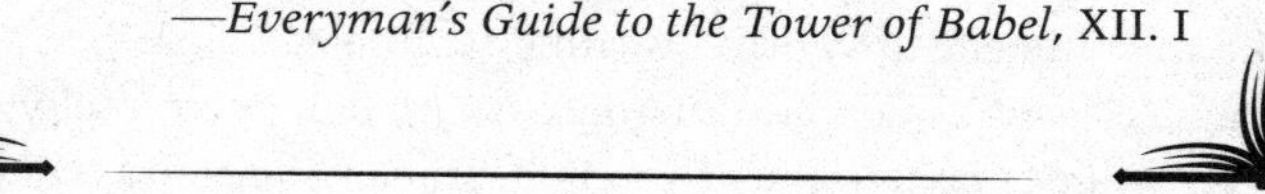

It looks like we've attracted an admirer, Captain." Reddleman jutted his lower lip at the magnovisor over his pilot's station. The vessel in question seemed no larger than an inkblot.

Edith left her captain's chair to see what he was pouting at. "Well, that's a funny-looking ship." She reached over Reddleman's shoulder to tune a garnet-studded dial, bringing the craft into closer relief.

Its massive green envelope billowed and bunched like the canopy of an old oak. The silhouette of the much smaller gondola that swung beneath it was unmistakably that of an acorn, though one composed of milky panes of glass, soldered together with lead and girdled by rings of tarnished brass. It called to mind a gaudy lamp, the sort of thing one might find hanging in the lobby of a bawdy house. "You must be joking."

"Is that *The Acorn*? Come to pick a fight? Seems a bit ambitious. Should I hail Mister Iren?"

"No, she needs to catch up on her sleep. Besides, I think we can handle this on our own. You see those flags in the rigging?" Edith cracked her back and swung her arms to loosen her muscles. "He's asking for permission to come aboard."

Reddleman gave a disbelieving scoff. "*Very* ambitious! Shall I fire a warning shot?"

"No need." Edith swept her hair back and screwed it down under her cocked hat. She strode to the weapons cabinet.

"What are you doing, Captain?"

"I'm going to meet him on deck with a knife and a fork and a napkin tucked in my shirt. I never pass up a free meal."

Edith stood alone above deck. A brisk wind whistled across the spout of her tricorne and raised the hair on her skin. She enjoyed the sensation—a renewed thrill of flight. That feeling had been blunted by days spent on an enclosed bridge staring at a painted sky.

At her back, the Tower erupted from the earth like the prow of a shipwreck, a monument to vanity, warning, and loss. Before her, the mountain range carved clouds into ribbons that spilled down rocky clefts and bunched against the tree line. Even midsummer she could still detect the faint scent of snow.

She had no doubt that if Iren knew of the meeting, she would've insisted on accompanying her, which was why Edith had not told her, nor indeed anyone other than her pilot, who'd expressed a little puzzlement over the secrecy. Edith could not quite bring herself to admit that she wished to meet the editor alone in case she felt called to violence. She did not enjoy being observed as she crushed hands, drowned men, or pinned men on her sword. She was ashamed, or more truthfully, she was protective of her crew's belief that she was a decent person, an illusion that her keenness for murder would someday surely dispel. But why hurry that grim revelation along?

Edith had selected from the armory a saber with a fearsome curved blade and a serpentine handguard, not because she was particularly fond of the weapon—she found it poorly balanced and unwieldy, and had always favored a rapier—but because of the impression it made, especially upon those unaccustomed to bloodshed, as she supposed the aging editor could only be. She wore the blade bare and tucked into a sash knotted about her waist. The arrangement was inconvenient and unsafe but absolutely daunting.

The fact was, she had not yet decided what she would do to the editor, but if her appearance rendered him a quivering, quaking mess, it might inspire in her feelings of mercy. She wore the naked scimitar not for her safety, but his.

The middeck of *The Acorn* bulged around a pair of bay doors, which now opened to release to the air a green box kite. When the kite swooped near enough for Edith to catch it with her boat hook, she brought it in and freed it of the tether it carried. She lashed the line to the ship's mooring mast before releasing the kite again. Once the tether was winched taut, a small carriage appeared in the mouth of the open bay. The ornately carved box slid down the sloped cord, its progress checked by a brake line. It was an impressive entrance that could've been spoiled by the swat of a sword. Edith couldn't decide whether the editor's boldness was a symptom of arrogance or lunacy.

Once the palanquin lighted upon her deck, Edith saw the little carriage was quite worn. Cracks marred the scrolls of ebony, punctures defaced the door's gilded screen, and rust shadowed its hinges. A faint coughing announced the presence of the person inside, a fit that continued as the door opened, and a slight woman in a gray silk robe stepped out. Her hair was black as candle soot, her skin was pale as tallow. She dragged with her a cumbersome cane that seemed to slow her advance rather than assist it. Then, at the discreet plying of a switch, the editor's cane sprouted legs. She unfolded a crowning plate and took a seat upon her stool.

"Forgive me for sitting," she said between chugging coughs. She lifted a handkerchief to her mouth, shifted something into it, swabbed her lips, and squirreled it away in one of her voluminous sleeves. Though she appeared to be Edith's junior by a decade, her eyes were sunken and her complexion waxy. Her chin was as prominent as the toe of a boot. Edith supposed she had been beautiful once, before the wasting illness had settled in.

Her visitor's miserable state left Edith feeling a little embarrassed by her own puffed-up appearance, and this sparked annoyance because she did not want to feel pity for the editor's emissary. It seemed an unfair ploy. "Where's Kilgore?" she asked.

"I am the editor," the lady said, drawing her collar up about her thin neck. She shivered nearly to rattling at the passing of a breeze.

"You're Samuel Kilgore? I expected someone older, more . . . bearded."

"My name is Imelda," she said. "I inherited the publication and the nom de plume from my father, who took it over from his father."

"Why not write under your own name?"

"People don't like change. No one wants to hear what Imelda Kilgore thinks."

"Why are you here, Imelda Kilgore?"

"I suppose you hate me."

"Oh, no. No, I'm very fond of being accused of devouring babies, cavorting with wizards, and kidnapping virgins. Tell me, what was I supposed to do with them?"

Imelda smiled thinly. "Slay them upon an altar so the Sphinx could collect their blood for his bath."

"Yes, of course."

"We have a friend in common who—"

"Believe me, we have no friends in common. In fact, the more you write, the fewer friends I have at all. You would turn the Tower against me."

The editor straightened on her perch, her shoulder bones jutting beneath her wrap. "That's not true. My words inspire no conversions. People only read what they already believe to be true, and if they encounter something that seems to disagree with their beliefs, they bend it into agreement, and if it cannot be bent, then they call it a conspiracy and cast it away!" The zeal with which the editor spoke appeared to exhaust her, and she was forced to pause to catch her breath. Once she had, she continued at a more constrained pace. "All I do is elaborate upon existing impressions. There are many who believe the Sphinx to be a sinister fellow. I did not make it so. Perhaps they find him suspicious because of his high address, his interloping influence, or his curious machines. Probably, they just believe what their fathers did.

"But for every reader who slaps the page and says, *See, I knew it all along!* there's another sort of person who looks upon my work and my audience with sorrowful disdain. They tut-tut the simpletons who have failed to realize I play to their fears. This discerning person knows the Sphinx is only an institution, a historical vestige. He is at worst a busybody, at best benign, and the only people who'd ever think him a cannibal are children and miscreants. So, the intellectual has his beliefs confirmed, as well. Everyone leaves happy and vindicated and feeling a little sorry for the poor cockeyed so-and-so who cannot see the truth even when it is laid plainly before him. As I said, I do not convert. I expound. I tell stories."

"Stories are not without consequence."

"Perhaps. The human race will march into the darkness singing songs and telling stories because that is who we are and what we do."

"I don't think you appreciate what's at stake here. I'm trying to stave off the end of civilization and you're not making it any easier with your talk of cannibals and rituals and witchcraft."

Imelda Kilgore coughed—three quick, wet claps—and again raised her handkerchief to receive the result. This time, Edith saw the gleam of blood. "Everything is always ending," the editor said.

"You shouldn't mistake longevity for permanence. The Tower could fall."

"Of course it could. And eventually, it must. How else could we begin again?"

"You're quite smug for someone who flies about in a chandelier baiting gunships."

"Well, we both know you can't kill me without proving my point. Besides, what's the rush? The job will be done soon enough."

"Why are you here?"

"As I said, we have a friend in common: the Mermaid, the Lady Pell-No-Longer."

"You know Marya?"

"I am what you would call an admirer. We have never met, but I have seen her perform on several occasions. I initially went with the intention of writing something awful about her. It's such a lurid little tale. But I lost my venom after hearing her play."

"Unnamed noble," Edith murmured.

"Pardon?"

"You wrote that I had maimed an 'unnamed noble.' But you knew who it was."

"Yes, I did. I hear things. I pay well for good gossip. I understand Marya is in your care."

Edith folded her arms in answer.

"Hmm. You should've killed him when you had the chance. The duke has not taken his humiliation well. The past two days, I have heard what I would call unsettling rumors. He is liquidating his fortune. Already his home has been sold. And he's been seeking out information about you and your ship, paying handsomely for any intelligence. I don't think he has learned much, but I know he is not done with her."

"I don't understand why you care."

"She is something rare for me; a truth I cannot exaggerate. She is a talent, entire, and purely of herself. She made me realize that I have wasted my short life. I've made a mark, but the mark was not mine. I told the stories people wished to hear, not the ones I wished to tell."

"What do you want? Pity?"

"I want you to be on guard. Your reputation protects you from the navies of the Tower, but not from him. He is mad, and rich, and may raise a fleet against you. If he can't have her for himself, I think Wilhelm would kill her and the child."

Her knowledge of Olivet seemed proof that the editor was good at mining secrets. Edith could not dismiss her warning as merely salacious. "Why don't you write about him? Drag the duke through the mud?"

"Because he would like it if I did. And it might rally more to his cause. Besides, I write about fictional monsters, not actual ones." The editor rose and turned her stool back into a cane. She returned to her litter slowly, her shoulders stooped with the fatigue of the effort.

Taking the seat inside, Imelda was about to shut the door when Edith stopped her, saying, "If you're going to make us ogres, could you at least make us more frightening? Say we breathe fire and spit acid and that we are as numerous as flies. We take no quarter, and we don't eat our enemies because they are unworthy of our table. And virgins? Really? Please."

Imelda smiled thinly, tilting her head in a vague gesture of understanding if not assent. Then she shut the gilded screen to conceal a fresh expulsion of her lungs.

Chapter Fifteen

The holdings of a ringdom's Lost and Found are auctioned off according to their perishable nature: lost milk, bread, and cut flowers are sold after a day; lost fruit and leafy vegetables are sold after three days; lost onions, tubers, and children after a week; hard cheese and smoked meat go on the block after a fortnight.

—*Everyman's Guide to the Tower of Babel*, I. VII

Marya leaned over the yoke of the *State of Art* as if it were the handlebars of a bicycle that she was pedaling uphill. At her side, Olivet slept in a wicker bassinet, buried to her cheeks in blankets. Over the bank of controls opposite them, gilded frames full of fluid shadows displayed the Tower cut into pieces by the ship's many eyes. In one, the great pillar of Ur stood stark as a butte, its many ornaments ironed out by distance. In another, a falcon preened its wings on a desolate ledge.

"Watch the wind. It's hitting your portside. You're drifting. You need to compensate. That's it. There you are. Straight as an arrow," Reddleman said.

Marya's green ensign's coat was buttoned to her throat. From its hem, the cream-colored skirts of her morning robe flowed. She peered over the jewelry case of indicators at the magnovisor above, then thrust her chin at the airship that lazed near the corner of the frame. "He's getting rather close, isn't he? Should I pass behind him?"

At her elbow, Reddleman rocked on his feet. "No, you're fine. This is a good tack."

"It's so big! Look at all those guns! I suppose we're fairly imposing ourselves. I always thought the sky was immense, but it seems a lot smaller when you're piloting a ship through it. The same is true of flying a kite, I'll have you know. Tom used to say if there was one tree in a field, I'd find a way to hit it."

Leaning forward in her captain's chair, Edith made a strangled noise.

"What was that, Captain?" Reddleman asked over his shoulder.

"Nothing. I was... Nothing," Edith said, pressing her mouth into her knuckles.

"What you experienced with your kite, Marya, is a documented phenomenon. It's called 'target fixation.' It's when you stare so intently at an obstacle or a hazard that you end up crashing right into it. Sort of a self-fulfilling prophecy."

"So, I shouldn't look at the other ships?"

"You certainly should," Edith said.

"Have you ever been to a party?" Reddleman asked.

Marya's mouth tightened about a rueful smirk. "Once or twice."

"You know how at every party there are always those people who you wish to avoid? Perhaps they're boorish or you owe them money or you prescribed them a silver tincture that turned their skin blue. Whatever the cause, you don't wish to bump into them. So, you keep track of where they are in the room. Now, you can't glare at them. No, that could bring them running. Instead, you glance, you cut your eyes, you take a peek now and again, and correct your course as needed."

"A helpful analogy. You're quite a good teacher."

"Thank you."

Voleta sat in the gunner's chair with her back turned to the controls. Her eyelids drooped over unfocused eyes. Her chin rested upon the mound of her hands, stacked one upon the other, on the open end of the diamond case. *The Brick Layer's Granddaughter* was almost always with her now. She leaned upon it like a staff. Edith thought of a young dandy she'd once known who used a cane as a jaunty prop, only to one day discover he could not walk without it. She frowned at the tin cup in her hand and the inch of rum that rolled about the bottom. Who was she to cast aspersions on another's crutch?

Edith had not been particularly pleased to see Voleta wearing the Red Hand's infamous cuff, but Reddleman's rationale for why she should have it was difficult to refute. They had already failed to administer her dosage once, a mistake that might have cost her her life. And what would happen if they were all incapacitated or she were separated from the ship? Wearing the cuff was the only prudent choice. Even so, Edith found it unsettling to see the young woman associated with such a dreadful instrument.

But it was not Voleta who was foremost in Edith's thoughts at the moment. No, the question that occupied her, and which had for many hours, was how to humanely ensnare an ambling, gnawing iron-plated fortress.

She had mulled over the possibility of raising a chain trip wire to catch the engine in its stride, but even if they managed to knock a few legs out from under it, would the Hod King stumble to its knees? Was it possible to trip a millipede? It seemed unlikely. She entertained the notion of greasing the floor and the Tower's spine, to rob the engine of traction and grip, but couldn't a man surmount great slopes of wet ice with a pair of cleats beneath him? A little oil would hardly impede a beast that walked upon spearpoint. Perhaps then, they could board the brute—jump on its back, get behind its guns, and force their way inside. Four against a hundred. It would at least make for a jolly suicide.

As each imagined scenario resolved in failure, it became increasingly apparent that Reddleman was right: If they wished to preserve the zoetrope panels, they would have to attack the crew rather than the craft. They could smoke the hods out, though that might merely move the lopsided battle from the ship to the streets. If Reddleman could somehow tap into the Tower's electrical system, they could electrify the Hod King, effectively striking all aboard with a single bolt of lightning. Or perhaps poison gas was the more humane option.

Such ghoulish thoughts to entertain while an infant snored nearby.

Then, for the third time in an hour, Edith saw again Tom's drowned face framed by her hands as she held him beneath the water. The longer he stared back at her, the less surprised he seemed.

She did not believe in premonitions or tea leaves or meaningful dreams. Ghosts did not fall from the ether or rise from the grave. No, those telling figments were the natural byproduct of head trauma and guilt. Why did she feel guilty for something she had not yet done? Because she knew with absolute certainty that when the time came, she would kill Marya's husband, Olivet's father, her friend.

And the Sphinx, indeed all the Tower, would call that result a *victory*.

Without warning, Voleta tugged the canvas from its diamond sleeve and slid from her seat onto the floor, muttering as she went. Ignoring Edith's questions about what she was doing or if something was wrong, Voleta smoothed the colorful scene out on the plated floor. She tightened a peg in her brass cuff and shuddered as a sanguine light swept down her wrist to her fingertips.

Voleta crouched over the painting as if to drink from a stream.

Voleta tumbled through the ghostly past. The smudged years seemed to billow like smoke from a stack. That boiling plume carried with it voices sped into a sort of birdsong and skulls that sprouted skin, that first tightened then plumped with the return of infancy. All the world was painted upon those fleeing clouds. She saw the monolith of Babel shed airships like spores, watched a wooded mountainside shrivel into saplings and turn at a flash into a lightning-scorched copse. She observed the strobing of the stars and the sun drawn out like a fresh weld across a twilit sky. This and more churned inside a passing wisp of wool.

From that pregnant mist, an interior emerged: well-lit, tidy, devoid of furniture, but full of people. The walls were lined with rows of gilded frames containing magnificent works of art. The brilliant and varied scenes hung in colorful conflict with one another. A crowd in formal evening wear scrutinized the collection. Among them was a man of modest dress, even more modest height, and ostentatious ears. His face seemed to have been warped by the passage of a hundred thousand smiles, an expression that appeared to radiate outward from his eyes.

The throng did not press upon him, though he did not seem to have commandeered the space. Rather, the gathered lords and ladies seemed a little awed by him. He stood with his hands in his trouser pockets, staring up at a painting of a girl in a white dress holding a paper boat in the shallows of the Baths.

A taller, exceedingly thin man, with blond hair tucked behind his ears and a cigarette pinched between prominent lips, stepped into the modest man's clearing. He spoke in a manner that implied a longstanding familiarity when he asked, "You like it?"

"I do. Very much," the modest man said. "The water almost seems to move. I think you see more colors than most men do. It's remarkable, Philip. Congratulations. Tell me though, who is the girl?"

"Oh, her. Yes, the girl with the folded boat. It's funny how much she peeved me at first. I'd been working on this piece for almost two weeks. Then the day comes when I could finally see the end in sight. I'm enjoying myself at last. I'm just daubing in the highlights, thinking of what I'll have for dinner. And then this little girl trudges out into the middle of my scene. She just stands there, arms hanging." The painter drew deeply on his cigarette. "Over the two weeks of working on this, I'm sure thousands of people had passed through my view. They'd swam and splashed, they'd fought and fondled, and moved along. But she posted herself like a sentry, an adamant blob of white. After an hour of waiting for her to get out of my way, I realized she wasn't so much irking my eye as drawing it in. She refused to be overlooked. She insisted on being seen. So, I saw her." He ashed his cigarette into a small dish he cupped in one hand and rolled the resulting ember to a point.

"I was sure she was going to wander away. There's no quicker way to chase off an unsuspecting subject than to include it in a piece. But three hours later, I had painted her in. And still, she lingered. I finally waded out and asked what she was looking at so fixedly. Then I saw the dried tears and the red eyes. She said she was watching the bridges. She was looking for her parents. She'd lost them, you see."

The modest man, who had listened to all of this attentively, drew from the loose collar of his shirt a silver eyepiece that hung by a chain from his neck. "Did she ever find them, her parents?"

"No, but I did. They were on the registry of a flight that had disembarked that morning. They had checked four bags and left one with the porter. The girl's suitcase. I can only suppose they left her on purpose. I wrote their names down if you'd like them."

"No." The modest man leaned nearer the painting, examining the hanging hair of the little girl through his loupe. He studied the back of her head as if it might show him her face. "Where is she now?"

"Staying with my sister. It's been nearly a month. We don't know what to do. It doesn't seem right to try to ship her back to the parents who abandoned her, but my sister isn't well enough to take care of a child. As for me... well, I'm no parent, you know that. We've plied all of our friends; none of them can take her. I suppose we'll have to put her in a common home. It's unfortunate. She seems a bright little girl."

The modest man stepped back, dropping the lens from his eye at last. "She's brilliant."

"Oh, is she?"

"Yes. A truly remarkable person, like yourself. I want to meet her."

"Of course. I'm sure you know, better than I, where the best orphanages—"

"She isn't an orphan, Philip. She's my granddaughter."

This seemed to surprise and amuse the painter in equal parts. He stubbed his cigarette out in the dish. "Well, I suppose you'll be wanting the painting, too."

The modest man dug his hands into his pockets again and turned to smile at the spindly artist. "Yes, this one and several more like it. I have a proposal for you. I think you'll find it an interesting challenge. A very..." The modest man's focus suddenly shifted past the painter's arm. Voleta, who had not thought herself present, suddenly found herself the subject of his attention. The modest man tilted his head and squinted at her. The painter looked around, but as one trying to see a buzzing fly. His gaze darted about, lighting on nothing.

"What are you looking at?" Philip asked.

The modest man raised the loupe to his eye, pinching the barrel with his brow and cheek. He stared at Voleta fixedly, as through the scope of a rifle. "You're not supposed to be here," he said.

Voleta tried to back away, but there was nowhere to go, because she was nowhere at all.

"Who are you talking to?" the painter said.

"Where are you from, young lady?"

"The Tower."

"Which Tower?"

"This one, I think. We're still in Ur, aren't we? Wait, you're telling me there's more than one Tower?"

Again, the painter began to speak, his face contorted with concern for this conversation between his companion and the empty air. But the modest man stopped him with a lifting of one hand. He said, "Is the Tower finished? Is it complete?"

"The Tower? I don't know. I haven't seen the top of it. My brother has, but he's—"

"Is there a cloud around the peak that never blows away?"

"Yes, of course."

"Good. Good, that means it's working, finished, or nearly so. But you shouldn't be here, young lady. That's a very concerning thing. So, if you please, come find me in your era so that I can—"

"I'm sorry, who are you?"

"I'm the Brick Layer."

"Oh. But you're dead."

"I am?"

"Yes, the Sphinx said so. You died a long time ago." Upon speaking the Sphinx's name, without thinking Voleta touched the lunar medallion that hung upon her collarbone, a gift from the Sphinx, a beacon that Iren had once followed to find her with a bullet in her head.

"Where did you get that?" the Brick Layer asked.

Voleta lifted the pendant. When it twisted, it showed both faces, one white gold, the other shadowy pewter. Both sides were pocked with minute craters and the scars of ancient collisions. "The Sphinx gave it to me to wear. That was before she stopped talking to us. There's someone trying to get into her home, and we're all concerned that she—"

"Listen to me, young lady. Listen to me. This is vitally important. There is a speck in the Tower's crown that contains an endless abyss: the Allonomia. It is a voracious hole, and a far greater source of power than anything the world has ever known; more powerful than all the wind and all the surf and all the coal in the ground. It is more energetic than the sun in the sky. The Allonomia is always hungry, but you must not feed it until the Nautilus is—"

Without warning, the gallery was gone and the Brick Layer with it, replaced by a great confusion of light; the kaleidoscope of edgeless color was like trying to look through tear-filled eyes. Voleta ascended through the years, passing through the murk of births and deaths, a storm of voices, the band of the sun, and the entwining garland of the silver moon. Time peeled away like fog from the beating wings of an owl.

Something seemed to burst inside of her. It surged outward under her skin to every extremity in an agonizing tide. The surge of pain fell away then came again, crested, diminished, and swelled once more. With each pulse the ache abated by degrees until at last, the thrum of her heart felt at home in her chest.

Voleta lay sprawled across Edith's lap on the floor of the bridge. Her captain stared down, teeth bared in fear. "You stopped breathing," she said.

"It was her," Voleta murmured.

"Who?"

"The girl in the painting. I thought it was her."

"What are you talking about?"

Voleta realized that Reddleman and Marya had abandoned their post and now stood at her side. She sat up to feel like less of a spectacle, though the movement made her head swim. "I thought if I could find her again, I could track her back to the present, ask what went wrong, ask what we should do."

"I told you not to go so deep," the pilot said.

"Who are you talking about?" Edith said, her frustration mounting.

"The Sphinx. She's the Brick Layer's granddaughter. Actually, she was abandoned by her parents, and he adopted—"

"The Sphinx is a woman?" Edith said.

"A very old one, now. I saw the Brick Layer, too. He's not what I'd pictured at all." Voleta looked to Reddleman. "And he saw me."

"Well, that *is* interesting," the pilot said.

"I know. The Sphinx could see me, too, in the conservatory. That was back when she had legs."

"She doesn't have any legs?" Marya asked.

Helping Voleta to her feet, Edith appeared to have reached the limit of her patience. "All right, what are we talking about here? Are you telling me you looked at the painting and, what—went back in time?"

"It keeps happening whenever I take a heavy dose of medium or whenever I'm suffering withdrawal from a missed injection. I can scarcely control it, but looking at an image or an object seems to help push me toward a particular moment in time."

"Did the Brick Layer say anything when he saw you?" Reddleman asked.

"He said something about there being a speck at the top of the Tower that's also a voracious abyss. He called it the Allonomia. He said it was more powerful than all the coal in the world and hotter than the sun. What does 'voracious' mean?"

"Ravenous. Insatiable," the pilot said.

"A gluttonous hole. That doesn't sound very promising," Marya said.

"There was something else he didn't quite get out. Something about a nautilus."

"What's a nautilus?" Edith asked.

"A type of ancient mollusk. It lives in a spiral shell and has nearly a hundred arms, I believe," Reddleman replied.

Edith frowned. "Just what we need: more sea monsters."

Chapter Sixteen

Inside the walls of the monolith, black water is stored in immense stacks and under great pressure to keep it from draining into the already overtaxed aquifers below. The arrangement has led some to call the Tower Ur's largest unflushed toilet.

—*Everyman's Guide to the Tower of Babel,* VI. I

From a distance, the ringdom of Cilicia looked like a window box in spring. Leaves wide as parasols burst from external balconettes, gathering sunlight and funneling life to the vines that crept above the city of vintners. Those vines, dense as a hedge and gripping as a cobweb, produced two crops each year. Upon the arrival of those fruiting seasons, berries pelted the rooftops, juice poured from the drainpipes, and pips and skins gathered in the gutters below. This sticky slurry flowed inward to the central Arcade of Pigeage, where great hoses sucked the sweet must into vats full of harvested grapes. There the two were milled together by the feet of eager youths. The local winemakers called the variety, which grew nowhere else in the world, Noir Cilicandry. The drunkards called it Ink Berry because it stained the lips and teeth a stubborn shade of blue.

Today, the south port of Cilicia was uncharacteristically busy. Gilded sloops, ivory yachts, and carracks railed in rosewood swarmed about the harbor. This grand flotilla of wealth crowded about marble jetties, each carved to resemble an immense leaf. The piers fanned from a central dock where twin limestone sculptures—sexless figures wearing crowns of berries—guarded the city's gates. The nymphs sat astride two monumental swans whose wings arched over great doors of winding iron.

A well-dressed and heavily burdened horde flowed from the city onto the port. Men carried framed paintings under their arms and knocked their heels on the ornate trunks they dragged behind them. Ladies cradled vases, lamps, cabinets rattling with curios, leading children who clutched beloved dolls or reassuring blankets. All wore handkerchiefs tied over their noses and mouths. They looked like bandits, an effect that seemed at odds with their opulent clothes.

All along the wharfs, soldiers in bicornes assisted longshoremen in the packing of luggage and loading of passengers. All appeared to be in a state of great agitation. The air roiled with quarrels. Children in white pinafores and shoulder capes wailed through lacy masks as their parents jockeyed for seats on already overcrowded ships. Someone cast a valise overboard to make room for an old hound. This started an argument with the suitcase's owner, who suggested he would have the dog fetch what his master had thrown. A brown-coated soldier threatened to give them both the heave-ho, a warning that seemed to dampen but not douse the tempers of either man.

Into this aspiring riot, Edith led her crew with her chin down and her cocked hat low. They wore their formal green uniforms, braided in yellow and buttoned in gold. In addition to her chain belt, Iren had a double-barreled gaming gun slung upon her back. Reddleman carried a satchel that bulged with something apparently precious; he held the burden like a pregnant woman might cradle her child-to-be. Voleta had dosed herself before disembarking so she could reload her brass cuff with fresh vials for the excursion. She walked as one in a trance, her gaze locked upon a subject, distant and unseen. Edith was glad to have both Iren and the pilot to help keep an eye on the unpredictable adolescent.

The docking of the *State of Art* had not attracted much attention, incredibly enough, though Edith had not given the natives time to gawk at her ship, having instructed Marya to retreat to the agreed-upon coordinates the moment they were ashore. Already, Edith had asked several men in russet-colored uniforms who was in charge of the port, a question that was met with a surprising amount of disagreement. Eventually, they encountered a harried young officer with several stripes on the shoulder of a coat that seemed too large for him. He was in the process of prying from a woman's arms a box of dining room silver. The lady wore three coats, one on top of the other, two of them fur. Gold chains festooned her neck; rings crowded her fingers. The officer said, "I told you, we can't carry the weight! Either the silver rides or you do."

"But it was a gift from my mother!"

"As was your life, madam! Which do you value more?" With a final heave, he wrested the box away and, before she could stop him, tossed it over the brink.

The officer had fine youthful features and hair that was as pale as porridge. Despite his white locks, Edith doubted he'd yet lived to see his third decade. "Are you in charge?" she asked as he shoved the lady onto a gangway.

"God, I hope not. Has the captain gone already?" He lifted the lip of the wooden walkway to help those aboard who were drawing it up.

"This looks like an evacuation."

"It feels like a stampede. Wait, did you just dock?"

"We did. I need to speak to the regent."

"Queen Hortensia? Oh, she's long gone. Don't expect we'll see her again. The generals are gone, too."

"What happened?"

The officer stooped to unwind a line from a cleat. He threw it onto the ship, then began untying the next. "Lights went out a week ago. The pumps stopped. Fans stopped. The air went stale. Then the real trouble started." He spoke quickly, automatically. He cast the last line onto the already drifting vessel, and in the same moment appeared to see a pair of soldiers standing on the departing deck. The two looked conspicuous and sheepish. "Boyard! Stockley! What are you doing? You can't leave, you cowards!" The pair shrugged, then sat down among the squatting gentry. "They'll have to court-martial half the navy before this is over with," he grumbled.

"You're abandoning Cilicia?" Edith asked, her shock apparent. Deserting a ringdom, especially one as prominent as Cilicia, was unheard of.

"It's more like we're escaping with our lives. Soon as the ringdom went dark, the city engineer took his spark-smiths to Pelphia to help repair the damage to the electrical system. He believed that was the cause of the disruption. Queen Hortensia disagreed, and decided to take it upon herself to get the lights back on. With the city engineer gone, she was allowed to exert her will, and unfortunately for all of us, she's as mad as a midge. Queen Hortie fancies herself a diviner. She has a magic wand. It looks like a stick. It is a stick, but she calls it a wand. She wandered around with it for half a day, then pointed at a spot on the wall and announced that was where the electricity had gotten clogged by a spirit that had been charmed by the current. Naturally. When the excavation didn't go quickly enough, she told them to blast. They ruptured the water stack that handles the sewage for half the Tower and collapsed the main city drain. In one fell swoop, she turned the ringdom into a cesspool."

Edith's eyelids fluttered with disbelief. "I'm sorry, she did what?"

"We were all huddled around candles, waiting for the lights to come back on, and instead we hear a boom, followed by the worst smell I have ever smelled in my life. The queen had the gall to tell us not to panic, even as the sewage began to lap at our doorsteps and spill into our parlors. Then, under the cover of darkness, she packed up everything, loaded it all onto the royal fleet, asked the port master to feed her pets, and abandoned us while her black tide was still rolling in. The brass took half the navy to retrieve her, but they haven't come back. No one has. Then, two days ago, the lights came back on and the fans began to turn. Still, everything is drowned in two feet of bog water. The city will be unlivable until the pumps are cleared, if they can be, and that's saying nothing of the clogworms."

"Clogworms," Iren said, doubling her usual scowl.

"Mmm. I'm given to understand they're essential to the process of breaking down waste. They're certainly hungry blighters. They can chew through a man, bones and all. They've made themselves quite at home." They were interrupted by a young private who arrived to inform the officer the entry tunnel was empty at last. The evacuation was nearly complete.

"What's your name?" Edith asked.

"I'm Sergeant—no, sorry. I keep forgetting I was promoted this morning. Second time this week. I am *Lieutenant* Thom Bassonette."

"That's a fine name. I'm Captain Edith Winters."

"You serve the Sphinx, don't you? Did you come to help us?"

"In a way. We came to warn you." Edith described in the briefest terms their belief that an engine of war would soon crack the floor of the city, climb up her spine, and burrow into the ceiling in pursuit of the Sphinx.

Lieutenant Bassonette laughed bleakly. "They're in for a surprise, aren't they? They're going to pop into the middle of a sump. Serves them right."

"We mean to intercept them."

"You want to go inside?"

"Have to, I'm afraid."

"I'd come with you if I didn't have to guard the port until the city engineer returns. We'll be shorthanded as it is."

"I understand."

"I'm glad someone does. Me, I had no idea my tribe was so soft. It's been an illuminating week. Anyway: mind the clogworms. They're slow and clumsy on land, so they mostly stick to the water. But they're surprisingly resourceful. Not a quality I usually associate with worms."

Edith nodded grimly. "I suppose we'll be back by morning or not at all."

"There's a stove in the guardhouse. I'll have a pot of tea waiting for you, Captain."

Edith had once in her youthful wandering come across a dead ewe half-submerged in a peat bog. Its exposed head and shoulders had been carved opened by foxes, the contents scattered by vultures, the result celebrated by flies who sired a generation in honor of the feast.

Cilicia's air smelled worse than that. The stench was nearly painful.

The passageway that carried them in was crowded at the corners with the evidence of the city's recently departed refugees. Makeshift bedrolls made from curtains, tapestries, and animal-skin rugs lay among empty wine bottles, pewter cups, and porcelain-lined pans. The flicker of electric sconces enlivened the friezes on the walls depicting the winemaking process, a tidy and organized parade that seemed at odds with the domestic chaff. Here and there, piles of bloody rags stood in memoriam of injuries, some apparently mortal, as they also passed more than one corpse hidden beneath a sheet. The result was so visually overwhelming, it came as a relief when the passage opened onto steps leading to the foul water that swamped the famed city.

Winding vines, some thick as a ship's mast, veined the dome above. Massive clutches of dark berries drooped nearly to the rooftops. The vines bore silvery leaves that were much smaller than the elephant ears that grew outside. If one regarded only the second and third story of any building, one would see an almost rustic structure composed of rosy adobe, framed in wood, and crowned with a rooftop terrace. The architectural style was both bucolic and familiar. Edith had seen such houses to the south of her father's farmland where humble winemakers scrabbled together a life, working and living in mud-walled communes. It was strange to see that modest aesthetic coyly echoed in such a lavish place.

And yet, the ringdom did not entirely conceal its wealth. The streets were lined with monumental marble figures lacquered in precious paints and alabaster lampposts that blazed with electric light. Fountainheads bubbled in fabulous pools about the city's perimeter. The mammoth trunks of vines dipped their roots into those unspoiled reservoirs that glowed like blue islands against the black water.

The addition of human mud to the avenues and alleys made the city look like a ballgown wicking up a puddle. The electrical system was plagued by numerous outages that left fully a third of the city's blocks in darkness.

The fact that this was a self-inflicted wound struck Edith as both tragic and infuriating. How could she hope to save a race that was so intent on and adept at sabotaging itself? And what should she conclude was the ultimate cause of the whole mess? Ignorance? Superstition? Privilege? Blind allegiance? Self-serving leadership? It was shocking how quickly the rulers had fled. If she survived long enough, she would seek out Queen Hortensia and haul her and all her ladies-in-waiting and chinless generals back to the mess they'd made. She would see to it that every last one of them was given a mop and a—

"Look there!" Reddleman said, pointing at the flooded boulevard before them. Even from the top of the stairs, they could see numerous shapes scything through the water.

"We played in the sewers when I was a kid," Iren said, drawing everyone's attention. "We'd go down to hunt for treasure: pennies, rings, that sort of thing. Some of the kids got lost and never found their way out. Some got sucked down a pipe and drown. All part of the fun. It was the clogworms that scared me most. A boy I knew had all his fingers bitten off by clogworms."

"How large are they?" Reddleman asked, adjusting the burden that rested on his belly.

"About the size of a rat's tail. But with more teeth."

"Do you think our boots are thick enough to discourage them from—"

Edith began but was interrupted by something wriggling onto the first step above the waterline. It was as fat as a man's thigh, and eight feet long at least. It resembled a headless pale-gray snake. The expanse of its rubbery skin was featureless except for the presence of short, fleshy whiskers that felt about as the monster writhed up from the bottom step to the next. In place of a skull, it had a maw like a leech, a round and active pore full of horrible banks of teeth, some shaped for tearing, some for gnashing, some for gripping in the throat. Slowly, it reached after a fur stole that lay abandoned on the stairs. The clogworm sucked the garment up like a noodle, then rolled back into the murk.

They all stared after it in shock. At last, Voleta asked, "Iren, how big were your rats?"

It took only a moment's investigation to discover how some of the evacuees had avoided the sunken streets. At the far end of the broad stairs, a wooden ladder leaned against the roof of the nearest building. Iren insisted that she test it since she was the heaviest. They all held their breath as they watched her ascent.

Though the ladder bowed like a riding crop, it did not break. In a moment, she had surmounted the parapet and waved for the rest to follow.

The terrace was as an incongruous jumble, like the pieces of a jigsaw puzzle rattling in a box. The mess included slippers, upholstered divans, mantel clocks, brocaded robes, punch bowls, bound manuscripts, stacks of bone china, and musical instruments. Blood pooled on the tile and gathered in the grout, hinting at even greater losses. Edith led her crew through the wreckage to the far side of the roof.

It came as some relief to discover that the buildings were not only snuggly arranged, but also connected by an impromptu system of bridges that had been cobbled together from boards and ladders by the fleeing natives.

Reddleman pulled from the inner pocket of his jacket a crisply folded map, a gift from Byron and the ship's library. Unfolding it, he quickly found their location from the starting point of the port. He'd already marked the location where he believed the Hod King would most likely erupt, a central mall called the Arcade of Pigeage. The route there had seemed rather straightforward while the streets had still been open to them. It was less so now, as they would have to circumnavigate the broader avenues to cross over the more navigable alleys.

"Can we get there in time?" Edith asked, peering over his shoulder at the city's grid.

"I believe so," he said, tracing a roundabout route with his finger. "We should be able to cross over here, to here, along this long roofline, which is the palace. Its eastern wing adjoins the arcade."

"Then what? Do we wade through the worms to greet the war engine?" Iren asked, reseating the strap on her shoulder.

Reddleman patted the top of the satchel lightly. "Well, it won't take the four of us to deliver such a small parcel. Maybe we can build me a boat."

In the end, it had been Reddleman who had suggested the means for incapacitating the Hod King. His study of the engine's blueprints had quickly convinced him that they stood no chance of piercing the head and reaching the bridge, which was reinforced with steel plates. The entire central deck of the engine, which extended out from the bridge, was encased inside a secondary frame, girded by curiously shaped stanchions. There was a conspicuous lack of detail around the midship, suggesting the existence of an additional set of schematics. Still, Reddleman could only assume this secondary fortification had been included to protect the excavator's vital stations. They might, of course, attack the hatches around the guns and castles, but that seemed akin to tackling a tiger by the teeth.

Reddleman had then turned his attention to the engine's undercarriage and its sixty-four legs. Separately, the limbs appeared somewhat vulnerable, but the question was how many would they have to break before the iron arthropod stumbled? It was impossible to know for sure, but his best guess was that they'd have to disable at least four sets. Given their small window of opportunity, attempting such a complex sabotage seemed imprudent.

The solution came when Reddleman had reflected on when he had seen the Hod King in motion. The legs of the engine had moved in a wave, much like the stride of a millipede. The individually operated legs stepped in perfect harmony. But how were those operators so well synchronized? Someone had to direct them, supplying the rhythm and tempo, much as the drummer on a dromon tells the rowers when to pull their oars. The thought of a drum reminded Reddleman of the rather innocuous label at the head of the galley, which read: MSTR. OF BELLS.

The solution came to him all at once.

When he'd gone to see the captain, it had taken him a little time to convince her that this obscure notation, which could only be short for "Master of Bells," marked a post and the person responsible for harmonizing the efforts of the individual operators.

"Lucky for us, the flooring is relatively thin. We could plant an explosive on the hull just here," he had said, pointing to one of the photographed diagrams that lay splashed across a table in the *State of Art*'s dining hall. "It wouldn't have to be a large bomb. I could fashion it easily enough. We have plenty of powder. Perhaps I could affix it to a magnet. That'd certainly make it a lot easier to apply. I'd just need to get through the legs, light the fuse, and get out of the way."

"You're sure this'll work?" the captain had asked.

"Well, nothing is certain, of course, but I do have a knack for knowing where to poke a man to make his knees buckle. If you want this beast to kneel, Captain, all we have to do is kill the Master of Bells."

Each terrace they crossed was much like the first: a confusion of possessions and footprints, both muddy and gory. Occasionally, they'd come to a taller structure that required them to enter and leave by a window or balconette. Passing through the bedrooms of strange homes and the private lofts above shops gave Edith the unpleasant feeling of being a prowler, a sensation that was hardly improved when Reddleman pulled a pair of electric candles from his pack, one of which he lit himself, before giving the other to Iren. The devices cast a yellow beam of light that made the private scenes they tramped through feel like spotlighted stages in a playhouse.

Still, she tried to observe as little of the environs as she could out of respect for the privacy of the absent owners. The effort was made difficult by Voleta's habit of dreamy dawdling. She gaped at portraits in the halls, read letters left out on dressers, and studied the rows of domestic totems displayed upon the mantels. She fell into dazes easily and repeatedly. When Reddleman suggested a slap to bring her around, Iren replied that if he laid a hand on her, she would throw him to the worms. Iren would allow no one else to bring Voleta back from her trances. Iren's restorative methods included vigorously rubbing Voleta's arms and hands and shouting into her slackened face or her softly shining ears. If there was any at hand, Iren would splash water on her neck, and failing that, she picked the young woman up and carried her over her shoulder until the jostling revived her.

When Iren suggested they blindfold her to block out the distractions, Voleta insisted that would only make matters worse because it would allow her to fall into her own memories, which were much more difficult to escape. The past was full of traps of guilt, dread, and bewilderment. It was better to be distracted by the lives of others; better to keep moving; better to run.

Even still, when they came upon the ringdom's palace—a six-storied structure crowned with goose-necked gargoyles on the corners and faced with tall, corbel arched windows—Edith realized that passing through its lavish interior would test both the young woman's concentration and Iren's nerves. To simplify matters, she ordered them to the roof, which was accessible from the third story balcony by an external stairwell. Those steps delivered them to a gate composed of wrought iron vines. Peering through the barrier, they discovered the entire length of the roof was enclosed by an eight-foot-tall parapet.

Scaling this gate, they found that, unlike the other terraces they'd seen, the palace's rooftop was unfurnished and barren except for an accumulation of fallen grapes. The long expanse was laid with small white tiles. Interrupting this enameled plain was a series of structures, sixteen in all, each separated by a gap of perhaps ten paces. They looked to Edith like mausoleums, and she wondered if this was not the resting place of the ringdom's former rulers. The crypts were enclosed by limestone walls and a single iron-studded door. The door of the first crypt they passed stood ajar, revealing a sliver of its unlit interior. It was an invitation that appeared to beckon Voleta; she began to stray toward the opening.

Reaching up to pluck a cluster of low-hanging berries, Iren tossed one at the back of Voleta's coat. The young woman turned to find the amazon cramming the rest of the bunch into her mouth. She spoke a single word through the inky mash: "Nope."

They soon learned to try to avoid treading on the grapes, which split easily, forming treacherous slicks. But it was already too late. By the time they were three-quarters of the way across the length of the roof, the crushed fruit had coated their soles so effectively, they were forced to adopt the shuffling stride of a fledgling ice-skater. Here and there, the fruit had gathered in larger piles. When Edith paused to try to scuff the grape skins from the bottom of her boots, Reddleman knelt to inspect one of the mounds more closely. "Interesting," he said. "These aren't grapes. Well, they probably were grapes, but this is scat."

"It's what?" Iren said.

"Droppings. Dung. There's rather a lot of it."

"Didn't that lieutenant say something about the queen leaving her pets behind?" Iren scanned the empty corners of the roof. "You don't suppose they—"

She was interrupted by what sounded like an untuned orchestra arguing inside a ravine. The deep and grating blat itched the ears and made the contents of Edith's stomach boil.

From behind the first crypt they had passed stepped a black swan. Its eyes were like egg yolks: orange and bulging. In place of feathers, large scales plated its neck, breast, and wings. Its head reached high enough that, if it wished, it could graze upon the fruited ceiling. Its wings, when it spread them, could have encompassed them all. The swan opened its black, pointed beak, and once more blasted its dreadful cry.

Even as Iren began to unsling her field gun, a second swan emerged from a nearer crypt. *No,* Edith thought, *not a crypt—a roost.* And there were sixteen of them.

Edith was about to order Iren to hold her fire, fearing it might agitate the flock, but already the stock of the field gun was snugged to her shoulder. The gun barked out a shower of shot.

The pellets struck the chest of the swan. It flapped its wings in irritation, but apparently not injury. Edith heard a spatter of lead rain upon the tile. The bird cocked its head back over its body as if it to draw a deep breath. Its head struck at the air, quick as an adder. Edith did not see the dart it spat until Voleta pinched it from the air not far from Iren's eye. The six-inch-long barb was black and coated in something viscous and yellow. Voleta dropped it suddenly, shaking out her fingers and wiping them on her jacket.

"It burns," she said.

"Some sort of acidic pile, perhaps? How interesting," Reddleman said as a second and third swan waddled out from their stony cotes.

"Run!" Edith said, then turned to lead by example.

Chapter Seventeen

Be leery of the agreeable grocer who bags your plums behind the counter. Be suspicious of the obliging clothier who offers to wrap your shirts in the backroom. Be wary of helpful persons, lest you go home with a bag full of rot or a box full of rags.

—*Everyman's Guide to the Tower of Babel*, V. X

arya couldn't help but think that if she blinked for too long the ship would fall right out from under her. The bridge's control panels shone forth like the footlights of a stage, while the distant engines murmured like an uncertain audience. At last, she had found a cure for her boredom. The terror was but a tax.

The *State of Art* lazed in the faux twilight of the Tower's midday shadow. Her waypoint had been selected by Reddleman, chosen for its distance from active ports and crowded trade currents. Initially, the captain had wanted Marya to steer the ship to a greater height, well out of the range of any craft or cannon. But doing so, Reddleman had pointed out, would place between the ship and their landing party the Tower's murky peak, which might obscure their signal flare. Should they need to beat a hasty retreat from Cilicia, the *State of Art* had to remain in view. And so, a nearer anchorage had been chosen.

Gaze leaping between screens as if she were following a badminton match, Marya gripped the steering yoke with all the attentiveness of a novice. While Reddleman could pilot the ship with one eye closed and an open tome on his lap, Marya was under no illusion that she could be so cavalier.

She had learned long ago that mastery sometimes gave the impression of indifference. The instructor who had taught music theory at the Bromburry Conservatory, Madam Alicia, was so skilled that when she played the piano at fancy dress parties, she would set a novel upon the sheet music holder and read while she enlivened the most intricate toccatas. Her nonchalance would sometimes entice overconfident amateurs into asking for her seat and the opportunity to delight the other revelers. Once enthroned upon her bench, they would fumble their way through an étude or butcher a minuet until they or the host arrested the cacophony, and Madam Alicia was allowed to take up her performance (and her book) once more.

Marya surveyed the vast display of dials, knoblets, and toggles, each ornate as a hatpin, reviewing again the few she had become acquainted with. She reached for a switch in a bank of many.

"What is that? What are you doing?" Byron asked from over her shoulder, his voice pinched by anxiety.

"Switching on the running lamps."

"And you're certain you have the right switch?"

"No, I thought I'd just start flipping until the lights came on or the bow fell off." She glanced over her shoulder, offering a reassuring smile that was wasted on the stag's back. Byron had already resumed his pacing. He had hardly stopped fidgeting since the captain, Iren, Voleta, and Reddleman had gone ashore. Marya knew he had wished to go, too, to fight alongside his friends in what would likely prove to be a bloody battle. But Edith had instead put him in command of her ship and a crew of three that was composed of an infant, a governess, and a very green pilot.

Byron's nose appeared over her shoulder again. "What's that noise? I haven't heard the ship rattle like that before. What's happened? What have you done?"

Marya nodded at the communication trumpet that flared from the bank above her. "It's just Olivet. She's snoring."

"Babies snore?"

"I think she's the first. A medical oddity. Perhaps she'll be my opening act, someday: Come one, come all. Hear the infant snore!"

"Feeling sarcastic this evening, are we?"

"I'm nervy. You're making me nervier."

"I'm sorry." Stepping back, Byron appeared to make an effort to leash his apprehension. He sat down in the captain's chair, or at least the very edge of it, and touched the arms as if he were checking a stovetop. He recoiled as if the rests were hot. Returning to his feet, he resumed his pacing.

Marya reviewed the gallery of magnovisors, letting her scrutiny rest upon each as she said under her breath, "Portside, aft, starboard, bow." Airships circled the Market like crows over a carcass. On the ground, lanterns flickered to life in the alleys between canopies: fragile protests against the Tower's roving shadow.

Tom's face flashed to mind, not as he'd been when she'd last seen him—wretched with guilt and keen for punishment—but bathed in the lamplight of a bedside table. He always wore such a concerted furrow during the day. Not precisely a frown, but a constricted sort of pucker. She might've thought it the natural preference of his features had she not observed him reading in bed by dim light. The act teased from him a serene expression of soft delight.

But the pleasant memory was quickly trampled by the thought of the Hod King erupting from its burrow with horn twirling and cannons popping, leaping into a trap that would spell either the end for all aboard, or the end of Captain Winters and her crew. The captain had continued to call it a rescue, and Marya had no choice but to hold out hope that Tom could be saved, though the conditions of the attempt were nothing short of—

The gentle pinging of a bell brought her attention back to the controls. Internally, she reproached herself for this lapse in focus, even as she hunted about for the source of the alarm. Byron was at her shoulder in an instant with one hand braced upon the dash. Her surprise slowed her recognition, but before Byron could pose the question, she answered it. "It's the proximity alarm," she said, flipping the switch that killed the bell. "There." She pointed to the frame that showed the aft view. The Tower's umbra muddied the picture, laying shadows over shade. She had glanced at the screen a moment before, marked the presence of an envelope that had seemed some distance off. A little further squinting now revealed that she had misjudged its distance because of its size, which she had assumed to be much larger. Byron tuned a knob under the frame, bringing the shape of the balloon into relief: an acorn.

"Another one! I warned Iren that if she kept letting them in, they'd keep coming back. They're like cats," Bryon said.

"I wonder if the editor changed her tune about us after the meeting."

"What meeting? What are you talking about?" Byron asked, and listened with appalled interest to Marya's account of Editor Kilgore's brief visit and conversation with the captain above deck, a story she had gotten out of Reddleman during their last session at the wheel. As she spoke, they moved to the periscope, where they took turns observing as the newspaper hawker cast out his grapple and hooked the railing above. "Well, what did they talk about?"

"Captain said Kilgore wanted an interview, but she wasn't interested in conversing with someone who had called her a cannibal. It wasn't a long chat. Apparently, the captain didn't go into much detail, but I gather she gave the editor some sort of warning. I wonder if he heeded it." They heard the stamp of landing heels ring the deck above. Marya peered at their waiting visitor. He wore a heavy cape, patched up like a quilt. Between the piles of his scarf and his knitted stocking cap, little more than the tip of his nose was visible.

"Do you know how to work the snuffler?" Byron asked.

"I do," Marya said.

"Well, if Kilgore's printed an apology, I for one would like to read it. Snuffle away."

The sensor soon completed its search and returned a clear result. From her station, Marya opened the hatch above while Byron approached the foot of the ladder to receive the young hawker. He fished about his waistcoat pocket for coins as the tick of boot soles announced the youth's descent.

From her station across the bridge, Marya watched the newsboy set foot on the floor. With his heels down, he seemed taller than he had before. He opened his coat. Byron said, "What are—" and then stopped at the sharp sound of a plucked wire. The Sphinx's footman fell backward stiffly, one hand still lodged in his pocket, the other wrapped about the end of a bolt that jutted from his chest. The newsboy's open cape framed a small crossbow. He dropped the weapon. Its stock and wooden limbs leapt and clattered like a caltrop beside Byron's lifeless form.

The intruder pulled down his scarf and swept off his cap. He'd shaved since she'd seen him last, a choice that made his cheeks look full and boyish, though the red rinds of his eyes had aged him a dozen years.

Duke Wilhelm Pell shrugged off his cowl. With a smile as ghoulish as a slit throat, he raised the hoary claw he bore in place of a hand.

Edith had never cared for long-necked birds and had never understood the wistful sentiments that writers and artists sometimes expressed for them, framing them as majestic or serene. Such persons had obviously never lived on a farm where imperious swans were allowed to lord the lake just because they kept the frogs and milfoil in check, and ill-tempered geese were given a free pass merely because they were good at weeding a berry patch. The favorite pastime of both birds was attacking small girls as they emerged from the back door of their home, or rounded the corner of a barn, or sat under a tree minding their own business. More than once, Edith had been left black and blue by the beat of wings and the snap of a bill. She would ball up in the grass, covering her face, and wait for the goose to tire of asserting its dominance over a crying child. How majestic! How serene!

Her father told her, again and again, that running away was the absolute worst thing she could do when confronted by a goose. Geese were like debts: not only was it impossible to outrun them, trying only made things worse. She had to stand her ground, make herself look big, tell the goose "No" in a strong and confident voice. Believing her father to be an expert in all things and circumstances, she tried his advice. The goose bit her nose so hard it drew blood.

The Swan War only ended when finally, at the age of seven, she got on top of a bird that had cornered her in the sow's pen. With knees dug in the mud, she had wrung its neck, and beat its head upon the slop trough. She choked it nearly to death, only stopping when two field hands pulled her off the creature, with her fists full of feathers. After that, the birds seemed to lose interest in her, which only convinced her that they were all in cahoots, members of some arcane bird society, hell-bent on giving little children black eyes and nightmares.

If her father had been on the palace roof with them, no doubt he would've told her not to run, to stand her ground and face the pod of eight-foot-tall swans that spat acid darts and ran on claws rather than webbed feet. And she would not have listened.

Still, she and her crew could not so much run from the beastly swans as flail and skid along, often falling to their hands and scrabbling onward like apes. Reddleman, who cradled a bomb, shouted barks of alarm between bouts of manic laughter. As they passed each roost, another swan burst forth, wings chuffing the air as they added the brass of their throats to the orchestral roar.

Voleta reached the locked gate first and was over it almost as quickly. Reddleman, close behind her, passed his satchel through the iron vines before summiting the creepers himself. Iren and Edith arrived a second later, finding the bars well-greased for them by the boots of their friends. Looking back at the closing flock of egg-eyed beasts, Edith saw at once they would not both be able to climb it in time. Rather than give Iren a chance to argue with her, Edith backed her way along the high parapet away from the gate. She waved her hands above her head and shouted at the birds, "Hey, you ugly hens! Over here! Look at me!"

To her surprise, the birds slowed their onslaught. From the corner of her eye, Edith saw Iren still struggling to get a foothold on the slickened gate. The moment the swans' attention drifted back to the amazon, Edith resumed her shouts and antics. The bird at the front tilted its head at her, blinking its lantern-bright eyes, the little abacus of its mind clicking through the primitive sum: Was she prey or predator? Arriving at an answer, the swan cocked its neck, thrust its head, and spat a quill at her.

She turned, and the barb pinged off her pauldron, scratching her ear as it passed through her hair. The surprising flash of pain made her draw her head in, her chin down. That seemed the signal of weakness that the birds had been waiting for, because they resumed their charge.

Turning, Edith leapt, reaching after the top of the barrier. She caught it with her fingertips and, strengthened by terror, pulled herself onto the parapet.

The top of the wall felt as narrow as a sawhorse. The view of the flooded street six floors below was unimpeded by the presence of a convenient sill or a useful balcony. If she fell, it would be a long dive into shallow water that seethed with omnivorous worms. To her left she saw her crew staring with open mouths at her from the landing. Edith was pleased to see that Iren had made it over, though the relief was short-lived. A swan jabbed her heel with its beak, touching off a brief unbalanced jig.

Edith thought of the bird she had throttled in the pigpen, and the secret society of swans that she had obviously underestimated, both in its reach and its patience for revenge. Then she pitched forward into the empty air.

"So, there was a devil after all." The duke lifted Byron's snout with the toe of his boot and let it drop again. Marya winced at the sight of Byron's tongue lolling from his parted lips, his dark eyes wide and devoid of life. The black bolt that staved his heart seemed too small to have felled a spirit so large.

"Why..." Marya said at a whisper, unable to finish. Her terror began to strangle her vision, ring the room in black and push it away. She watched her unwanted husband as if from the bottom of a well.

"Only one man survived the boarding of this ship with his brains intact. Well, mostly so. He sounds drunk even sober and dribbles his soup. Said he was needled in the nose. But he insisted the ship was empty except for a walking boiler, a froggish man, and a horned devil. No one believed him." The duke lifted Byron's remaining antler with the toe of his boot. "What a strange beast. I wish I could've given him a proper chase. Such a pity."

She shook her head to clear it and pushed herself to her feet. She would not face him sitting down. "There was more humanity in him than there ever was in you."

"Darling! You seem unhappy to see me. Don't you understand? This is a rescue."

"Said the spider to the fly."

"Oh, come now! You were never a prisoner, never trapped. I didn't lock the doors. I opened them! I gave you a house, a stage, a fortune." He flicked out a finger as he enumerated his gifts.

"You locked the nursery."

"Only for her protection."

"Please, go away."

"Is it this that bothers you?" he said, raising the three-pronged rake. It was old, its digits nicked, its coloration so mottled she could not guess its material. Between the cuff of his jacket and the base of the prosthetic, the straps of a leather harness crossed over bandages that were inky with blood. "It is a wicked-looking scratcher. There wasn't time to make a custom one, but I like it well enough. I could've had a ball or a hook, but this reminded me of the talons of a hawk. Still—" He dropped the arm and straightened his collar, showing some of his old preening habits. "It's only temporary. I intend to hire the Sphinx to make a better one, one as strong as that wagtail who ambushed me."

"She's downstairs. For your sake, you'd best be gone before—"

"No, she's not." The duke dismissed the notion with a sniff and took a step nearer. She refused to give him any ground. "I saw them all get off: her, the old gorilla, the brush-headed girl, and the potbellied mangler who takes bullets like a stump. No, I suspect we're very much alone, and if not, well, there's always my faithful companion, here." He swung around from his back a much larger, heavier crossbow that she recognized at once. Its limbs were made of golden hedge apple, a fact he had often bragged about. It had cost him as much as a carriage. At night, he liked to oil it on his desk while she was forced to sit and listen to his hunting stories: the bears he'd treed, the cats he'd tracked. He was famously wretched to his hounds, but he would pet and caress that crossbow for hours.

He propped it now upon his forearm and aimed it at her core. "You look like a cabin boy dressed like that. It doesn't suit you. What are you supposed to be?"

"I'm an ensign."

"Aye, aye, and aren't you, though? On second thought, perhaps I like it. We could play disappointed captain and naughty ensign." He laughed, then winced and looked again at his new talons. "The doctors said she broke every bone in my hand. They said it might be saved, but it would always be a withered knot. It would never make a fist again, never grip a ramrod, or lift a glass. The pain was unbearable. I begged them to cut it off. They did, but it still aches. I can feel the ghosts of those fingers throb even now."

"Good," she said.

He voiced the melody of his fake laugh, a birdsong she had come to hate. "But those ghosts are nothing compared to yours, darling." He came nearer, his steps unhurried, judicious, a cat stalking its prey. "How I have ached for you. How my blood has thumped through my veins. If you had been anyone else, I would've drowned you like a runt months ago, but you have been such an interesting quarry. We've had such fun kissing in public and clawing in private.

"Remember when you got your hands on a vial of poison? You ruined a perfectly good bottle of port. So clever. Then there was the time you promised that composer an original composition in exchange for airfare for one adult and one child. Of course, he came to the club straightaway. We laughed about it for hours. He liked the song you wrote for him, by the way. There's no sweeter music, I think, than when we sing for our lives. How many knives did I find under your pillow? How many scribbled maps of the sewers? Oh, you will always be my favorite chase. Though I admit, I'm a little disappointed you aren't running now. I'd hoped for one more hunt."

He had caught her by surprise again, as he was so apt to do. The night before her escape when she stood offstage at the Vivant for the last time, the duke had found her listening for her entrance queue, alone, distracted. He had seemed to materialize from the folds of a curtain, had grasped her like a net, making her shout in alarm for none to hear over the bellow of tubas and rumbling kettledrums. Before she could wrench away, he whispered in her ear that he had waited long enough. Never mind the doctor's orders: He'd have her that night on the nursery floor so the little whelp could listen to her mother cry out for a change. Robbing her of the chance to offer a rejoinder or throw him an elbow, the duke then shoved her into the spotlight. She'd stumbled to her piano bench, rendered defenseless by the eyes of a nation.

Since she could not fight him there, she turned her curses into a melody and formed her fists into chords. As was his preference. He liked to goad her and flit away, like a bullfighter torments a bull.

Marya made as if to wipe sleep from one eye, an act of indifference she knew would infuriate him, though of course part of the game was to appear unaffected. "I've met so many bullies in my life, but you are by far the most frightened of them. You call yourself a huntsman but take forty hounds and a dozen men to kill a sickly fox or an old hog. You come back and crow about how brave you are, how intrepid, then you go to your club and wager on the backs of much larger, tougher men. You want to believe you are superior because you have a purse and a box seat, but if any of them ever got you in a corner, they would wring you like a rag. You preyed upon me when I was desperate, you hemmed me in and threatened my child not because you are a mighty hunter but because you are afraid of me. And you should be afraid."

"I love it when you growl. You have such pretty hackles!" he said through his teeth as the veins in his neck plumped like welts from a whip.

A gasp in the hatchway brought their heads around. Ann stood in a long, white nightgown, a basket of laundry in her hands. She dropped her burden in shock, turned on her bare heel, and fled.

"Ho, ho!" the duke said with grim merriment. "It looks like I'll have my chase after all!"

Chapter Eighteen

Leapt fences have spoiled many trousers. Often it is while skirting inconvenience that we encounter catastrophe.

—*Everyman's Guide to the Tower of Babel,* II. I

Upon seeing the captain flail from the top of the wall, Voleta again experienced a curious bloating of time, as each second fattened into a minute. When the clocks had seemed to dawdle on the betting floor of Oyodin, she had felt empowered by the deliberation it allowed her. She could trot across the heads of the crowd as if they were stepping-stones fixed in a stream rather than a collection of undulating, unpredictable flotsam upon the sea. What a gift it had seemed!

Though now, as she watched Edith fall, she realized it was a curse, too, because all she could do was absorb the excruciating minutiae of her friend's plummet and end.

And so, when for a moment, Edith's fall appeared to entirely halt, Voleta wondered if she had not entered a new purgatorial state, one where time had stopped, leaving the captain to hang upon death's door forever. But then Voleta realized Edith's fall had indeed stalled. One of her raised hands stood plunged into the foliage overhead. She had caught hold of a vine.

Time began to gallop again as Edith dangled by her engine over the precipice. Her legs kicked the air, reaching for the lip of the wall, but only grazing it with grape-slicked toes. Voleta was about to climb onto the wall and run out to her aid when Edith's salvation began to pull like a thread from a sweater. They watched her drop a dozen feet as berries and leaves rained upon her head. As the vine lost its grip on the ceiling, it carried her farther from the palace, out over the foul waters of the flooded arcade.

Even as Voleta tried to calculate how long a boathook they'd need to pull her back in, the captain's growing tether continued to tear through the canopy. She plunged again, swinging farther out, then back again, and finally beyond the edifice of the palace altogether toward the adjacent building. Even if they put a hook on a flagpole, it wouldn't be long enough to reach her. Iren pounded down the stairs, and Voleta followed her to the broad fourth-story balcony where they rounded the palace's corner. Not far off, they heard something slap the water, though they couldn't say if it had been the captain or just dislodged fruit, because Edith had fallen out of view. Iren climbed onto the balustrade. The neighboring roof was nearly level, its terrace crowded with cane chairs and café tables.

When Iren landed, she tipped nearly half the tables over and broke the legs from four or five chairs. Voleta and Reddleman followed with fewer casualties and joined the amazon at the front of the building, where she stood staring out.

Edith hung mere feet above the black water. The vine she clung to dragged in the murk, appearing to have finally struck upon a firm enough rooting in the domed ceiling. Her boots were wet. Voleta supposed she had touched down in the water, then climbed the vine to escape it. She dangled, stranded over open water some thirty or forty feet away from the facade of the building they stood atop.

Through cupped hands, Iren shouted, "Are you all right, Captain?"

"Fine! Just fine. I think I swallowed a few leaves." The surface of the water beneath her began to froth with activity as the clogworms converged to feast upon the woody rope. "Seems I've attracted some admirers."

"We're coming out to get you!" Voleta shouted.

"That would be nice."

They found the hatch to the internal stairs and descended to discover a hallway with doors to a darkened kitchen and, a little farther on, a brightly lit scullery closet. Glancing inside as they passed, Voleta saw beaming copper pots, stacks of clean china, and a spotless sink. Voleta thought it strange that, faced with evacuating a sewage-flooded city, someone had gone to the trouble of tidying up.

But it proved to their advantage that the proprietor of the Maundering Benison Wine Bar was so devoted to his property. When they reached the ground level, they were pleased to find the terracotta floor dry and clean swept. Beyond the grape wood chairs and wine barrel tables, they saw the sandbags that dammed the restaurant's doors. The long bar, backed by a library of wine bottles, was set with tall wrought iron stools. With scant deliberation, Iren heaved one through the café's front window.

The crash and splash were quickly followed by the sound of Edith cursing outside. Voleta ran to the sill, Reddleman close behind her, to find the captain twisting on her leafy line, her heels pulled up to evade the reach of the churning clogworms. They had finished eating the grapevine that had touched the water, but now seemed to sense a larger meal was nearly in reach. There were dozens of the pale worms. They knotted, writhed, and piled upon one another, their teeth chewing air. Every flagellum on their bodies quivered like a salted leech. Edith attempted to climb higher, but when she did, the vine lurched downward.

"Moving makes it worse!" Voleta shouted.

"Everything makes it worse!" Edith called back.

Just outside the window, the seat of a bench stood above the dark water's reach. To one side of it, a decorative lamppost lit the murk well enough for them to see shapes carving past, moving to join the congregation gathering in Edith's shadow.

"We need a raft," Iren said, looking about. "One of the wine barrels, maybe?"

"They don't seem to mind eating wood, though," Reddleman said.

"I have an idea." Voleta picked up the nearest stool and negotiated it, feet first, through the burst window. Setting it down just past the slatted bench, she crouched upon the sill and rocked the stool back and forth to test its footing. Satisfied, she began to climb out, when Iren gripped her by the arm.

"I'll go," the amazon said.

"Sorry, Iren. This is nimble work. Reddleman can pass me the stools. Why don't you try shooting one or two of those worms? Maybe they'll turn on each other if you put a little blood in the water."

The muscles in Iren's jaw jutted like knuckles, but rather than argue, she unslung her field gun and used the butt of it to knock out the window on the far side of the dammed door.

Voleta climbed out, planting first one foot, then the other on the stool top. She turned, hands out expectantly, and gripped the round seat

Reddleman held out to her. When she tugged upon it, he held it a moment longer till she met his gaze.

"Are you afraid?" he asked.

"No," she said.

"Then you've taken too much."

"I know."

"Don't take any more," he said, and let go. She turned and planted another stepping-stone into the putrid lake.

Ann had changed into her nightdress after Olivet had spit up on her blouse for the second time that day, leaving her with no clean alternatives. She meant to pass by the bridge on the way to the laundry room to make sure Marya could still keep an ear out for the sleeping infant. When she'd heard a man's voice from the corridor, she had assumed it was Byron's, but then she saw him lying on the floor, apparently unconscious or worse.

She recognized Duke Wilhelm Pell the moment he turned to face her. She'd seen him on several public occasions while chaperoning Xenia. He had always beamed such perfect health and vitality. Now, he looked peaked. His skin was drawn and ashen. There was a tint of madness about his eyes.

She fled out of instinct, running barefoot down the carpeted corridor, onto the cold parquet floor of the conservatory. In the map room, the dominating model of the Tower shimmered and shone like a mountain of tinsel. She'd nearly crossed the chamber when conscious reflection finally outshouted her primal urge, and her pace slowed. She realized with a pang of shame that she'd left Marya to confront the duke alone. Not only was it cowardly, but also unwise. Surely, their only hope was to fight him together.

Turning about, she scanned the room for something with which to arm herself. The six dining chairs were still arranged in a crescent, but they were too heavy for her to use as a ram. Then she recalled the diamond tube that contained the Sphinx's painting. The captain had told Voleta it was too precious to take into battle, and so the young woman had left it behind, tucked under her chair. The cylinder was supposed to be indestructible. If Voleta could get a grip on it, then so could Ann.

The instant she took a step toward the row of chairs, she heard what sounded like the breaking of a piano string. Something whistled past her ear. A curious cracking sound behind her made her turn. A bolt of black steel had pierced the wooden frieze, pinning the haunch of a long-eared hare. She came about again in time to see the duke emerge from behind the doorway with crossbow lowered. Setting the toe of his boot in the stirrup, he drew the string back with his good hand. The string clicked into the latch, and he reached for the quiver strapped to his thigh.

"Oh, don't wait around on my account. I'll catch up," he said.

For the second time in as many minutes, Ann took flight.

The fountains at the center of the Arcade of Pigeage bowed out from the spine of the Tower like the leaves of a clover. Monumental nymphs presided over these crystalline pools. They poured water from urns held high on their shoulders and looked down admiringly at the ripples their dribbles made. Twelve titanic chalices ringed the fountains—the famed Cups of Plenty, where generations of youthful feet had churned the ringdom's bounty. The exterior of the marble bowls were carved with the faces of beautiful men bearing thorny beards and women with tangling locks, their hair all knotting together, their eyes narrowed by delight, their mouths wide with laughter. Golden vines coiled about the fat stems of the cups, snaking down to bases so grand the natives would lounge upon them like a public bed.

In other circumstances, Iren might've sat and savored the view. On a different day, in a different life, she might've brought Ann there. They could've picnicked on the long wall of the fountain. Iren would've rolled up her trousers, Ann would've knotted up her skirts, and they'd cool their feet in the water. They'd hold hands and listen to the musical trickling until they fell into a trance.

But instead, Iren was about to watch her friend get eaten by toilet worms.

Kneeling on a sandbag, she let the barrel of her field gun rest among the ragged teeth of the popped-out windowpane. Twice already she had fired both barrels into the mob of clogworms that boiled near the captain's toes; both times the result had been the same. The pierced worms spurted oily blood that inspired a frenzy among the rest. The swell of worms would then shrink beneath the surface as their attention turned to devouring the wounded, a feast that took mere seconds to finish. Then the wriggling mound of ghastly maggots would rise again, only a little higher now, because more worms had been summoned by the bloodletting. For each one she killed, two more took its place.

Luckily, Voleta was making good progress on her stool-top archipelago. In the span of a minute, she had already laid down ten iron islands. Another four or five trips, Iren estimated, and she'd reach the captain.

With a barstool held balanced atop her head, Voleta again hopped from the café window, to the bench, then sprang onto the first foothold. The young woman hummed loudly and without melody as she bounded from stool to stool. Iren had to admit Voleta had been right: it was nimble work not suited to an amazon.

Voleta was in the process of setting down her eleventh stepping-stone when the stool behind her abruptly toppled and landed on its side with a splash. From the café window, Iren could see the fat-bodied culprit winding over the rungs of the sunken barstool.

"You cheeky devil!" Voleta cried and replaced the missing step with the one she carried. But the moment she straightened again, a pair of clogworms rammed into it. The stool toppled, clanging into the next in line, tipping it over, too. The water began to riffle and luff as if caressed by a gust. Two more stools were overturned by the thickening school of worms. Iren couldn't tell whether these were acts of sabotage or just the result of overcrowding, but the result was the same: Voleta was quickly becoming stranded.

Realizing this, Reddleman snatched up another stool and ran to the window to begin rebuilding what the clogworms had knocked down. Iren hastened to help, but before either of them could climb onto the bench outside, a chorus of splashes announced an end to what remained of Voleta's bridge. All the stools had been felled except for the one under Voleta, and it quivered and danced with the collisions of passing worms.

"There's not enough stools left to reach her," Reddleman said.

Iren turned and counted six remaining seats at the bar. "Then we'll use barrels."

"The worms eat wood."

In a flash of temper, Iren flung the stool over the bar, shattering a score of bottles at a stroke. "Then I'll wade out and get her myself!"

Reddleman clapped her broad forearm with a thin hand. "Your sacrifice would be but a dinner bell, Mister Iren! More will come. Wait a moment. We must think."

Mounting the windowsill, Reddleman leaned out over the flooded street. He craned his neck, appearing to search for some solution. Helplessly, Iren watched as Voleta rode the bucking stool, her arms thrown out and pumping in pursuit of balance. Still, Voleta did not seem afraid; only resolute. Behind her, the captain bared her teeth at the worms who'd piled high enough to nip the frayed ends of the vine beneath her lifted heels.

Reddleman gave the ornamental lamppost beside the bench a speculative shake. The green copper post wiggled as the panes of glass that boxed the filament rattled. Climbing onto the top of the bench, he wedged himself between the facade of the wine bar and the lamppost.

"What are you doing?" Iren asked.

"Something a bit desperate. The worms are all so tangled together they should make a fine circuit." Reddleman set his toes near the lamppost's head. He called out to Voleta, "You're going to get a shock. It'll hurt, I'm afraid, but your blood should hold it. It might push you out of time again. Don't stray too far."

Voleta looked to Iren, forcing a smile. "I'll be right back."

Reddleman kicked out his legs, shearing the post near the base. The lantern splashed into the reeking murk with a crack of glass and current. The surface went still then began to boil softly. Atop her meager island, Voleta appeared to stiffen as if in anticipation of a blow. Yet her expression was almost serene. Just as Iren began to think that perhaps she had escaped any ill effect, Voleta's neck started to glow with a ruddy light that rose to her lips, her nose, her eyes.

Something in the distance popped.

The city block went dark. And still, Voleta's head and outstretched hands glowed like the stems of a candelabra.

When the duke charged from the room after Ann, Marya had suffered a surprising flash of indignance. How could he still believe she was so harmless after reciting just a few of the occasions when she had tried to kill him? She had very nearly succeeded more than once. He had survived her attempts on his life by dint of luck, cronyism, and a staff who'd been terrorized into loyalty. He would've drunk the poisoned port she'd prepared had he not been entertaining a guest who had the unlikely ability to smell cyanide. The knife under her pillow was discovered not by the duke but by a maid who'd gone to change the bed linens late in the day after her morning routine had been disrupted by the duke's unwanted attention. There were other close calls as well, and none of her failures had eroded her resolve.

And what the duke had failed to understand was that she had spared him when she'd left his home in Captain Winter's company. She would not be so merciful again.

No sooner had the duke's cloak fluttered behind the bulkhead than her thoughts turned to his discarded crossbow. Wil's evening fondling of his crossbow had revealed to her the means by which it was loaded, aimed, and fired—knowledge that she intended to put to use now.

She ran to it and Byron's side, her jaw locked to cage her grief. This was not the time to mourn. Though she had a weapon, the only ready ammunition jutted from Byron's chest. With an apologetic grimace and averted eyes, she placed one hand on his vest and wrapped the other about the stub of the bolt. She pulled with all her might, quickly adding her other hand to the effort. Rising to stand astride the footman, she heaved as if it to dislodge a stubborn weed. The anvil of Byron's chest rose half an inch from the floor, but still the arrow held. She surrendered the effort with an irate grunt.

Through the communication horn at her pilot's station she heard Olivet bleat in her sleep. She would wake hungry, would summon the duke to her crib with her cries.

Abandoning the effort to strike the dart from Byron's heart, Marya hurried to the weapons cabinet and pulled open the glassless doors Iren had cobbled back together. Pistols hung from pegs above racks of rifles and scatterguns. None were loaded, though she wasn't certain she could've reliably fired one anyway. She rummaged through the rows of sheathed sabers, tucks, and rapiers, even as she tried to imagine herself swinging a sword. It hardly seemed the time for imagination. She needed something simple, something crude and deadly. Beyond the tiers of swords, a long and formidable shaft leaned against the back of the cabinet. As Marya extracted it, she heard the distant twang of a crossbow.

Gripping the harpoon as if it were a spear, Marya ran after the retreating footfalls of the hunter.

Ann's experience working in a variety of domestic situations had exposed her to a seldom-discussed truth about domiciles. It was common enough for garden poets to embellish the notion of *home* with sentimentality and cliché. A home's blemishes were always charming, its odors undetectable, its clutter quaint.

But those same poets were virtually mum on the fact that a home was also a closeted sadist and an aspiring killer.

It took a few weeks, perhaps months, for Ann to discover the shady side of a new home, but sooner or later, she would happen upon the abode's secret arsenal. The murder weapon sometimes came in the form of an uneven board at the head of a staircase, or a scalding hot furnace that could not be tamed, or a pilot light that had the bad habit of going out and gradually filling up a room with gas.

Ann knew that a home would warm your dinner, echo your laughter, then knock you on the head and drown you in the bath.

In the case of the *State of Art* it had taken mere hours for Ann to discover the ship's most perfidious snare. It lay between the main dining room and the brass-railed bar, the far end of which concealed the galley entrance. There was a single step down to the bar area that was rendered nearly indiscernible by a confluence of dim lighting, dark flooring, and an optical illusion caused by the fact that the sunken stools appeared to be the same height as the elevated dining room chairs.

Mere hours after joining the crew, Ann had been trotting along with a stack of dirty dishes when she encountered the trap for the first time. Missing the step had sent her sprawling onto her hands and knees amid the applause of popping porcelain.

Despite the bruises and mortification of the lesson, she was forced to learn it a second time when two days later she met the step coming the other way, and stumbled so completely she upset a table on her way down.

Thereafter, she made a point of addressing the step whenever she approached it. She'd say, "Good morning, Mr. Tumble!" or "So nice to see you again, Mr. Tumble." Or "No time to chat, Mr. Tumble. Little Miss needs a bottle!"

But today, Mr. Tumble would have to come to her rescue.

Ann didn't allow herself to look back, not only because it would impede her negotiation of the tables and chairs in the dining room but also because, all things considered, she'd rather be shot in the back. She suspected that if she had to face her end she might have time to think things like, *Oh, I wish I'd spent less time ironing out creases and more time making them!* So, she charged ahead and spared herself (or very nearly did) bearing witness to a parade of regrets.

She cleared Mr. Tumble as quietly as she could and reached the far wall of the dining room where the pale green of alabaster lamps painted her nightdress a ghostly hue. To her right, the door to the galley promised access to its armory of knives, skillets, and rolling pins. But what good would any of those do to repel a man armed with a crossbow? If she disappeared into the next room, wouldn't he be more likely to proceed with caution? Wouldn't he mind where he stepped? But if she stood like a target, perhaps he would train all of his notice on her and neglect for a moment his feet.

If Mr. Tumble were the snare, she would have to be the bait.

When she turned around, she found the duke had just crept into the room. He appeared to see her the same instant she marked him and lowered his eye to the sight of his weapon. Advancing upon the balls of his feet, he navigated the forest of furniture without stirring a single stick. She raised her hands, a useless gesture that only made him smile. She knew the moment she ran, he'd nail her to the wall, yet the urge was quite profound.

"Would you like a cup of tea?" she said, her voice quavering. "I was just going to make one for myself. We have red, black, or green."

"You're a funny old thing, aren't you?" he said, drawing nearer the step that Ann steadfastly refused to look at.

"Or something stronger, perhaps? There's brandy."

"You know, some men don't like the heel of a loaf of bread. Say it's too rough on the mouth. But I never minded it. Sometimes it's nice to have something tough to chew."

"Or sherry."

"Yes, a good heel of bread works the jaw, hones the teeth. If you eat nothing but young, soft cake it begins to spoil your—" He tread upon the open air. With cheek still pressed upon the stock and eye to the sight, he pitched forward. Ann heard the horrible twang of the bowstring and felt a fiery sensation run the length of her body. The duke landed hard on his elbows, as his weapon clattered away from him and his quiver spilled across the floor.

Ann thought to run to the kitchen, to find a knife, to return and spring upon him while he floundered, but it was as if she'd grown roots. Looking down, she saw a bolt staked her right foot to the floor. The sight of it drew the blood from her head, and she slumped back against the wall to keep from fainting. The duke had already gotten his knees under him. He reached after the nearest of the scattered quarrels, then seemed to think better of it. He left his crossbow on the floor when he drew himself to his feet. Gripping the wrapped wrist beneath his claw, he observed her through the talons.

Marya charged him with her harpoon held level; the sound of her feet brought him around in time to catch the barbed blade with his shoulder rather than his back. He shouted and pivoted away, dislodging the point of the harpoon as Marya continued past. He clapped his good hand over the wound, hissing and spitting as Marya hurried to Ann's side.

Perplexity crimped Marya's brow as she took Ann's elbow to pull her toward the galley. Ann shrugged her off, grabbing at the knee above her pinned foot. Through gritted teeth she said, "Never mind me. Get him!"

Marya faced the duke, who stood examining the blood in his hand, testing the wound again to gauge the flow. "You really stuck me, darling. Oof, that smarts. I wasn't going to kill you, you know, but now I can't remember why. I suppose I just enjoy flirting too much. It's hard to know when to quit." He threw out his cuff, and the hilt of a long knife sprang into his open hand. "You certainly never knew when enough was enough." He scraped the blade upon his claw like a man clashing knife and fork together over a crowded plate.

"Pardon me, sir, but you dropped this."

The duke spun about to see Byron standing above him. He pointed the small crossbow at the duke's head. "But I shot you in the heart," Wilhelm said.

"I haven't got a heart," Byron said, and fired the bolt he'd plucked from his chest into the duke's green eye.

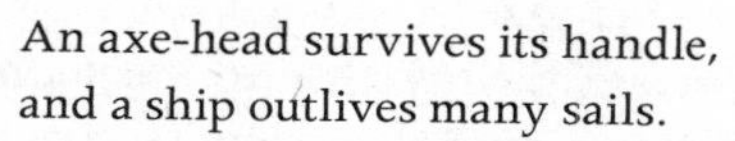

Chapter Nineteen

An axe-head survives its handle,
and a ship outlives many sails.

—*Music for Falling Down Stairs* by Jumet

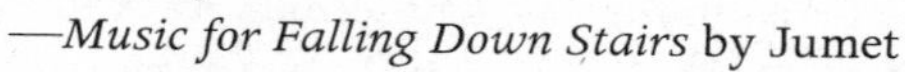

Agony seized Voleta like a shiver that would not subside.

A fire ran up from her feet, turning her blood to steam. She felt like an overfed boiler preparing to explode. She tried to open her mouth to scream but discovered her muscles had fused to her bones.

Then, as quickly as it had come, the pain abated.

For a fleeting moment, darkness swallowed Cilicia, then the streetlights flickered on again to reveal the black waters had vanished. The rosy city stood unstained.

Above her, the fat grapes shriveled into frond-like flowers that then shrank among retreating leaves. The great canopy withdrew into emerald-bright buds that vanished the next instant. But this retreat into winter was short-lived. Soon, the brown stems and bare vines gathered up their fallen leaves and picked up their fruit. The vision of the reversing season played again and again at a quickening pace. Bunches of berries erupted and evaporated; the greenery strobed like the light between passing train cars. The city streets about her coursed with pedestrian ghosts, their features indistinct, their presence thin as a morning mist. They flowed about her and through her perched atop her post.

The only thing that changed little was the architecture. The round edges, scant features, and smooth faces of the buildings reminded her of sandcastles lined up on a shore. The sign that hung over the double doors of the wine bar changed every few seconds. First, the Maundering Benison became the Punt and Collar, which turned into the Swan's Leg, then the Fat Abbot.

She could not guess how many years she had fallen through already. It occurred to her that she ought to try to slow her recession. She focused harder upon the sign, attempting to block out the swirl of indistinct figures who surged and ebbed with the tides of the passing days. She traced the Abbot's curling *A* with her gaze, stroking it like a cat, willing it not to change. Just a moment before, the streetlamps, which dimmed at night and flared in the day, had seemed stuck in a gloomy sort of twilight, but now she could distinguish their strobing, which gradually began to slow.

Something fluttered before her face, calling her attention away from the sign. It was a moth. No, not a real moth. One of the Sphinx's insects. Its white paper wings were unpainted; its brass head horned with feathery antenna, a feature she'd never seen on them before. It seemed to light upon her chest, but when she tried to look down, she found she could not move her head. Still, she felt the moth's legs touch her jugular notch and crawl down to the medallion of the moon she wore about her neck.

All at once, the people in the street were moving at a regular clip. They seemed unaware of her, floating in their midst. It was strange to feel so obvious and yet be so readily overlooked.

Then, from the corner of her eye, she saw the Sphinx approach with the Brick Layer at her side.

The Sphinx was much as she had appeared to Voleta in the ship's conservatory. Her black-hosed legs were visible through the break in her inky robes, and her face was obscured by a small mask, one no larger than a hand mirror. The Brick Layer was as modestly dressed as ever and might've seemed entirely unremarkable had he not strode along with a loupe pinched to his eye by the pressure of his hairy brow.

The pair came at her with such purpose, she was sure they could see her even before they spoke.

"Is that her?" the Sphinx said, her voice still full of the music of youth and hardly recognizable from the rasp Voleta associated with her.

"It is indeed," the Brick Layer said. "I've been looking for you, young lady. You left before we could finish our chat."

* * *

"Catch her!" Reddleman shouted the moment the building's lights went out.

Iren was about to vault the window when Edith shouted at her, "Stay there! That's an order." The captain lowered her feet through the dead bodies of the clogworms until her heels found the street beneath the flood. Resisting the urge to look down, she waded toward Voleta, still standing rigid on her stool, still shining bright. Then, as if she were a marionette whose strings had been cut, Voleta fell.

Edith caught her just above the floating bodies of colorless worms, crowded as noodles in a bowl. Cradling her from knee to neck, Edith slogged on through the toppled stools and unspeakable mire.

"Good day for tall boots," she said between hard breaths.

"Quickly! More may be coming!" Reddleman said.

Edith passed Voleta to Iren, then surmounted the windowsill herself. Iren licked her knuckle and held it under Voleta's beaming nose. "She's breathing," she said. "Why isn't she awake?"

"She'll be all right. She's finding her way back to us. Give her a mo—"

One of the bottles shelved on the wall rattled against its neighbor. Then, as if picking up an alarm call, a second began to chatter, then a third, a fourth, until the assembly cried out as one.

Turning back to the glassless window, Edith saw the water that flooded the Arcade of Pigeage begin to ripple and moil.

"It's here," she said.

"I think we should get away from the window," Reddleman said, and no sooner were the words out of his mouth than the water swelled, pushed out by a growing mound of pulverized stone. The tip of the excavator's mighty trident pierced the growing boil, even as a black wave rose and rolled out in every direction, including theirs.

They rushed to the stairs, Iren at the fore with Voleta squeezed to her chest. The amazon kicked through the chairs like a snowplow clears a track and leapt onto the first step even as the wave broke against the front of the building. The force of the flood blew the doors from their hinges. Water streamed through the breach and gushed over the sandbags. Edith was the last in line, and just managed to evade the splash of rank water as it slapped the back wall.

Voleta's glowing body illuminated the darkened stairwell, guiding them back to the corridor that held the kitchen. Even through the earthen walls, they could hear the monstrous gears.

"Leave her here. She'll be safer," Edith said and helped Iren lower the young woman to the floor. Reddleman pulled off his jacket, balled it up, and braced it under Voleta's feet. When Iren scowled at him, he explained, "Encourages blood flow. It'll help revive her."

Iren knelt over her, kissed her on her pale forehead, and said, "Hurry back."

Then all ran for the roof to see the ironclad beast.

"But who is she?" the Sphinx asked.

The Brick Layer folded his arms high on his chest and leaned in a little closer to inspect Voleta's half-lidded eyes. The wrinkles on his brow made her think of a freshly plowed field. "Perhaps the less we know about her the better. We don't want to interfere needlessly. You trusted her enough to give her your necklace; that's enough for me."

"What if I didn't? What if she stole it?"

"I suppose we could ask her for some reference. Young lady—"

"My name's Voleta." She spoke in an inflectionless mumble like a shy student forced to read aloud before a class.

"How do we know you're a friend?" the Sphinx asked.

"I nearly killed you once," Voleta said, a statement that made the Brick Layer's eyebrows leap. The loupe popped out, though he caught it awkwardly in the basket of his folded arms and returned it to his eye. "You took me to see your lightning crèche, asked me to change your batteries. I was nervous. The lightning startled me. I dropped the vials. The way you looked at me with your good eye—I'll never forget it. When I finally had your batteries in again, you told me all your clocks had stopped. It made me cry. I still haven't forgiven you."

"Well, I'm satisfied. Are you?" the Brick Layer said.

"I am," the Sphinx said softly. A fat gentleman in suspenders with a mustache like two kissing doves stopped to stare at the short Brick Layer and the willowy Sphinx, who must've appeared to be interrogating a ghost in the middle of the street. "Move along, vintner," the Sphinx said in a more confident tone.

"You seem to be falling," the Brick Layer said, tilting his head at Voleta, who found she was no longer upright but drifting to one side.

"Hmm. Strange. Well, we can't waste any more time. There's too much to say."

Voleta could only watch as her hands rose nearer her face, crossed at the wrist, and then settled upon her chest. Feeling as if she were being cradled by absent arms, she drifted toward the doors of the Fat Abbot. "I don't know how you died," she said, presuming that was what he would ask.

"And I do not wish to know. Please, listen carefully, Voleta. You don't have to understand everything I'm about to tell you, but you must remember it and tell those who need to know. It is essential that you not open the bridge before the attic reservoir is full. If you do, you will eventually be stranded upon an endless sea. The light of the pyramidion will fail. You will starve or freeze to death or go mad in the dark."

Voleta found this information, though obviously dire, too obtuse to be alarming. He might as well have told her there were sharks in the cornfields or cannonballs in the bath. She tried to focus on one part of his message, which seemed a little familiar. "The reservoir? Do you mean the lightning sea? That's what the captain calls it. Captain says the sea is boiling. It could explode."

The news obviously concerned the Brick Layer. "It's past time, then. You must act, and soon."

"The Sphinx isn't answering us. The gates are sealed. We're locked out."

Voleta passed through the closed doors of the Fat Abbot as if they were a shadow. A quarter of the barstools were occupied by patrons who leaned on elbows over short pours of wine. All the tables were empty. The Sphinx and the Brick Layer opened the doors to follow her. Without looking, the bartender shouted that he was about to close for the afternoon. Then he saw who he'd barked at and began to apologize until the Sphinx finally managed to wave him into silence. The Sphinx bent and whispered into Voleta's ear.

When she was finished, Voleta murmured, "A bottled storm? A skylight? What—"

The Sphinx touched Voleta's forehead with a velveteen finger. "Remember."

Voleta floated just low enough for the diminutive Brick Layer to look her in the face as he walked backward, bumping into chairs, retreating as she advanced. His voice was suddenly very close, pervasive, inescapable. His voice felt like water trapped within her ears.

He spoke in a desperate rush: "Listen to me! Before you open the bridge, the windstiles must be shut; the Nautilus, sealed. The Allonomia is being kept in a state of suspension by the slow water, but once you flood the Nautilus, it will awaken. When it does, there's no putting it back to sleep. You must be ready. You must—"

He vanished, his voice draining from her head. The lights above began to flash; the patrons turned to smudges. She continued her slow, bobbing transit to the stairwell, then upward through a cascade of ghosts. She passed through the onslaught of time tucked up like a fetus in a womb.

From the rooftop of the Maundering Benison, Edith peeked over the thick parapet at the head of the iron trilobite. It rose from the black water like a drowning worm, struggling from its hole. The plates of its articulating shell shifted, and the engine curled down, its legs marching in the air in search of the ground it could not yet reach. Its drilling horn continued to whirl, slinging muck into the fountain's pools and lashing the Cups of Plenty with filth. The drill clipped one of the storied vats. The laughing faces turned to gravel as the Hod King continued to thrash.

At last, the spear-tipped legs of the engine reached the ground, and the Hod King pulled its tail free of the bore. As it came, so the waters went—draining into the gravel-filled well so quickly it frothed and bubbled like the maw of a rabid dog. As the flood receded, the colorless worms fled outward in search of water, though many were left stranded and slapping in puddles.

The trident's churning slowed; the gnashing of its teeth faded. The dripping engine turned in place, seeming to survey the befouled and lifeless city.

"What's he doing?" Iren asked.

And as if in answer, the siege engine's battery of portside cannons fired in quick succession. The balls whistled above their ducked heads and struck the palace. Rows of voluptuous pilasters were cut down to their plinths. Craters appeared in the grand facade, long-necked gargoyles surrendered their heads, and the panes of windows popped amid a great squall of glass, wood, and plaster. Somewhere inside the palace, a curtain-wrapped cannonball crashed through a piano. The instrument gave a final, atonal shout.

"He's probably testing the waters. Making sure there isn't an army lying in wait." Edith brushed masonry dust from her shoulder. Then, to the surprise of all, the Hod King produced what seemed an emphatic fart: a great expulsion of wind that was immediately followed by the whine of fans and the chugging of pumps.

"They're cycling in new air. Picked a bad spot for it, didn't they?" Reddleman's smile was as brief as a wink. "Soon as that's finished, I imagine they'll be on their way."

"Then it's time we played our hand," Edith said.

Reddleman had the craning appearance of one looking for an empty seat in a crowded café. "I'd thought there'd be more people here to divide their attention. There's no way to cross the arcade without being seen. I'll need a distraction if I'm going to put a bomb on its belly."

"Did you have something in mind?"

Reddleman produced the electric candle from his pocket. "Perhaps you should just keep it simple, Captain. Turn the candle on and lead him away."

"Won't he smell a trap?"

"Try to be subtle. Well, I mean, you'll want to be obvious enough to get their attention, but not so much as to rouse suspicion. Be modestly obvious."

"Just be ready with the bomb," Edith said, and snatched the candle from his hand like an unhappy customer accepting a bill.

Not wishing to call down the Hod King's wrath upon an entranced Voleta, Edith endeavored to put as much distance between them as possible before switching on the candle. She crept across the unlit rooftops, furtive as a fox, listening to the gulp of the Hod King's pumps. The noise made the leaves above her shiver and the ripest grapes fall. They pelted her shoulders and the brim of her cocked hat as she straddled the half walls between terraces and tiptoed across impromptu bridges. She kept the Arcade of Pigeage on her right and within sight. The Hod King stood nearly four stories tall.

She came upon a sturdy trellis that had been turned into a gangplank. Withered vines drooped from the lattice. The sight made her temper spike in a way she found perplexing. Why should a few shriveled leaves make her blood boil? In fact, why have any feeling for this spoiled metropolis at all?

Since the Sphinx had given her the *State of Art* to command, there had been occasions when Edith wondered if the Tower was even *worth* saving. It was only a structure, after all, an environment that seemed to permit, if not court, corruption and exploitation. It was a place where natives preyed upon the displaced and ringdoms made their fortunes by bilking the vulnerable. The administrators were inept, the guardians treacherous, and the regents unmoored from reality.

Edith's father had taught her the dangers of exhausting the earth. It was possible—in fact, almost easy—to suck all the life from the soil, to deplete it so completely that not even weeds would grow. Her father had taught her that to keep a plot of land vital, a farmer had to sometimes silo his seeds, plow the earth, and let the field go fallow. Perhaps the same was true of the Tower. Perhaps the negligence she saw in evidence everywhere was not some wicked conspiracy but rather an ancient instinct to harrow the ground, to let the earth rest for the benefit of future generations. Perhaps it would be for the best if the old stalk was mown down.

But looking at those flaccid vines, she did not feel cynicism or despair. No, she felt angry. The stupidity, disregard, and entitlement of Queen Hortensia would not bring about a greener spring. Having escaped all consequence, the queen would loaf upon a cloud until her city manager, conscripted airmen, and unlucky hods could mop up her mess. Then she would return and, with the long guns of her navy bristling at her back, assure her remaining subjects that they had all suffered the inconvenience equally. She would defer any responsibility for the spill but would certainly accept credit for the recovery.

So it went. So it always went.

Since she'd taken up the mantle of Wakeman, Edith had felt only the burden of her duty to the Tower, but glancing up at the great and bursting crop overhead, she realized why she was so irate. She was mad because she cared, and she resented those who did not. The Tower was more than a structure, just as a farm was more than a patch of dirt. A farm was also its crop and livestock, and the sustenance they provided to the women and men who devoted their lives to them. A farm was the children who grew there, the happiness they inspired, the music they made, the traditions they learned. A farm was the love of the land and a keen regard for the stellar bodies that wheeled through the heavens, shepherding in seasons of birth, growth, death, and rebirth. The Tower was not a structure; it was a farm.

Though she had hoped to find affection elsewhere, it came as something of a relief to find there was still love in her heart and a purpose worthy of that passion.

Then the Hod King's pumps fell silent, and she realized she was out of time.

Stepping from the trellis bridge, Edith probed her pocket for the electric candle. Finding it, she thought to shield it with her engine hand to make it appear, as Reddleman had suggested, "modestly obvious." She thumbed the switch on. The brash light flared to life in the same instant that the steely cylinder slipped from her grasp. She tried to catch it in the air, but again it eluded her. It felt like she was trying to get ahold of a fish she'd just pulled from a lake. It leapt between her hands twice more, flashing in every direction along the way, then tumbled toward the tiled floor beneath her. She threw out the toe of her boot to catch it, but only succeeded in kicking the electric candle over the low parapet. It turned end over end, falling three stories, before popping upon the cobbles below.

With a breath stuck in her chest, she looked out at the broad side of the silent, hunkering Hod King. She wondered if her spectacular display had gone unnoticed. Then the siege engine's legs began to march, and its horn swung toward her. Near the base of the trident, two black half-moons rose. They resembled nostrils, or so Edith thought before they shone forth like beacons on a rocky shore. She raised a hand to shield the light from her eyes. The tattooing of spear-tipped legs commenced a quicker march. Between the crack of her splayed fingers, Edith saw the devilish pitchfork begin to whir once more.

Chapter Twenty

True conspiracies are inflexible and susceptible to discovery, but imaginary plots are ever evolving and, as a result, invulnerable. That is to say, conspiracies are perishable, paranoia is not.

—*Everyman's Guide to the Tower of Babel*, VIII. I

From behind the gold-vined column of one of the Cups of Plenty, Reddleman watched the captain leap from roof to roof. She appeared no larger than a fly ticking against a window, and her movements were almost as lively. When the Hod King's pumps fell silent, she halted, switched the beam of her candle on, and waved it about wildly before casting it into the street. He wondered whether his advice had been unclear, or if the captain had simply decided upon a less subtle tactic.

For a moment, it seemed her antics had gone unnoticed. Then the mighty trilobite turned and began to march upon her position. Reddleman smiled. The titan had taken the bait.

A thorough study of the Hod King's schematics had convinced him that the walking fortress had a blind spot. The dead zone extended from the aftercastle, where the fierce Quibbler was housed, and winnowed to a point some hundred paces behind. Reddleman had already managed to flank the engine by circling around the spine and keeping either the fountains or the chalices between himself and it. But now, he had no choice but to test the existence of the blind spot. He would have to break cover and make a dash for the Hod King's undercarriage.

With match in hand and bomb underarm, he charged into the dead zone.

Dancing through puddles and over tangles of expiring clogworms, he bounded for the drumming feet of the engine as they rose and fell in rolling order. He suffered the fearful giddiness of a child rushing into ocean surf. He had to stop himself from shouting in delight.

Then the sterncastle, which warted the engine's shell like a barnacle, came alive with activity that dispelled the hope that he could skirt detection. Scowling faces appeared in the notches of the crenelated turret. The woolly and wooden heads of cannon sponges and rammers flitted about behind them. They were loading the guns. But already he was under the range of their cannons and closing on the shelter of the stalking engine.

The first cannonball to fall nearly landed on his foot. It shattered the marble tile, tilting it upward and causing him to stumble—though not fall. Another missile thudded just behind him. He looked up in time to dodge the third ball by springing to one side. The hods above had abandoned their barrels and black powder in favor of gravity, which could deliver a twenty-pound shot violently enough.

The need for evasion made the distance expand as he was forced to run like a stitch, juking and jinking this way and that. The balls rained all about him, popping the marble floor like a bootheel breaks thin ice. The pistons of the engine's legs churned more quickly, and the Hod King began to pull away as its horn roared to full speed, its head lowered like a charging ram's. From the aftercastle above, some clever goon poured out a bag of grapeshot. The pellets cracked Reddleman's head, bruised his shoulders, and rolled underfoot. It was all he could do to keep his ankles from buckling as he bent forward to shelter the bomb with his back.

When the Hod King's drill touched the building that the captain had been standing upon a moment before, there rose a crash of rending earth and grinding metal. The excavator's jog slowed to the deliberate trudge of a plow horse; its feet gouged the marble like hooves sink into mud. The Hod King ground the three-story home down to a ragged stump in a matter of seconds, then pressed forward to demolish the next building in the block.

At last, Reddleman passed under the shadow of the carapace and clear of the bombardment from above. A rivulet of glowing red ran down his nose. He did not stop to daub the wound on the crown of his head, but ran faster down the colonnade of iron legs, counting under his breath as he went. Glancing up, he saw the underbelly was a patchwork of scrap metal, welded together, and only occasionally reinforced with a thicker girder. The sight filled him with relief: He had been right; its armor was penetrable here. His bomb would break through.

Past the great churning confusion of the drill, which whipped wall into rubble and rubble into dust, he saw yet another building crumbling before the engine's advance. He could only hope the captain had gotten clear. She just needed to run a little while longer. He had reached the spot. The Master of Bells stood above him, though Reddleman could not hear his music over the clamor of the drill. He lifted the match to his mouth and struck it upon a tooth. He held it to the fuse, which he had braided and trimmed himself, a precaution that only served to make the premature explosion especially disappointing.

Edith found the Hod King's speed astonishing. When it had beetled along the face of the Tower, she had been impressed by its armor and artillery, but its swiftness had been subdued by distance and perspective. Standing in its path now, the excavator seemed less like a scurrying crab and more like a thundering train.

She reached the back edge of the terrace the same moment the churning drill touched the front of the house. The rooftop leapt, throwing her to one side, onto an upholstered divan. She rolled back to her feet and jumped onto the perimeter wall just as the floor caved in behind her. The sofa slid into the advancing propeller and burst into a swarm of wood chips, springs, and batting. The adjacent building appeared scarcely within reach, but seeing no choice, she hurled herself over the void. She caught the lip of the neighboring wall with the toes of her boots. Teetering backward, she swung her arms and reeled herself onto the roof. Stumbling across a disheveled, lumpy rug, she bowled through a dining set. She didn't need to look to know when the Hod King's lance staved the house beneath her. The sound of shattering glass and splintering furniture burst from the windows like screams from an asylum. Again, the floor beneath her cracked and drooped. And again, she reached the opposite wall a second before the house fell in on itself. She sprang onto the plank that spanned the alley, heard it fracture beneath her heel, and half expected it to break. But the board held long enough to deliver her to the next rooftop. She landed on surer footing and crossed the terrace in six quick strides, before being confronted by the tall bare wall of the adjoining structure. She cast about for any sign of ladder, window, or scalable gutter, but found none. On one side of her stood the gap of a courtyard, on the other yawned a broad avenue. She was trapped.

Facing the engine once more, she found it had raised the central tine of its monstrous drill level with her. The outer prongs devoured the upper story, roaring like a chorus of buzz saws. Turning away from the omnivorous maw, Edith cocked her engine arm and struck the wall. Her fist shattered the outer coat of plaster, pocking the adobe beneath. While her ribs still rang from the first blow, she applied a second, then a third. The crater grew, the cracks spread out, but too slowly to inspire hope. She felt an unnatural wind at her back, and the floor of the roof began to slope. Feeling the sudden exhaustion of acceptance, she rested her forehead upon the wall and, raising her human hand, knocked the faithful pattern: hard, soft, hard. She wondered where this door would lead her, and whether she would one day see Tom there.

The muffled whoomph of an explosion rumbled through Edith's chest, and she turned in time to see the Hod King's horn lunge away, over the avenue. What seemed at first a flinch turned into a full stagger as the engine's legs buckled, crossed, and fell out of step. The colossal drill swung toward the ringdom's royal bank, a conspicuously august structure amid the mudbrick city. An ornate rotunda crowned the institution, or did, until the drill split the dome like a spoon opens a soft-boiled egg. The engine's broad bow crashed into the bank's pillars, then the drunken locomotive lurched back toward the half-demolished house Edith stood atop. When it clipped the facade, the ground under her opened like a trapdoor. She fell through a great storm of detritus and grit into the crushed and jumbled remnants of a dining room. She landed on a tilting cabinet that pitched forward, vomiting fine china into the crumbling world. Feeling like a card being shuffled into a deck, she tumbled into the bewildering dark.

When at last she came to a rest, Edith found herself a little buried, but not crushed. She felt around blindly, finding a way forward through the wreckage. She crawled and wriggled without any sense of where she was going. Something blocked her way; it felt like an empty bookshelf. Punching through its back, she uncorked a shaft of dim light. Following the promise of an exit, she soon muscled her way free of the ruin.

Coughing into her fist, she shuffled through the haze into the avenue where the Hod King continued to reel like a stung scorpion. On shaky legs, she followed its retreat past the rubble of the homes it had demolished, back to the edge of the Arcade of Pigeage. The excavator crashed into four more of the immense marble cups, bowling them over like pins on a lawn. The drill carved a trench in the floor, clattering and leaping as it slowed. Then all at once, the wicked horn popped free of the Hod King's head.

Edith could hardly believe her eyes as she stood bearing witness to the death throes of a giant.

They had done it. They had won.

Unfamiliar, fluttering hope stirred the currents of her heart.

Reddleman rushed to her side, his face streaked with ashen blood. Despite his own injury, he presented himself as a crutch; she accepted as she continued to clear her lungs.

"It worked. You did it," she said between coughs.

"No, indeed." Reddleman lightly patted the bulge in his satchel. "Someone set off a bomb; it just wasn't me. In fact, I was almost trampled when—"

Amid the broken halo of stone vats, the Hod King collapsed in a wave. The buckling began with its head and carried on down its length, each thudding section seeming to pull down the next in line. The echo of each resounding clang splashed back and forth across the domed city until the beast lay flat on its belly and the clamor rolled away like thunder into the distance.

Silence came, a calm so entire they could once again hear the trickling of the fountains.

"What happened?" Edith asked.

"Given the progress of its collapse, I think the explosion may have originated in the engine room."

Unhooking her arm from his neck, Edith cleared her throat and said, "I suppose we should be ready for a fight."

"Perhaps. Or perhaps the blast was sufficient to cook the crew."

As they marched upon the iron carcass, Edith scowled at the possibility that Tom was dead or dying. But their advance was soon broken by the popping of ten thousand rivets, each sharp as the crack of a pistol. The hull broke along its circumference, the segmented shells of the carapace parting from the base. The excavator's bow opened like the mouth of a whale, and a second engine scuttled out of the head of the fallen King. The machine was much smaller, not even a quarter the size of the outer shell. Skittering on six quick legs behind a blunt, round nose, the machine seemed as slender and lithe as a silverfish, albeit one plated in burnished steel.

When the newborn vessel turned toward them, they saw a mouth of burr grinders circling around a darkened hub. With a grunt of fascination, Reddleman said, "Well, aren't you a curious fellow!"

The bark of a field gun proceeded a splash of pellets upon the hull of the nascent engine. Edith looked around to discover the source and saw Iren reloading her gun on the roof of the wine bar. The heir to the Hod King seemed to regard Edith a moment longer before curling about. It crawled over the husk of its former self, splashed through the pool, and climbed onto the Tower's spine. Coiling around the prodigious pier, the engine soon reached the roof of the ringdom. It buried its head among the leafy vines and began to dig.

They could do nothing but watch falling gravel boil the fountain's waters as the engine opened a burrow that would end in the Sphinx's parlor.

Edith was surprised when the first shorn head peeked from a smoking fissure in the Hod King's husk. Then a second popped up like a prairie dog, eyes wide and staring. More followed—their number grew to a dozen, then a score, until soon nearly a hundred men and women had clambered through the ribs of the fallen beast.

She had to fight the urge to rush forward in search of Senlin. She assumed Marat had escaped aboard the silverfish. Hope had fled. She had failed to save the Tower. But if all was beyond redemption, she wished at least to have rescued her friend.

She had already settled upon what she would do when they were reunited. She would offer him a companionable handshake, perhaps cap it off with a slap on the shoulder. She would tell him he looked well whether he did or not, then say that Marya and his daughter were waiting for him aboard the *State of Art*. And that would be that.

If she allowed herself a more familiar gesture—an embrace, for example—she was afraid she might blurt out the truth and say, "I destroyed the record of your affection in the hopes that it would purge what you said from my memory, but it did not, and no matter how I try, I can't extinguish this stubborn feeling I have no right to feel. I know I must trade love for duty, but I'm afraid that will only work if I do not hold you like this or let your voice warm my ear."

No, they could not commiserate, or celebrate, or review the past. In time, whatever affection lingered in her heart would fade into fondness.

In time, his voice would rattle out of her head. Today, she would shake his hand, slap his shoulder, deliver him to his wife and child, and then, as soon as possible, deposit them in a safe harbor and never look back.

The hods gathered upon the hull like sailors climbing onto an overturned boat. To Edith's relief, they appeared unarmed. She would come to learn that the pistols and rifles were stowed inside the nested engine. Even so, the men and women presented a less-than-toothless foe. They bore the tempered physiques of long, hard labor, and they numbered well over a hundred. If they attacked with only their fists, Edith knew she'd not be able to rebuff them all.

She had to address them and dissuade them from violence.

Climbing onto the base of one of the Cups of Plenty that the Hod King had relieved of its basin, she scanned the crowd for a familiar face. Failing to find it, she said, "Look around you, my friends. Luc Marat has abandoned you. I do not know how many of you were willing crew and how many unwilling slaves. It hardly matters now. You are all castaways. Perhaps some among you will think Marat's willingness to sacrifice you is somehow fitting or honorable. I promise you, it is neither. You are not chattel. You are not cogs. You are men and women who deserve better for your loyalty. You deserve better from the Tower and better from me.

"Cilicia's royalty has fled. They drowned their city in sewage, then took to their heels rather than confront the consequences of their mistake. As a result, they have surrendered their claim to this ringdom. I will not allow the queen or a single member of her court to return. If they try, I will strike down their ships. This ringdom will operate under the guidance of the city engineer until such time that new leaders can be elected. If you are willing to stay and help rebuild, you will have a home and a vote going forward. Until then, you can lodge in the palace. Eat down the queen's pantries. Drink up her cellars. Or, if you wish, you may return to the black trail and wait for Marat to come collect you. The choice is yours. I suggest you choose to serve yourselves rather than a man who has used you like a steppingstone and left you with nothing but a boot print on your head."

She'd not expected cheers, and so was not disappointed when none came. She was, however, relieved to see that no one seemed interested in a fight. Judging by their dazed appearance and their slow dismounting, they looked hardly up for a brawl at the moment.

"Rousing stuff," Reddleman said. "Can you do that, though? Banish queen and court, I mean? Won't the Sphinx object to such an obvious interjection into ringdom politics?"

Stepping down from her cracked stage, Edith said, "Then I'll just have to convince him... *her*."

"The last time I offered a suggestion to the Sphinx, she suggested she might return me to the Baths for re-drowning."

The corners of Edith's mouth tightened, a vestigial smile to conceal her racing and increasingly bleak thoughts. *Where was he? Was he trapped inside the mangled wreck—bleeding, dying, dead?*

"Edith?" The deep voice rose above the muttering of the disoriented crowd. She found its source: a man who resembled an emaciated bear—tall, with a broad and hairy chest, and a hollowed-out stomach. The soot on his face made his wide and wondering smile seem to glow.

"Do I know you?" she said.

"My name is John Tarrou. I'm sure Senlin told you all about our escapades in the Baths. He helped me out of a deck chair once; I'd gotten rather stuck. I helped him steal a painting." He wiped at watering eyes, making mud on his cheeks. "And I was so looking forward to a breath of fresh air. What happened here? It smells like someone burned down an outhouse."

"Where is he?"

As he spoke Tarrou turned halfway about, surveying the fallen engine. "The headmaster landed a plum position. While I was sweeping out cannons and Finn had his head in the furnace, ol' Tom was..." His gaze followed the snow of mortar to the hole in the ringdom's roof. "What is that? What happened here?"

"It appears the Hod King was something of a nesting doll," Reddleman said, presenting himself to John, who'd not yet noticed him.

When Tarrou saw the Red Hand, recognition dawned at once. He raised his hands to his chin like a startled sleeper pulling up a sheet. "You!"

"Me. Well, somewhat me." Reddleman grimaced and stroked the air as if a pantomime might calm the big man's nerves. "I've had a change of heart."

"There's a lot of that going around," someone else said from behind Tarrou. Edith found the voice dimly familiar, and yet when Finn Goll stepped out from the bear's shadow, her heart leapt and her hand fell to her sidearm. Though his head was shaved, Goll's eyebrows were as stark and active as ever. He drew them together, steepling his forehead with wrinkles of contrition. Though she did not find the expression altogether convincing, he sounded sincere when he said, "No need for that, Winters. We're all friends here."

"Are we?" Iren said from over Edith's shoulder. Edith turned to see the amazon striding across the arcade. She held Voleta over her shoulder like a sack of flour.

Goll leaned back as if pushed by a wind, though he kept his feet planted. "Hello, Iren."

When she stopped, Iren pushed out her jaw and fattened her lower lip until she looked like a pensive bulldog. "How're the kids?" she asked at last.

"Driving their mother mad, I'm sure. I haven't seen them in a while."

"You can put me down, now, please. Really, I'm fine," Voleta said, twisting about. Iren set her down, and the young woman dusted her jacket to reclaim some dignity.

"Voleta?" Finn Goll said, his voice light with disbelief. "What did you do to your hair?"

Scrunching her chin into her neck at the sight of her old slaver, Voleta said, "I ate it. What are you doing here?"

"Just taking in the sights."

"All right, that's enough," Edith said sharply. "I'm so glad we could have this lovely reunion, but honestly, the one person I wanted to see isn't here. Where is Senlin?"

"He was on the bridge with Marat," Tarrou said, his eyes again straying to the borehole above. "Looks like he's gone on without us—an unmasked traitor."

"Tom? A traitor?" Edith squinted at the absurd suggestion.

"Oh, yes. Tom stabbed the old zealot in the back. But it looks like his timing was bad. We were all supposed to have been buried alive. We're all supposed to be sharing a coffin with Luc Marat." Tarrou looked to Finn Goll, whose expression had turned as haggard as a pallbearer. "But we're alive, and Luc's escaped. And I'm afraid it's all your fault, Edith Winters."

From the Belly of the Beast

4

Souls are like sails. Without a mast to cling to and a ship to pull, the ocean winds will whip them to shreds. It is constraint, purpose, and labor that gives a soul its shape.

—from the sermons of Luc Marat (translated from hoddish)

~~In my time as a thief, I've carried many tools of the trade: lockpicks, marked cards, grappling hooks, and a cigar box full of false noses. But none were as important as how I carried myself. Confidence is the crook's shield, and bearing is her sword. If one slouches into a gamble, one can expect to~~

As it turned out, heaven smelled absolutely foul.

When the Hod King breached the floor of the penultimate ringdom of Cilicia, a ringdom that Thornton had described as the cask of the gods, the external vents of the siege engine began to gasp in air that was beyond noisome.

Upon his throne in the wheelhouse, Marat masked his mouth with his hand. The crew gagged and coughed. Even with the stench of the black trail fresh in their nostrils, the incoming fumes still made their stomachs churn.

And yet Senlin smiled. He smiled because his official performance that morning had been moderately improved, passible, even. He had not forgotten the names of numbers or stammered into the brass ears of his superiors. He'd been surer of his readings and quicker in his responses.

In fact, when the engine reached the mid-burrow point, with a hundred feet of rubble behind it, and a hundred feet of block afore, Senlin had felt so confident in his command of the moment that he had very nearly delivered the password to Finn Goll.

But he had reined in his hubris, had held fast because he'd heard the chief navigator lay out the day's course, the final stage of the Hod King's ascent, revealing that the last leg of their long climb would be the most precarious, the slowest, with the narrowest of margins. There'd be no black trail to escape to, no alternative to suffocation. They would have to creep between lead plumbing and a column full of unzippered lightning. And that was when he would strike—when the blow would be most certain and fatal.

The fact that his adventure would soon come to an end filled Senlin with a dreamy sort of serenity, a magnanimity of spirit, the likes of which he had not felt in many, many months. In days past, Tom had done his best to avoid making eye contact with Marat's formidable bodyguard, but reconsidering him now, Senlin found his beetled scowl theatrical and his probing squint a little nearsighted. Hanif's habit of folding his arms in a muscular knot over his chest now seemed a pose of self-consolation rather than domination. The cleaver at his hip seemed better suited to hacking weeds in a garden than limbs upon the battlefield. Senlin recalled the tenderness that the strong man always showed his master as he shifted him from wheelchair to throne and back, a ritual that seemed almost maternal.

Looking about at the rest of the officers on the bridge, Senlin found them similarly abloom with sensibilities. What had seemed an indistinguishable gathering of background actors before now flowered with personality and foible: He saw in them insecurity, cheerfulness, waggishness, and thinly veiled anxiety. All at once, they were as diverse and contradictory as the crew of the *Stone Cloud*.

Once more, he was visited by doubt. Was all this—this wrangle, this plot—was it righteousness or was it vengeance? Wisdom or madness? There was recognizable humanity here, and sympathetic flaws. Must those redeeming qualities be extinguished, too?

Though what did he expect? Tyranny had many victims, and rarely spared its own. He hadn't time to resurrect the consciences of those who'd chosen to serve one who only served himself; he could not reason with those who had dismantled their own minds from ratiocination down to alphabet. It was possible to mourn the loss of potential—including his own—while celebrating the world that would survive them.

The zealot, though closing upon his final goal, was not in a winning mood. The fact that the Hod King had broken upon a half-lit, apparently abandoned ringdom filled Marat with dread. He ordered a careful survey of their surroundings and the investigatory volleys of many balls and grapeshot, the result of which he watched with undiminished suspicion.

As the pumps worked to cycle in fresh-but-foul air, Senlin set his eye to his station's pentascope. He beheld a dim ringdom canopied in greenery and fortified in pink stucco. Festoons of foggy grapes drooped over a metropolis of stout vigas and florid terraces. The architecture was at once quaint and conspicuous, like a paper crown set with an authentic jewel. And yet, this facade was eclipsed by a midnight of mud: the malls and streets of the ringdom were drowned in dark sewage, a grotesque sea that crested with the humps of pale worms. It was at once a terrible and incredible sight.

The Hod King seemed to have surfaced near the midpoint of the central plaza. Even as Senlin began to scrutinize the monumental goblets that ornamented the arcade, a flicker of light from the periphery caught his eye. With a twist of his eyepiece, he enlarged the various views of his pentascope and, focusing his attention upon a single cell, he beheld the rooftop of a manor. The flash of light obscured the culprit, who seemed to be juggling an electric candle of some sort. Then the masking light fell away, and Senlin saw her: face aghast, cocked hat knocked back, arms out as if she were bowing before an encore.

Thoughtlessly, he leaned forward, depressing a bank of switches with the bar of his arm. He murmured into the ears of the broadcasting horns, "Edith. You're alive. My god, you're—"

"The Arm of the Sphinx," Marat said, his eye pressed to the cup of his periscope. Pulling back from a barrel that bore the dimples and rivets of repair, Marat said, "Or Edith, as she's known to her friends."

Senlin swiveled about to face his unwanted captain. His guile exhausted at last, Senlin could not contrive a pacific face. His eyes watered with relief at Edith's survival and his cheeks flushed with anger at the sight of her would-be murderer. Finding he could not concoct a lie, Senlin watched Marat's expression flatten with comprehension: *His Tom was not the toady he pretended to be.*

"Someone's advancing on our aft, sir," the tactician said at a heightened pitch.

Annoyed by this interruption of his murderous stare, Marat said, "Well, open fire."

"He's already under our range, sir. He appears to be carrying some sort of . . . parcel."

"Well, use your imagination. Pelt him with iron! Lambaste him with lead."

"Lambaste, sir?" the tactical officer asked.

"Throw balls at his head! And fire on the woman—no, *wait*." Marat smiled at Senlin. "Mow her down."

The navigator quickly piped up, "Sir, the Master of Bells is asking for clarification on—"

"Charge!" Marat shouted into his horn.

Taking what he imagined would be his final moment of liberty, Senlin leaned to the trumpet that wound down to the furnace room and said, "Marya, Marya, Marya."

Even thinned by the distance and distorted by the plumbing, Finn Goll could still hear the awe in Senlin's voice when it bled from the battered trumpet above the furnace: "Edith. You're alive. My god, you're—"

Then, all at once, they were at war. All stations were called. The engineer on the bridge shouted for more heat as the Hod King rolled and pitched beneath them, upsetting the precarious mounds of books from uncapped carts. The long-limbed fireman swung upon the arm of the bellows like a bellman on his ropes, making the flames leap from the coals and out the furnace door. The fire licked Finn's shovel and the fuel it carried.

When Finn heard the instigating phrase tumble from the communication horn, it sounded comically pedestrian. Though, in fairness, what had he expected of the headmaster? Tom couldn't muster a battle cry if he were leading the cavalry and his horse was on fire. It sounded as if Senlin was calling his wife's name from the living room. It didn't help that his pitch suggested an unfinished question, as if he'd been interrupted while trying to ask, "Marya... have you seen my reading glasses?" or "Marya... is there any more butter?" or "Marya... has the post come yet?"

But what did it matter? Even a humble, hissing fuse could touch off a mighty blaze.

While the man on the bellows gave a wheezy shout for Finn to get back to his post, the lord of port squeezed past the overloaded fuel carts. He reached under the carriage of an empty wagon and extracted a trio of books, robust volumes that he had hollowed out and filled with black powder smuggled out from Tarrou's gunnery station. Finn had glued the tomes shut with beetle porridge and reinforced the seal with thongs torn from the hem of his own sarong. They were crude incendiaries, and yet when laid inside a sealed oven, he hoped they would be enough.

He threw the wrapped bombs into the fire, then, using the butt of his shovel, closed the furnace door and knocked down the heavy latch.

"I'd run if I were you," Finn said to his peer as he hastened to the door.

Still plying his bar, the bellows man rasped over his shoulder, "Lely will skin you alive and make gloves out of your hide!"

Then the furnace door burst from its hinges, and the lungs of the bellows exploded, and the fire that had been dawdling about the threshold of the oven strode into the room.

"Look, Tom! I want you to witness the end of your infantile hope, your dumb luck, and all your feckless plans. Put your head down, or I'll have Hanif bow it for you! You steered us here, now watch her die!" Marat roared, leaning to the edge of his throne.

Again, Senlin lowered his eye to the pentascope and the bouncing image of Edith's back, growing larger even as she fled across the rooftop and leapt into the air. Swift as she was, the Hod King was quicker. He saw at once she would not get away.

He felt the lurch of the collision with the manor, like a wave breaking upon the bow of a stout ship. The Hod King slowed, but only just. He saw her panic grow and then be eclipsed by her anger as she reached the limit of her retreat. With her back against a wall, she turned away and he thought at first she did so to spare herself the morbid view of the trident coming to stir her life from her bones. But rather than cower, she began to beat upon the wall with her indomitable engine. The mortar cracked, a divot formed, but it was clear the brick would hold. Her desperate effort to pummel her way to freedom turned cloudy as tears gathered in Senlin's eyes.

A boom ran through the engine's girders like a finger down the strings of a harp as the Hod King heaved violently to starboard. Even strapped to their stations, the limbs of the crew leapt and waved as if attempting to escape the trunks of their bodies. The noxious fug of the air was abruptly spiced with smoke. Even before the thunder of the explosion had rumbled out, panicked voices from all the ship's stations crowded the communication horns. Four cannoneers—no, five—had been bucked from their castles. The furnace room was aflame; the fuel carts roared like pyres. Three of the four air pumps had failed. Smoke was already flooding stepper's galley, and the Master of Bells had been grievously injured, thrown into a girder, though Hodder Lely continued to shout between violent, wet coughs. She asked for orders even as her capacity for hearing them failed and her effort to keep the rhythm of her chimes faltered. Hanif, who had not been prepared for the deck to pitch so violently, was thrown to his knees. He slid to the back of the wheelhouse, grasping for and missing the spindles of the railing. The bridge lights flared, then vanished when the prow broke awkwardly upon the facade of some unforgiving structure. The rending of metal that followed in the darkness was as violent as a train leaping from its tracks. Still, the titan continued a seemingly endless, disorienting collapse. Senlin, who'd thought himself ready for death a moment before, discovered at a stroke the absolute petulance of such thoughts. More than anything, he wished to survive, to walk free, to hold his wife and kiss his child and watch the Bay of Isaugh grate the evening sun into a fleeting galaxy.

When at last the stillness came, it brought with it the electric lamps, though the light from them seemed thinner and less certain. On either side of him, the crew cradled their heads, kneaded their abused limbs, and tugged dazedly at their harnesses. The voices from the ship's plumbing had turned into an insensible moaning. Hanif stood, sliding his back up the bulkhead like a man in need of a crutch. Touching the back of his head, he drew away a bloody hand. He seemed bewildered; his eyes were hooded with pain as he surveyed the bridge. Then he stiffened and the whites of his eyes grew large. His shock seemed contagious. Senlin watched as the rest of the strapped-in crew, one by one, began to gape upon a single object.

Grunting at the pain, Senlin twisted his head to follow their fascination.

The zealot stood before his throne on bent golden legs laureled by geysers of steam. He had the posture of one who'd been thrown from his saddle but somehow managed to land on his feet. For a flitting moment, he seemed nearly as surprised as his followers.

But then, while the crew continued to gawk at their risen lord, Marat's own focus turned toward Senlin, even as he bent down to his communication horn and said, "You were right about Tom, Mr. Gedge. Ready the Ardennes quick as you can." As he spoke, Luc held Senlin with the level gaze of an adder cocking its head for a strike. When he spoke again, his voice was flat as a shingle. "Hanif, I'm afraid we have a traitor among us. Your sword, please."

With a heavy, unstable gait, the zealot's bodyguard crossed the wheelhouse and mounted the stage to the captain's chair. Standing for the first time at eye level with his would-be king, Hanif seemed ready to embrace him, though Senlin couldn't say whether the urge arose from joy at his sudden recovery or forgiveness at his deceit. The big man quickly collected himself, squared his jaw, drew out his long knife, and presented the handle to his master.

Taking the blade, Marat continued to gaze at Senlin, his eyes as piercing as a lighthouse. He said, "Thank you, Hanif. Your service has always been absolutely and impeccably adequate."

With a jerk of his arm, Luc Marat dismissed his enforcer's head from his neck.

As Hanif's severed head splashed upon the floor like a dropped wineglass, Marat swept up behind his engineer, who sat agog, petrified, and still bound to her station. With his borrowed cleaver, he swatted her head from her shoulders, spraying Senlin with the warmth of her wasted life.

This seemed to break the spell that held the rest of the crew, who frantically began to grapple with their harnesses even as they vocalized their terror.

Wagging his bloody machete at Senlin in a manner far too casual for the occasion, Marat said, "This is your fault, Tom. I told you they were not ready to see me as I am."

~~Be friendly to your warden. Make your ear an open drain for their worries and complaints. Most of the jailers you'll meet will have spent more of their lives staring at bars than you. If they are not ambitious, imbecilic, or an unapologetic sadist, they may become an ally. Don't rattle doors you cannot~~

Senlin had never approved of the tired old fallacy that began, "There are two types of people in this world—" Whenever he heard someone begin to roll out the maxim, Senlin would chuckle them into silence before they could finish, and say, "There aren't just two kinds of fish in the sea or two variety of clouds in the sky or two species of trees in the forest. Why should there be only two types of people?"

And yet, amid the bridge's seizing light, as he watched Marat systematically slaughter his crew—women and men who he'd spent days and weeks praising, disciplining, and instructing, only to cut them down where they sat or pull them onto the floor so that he could better crush them underfoot—Senlin wondered if he wasn't wrong. Perhaps for Luc there really were only two types of people in the world: *himself* and *everybody else*.

Disarmed by trauma and despair, Senlin could do nothing but watch and wait for his own execution. When the last engineer had begged for and been denied the gift of his life, Marat panted like a marathoner at the end of a race. He stamped toward his treacherous confidant, his gilded legs chapped with gore and sarong sodden to the point of nakedness. Senlin willed himself to say something biting or profound, but discovered that his wit had at last been exhausted. He could do nothing but hold his eyes open in anticipation of the end.

Marat grasped him by the shoulder as if they were friends in a crowd. "Come on, Tom, unbuckle yourself. There isn't much time."

The unanticipated mercy and the familiar manner of address had a dazzling effect upon Senlin's senses. All his appendages turned reluctant, heavy, and strange. He felt as if he were trying to sign his name while wearing a mitten. Fumbling with the latches at his chest and groin, he eventually managed to extract himself and rise, only to feel the steely crozier of Marat's hand. He stumbled after the zealot, whose over-the-shoulder smirk seemed at odds with his unforgiving stride and grip.

Tripping up the stages of the bridge, Senlin cracked the tops of his toes on the threshold of Marat's private quarters. Here, the zealot hesitated, muttering a curse as he surveyed his private effects. He dallied over his desk, gathering a stack of books and tucking a bottle of wine under his arm before seeming to suffer an epiphany. Speaking to himself, he said, "Second editions and sour wines. Where's the loss?" He dropped it all on his unmade bed. "Never liked this squalid little closet anyway."

Pulling Senlin into the neighboring chamber, Marat sealed, then inspected, the hatch between his cabin and the vault of zoetrope panels. Behind the inner brace of drawers, Senlin heard the ascending whine of a turbine, a sound that seemed new to the Hod King's mechanical philharmonic.

In the wardroom, Gedge, Thornton, and Cael sat at their stations at the copper crescent, the surface of which was entirely changed. The level expanse where they'd thrown cards for hours on end had sprouted blinking lights, switches, and throttles, instruments that seemed at a glance more refined than the cranks and handwheels that crowded the neighboring bridge.

Harnessed to his chair at the apex of the curve, Mr. Gedge wore the serene expression of a man in his element, a man made confident by his communion with unfeeling machinery. On his left sat Thornton, bloodshot eyes bulging under indigo lids. One of his gaunt cheeks bore the blush of a recent slap, though the blow seemed to have only half-revived him. Even as his lips trembled with the reassertion of an unquenchable thirst, his silvery hands pecked at his section of regulators, making fine adjustments here and there with the rapidity and confidence of a veteran typesetter. On Gedge's right, Cael, still in his narrow nightshirt, gripped a pair of enormous squeeze levers that entirely consumed his station. His eyes flitted back and forth between the stout throttles to Mr. Gedge, betraying all the anxiety of a scolded child.

"Now?" Cael murmured.

Mr. Gedge did not look up when he replied, "Don't ask me again. I'll tell you when."

Dropping Senlin's arm at last, the zealot cleared his throat. "Gedge, would you mind pulling out my chair?"

At the focal of the crescent table, the swirling engravements that scarred the floor first swelled into welts, then grew into plates, each rising from the ground like a card from a magician's deck.

For a moment, the erupting panels looked like a cabbage cut in half, a maze of blades that had symmetry if not form. Then the shelf of a seat emerged; armrests appeared; a chairback grew to a high peak. The design was strange. It reminded Senlin of a conch shell—a twisted cone, knobbed with blunt horns... No, that was not quite it, it was more like a ragged hill, warted by a thousand odd rocks and shrubs, and ribboned by a foot path.

Then all at once, Senlin saw it for what it was: a mockery of the Tower, wreathed with parapets, minarets, and the piers of skyports, framing a seat carved out for its aspiring king.

"If you don't want to get tossed about, Tom, I suggest you belt yourself in," Marat said, nodding at an empty station even as he settled upon his ridiculous throne.

Sliding into a seat before a rack of throttles and a score of shining diodes, each bright as the eye of a dragonfly, Senlin had just begun to do up his harness when the whole panel somersaulted away from him. The table swallowed up the instruments and replaced them with a featureless surface. Astounded, he looked up to find Mr. Gedge regarding him with level brows and a hooded glare that was only somewhat spoiled by the cheerful lights that animated his round spectacles.

"What is all this?" Senlin asked.

Feeding his arms into the shoulder straps that accompanied his throne, Marat said, "We always knew there was a chance that the Hod King could be damaged, either by attack or malfunction—"

"Or *sabotage*," Mr. Gedge said pointedly.

Marat clicked the buckle together over his chest. "Indeed. So, we designed this as a fallback, a lifeboat. Her range is limited at the moment, but that's because we've had to fuel her with the blood of ten thousand moths. Still, we should have enough power to complete the final leg of our journey."

"First lifeboat I've ever seen with a throne in it," Senlin said, enjoying the fact that he no longer had to indulge Marat's ego. "Don't shipbuilders usually try to leave a little more space for the living?"

The pert nature of Senlin's question appeared to amuse the zealot. "I admit it's a tad facetious to call it a lifeboat. The Hod King was a functional, if blunt, instrument, but ultimately not something befitting a king. Once I have access to the Sphinx's reservoir, this will be my royal chariot." He stroked the steel of his armrest as if it were a beloved cat. "No need for steppers; no stink of burning glue. I can ramble about as I wish. I have yet to christen her, but I was thinking something like the Palatine. It has a nice ring to it, don't you think?"

"Brace for decoupling." Gedge flipped up a line of switches, one after the next.

The bulkhead tolled with a series of small explosions, pops that ran down the length of the deck. Gedge plied the controls before him as he peered into the lens of a pentascope barrel that grew to meet his eye. In a voice as commanding as a train conductor calling the last aboard, he said, "The Ardennes will ignite in three, two, *one*."

The stillness that followed was conspicuous, the anticipation profound.

Brushing his spectacles onto his forehead, Mr. Gedge pinched the bridge of his nose and said, "Now, Cael. Now."

The moment Cael threw his throttles forward, the cabin leapt like a startled horse. The straps of Senlin's harness sawed at his neck as the deck cornered from horizontal to vertical with the abruptness of a precipice. Their corkscrewing ascent was alarmingly swift. When the craft struck upon something more resistant than air, something Senlin could only assume was mortar, she slowed, but did not gnaw and gnash as the Hod King had. The Palatine swallowed stone like spring rain carves the snow.

Steering the ship appeared to require the sum of Gedge's attention, but no one else's. Thornton nipped from a flask and swatted at the unreal gnats that orbited his head. Cael, who loathed ascents, clutched his harness with his anvil hands and squinted his eyes tight as a stitch.

Head rocking with the gentle sway of their progress, Marat smirked at Senlin. Over the low rumble of dissolving rock, the zealot said, "She is a lithe little sloop, isn't she?"

"I'm all out of pleasantries, Luc. I know I'm only here because you still need me."

"Well, obviously. I need those memories in your head, and I can't squeeze them out with my heels. Though, honestly, it has occurred to me to try." Marat extended his throat, stroked his stubble, then examined his fingernails. Senlin could tell that his successful sabotage had deeply irked the zealot. Marat had struck down his most faithful and essential staff out of ire rather than consideration, and now he felt the need to compensate for that loss of control with conspicuous detachment. He was attempting to shrug and preen his way back to a position of dominance.

Senlin snorted at the transparency of the performance.

The insult only made Luc's composure grow more aloof. "But—and I hope you believe this, Tom—I do not hate you. I feel sorry for you. I pity you because even when you are offered security, utility, and good company, you cannot accept the opportunity, because to grasp it would first require you to relinquish your grip on your insipid virtues. But what has your high-mindedness and uncompromising self-righteousness gotten you? What have you gained from following your nearsighted heart, from letting your facile little principles tug you about by the nose? What has been your reward? Misery, loss, degradation. I did not inflict these upon you. I am not the tyrant who ruined your life. *You* are, Tom. And you know this to be true."

Senlin rocked his head back and laughed. It was the deep and ringing laughter of long deferred honesty, though he pinched off the release of pressure before it could devolve into mania. "Luc, you are the first hound I've ever met who wags his tail as he retreats. This isn't a coronation. No, you are running away. Because you are afraid of the Arm of the Sphinx, and you should be. You may have cobbled yourself a throne, but she will not let you sit on it for long. And you know *this* to be true."

~~New arrivals might find themselves perplexed by certain conventions for ordering tea in the cafés of the lower ring domes. "Gray tea," for example,~~ wh~~ile a frugal alternative, is steeped in recycled bathwater. Though boiled, the brew maintains distinguishable notes of its original steep. "Beige tea"~~

In his tenure as headmaster, Senlin had more than once been the object of concerted sulking. When he gave a clever student a poor mark for a half-hearted effort, or reprimanded a pupil whose eyes wandered to their neighbor's slate during a quiz, or when he confiscated a slingshot, firecracker, or (on one occasion) a lewdly decorated deck of cards, he could reliably expect to be scowled at, snubbed, and made the subject of graffiti and salacious rumor. He'd once seized a girl's whistle after she'd spent a morning blowing it the moment his back was turned. He'd identified her as the culprit by her exaggerated pantomime of innocence and her suggestion that perhaps an exotic jungle bird had taken roost in the rafters of the schoolhouse. Mere hours after locking up her instrument in the supply closet, Senlin was informed by the patrons of the Blue Tattoo that they had it on good authority he kept dead frogs in his desk drawer to snack upon during study hour.

Such was the petty revenge of children.

And so, he found it amusing when Marat, the would-be king of the Tower of Babel, spent their relatively brief ascent shouting over the roar of cracking stone a litany of Senlin's embarrassments. Humiliations that included the fact that he preferred to scribble himself to sleep, broke wind when he partook of hard cheese, and had abandoned his wife to a kidnapper because he knew in the end she would be better off.

Senlin understood that this was all recompense for his suggestion that the zealot was frightened of the Arm of the Sphinx, who had eluded the tines of his siege engine, and who would doubtlessly return again to thwart him.

Underneath all of Luc's bristling and pouting, Senlin perceived the familiar symptoms of fear.

Then, like the abrupt conclusion of an earthquake that seems at the outset to be inexhaustible, the juddering and roaring of the Palatine's ascent came to an end. Mr. Gedge announced they had arrived. The Sphinx's defenses had been pierced; the Palatine had broken upon the vaulted halls of the Brick Layer's former home. The siege had begun and concluded before any among them could mark the occasion.

Even as Senlin unbuckled himself from his station, Marat, still nested in his ridiculous throne, said: "Cael, you have one job going forward, and that is to monitor the traitor. We need his head intact, but the rest of him is gratuitous. If he tries to run, crush his feet. If he raises a hand, ruin it. Do you understand?"

Releasing the mighty throttles that he'd gripped throughout their brief ascent, the pale and seasick Cael said, "Got it, boss."

Marat barked at a groggy Thornton to fetch the luggage. It wasn't a moment before the statuesque drunk returned with an oversized valise that, when opened, revealed an accordion of attached sleeves. Carrying it into the adjacent vault, Thornton began, with shaky ceremony, to shift the paintings from their steel drawers into the papery gills of the suitcase.

Marat announced that he was leaving Mr. Gedge to oversee the "bridling" while he took a moment to dress himself for the occasion. The zealot then vanished through a hatch in the corridor that Senlin had never seen cracked before.

While Thornton moved the paintings as warily as an egg thief, Mr. Gedge smirked at Senlin. "I saw through you from the start. I told Luc you would betray us. But he was too amused by your fawning and buffoonery to listen." Gedge groomed the thin fringe of his hair with a small tortoiseshell comb. "Do you know how I knew you were a traitor?" He chimed the shell of one ear with the shaft of his grooming tool. "You mutter. I heard you in your bunk sounding out coded phrases, heard your lisping to your coconspirators about plots and fallen friends.

"Some people think muttering is a symptom of genius. I assure you: It is not. It is a sign of an unfinished intelligence, a primitive mind. Having to mumble your thoughts aloud is one step removed from counting upon your fingers and toes. You, sir, are an imbecile. And like most dullards, you believe that you are quick-witted—the master of unfathomable designs. In truth, you are a slow and shallow stream. I see right through to the bottom of you."

Senlin smiled back. "And yet, somehow, I managed to destroy your siege engine, save my friend, and spoil your master's hour of triumph. Not bad for a trickling brook. And I'd thank you to stop looking at my bottom."

The rejoinder appeared to spoil Gedge's revelry, and he leered as he stomped back to his station. After rummaging through an obscure cubby, Gedge returned brandishing two copper pipes that were bent at one end to form an L. Senlin, who had more than once been whipped with a switch in his childhood, had to resist the urge to shrink from the approaching punishment.

As soon as he was in reach, Gedge menaced him with one length of pipe, but stopped short of striking him.

"Even the seed of a mighty tree may travel through the bowels of a rat! Don't think yourself exceptional because you seduced Marat! He's not the bulwark he pretends to be."

To Senlin's relief, Gedge then lowered the rod.

Slouched in the middle of the wardroom, Cael wore the beleaguered expression of one who'd recently watched his house burn down. It seemed all this internal conflict had taken a toll on him. When Gedge spoke his name, Cael did not immediately harken to it until it was said again, and more forcefully. The anchor-armed Wakeman shook his head as if rousing from a daydream. Gedge collected his wandering gaze with his own and said, "It's time we took a walk."

Gedge beckoned, and Cael nudged Senlin forward with the railcar buffer of one round knuckle. The engineer led them to the hatch across from his workshop, another portal in the long corridor that Senlin had never seen unlocked before. Behind it lay a small vestibule that was further cramped by the steel ribs of the outer hull and the bulge of a windowless hatch. Its prodigious lock looked as if it would require at least two burly men to unseal, but reaching over Senlin's shoulder, Cael turned the wheel as if it were the tap of a bath.

When the door swung out, the light of their lobby did little to cut the murk outside. Mr. Gedge said, "Here, let me shine a light," and the dishes of his ears beamed forth with a pair of pale blue spots.

Suddenly, the silhouette of warhorses, their ears stiff as horns, appeared to gallop over a mountain range, and for an instant, Senlin imagined a silent cavalry had arrived. But then he saw the painted hobbyhorses that cast those fearsome shadows and beheld the row of cribs beneath the highland mural.

The nursery, which lay in some sublevel of the Sphinx's home, was furnished with a number of changing tables, toy chests, and rocking chairs, all of which bore the dust of disuse.

"Never would've pegged the old snake for the fatherly type," Thornton said, adjusting his grip on the now full suitcase. He seemed uncomfortable with the invaluable burden, or perhaps he was only getting used to his new foot, which was fashioned out of darker metal and not as shapely as its counterpart. He looked like a man who'd dressed in the dark, donning unmatched shoes.

"More likely it was for the offspring of the Sphinx's guests, back when he had the temerity to entertain them." Gedge crossed the copper pipes, holding them out as if to hex the darkness. "Stay close, boys, and keep the traitor between you."

The short leap down to the nursery floor was made a little treacherous by the rubble of stone and plaster that the Palatine had cast out on its arrival. Looking back, Senlin saw that the portside of the burrowing engine had replaced the wall of the nursery with its steely barrel. A pair of the engine's immense legs staved the floor. He was still marveling at the refined, sculpted curves of the vessel, which seemed a perfect opposite to the pocked and hulking Hod King, when Cael cupped him by the back of the neck and dragged him farther into the spacious crèche.

Gedge slowly swung the pipes before him like a well sniffer scouring a field with his divining rods. Senlin had never seen any evidence that dowsing was anything but a trick of traveling charlatans, a performance that, as often as not, resulted in the digging of many errant holes. It was something of an amusing surprise to watch the paragon of science sleepwalk over abandoned dolls, blocks, shoes, and toy wagons, enthralled by two lengths of copper tubing.

When the rods crossed, Gedge gave a triumphant whinny. "Here we are. X marks the spot! Cael, if you would."

Cael knelt, raised one hand, and chopped at the old varnished planks. The blow was more effective than an axe, snapping six boards at once and raising a little plume of dust. Jamming his fingers into the gash, Cael peeled the boards back as if opening a stubborn cellar door. The thunderclap of breaking wood made Senlin wince. The moment the hole was opened, Mr. Gedge rushed forward, turning the light of his ears downward. Senlin peered over his shoulder into the void.

There was nothing there. Just a gap of dusty air and the lathe of the ceiling of the room below. Senlin chuckled. Gedge muttered a schoolyard obscenity, then dropped to his hands and knees and stuck his head into the hole. He looked this way and that, before returning to his feet. Marching several paces to the right, he kicked aside a child-sized dining set and pointed at the ground. "Here, Cael. Dig here."

Again, Cael opened the floor with his steam-shovel hands, and this time Gedge seemed to find what he was looking for: a network of cloth-wrapped wires, each fat as full-grown bamboo, and all twined together. Gedge dispatched Thornton to fetch "the reins" from the Palatine, and the drunkard soon returned, dragging the heads of two robust cables behind him. With tools brought from the ship, Gedge cut into the cords in the floor of the Sphinx's home and spliced them to the umbilical hauled out from the ship. The patch complete, Gedge then directed Thornton to "snap the reins."

The gloomy nursery was briefly lit up as if by a flash of distant lightning. The filaments in the chandeliers and sconces blazed, dwindled, and flickered on again, though not as brightly as before. The character of the resulting light was almost candle-like.

Wiping his grimy hands with a rag, Gedge surveyed the newly lit nursery and said, "There. She is ours. The Sphinx's home is ours."

"You're powering it with the ship?" Senlin asked.

"The Ardennes can carry quite a load. Still, we'll only have twelve hours, give or take, before the fuel runs dry and the lights go out."

"It should be more than enough," Marat said from behind them.

Senlin turned in time to witness the zealot climb down from the ship, his feet crunching clods of plaster into powder. He was almost unrecognizable. He wore a silvery breastplate, piped in rosy gold and pounded into the idealized musculature of a torso, and at its center—a golden medallion emblazoned with a wide, lidless eye. The tops of the pauldrons on his shoulders bulged level with his jaw, which was one of the few stretches of flesh left open to the air. The smooth-crowned golden helm he wore stretched from the point of his nose to the nape of his neck, but left his ears, mouth, and eyes exposed. He gripped a short falchion, its blade tipped like the point of a holly leaf, an elegant flourish for a crude instrument: the single-edged sword, a glorified machete, was forged for hacking and dismemberment.

Marat made no effort to conceal his pleasure at Senlin's astonishment. Jangling like a bag of broken glass, Marat approached the frozen headmaster, who was too cowed to emote. Senlin wore the sullen expression of a thoroughly shocked man.

"I told you I would stand for my crowning, didn't I?" Marat said, clapping Senlin on the cheek with the familiar force one might administer to the haunches of a horse. Senlin's teeth ached and his ears rang. "Now, Mr. Grudge, I believe it's time you woke up Delyth and got yourself dressed. First, we open the bridge. Then, we open the Sphinx."

~~The traditional condiment of Oyodin, known as~~ "h~~orcum,"~~ ~~is composed of preserved soft shelled crayfish. The pickle is roughly milled before being ladled over boiled filets of iffy haddock. Some believe it delicious; all agree horcum reeks of an old boot left in a warm swamp.~~

Senlin felt like an ambitious weed growing in the deep shade of old trees.

Behind him, Cael loomed, square and impenetrable. At his elbow, Thornton's silver corpse stood rigid while his head drooped and snapped like a flag caught in a changing wind. Delyth, who'd been roused after days of sedation, was restless, not because her joints were stiff and required loosening, but because she had taken the news of Senlin's treachery poorly. If the knightly zealot had not braced his thigh against the rim of her carriage and shored up her glass bell with the palms of his hands, Senlin had no doubt that the spider-legged Wakeman would've leapt upon him and staved him to the nursery floor with the spearheads of her feet. Even with Marat standing between them, Delyth had no trouble broadcasting her rage. She whitened her bubble with her breath and wrote upon that foggy slate the words *Bite. Chew. Swallow.*

Seized by a sudden chill, Senlin crossed his arms over his naked chest. He felt conspicuous in his sarong and sandals, though he supposed his discomfort was Marat's goal. Still, the Sphinx's house was too cold now to walk around half-naked. Senlin retrieved a quilt from the back of a rocking chair and wrapped it round his shoulders. It was only then that he saw it was paneled with a collection of yellow ducks in a variety of poses, some wearing bows, some in galoshes, and all done in meticulous needlepoint.

When Marat saw it, he chuckled and said, "Quack, quack."

They stood huddled about the nursery's exit: one of the home's many indistinguishable doors. All around its white frame a painted parade of red ants marched, each large as a hot water bottle, and all carrying different colored gumdrops on their heads.

Impatient, Marat once again pressed the button in the wall plate beside the door, summoning the elevating hallway that serviced the central canyon of the Sphinx's home. The progress of the traveling corridor was slow and, according to Gedge, for much the same reason that the lights of the nursery were dim. The Ardennes could power the Sphinx's home, but not perfectly.

In addition to waiting for the lift, they were also anticipating the arrival of Mr. Grudge, Gedge's armored alter ego. Marat murmured to Thornton that he wished he could be a fly on the wall while the engineer stripped to his long underwear, climbed the step ladder, and crawled into the womb of his coal-black golem. When Cael asked how in the world Gedge would walk in such a thing, Marat explained that the engineer would operate the engines of the knight's limbs like a puppeteer: an art form with which Gedge had little practice. "But he's determined," Marat said with a condescending chuckle. "Some men have their cobblers tack on a bit more heel to lift their height; Gedge has decided to append an entire leg."

In response to this vague witticism, Thornton leaned to one side and vomited upon the head of a stuffed bear who sat slouched in a toy rocking chair.

Swiping bile, first from his chin and then from the corner of the valise that held the keys to the Bridge of Babel, Thornton rasped, "Sorry about that, Hodder Luc. Climbed a little too deep into the jug last night."

Marat scowled and briefly squinted in Senlin's direction. That glance was sufficient to express the zealot's grief over their lost camaraderie. Who could the king talk to now that his fool had perjured himself?

When at last Mr. Grudge appeared in the hatch of the Palatine, he seemed as encumbered as a man trying to exit a carriage with an open umbrella. The couters at his elbows clattered against the jambs, and the birdlike comb that crowned his visor banged upon the lintel. It took him several attempts to successfully navigate the portal, and when at last he was free, he stumbled on the step down.

Catching himself, Mr. Gedge rallied, straightened, and stamped the heel of his sinister halberd upon the floor, saluting a crew who gaped at him with more amusement than awe. Rather than a knight in a suit of armor that evoked a fierce raptor, he looked like an infant who'd been swallowed by a blackbird. His chin barely reached the visor's open beak. Even so, his round cheeks were pink with pride. He seemed about to say something suitably exultant, but then, as if compelled by a tic, he brought one colossal arm around to push his spectacles up his nose. In doing so, he nearly drove the peen of one steel finger through his own forehead. He had to duck down into the suit to avoid killing himself. Once he'd successfully removed the digit from his empty helm, he extracted his flesh and blood arm from its rigid sleeve, wormed it up through the neck of his suit, and pushed up his glasses with a stubby, unsteady finger.

"You sure about this, Gedge?" Marat asked.

The engineer beamed. "I've never been surer of anything in my life, Hodder Luc. I finally appear on the outside as I have always felt within."

Marat shrugged. "As you like."

The clack of the releasing bolt in the nursery door announced the arrival of the elevating corridor. Filing out into the hall, the more heavily shod among them found they had to mind their toes to keep from stumbling on the thick collection of tattered rugs that padded the passageway.

The pink paper on the walls of the chasm took on a dusky aspect in the light of ten thousand half-lit candles. Yet the valley of doors was made no less astounding by the gloom. If anything, the underpowered sconces glittering above them seemed to evoke an orchard of stars, a cultivated galaxy.

Mr. Gedge clomped into the broad hall, stamped the butt of his halberd into the loam of aged carpets, and raised his left arm. The black gauntlet broke at the wrist, cocking back over the forearm, revealing a rosette of gun barrels. They began to spin, rattling and whining as they picked up speed. When the bullets began to pour forth, they carried the fury of grapeshot spat from the bore of a cannon. Geysers of shredded carpet and molding and glass erupted from all sides of the hallway, mingling into a cloud of dust and debris that billowed and was punctured by the arrival of a second volley of lead.

Ending his barrage, Gedge let the bark of his rotary gun roll into silence before shouting down the hazy passageway, "I'm ready for you, old boy! Come at me again! If you're not dead, come at me!"

The silence that answered him seemed somehow more profound than the thunder he had wrought.

"Never understood why you hated him so much." Thornton shifted the plug of tobacco from one end of his lip to the other. "Old Ferddie was just a rowdy pup."

"A pup!" Gedge quit his menacing stance to better pin Thornton with a sneer. "Ferdinand was responsible for the destruction of more invaluable scientific instruments, experiments, and documents than the devastation of any earthquake, inferno, or storm on record. *Old Ferddie*, as you call him, set the human race back a century!"

"Because he dropped your luggage? When was that...sixteen years ago? You really think that one bungle cost all of us a century?" Thornton spat on the floor.

"Well, he ruined the hinges on my trunk in any case. And the fact that he isn't here now makes me think the Sphinx must be dead himself. An unlit house, an unguarded hall. We've already won!"

"That's enough," Marat said, his heavy footfalls on the carpet sounding like the stifled report of distant guns. "A beheaded snake can still bite. Don't celebrate yet, Gedge."

Privately, Senlin marveled at Ferdinand's nonappearance. The childlike locomotive had seemed so terrible and wonderful and impervious to harm. It was his absence from the hall that at last made Senlin confront the idle hope that he'd been concealing like a self-inflicted wound: the hope that Marat's intelligence was wrong, his assumptions misguided, his confidence misplaced. Senlin had known the Sphinx's influence was waning, her powers abating, and yet, he'd hoped that if Marat ever broke down the Sphinx's door, he would be met by a crawling army of insectoid engines, would be lanced by a bolt from the Sphinx's wand, and trampled under the feet of her doting doorman.

When the zealot turned to Senlin, he caught him wearing his grief upon his sleeve. The sight made Marat glow.

His armor jangling like the loose spurs of a rider, Luc approached his former confidant. "All right, Tom. Here we are. It's time to earn your keep. Obviously, we need to find our X axis first. You say you remember the patch of carpet outside the elevator? Well, let's start there." Reaching around to his back and the small purse that dangled from his sword belt, Marat extracted a stopwatch that nearly filled the well of his palm. "Now, I do realize you have ample incentive to dally, to feign uncertainty, to lead us to dead ends, in the vain hope that your friends will burst in to rescue you.

"So, by way of motivation, I'm going to give you an hour." Marat twisted the winding knob of the stopwatch, eliciting a cheerful ribbit of gears. "But, *Oh,* you say, *you can't threaten me! You need me!* But do I? Do I really? Look around you. Might I not just kill you and then the Sphinx, wherever he's hiding, leave his fortress sealed, and explore the bowels of his manor at my leisure? Yes, such a survey might take days, weeks perhaps, but certainly not forever. And what is not-forever to a man who's spent so much of his life in exile?

"So, I give you an hour, Tom. At the end of an hour, if you have not found my elevator, Cael will crack your head like an egg and pour at my feet the yolk of your brains." Marat clicked the start button on his timepiece. Senlin glowered at him as if he might stare him from existence. Marat laughed. "Personally, I find that anxiety often confuses one's internal sense of time. Soon, you'll start to wonder whether you truly grasp the substance of a second, wonder how many heartbeats fit within a minute, wonder why you're still standing here wasting your final hour when you could be searching for my door. Ah! That's the spirit, Tom! There you go! That's a brisk pace. Good. Don't even think about the tick-tocking! Let the clock do the wondering! Time thinks only of you!"

Trotting down the center of the Sphinx's corridor, the quilt on his shoulders flapping like a cape, Senlin had the halting gait and searching gaze of a man who'd dropped his wedding ring. Once again, he stopped, crouched, and squinted at a rug and its pattern of blue-green fronds. The peacock-themed paisley that had once been emblazoned upon his memory now began to quiver and stretch like an amoeba under a microscope.

"Is that the one?" Cael asked, looming over his hunched back.

"Maybe. It does look a bit like... No, no, this isn't right; these paisleys are too broad." Senlin duck-walked a step to get out of Cael's shadow, then straightened once more.

"You're running out of time," Cael said quietly, his face clouded with concern. Senlin couldn't tell whether his misery arose from a genuine amity, or if Cael's dislike of discord among the crew was wholly responsible for his distress.

Whichever it was, Senlin still felt compelled to reassure him. He said, "Oh, there's plenty of time," but his voice lacked any conviction.

In the dim distance, Senlin beheld the end of the corridor. He tried to remember if it been in view when he had last exited the elevator. Though he couldn't be sure, he thought not. Perhaps he should return to the nursery and try the other direction. His original choice had been arbitrary, after all. How fitting that would be: A man of letters undone by a wild guess, an impulse, a thump of the heart.

Behind them, Marat and the rest of the crew were delighting in Mr. Gedge's efforts to acclimate to his new suit. Even as Senlin watched, Mr. Grudge attempted to perform a quick about-face. The toe of one foot tangled upon the heel of the other. Trying to catch himself, Gedge stuck his arm through a painting and a portion of the wall behind it. Thornton grabbed his knees and hacked out a long, unwholesome laugh.

Feeling abruptly depleted, Senlin leaned against the nearest door. He wondered why he continued to fight. His fate was sealed. Whether or not he found the elevator to the lobby of the zoetrope theater made no difference. Perhaps Marat would keep him alive long enough for Senlin to witness his moment of triumph. But sooner or later, the zealot would tire of gloating and take his revenge.

His downcast gaze, which had been inward-turned a moment before, was called outward again. The rug he'd just scrutinized and dismissed looked different from the side. As the mind sometimes does with a forgotten song, or the misplaced names of an acquaintance, or a dream that evaporates with the morning sun, his memory suddenly produced, full and vivid, the scene of his emergence from the elevator. He saw Edith's uncertain smile and pronounced relief, her wet hair, her new arm, angled slightly away as if to conceal it from him, and the paisley under her bare feet.

Pushing himself from the door, he called to Marat. "This is the spot. I found it."

Grimacing at his stopwatch as he approached, Marat examined the rug with an air of boredom. "All right. Which way now? Up or down?"

"Up," Senlin said quickly.

"Are you sure?"

"Not at all," he said, and felt surprisingly untroubled by the admission.

~~The Tower's notoriously unreliable postal system, the Trans-Ringdom Express, rather than address its organizational inadequacies has elected~~ to ~~limit its services. Items that can no longer be sent through the post include valuables, currency, perishables, and stationery. Customer satisfaction has~~

The painting that paired with the paisley was much more easily found because the subject was so odd. The bucolic scene featured a dark bear standing on its hind legs, with paws raised to the shoulders of a gray-haired country gentleman in a pale blue cloak. It was not clear whether the bear was attacking or waltzing with the man, a fact largely owed to the bear's closed mouth and rather placid expression. Since the back of the gentleman was turned to the viewer, the question of whether his expression mirrored the bear's was left a mystery, but Senlin liked to think he was smiling back at his shaggy dance partner.

After a few minutes' ascent, Senlin spied the bear embracing his country lord, and pressed the cancel button when the next call panel came into reach. The slothful corridor clanged to a halt and the wan cosmos of sconces briefly dimmed.

Senlin swept a hand toward the door that concealed the elevator to the zoetrope theater like a waiter introducing diners to their table.

Marat peered at his ticking stopwatch. "Care to take a guess?"

"Fifty-six minutes," Senlin said.

Marat clicked the stop and turned the dial out for Senlin to see. "Nineteen minutes. Isn't time a funny thing?"

Despite its Bottomless Library, endless wardrobe, and thousand other wonders, Senlin did not think the Sphinx's home was capable of vanishing an entire elevator shaft. Still, it came as some relief when the bland white door opened upon the brassy gates of a lift.

The car was too small for them to all take at once, so they descended in pairs. Marat and Gedge first, and Thornton and Delyth last. During

Senlin's descent, Cael filled the car like dough possesses a loaf pan, leaving him breathless and pressed against the egress. The interminable journey ended with Senlin being ejected through the doors the moment they began to crack. He landed on his hands and knees on the fine carpet of the broad theater lobby. He might've lingered there longer had Cael not hoisted him back to his feet.

The low electric chandeliers that had once radiated a flattering candlelight were now as faint as banked coals. The formerly inviting sofas and club chairs had taken on a mournful aspect. A space that had struck Senlin as merely unused upon his first visit now seemed utterly abandoned.

When the rest of the crew had ferried down, Marat dispatched them to their duties. Thornton and Mr. Gedge would install the panels into the zoetrope's carousel and get the projector running. The activity required Gedge to abandon his new stygian skin for the moment. Watching Mr. Grudge's breastplate break open like a saloon door was almost as incredible as observing the usually fastidious Gedge climb out of his golem wearing a pair of tatty long underwear. Before anyone could crack a smile, the mouse-eared engineer raised a tightly balled and trembling fist, promising that all smirks and jokes would be repaid in full once he repossessed his aptly named engine.

Cael and Delyth were made to stand guard at the lobby doors and to be on the lookout for a flanking attack.

Which left Marat and Senlin to receive the encoded numbers from the snowy slopes of the auditorium.

Above them, the shell of a nautilus filled the plaster ceiling with its uncoiling chambers. The crystal fronds of a chandelier that Senlin had once likened to seaweed now evoked cobwebs, and the intermingled spherical lamps called to mind the knitted egg sacs of a spider.

Shuddering at the thought, Senlin turned his attention forward. Before them, an inky proscenium framed a silken white screen.

As Marat moved to the middle of a central row, his new armor clanged against the old. He seemed as ungainly as a man who, upon arriving late to the theater, is forced to navigate a gauntlet of knees. Coming to his chosen spot, Marat removed his helmet and placed it on the seat beside him, a chaperone between himself and Senlin.

The two men then engaged in the timeworn practice of trying to settle into a seat whose beauty belies a host of old, unoiled springs. Their shifting and squirming enlivened a chorus of squeaks as Marat tried to level his great weight and Senlin experimented with whether it was more uncomfortable to have his legs crossed or uncrossed. In the end, it seemed to make no difference.

When quiet returned at last, Marat raised his chin and said with quivering grandeur, "I'm going to turn the lights down now. Do not be afraid!"

"I'm not afraid of the d—" Senlin began, then halted as the phrase sparked a memory. "That's what the Sphinx said the last time I was here."

Marat chuckled and brought his chin in. Even the wrinkles of his wattle were handsome. While many men of his age developed a fatty dewlap, his rolls were thin and pleasing as the wrinkles of a smile. "He said as much to me, once upon a time. The Sphinx always seemed to have a speech up his sleeve. 'Oh, Luc, harken to me, my boy: When humanity ceases to aspire, it begins to decline!' " Marat raised a finger as if to punctuate the recitation, sneering happily at the joke. "The Sphinx loved to bang on about cooperation and harmony and how the Tower is really a bridge to the heavens. And the hods—my god!—always going on about the hods, but never doing anything about them because the hods were not victims of the Brick Layer's lofty enterprise. No! No, their suffering was owed to the profane interlopers who filled up the ringdoms and built up their navies and established one monarchy after another. It was the ringdoms who tainted the Brick Layer's magnificent vision with purposeless greed and avarice, not the h—"

From near the foot of the empty screen, a discreet door opened and Thornton's miserable head popped out, a cancerous mole against an alabaster backdrop. "Going to be a few more minutes, Hodder Luc. Just put the last panel in, but Gedge says he needs to boost the current to the machine. So, we need to—"

Marat waved at him dismissively, irritated to have been interrupted. The lout spat on the floor and retreated.

"You know, looking back on it, Tom, I think sitting here in this empty theater with the Sphinx was the moment when I first hatched my plan to activate the hods. The Sphinx thought they could be placated with promises of progress, that they would welcome a kid glove revolution of incremental betterment. But it wasn't aspiration that the hods longed for. No, they wanted *action*, they wanted *organization*."

Marat went on to elucidate his designs while they waited for the light show to commence. Senlin suspected that he was merely a practice audience for a lecture whose ultimate target was the Sphinx, and so he thought better than to interrupt.

The zealot began with the rather lackluster epiphany that he had always found it notable that while the ringdoms flourished with unique and coherent cultures, the Old Vein, despite drawing from those same vibrant sources, quickly ground down any tradition or customs and provided very little by way of replacement. The tumultuous nature of the trail—the hazard of the climb, the scarcity of resources, the fracturing of families—made it almost impossible to hold any group together for long. The black trail was a perfect whisk of suffering and confusion.

Even the hods who tried to cling to the forms and habits of their past found themselves increasingly alienated from their prior lives. In illustration of this point, Marat described a time when he had first begun to explore the black trail, not long after leaving the Sphinx's nest, but while he still had the residual resources to power his legs. He had come upon a group of thirty or so Algezian hods who had, quite literally, carved out a little space for themselves near one of the more reliable drinking fountains that serviced the black trail. They wore red rags in tribute to their ringdom's herald and insisted upon a strict adherence to all the old teatime rituals even though there wasn't any tea to be had. They played dominos with tiles they'd fashioned out of clay and candle black. At first, it had all struck Marat as rather quaint. *Good for them,* he had thought, *for shielding the wick of civility from the lugubrious drafts of chaos!*

But the true revelation came soon after when a freshly minted hod from the Algezian ringdom discovered the camp of his purported compatriots. The new hod found his former countrymen entirely alien and their society anything but charming. He ridiculed their crude tributes to the venerable house of Algez and mocked their outdated pastimes. Dominos had not been popular in years! They were all engaged in a pathetic pantomime of a society they would never be allowed to rejoin.

In return, the camp of sham-Algezians shunned him. He gladly fled their company. But the damage was done. The little clan drifted apart, hiding their shame within the indifferent throng.

And that was when Marat had realized an essential truth: What the hods lacked most was a sense of themselves.

Marat described the identity of the hods before his intervention as *impoverished.* Yes, there were hod poems, and songs of hoddery, and eerie tales of the Old Vein, but these passed back and forth between ringdom and trail with such alacrity that new arrivals to the dark came knowing many of the hod's hymns and yarns. Invariably, those newcomers were disappointed to find that the whiff of romanticism and tragic beauty that clung to the hod songbook was entirely false. Those jolly old melodies were at best *ironic*—the one thing an anthem can never be.

The hods had developed a few mores that were unique to the trail—such as those that governed the tattle post—but they had little appreciation of who they were or what they had built, this despite the fact that they had raised the Tower itself. The hods were so scalded by misery, so disoriented by the churning of the trail, by the frequent additions and morbid subtractions, by the dearth of consistency, and a lack of hope or prospect that they could not see themselves as an entity, an entirety, a *nation*.

What the hods required was a separate and distinct culture, and it was that which Marat had set out to provide.

"The wonderful thing about creating a culture from whole cloth, my dear Thomas, is that you can begin with the desired outcome and work backward. I wanted a devoted and fanatical core of uninquisitive drudges who perceived all outsiders, even other hods, as being either gelded or sinister. One way to accomplish that was by cloistering them with a new language. Those who spoke hoddish would feel included, those who didn't, shunned. From there, it was easy to discredit all other opinions with the broad stroke of illiteratization and the destruction of books. Then, having extinguished voices both present and past, I fashioned myself as the only luminary, leaving them neither alternative nor the capacity for dissent.

"And the truth is: It wasn't even that hard. It just required a little will and the realization that the human race is motivated not by aspiration with all its sharp edges and long drops but by the desire for certainty, inclusion, consistency. The Sphinx's mistake was that he projected his noble-mindedness upon everyone else. My genius is that I understand the wellspring of human desire. It bubbles up, not from some buried stream of hope, but from a great aquifer of fear."

Exhausted by Marat's self-congratulatory cynicism, Senlin sought to change the subject. "So, what do you think is behind the vault door?"

"That's been a beloved subject of speculation for quite some time. Gedge believes that the Bridge of Babel is like the bridge of a ship: a central station from which all commands flow, all measurements are reported, all power is dispatched. There are so many fragmented systems within the Tower, he believes the Brick Layer must've fashioned himself some sort of helm that overrode it all. It is, admittedly, quite a fetching thought."

"And what do you think?"

"I think it's a literal bridge, or more specifically, a lift of some grand variety that will deliver me to the crowning city, Nebos, where the gardens are unspoiled by winter and the vines bear fruit all year in the shade of golden spires. I think the Brick Layer built himself a paradise. That's what all this was really for, but he died before he could enjoy it."

"Why not go there directly, then? Couldn't the Hod King just have—"

"No, no. It's an impenetrable fortress, walled up in diamonds with a foundation made of steel. And that's to say nothing of the lightning mortars that guard it."

"Oh," Senlin said, fretting once more over Adam's fate.

Sighing deeply, Marat rested his hands on the sculpted belly of his breastplate with all the contentment of a glutton at the end of a feast. "I don't wish to retire just yet. But when I do, I'd like it to be to a city befitting an emperor. I want to live out my twilight years in a tower atop the Tower of—" The abrupt illumination of the theatrical screen interrupted him. "Ah, here we go."

What had in Senlin's memory been an imperfect image of juddering color now coalesced—almost unblinking, almost entire—like a vivid window into another's imagination. The waters of the Baths rippled and coruscated; the blue-green-purples broke about the thighs and waists of waders in azalea-bright bathing suits. These out-of-focus figures splashed and gamboled around the periphery of the girl in white, doused to her ankles in a shadow that seemed to gulp at her like a living thing. The tails of her braids swung; the paper boat in her hanging hand twisted softly in a draft. It was the most beautiful and delirious thing Senlin had ever seen.

"The Sphinx would've liked to get an eyeful of this, I bet," Marat said, spoiling Senlin's trance. "It brings me pleasure that he never will."

"It's stunning," Senlin murmured.

Marat shrugged. "I suppose. If I was going to commission the Tower's greatest talent to create a masterpiece that would consume a quarter of his life, I would've picked a more auspicious scene, I think. An airship battle, perhaps, with the Tower as a backdrop, and the sun crowning the monolith like a candle flame. But, alas I was not consulted. And now, it's time to get to work."

The numbers that Senlin had glimpsed in the water beneath the bow of the paper boat were more distinct. Where before there had been a great flash of white in the image, there now followed a second number a moment after the first.

Marat asked him what he saw, and he reported the location and the numbers: nineteen and thirty-two.

"Yes, that's the same spot the Sphinx showed me. But it doesn't make for much of a combination," Marat said. "There must be more to it."

So, they stared into the flood of color and waited for more numbers to appear. The duration of the animation was not quite five seconds, and yet in that span, the amount of variation caused by the minute difference of individual brushstrokes made all seem to waver, wrinkle, and leap like rain falling upon a lake. It wasn't long before Senlin's eyes ached with the effort.

Soon, Gedge came and joined them in their gawping. With grease on his nose and smudged across the belly of his union suit, Gedge still carried himself with a new sort of confidence, a poise that seemed to have emerged from his short time inside his dynamic armor. He mused aloud what a pleasure it was to have a little brain teaser to break up the afternoon, before cracking open his trusty pad and licking his pencil lead. At first, he seemed rather amused by the zealot and headmaster's puzzlement.

But soon enough, his effort to stare the secrets from the zoetrope's light was foiled by the same frenzy of details. After another ten minutes of searching, Senlin spotted a second set of evanescing numerals between the stout legs of another bather. This time instead of two, there was only one number. He and Gedge jotted it down, even as Marat identified the problem they were now facing.

"But how will we know the order of the numbers, or how many of them there are in all? You can't open a vault with an incomplete combination that's out of order," the zealot said, puffing his cheeks to punctuate the sigh. "I suppose we'll just have to squeeze the answer out of the Sphinx."

"Assuming he's still alive," Gedge muttered unhelpfully.

Shutting eyes that felt as dry and rough as sugar cubes, Senlin slouched in his seat. He rested the back of his neck upon the ridge of his chairback and attempted to squeeze some moisture back into his eyes.

While the zealot and the engineer bickered about the probable fate of the Sphinx, Senlin ignored the screen and focused instead on the gloomy coil overhead. He followed the central vein of the shell as it flowed out from one of the corners, and lazed around the ceiling in a wide turn that brushed the box seats, and passed the corner pieces that resembled flowering cephalopods—a cuttlefish whose tentacles bloomed into carnations—and on the bony ridge went, tightening toward the center of the ceiling, passing under the spider-egg lamps, until the coil at last clenched its axis—suddenly, decisively, like a hawk strikes a mouse.

"A logarithmic spiral," he said to himself, identifying the curve. The resurgence of his idle habit reminded him of how he had once noted the genus of a desert bird to Adam on their first meeting. He smiled to think how often he once conflated classification with understanding.

Only then did Senlin realize that the sparring dialogue had ceased. He lifted his head to find Marat and Gedge squinting at him.

"What did you say?" Marat asked.

Tightening the quilt about his throat to warm himself, Senlin said again, "A logarithmic spiral." He pointed to the ceiling; the gaze of the two men followed. "You know, the natural gyre."

Gedge poked the air above him with his pencil, muttering under his breath as he counted each egg-like globe in the unusual chandelier. "Sixty-four lamps, sixty-four ringdoms. That can't be a coincidence."

Head back, Marat drew lines with his finger across the heart of the ceiling. "And those glass fronds . . . they form a radial grid, do they not?"

"Now, if we can just find the axis in the painting, we can orient our search," Gedge said.

"But we have that already, don't we, Tom? That was the gift the Sphinx gave us—a starting point. We begin at the prow of the paper boat and wind our way out."

Even with a map to guide them, finding the coordinates in the zoetrope projection required the sketching of a grid and much squinting at pencils held out at arm's length. In all, it took nearly an hour to assemble the numbers and untangle them. Generally, each point in the painting produced two digits, though on a few occasions, one of the figures was broken or incomplete, and these they noted with an X.

It didn't take long for them to discern a pattern. The second number of any given coordinate was repeated as the first number in the following set. So, if one spot in the logarithmic spiral surrendered the numbers nineteen and thirty-two they could expect for the first digit in the next series to be thirty-two. This was the Sphinx's, or rather the Brick Layer's, insurance against lost or defaced paintings—a simple backup to account for minor gaps. So long as the zoetrope was not missing too many panels in a row, it would still be possible to extract the combination. With the addition of his own collection to the Sphinx's, Marat now presided over a zoetrope that was missing only three of the sixty-four panels.

It proved more than sufficient.

Soon, Marat led them to the lobby, his pace quick enough to force Gedge to jog, an indignity that usually would have invited a protest, but now inspired the small engineer to skip and grin.

All huddled about the grand dial of the vault, Marat patted the plaque that said The Bridge of Babel as if it were a familiar totem of good luck.

"Gedge, would you do the honors?" the zealot asked.

With a page ripped from his notebook rattling in one hand, the Ingeniare in chief stepped forward in his long underwear and laid the moon of one ear against the expanse of steel. Setting his hand to the dial, he took a breath, held it, and began to turn the tumbler with the care of a man afraid of overwinding a clock.

It took several minutes for Gedge to enter all sixty-four digits in the combination. As he worked, the only sound was the thin rasp of the dial against its beveled collar and Thornton's nose, which had developed a whistle.

At one point, when Gedge paused to look for the next number, Marat asked if he could hear whether the tumblers were aligning. The keen-eared engineer admitted that he could not. The door was too thick or the safe's sound dampeners too advanced for his hearing to pierce. "Though the flute in your head isn't helping, Thornton. Could you blow your nose before I blow it off, please?"

When at last he arrived at the final number, Gedge waved Marat forward and, with a little bow of his head, offered him the sheet of paper. The zealot glanced at the final number, returned the page, and arranging his limbs and spine into a most imperious posture, said, "Friends, I shall not forget your contributions or sacrifices which helped bring us here. The day is nigh when you shall each collect your reward. And well deserved will your lucre be.

"But this moment is mine. And so, I ask that you genuflect before your king."

Cael was the first to drop, his apish fists knuckling the rug, his devout expression eclipsed by the black cloud of his hair. Delyth's glass bell sank among the peaks of her joints, a pose that evoked a spider preparing to jump. Thornton followed her down, his limbs venting steam in a shush, the song in his nose ending at last. Gripping the back flap of his underwear to keep an unseemly gap from opening, Gedge squatted, wincing when the main of his weight shifted upon his middle-aged knees.

Marat looked at Senlin, who stood clutching the neck of his quilted cape with a stormy look on his face. "Too proud to kneel, Sir Duckington?"

"I have nothing left but my pride. And I don't understand why you'd wish to show me this."

"Is it not a fitting reward for your efforts? It was you, after all, who helped Gedge and me unlock the mysteries of the zoetrope."

Senlin recognized in this a common trick that bullies used to recruit cretins and manipulate their victims: first, they gave you no option, then they celebrated your complicity. Senlin smiled like a horn-mad hound. "Oh, please! Don't pretend I've enabled in any way this spree of arrogance and avarice. Whatever victory you enjoy today, it won't last, because you have cobbled a kingdom out of treachery and deceit, and you shall be repaid in kind. The Sphinx—"

"Thornton, if you wouldn't mind." Marat swatted a finger through the air as if to clear the rail of an abacus.

Thornton chopped at the back of Senlin's knees with the steel bat of one arm, and he fell as if legless to the floor.

Scarcely getting his hands up before his cheek struck the rug, Senlin pushed himself back onto his haunches, ignoring the great throb of pain that the effort inspired. He was determined to reclaim what dignity he could, to show Marat that the captain of the *Stone Cloud*, the headmaster of Isaugh, the husband of Marya and father of Olivet would not go out groveling upon the carpet.

But Marat had already turned his attention to the door of the vault. With a decisive twist of the dial, he brought the final tumbler into line.

In the muffled distance above, they heard a mighty clangor like a long anchor chain being poured into a pile; then came an arrhythmic knocking like warming lead plumbing, punctuated by a thunderous roar that rumbled and rolled and refused to break.

Sneering down at Senlin, Marat said, "I am the Sphinx."

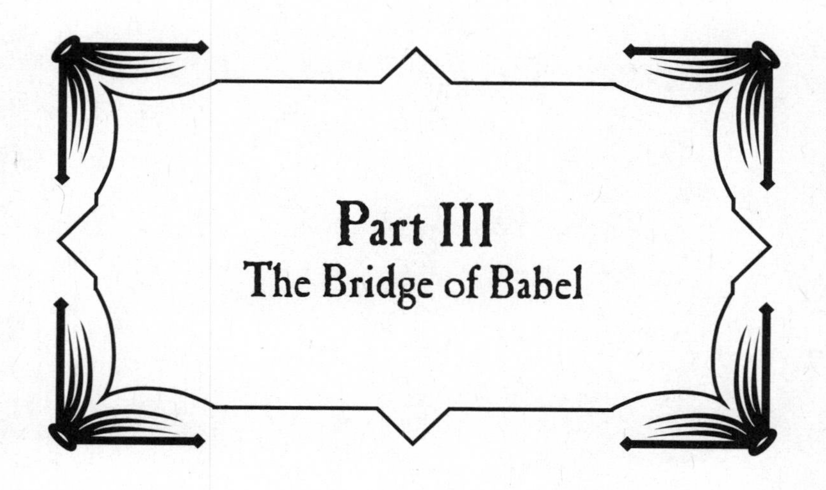

Part III

The Bridge of Babel

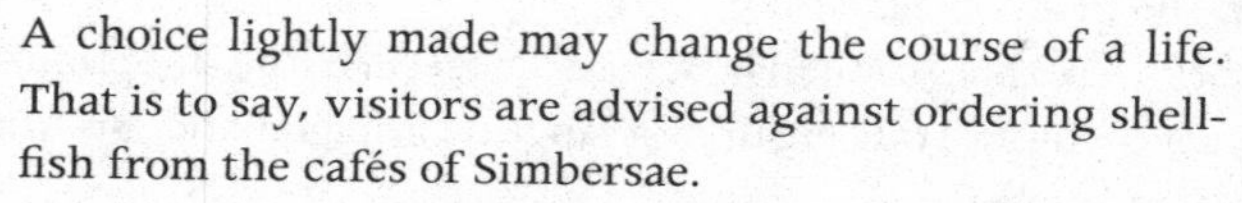

Chapter One

A choice lightly made may change the course of a life. That is to say, visitors are advised against ordering shellfish from the cafés of Simbersae.

—*Everyman's Guide to the Tower of Babel,* VIII. II

Catherine Evreux, private second-class in the lumenguard of the crowning ringdom of Nebos, had never been so grateful to be on sentry duty in her life. She sat upon a wooden stool that rocked on the soft lawn, reading a book she did not particularly like, with only a thermos of hot chocolate to sustain her. Her ionastra and battery pack leaned against a nearby trellis where the vines of spring peas withered, and a pair of disappointed wasps probed her weapon for nectar. Her tall boots lay deflated upon the golden path that ended, or rather began, at the western windstile.

Technically, her post was on the road where she could peer through the fish-eyed lens into the airless chamber to visually inspect the returning patrols, but the next troop wasn't due back for hours, and there seemed little point in spending that time staring into a literal vacuum, especially when there was such a pleasant view just around the corner. She sat where the green of the ringdom broke upon the crystal dome and looked out at the clouds as they folded and rolled like cream whipped in a bowl. The tall grass pricked her feet and kept her awake since her book was failing in that regard.

Her hot chocolate had gone cold almost immediately but not before developing a scum upon its surface that bumped against her lip whenever she took a sip. And yet Catherine Evreux wore a contented smile because at least she wasn't having to sit through another blasted accord.

She had always loathed those ringdom-wide assemblies, with their pomp and circumstance. They were contentious, catty affairs where the majority of generally agreeable Nebosans were held hostage by the same gabblers and grandstanders time after time for hours on end. It seemed to Catherine that her true civic duty had always been to refrain from leaping from her seat and rushing the podium to slap the teeth out of the mouth of whatever self-important elder was presently fogging the stage with vitriol and halitosis.

So far, she had succeeded.

The fact that this particular accord concerned the adoption of some five thousand young hods ensured a lengthy, antagonistic, but ultimately unnecessary debate.

The moral choice was plain enough.

Just hours earlier, Catherine had listened to her old friend Runa succinctly articulate the heart of the question at hand. The Brick Layer had been blunt about the ringdom's charter as a safe harbor to the hods. The opposition could appeal to no higher authority than the creator of their ringdom. Even setting the Brick Layer aside, turning away half-starved children was indefensible. And then there was the practical fact that Nebos was aging more quickly than it was repopulating. The ringdom needed the bantlings as much as they needed Nebos.

No, Catherine was not concerned. The accord would come to the right conclusion with or without her vote. Soon enough, Runa would climb down from her purgatorial stool—that ridiculous and unjust practice that seemed to have begun as a prank and somehow transmuted into custom—and the children would find a home in Nebos. The future would be strange, but their consciences would be light.

Catherine discovered she had reread the same miserable paragraph of her unlovable novel several times without absorbing a single word. She snapped the book shut and yawned.

The pumps of the western windstile hummed to life, engaging a regular cycle that had become as familiar as the purr of a cat.

She pressed her shoulder against the diamond wall to stop her stool from wobbling. Outside, the fog continued to churn as it always did. Or nearly so. At a second glance, it seemed sparser than usual. Catherine could now make out the head of the nearest bolt cannon, some fifty strides away. On most days, even the base of the keep was barely visible. Now, she could make out the folds in the robes of the colossal beggar. Even as

Catherine stared, the entrance at the base of the keep swung open. One of the two gunners on duty slouched through, plucked the smirking helmet from his head, and tugged a cigarette from a pocket in his rubber armor.

Catherine was about to return to her contemptible book when the head of the monumental supplicant began to twist and nod, vomiting lightning at the sky. The exposed gunner dropped his cigarette and fled back inside, even as the murk above him flashed with the fleeing bolts. Catherine felt a vague sense of excitement, but not urgency. Nebos was like honey, and honey attracted flies, though they were swatted away easily enough.

One of the cannon's missiles struck its clouded target. The ball of blue light splashed upon the unseen hull. Sparks blew out in a thousand directions like an electric dandelion.

But the burning rain of eviscerated silk Catherine expected to follow did not. Instead, the head of the ringdom's defender tilted farther back, to the very limit of its throat, and cast another bolt into the clouds. Again, the energetic missile burst and evanesced. A curious red light illuminated the haze above the keep. A prow like a plowshare cut through the clouds. The long ship that followed rode upon a slip of light. The ringdom's cannon had failed to burst its bubble because it had no silks to burst.

The silvery warship settled in the gap between the gun turret and the windstile. A hatch in its lower deck opened. Figures began to emerge.

The stool toppled under her as Catherine leapt to her feet. Deciding she'd rather be caught by Captain Dyre barefoot than unarmed, she snatched up her wand and pack and trampled through a bed of marigolds to return to the road.

There was no reason to panic, of course. Outsiders couldn't open the windstile, and their weapons could not penetrate the dome. Even if they had slipped past the ringdom's cannons, they would never get inside.

The clang of the windstile's outer latch made her jump. Peering through the fish-eye porthole, Catherine watched as four interlopers strode into the vacuum chamber. One was a broad-shouldered beast of a woman with a neck like a tree stump. To one side of her was a small, potbellied man with skin like a candle and eyes like flame; on the other was a young woman with hair like a boot brush. She looked oddly familiar, though Catherine could not imagine how. Leading them was a woman with skin the color of dry earth, a cocked hat, and an iron arm. The outer door swung shut behind them, and the air pumps began to whine. Catherine felt almost sorry for them. The outer door must've malfunctioned, and now these lucky marauders would have the air sucked out of their lungs.

The woman with the engine arm raised her palm even as the windstile's fans above began to suck at the braids of her forest-green coat.

The inner hatch gasped. Catherine's retreating heels tangled upon her abandoned boots. She stumbled and nearly fell. But, keeping her feet, she raised the wand of her ionastra as the pumps of the windstiles wound down and the western gate of Nebos swung open.

"I am the Arm of the Sphinx. We have come to use your basement."

"And also..." the young woman with a familiar face prompted.

"And also to inquire after a young man named Adam. I believe he's your pris—"

"Go away, please. Go back. Right now. This...this is called an ionastra. It spits lightning. And it can...it will turn you to dross."

"We're not here to pick a fight," the young woman said, stepping forward, raising her hand. Catherine marked the enormous bangle that consumed her wrist; it seemed to shine with a dozen rubies. "The Brick Layer said that you'd be—"

"The Brick Layer is dead. Go back!" Catherine felt her body curling about her weapon. She never would've guessed that she'd be the one to defend the gates alone. Every muscle in her body seized.

"We just want to—" the young woman began before her voice was drowned out by the crack of a thunderbolt. The spark caught her full in the chest. The wool of her lapels blackened and fumed as the electricity vined down her arms and up her neck. Her eyes shone like the beacons of a spire, and the garnets in her brass cuff grew enflamed.

Catherine lurched back, expecting the girl she'd just shot to collapse or erupt into flame or cry out in agony, but the young lady seemed to have been only pinned by the spark that ran through her.

Then, to Catherine's great surprise, the young woman shook out her limbs, rousing as if from a daydream. Brushing past her would-be executioner, she began to chase down the empty lane that curved off through the gardens.

"Wait!" the young lady cried, cupping her hand to her mouth. "Hey! Don't you walk away from me. I know you can hear me, old man. Come back here!"

Catherine turned back around when she felt her weapon leap from her hands. She looked up to see the amazon clutching the wand of her ionastra.

"I'm going to borrow this," the scowling hillock of a woman said.

In a daze, Catherine pulled her arms from the straps of the battery pack.

"Probably going to need it for a little while," the amazon said, examining the scrollwork around the bar trigger.

"Of course," Catherine said numbly, even as she tried to digest what had just transpired. When the history of Nebos was written, the record of the first intruders to break through the gates would doubtlessly fill a page or two and inevitably include the name of the guard on duty. The biography of her entire existence would comprise a single line: *Catherine Evreux was barefoot and reading a bad book when she let the buggers in.*

The amazon looked down the length of the barrel, sighting the high branches of a nearby tree. "Probably won't give it back, if I'm honest."

Catherine smiled bravely. "Oh, I don't think they'd let me keep it even if you did."

Mere hours earlier, Byron had sat on his heels rubbing a mixture of beeswax and orange oil into a gouge in the barroom floor. It had not escaped his attention that of late he was spending a great deal of time on his knees—scrubbing, daubing, polishing. In the past he'd complained about the disarray that resulted from hosting dinner parties or catering to a pirate crew, but neither compared to the outright disaster that resulted from acts of violence.

Tellingly, none of the adventure stories Byron had ever read mentioned just how messy the adventuring business was. The hero never swept up the broken glass or mended the curtains after a brawl. No, duty called! The Sphinx's footman suspected the hero's true quest was to be on the road before the brooms came out. Byron liked to imagine that if every knight, soldier of fortune, and buccaneer were forced to scrub blood from a single area rug, that the tedious, unpleasant experience would usher in an era of peace. Let the generals mop up the battlefield for a change, then see how long they'd go before waging another war!

The uneven beat of a hobbling gait brought his head up. He watched the former governess wend through the maze of dining room tables, straightening chairs as she came. It was the absentminded tidying of a lifelong professional and a trait Byron adored in Ann.

"Iren's waving the flag. They're back out at port," she said.

"All of them?" Byron rested on his heels.

"Yes, thank heaven. And it looks like they've picked up a couple of guests, as well."

Byron sighed, giving the gouge one final pass with his rag before folding the cloth back into a square. "And you're sure you're all right to be jogging about?"

"I'm fine." Ann lifted her bandaged foot, twisting it to inspect the gauze. She had been lucky; the duke's bolt had passed between the bones and tendons. "Fortunately, my feet have been toughened by years of pacing nursery floors. I've stepped on a thousand blocks, a hundred jacks, and a dance company of porcelain ballerinas. How are you holding up?"

Byron touched the back of his head tentatively. "I have a lump, but there's a bigger goose egg on my pride. It was a devil of a time to faint."

"Seemed a perfectly reasonable time to me. Besides, no one can say you didn't redeem yourself. By the way, thank you for mopping up my..." Ann waved at the floor and looked a little pale.

"Of course. What are you going to tell Iren?"

"That I dropped a kettle on my foot."

"How clumsy." He rose and screwed the lid back onto the tin of wax. "And Marya... she still doesn't want to tell anyone about what happened?"

"It makes sense, when you think about it. It'll just upset everyone, and this is hardly the time to be piling anxiety on grief. The captain would feel guilty she left the duke alive, and Iren would never want to leave me alone again. The captain will need Iren at her best. We all will."

Byron's thoughts drifted back to the moment that he, Ann, and Marya had stood with the duke's body slumped before the ship's main hatch. A frigid wind had whistled past the open portal, sucking at the rags of the duke's disguise. Marya had asked to do the honors, and so it was she who rolled him out upon a cloud using her harpoon as a lever. His body would've landed somewhere in the barren pan of the basin floor, far away from the Market, out where the buzzards and flies could undress him without fear of interruption.

Byron took his jacket from the back of a barstool and shrugged his arms into the sleeves. "I must admit, it is fun to have our own secret."

"I like it, too," Ann said, reversing her course. She spoke over her shoulder. "I'll turn down the beds. Marya said that our two guests look a little lean. Perhaps an early tea would not go amiss?"

"I'll put the kettle on."

"Mind your toes."

Chapter Two

It is true that what distinguishes the amateur from the professional is not a single stroke of success but rather the lengthy education of repeated failure. Even so, visitors are advised to beware the captains who boast about the many shipwrecks they've survived.

—*Everyman's Guide to the Tower of Babel*, II. VI

Though Byron heard the distant plash of voices, his crewmates and their guests were slow to filter up from the crew quarters. Frankly, he felt a little relieved to be alone in the refuge of his kitchen. The orderly stacks of crockery, the beaming counters, and the racks of balloon whisks, strainers, and spatulas all had a soothing effect on his nerves.

He distracted himself by trimming the crusts from slices of white bread, a mindless effort that allowed him a moment to thumb through the filing cabinet of his feelings. Wedged right at the front of this emotional drawer was the thrill of survival: He was lucky to be alive. The duke's bolt had shattered one of the vials of medium that powered his limbs, but Byron's remaining cells had been left untouched and sufficient to sustain him.

Still, just before Byron had lost consciousness, his last thought had been rather unceremonious: *Uh-oh, I've died.*

He'd been wrong about that, happily. Byron could only hope the duke had suffered a similar banal epiphany on his way out.

That bleak thought perhaps explained why the next drawer in the cabinet of Byron's emotions was so overstuffed with anger. Rather than guilt or regret, he felt only fury that this stupid, petty, unworthy man had cornered him into committing such a profane act. How dare that spoiled brat make him a murderer!

But the final file Byron touched while thumbing through the archives of his heart went a long way toward allaying his rage. What he felt underneath all else was love: love for these friends he'd unexpectedly found, love of a life that was much more profound than anything he'd ever allowed himself to hope for.

As his eyes welled up like a plugged sink, Byron peeled the cucumbers, and spread the cream cheese, and chiffonaded the mint, until he felt as if all the drawers in his soul had flown open at once, and the pages of his timid hopes and immodest fears were soaring about in a joyful, unorderly flock.

After half an hour, Ann popped her head into the galley and said that she had sent everyone straight to the bath, adding that the state of their clothes fell somewhere between unreasonable and unspeakable. "And I think Marya might've undersold the emaciated condition of our guests. They look like they haven't had a proper meal in weeks."

Byron surveyed the pallid finger sandwiches he'd just stacked into a ziggurat. "Well, this certainly won't be enough to sate a starving man. All right. Let's see: I've been aging a strip loin, and I still have some fresh beans. Ah! I could make a béarnaise sauce!"

"Byron, don't feel like you have to fuss."

"It's not a fuss; it's affection."

"I had no idea you liked guests so much!"

"Not affection for them—affection for you and our crew and for myself. We can't take anything for granted. Each and every tea could be our last together. Why not make them all memorable?"

Ann dipped her chin and raised her eyebrows. "You've got a theatrical streak."

Byron flattened his ears. "I've killed a man."

"And only fainted the once."

He dashed a dish towel at the air as she retreated through the swinging door.

Byron had just set the last caper berry upon the plank of smoked salmon when voices, familiar and strange, overtook the dining room. Ann limped in to collect the first course.

"So, what do you make of our guests?" Bryon asked as she collected the fish board.

"They're friends of Thomas Senlin, apparently. They were all aboard the Hod King together."

"They escaped? How?" Ann quickly recounted what she had gleaned while finding the men something to wear from the ship's wardrobe. The revelations she shared made the stag frown. "So, there's another engine, a smaller one?"

"Sort of a Hod Prince, I guess. And that's where Senlin is. Or where they hope he is."

Byron closed his eyes. "Marya."

"She doesn't know. Still at the wheel. Captain asked me to leave it to her to deliver the bad news. Is there any butter?"

"Is there any butter? This isn't a shanty! Of course there's butter!" He stamped the butter pot upon the fish board and Ann bustled out the door again.

Byron busied himself plating the next course, though he'd scarcely finished dressing the haricots verts when Ann returned, her eyes wide and staring over an empty platter.

"Did they like it?" Byron asked.

"They fenced over the fat with their forks. I've never seen Iren's stomach meet its match, but the big one, John, can unhinge his jaw. I think we might want to pick up the pace."

"What manners!"

"They're ravenous, Byron. Carve the steak."

Byron could scarcely garnish the courses quickly enough. Ann's cheeks grew pink from ferrying out platters of fennel-crusted chops and dishes of niçoise salad and bowls of mushroom bisque and shingles full of fruit chutneys and soft cheese. After this submission to the bottomless pits of their guests' stomachs, Byron asked, "Did they like it?"

Ann replied, "They did; I just hope no one swallows a finger."

"Excellent, and did you happen to prepare them for . . . ?" Byron waved a hand before his snout to indicate his face, though he imagined it looked like he was trying to shoo a gnat.

Ann adopted her most diplomatic smile. "I may've mentioned that you were a most handsome stag who sometimes has a dazzling effect upon the uninitiated."

"*Dazzling*. That's a nice word for it. Thank you."

When at last Byron emerged from his depleted galley carrying a tray of immaculate chocolate profiteroles arrayed upon a doily, he saw that the dinner party had split into two factions. The captain and pilot sat at the bar, and beyond them, the guests and the rest of the crew occupied a table crowded with dishes and glassware. He was about to approach Edith when someone in the dining party noticed him and bellowed the phrase "Sir! Sir, are you the genius?"

Byron's head swung around to behold one of the largest persons he'd ever seen. He was taller than Iren by half a head, and his shoulders were just as broad. His size was further exaggerated by the clothes Ann had provided him. The buttons on his white blouse strained to hide the breadth of his chest, and the sleeves, tight as sausage casings, only reached halfway down his forearms. Above his gaunt cheeks, his dark eyes shone with a giddy light.

"I beg your pardon?" Byron said, mounting the dining room step.

The goliath stood, napkin falling from his lap. He spread out his arms as if to embrace the room. "This food! This magnificent food! Did you prepare it?"

Byron felt uncertain. He appreciated commendations, but only in small portions. Praise was like chocolate; a little made you euphoric, too much just made you sick. Yet it seemed silly to lie. "Yes, I did."

The giant approached, bringing his hands together, a gesture that seemed to necessitate Bryon offering up his own, which were immediately clasped and worked like a pump handle. "You are the most talented chef I have ever met, and you are looking at a practiced gastronome! My good sir, your chops were as tender as a mother's kiss. The potatoes in your niçoise had just the right amount of tooth, but still crumbled on the tongue. Your loin should be framed and hung in a museum!" Byron blushed beneath his fur, but the giant was not done. "And your béarnaise! A revelation! So often it's too salty or the cook stuffs it so full of tarragon it tastes like lawn clipping or there are lumps—"

Byron couldn't help but interrupt here: "You can't have lumps in a béarnaise sauce."

"No, you cannot! Then it's just poorly scrambled eggs! But, chef, hear me: You are a gift to mankind. How can I ever repay you?"

As graciously as he could, Bryon withdrew his hands from the giant's grip. "That's very kind of you, but you are my guest and—"

"I insist!"

"Well, we have made a dish or two."

"Say no more! I shall lick them all clean."

"Ha-ha! Yes. And wash them, too, yes? With soap and water?"

"Naturally! Sir, I would wash every dish that you make for the rest of my life! My heavens, are those profiteroles? Would you mind terribly if I . . . ?"

Feeling somewhat dazed by the outpouring of praise and carrying a platter that had been snatched empty by the famished diners, Byron veered toward Edith and Reddleman, still conferring in low tones at the bar.

"No, I don't think so," Reddleman said, his voice weak but articulate, in answer to a question Byron had missed. The pilot leaned bodily upon the bar like a drunk at the end of the evening, this despite the fact that the only liquor in sight sat in front of Edith. "I gave them both a quick physical after their baths. The large one, John, he was shot in the thigh nearly three weeks ago. The wound has not healed well. In fact, it's hardly healed at all. I'm sure he's in considerable pain, and if he keeps walking on it, he'll either lose the leg or himself. The other one, Finn, he seems to have what I'd call walking pneumonia, probably brought on from either months on the black trail or standing too near a poorly ventilated furnace. Even if you wished to trust them with a sword, neither is fit to swing it." And with that, Reddleman's face fell to the mahogany, a collapse that did not seem to inspire concern from the captain. A farting snore whiffled out from the sides of his flattened cheeks.

"Well, that's disappointing," Edith said, her gaze roving over Byron's empty tray.

"Might I ask what the plan is, Captain?" Byron said.

"The skylight! It has to be the skylight." Voleta hopped down from the dining floor gripping a rack of rattling, glowing vials.

Edith picked up Reddleman's head, rolling it to one side to ease his breathing. "You keep saying that. What skylight?"

Voleta set the brace of batteries upon the bar top. "That's our way into the Sphinx's lair—"

"Not a lair," Byron corrected.

Voleta conceded the point with a bow of her head. "The Sphinx called it a skylight."

"When did you speak to the Sphinx?" Byron asked.

Voleta squinted at his chest, leaving him to wonder if there was a stain on his vest. "A very long time ago, actually. I bumped into her and the Brick Layer in Cilicia. I told her we were locked out of the house; she told me how to get in." With a wrinkle of a smile, Voleta poked Byron's cravat, or rather she hooked her finger through the hole the duke's bolt had made in it. Byron swatted her hand away. She shrugged and said, "There's a sort of... ladder that leads down to the attic, and the attic connects to the Sphinx's workroom."

"And how do we access the skylight?" Edith asked.

"Through Nebos. That's what the summit is called, isn't it, Byron?"

"Yes, Nebos."

"That's where Adam is. I'm looking forward to seeing him. He's missed so much. To be fair, I've probably missed a lot, too." Voleta turned her attention to the snoring pilot. She threw the tails of his jacket over his head and began tugging up his dress shirt, revealing his forged spine and the diminished crimson bulbs that illuminated it.

"Don't forget the sparking men. They're up there, too," Edith said darkly. "Do we know if the ringdom still respects the Sphinx?"

Byron clucked his tongue. "Perhaps. They used to be quite fanatical about the Brick Layer's wishes, but it's been more than a generation since the Sphinx paid them a visit."

"Will the ringdom still have electricity?" Edith asked, watching as Voleta unscrewed the vials from Reddleman's vertebrae.

Byron's lips gathered in thought. "Probably. I remember an occasion when Marat suggested to the Sphinx that she shut off power to the peak—turn off the tap, as it were; remind the Nebosans who their landlord was. The Sphinx said the notion was both unlikable and impracticable because Nebos had its own generator, independent of the Tower."

"Really? That's surprising. Still, should make things easier for us."

"How so?"

"If the gates of Nebos opened for the Sphinx in the past, they might open for her arm in the present."

"What exactly *is* your plan, Captain? You enter Nebos, you go through the skylight, you access the house—then what?"

"I saw the size of Marat's new weevil. It's scarcely bigger than a longboat. He can't have more than two dozen men in there. Even if he manages to dig his way in and unlock the bridge, that doesn't mean he has the strength to keep the castle."

"Have you forgotten the last time we crossed his toadies, Captain?" Voleta extracted another murky cell from the pilot's back. "He won't need an army if he's still traveling with those Wakemen."

"We'll be ready for them this time. First, we find the Sphinx, make sure she's safe. Then we rescue Tom, and beat the zealot back."

"Captain, if I may offer a piece of unsolicited advice," Byron began, clasping his hands behind his back and raising his chin to signal a moment of sincerity. "You know I don't have a taste for blood, but if you have the opportunity to reason with Marat, to hear his sympathetic explanations for these horrific machinations, please don't. Don't listen. Kill him. He will never coexist with the human race because he is a race of one. He does not believe in us. He believes in nothing and no one outside himself. He is a fire burning through the world: If you let him go, he will not repent; he will just burn hotter and make more ash."

Edith patted Byron's epaulet. "I understand, Byron. Believe me."

Reddleman heaved a sharp breath as he sat bolt upright on his stool. His lashes fluttered, throwing small tears from his eyes as he grinned and craned his head about. "What a terrible nightmare! I dreamed I had died and become a machine, a mind like a honeycomb, a fearless gear! And now, here I am, back in this old pudding." He slapped his round cheeks and laughed. "What did I miss?"

"We've agreed to go in by the skylight," Voleta said, pulling down his blouse and coat.

"Fine, fine! Have you puzzled out all of the Brick Layer's riddles yet?"

"No, not at all."

Reddleman spoke in a rush as he stood and began to pace in short, hot-footed steps. "The 'endless sea' alludes to death, perhaps? And that other phrase, 'go mad in the dark,' could refer to being in a mausoleum, though of course madness suggests awareness, and if you're alert inside a crypt, something has gone terribly, terribly wrong. Buried alive? Does that ring any bells? No. A pyramidion is the capstone of a pyramid, as we all know, but I don't understand how a capstone can fail. Surely it's the base that fails if anything. If you lose the point of a pyramid, the rest endures, does it not? And we can't forget the Nautilus and the Allonomia. We know, of course, that a nautilus is a mollusk, but an Allonomia—"

Captain Winters waved a hand to interrupt his manic review. "Reddleman, this is all very interesting, but if you are well enough to relieve Marya on the bridge, I do need to speak to her."

"Of course, Captain."

"I'll go with you," Voleta said. "We can puzzle as we walk."

"And how *does* one put a mollusk to sleep?" Reddleman said as he and Voleta leaned their heads together and marched toward the dining hall's exit.

"What are you going to tell Marya?" Byron asked as the pair retreated from earshot.

"The truth," Edith replied, knocking back the last of her rum.

"The whole truth?"

"The hopeful truth."

Chapter Three

The Shadowless Hour, when the sun shines directly above the Tower, is commemorated that night by a great dispersal of sky lanterns, the scattering of which briefly resembles the birth of a galaxy, an impression that is somewhat spoiled by the resulting widespread fires.

—*Everyman's Guide to the Tower of Babel*, VI. XII

hen Marya entered the dining room, she carried in her a tempest of conflicting feelings beneath a tempered calm. It was her placid mask, a face she'd learned to compose when accompanying the duke on his social rounds. Strange to think how much more of an act it had been to stand at his side than to play on a stage where she could veil her moods behind theatrics and camp.

She felt the ambivalence she once had upon attending her own surprise party, an occasion that had been spoiled in advance by an indiscreet cousin with a carrying voice. In the days before her friends and family tried to stun her with birthday wishes, Marya had felt giddy over their sincere expression of affection, nervous about her ability to act suitably astonished, and irritated that what should've been a pleasant surprise had become an anxious act. When her loved ones finally popped out from behind her mother's couch, Marya shouted in relief rather than surprise.

There was nothing quite so exhausting as opposing emotions in equal supply.

Every atom of her being still hummed with what she had done. Again, she relived the arc of her harpoon as it carved open the wound, watched the look on Wilhelm's face evolve from disbelief to anger to perverse arousal. In that moment, he'd still thought it a game, still believed himself a huntsman and her a doe. He'd always said he did not trust a man who came back from a fox chase with unspattered britches and clean boots. Filth was proof of pursuit.

Then Byron had appeared and stolen at a stroke all of Wil's pretension and poise—indomitable powers that for years had inspired ladies to paw at his elbow, and maids to fly from his office, and noblemen to bay at whatever quarry he suggested because they, as so many had, mistook his confidence for wisdom, his decorum for decency, his malice for courage.

And the entire charade had vanished at the twang of a crossbow string.

Which was the genesis of her disappointment. Because the life of excess and ease, of casual tyranny and habitual torment that Wilhelm had enjoyed for decades could never be taken from him now. For all the suffering he had inflicted upon others, *upon her*, his own discomfort had been but brief. Now, there was no correcting the account. The duke had, in fact, won. And he would continue to win so long as she did not devise some means for keeping him from living and dying in a corner of her mind, over and over, for the rest of her life.

And still, when she sat down before a cleared space at the crowded table across from two men she did not know, Marya appeared perfectly composed. Since the rest of the table was engaged in conversation, she made no effort to interrupt them with an introduction. She thanked Ann for the plate of food, a portion that Byron had sagaciously held in reserve just for her.

Taking up her fork and knife, Marya said to the governess, "I checked in on Olivet on my way up. Still fast asleep. But if you wouldn't mind keeping an ear out?"

"Of course. You eat. I'll catch her when she wakes," Ann said.

Marya cut the filet and, raising a pink morsel to her lips, again pictured rolling Wil out the open hatch, his lips blue, his tongue protruding, his punctured eye still flowing down his sculpted cheek.

"Madam!" The large man across from her pushed himself back from the table and stood. It seemed the teetering ascent of a camel rising from its knees. "My name is John Tarrou."

The small man at her elbow, who'd been scraping gravy from his plate with a spoon, paused the effort long enough to say, "Finn Goll."

"A pleasure to meet you, Mr. Tarrou and Mr. Goll. Marya Senlin, at your service."

The cymbal-like crash of a dropped spoon made Marya hop in her seat. Finn Goll squinted at her as if she were the sail of a lost ship rising over the horizon.

The giant John seemed likewise astonished. For a moment, Marya wondered if her fame in Pelphia had reached so far, but something in the strain of their gazes suggested they were more than just starstruck. "You must forgive us," Tarrou said at last. "We are better mannered when we are not so starved."

"Of course," Marya said, nodding to them both in turn. "Byron's cooking has the same effect on me."

John sat down again, gripping the table as if for support, though he continued to hold the edge even after he was safely seated. He ducked her eyes when he spoke again. "I have listened to Tom reflect upon your noble visage and generous character for hours on end; even still, it is very strange to sit across from you in the flesh. At least I understand now why you were the only subject that never failed to rob Senlin of his eloquence."

Marya put down her fork, her appetite receding so quickly it turned the morsel in her throat to straw. She coughed hoarsely and said, "You know Tom?"

"I met the headmaster while there was still a whiff of train smoke on him. He found me in the Baths; he was looking for you. I'm ashamed to say, I impeded his search, distracting him with wine and cynicism and my own indolence. But Tom persevered and was still persevering the next time I met him with a bucket on his head and his heart in his hands in a Pelphian sewer. When I wished to lay down and die, Tom carried us both. He kept me awake with talk of you, your humor, your magnificent voice, your wonderful child, who he had not yet met, but who'd already become the object of an hourly catechism for why he had to survive. I've never met such a stubborn fellow, nor one more adoring of his wife."

Marya attempted to absorb the breadth of these sentiments and their history but soon felt compelled to brush the past aside. "Then you were aboard the Hod King? Where is Tom? Why isn't he here with you?"

As if on cue, the captain came and sat down beside Marya, angling her seat to face her.

Edith wore a smile so tight it nearly seemed a frown. "The Hod King has fallen. Marat escaped. I think he took Tom along with him."

Marya saw at once there was more news to come, and it did not seem that it would be happy. She pushed her plate away and looked to their new guests. "All right. Tell me the rest."

It took several minutes for Finn and John to acquaint Marya with the broad strokes of Tom's passage through the black trail, his induction into Marat's army, his aspirations of sabotage, and unlikely ascension in the ranks of the Hod King's crew. The end of the story, it seemed to Marya, was rather hopeless. Tom had succeeded in signaling his conspirators to detonate their bomb, but then had been carried away by the unexpected emergence of a smaller boring engine.

John Tarrou, who had been studying the salt and pepper cellars like pieces on a chessboard, abruptly leveled Marya with a most earnest stare. "But you should know that Tom chose your name to be the starting pistol for our escape. Of course, he knew there was a chance that we'd all be killed, so he chose to use what might've been his last breath on his first love."

From the corner of her eye, Marya saw Edith tip a near empty bottle of wine into a glass, then add the leavings of a second to the collection.

"But you really believe he's still alive?" she asked.

John did not so much nod as roll his head in answer. "In one of his last secret missives, Tom remarked that Marat needed him to guide him through the Sphinx's maze. The headmaster is still useful, and that should protect him."

Marya asked what the plan to rescue him was, and Edith explained how they would intercept the Hod King's progeny. Its destination was not in doubt. They would find Marat and Tom in the Sphinx's home, which they would have to enter from above.

"And Nebos—it's a safe harbor?" Marya asked as Byron arrived with a tray to begin clearing the table. She looked to him for an answer.

Hands moving quick as a whisk, Byron said, "Nebos is a wonderful place. It's full of flowers, fruit trees, and gardens. It's an oasis teetering on top of a desert. And the populace is, I believe, still loyal to my master. We expect a warm welcome." He smiled at Edith as he hauled the heavy tray away.

John stood with a theatrical groan. "Ah, my destiny calls to me, and I must answer. I have suds to agitate! Crumbs to liberate! My gracious hosts, thank you for this warmest of welcomes. I am hardly worthy but am exceedingly grateful. Mrs. Senlin." The giant managed a rusty bow and shuffled after his retreating chef.

Marya did not look at Edith when she posed the question suddenly, hoping to jar an honest answer from her: "He's dead, isn't he? I think you're all trying to spare my feelings, but it's not a kindness to let me hope."

Edith had been in the process of tilting her glass back, but made a dam of her lips, and brought it down again. Wiping her mouth, she said, "It's impossible to say, of course, but you should prepare yourself for—"

"Excuse me, Captain," interjected the half-forgotten man with eyebrows as proud as a general's mustache. Marya and Edith twisted toward Finn Goll. "I don't want to be crude, but in case you've forgotten, your Tom is a tick. Just when you think you've crushed him between your fingernails, you haven't. You haven't even creased his shell. Believe me. I tried. When I met Tom, I was king of a fiefdom, a lord of port. Now look at me! My fineries, fortune, family, all gone, taken from me by a green tourist from a fish-piss village a hundred miles east of the end of the earth. He humbled me not because he held a grudge or wished to fleece me, but because I tried to keep him from finding *you*." Finn nodded at Marya with a rueful smirk. "Luc Marat will underestimate him, just as I did, and he won't realize his mistake until his port is on fire and his debtors have foreclosed on his home, leaving him nothing, nothing but wistfulness for a time before he met that tick of a man named Thomas Senlin."

In the misty streets of Nebos, Voleta finally caught up with the Brick Layer as he stepped backward over a golden curb, through a hedge of azaleas, and onto the verdant lawn of a park. He walked with his head thrown back, his mouth agape, marshaling the lumbering progression of the largest crane she had ever seen.

She had grown up around outriggers and wreckers that shifted freight and reseated derailed train cars. But the immense machine the Brick Layer shepherded made him look as inconsequential as a flea. The rumbling crane's towering neck, latticed with a thousand iron struts, soared over the blocky operating cabin to a pulley that was as fat as a millstone. The machine moved on a ribbon of steely teeth that carved the ground like a plow. Dangling from the crane's lofty boom hung a most curious payload: a black pyramid. It swung lazily as the charm on a hypnotist's chain.

The Brick Layer, who had held his loupe clenched to his eye, seemed to drop his gaze in Voleta's direction by accident. She did not give him a chance to retract his attention. He only had time to scowl as she chased down the lane after him. The moment he thought her near enough to hear, he said, "This is an inconvenient time."

Voleta panted as she came to a halt and dug her fists into her hips. "Oh, just stop. Stop pretending."

The Brick Layer mopped his brow with a handkerchief. "Pretending? What am I pretending exactly?"

"Obviously, you're the one who called me here. We keep crashing together. Once is a coincidence. Twice, a contrivance. But again and again—that has to be a summons, surely. So, what do you want?"

The Brick Layer snorted in brief amusement, but even then, Voleta perceived a tone she had not heard before. He was nervous. "There's no subterfuge here, young lady. We bear the curse of the same braid. We are drawn together because we share a fate. Even so, today is not a good day for me to be nattering with ghosts. Look around you." The Brick Layer lifted his chin toward men who lurked around the crawling treads of the crane like porters about an arriving train. Voleta saw in their expressions an unsubtle loathing. They bore the scowls of drudgers who hadn't been paid in weeks. "I have to put a candle on this cake," the Brick Layer said, discreetly shielding his mouth. "Though no one is in much of a celebratory mood."

"What are you talking about? What is that thing up there? A gravestone?"

The Brick Layer looked up at the dangling onyx square. He smirked, seemingly at some private achievement. "That... that is the Wick of the Sun. It will warm the dark, feed the greenery, and keep the world a—" The Brick Layer broke off, waving his arms above his head, vying for the attention of the crane's operator. "Mind that bed! We'll miss those peas come winter! Keep to the lawn." He spoke again to her behind the cup of his palm, "Do you remember all that I told you?"

"Of course." As the Brick Layer continued his backward march, Voleta looked out ahead. Above the leafy cumulus, silvery and gilded towers rose, their shapes as diverse as the stalks of a garden with lines that twisted, swelled, and swooped. Nestled at their apparent center was a golden pyramid, seamless and perfect but for a blunted pinnacle. "This rock—it's bound for that pyramid?"

"It is. And once the Wick of the Sun is in place, the Tower will be complete, and my work will be done. I can retire."

"What does retirement look like for a brick layer? Especially one who never seems to get any older."

"Oh, it's quiet. There'll be a hammock soft as a cloud. No trowels, no grout, no blueprint for the day... I've been at this a long time."

"Why?"

"Pardon?"

"Why? Why be at this for a long time? I don't mean to blow your candle out, but the Tower is an *awful* place."

"Yes, I suppose it is, isn't it?" The Brick Layer waved to a frowning fellow who appeared to be his second-in-command, a foreman with eyes as flat as a lead plug. "Oh, what does it matter now anyway." The Brick Layer briefly engaged the man to give over the reins of their procedure. He then turned to walk beside Voleta, his hands shoved deep into the pockets of his rough trousers, his mouth no longer veiled. "You know, that has often been the case with the Towers: they are perfect, if unwanted, distilleries of nature."

"Towers? As in more than one? How many are there?" Voleta said as she leapt over a row of pansies.

"Tell me, are you familiar with the concept of evolution—the broad notion that change happens gradually as traits are rewarded with survival? Yes? No? A little? Well, the thing to understand here is that there are many different tracks of evolution. There's biological evolution and societal evolution and technological evolution. Those are what I call the primordial three. There are, of course, seven in total. Anyway, the trouble often comes near the introduction of each branch of growth. Those who are first to emerge from the puddle of unconsciousness tend to dominate the weak; the first social collectives are usually ruled by bullies, who naturally gravitate toward tyranny; the first technologies are turned toward destructive efforts almost at once. In other words, the discovery that fire could cook your food was quickly followed by the revelation that it could also cook your enemies." The Brick Layer's demeanor had entirely changed. He seemed like a conductor at the end of his shift: unguarded, frank, tired. "Life begins in violence. It always starts that way. But it does not have to persist so. I can tell you that the cruelest confluence is when society is in its adolescence and technology in its nascency. That pairing of uncompromising gears, gnashing together at two different speeds, is a meat grinder. The longer it goes, the freer the blood flows. If your race survives this period, I think you will have something of value to contribute to the rest of us. And if you do not, you will join the ranks of the beautiful extinct, those who ran too fast for their bones to bear, those whose plumage was too bright to hide."

"I hope you don't expect me to recite all of that."

The Brick Layer laughed dryly. "You're not the messenger, Voleta. You are the addressee."

Voleta felt the sudden tug upon the skin beneath her skin, felt the gust of time pulling her forward by the heart. Realizing that she had little time left, she shouted, "But what's the point of all this? What's the point, really?"

The Brick Layer squinted like a man trying to hear through a roaring wind, and said, "The point is to try! The only enemy is complacency; the messy rest serves the cause!"

Chapter Four

Not all political feuds are heated. The diplomatic bond between some factions is like the unhappily wedded pair who, having endured many decades of infraction and contention, no longer see the need to vocalize their revulsion. They can bicker well enough in silence.

—*Everyman's Guide to the Tower of Babel,* VI. VI

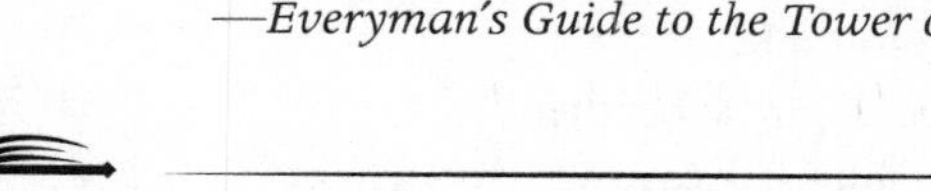

Charging again through the maelstrom of time, Voleta watched the ghostly hosts seethe through their lives like embers from a smokestack.

She felt perfectly serene.

The more she fled through the ages, the less frightening the trial became. There was something soothing, almost drowsy, about the experience. It reminded her of stormy days in the Depot of Sumer when her mother would have to bar the door to keep her inside. Voleta would climb into the attic to pout and lie with her face scant inches from the rafters, and there would listen to the rain rumble down like the muted applause of ten thousand gloved hands. That drumming would turn a day into a daydream. And her mother, who'd had to bolt the windows in the morning to coop her up, by evening would have to promise bread pudding to lure her down.

But then a shiver ran through her from the crown of her head to the soles of her feet as she realized what was happening. She was losing her way as Reddleman had warned she would.

Gathering her vigilance, Voleta focused upon the first static object her eye fell upon: the Brick Layer's crane. She watched that polished cabin tarnish and darken as vines advanced up its sides, shaded its windows, and snaked up its soaring trestle like a garden trellis. The ivy climbed higher and higher, until the great engine was sheathed in green from tread to pulley. And far beneath its bearded pinnacle, the Brick Layer's last brick, the capstone of which he'd been so proud, sat abandoned and half-sunken in the lawn.

Then, all at once, the peripheral flutter of life and the strobe of light subsided. She was standing in the present again and swaying in its stillness.

"Voleta?" a familiar voice said. She turned to find her brother standing upon a kitchen stool with his neck in a noose. The sight of him inspired a flurry of memories, discrete as confetti. Seeing Adam shattered across seven thousand days conjured a hundred quick and conflicting emotions that left her feeling rather numb.

She said, "What'd you do, little brother?"

"Oh, the usual." He sounded cavalier, though his face beamed with relief.

Edith and Iren jogged past the woolly-headed Voleta. Iren cut Adam's anchor as Edith steadied his perch. As soon as Edith had helped him to the ground, Adam hurried to grip the uneven pedestal of the young woman who toed a similar fate. Appearing to take Adam's cue, Iren hacked through the end of the stranger's noose, and the young woman tumbled into his arms. Though their legs seemed weak, their embrace was not.

"I told you I had a plan," Adam said to the young woman with bright, close-set eyes.

"Very dramatic." She patted him on the check and said, "Now let me go. I have to find a privy before I burst."

Adam leaned upon his hangman's stool and watched her flee through the park.

"What happened? Why were you being hanged? Who was that?" Edith asked.

"It is a bit of a yarn, Mister Winters," Adam said.

"*Captain* Winters," said Voleta, her attention drifting again toward the pyramidion crashed upon the lawn.

"Captain? Well, congratulations. Where's Senlin?"

Edith smiled, though her brow frowned. "I shouldn't have left you."

"As I recall, I was the one who went looking for adventure."

"You seem to have found it," Edith said.

"Yes, indee—Is that who I...Is that the Red Hand?" Adam said, and Voleta turned her attention back, hearing the sharpening edge in his voice. He stared at Reddleman, his shoulders rounding, his stance widening.

Voleta quickly intervened. "The Red Hand is dead. This is Reddleman. He's our pilot. A friend. He's saved our necks a time or two."

"And wrung Senlin's neck in the bargain. Or have you forgotten?" Adam seemed to be glancing about for a weapon.

Reddleman said, "Iren, do you recall what you did when you first saw me again in the Sphinx's lair?"

"I threw a cart at your head."

"Yes, you did. And it seemed a very reasonable thing to do. I did not blame you. But do you still wish to throw furniture at me?"

"A little bit," Iren said, and Voleta cleared her throat. "No. I vouch for the man, Adam. He is different. Not exactly good, but better."

Interrupting the awkward reunion, Edith said, "Where is everyone? Where are the guards, the magistrates, the crowds?" Edith waved at the empty park, the inactive roads.

Adam answered: "They've been called to the pyramid. They're voting on whether to send five thousand children back to the black trail. Runa and I brought them in without permission because, well, there's plenty of room for them here, and it's what the Brick Layer wanted, and...wait, Mister Win—*Captain*, where are you going?"

Rocking the pommel of her rapier forward on her belt as if it were the throttle of her legs, Edith marched for the gilded temple. "You said there's a ballot. I'd like to cast my vote."

They all jogged after her as Adam cried, "Wait, there's more!"

"Talk quickly."

The sloping shaft into the pyramid was a seamless aqueduct of light. The radiance that streamed up from the chamber beyond was almost blinding. Edith and her crew squinted and shielded their eyes as they descended into the hurly-burly of overlapping voices that was further muddled by a competing drone that called to mind grain pouring into a hopper.

Breaking upon the vault within, they found themselves standing at the mouth of a long, broad aisle that flowed down to a stage dominated on either side by two immense urns. Each was as capacious as the water stop of a train yard, but with walls made of unblemished glass. The silver mouths of the austere cylinders stood uncapped, and inside each, a swarm of bumblebees churned. One school shone with a pale blue light; the other glowed a saffron yellow. Suspended over either cistern was what seemed a brass chandelier, though dark and shallow as a saucer.

The ceiling above was both flat and much lower than Edith would've expected from such a grand facade, and yet it was far from humble; the great golden expanse was divided into a honeycomb of tiles. The air of the chamber teemed with unlit bees, rising from the elevated hands of the parishioners on either side of her, where they sat on long and curling pews. Those benches descended in tiers and winnowed as they approached the stage, or perhaps it was more accurate to call it an apse. Certainly, the figure who stood between the urns behind a lectern of glassy obsidian seemed to be wearing the embroidered vestments of some sort of vicar.

"You're just in time." A creaky voice at Edith's elbow brought her head around. An ancient woman in white robes stood by the entrance. A covered hamper dangled from the crook her arm. From it, she drew forth a clockwork bee as large as a plum, which she offered to them. Judging from the cataracts in her eyes, the woman seemed to perceive Edith only dimly.

Clasping Iren's shoulder, Edith said, "You four stay here for the time being, but please don't hesitate to join in if the mood sours. And keep an eye on our little dreamer; the last thing I need is a sleepwalking Voleta."

Edith graciously accepted the dormant insect and strode down the aisle, gathering the notice of the attendees as she went. Though she did not give any particular one of them her attention, she did perceive the bizarre nature of their general appearance. There seemed to be no rhyme to their fashion; indeed, they looked like a shuffled encyclopedia of textiles and garments. Their clothes ranged from the ostentatious to the reserved and looked to represent several centuries' worth of trends. A not inconsiderable number of the mob wore transparent masks that had the odd effect of making them look like porcelain figurines. The only thing they all held in common was pallid skin and hair that was similarly pale. Though there were thousands in attendance, the assembly hall stood not even half-full.

To her surprise, no one moved to intercept her. Nobody raised the alarm. They seemed like a secluded island species who, having never beheld a human before, were uncertain whether she was friend or foe. Which seemed fitting, since Edith wasn't yet sure on that point, herself.

By the time she reached the edge of the elevated platform where footlights beamed upward, casting dramatic shadows, the only person who hadn't seemed to have noticed her yet was the celebrant behind the pulpit. The young woman stared fixedly at a draining hourglass on the forward edge of her lectern. When the last grain of sand fell, she flicked a switch on her station, and a gong bellowed a dour note. What Edith had originally mistaken for chandeliers lowered to cap the mouths of the crystal urns, rebuffing the arrival of a few delinquent bees. Those unlit mechanical insects tinked stubbornly upon the shut lid like flies upon a windowpane.

When the officiant spoke, it was without conviction or confidence. Indeed, all had to strain to hear her stammer and swallow and rub her tall forehead as if she were trying to polish up a thought. "That's the end of the voting. Thank you for your patience as we... uh... the accord is tallied by the... as the Cauldrons make their count. Just to remind everyone... blue is, we agreed, for the expulsion of the invaders, as some prefer, *refugees*, the term not being, I think, so important as the result, and the subsequent... exclusion, I'm sorry, *execution* of Adamos Boreas and Runa La-lod, uh, Allod. While the yellow pot... uh, is for those who wish to—"

"Excuse me," Edith said, climbing onto the stage. The young officiant leapt in surprise, upsetting the emptied hourglass. It rolled toward destruction, and she scarcely managed to save it. Her brocaded shawl slid from her shoulder in the doing, and Edith stooped to retrieve it.

"Here you are. Are you the leader here?"

"No, I lost... I won... I *drew* the lot to lead today's accord. It's my first time. Have I done something wrong?"

"I'm sure you're doing a perfectly fine job. Would you mind if I said a few words?"

"I suppose that would be okay," the officiant said, slipping backward toward the dramatic shadows behind the urns with an expression of relief.

"Thank you." Edith tapped the brass-ringed abdomen of her dormant bee upon the podium and surveyed the stunned faces of the denizens of Nebos. "I am the Arm of the Sphinx, Captain Edith Winters of the *State of Art*. I have come in an official capacity. I need to traverse your city to access the Sphinx's home. There's been an outage of power in the Tower, which you might not be aware of, but which has been of some concern to the rest of us."

She paused, perhaps hoping for some noise of affirmation, but they all continued to blink and stare like a pond full of frogs.

"Since arriving here, it has come to my attention that you have arrested one of my crewmen, Adam Boreas. Further, I've been informed that there has been some debate about his fate. As I understand it, he stands accused of enacting the Brick Layer's vision for the ringdom by allowing young hods into the garden, as is their right."

A flushed man with a bulbous jaw and hair as thin as frost stood from his pew near the front of the proceedings, though it seemed more out of obligation than passion. "Excuse me, how did you get into the city? How did you get past our mortars, our windstiles, my guards?"

"And who would you be?"

"I'm Captain Dyre..." He looked suddenly uncertain. "At least I'm captain for the moment."

Edith decided to let that point lie. "It's quite simple, Captain: Your cannons will bow their heads and your gates will genuflect whenever I come to Nebos because your ringdom falls under my jurisdiction, as does all the Tower. Now, back to the question at hand: Why are you debating whether you will obey the Brick Layer's explicit and standing order, even after, as I've just been informed, you have again witnessed the command coming from his own mouth?"

A sharp-nosed woman in a brown architectural bonnet popped up and said, "Because he charged us with protecting Nebos, and we can't do that if we're all dead. The hods bring disease. They are violent. They can't be trusted!"

A man in a silver wig and white dickey leapt up to offer a rebuttal even before Edith could reply. "But we have reveled in the fruits of their suffering for generations! How many hods have toiled and died just so you can walk around with a poorly stuffed owl on your head?"

"It's a genuine Vanholt!"

"It's an abomination!"

"Will everyone please shut up!" Edith all but shouted.

Again, a gong rang a deep and solemn note. All at once, the bees in the urn that shone blue flared brighter as the light of their yellow compatriots dwindled into darkness.

"There you are!" The bonneted woman's voice warbled with triumph. "It's settled, then. We are in accord. The hods must go."

"Mmm." Edith's gaze swept back and forth between the swarms in the two pots; the one vibrant, the other dark. "It seems to have been a close vote. That's a razor's margin if ever I saw one. Perhaps the count is off." She tapped the dead bee upon the podium as if just striking upon a solution. "I have it! Why don't we vote again—just to be sure. A show of hands should suffice."

The bonneted woman seemed to turn a sicklier shade of pale. "This is an outrage. You can't cancel an accord just because you don't like the results!"

Edith smiled as she draped her iron arm over the podium. "It's just a show of hands. All those who wish to hang one of the Sphinx's emissaries and expel thousands of malnourished children, in defiance of the Brick Layer's will and the bounds of basic decency, please raise your hands."

"This is intimidation!"

"I can't help it if your conscience has embarrassed you. Surely what you believe in private you can also espouse in public? There's no cause to feel intimidated!" Edith spread out her arms in a gesture of welcoming. Though it was short-lived as again her arm clanged upon the pulpit, and the beam of her smile seemed to pass behind a cloud. "But, I would caution you that the Sphinx expects faithful adherence to the Brick Layer's edicts, and anyone who defies those decrees must necessarily have their citizenship reviewed." She grinned again and brushed something from the front of her coat. "That should only take a few weeks, months at most. In the meantime, you will be my guest. And I promise you, what the Sphinx's jail lacks in luxury, it more than makes up for with capacity. I'm sure there's room enough for everyone."

The woman's lower lip quivered, and yet she was not ready to relent just yet. "You can't threaten us. You can't force us to open our homes against our will!"

"You are under the misapprehension that the privileges you enjoy are owned rather than rented. You do not hold the keys to the ringdom; the Sphinx does, and therefore, I do. If you are unable to fulfill the terms of your inhabitation, there are plenty of other willing tenants waiting in the wings to take your place."

"You're threatening us with genocide?"

"Madam, I am merely reminding you of the vows you made, and I'm asking you one final time if you are absolutely sure that you wish to break your oath. Now, a show of hands, please."

Edith did not rush the moment. She let the weight of her words settle upon each soul in turn. As she surveyed them, she marked the evasion of eyes, the slouch of shoulders, the reluctant acceptance of a new reality. Perhaps it was unwise to bully them. There would be consequences, of course: tensions, the possibility of violence. She would have to deal with each crisis as it came. But if she were to be the Tower's ward, it could not be only in service of the wealthy squatters, the leeches of prosperity, and the careless regents who tormented their constituents with wars, inequity, and mismanagement. Because as corrupting and vile as Luc Marat was, he would not be the last to invigorate the anger of the hods, not because they were a wicked or temperamental race, but because they had a sensible grievance that, left unaddressed, would someday lead to bloody revolution.

Though some of the people sitting before her in an affluent stupor would never believe it, she was trying to save them from a far worse fate.

Seeing not a single palm rise, Edith clapped iron to flesh, and said, "Good. Then we are in accord. Go to your homes. Prepare for guests. Busy days lie ahead."

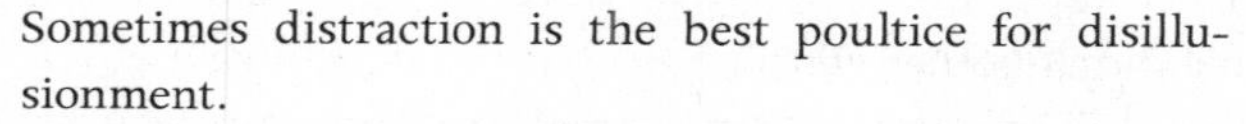

Chapter Five

Sometimes distraction is the best poultice for disillusionment.

—*Everyman's Guide to the Tower of Babel,* I. IX

Iren and Adam walked hip to hip out from the pyramid, across the golden cobbles, under streetlamps that curled like the ribs of a whale. They began to ascend the shallow cant back to the oak that had nearly been Adam's hangman.

"You'll like her—" Adam was in the midst of saying in a smiling, bashful way that Iren was not accustomed to hearing from him. "She's blunt, honest, droll . . . a little like you, now that I think about it. And beautiful, of course. Her name's Runa. She likes to paint skulls and she lives in a ruin with a sleepy old dog."

"She sounds nice. I met someone, too."

Adam gaped up at her with an expression of apparent delight. "You did? That's wonderful. Who's the lucky man?"

"Ann."

"Oh, who's the lucky Ann, then?"

Iren snorted. "She's the kindest person I've ever met. Patient. Strong. Warm. Smart. She picked up where Senlin left off with my reading lessons."

Adam chucked her on the arm. "Good! She sounds perfect. But where is Senlin?"

The ground beneath them began to buck and jounce. Birds burst from the bushes and coursed over the gardens, trilling and shrieking. A steel plate popped free from the steeple of a spire and clanged down its edifice to splash upon the street. Iren dropped into a crouch like a sprinter on a starting block. She had the urge to bolt, but no sense of which direction to run.

Unperturbed, Adam stood beside her with his hand on her shoulder until the ground fell still and the distant rumble of mechanical thunder dwindled into silence.

She popped up quickly, slapping the dampened knees of her trousers, both to clean them and to shake off his reassuring hand. Frowning, she said, "That didn't bother you?"

"Not really," Adam said, then seemed to realize the absurdity of such a claim. "I mean, you get used to it. The quakes have been happening for years; nothing has come of them so far. Though to be fair, they have been growing stronger, more frequent. But I figure since we never felt them in the lower ringdoms, they must be isolated events. The Tower isn't going to tip over. At worst, the top bit might fall off."

"But we're standing on the top bit."

"Yes, we are." He made a show of looking about them. "What do you think? Spectacular, isn't it?"

"A little showy." Iren slapped the side of her neck and grimaced. "And buggy."

"Is that all?" Adam scoffed.

"The carpet's nice."

"It's called grass, Iren."

"This shouldn't be here," Voleta interrupted them. She was again standing beside the black pyramid that looked to have been dropped upon a flower bed. Iren didn't find her obsession with the block remarkable—Voleta had been drawn to stranger things in recent days—but Adam was obviously perplexed. He was used to his sister scaling the world, not scrutinizing it. Or perhaps he was still confused by Voleta's cool reception of him. She'd said hello, and little else. As the amazon watched Adam pace after Voleta while she stalked about the foot of the gloomy ornament, Iren couldn't help but feel sorry for him. He had not yet discovered that the sister he'd known had been replaced by someone of tickling familiarity and shivering strangeness.

Edith, who had been conferring with Captain Dyre near the mouth of the pyramid, now rejoined their group. "No time for sightseeing, Voleta. Marat might've broken through already. We need to get to the skylight."

Trampling the flowers and feeling along the sleek, featureless stone with her fingertips, Voleta shook her head. "He said this was important. He called it the capstone of the Tower. He called it the sun wick or something. It lights the darkness, he said. For all we know, the tremors might be caused by it being here rather than up there." Without looking, she pointed at the golden pyramid.

"What are you talking about? And what's the matter with your eyes? Did someone blow pepper in them?" Finally catching her by the shoulder, Adam turned his sister around.

Voleta gave a tipsy smile. "I've been chatting with the Brick Layer, and—"

Only then did he seem to see that what had been the whites of her eyes were now not only red but glowing. Adam pulled his hands back, his expression baffled and frightened as a kicked pet. "What happened to you?"

"Well, I suppose it all started when I was shot in the head . . ."

Marya filled a shoulder sling with a few essentials: two burp cloths, a swaddle, six diapers, three pins, a shaker of powder, the precious tin of ointment, a few rags, and a flask of water. She dressed herself in a knee-length khaki shirt and white blouse, pulling on her tall leather boots that had grown a little dry from neglect. With provisions slung over one shoulder, she scooped up Olivet from her bassinet, kissed the white down of her nascent hair, and strode from her stateroom.

She had just set her hand on the wheel lock of the ship's main hatch when she heard a shuffling of heels behind her.

"Where are you going?"

She turned to find Byron with his shirtsleeves rolled and a fine paintbrush in hand. "We're going for a walk."

"A walk where?"

"You said there were gardens, fruit trees, flowers. Captain said it was safe. We all saw they had no trouble at the gates. So, I'm taking Olivet for a stroll."

He sighed sympathetically. "You're feeling cooped up. We all are. But if we keep calm and stay the course, we—"

Dropping her hand from the wheel lock, Marya turned and laid it upon Byron's shoulder. "Byron, I have spent so many months building up a cordial and indifferent front. I built a seawall out of a smile. I meant it to protect me, and it did. Too well, I think. Because the more distant you grow from everyone else, the stranger you become to yourself. It's easier to be formal, yes; there's a sanctuary in the *pleases* and *thank-yous*, a refuge in the customary. But you can't live inside a smile."

He looked to the carpet as a furrow scored the length of his snout. "It... it may not be *perfectly* safe."

"It's not perfectly safe anywhere, not even here. And you have to understand, I haven't seen a tree that wasn't growing out of a pot in a year, haven't walked on grass in as long, or smelled the earth, or heard the hiss of insects. I've been living in a bottle, and I need to get out, Byron. I *need* to. We'll be fine. I promise. It's just a walk."

Byron opened his mouth to argue, then something inside him seemed to refute the argument before he could make it. He gave a rueful snort, a self-effacing shake of his head, and said, "Well, I wish I could join you."

"You can."

"No. No, not yet. Soon. Perhaps." He edged past her. Sticking his brush in his mouth like the stem of a cigarette holder, he turned the wheel lock and opened the hatch. He held his arm out, the invitation of a doorman. "Enjoy your stroll."

"Thank you," Marya said, kissing him on the cheek. Then, cradling Olivet's head to her breast, she stepped out onto the silvery shore.

"And, Marya," Byron called after her from the hatchway, even as the blown mist snagged upon her feet. "If the captain asks, you sneaked out."

"I am clever like that," she said, and strode toward the bubbled metropolis.

Edith insisted that Adam be enlightened on the broader points of his sister's calamities and Senlin's ongoing misfortunes while marching at a brisk pace toward the entrance of the Warren. They followed in a pod behind Captain Dyre, who proved to be both surprisingly unterritorial and quick to help. When Edith asked him to deliver them to the lowest reach of the ringdom, a point she could only presume would bring them nearer the Sphinx's skylight, Dyre had offered to take them there himself.

Naturally, she had expressed some astonishment at his enthusiasm. Surely he must harbor some ill will against her for impinging upon his territory. But the captain of the lumenguard had replied, "My tenure is nearly over. I have brushes to empty and canvases to fill. A peaceful end to my term will hopefully bleed on into my retirement."

And so, Adam learned part of what he had missed at a trot behind a pigeon-breasted, red-faced captain who summoned to his side the uniformed guards they encountered along the way. The empty streets they'd been met with before now flowed with strange two-wheeled chariots and jogging natives, all rushing to get home ahead of the coming wave of refugees.

As a girl, Edith had learned that difficult news and confusing information were sometimes best imparted and absorbed while busy with some unrelated chore. When her father had informed her that the colt that had been promised her had taken ill and perished suddenly in the night, he did so while they were both engaged in the exhausting work of shoveling a path to the barn after a heavy snow. There'd been no time to elaborate or console. Her tears and sweat froze to her scarf in a uniform frost as she shoveled all the harder, letting exertion blunt her sorrow.

Nevertheless, the news that his sister had been first shot, then resurrected by the same menacing ooze that supplied the Red Hand with his power even as it drained him of his humanity clearly affected Adam. Moments earlier, he had seemed self-possessed, free, and in love. Now, the more familiar downcast youth resurfaced. Voleta seemed completely blithe to his misery, but Edith could only suppose he was tormenting himself with condemnations: *He had abandoned her, and look what had happened!*

Even when the young woman named Runa rejoined their retinue, her presence did little to elevate his mood.

But there was little time to address his misery, to correct the record, because even as Voleta finished her hurried explanation of her slippages through time, they arrived at the mouth of the Warren. The entrance was braced by four lumenguard in smirking visors, sparking wands held crossed over their chests. They dammed a standing crowd of children whose crowns and shoulders were lit by the frozen lightning of an electrified underworld.

At the fore of the immature mob, a man with a cornucopia of recently tightened white locks leaned upon an axe handle. When he saw Adam's expression, he said, "It's bad news, then?"

Adam composed a brighter demeanor. "No. No, Faruq, far from it. I'm just a little... *stunned* by our victory. You have a home, at last. You all do."

Faruq's eyes filled and his chest swelled to trumpet his Joy. Then Captain Dyre stepped forward, with palms clammed together and pressed to his lips; a calming gesture and a signal for discretion. "Sir, let's not excite the children. Perhaps we should take advantage of the order that we have. After all, they are already in a queue. Why don't we take this opportunity to mete out their lodgings a troop at a time, and—"

"Our... *lodgings*?" The word tickled the old shepherd, who was obviously overcome. Faruq seemed to have been bracing himself for rejection, only to be met with a welcome. He clasped the captain's hands, and Dyre did not reject the embrace.

"There are several empty neighborhoods. I suggest you should start with the Aster-Lamb block, and then—"

"The what?"

"Ah. One moment." Captain Dyre turned to Edith. "I should've anticipated that I'd be needed here. I have an invasion to oversee, after all. But..." The captain scanned his surroundings and lighted upon a man in a knitted cap who, Edith thought, resembled a recently raked together pile of autumn leaves. "Ossian! There you are. Ossian, could you please escort our esteemed intruders to the Fundament?"

Ossian elbowed through a squirming wall of children to hook his arms over Runa's shoulder. "You did it! My god, how did you—"

Again, the ground shuddered. The children in the throat of the grotto cowered in a wave; the smallest among them whimpered, though none cried out. Edith's heart broke to see such resignation in ones so young.

"They're getting worse," Adam said.

"Then we should hurry," Edith said.

Voleta seemed to pop out of the ground before Edith, her red eyes brighter in the shadow cast by the mouth of the cave. "More the reason to put the capstone in its place, Captain. We can't leave it where it is." Edith took a deep breath to answer, but Voleta hurried on. "Please, Edith. Edith. Listen to me. This is important. As important as saving the Sphinx and finding Senlin and stopping Marat. We have to put the last stone in place."

"I could do it," Adam said.

Voleta pounced upon the offer. "Yes! Wonderful! See, Captain? Adam can do it. There's a crane buried underneath all that—"

"We know," Runa said.

Seeing that Voleta was not going to let the matter go and accepting the fact that the young woman was privy to secrets she was not, Edith said, "All right. If you think you can raise the capstone, Adam, then do it." She was about to turn away, but again perceived his torment. It was a private suffering to which she could relate: the failure to save those you cared for from needless cruelty. Composing a cheerful scowl, she said, "But I will be back to check on your work, pilot. Mind your knots and lines. I don't want to see any sloppy halyards."

"Aye, sir," Adam said with glum constraint.

He seemed about to break away, but Edith held his shoulder, leaned near his ear, and said, "We were all there. We were all huddled around her, all chasing after her with butterfly nets. We tried to catch her. Iren made it her life's work, and still, she . . . There's nothing you could've done. If this is the last thing you ever hear from me, I hope you remember it: I'd trade both of my brothers for one brother like you."

Chapter Six

Ambivalence is the midwife of happiness. Do not make promises when a shrug will suffice.

—*Everyman's Guide to the Tower of Babel,* IV. XVI

arya was a little surprised to be so soundly rebuffed by the ringdom's crypt-like door. When the captain had approached it, Marya had watched the gate yawn open for her at the wave of a hand.

But the hatch proved much less impatient to swing open for her, despite her many attempts to flag it into action.

Undeterred, she followed the wall of the steel gatehouse, which bulged with bound wires and a maze of pipes, to the crystal boundary. She rubbed her sleeve upon the foggy glass and peered at the land within. Trees erupted above the golden roofs of half-moon homes; gardens burst with colorful harvests between gilded lanes and emerald lawns. Beyond the crowns of maple and cherry, the heightening spires of a city rose like notes on a musical staff.

Olivet, who a moment before had been perfectly content, began to squirm and mewl. A quick inspection of her diaper revealed the cause of her unhappiness, and Marya wondered if that wouldn't mark the end of her expedition. Then she saw a young woman, barefoot and sitting on a stool. A novel drooped in her hands while she stared off with an expression of dozy enthrallment. Instinctively, Marya knocked upon the dome, but it was like rapping on a cliff face. Jogging a few steps along the milky wall, Marya stopped and again cleared the condensation, unveiling a much closer view of the young woman, who seemed to spot her at once. She frowned, and Marya waved peaceably, then turned to introduce Olivet's fisted eyes, pink nose, and bawling mouth. The young woman's expression softened, her brows rising in sympathy. Marya motioned toward the gate and, with a little leading, convinced the stranger to trot in that direction.

The outer gate opened with the slow and heavy portent of a stage curtain, revealing a room like the inside of an oven. Marya might've turned back had she not seen the young woman's face appear in the round window of the opposite hatch. Answering her enticements, Marya entered the steel gatehouse. The moment the gate behind her shut, the hatch before her rolled open.

"Hello," Marya said, her smile flickering as Olivet's bawling grew more determined. "My daughter needs a change. Do you mind if I...?"

Apparently confused by either the request or the passage of an infant through her gatehouse, the young woman said, "There are cots in the barracks."

"Oh, the lawn is more than fine," Marya said, and carried Olivet to a nearby patch of plump clover. She spread out a swaddle, demurring help when it was offered. As she changed Olivet's diaper, she said, "My name is Marya. This is Olivet. What's your name?"

"Catherine. I suppose you're with the rest of them, the others who came through?"

"Yes, but we're on our own expedition. We wanted to stretch our legs a bit. We've been cooped up for..." Marya tilted her head to one side as she searched her memory for the last time she had felt free to pursue her own whims. "A long while." She finished pinning Olivet up and gathered her supplies. "Could you point us to the nearest park? I'd like to introduce Olivet to a tree. She's never met one before."

"Do trees talk where you're from?" Catherine asked with some amusement.

"Oh, I think all trees can talk, it's just that hardly anyone ever listens."

Though the walk was brief, Marya's awe stretched the minutes. The Tower's crowning ringdom seemed to resemble a greenhouse more than a city; the density of growth, the diversity and vitality of vegetation was like nothing she had ever seen. Among the rows of squash and peas strode machines, serene as stick bugs, large as scaffolds. For reasons she could not articulate, she did not find their presence dreadful, only a touch surreal. She felt as if she had wandered into a whimsical production of some outlandish fairy tale. The props were inarguably odd, but they were props nonetheless.

The trees, however, were familiar. She could've sworn she had once climbed their branches, and read in their shade, and composed tunes in the cradles of their roots. The sight made her homesick. No, worse—it made her nostalgic for her former self, for those days she had felt so self-assured and dreamily bored and full of anticipation.

Yet, curiously, she found she had no desire to go home.

She plucked a red amaryllis from a crowded bed. The bloom was so large it could've served as a bonnet for Olivet. Marya tucked its stem behind her own ear and inhaled its grand perfume as she gazed up at the curling tusks of a lordly live oak.

"You know, your mother is a climber. Granny Berks was, too... and both your great aunts and most of your cousins. The Berkses are a squirrely clan, I suppose." With her free hand, Marya tugged her boots off by the heels. She hopped, teetered, and bounced as she did, all of which Olivet seemed to enjoy. "Now, the trick to climbing a tree is that, first, you have to give it a good look up and down." Now barefoot, Marya felt the grass, soft as fur, beneath her toes. "You have to picture your trajectory, plan your ascent. It's good to be prepared. Of course, there are some risks you can't take while standing on the ground. Branches snap. You lose your grip."

Olivet frowned and gummed upon her tongue.

Though Marya knew the display was unrelated, she couldn't help but respond conversationally: "Oh, I *know.* It'd be nice if you could just leap straight to the top or be carried up the whole way. Honestly, the easiest way to surmount a tall tree is to be born in a high nest. But for ones like you and me, the only thing that happens quickly is a fall."

The phrase, though lightly said, seemed to mute the warbling birds in the branches above her. The green of the leaves seemed to dull; the perfume of the flowers soured. Marya suffered a sudden sense of loathing, a curdling misgiving of this spectacular gift. It must be a trap. It *must* be. Happiness and beauty were like the color and nectar of a pitcher plant: a sweet, alluring pretention that masked a slow and strangling death. This was not a garden; it was a snare.

She pressed Olivet to her bosom and glared at the tree as if it were a rearing viper.

"Can you help us?" a small voice asked.

Turning about, Marya found she'd been snuck up on by two wide-eyed children. They held hands in the determined way of siblings. The eldest could not have been more than seven or eight years old; the younger was perhaps five, though it was difficult to gauge her precise age because she, much as her brother, suffered from the aging effects of malnourishment. And yet, their gaunt and sallow complexions were at odds with their noble dress. They wore the uniforms of private academies: black stockings, white collars, and tartaned neckties, clumsily knotted.

"Of course I can help you. What's wrong? Are you lost?"

"Uhm, the man said we should come this way, to look for a house with the number 4...9...0...8 Peony Drive." He recited the address with the care of one who'd spent some effort memorizing it.

"Oh, are you paying someone a visit? A cousin or grandparent, perhaps?"

"No. We just got here. We came from the trail, and the man said that 4...9...0...8 Peony Drive is where we live now."

"Well, it's a very nice address. When you say, 'the trail,' do you mean...?"

"The black trail, ma'am."

A shiver rattled her spine as Marya thought of how often the duke had used the threat of the black trail to throttle her hope or correct her defiance. He'd say, "You know, there's always room for two more on the Old Vein. You think I'm a brute? The hods sleep on beds of bones, they drink their piss and gnaw upon what's left of their children. Challenge me again. I beg you. Challenge me."

"What are your names?" Marya asked around the hard lump that had formed in her throat. She saw at once that the question made the boy nervous. His hair appeared to have been recently and inexpertly cut. It glistened with a new slather of wax that lustered like a fingernail when he looked down at the grass. Trying to dispel his torment, she said, "My name is Marya. And this is little Olivet." She turned the swaddle to present her infant's uninterested face.

Seeming to gather his courage, the boy said, "My name is Kapil and this is my sister, Nia."

"Hello, Kapil. Hello, Nia." Marya knelt and stuck out her hand. The boy gave it a single rigid pump, but Nia stroked it gently, carefully, as if it were the snout of an unfamiliar dog. Nia's hand was as dark as print against Marya's papery complexion. The girl smiled at her shyly. No, not at her—at Olivet, who had managed to form and hold a bubble upon her lips.

"We're new here, too. Why don't we look for 4908 Peony Drive together? It's a pretty day for a walk."

"It's very bright. Is it always this bright?" Kapil asked.

"Not always," Marya said, looking up at the murky cataract of banked clouds. She slid Olivet into the swaddling wrap that held her pressed to her chest, a position that often invited a doze. "Tell me, what's your favorite song to sing?"

"'Ten Toes on a Toe'tool,'" Nia said, her words hazy with novelty.

"That's her favorite. 'Ten Toads on a Toadstool.' Do you know it?"

"I'm sad to say I don't. But I do love learning new songs. Could you teach it to me?"

No sooner did Marya ask than Nia began to sing. She sang with the pitch of a rusty hinge but the confidence of a soloist.

Marya felt the flying birds of her anxiety quiet once more. Rediscovering that she could be of some help and cheer to others tempered her sense of being caught in another ruse. Perhaps the world was not floored with trapdoors. Perhaps not everyone was fake, nor everything false.

As Olivet snored in her sling, Marya offered the children her hands, and singing in a key all their own, they accepted them with a courage she found most heartening.

"I think this is it," Marya said, staring over a shorn lawn at a golden igloo with two windows like smiling eyes. She tried to appear nonchalant for the benefit of the children, but in fact, she felt more than a little awed.

At least they were not alone in their wonderment. All down the glittering lane, children of every age, many in the company of hunchbacked elders, approached new homes with a mixture of excitement and worry. Some of the children sobbed upon being confronted with the alien fixtures of doorknobs. Others carried mounds of ripe fruit in their shirttails, cheeks and chins gleaming with the juice of recent feasts.

There were soldiers, too, dressed in the whites and yellows of a fried egg. Some of them wore eccentric helmets, coned like a bullet with eyes like telescopes. Several doors down, a robin-chested woman in a dressing gown stood in her front yard, snapping like a dog at the passing juveniles.

She said, "Mind my flowers! Mind them! You're in Nebos, now. You can't tramp around like billy goats. Maybe that was acceptable down where you're from, but up here, we respect our neighbors!"

Sensing that she had stumbled upon some significant and unusual tide, Marya squeezed the hands of Kapil and Nia. Mounting the home's stoop, she knocked upon the front door. They endured the nervous moment of silence together.

"Maybe no one's home," Marya said.

"They told us it was *our* home," Kapil said.

"Did they?" She cracked the golden shell, poked her head in, and voiced a practiced, friendly hello.

When it became apparent that the home was unoccupied, they entered with the hushed reverence of archeologists unsealing a tomb. Here was an unflickering candle in a closed jar; here was a winter wind caught in a box that was stocked full of food; here were rugs and sofas, beds and pillows—all plump and colorful as dusky clouds. In nearly every room, crystal clear water waited to flow at the twist of a knob.

The duke and his stately manor had acquainted Marya with certain luxuries that would've been considered nothing short of wondrous back in Isaugh. In Wil's glamorous prison, water and light answered her beck and call, but the pipes knocked and sputtered, drawing from a well that stank of sulfur. The lights were more unreliable still, frequently flickering and dimming as if blotted by a passing cloud.

This technology was something else. The light beamed like the highlights of a painting; the water gushed forth and was hot or cold at an instant as one pleased. There was a closet in the privy dedicated to the containment of a rainstorm. Poised outside the shield of glass, she turned the spigots on, and the three of them marveled at the torrent that quickly fogged the mirrors.

After the third or fourth miracle, the children's caution broke, and they began to own the home with their excitement. They lorded the furniture with their feet and humbled the icebox with their hunger. What had been a tidy and tranquil domicile minutes before quickly became a home as their enjoyment rumpled it to life. Even Olivet contributed a little spit-up before falling asleep in a well of pillows on one of the lavish beds.

They had, as a trio, just discovered the battery of pictorial buttons in the kitchen, which appeared to promise an assortment of savory possibilities, when there came a firm rap on the front door. Before Marya could answer it, the door swung open, and in tramped a pair of helmeted guards.

Kapil and Nia stuck themselves to Marya's legs like a wet skirt, and she hooked her arms around their heads defensively. "Hello, what do you want?" she said.

"Just doing a headcount, ma'am. Have to make sure that—"

"I'm sorry, would you mind taking that off? I think your helmet is frightening the children."

The foremost guard, the shorter of the two, twisted the chin of his visor sharply, like one attempting to crack his neck. Raising the loosened hood over his face, he revealed a visage much younger than Marya had expected. The soldier couldn't have been more than eighteen or nineteen years old. His cheeks were flushed pink and furless; his eyes were expansive, his eyelashes white as frost. He said, "Sorry, ma'am. We don't mean to scare them. I'm supposed to mark down how many children are at this address, their ages, names, and whether there's someone looking after them."

Marya reported their names and her guess as to their ages, a supposition that neither child corrected, seeming not to know themselves.

The guard jotted the information down on a small pad, saying, "All good; all in order." It seemed the phrase of one unaccustomed to their duty. He appeared as uncomfortable in their presence as she felt in his. "And are you their guardian, ma'am?"

He posed the question without looking up from his scribble, and so did not see the flurry of misgiving that passed over Marya's face. Though Nia seemed unconcerned by the query, Kapil appeared more attuned to the fact that something important had been asked, even if he did not quite understand the scope of it.

And all at once, Marya knew she could not go on living aboard the *State of Art*. It wasn't only the confinement, or the constant threat of bloodshed, or the straps on her bed and Olivet's gimbaled crib, nor even the recent trauma of the duke's invasion and his violent end. As trying as all that was, and as much as she cared for the crew who had rescued her, embraced her, given her back some sense of herself, Marya knew she could not reunite with Tom while sharing a ship with his former first mate, his adopted spouse.

She did not blame Edith for Senlin's failure. She had found Edith's remorse authentic, but even so, Marya knew that an honest reconciliation between her and Tom, if such a thing were even possible, could not happen in the presence of . . . the alternative.

Marya heard Nia sigh like a gust before a gale; the pregnant silence was upsetting her, and she would break soon.

Even as Marya knew what answer she would give, she saw the absurdity of it. She had just gone for a walk. And while a walk was always an adventure, one usually returned home with, at most, an empty bird's nest or an orchid clinging to a bit of moss. Just that morning, she had felt overwhelmed by the prospect of caring for one life. Now, here she was, volunteering to be responsible for two more.

But if not her, then who? Had misery ever been cured by selfishness?

Smiling down at Nia and Kapil, she said, "Yes, of course, put me down as their guardian. My name is Berks, Marya Berks."

Chapter Seven

In a tower full of farewells, eloquent goodbyes are surpassingly rare. Many go unmarked amid a gradual parting of ways, like a receding hairline or a fading tattoo. Though, there are those grand bon voyages that fly forth like a knocked-loose tooth: abrupt, inarticulate, and aching.

—*Everyman's Guide to the Tower of Babel*, III. IX

In the moments before Iren had followed the captain down from the *State of Art* and into the fog that crowned the Tower, Ann had become suddenly elusive. Iren hunted for her even as the captain adjured her to hurry, saying time was of the essence. As if Iren, an unyoung woman marching into battle having recently fallen in love for the first time, did not understand the scarcity of time. She scoured the cabins, privies, and closets for Ann precisely because she knew how precious a single minute could be.

Iren finally discovered Ann in Byron's pantry, sitting on a drum of olive oil, fretting with the fetters of her apron.

"I've been looking for you," Iren said, kneeling before her among the sacks of sugar and salt.

"And I've been waiting for you to find me and wishing that you wouldn't." Ann addressed her lap and the loose ties she continued to torture. Judging by the curl of those strings, Iren imagined she'd been tormenting them for some time.

"Why?" Iren asked.

Dropping her apron strings, Ann looked up, a suppressed grimace dimpling her cheeks. "Because I know you want to say goodbye before you go, and I don't want to say goodbye. I don't want to admit there's a chance, even a very small one, that I won't see you again. Can't we just say hello? We're so good at hellos. Good morning! How do you do! It's been too long! Oh, it's so good to see you again." Ann touched Iren's cheek and then pulled away, straightening her back toward a more formal posture. "Here, let's shake hands." She grasped Iren's hand and tried to pump it, though she only succeeded in waggling her own elbow. "My, that's a firm grip!"

"Ann."

"Please, Iren. Please. I love you too much to say goodbye." Ann tucked a wisp of loose hair behind her ear.

Iren's chin dropped as she huffed out a breath—a slow and mirthless chuckle. "I'll never understand how you could love someone so unlovable."

"Unlovable? You? Iren, dear, as far as I've ever seen, in this world there are two great nations of the Unadored. There are the Love Gluttons who feel they cannot dote on anyone for fear of stealing some small measure of kindness from themselves, and there are those Paupers of Affection who refuse to care in retribution for the love they feel they deserve and have been denied. Both think the feast of human kindness small, the table settings but few. That has never been you, my dear. *Never.* Your heart is bigger than your chest. It drums so loud I can hear it from across the room. I hear it through doors and down halls, hear it beat in my sleep and throughout my dreams..."

"You sure that's not just my snoring?" Iren said, and the corners of Ann's eyes beaded with tears.

Iren stood, scooping Ann up, one hand under her, one hand behind her, raising her to eye level. She could feel her scars were bright and shining when she said, "Ann, you make me wish I was more elephant, element, elo—"

Ann laughed a small sob and said, "You're perfectly eloquent. Here, let me read your lips."

When they finally arrived at what Captain Dyre had called the Fundament, Edith felt as if she had again been jerked from wonderment to disillusionment, a whiplash that she had already suffered several times since arriving in the crowning city. She had been astounded by the ringdom's lightning mortars and impermeable shell, but disappointed by her gaudy spires that seemed as fussy as the fingernails of a country dame. The gardens had been a source of absolute awe—lush as a hothouse and roving as a ranch—but the underground tunnels, streaming with destitute children, had filled her with anger and revulsion. Descending through the Warren, aboard an electric chariot that flashed past dazzling mosaics of exotic animals shepherded by glass pipes full of effervescing blue fluid, had been nothing short of spectacular. It had felt like riding through a painting upon a paintbrush.

But standing now in the bottom-most unlit chamber, a room stripped to the strut, with exposed wires cobwebbing the corners, Edith suffered again the revelatory frisson of disappointment.

Heaven's root cellar was a rotten place.

All they had to cut the dark was a pair of electric lanterns and the eerie glow of Reddleman's and Voleta's eyes.

"And you're sure the Nautilus is sealed?" Voleta asked Ossian for the third time since their journey had begun.

Ossian's answer was the same, but this time he gathered Voleta's cheeks in his leathered hands, touched the soft radish of his snout to her pointed, poreless nose, and said, "Yes, young lady. Once again, yes. You don't leave the oven door open, and you don't walk away from an unsealed Nautilus. I can tell you've never seen it, because if you had, you'd know it is impossible to ignore the greasy static that pours from it. I'd sooner forget my boots in a blackberry bramble, sooner fall asleep on a bed of fire ants, than leave the door of the Nautilus ajar!"

"What is it exactly?" Edith asked.

"I don't think anyone knows the nature of the Nautilus *exactly*, but it serves as a holding tank for a very strange and rare phenomenon. The Allonomia is a—"

Voleta interrupted in a voice that had the dreamy quality of a recitation: "A voracious bottomless speck that's as potent as the sun."

"How on earth did you know that?" Ossian asked, his astonishment doubling the furrows on his brow.

"What happened here? A skirmish, perhaps?" Reddleman ran his hand over the devastated number plate that appeared to have been savaged with an axe. "No. Sabotage?"

Releasing Voleta, Ossian swung the beam of his lantern about, enlivening the murky corners with vaulting shadows. "This was once the most handsome and inviting immigration bureau the Tower has ever known. I've read about the nightmarish customs offices of the lower ringdoms: the iron collars and cages, the shakedowns and bribes. This was meant to be a celebratory place, a Welcome Home to the weary traveler, a finish line. But that was back when there was still a bridge, a dedicated avenue between the Old Vein and the Tower's crown. I'm sure you noticed how empty the Warren is. It was not meant to be so. But the natives who inherited this duty, my step-forefathers, decided that Nebos would be better protected and the Tower better served if the muddy ground and our cloudy heaven were decoupled. They gutted this place, turned it into a garage for a scow, something just large enough to ferry treasure over a gulf of broken promises."

Edith kicked a snuffbox, one of the many trinkets and garments that lay strewn upon the floor. The ground about her resembled a beach dressed by a shipwreck. "We will reopen it. We'll rebuild the bridge and renew the Brick Layer's commitment to the hods. It's not right for so many to suffer for the comfort of so few. But, for now, we have to press on. We need to go lower."

"This is the lowest point, I'm afraid."

"What's outside those doors?" Edith pointed at the seam in the steel barrier.

"A cyclone trapped inside a canyon. Behind those shutters is a storm that has blown for more than a century. It is one of the wonders of the Tower, though few have ever seen it. It is a coiling leviathan of unending wind." Even as he announced this dramatic evocation, Ossian attended the undamaged panel beside the bay doors. He poked at the aged number pad, his jabs quick and sure. Then pausing, apparently over the last key, he said over his shoulder, "I would hold on to something if I were you."

Doing as they were told, the crew of the *State of Art* gripped the guardrails of the central platform.

Before Ossian could punch the final digit, Edith intervened. "Wait." She raised her engine, uncurling her fingers to show the medallion of her palm. "Let me try."

Though he gave a huff of confusion, Ossian conceded. "As you wish." He braced himself against an exposed stud beside the control box and observed her with a dubious sort of curiosity.

As she had done while approaching the sealed windstile of the city of Nebos, Edith pressed her will down her arm and into her hand as a child pushes a wish through a breath into the candles of a cake. She bade the bay door to open for her.

The hatch broke with a spectacular groan of uncared-for gears. She turned her head in anticipation of the coming onslaught.

But the whirlwind did not materialize.

The air outside was placid, voiceless, and dark except for the mouth of the black trail where pads of gloamine shone wanly as a distant galaxy.

Ossian's chin balled in disbelief. "That's impossible. I saw the gale with my own eyes just yesterday."

Iren shrugged. "Storms break."

"But the timing is conspicuous, isn't it?" Reddleman said. "It's as if something essential has changed."

"You think he's done it already?" Voleta asked.

"Who's done what?" Ossian squinted at them like a guide who'd unexpectedly become a tourist.

Ossian did not get an answer. Instead, Edith stooped and plucked a trampled bonnet from the domestic loam. "This chaff, all this stuff, where did it come from?"

"I call it windfall. It's spilled treasure. Gifts dropped between barge and bandy."

Coming alongside him at the sill of the void, Edith peered down into the murk. Stretching her lantern into the ink, she saw nothing beneath them but the occasional page coasting like a lost gull above a field. "And what's down there?"

"I don't know. The Tower, I suppose," Ossian said.

"We'll need rope." With the toe of her boot, Edith nudged a silver baby rattle over the precipice. Her father had taught her how to estimate the depth of a well by counting the journey of a stone from release to impact. She counted as the rattle fell, hearing a distant clink halfway between the count of three and four. One hundred and fifty feet, or thereabouts. She scowled at the result. "We'll need a lot of rope."

"That's no problem. I have miles and miles of cord—good, heavy jute. But..." Ossian hobbled to the guardrail of the steel-sided platform. When he hunched over, he looked like a pile of unwashed laundry. He opened a panel in the stage and made several quick, practiced adjustments to the controls held within. A crepuscular light began to seep from a fissure beneath the stage, a crack that had not seemed to be there a moment before. Iren snatched her hand from the guardrail in surprise. The crack quickly grew, the light swamping the floor as the slab rose into the air. "If you don't feel like climbing, you could always take this."

"What is it?" Iren asked.

"It's a windscow. I almost scuttled it after we brought the last of the children over. I suppose it's a lucky thing I didn't."

As the four of them stepped aboard, Ossian asked Edith if she wanted him to pilot them.

Edith looked to Reddleman, who already had stationed himself before the ship's modest throttles. "Can you steer her?" she asked as he inspected the controls.

"It shouldn't be a problem, Captain." He nudged the regulator and the sled slid forward a few feet. "Aha!" he said boastfully, shortly before the skiff sloped and lurched backward, nearly casting all aboard over the rails.

Bringing the scow level again, Reddleman said, "It's a bit more ticklish than the *State of Art*."

Squeezing the taffrail before her, Iren said, "If you crash, I'll make sure the last thing you feel is my foot."

"If there were two of me, you could make a nice pair of slippers," Reddleman said, looking over his shoulder with a wide, inhuman grin.

Addressing their guide, Edith said to Ossian, "Seal the door after us. Help with the children as you can. I expect we'll be back soon, or not at all."

Despite an inauspicious launch, their descent aboard the windscow was remarkably temperate. They drifted through the gloom like a lure into a lake. Voleta found that, with a little squinting, the darkness thinned for her, and she could make out the distant walls that encompassed them. She saw the curvature of rough monolithic stones and the titanic vents that broke them. Those iron blades seemed large enough to accommodate the passage of an airship, though imagining the *Stone Cloud* lacing through that monstrous baleen made her shudder.

She shared her observations with the others. Reddleman, who appeared to be similarly sighted, said, "I used to assume the Tower's woolly cap came from the same bank of steam that filled the Baths. What a pretty symmetry that would've made! To think the fog that dressed the ground was cut from the same cloth that heaven wore!"

"But that's not the case?" Edith asked.

"No. We know that the steam that rises from the fires of the Parlor is used to create the lightning in New Babel, which, in part, charges the Sphinx's medium."

"But if the fires of the Parlor didn't blow the Collar of Heaven, what did?"

"The Brick Layer said the Allonomia was being kept in a state of suspension by something called 'slow water,'" Voleta said.

Reddleman raised and shook a finger to punctuate the revelation. "Well, there you have it! What do you get when you douse a coal that's as hot as the sun with water?"

"Steam."

"And a lot of it. My supposition would be that this superheated steam, if it were allowed to blow directly to the open air, would've boiled alive the crews of any ships that were unfortunate enough to pass through it. So, it had to be cooled, given a chance to expand, a process that required the application of cold air, a whole tempest's worth."

Edith frowned and reseated her sword belt on her hips. "But if the Allonomia is no longer being cooled, what's happening inside the Nautilus?"

Reddleman's quick laugh sounded like the caw of a crow. "Ah, now that *is* the question!"

"Look!" Iren pointed through the railing.

Much as a sunset makes a landscape blush, the crimson light of the scow's turbines brought the chamber floor into view. There, dunes and dells, alien as the ocean floor, rolled out as far as the light could reach. From a distance, those hills seemed to be composed of a piebald rubble, but as they drew nearer, nuance emerged. They saw antique lamps, rotting furs, burst-open books, cracked drawers, and shattered mirrors—a whole desert of broken treasure.

Reddleman steered the windscow into a valley of domestic debris close to the Tower's center, though unlike the ringdoms below, here there was no spine to mark the spot.

Even before he'd throttled down the engine, Voleta leapt from the deck onto the underside of an upturned table. Her raft tottered beneath her, and she had to dance to keep from falling into a confusion of toys, crockery, and curtains. She marveled to think that every stitch of clothing and stick of furniture in the wasteland that surrounded them had been carried up from the ground on the back of a hod: a soul born and worn down just to cast a single pearl upon an unwanted trove.

Stepping down, Edith crunched up a hill of broken china, raising her lantern to survey the junkyard. "I was hoping for a hatch. I don't know where to go from here."

"I have something that might help," Reddleman said, digging into the pocket of his jacket. The activity seemed to bring the captain's attention to the current state of his uniform.

"Your shirt is unbuttoned, airman."

"Is it? Must've been the change in pressure."

"That's not how buttons work." Edith massaged her forehead. "Or air pressure."

"Ah, here we are!" Reddleman twisted a small something in his hands as if he were unwrapping a candy. Then the mechanical moth shook the wrinkles from its uncolored wings and looked about, its wiry antennae probing the air. "I paired this moth with the beacon inside your friend Senlin. I thought it might help us find him, presuming he's still with Marat and . . . relatively intact."

"You didn't tell me you'd done that," Edith said.

"To be honest, Captain, I'm not entirely sure it'll work. But it's worth trying. Perhaps it can help us find a clear passage through this bog." He hiked up his hand as if to launch a falcon, and Reddleman's moth bumbled into the air uncertainly, dove at the ground, rose again, peaked, and then drifted downward to light on the hook of an umbrella only a few paces away.

"What's wrong with it?" Iren asked.

"Oh, it could be anything." Reddleman stumbled and slipped as he traversed an uneven morass of shoes and belts. Approaching the perched insect, he collected the moth onto his palm and carefully settled it upon the thin bristles on his crown. "Or perhaps it's working perfectly." He pulled the tattered umbrella free and threw it to one side. Stooping, he gripped a mantel clock and heaved it between his legs like a dog digging in a yard, an action he repeated after putting his hands to a half-buried bust.

Taking off her greatcoat and rolling up her sleeves, Edith said, "Never crossed my mind to bring a shovel to a sword fight."

A half hour of heave-hoeing later, they were nearly ready to give up. After carving a seven- or eight-foot well down into the wreckage, a process that required slicing through carpets, breaking the spindles of a crib, and shoring up the walls of their deepening pit with coatracks and croquet mallets, Iren asked Reddleman if he was absolutely sure that his moth was not wrong. When he reiterated his cautious faith in the device, Iren suggested that perhaps the moth wouldn't mind helping them dig then.

Edith would've called an end to the exercise earlier if she'd had any alternative in mind, but if this failed, they'd have no choice but to return to the ship and try knocking upon the Sphinx's gates with the prow of the *State of Art*.

So, it was not out of an excess of optimism but a paucity of options that they finally uncovered the great wheel lock buried beneath that crust of rubbish. Since the hatch was as wide as a captain's wheel, it was another half hour before they managed to broaden the hole enough to clear the entrance and ensure the walls of their pit would not collapse upon the portal once it was opened, a feat that Edith was disappointed to discover could not be remotely accomplished by a wave of her iron hand. In the end, it took all four of them to unfreeze the ancient screw.

Lifting the hatch, they were beset by the deep-throated roar of what sounded like a waterfall and, under that, a mechanical drumming. A strange agitation suffused the air; static seemed to cling between the hairs on Edith's arm. She could only think to describe the sensation as a sort of energetic humidity.

All that was immediately visible beyond the hatch was an enclosed and unlit winding stairwell. Leading the way down the coil with her lamp raised to guide them, Edith was the first to see the gleam of red light on the lips of the steps. The roar that had greeted them at the mouth of the portal now seemed to be nearing a climax. Edith's eyes teared and her ears ached as their destination became more familiar if not any less strange.

At last, the stairs ended upon an iron grate floor, a round island held over a vast chamber by a central column like the rod of a plunger. The base that clung to that post was spacious enough to accommodate them, though scarcely any more. It was sparsely railed and felt a little rickety, though it was not the balcony but rather the view that commanded their attention.

Beneath them, a sea of crimson light pitched, peaked, and bubbled. Beneath the surface of that surging expanse, lightning forked, but slowly and in jerking, hesitant leaps. The ends of the bolts unraveled like a sawed rope, brightening the ruddy flow with brilliant ruby threads.

Only Edith, who'd seen the reservoir before, perceived something was different, wrong, worse. Gone was the chaotic chop of crossing waves. There was a uniform course to the waters now. What had seemed a stormy sea before was now a sucking vortex. The level of the reservoir appeared to be falling. The violent, unstable lightning sea was slowly draining away.

Chapter Eight

The mind is ingenious at finding itself expressed in secret everywhere. We detect human faces in wood grain, countenances in cloudbanks, and profiles in the moon. It is comforting to think our visage is so ubiquitous; but alas, we are only vain.

—*Homage, Vol. II* by Jumet

The lighthouse from which Edith had first glimpsed the boiling reservoir was directly beneath them, and yet entirely out of reach. "We should've gone back for rope," she murmured.

"Captain, look." Reddleman pointed into a panel he had opened in the central column that held their little stage aloft. "I believe this is an elevator. Should I take us down?"

The descent, which was accompanied by the squeal of parts unaccustomed to the effort, was not unlike being lowered into a volcano, or so it seemed to Edith. The closer they drew to the violent flow of scintillating medium, the louder the roar of the torrent grew, and the more the ambient energy prickled them.

At Edith's side, Iren yelped and swatted her hand as if to brush off a spider. When she stopped, they all saw the pink plasma roiling over her knuckles and climbing up her fingers. "What is it?" Iren asked.

"It's perfectly harmless. Just a side effect of the medium." Edith examined the rosy flames that feathered down the sleeve of her coat. She failed to add that the last time she'd been exposed to the cheerful fire, she'd been wearing rubber armor. She could only hope that neither they nor their organs would begin to sizzle and foam like butter in a pan.

At last, the foot of the platform touched down on the widow's walk. They disembarked, and Iren, apparently mistrusting the iron grate of the floor, pressed her back against the inner wall. Meanwhile, Reddleman and Voleta flocked to the golden rail to improve their view of the medium that coursed about the silver lighthouse.

"Where is it all draining to? Will it flood the Tower?" Voleta shouted over the furor of fluid and static.

Reddleman shook his head. "That droning we heard in the stairwell, it sounded like pumps to me. Pumps would mean it's going up, not down."

"To the Nautilus?"

"That would be my guess."

Iren was the first to locate the lighthouse's service elevator and the first one in. Reddleman followed, his face lit with patent delight. "Wasn't that the most incredible sight! Like watching an eclipse! Like seeing an island bubble up from the sea! Marvelous. Absolutely . . ." His expression clouded when he appeared to notice Iren's nervous frown. "What's the matter, Mister Iren?"

Iren continued to try to dislodge the licking lights from her hands. "Don't like magic."

"I don't think it's magic. In fact, I think it's—" Reddleman began, but Iren cut him off.

"Can't stab magic. Can't strangle magic. Can't shoot magic in the head."

"Ah, but you can shoot the magician!" Reddleman said.

Edith grimaced at the implication.

Finding herself standing before the control panel and the two clearly labeled options, ROOF and ATTIC, Voleta asked, "We're bound for the attic, I presume?" Edith nodded.

It was only after the elevator commenced its descent that the fairy lights finally flickered out of existence, and Iren's distress abated. Edith perceived in her first mate a caution approaching wariness that seemed unlike the mad amazon who'd once leapt from the bow of an airship to open a stuck hatch with an axe, who'd skewered a prince and trampled a general. Edith suspected that this new reticence had something to do with Ann and their deepening bond.

Edith drew her sidearm, a four-round cartridge pistol with a spur trigger that she had initially overlooked in her perusal of the *State of Art*'s gun cabinet. Reddleman had recommended it, saying that its small size belied a powerful blast. She hoped she had not made a mistake in taking him at his word, but if it failed, she had her rapier and her arm to fall back on. She addressed her crew over her shoulder as they all faced the lidded elevator doors. The scrape of pulley wheels accompanied her speech. "We all should be on guard. Marat and what's left of his crew could be hiding behind any corner. If we run into them, let's try not to scatter to the four corners. Last time they thumped us because we were divided. Let's not allow them to carve us up again. If we can avoid an encounter, we will, at least until we've got the Sphinx with us and have had time to agree upon a strategy. My hope is that we'll be able to extract Tom before the fighting starts. So, let's do our best to be discreet."

In the warped reflection of the elevator doors, she watched Voleta adjust one of the pegs in her arm brace, injecting herself with a little more of the Sphinx's medium. The young ensign unslung her crystal bat, its prized contents having been left aboard the ship. Voleta slipped the cloth strap (a gift from Ann's sewing box) into her pocket. Reddleman pulled the snub-barreled scattergun from the holster that held it between his shoulder blades, cracked open the breach, and fed a shell into either barrel. Eschewing the chains about her waist for the moment, Iren drew the wand of her lightning caster and again familiarized herself with the weapon's curious trigger.

Their descent slowed to a stop, and a dulcet bell chimed to announce their arrival. The doors slid open.

The crystal-belled spider loomed outside the entrance, its pickaxe legs compressed as if to pounce.

With a bellow of fright, Iren loosed a bolt of cracking lightning at the apparition. The spark broke about the bubble. The split tendrils popped like fireworks, scorching the red carpet and blackening the white plaster of the ceiling like candle soot.

In the thin light of the elevator lobby, they beheld the glass of a spidery carriage marred by a new blot of soot. The Sphinx's walker was just where she had left it after their tour of the lightning sea.

With a calm but firm stroke, Edith pushed the barrel of Iren's lightning caster down.

Edith dispatched Voleta and Reddleman to check the adjacent changing room where the rubber armor and some of the Sphinx's instruments were stored. The moment they were out of earshot, she said to Iren in a low voice, "Are you all right?"

"I'm fine," Iren said without meeting Edith's eyes.

"You seem a bit jumpy."

"I'm not scared."

Edith cupped her first mate's shoulder; the uncommonness of the contact was enough to bring her gaze up from the floor. "Well, I'm scared. This is scary stuff. And there's nothing wrong with being afraid, though it is exhausting. We're all going to need a break after this, I think. I'm sure you and Ann could use a little shore leave. You could take over one of those golden bungalows, nap under the trees, bake pies, and putter around the garden. There really is nothing more restorative than a garden."

Iren chugged out a low laugh. "You mean peas and carrots? That sort of thing?"

"Exactly. And if you find you like it, if you find there's always one more weed to pluck, one more stalk to stake, you could stay longer. You could stay as long as you like. You've taken care of all of us for far too long. It's past time someone took a little more care of you. So, let's get through this together. One last terror. One last time. Then it's off to shore with you."

Interrupting their aside, Voleta and Reddleman returned from their short scouting of the antechamber. The pilot held aloft a familiar device. "The dressing room is empty, Captain, but look what I found." He showed and then scrutinized the instrument's clockface and the golden tuning fork that horned the dial. "I have no idea what it is, but when you squeeze the trigger... look, the needle twitches."

"It's an ammeter. It measures the intensity of the current stored in the medium." Edith's knowledge of the esoteric device seemed to both please and puzzle Reddleman. "Don't drop it. I'm told they're expensive."

Reddleman pointed the ammeter at Voleta and took another reading. The needle danced farther to the right of the dial the closer he brought the prongs to her brass cuff. "Fascinating."

Edith cleared her throat. "Fair warning, everyone: The next room is a little... *unsettling*."

The hall beyond the lobby was much as Edith remembered it, except dimmer, and perhaps more haunting for the absence of the Sphinx's cheerful nattering. Her titans stood on platforms behind swoops of velvet ropes under spotlights that only added severity to their strangeness. Edith recalled the friendly names the Sphinx had given her automatons: Zoë, Penelope, Mr. Ekes. And she remembered the humanoid footmen with the picked-clean skulls of a wolf, a lion, and a ram—Byron's predecessors, whose inclusion in the gallery had seemed more than macabre. If the Sphinx had been in charge of Ferdinand's funeral, would she have applied the same taxidermy to the hound's body inside the belly of the dead engine? Edith could hardly imagine a less tasteful tribute to such a faithful companion.

And yet it was not the exhibits, grand nor gross, in the Sphinx's opus of utility and oddity that stirred Edith's anxiety. No, what she dreaded most was confronting the final showcase, the waiting space that the Sphinx had said stood in reserve for her own eventual display. Edith was not ready to lose her mentor, not ready to accept the full weight of the Sphinx's curse—the curse of caring for a mountainous tower that seemed determined to court tyranny, inequality, excess, and decay. It was a weight that Edith worried would be too much for her to bear.

When she turned the corner and found the final platform vacant, she felt like shouting her relief, though she only permitted herself a sigh. The Sphinx had not yet assumed her place in the museum. The Tower was still a burden shared.

Reddleman lifted his chin at the three skull-headed footmen in their trim waistcoats and brushed epaulets. "Intriguing."

Voleta seemed to take a dimmer view, replying, "Awful, is what it is!"

"No, no, look at their hands. They become more elegant as they go. See the ram's knuckles are big as walnuts, but they're smaller on the lion, and finer still on the wolf. Now, think of Byron's hands: delicate, adroit... perfected." Reddleman rocked onto his toes to look the wolf in his empty eyes.

"But Byron is more than just a pretty pair of hands!"

"Of course he is! I'm just pointing out that perhaps the Sphinx's intention wasn't to be outré. Perhaps she preserved these specimens of increasing complexity to demonstrate *how* she learned to outfit them. Perhaps this is just her way of *showing her work*, as it were, to guide those who come after her. What if one day we had to repair Byron? Would you know how?"

The point seemed to catch Voleta off guard, and while she pondered it, Edith took the opportunity to shepherd them onward.

She tried to be patient with the slack-jawed progress of her crew down the airy hall. They muttered their astonishment at each monstrous engine.

Contemplating the Sphinx's collection once again, Edith was reminded of a game she had played as a child with her brothers on rainy days when they were all feeling well disposed toward one another. One of them would take a sheet of paper and draw at the top the head of some person or animal. When they'd finished, they'd fold the sheet over the face, leaving only the lines of the neck exposed. The next sibling would draw the arms and torso of one creature or another before folding the sheet again down to the waist, allowing the legs to be added by the final player of the game. Then, they'd unfold the sheet and laugh at the absurdity of their creation, which might have the head of a parrot, the body of an ape, and the legs of a dragon, or any number of wild combinations.

The Sphinx's work had something of that incongruity to it. Edith stared up at Horace, large as a bull elephant who, rather than feet, traveled upon a rolling drum studded with enormous spikes. Bolted to this was the body of a man with swollen arms that bowed away from an unnaturally broad chest. The head of an ox sat atop a rivet-warted neck with horns as broad as his shoulders. If the Sphinx's intention had been to make her farm equipment appear more friendly than a tractor, the effort had failed.

Iren had done an admirable job of appearing unaffected by the bizarre golems she paraded past until she caught sight of the engine that roughly resembled a praying mantis, one that had grown to the size of a cottage and shelled itself in foggy steel. The machine's scythe-like forearms were somehow made more menacing by the face that hung above them. The hairless head of a woman sat at the top of the engine's long neck, wearing a painted expression of placid amusement.

"Well, I don't like that one bit," Iren said, crossing her arms. "Why the doll's head? Why the blades? What was this thing even for? Harvesting nightmares?"

"The Sphinx called it... called *her* Penelope." Edith quickly explained that she was built to manage the flocks of spider-eaters in the Silk Reef, but then there had been some sort of accident where Penelope killed several people, and the Sphinx was forced to decommission her.

Reddleman pointed his ammeter at the towering mantis. Watching the gauge swing, he said, "Actually, Captain, I think—"

"Miss Adelia?"

The voice made them all start and raise their weapons. A figure stalked toward them between the gloom of the spotlights. His voice was garbled like a parrot's imitation of a man, but more mechanical and inflexible.

When the moon-faced Mr. Ekes emerged from the shadows, Edith had to throw out her arms to keep her crew from firing upon the ambling scarecrow. His limbs rattled inside the tattered sleeves of his coat and the legs of his trousers as he came to a halt in front of Edith. He stooped toward her. What Edith at first took for a bow turned out to be an inspection. His black, painted-on eyes and smiling mouth inspired little comfort.

The music box in Mr. Ekes's throat said, "No, you're not Miss Adelia. You're Miss Adelia's friend."

"That's right, Mr. Ekes, we are friends." She touched his shoulder again as she once had upon their introduction when he had seemed nothing but an inanimate relic. Now, she felt the warmth of kinship and familiarity pass through her arm.

"Who's Miss Adelia?" Iren asked.

Mr. Ekes swung the tambourine of his head toward the amazon. "Miss Adelia is the master of the house."

"The Sphinx's name is Adelia?" Voleta said.

"I have made tea," Mr. Ekes said. They looked about for evidence of cup, saucer, or pot, but saw none.

"Tea for Miss Adelia's friends?"

"No. Tea for unexpected guests."

"What is he talking about?" Iren asked.

Edith rested her hand upon the pommel of her rapier. "Mr. Ekes, is someone else in the house?"

Mr. Ekes rattled like the lid of a boiling kettle. "Good morning!"

Edith tilted her head. "Mr. Ekes, where is Miss Adelia?"

"Good morning!"

Reddleman circled the gaunt butler, examining the lengths of his steaming, shivering limbs. "I think we may have found the limit of his faculties, Captain."

Voleta's brows rose with the dawning of a thought. "But if the Sphinx is still giving out orders, asking for tea or whatever, that's a good sign, isn't it? It means she's alive. We just have to find her."

"It's a big house," Iren said.

Lowering the pointed brim of her cocked hat, Edith said, "Best we start looking, then."

* * *

Returning to the Sphinx's workshop revived in Edith memories she hadn't wished to revisit. Once again, she felt the Sphinx unbolt her damaged arm and remove it as casually as the sleeve of a coat, as if it were not an extension of Edith's personhood, a part of herself.

As assiduous as the Sphinx always was with her gifts, she too often gave little thought to the feelings of those who bore them. Having suffered the Sphinx's callous handling, Edith had decided long ago to lead with compassion and to never confuse her crew for implements.

The Sphinx's study gave a mixed impression of whether or not it had been recently occupied. Books, tools, and half-assembled machines filled the expansive desk to its corners. Behind it, a stack of dishes consumed a cubby between a jade egg on a golden stand and an exotic thermometer full of jewel-like bubbles. Voleta took these as positive signs that the Sphinx was nearby. But then Reddleman found on a side table a cold reef of wax beneath a three-armed candelabra. The candles had been allowed to burn themselves out—surely not a good sign.

Edith noted the vacant copper dome. The absence of the Sphinx's fluttering spies suggested that Byron had been right to suppose that the home had been entirely sealed and that none of his dispatches had reached his master. She paused before the aged tapestry that hung on a long rod beside the vault-like door. That arras, some fifteen feet long and just as tall, depicted a more detailed vision of the Brick Layer's seal: the lithe-limbed men and women who comprised the harmonious wreath of hods marched about a continent that was crowded with docile animals and fruiting crops. The idyllic vision was a little spoiled by a thick film of dust that made the openmouthed expressions of the hods evoke not laughter but anguish, not song but shrieking. What once had been a herald now seemed a pall, a shroud that betrayed the shape of the Tower's failure to revere and reward those who had raised it. Edith scowled and looked away.

They were preparing to advance on the adjoining conservatory when their forgotten escort crawled out from under Reddleman's lapel and bounded into the air. In the stillness, the moth's wings seemed to glow like an apparition. They followed it across the Sphinx's study in a shared trance and gathered around to see where it had alighted behind a high-backed chair.

The moth clung to the brass gills of an air vent.

Edith found Voleta beaming up at her with a speculative smile; she read her thoughts at once. "Absolutely not."

Voleta scowled. "Why not?"

"Have you already forgotten the speech I gave where I reiterated the importance of us all sticking together? You crawling around the ductwork on your own is the exact opposite of that."

Reddleman raised a hand to volunteer. "I could go with her."

Voleta pointed at his round belly, straining against his shirt, proud as the throat of a bullfrog. "I don't think you can."

"No one's going anywhere," Edith said with a definitive chop of her hand.

Voleta scrubbed her cheek with her palm, eyes wide with contemplation. "But think about it, Captain. Say we find the Sphinx, then we come back here, and our homing moth is still sitting right where we left it. I'll still be the only one who can follow it. I can go now, or I can go later, but either way, I'll be going alone. That is, assuming you still *want* to find Senlin..."

"Don't do that."

"I'm sorry, Captain. That was uncalled for. But it doesn't change the fact that I'm right."

"What are you going to do if you find Senlin? I'm sure Marat will have both eyes on him. Tom will probably be under heavy guard, perhaps under lock and key. What will you do then?"

"Come right back here and tell you where he is and what we can expect when we all burst through the door together to rescue him." Voleta reseated the loops on her diamond bat.

"A little reconnoitering wouldn't hurt," Reddleman said with a thoughtful pout.

Edith was less than delighted with the growing consensus, though she couldn't deny the sense of it. "What do you think, Mister Iren?"

Even as Voleta drew a breath, apparently preparing to protest the amazon's inevitable refusal, Iren surprised her by saying, "She has a point."

Voleta's brows rose. "I do?"

Iren gave a slow, one-shouldered shrug. "Her running off on her own—it was bound to happen eventually."

Handing the electric torch over to the lucent ensign, Edith delivered yet another disagreeable order. "All right. Take a look about. Get eyes on Tom if you can. Don't engage Marat or his men. But don't dally. We're going to need you."

Chapter Nine

Pilgrims are encouraged to remember that the principal consumer of sheep is not wolves but shepherds.

—*Everyman's Guide to the Tower of Babel*, IV. IX

The conservatory was as cold as wet clothes. Only pallid ashes broke the darkness of the hearth. The light that bled down from the orange bowl in the ceiling painted everything in autumnal shades. The tree's leaves seemed scarcer upon the branch and more abundant upon the floor. A shower-headed watering can rested upon the shattered soundboard of a piano that was lanced through by an age-gnarled trunk. Beneath it, cradled among the erupted roots, sat an old woman apparently napping on a bedizened tea tray.

"Who's that?" Iren asked, gesturing with the tip of her lightning caster.

Shaking her head, Edith answered in a near whisper, "I don't know. Could be one of Marat's people, could be..." An object propped upon the mantel caught her eye. From the side it looked like a platter, a shallow silver bowl. Another step in, and she saw the room turn onto its head inside the hollow looking glass. It was the Sphinx's mask.

Ears buzzing from a sudden and dreadful pressure, Edith approached the motionless woman. Her head was bare but for a few threads of colorless hair; her skin was a motley quilt of wrinkles and tarnished copper plates, all held together with scars and screws. One of her eyes had been replaced with an aperture like a peephole. Colorful rags draped her shoulders and hung down her rail-thin arms. The delicate engines of her hands lay in her lap. In one, she gripped her forked wand. The other curled about something Edith could not quite see.

"It's her, isn't it?" Iren asked.

Against her wishes, Edith's thoughts fled to a distant, sunny room where large, open windows ruffled sheer curtains with a sweet spring breeze. Her mother lay tucked in her wide bed like a doll. Her lips were rouged, her eyelids tinted, her dark hair brushed and splayed upon her pillow. She had wanted to look her best when she said goodbye to her children.

Edith and her brothers were made to stand in the hall and wait to be called in, one at a time, to hear their mother's last words to each of them. Pressing her back against the wallpaper of the corridor, Edith had wished to fall into the pattern, to escape what was coming. She had felt as if she were anticipating a punishment. She did not enjoy talking to her mother, who did not seem to like her or the dirt under her fingernails, or the leaves in her hair, or the bloody scrapes on her knees, or her reluctance to admit that her childhood was coming to an end.

When it was her turn to say goodbye, Edith found she was unable to raise her chin, or straighten her back, or unhunch her shoulders, all things her mother had commanded her to do a dozen times a day for as long as she could remember. Standing at her bedside, Edith waited to receive her mother's final rebuke.

In a drowsy voice that had none of its usual forceful elocution, her mother said, "Edith, we never got along. If I had lived to be a hundred, I don't believe we ever would have. But that's all right. The truth is, I've gotten on famously with so many people I did not care for or admire or enjoy. And I love you. I love how close you are to your father. I would ask you to take care of him, but I know I don't need to. There's really only one thing I wanted to say, something you might find useful someday. It's something my mother told me when I was about your age. It's this: When you think little of yourself, everyone else's opinion of you becomes more important than your own. I hope you don't slouch your way through your life, trying to hide the greatness in you for fear of putting someone else off. You will do great things, Edith. I know you will. I'm only sorry I won't be here to see them."

Through the receding memory, Edith heard Reddleman clear his throat. "Captain, if I may?" Brushing past her, he felt under the Sphinx's jaw and pulled back her remaining eyelid. He licked the side of his knuckle and held it under her nose for a moment. Probing about the base of her tray, which seemed to be an inseparable part of her, he found and opened a small drawer. The oven glow of the Sphinx's charged batteries underlit his face.

Feeling as if either her tongue had lost all its strength or the words had grown too heavy, Edith said, "She's dead."

"For several hours at least." Reddleman undressed one of her arms. The skin he revealed was as dark as pitch. "It's hard to say for sure; parts of her seem to have mummified years ago."

"What killed her?"

"I think the question is, what was keeping her alive?" Reddleman unrolled the Sphinx's closed hand, exposing the bare thorax of a moth. "Ah. Perhaps she can tell us what happened."

Amid the lull in their conversation, the mantel clock seemed to tick louder, the shade of the tree thickened. The three of them huddled around the recorder. With the poise of a surgeon, Reddleman pinched the moth's head and twisted it to the right.

A deep, unearthly moan swelled to fill the room.

When Voleta had first explored the airshafts of the Sphinx's home scant weeks earlier, she had felt intrepid and roguish and a little giddy. The sharp edges of the sheet metal were entertaining hazards. The tight corners she encountered were an opportunity for her to play the contortionist. She didn't care if her nightgown snagged on a loose nail because it could be easily torn free. And since she only had to answer to the whim of her curiosity, if a section seemed too steep, too dark, or too clogged with cobwebs, she could just go another way.

Now, she didn't have that luxury. The moth had her on a leash.

When it glided down a treacherous slope, she had to go headfirst right after it, and grate the meat from her palms along the way. The moth did not slow its bouncing course when it encountered a tortuous sequence of turns, nor did it wait for her at gloomy intersections, where the light of external vents was thinnest. She sometimes found she could not spare a hand to hold the torch, so it was in her pocket when she lost sight of the moth entirely and was forced to scout some distance down three different chutes. Just as she began to panic that she had lost her guide and Senlin's only salvation, she found the moth snagged and twitching in a spiderweb. She had to resist the impulse to swat it like a mosquito.

The only positive thing Voleta could say about the experience was that at least it was keeping her rooted in the present. There was no time to go traipsing off into the past while scrambling after an inconsiderate moth.

But she sensed that it wasn't just the frenzy of the chase that was causing her to feel increasingly anxious. Her breathing had turned short and sharp; her fingers trembled; a cold sweat dripped between her shoulders and ran down her back. She was fighting the onset of a suffocating dread. It was all she could do not to find the nearest vent opening, bash it out, and escape the tightening walls of the airshaft.

Though it had been only several weeks since she had last crawled through the walls of the Sphinx's home, she felt entirely transformed. Which was strange in and of itself. She had felt more or less the same for so many years: She was Voleta the daredevil, Voleta the invincible, Voleta the escape artist! But then she had failed to get away. She had fallen. She had died.

Suddenly, she wished she had not parted company with the rest of her crew, nor been so cavalier about her reunion with Adam. The truth was, she'd been so dosed on medium, so literally absentminded, that she could not... *had* not adequately expressed her relief at seeing him again. She wondered how long he would continue to care for a sister who was so often ambivalent, inconsiderate, and unaffectionate. She had just taken it as rote that his patience and love for her would never dwindle, but why should that be the case? Why would he persist when she had made it abundantly clear that she preferred her own company to his?

She did not want to escape anymore; she wanted to converge, to tighten, to knot together. She wished to make a safer center between them all, something bright and warming like a campfire, something to hold back the endless and somehow still growing darkness. She on her own did not feel sufficient, not least of all because her new sense of mortality brought with it the utter certainty that she did not wish to die alone.

Such was the bleak nature of her thoughts when she folded herself around a tight corner and saw the moth perched upon what appeared to be a dark curtain blocking her way. She grasped after the insect, hoping to catch it before she lost it among the folds. Putting her other hand down to increase her reach, she was surprised to discover she had run out of floor.

With a startled yelp, Voleta tumbled headlong into a pitch-black gulf.

* * *

The mechanical moth in Reddleman's hand continued to moo like an unwell cow.

"What's wrong with it?" Iren asked.

"Shh." Reddleman cocked his head and squinted as if to better tune his ear to the spooky noise. "I believe it's a voice. Yes, it seems to be someone speaking, just very, very slowly."

"Perhaps the recorder is running out of power," Edith said.

"One moment, please." Holding the moaning instrument nearer to his ear, Reddleman strode back into the vestibule they had come by and shut the door behind him, muting the mournful groan.

The two women exchanged a scowl of bewilderment.

Reddleman flung the door open and switched the recording off. "I can hear the clock behind the voice."

Though the discovery seemed to please her pilot, Edith did not immediately understand why. "Meaning what?"

"The ticking is the same. It's not the recording that's running slow; it's the speaker."

Edith found the thought of the Sphinx moaning out her last words to an empty room as she unwound like a clock too upsetting to entertain. She shook her head to dispel the vision. "Can you—I don't know—speed it up?"

"An intriguing thought, Captain! I could give it a tinker." Her pilot all but skipped back to the workshop as he called over his shoulder. "At least the Sphinx has left me no shortage of tools!" His insensitivity aroused Edith's disgust, and she could not keep the grimace from her face. How could he be so unaffected by the death of someone who'd saved his life, not once, but twice?

Or perhaps his tactlessness just reflected an unhappy truth: the Sphinx, in wishing to remain a mystery, had made herself a stranger to those around her. Edith could claim that her own sense of sorrow was legitimized by intimacy; certainly, it was not uncolored by self-pity. If there was such a thing as righteous mourning, she had no claim to it. And yet, she could not help but feel responsible for the Sphinx's memory and protective of her tragedy.

Turning her attention again to the wilted woman nestled under the wizened tree, Edith wondered if she were not peering into her own future.

Kneeling before the Sphinx, Iren reached out as if to caress her jigsaw cheek but stopped short. Capping her knee with the hand, she turned her head in Edith's direction. "What do we do with her?"

Edith composed herself with a deep breath. "Exactly what she asked."

It felt a bit like falling from a tree—a sensation with which Voleta had some experience. And as anyone who has ever tumbled from an oak or magnolia knows: It's not the fall that smarts; it's all the interruptions.

She bounced from one unyielding limb to another, battering first her ribs, then her hip, her back, her chest. In between each collision, she passed through a yielding layer that felt a bit like a canopy of leaves, but softer. After a few such transits, she realized she was passing through a bank of hanging clothes. She was careening through coats, frocks, shirts, and trousers, rattling their hangers, and caroming off the rods they swung from. She was falling through the Sphinx's bottomless closet. She was falling through the Fardrobe.

She pulled upon the reins of time, slowing the charge of the clock down to a fanciful trot. Her environment emerged from the blackness, and she saw the garments tangling about her, tumbling after her, all drawn in crimson lines, not sharply, but clear enough. Looking down, she saw the next bar, which held the squared shoulders of dozens of dining jackets. She endeavored to light upon it as if it were a tightrope, but the moment one heel was down, she felt the hooks of the hangers roll under her weight. Reaching up, she grasped the train of a dress above her to steady herself. With some sawing back and forth, she at last found her balance.

Posed there like a caged bird on its swing, she felt the listless instant begin to harden. She was caught between heartbeats, between breaths, between blinks. The torpid second stretched into a year that stagnated into an age that sprawled on and on all around her, a petrified forever.

She found the prospect of being frozen in time untroubling. In fact, she'd never felt more at peace. She could not recall why she had been anxious a moment before. Nothing could touch her here. She was safe at last. And alone.

Horribly, inescapably alone.

Something tickled. She tried to turn her focus toward it but discovered that gathering her concentration was like trying to sweep up sunshine. And there was so much light—womb-like, edgeless light. She realized she had fallen too far into the chasm of the present. There would be no climbing out. Though why would she ever want to leave?

The tickling persisted. She wondered where it was coming from. The charges of lightning that leapt between her nerves had nearly frozen. And yet, she could still feel her distant hand, her closed fist, the bite of her fingernails upon the heel of her palm, and the tickling. Just *there*.

Her heart thumped and she gasped in darkness, reeling wildly on her perch. The hangers clattered, and the coattails shushed, and her heartbeat reverberated like thunder through a roof. The resurgence of her panic made her pant like an overrun hound, and she thought for a moment that her lungs would burst.

But then, little by little, she calmed, consoling herself with several important truths. She was alive; she had work to do; she had to help her friends, had to survive to see Adam once more and make certain he knew the truth: His wretched sister loved him dearly. She did not wish to be alone.

Once she was certain her legs were steady enough and her balance was secure, she let go of the dress above her and felt around inside her pocket for the electric torch. Switching it on, she raised her closed hand into the beam of light and opened her fist to find her tickler: Reddleman's unpainted moth. She closed her hand again before it could fly off.

"Right," she said, swinging the beam of light about to get her bearings. "Now where did I park my trapeze..."

The Fardrobe's layout was a bit like a circulatory system, in which smaller avenues wound toward wider thoroughfares. The tracks were serviced by a staff of mechanical tentacles, which Byron had called "couture flukes." These arms retrieved articles of clothing by grasping the relevant hanger with all the alacrity of an octopus. The flukes then set the hanger upon the right track for delivery to the cabinet in Byron's fitting room. These hardy bars slid down greased rails that wended and coiled and were carried up inclines by an elaborate, jangling system of sprockets and chains. The frequent intersections where tracks gathered and forked were also operated by the intelligent tentacles. Voleta had discovered these crossroads also included a "manual override," which was what she called kicking the track switch out of the fluke's grip.

Fortunately, she had some experience with this violent manner of steering her way through the yawning depths of the Fardrobe, though this particular tour was made somewhat more difficult by the addition of a winged guide. Since her torch occupied one hand, she was forced to depend entirely upon the grip of the other. Each time she kicked a switch to chase the moth down a new track, the blow set the swiveling hook of her hanger spinning, and her along with it. She felt a bit as if she were chasing a snowflake through a blizzard.

The moth fluttered past rows of busts in hats and bonnets, deeper into the recesses of the closet. Though she had set her grip near the neck of the hanger, it had, after several knocks, slipped down the shoulder. When the moth dove suddenly into a crag walled with the skeletons of crinolines and bustles, Voleta was forced to kick the switch plate more recklessly. The shock traveled up her arm, into her hand. Her grip loosened. Voleta gritted her teeth, realizing she would either have to surrender the moth or her life.

She was still wrestling with the decision when it was made for her. The moth vanished into a grove of long-sleeved gowns that abutted the end of her track. When her hanger struck the end of the line, she flew from it into a gauntlet of hanging arms, none of which made any effort to catch her, though she pulled several of the blighters down with her.

She struck the bottom of the Fardrobe in a tumble, a rolling spill made more painful by the buttons, clasps, stays, and clips that littered the floor. The electric torch flashed wildly as it cartwheeled ahead of her and thumped upon a wall shortly before she banged against it herself.

Lying in a tangle of torn dresses and hangers, Voleta followed the rolling yellow cone of her torch to where it painted a halo upon a grate in the wall. The moth clung to the vent, its wings trembling lightly in the flowing air.

As she turned the screws that held the vent plate with the point of her knife, she said, "I'm sure I deserved that dose of my own medicine, but if it wouldn't be *too* much trouble, would you terribly mind slowing down a bit? Why not take in the sights; smell the roses; have a spot of tea?"

The instant she moved the vent aside, the moth darted into the ductwork.

Voleta sighed heavily. "All right. Have it your way."

Chapter Ten

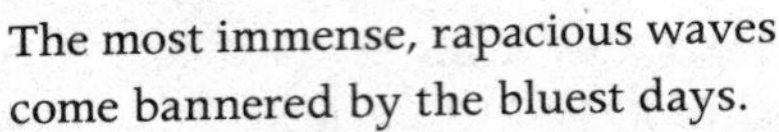

The most immense, rapacious waves
come bannered by the bluest days.

—*Music for Falling Down Stairs* by Jumet

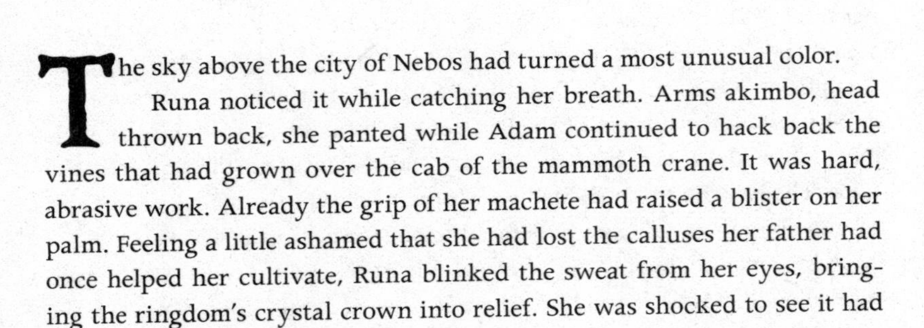

The sky above the city of Nebos had turned a most unusual color.

Runa noticed it while catching her breath. Arms akimbo, head thrown back, she panted while Adam continued to hack back the vines that had grown over the cab of the mammoth crane. It was hard, abrasive work. Already the grip of her machete had raised a blister on her palm. Feeling a little ashamed that she had lost the calluses her father had once helped her cultivate, Runa blinked the sweat from her eyes, bringing the ringdom's crystal crown into relief. She was shocked to see it had turned a dazzling shade of cerulean.

Academically, she knew that the sky that lay beyond the enduring veil of clouds was blue, much as she knew the seas were also blue, and the desert red, though she had never seen any of those natural wonders in person. She had only been exposed to the heavens as depicted in Ossian's collection of paintings, and those skies were all varying shades of sallow brown, the result of rough storage and old varnish. Even when her own experience with paint had revealed to her the cause of those discolored firmaments, the impression was too deeply imbedded in her. The sky was not *really* blue. How wrong she had been.

"I wonder what it means," Adam said, shucking the sweat from his brow with the back of his hand.

"I suppose something's changed. Something important. Do you think this is what your friends were worried about? Are we about to be invaded, or does this mean the Tower is going to..." She could scarcely finish the thought and was relieved when Adam hurried to answer.

"Voleta thinks we need to get the capstone up, that it's important, so I'm just going to focus on that for now. Who knows—maybe finishing the pyramid will bring back the clouds." He targeted a long train of ivy and chopped it, clearing the engine's entrance at last. The glass of the cabin door was foggy with condensation and grime. He grasped the handle and twisted; the bolt released with a creaking complaint, and the sliding door budged a little before miring again on its rail.

"I don't know that I want the clouds back. Is it always so blue?"

Clapping his hands together to knock loose the sandy rust, he said, "Oh, I think I've seen the sky done up in about every color."

"*Every* color? Even purple? What about orange?"

He took a shovel from the tools they'd gathered and worked its blade into the door crack. "Absolutely. Here, help me push." Together, they leaned upon the shovel handle and levered the door open at last.

The interior of the crane's pilothouse was a snarl of roots. They trailed from the ceiling and burst from the floor, crowding every seam, handwheel, and throttle casing. The machine's control bank was scarcely visible beneath the tendrils that swarmed it.

"Do you think you can get it running again?" Runa asked.

"I think I'd have more luck trying to start up a hedge."

"Oh, come on. You're a wonderful mechanic!" Runa slapped him on the back.

"Maybe. But we don't need a mechanic. We need a goat."

In the end, Adam decided to focus his restorative efforts on the main controls. While he did, Runa worked to clear the windscreen, a process that gradually brought in more light. He discovered mold on the pressure gauges and mushrooms growing among the hydraulic lines. The deeper he looked into the recesses of the control cabinet, the more he was convinced that the crane was closer to a flowerpot than a functioning engine.

Though there were some positive signs. The boiler registered as half-full, and when he thumped the bottom of the tank with one knuckle, it made an encouraging muffled gong. The oil indicator wasn't empty, and the fuel lines that ran to the winch at the rear of the cabin were intact; he could tell because they still ran with the Sphinx's luminous medium.

By the time Runa rejoined him in the cabin, his expectation that the crane would start had improved from *completely impossible* to *exceedingly doubtful*.

And so, when he turned the ignition key, he was only slightly disappointed when they were met with stony silence.

After repeating the process several more times and jostling all the levers he could think to jostle, he gave Runa a brave if rueful smile. "Perhaps I'm a mechanic to the same degree that a house painter is an artist. This is well beyond my abilities. I'm used to boilers, not"—he waved his hands over the controls—"whatever this is."

"What did you used to do when one of your boilers wouldn't work?"

"As a last resort? I'd hit it with a spanner. Sometimes you just need to give a machine a good knock." Adam saw Runa's expression writhe as she tried to conceal her doubt. "That actually gives me an idea." He searched the levers that crowded the panel before him, swiping years of dust from the labeling plates. "Ah, here we are." He gripped the throttle by the head.

"What's that?"

"The brake for the hoist. I'm guessing there is a hook ball at the end of the line up there. I'm going to drop it and see if running the cable doesn't rattle something loose."

For a moment after Adam pulled the lever, nothing happened, and it seemed that he might have no choice but to apply a little shovel therapy to the side of the pilothouse. Then they heard the drone of unspooling cable, felt the winch vibrating through the floor. When the hook struck the lawn, it raised a thump like a bass drum. Leaves and torn vines rained down after it.

Squeezing his eyes shut, Adam held his breath and turned the ignition once more.

He had thought that if there were going to be a resurrection, it would be dramatic, one full of explosive chugging and billows of smut, because such was the violence that filled the garages of New Babel. So when the Brick Layer's titanic crane merely began to hum, Adam didn't know what to make of it. The noise was as innocuous as a purring cat. He gave one of the throttles a tentative nudge.

Neither he nor Runa was prepared for the floor to lurch beneath them.

They grasped each other, even as the pilothouse swiveled, causing the ball hook to carve an arc in the lawn.

Bringing the throttle back to the neutral position, Adam laughed to dispel some of his nervous amazement. "There. All fixed." Surveying the control board before them, he quickly sobered. "This is going to require a little trial and error."

"We're about to wreak a lot of havoc, aren't we?"

"No, no. Just a little havoc. There are, what, maybe three park benches and a half dozen lampposts between us and the pyramid. I probably won't hit all of them. At least everyone is busy with the children, so we don't have to worry about witnesses—I mean, an audience."

"But how are we going to lift the capstone?"

"You know, I had a chance to ponder that very thing once when I was waiting to have my neck wrung by a tree. I have a plan. Come on."

Adam had spent enough time in the Port of Goll to learn the basics of hoists and cranes, and in particular the utility of a spreader bar, which provided stability to the lifting of ungainly objects. It had occurred to him once while he was standing upon the purgatorial stool that the modest hole that pierced the capstone two-thirds up from the base might've been meant to accommodate a spreader bar, and studying the stone again now, he was sure such was the case.

It took them half an hour to find a suitable length of steel, and another half hour to get everything rigged up. Then, with Runa playing spotter on the lawn, Adam bid the crane raise the ancient capstone. Plucking the pyramidion from its flower bed, Adam was struck by how serene the stone looked swaying gently in the air. It was a calm that was cut short by his engagement of the crane's treads, for while the heart of the machine purred like a cat, its tracks roared like a lion. The clattering squeal of unready wheels filled the pilothouse to the exclusion of all other sounds. He gritted his teeth and steered the crane through the park to the utter devastation of the lawn and two park benches. To reach the street, he first had to pass between a pair of lampposts. After he succeeded in knocking both posts down, and a neighboring third, Runa asked if he wouldn't like to back up and take a crack at the rest of them.

His relief at reaching his destination and bringing the engine to a halt was soon spoiled by the realization that the more difficult task still lay ahead. He had to raise the capstone, position it over the pyramid, and bring it down in perfect alignment. It seemed a job that would challenge a veteran crane operator. Visions of him cracking the sacred pyramidion or denting the gilded facade played out in his head in vivid detail.

And yet a curious thing occurred. The closer he brought the capstone to the pyramid's peak, the more the stone seemed drawn to its perch. At first, Adam thought he was imagining the attraction, but even from ten feet out, he could tell that the pyramidion was bending the cable, straining as if magnetized. When the stone began to spin, Adam was briefly alarmed, but the turning ended as abruptly as it had begun with the capstone aligned to its destination. The last few feet of the descent passed in an instant. The pyramidion stamped into place, prompting a cannon-like report that bounced between the city's spires and roiled through the treetops.

While the boom still rang in their ears, the black capstone blazed forth with a light as profound as an apogean sun. It lit the city like a sheet of lightning that refused to break or fade.

Adam stumbled from the cab of the crane to find Runa shielding her face as she backed into the park, not, it seemed, to escape the glare, but to get a better view.

Even squinting, Adam found it painful to look directly at the incandescent stone. His gaze dropped down the face of the pyramid for relief, which was when he saw it: a break in the golden slope, a third of the way down the monument, an unadorned rectangle, an open, unlit door.

From its inky threshold, unrailed stairs emerged, each sliding out from the golden facade as if pressed from behind by a monolithic finger. Returning to the boulevard, Adam and Runa followed the surfacing stairs as they knuckled around the pyramid's corner and continued down to the street. The steps seemed to beckon and threaten, to exalt them and daunt them like a wedding altar.

Trembling at the foot of the invitation, the unready pair gripped and wrung each other's hands.

Chapter Eleven

Some fear the desolation of a broken heart; others dread the chronic suffering of an injured back. Both grievances benefit from a division of burdens. Lift your sorrows with a friendly ear and your luggage with a brawny porter.

—*Everyman's Guide to the Tower of Babel*, VII. I

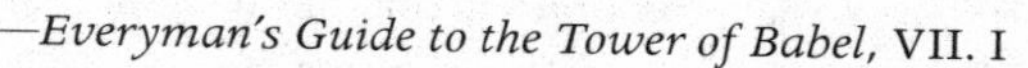

For an old woman on a plate, the Sphinx proved to be surprisingly heavy. At first, Edith had thought that she would carry the Brick Layer's acolyte on her own. She pictured a solemn and lonely funereal march up the winding stairs and down the Sphinx's gallery of miracles—a fitting gesture, Edith thought, to mark the shifting of the existential burden of the Tower's stewardship.

But after several straining steps, it became apparent that while the gesture might be possible, it was certainly unwise. Edith didn't wish to risk a self-inflicted injury shortly before confronting her nemesis in combat, and so decided to share the load with Iren.

While the amazon tottered forward like a penguin, Edith shuffled backward after her, carrying the weight of her half with her engine arm while her other hand held the Sphinx's body upright. The old dame had already surprised them once with an unanticipated backward slump that had nearly sent them all tumbling into the fireplace. Still, it felt strange to hold the Sphinx by the shoulder; it was an intimacy they never could've shared while she was still alive.

They crossed the workroom slowly, navigating the decorative furniture and ignoring the pilot who sat at the storied desk muttering exclamations, both delightful and troubling, as he eviscerated the Sphinx's mechanical messenger. When they reached the foot of the spiral stair that led up to the attic, they adopted the ancient argot of furniture movers, communicating in grunts, head bobs, and monosyllabic chants: *up, up, turn, turn, ow.* They crested the final landing in a state of heaving exhaustion, barely managing to set their fare down before collapsing around her.

"Maybe this is good enough. She looks happy in the stairwell, don't you think?" Edith said between gasps.

Sitting on the top stair, Iren knuckled the sweat from her eyes. "And you thought you could do this on your own."

"Only briefly."

"No, I mean the peas and carrots thing—all that shore leave talk. Sounded like you were trying to get rid of me."

"What? No! Iren, you know I'm still going to need you a week after we're both dead. I'm *always* going to need you. But I also want you to... to have a life."

Iren cleared her sinuses with practiced efficiency. "I have a life. I like it. I don't want to sit under a stupid tree on"—she made a face of great revulsion—"wet grass."

"I take it you weren't particularly charmed by Nebos either?"

"I'd rather live with the clogworms."

"There must be something wrong with us," Edith said.

Iren gave an indolent shrug. "Eh. I feel all right."

When they at last settled the Sphinx onto her lonely stage at the end of the gloomy gallery, Edith found she could think of nothing suitable to say. As they stood shaking out their arms and stretching their shoulders before their former master, slouched in her unflattering spotlight, Edith wished for some elegiacal inspiration. Lacking any, she instead gently arranged the Sphinx into a more flattering pose: shoulders even, head bowed, hands folded in her lap upon her wand.

An eerie creaking rose from somewhere in the expansive dimness. They peered into the shadows between the spotlighted exhibits but could not discern the source of the sound.

"Mr. Ekes?" Edith called, her voice echoing until she hardly recognized it. Mr. Ekes did not answer, and the lack of his smiling presence seemed to change the character of the room. The Sphinx's industrial titans loomed on their platforms like the carved pillars of a king's tomb. It was an august and uneasy sight. She said, "We should get back. I'm sure Reddleman has either fixed the moth or repaired it to death."

"Can I say a few words first?"

Surprised, but glad to have the occasion marked in some fashion, Edith said, "Yes, of course." Feeling suddenly self-conscious, Edith dragged the cocked hat from her head.

Iren clasped her hands together and shut her eyes, lifting her chin as if she meant to speak to the ceiling. Not knowing where to look, Edith bowed her head.

"You were an awful boss. I've had a lot of bad bosses. But you were the worst." Edith glanced at Iren to see if she were joking, but the amazon's expression was quite earnest. "I didn't like how you treated Senlin or Voleta or the captain. You could've been nicer to Byron, too. He really loved you. I think you made a lot of mistakes. Me too, I guess."

Iren paused, and for a moment, Edith thought that was the end of it. Then her first mate spoke again through the phlegm of congested emotion. "I also wanted to tell you, you were right about me. I did have a lot to lose, and now I have even more. But I'm not as scared as I was. I think I've learned to fight with my heart as much as my fists. I'm happier for it. So, thank you. And goodbye."

In the Sphinx's workshop, Reddleman was having a splendid time.

So many of the Sphinx's tools were a marvel in and of themselves. There were spring-loaded hammers, automatic drivers, electrified snips, and self-heating irons, no bigger than a knitting needle, that could melt gold on contact. Applying these instruments to the repair of another technical miracle was like bowing a cello with a piccolo or touching off a cannon with a pistol shot. It was heady work.

Still, there was no denying the effort itself was going miserably. The Sphinx's final message was almost certainly unrecoverable.

The recording was transcribed upon a minute spool of black ribbon composed of some exceedingly fragile material. The very act of speeding it up could very well cause the ribbon to break. This fact left him with little room for experimentation. He had settled on two possible solutions. He could manually swap out the minute dynamo that pulled the tape for a slightly larger one he'd found among the Sphinx's extensive collection of parts. Doing so would require him to remove and reseat the ribbon, a daunting prospect that seemed bound to end in tatters. The second option was much cruder: He could simply increase the current to the existing motor, which in theory might quicken the playback, if it did not melt the engine itself. And either outcome could be superseded by a failure of the—

"Reddleman." He looked up from the desktop to find the captain and first mate standing before the Sphinx's desk. The lamp at his elbow, which underlit their faces, made them both look a little skeletal. He wondered if they saw the skull behind his face, too. The thought made him smile.

"Good news, then?" the captain asked.

"No, no. Just the opposite. Horrible news, I'm afraid."

"Then why are you smiling?"

"Well, just because it's disappointing doesn't mean it's not interesting." Reddleman saw at once that neither the captain nor her first mate were in the mood for such reflections. He hastened to reassure them. "The best I can do is offer you two rather poor options, either of which may result in the destruction of the message. One option is that I—"

The captain held up her hand. "No need to regale us with the technical details. Just use your best judgment."

With a deferential nod, he delicately pinched the wire cage of the exposed recorder, raised it to eye level and, with elbows braced on the desktop, applied the stripped tip of a wire to the heart of the machine.

A tiny spark popped at the contact, and a deep and resonant voice pressed into the room. Though her speech was still sluggish, her words were now at least intelligible. The bass tones of the Sphinx's voice gave her words an unneeded additional gravity.

"I thought I had more time. No, that's not quite right: I wanted more time. But some clocks cannot be rewound.

"I should've begun arrangements years ago, but it's so hard to surrender unfinished work. You'll understand someday if you don't already.

"Of course, I don't know which *you* I am presently addressing. If this is you, Luc, as I fear it may well be, you're probably crowing and strutting about, celebrating your victory. You always were an overweening young man. But I'd like you to know two things: First, I see potential in you still. You may change the course of your life and the arc of history yet. You have already done some good, I think, in trumpeting the plight of the hods, in bringing their suffering to the attention of the myopic ringdoms. What began as a selfish pursuit, young man, could still become egalitarian. You could finish the Brick Layer's vision: open the ringdoms to the hods, empty the black trail and seal it up. It was meant to be a ladder to prosperity, not an inescapable cul-de-sac. Instead of posing as a savior, you could behave as one.

"Second, you should know that if you choose to be a tyrant, you are conscripting yourself to a life of paranoia and isolation. Your reign will be defined by treachery, rebellion, and terror of your own dwindling faculties. I have conducted a survey of history and found that the most common causes of death among dictators are beheading, dismembering, disemboweling, hanging, and poisoning. Have you never wondered why the bullies of the past are always anemic, impotent, depraved, incestuous, deformed, bedwetters? It's because their obituaries were written by their victims, written by the very men and women who pulled down their pants and chopped off their heads. So shall it be for you. You will live in fear, die in violence, and your name shall be scorned for generations.

"Ruminate upon your fate, young man. That is all I have to say to you.

"And if the *you* I'm speaking to is Captain Winters, as I sincerely hope it is, I'm sorry to have left you with such a mess. Before I give you my blessing and parting advice, I must first give you a warning. Do not open the Bridge of Babel until you enter the crowning city and ensure that the Nautilus is sealed. If that door is ajar, then the nation is lost. You must also seal every windstile into Nebos and clear the surrounding verge. Anything that lies outside the city gates will be lost and irredeemably so.

"Now, as to my advice. Edith, when you—"

Silence swallowed the Sphinx's voice. The recorder in Reddleman's hand began to fizzle and smoke. A candle flame burst from one end of it. Reddleman dropped the device onto the desktop and fanned the wreckage with his hands, as if that might somehow salvage the loss. A moment more, and the recorder had burned itself out.

When he looked up, the captain was wearing an openmouthed, wide-eyed expression of horror, and the amazon was charging across the room. The first mate had her foot on the first step of the spiraling stair to the attic when the captain at last found her voice.

Without pulling her eyes away from the molten ruin of the recorder, the captain shouted, "Wait, Iren! Wait."

Hesitating on the stair, Mister Iren replied over her shoulder, "You heard what she said. The ship's in trouble. We have to go back."

At last, the captain pulled her eyes away from the recorder. She turned to face her officer. "You mean Ann's in trouble."

Iren's face contorted with anger. "That's not fair. Byron, Marya, the baby . . . they're all on the ship."

The captain approached her with the poise of an animal trainer, Reddleman thought.

"And Voleta and Tom are here. Think a moment. Marya can pilot the ship. If there's danger, there are few places that are safer than a warship that cannot be shot down and can retreat as quick as a deer fly. The minute Voleta comes back and we know Senlin's fate, then we will make for the ship with all possible haste. I promise you. But in the meantime, we wait."

Her shoulders rounding with acceptance, Mister Iren took her foot from the stairs and turned back to the room. Her thick arms hung heavy as the pails of a milkmaid's yoke. "And what do we do if she doesn't come back?"

Edith opened her mouth to answer but was arrested by the intrusion of a deep mechanical grumbling. They rushed to the great vault door that sealed the Sphinx's workshop; Iren plied the cross wheel before shoving the bulky slab open.

Gathering in the threshold, they gazed out over the pink-papered canyon full of shut doors and white sills and ten thousand sunken sconces. Far beneath them, the long floor of the corridor engulfed a row of lit sconces at a stroke.

The valley was shrinking.

Someone had activated the elevator.

Someone was coming.

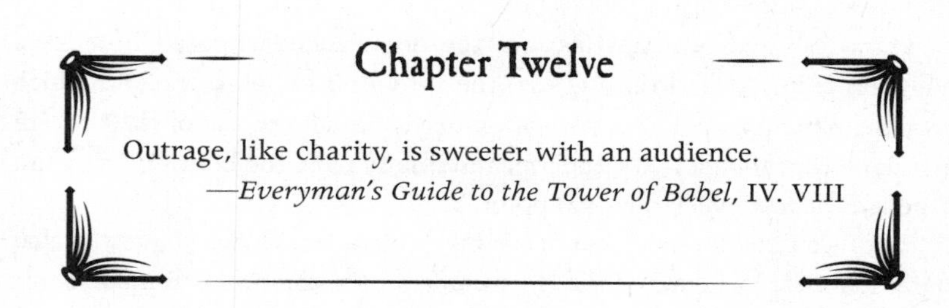

Chapter Twelve

Outrage, like charity, is sweeter with an audience.

—*Everyman's Guide to the Tower of Babel*, IV. VIII

Senlin had not expected to smile again for the remainder of his life, what little there would be of it. And yet, he was having a very hard time not beaming at the scene before him. Never before had such triumph soured so quickly.

Despite the ominous fanfare that had succeeded the unlocking of the bridge, the door had failed to swing open.

So many aspects of the Sphinx's home were automated; it struck Marat as an unfortunate oversight (verging on an outrage) that the home's most auspicious door had to be yanked open like a common cupboard. Appearing to tamp down his annoyance in an effort to preserve the grandeur of the moment, Marat laid his fingers to the smooth, round lip of the vault and pulled.

At first his exertion was modest, but it soon mounted as the door resisted his efforts. He began to tug and heave until his armor rattled like a tinker's cart on a rough road.

When at last he turned around, Senlin saw the sweat beaded about his perfect dimples. The zealot ordered Cael to unstick the door. Taking the rind of the vault in his steam-shovel hands, Cael pulled with a long, constipated grunt. His fingers slipped, and he tumbled like a dizzy drunk over the back of a nearby club chair.

They reorganized. Mr. Gedge crawled back into his black golem and Thornton spat on his steel hands, while Cael scowled at the vault as if it had ambushed him. The three packed themselves against the door, their heads piled up like faces on a totem pole and their hands crowded upon the lip of the vault. On a count, they made a concerted bid to peel the door back. Iron rattled, steam hissed, the men and their gears groaned. One by one, they lost their purchase and fell away until the vault stood bare, unmoved, and perhaps a trifle smug.

Marat pointed out that because the door lacked exposed hinges—a common security feature of safes—they couldn't know for certain which way the hatch swung. This revelation necessitated a repeat of their recent attack on the left side, then the top, and finally from the bottom. The vault repelled them at every cardinal point.

Red-faced inside the throat of his black bird, Mr. Gedge suggested that perhaps Marat had entered the last number of the combination incorrectly. He had, after all, "spun the dial as roughly as a roulette wheel."

Infuriated by the suggestion, Marat wanted to know what all the ruckus above them could have been if not proof that the combination had been correct. Gedge pointed out that the tumult might've been unrelated or, for all they knew, the result of a failed attempt. The din might've just been the Sphinx's version of alarm bells. To this, Marat said he would be more than happy to remind Gedge what a bell sounded like: the engineer's ridiculous helmet could be the bell, and his thick skull its clapper.

Senlin was enjoying having been entirely forgotten for the moment. While Marat and his marauders attacked the impregnable vault with pry bars, hammers, and a blowtorch retrieved from the Palatine—squandering hours and tempers to no avail—Senlin leaned upon the back of a musty sofa with his legs out and his hands in his lap. Seeing the zealot flustered and frustrated filled Senlin with such a warm sense of satisfaction. From lectern to court bench, how illusory was the equanimity of power!

He was then surprised by the arrival of a visitor. A moth crawled up the yellow-and-white mountainside of his quilt. Though its wings were unpainted, he recognized its ilk at once. It was one of the Sphinx's little spies.

A glimmer caught his eye, or rather, a sharp gleam of light burned upon his face. He looked for the source, found it against the wall, near the floor, some fifteen yards away. The beam came from an open vent. The moment he located the light's origin, its target changed, turning upward to illuminate the face of the person hiding in the shaft.

Voleta.

She beckoned to him, her mouth bunched tight as a little fist.

Half believing her to be a figment of his imagination, a shimmering oasis in a brain cooked to madness by the desert sun, he began to crawl toward her. His heart corked his throat. His limbs trembled with excitement and fear. His quilt slipped from his shoulders. He did not stop to retrieve it. His sarong loosened at his waist, and this he could not abandon. He gripped it with one hand and limped along on three points. Never had fifteen yards been so many miles. As he approached, Voleta or the mirage of her retreated to make room for him in the wall.

The muted but rapid *tock-tock-tock* of feet brought his head around. Delyth was charging him, her hair writhing like a disturbed nest of snakes about her bandaged face.

The closer Senlin came to the opening of the air duct, the narrower it seemed to grow. He began to doubt that he would fit, and wondered if he'd rather die facing his attacker or be skewered in the back with his head stuck in a wall vent.

Hoping he would not regret his choice, Senlin sprang at the opening with arms steepled overhead as if he were diving into the sea.

Though he made it through, the shaft beyond proved just as narrow as the aperture, and it quickly pinched him, stealing any momentum. He wriggled onward into the dark like a newt, palms flat and pulling upon the tin sheeting, toes digging first into carpet and then slipping upon metal. He could not see where he was going, but it did not matter. He wouldn't stop until something grabbed him from behind or blocked him from ahead.

The bellow of voices that pursued him began as a confusion, but soon resolved upon a single source. Marat's voiced washed about him, raising goose bumps on his skin as if his very breath lapped against his ear.

"Go on, little mouse! Scurry, scurry quick as you can. Don't you dare die in my walls! I don't want to smell your rotting corpse. Eat your crumbs! Hide your tracks! Every house needs a little mouse, and you shall be mine."

Voleta waited for the headmaster in the foot of the Fardrobe under a great, unlit canopy of hanging frocks. She sat with her legs crossed, staring into the dark of the vent she'd lately vacated. She felt much as she had as a child in the bottom of her mother's small closet, nestled among the hems of her handsewn dresses and winter coats: safe. She felt safe. The intruders with their bulbous armor, unwieldy poleaxes, and crystal carapaces could not follow her into the walls.

Even the gaunt headmaster was having some trouble in that regard.

When at last he squirmed free of the ventilation shaft, he was dewed with sweat, and his knees were carved and bleeding. His limbs shook, from either the exertion or exhilaration, she wasn't sure which. He tried to stand, was immediately enveloped by hanging gowns, and crouched down again before her.

In the harsh light of her electric torch, with his shorn head haloed by the tulle of a skirt, he looked like a ghost. She scarcely recognized him.

He made a sound somewhere between an anguished sob and a guffaw of relief. She wondered if he weren't succumbing to some sort of manic fit, wondered if Marat had succeeded in breaking a man whose spirit had always seemed indefatigable. There were tears in his eyes when he gripped her bent elbows and said, "You *are* real! For a moment, I thought I'd been dosed with Crumb again, but you are real. Voleta, you saved my life. You..." The side of his hand touched the hard edge of her brass cuff. He lifted her wrist and the sleeve of her coat fell away, revealing the instrument that had once fueled the Red Hand's carnage. He recoiled from his embrace. She met his gaze, smiling weakly at his horror. "Your...your eyes. No, Voleta. Not you. What happened? Who—"

"There's not really enough time for all that right now, Mr. Senlin. The captain is waiting for us upstairs."

"Edith."

"Yes. And Marya and little Olivet are waiting for you on the ship."

"M—" he began, but her name lodged in his throat. He clapped a hand over his mouth, a pressure that seemed to milk more tears from his eyes.

"But the captain needs us right now. She and Iren are looking for the Sphinx. We're hoping she'll know what we should do about Marat. We should hurry back."

With apparent effort, Senlin composed himself, swiping away the tears and clearing his full throat. "Yes. Yes, of course. Lead the way."

"I think we have time for a quick stop, though."

"A stop? Stop for what?"

"Well, Mr. Senlin, you can't very well show up for your reunion with your wife and child dressed like...well, like you've just crawled out of a sauna."

Looking down at himself, the old headmaster chuckled. "Quite right, Voleta. Quite right."

* * *

The tufted sofa leapt into the air, its broken back spilling splinters and batting. It crashed down on a floor lamp, turning its glass shade into jingling shards. Luc Marat flattened a footstool under his golden heel, then kicked the crushed mass into a chandelier, inspiring a rain of crystal pendants.

The zealot was humoring his ire. He was still very much in control of himself; he could end his rampage whenever he wished. But he did not wish to. Not yet. He cleaved the oval back of a bergère chair in half, then turned the blade of his falchion to its twin.

When Tom had wriggled into the wall, Marat had initially taken out his rage on the door of the stubborn vault. Though his toes made the metal ring a little, his blows left no mark. Irked by its imperviousness, he began to lavish the lobby furniture with his wrath. Since he could not chastise the Brick Layer himself, he would punish the Brick Layer's house for displeasing him.

He was very much aware that his crew was watching him. From the corner of his eye, he saw them huddled together, nervous and cowed. *Good*. He wanted them to be alarmed, wanted to remind them of the consequences of disappointing him, to show them once more his willingness to vigorously punish unsatisfactory efforts and unacceptable results. He would not allow their botches and blunders to cast a shadow upon his radiance. Not today, of all days!

He stopped all at once like a dancer who's come to the end of a song. He sheathed his sword, walked back through the debris he'd made, and addressed his crew as if he were continuing a conversation. "Come to think of it, I have an excavator at my disposal. Why knock upon the door when we can walk through the wall?" Marat popped his fist into the cup of his hand. Mr. Gedge, Thornton, and Delyth all nodded mutely.

Only Cael was unresponsive. He wore the wide-eyed, drawn expression of a man shaving his upper lip. Recognizing this as his contemplative face, Luc sighed and asked, "What is it, Cael?"

"I was just wondering if maybe it isn't a door."

"What do you mean?"

"Maybe we can't open it because it doesn't open. It looks like a lock. Maybe it's just a lock."

"Huh," Marat said, frowning at Gedge. This was the sort of useful musing he expected of his chief engineer and strategist rather than his knuckle-dragging tank. "Now, that is an interesting question—one that I think we should pose to the Sphinx. We've tarried long enough, my friends. It's time we paid our maker a visit."

Chapter Thirteen

Should you ever feel dread at the prospect of where your adventures have carried you, take solace in the fact that the vast majority of mortal accidents occur in the home. Perhaps the secret to longevity is absenteeism.

—*Everyman's Guide to the Tower of Babel*, IX. II

enlin tumbled from the cavernous Fardrobe into Byron's fitting room and collided with the headless sewing form that tipped and toppled backward. Recovering his footing in the nick of time, Senlin caught the dummy like a dancer dipping his partner and brought it upright again.

Voleta, who had arrived first, picked up the top hat that sat cocked on the handwheel of Byron's sewing machine. Pulling it onto her head, she said, "Enjoy the ride?"

"No, it was awful. Didn't you hear me screaming?"

"I thought you were just...giddy." Voleta shut the Fardrobe's doors and turned her attention to the baroque controls of the immense purring closet. Muttering under her breath, Voleta hunted after and adjusted a selection of the many dials that crowded the door of the Sphinx's miraculous armoire. "I hope you know your measurements."

Senlin rattled the numbers off, and crossed his arms over his chest, feeling both cold and a little conspicuous. "Do you know how it works?"

"More or less. I helped Byron pack for our trip to Pelphia. What should we dial up for you?"

"Gray or black trousers, braces, a white shirt, socks, and shoes, of course. A gray or black jacket, if you can. A necktie would be nice."

"Oh, you *are* dressing for battle. And drawers, too? Long or short?"

"Long."

"Coming right up."

A few minutes later, Senlin's ensemble had been assembled, and he set about changing while Voleta faced the door. She whistled dryly and every few seconds jabbed the call button for the elevating corridor. The slow clack of distant gears rattled the doorknob like a burglar.

Voleta's plumbing of the Fardrobe's great bounty had produced imperfect results. While the sizes were correct, her familiarity with the color codes proved to be skewed. What she was certain was the numerical code for black was in fact white, resulting in the delivery of a white jacket, white trousers, white braces and tie, and cream-colored patent leather boots. The only colorful article of clothing was his collared shirt, which she had believed would be white, but had come out pink.

"I look ridiculous," he said, pinching the knot of his tie, as if a dimple might improve the overall impression.

Voleta turned around, her mouth opening about what promised to be a laugh, but she swallowed it, gathered her brows into an earnest furrow, and said, "You look like a nice country gentleman."

"I look like a country gentleman's grandfather."

Dropping his hands, Senlin regarded his likeness uncomfortably. The mirror's diagnosis was frank, expected, and brutal: He had aged a decade in a year. Scars crosshatched his wrinkles; moles stippled his sunspots. His once bright eyes were now dull as pencil leads. He looked like a regent's visage printed on a bank note, softened by a thousand pockets, halved by as many wallets, creased and broken by repeated exchange. He looked as if he should be removed from circulation.

He spoke without inflection when he said, "Do you ever wish you could travel back through your life? I do. I wish I could find myself when I was younger, carefree, cocksure, happy—*perfectly*, entirely happy. But never quite satisfied. I wish I could find that fool and just flog him up and down the street. I took so much for granted."

Voleta knocked back the brim of her hat, which had sunk nearly to her eyebrows. "I suppose you could look at it that way, Mr. Senlin. You could resent yourself for your imperfect enjoyment of your life, but that seems to me like a never-ending chore. A thankless one, too. I think that if we really knew how good our lives were *while* they were good, we'd be too scared to do anything, change anything. We'd never take a risk, or explore, or grow. You can hate yourself for not fully appreciating your happy days while you had them, or you could look back and be warmed by the memory, couldn't you?"

Senlin tucked in his chin and frowned though it seemed a smile. "Look at you: getting wise in your old age."

Voleta swatted the air dismissively. "I've just been thinking about time a lot recently. And I think I know what you're *really* fretting about, Mr. Senlin. I think she still loves you. I truly do. And the two of you made the most beautiful little girl. I don't particularly like babies, but she's as good as they come. Sweet tempered, watchful, healthy. Marya won't care if you're dressed like a country gaffer. I'm sure it's not your fashion sense that she missed."

Senlin smiled at the floor, blushing at the thought of meeting his child. He had lost and scrounged hope so many times he had begun to worry that his heart had grown calluses—impenetrable, implacable, unfeeling bark. But he could think of no more optimistic event in the world than the birth of a child, and he could imagine no greater gift to that child than to have Marya for a mother.

The rumble of the traveling corridor ceased, and the lock on the door released.

Voleta put her hand to the knob, then stopped. She turned around sharply, knocking the heel of her hand against her forehead as if to punish her forgetfulness. "You're unarmed!"

"Oh. Right." Looking about, Senlin's eye fell upon a large pair of tailor's scissors jutting from Byron's sewing box. He took them up and snipped the air tentatively.

Voleta made a face. "You really want to have a go at a bunch of knights in plate armor with a pair of scissors?" Wagging her head, she pulled the pistol from the holster at her hip. Its barrel was elegant and slender, its pommel was made of polished burl wood and braced with brass plates. Rather than a flint and frizzen, it had a simple hammer that rotated a chamber of six cartridges. Accepting the wondrous gift, Senlin was surprised by its heft, given its relatively small size. "But what about you?" he said.

Passing him a handful of jingling ammunition, she answered, "I don't need a pistol, Mr. Senlin. I spit bullets now."

The rising corridor ground along like an old funicular. The jaundiced light of the receded sconces painted the rosy paper a rusty shade of umber. The thickly framed paintings were as gloomy as windows facing the dusk of an evening. The atmosphere was intimate and cloistered—a strange effect considering the great volume of space behind them, a yawning vacuum that faded into aseptic shadow. Still, there seemed no reason to hurry. The conclusion of the hall was in sight. They'd reach it long before the underpowered lift finished its ascent. They strolled like friends prolonging a visit that soon would come to an end.

"Where do you think the Sphinx is?" Senlin flexed the stiff soles of his new shoes.

"If I know her, she's laying some clever trap for Marat and his gang. I for one hope to be there when she springs it. I want to see the look on his face."

"I just want to see the faces of all my friends again." Senlin adjusted his gun belt to keep the heavy holster from banging against his thigh. "You said you came in through the attic; does that mean you saw Adam?"

"I did. He's met a girl."

"Good for him!"

"Iren did, too."

"*Really?*" They came to a halt, having reached the limit of the corridor, though the vault to the Sphinx's workshop still lay four and a half stories above them. The doors on either side continued to sink sluggishly into the floor. Senlin folded his arms to better enjoy the revelation of Iren's new romance. "Tell me everything. Spare no detail."

"Well, it all began when King Leonid decided to foist me and Iren upon a young duchess named Xenia. She had goo for brains. Every time she blew her nose, she got a little dumber. Anyway, Xenia—"

The gears beneath them squealed, and their ascent lurched to a stop.

Senlin and Voleta looked at one another in puzzlement, then at the remaining four floors above them, before turning their attention down the empty corridor.

The angle of their view made it impossible to observe when, some fifty paces off, the doors of an elevator slid opened. To them, Delyth seemed to walk out of the wall. The daggers of her legs further carved the tattered carpets; her thin hair floated like cinders in a draft.

Senlin felt Voleta tense toward action, and he gripped her shoulder to give her pause. "You can't break her crystal bell," he whispered. "I've seen her ram it against a steel bulkhead without so much as a crack."

Unslinging her diamond club from her shoulder, Voleta said, "I know. That's why I brought this."

"I don't think you understand." Senlin tried to pull her toward the shelter of a doorway. "She hasn't seen us yet. Perhaps we can—"

Thornton entered the corridor with his head already swung in their direction. He raised a steel finger at them. Though muffled by the distance, they could still hear him say, "Sic 'em."

Delyth turned on her tiptoes. Her carriage swayed one way then the other; she seemed to be savoring the moment. Then the pariah of the Silk Reef began to charge.

"Stay behind me." Voleta rested her bat upon the crook of her arm as she tuned her cuff to release a little more of the medium into her veins.

"I most certainly will n—" Senlin began to say, but in lieu of argument, Voleta put her palm to his chest and gently shoved him back three steps against the hall's dead end.

She ran to meet Delyth with her diamond bat raised over her shoulder. Voleta was disappointed to see that the leg Iren had broken off had been replaced. The image of her own severed hand pressed to the fore of her thoughts. Her wrist ached in sympathy, perhaps, or in anticipation of revenge. At least the amputation had taught her the limitations of the fiend's elbowing arm. Assuming it had also been repaired, she knew its reach, knew it could flex in many directions, but not all. The chimera had blind spots, and Voleta meant to exploit them.

Inside her crystal bell, Delyth held her rag-clothed fists balled on either side of her chin—the posing of an excited child. As they closed, Voleta waited for the knife-fingered limb to unfold, but Delyth kept it stowed away, no doubt delaying until Voleta was within range.

When they were mere strides apart, Voleta put her foot to the wall, launched herself to the opposite side of the hall, and back again, zippering upward. Delyth appeared to try to veer off, but her momentum was too great, and Voleta too quick. She landed on her rump on the peak of

Delyth's bell. Feeling as if she were riding a horse backward, Voleta swung her bat at the base of the crystal dome. The first blow made her arms shake like jelly on a spoon as the bat bounced harmlessly back the same way it had come. She shifted her stance on the now bucking carriage, centered her weight, and hammered upon the shell once more. The sound that followed was brief but unmistakable. She knew it would be there before she looked: a finger-long crack forked up from the base of the diamond dome.

Voleta yipped in triumph and was at nearly the same instant puzzled to see the long point of Delyth's stiletto protruding from her shoulder. Then she found herself lifted up like a hooked fish, and before she could look around to assess her chances for escape, she was flung back down the hallway. She tumbled hard as if rolling down a hill, her top hat flying from her head. Her vision continued to spin even after she came to a rest on her back. Her head rolled in the fiend's direction.

A dark tentacle curled up from the fender of Delyth's carriage. Voleta could only guess that whoever had repaired her leg had also decided to fit her with the new arm, or rather, a jointless, eight-foot-long black whip that was tipped with a silvery stinger.

Reaching for her pierced shoulder, Voleta was surprised to find it suddenly extended. Senlin pulled her by the arm as if it were a string and she a grounded kite. Though her wound did not hurt exactly, she could feel his efforts squeezing the medium from the puncture, and she cried out so he would stop.

He helped her to her feet, and she retrieved her dropped club before continuing their stumbling retreat. Over her shoulder, Voleta marked the black spider's deliberate advance. Delyth flayed the walls with her tendril, hacking paintings from their frames, puckering the wallpaper with meandering scars. Voleta braced one hand against the dead end of the hall, which suddenly seemed much closer than where she had left it.

Her lungs felt as if they had shriveled inside her chest. Every breath became a gasp. Her heart throbbed with heavy, silted blood. The petals of the pale fleurs-de-lis that patterned the paper before her began to wither as a tunnel of insensible darkness choked her vision.

She was dying. She had no choice. Reaching for her cuff, Voleta opened each valve as her fingers found them. It felt like opening the spillways of an overburdened dam. The gash in her shoulder began to boil. The shadows of the corridor thinned as she beheld the floating ghosts of ten thousand visitors to the Sphinx's home streaking overhead. She refused to consider them, refused to take her eyes off the prowling arachnid and her adder-like arm. Voleta would not retreat into the past. She would not leave Mr. Senlin to face the present alone. She would *not*.

Senlin drew the pistol Voleta had given him. Delyth, not ten steps away, had cocked her stinger high and back like a cobra preparing to strike.

"That won't stop her," Voleta said, her voice sounding unusually forceful for someone who'd just been run through.

"I know. I just mean to be a disagreeable corpse." Senlin glanced back at her and was shocked to see her eyes were as red as the rising sun, and just as uncomfortable to gaze into. He wondered again what had happened to her. Whatever the nature of the misfortune that had driven her to such desperate ends, he felt a searing guilt for having been absent when she needed him most. At least he could be certain that he would never abandon her again.

Leveling his sidearm down the hall, he took aim at the wretch's unreachable heart and shifted his finger to the trigger.

Something tickled his ear, and he recoiled to one side. Craning about, he found the culprit: the loose threads of a torn curtain brushed the top of his shoulder. He looked up.

The bolt of lightning that crashed down from above struck the receded lamp beside Delyth's dome. The crystal shade exploded with a flash, spraying her inky carriage with shrapnel and molten glass. A second fizzing barb of electricity fried the carpet at the chimera's feet; a third narrowly jagged over her head. Delyth turned and fled as the lightning continued to seethe down around her.

Iren peered from the open doorway high above them, still gripping the wand of a lightning caster. "Grab the rope!" she shouted, before resuming her sporadic fire at the fleeing spider.

Holstering his pistol, Senlin grasped the fringed end of the drape that slapped at his cheek, the last strip in a knotted chain that swung from the entrance of the Sphinx's workshop. With his nose pressed close to it, he recognized the woven features of a hod, bent under a great stook of wheat.

He was about to tell Voleta to grab hold of the riven tapestry when she scrambled up his back, stepped lightly upon the crown of his head, and began rapidly pulling herself, arm over arm, up the makeshift rope.

Iren bellowed over her shoulder the word *pull*, and Senlin felt a jerk in his shoulders as his feet left the floor.

As Senlin twisted like a barber's pole and bounced upon the wall, his ascent was celebrated by the arrival of gunfire. The plaster by his ear burst, stinging his skin with ejecta. When his spinning brought him around again, he saw Thornton ducking out of the elevator once more to fire on him with his pistols. A blaze of energy from Iren's barrel sent him ducking behind a doorjamb before he could get off another shot.

Hands wrapped around his wrists and hauled him over the sill of the Sphinx's vault. Dizzy and abuzz with the exhilaration of his ascent and his survival, Senlin felt a great muddle of emotions: delight at the sight of Iren; wonder at the whoomph and crack of her lightning caster; melancholy at the sight of the Sphinx's subdued workshop where, not a month prior, he had refused her offer of a quick reunion with his wife rather than abandon his friends. Then he saw who had pulled him up.

He hugged Edith as if she were the mast of a storm-thrown ship.

Though the nature of the storm would not let him linger for long. She prized him away from her and held him at arm's length to examine him, head to foot. "Are you hurt?"

"Incredibly, no. I don't think I am. But Voleta—"

Edith cut him off. "Good, because we need to hurry. Iren, seal up the h—"

Iren flung herself from the open door, flattening the pair of them ahead of a bombardment that tore the air above their heads. The gunfire shredded the top shelves on the far wall, atomizing a set of glazed vases, an alabaster pestle, the bust of a young boy, the death mask of a composer, and a dozen other irreplaceable artifacts.

Senlin rolled onto his stomach and laced his fingers together to shield the back of his head. Glancing to either side, he saw that Edith and Iren had done much the same. Voleta crouched ahead of them with her fingers in her ears, her cheeks balled tight under her eyes, and her jaw clenched.

When the torrent finally broke, Iren said, "Reinforcements. A big black knight."

"Mr. Grudge," Senlin said. "He has a cannon up his sleeve."

They heard the groan of the elevating corridor and knew it wouldn't be long before their adversaries were through the door.

"I'll lock us in," Iren said, but even as she thought to return to the hatch, a second onslaught drove her back again.

"Make for the attic!" Edith shouted over the bedlam.

They crawled on their stomachs. Snaking around the furniture, sliding over the fresh shards of antiquity, they did their best to ignore the fact that the devastation that wracked the Sphinx's shelves was slowly descending as the corridor lifted the artillery to their level. The leather-clad tomes of the middle shelves were reduced to pulp by a single pass of Gedge's gun. Pages flitted about them, piling upon the ground like the petals of a cherry tree.

Voleta reached the foot of the stairs first. She scrambled through the open door and up the coiled steps where Mr. Grudge's bullets could not reach. Senlin followed, his nails grating upon the timeworn treads, then turned to see Iren and Edith charging up behind him, shoulder to shoulder, their heads ducked as a chorus of bullets pocked the outer wall of the well.

They climbed on slowly enough to catch their breath. Though Voleta and Senlin initially led their party, Edith soon tapped Voleta on the shoulder and asked her to swap places. Before relinquishing her spot, and while she stood nose to nose with Edith, Voleta asked, "Did you find her? Did you find the Sphinx?"

"Yes."

"Well? Is she all right? Where is she?"

"Precisely where she wishes to be. I need to talk to Tom."

Voleta scowled, but it seemed an expression born out of worry rather than sedition. She surrendered her step, and Edith clambered up beside Senlin.

He suffered a sudden foreboding, a premonition that she was about to confess something terribly intimate, compelled either by the direness of the situation or encouraged by the last message he had sent her, in which he had confessed his tumultuous feelings, believing as he had that Marya was happily ensconced in a new life. But much had changed, and he found that he was afraid of what she would say, afraid of how he would answer, huddled there in the intimate corkscrew of a stairwell with death at their heels.

She said, "How many are there?"

He cocked his chin in surprise. "I'm sorry?"

"Marat. How many men does he have? How many survived the trip?"

"I, uh...I..." he said, floundering with her unexpected, though entirely predictable, question. He was glad it was dim where they stood so she could not see him blush at his own melodrama. "There are four others beside Marat. All Wakemen. Very dangerous."

"All right. The stairs should slow them down a bit, I think. Let's go."

"Edith, I just want to say—"

"It's not the time, Tom." Her expression was as opaque as a sealed envelope. Even when they had conversed through walls, he had not felt as shut out as he did now. Though of course she was right; she was behaving as a leader should and projecting the sort of poise that he had always found difficult to affect outside of a classroom.

He smiled bravely and said, "Aye, Captain."

The sound of descending footsteps snapped his head around. Polished boots preceded a pair of forest-green trousers, followed by an unbuttoned shirt and a green jacket of a military uniform like the one Voleta and Iren wore. Then Senlin saw the thin, frog-like smile and blazing eyes.

Senlin had drawn his pistol and fired before Edith could get out a word. The shot caught the Red Hand in the arm and spun him about. Senlin cocked the pistol's hammer to send a second slug into his back when Edith wrenched the weapon away with her engine.

Senlin was astounded, a surprise that was compounded by the outraged look Voleta gave him as she squeezed between them to attend to the Red Hand. Voleta pressed her hand to his wound.

Edith turned the pistol's grip toward Senlin, but held the pistol fast, apparently waiting for him to prove to her that he understood and accepted what she said next: "He's with us, Tom. He's part of my crew. You've missed a few developments."

"I didn't think you were the sort of man to shoot first, Mr. Senlin," Voleta huffed at him, as the injured assassin blinked his eyes and moistened his lips with a tongue that seemed too large.

With his hand resting upon his confiscated pistol, Senlin said, "But it's the Red Hand! He tried to kill me. He tried to kill all of us!"

"A completely understandable and justifiable reaction," the Red Hand said, feeling along the back of his arm. "Oh, good. It went right through. See! No harm done."

"*No harm d—*" Senlin began with incredulous ire before Edith cut him off.

Edith said, "Later, Tom. We need to hurry. The ship's anchored in a bad spot, and Marya and Olivet are aboard." The revelation put a seal on all of Senlin's questions. He nodded, and she finally relinquished her grip upon his pistol.

Voleta put the Red Hand's uninjured arm over her neck to help him up the stairs, though he hardly seemed to require the assistance. Senlin's bullet had apparently been as bothersome as a bee sting.

Iren clapped Senlin on the back and said, "Don't feel bad. I threw a cart at his head when I first saw him. At least you didn't miss."

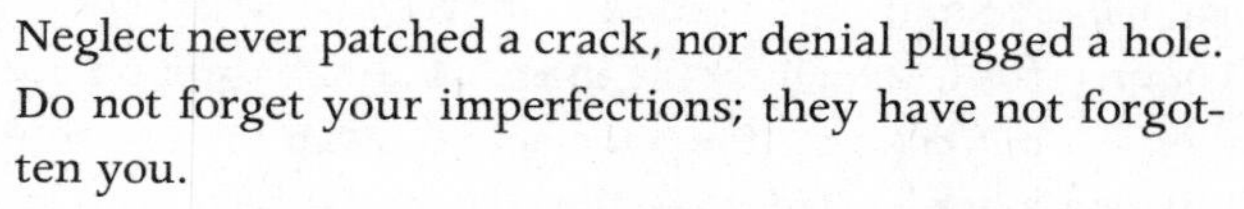

Chapter Fourteen

Neglect never patched a crack, nor denial plugged a hole. Do not forget your imperfections; they have not forgotten you.

—*Everyman's Guide to the Tower of Babel*, II. VII

With the door to the attic in view, Senlin became aware of the riotous commotion that lay before them. The madrigal of heavy machinery, like a factory in full swing, broadcast its lumbering tempo through both air and floor. At first, he presumed the others would know the cause of the clamor, but they seemed just as uneasy as him, all except Reddleman, who smiled with his hand upon the shut door of the attic, giddy as a parent unveiling a birthday surprise.

"My suspicions were correct, Captain. The noises I'd heard were not coming from the reservoir." With that, Reddleman pushed open the door, revealing a voluminous spotlighted gallery. A colonnade of stately pillars with capitals like overflowing jardinieres held up a darkened vaulted ceiling. A score of exhibition stages stood in the recesses between columns, their perimeters outlined by swooping velvet ropes and brass stanchions. At first, the space reminded Senlin of summer break during his years at university when he would retreat to the cool of the natural history museum to marvel at the posed dioramas and quibble with the grammar of the explicatory plaques. The Sphinx's attic might've seemed such a refuge had it not been for the milling passage of more than a dozen iron-sided beasts.

"It seems our slumbering cousins slumber no more," Reddleman said.

The engines roved the great hall on wheels, hooves, and treads that cracked the polished marble and tore up the railed carpets. The smallest automaton had the girth of a hippopotamus; the largest would've strained the rafters of a barn. Each seemed an unlikely pastiche of animal and machine. Most were horned with the armaments of industry: threshers, grinders, augers, and plows. The nearest behemoth, big as a covered wagon, was plated like a pill bug, and just as apparently headless. Its numerous stout legs pushed a shovel that was wide enough to grade a country road, though at the moment, it only ground against one of the gallery's stout pillars. After a moment of straining and slipping, the mammoth wood louse backed up to the edge of its abandoned stage, then repeated the hopeless operation once more.

Crowding with his former crew about the entrance, Senlin asked, "Are they dangerous?"

"I don't think they're malicious, but I wouldn't get in their way, if I were you." Edith raised her engine and groped the air as if testing the fingers of a new glove. "I'm surprised they're operational. The Sphinx said they had been decommissioned."

"Why?"

"Apparently, there were accidents. Inadvertent beheadings, that sort of thing."

"Accidents happen, I suppose." Senlin winced as the pill bug's broad scoop once again ground into the notch it had carved in the pillar's side. "What are you doing with your arm?"

Edith raised her iron hand a little higher. "Seeing if I can control them."

"And?"

She dropped her engine with a heavy sigh. "No. I'm afraid not. I can feel their presence, but I can't move them one way or another."

"Perhaps their minds are too primitive," Reddleman suggested gamely. Senlin edged a little farther away from the rehabilitated assassin.

The clock-faced scarecrow seemed to materialize from the shadows at Senlin's elbow, and he barked in surprise, though his fright was somewhat blunted by the boogeyman's features. They seemed to have been painted on by a youthful hand. The cheerful, if tuneless, quality of the automaton's voice sounded like an eloquent bicycle bell. "Good morning, Miss Adelia!"

"It's us again, Mr. Ekes. Miss Adelia's friends."

"I've poured the tea!" the scarecrow said, drawing something from his tattered pocket. Uncurling his hand, they saw the empty glass vials that rolled in the cradle of his tarnished palm.

"Yes, we see that you have, Mr. Ekes. My friends and I need to get to the lift on the far side of the hall. Do you think you could escort us?"

"Good morning!" he said again.

Iren, who stood poised with her ear to the open door, said, "They're on the stairs."

"Right. Mr. Ekes, the unexpected guests are right behind us. Let's not make them too comfortable."

"No, miss."

"Very good." Clapping the dusty footman on his high, thin shoulder, Edith then looked to the rest of them. "Stay close, stay low, and try to keep away from the exhibits."

They waited until the shovel-nosed wood louse crashed again into the pillar before snaking in a tight line around its back. Once on its far side, they discovered just how many of the other engines appeared to be caught in similarly unproductive loops. They turned in circles, and bumped against walls, and collided together, all heedless as sleepwalkers and subtle as train wrecks, but predictable, at least.

Or nearly so. A few of the engines appeared more aloof than the rest; they lurked on the periphery, though Senlin couldn't say whether this was out of inability, an abundance of restraint, or the anticipation of some as-yet ungiven signal. Whatever the cause, it was the engines that loomed just outside of the pools of yellow light that made him the most uneasy.

Their progress was necessarily halting. It was like navigating a crowded gymnasium. They ducked under the swinging claw of a crane that dangled from a lattice boom molded to resemble a giraffe's neck. They skirted the circular brushes of a goat-headed street sweeper that called to mind a siege engine. They were in the midst of darting through the slowly scissoring legs of a mortar-splattered, gargantuan stick bug when they heard Mr. Ekes's unmistakable warble in the distance behind them.

Peering through the crossing traffic of the Sphinx's relics, Senlin saw the spangle of Marat's armor and the bleak crest of Mr. Gedge's golem. At their backs, Thornton and Delyth pulled on Cael, who appeared momentarily wedged in the entrance.

Standing in the zealot's way, the Sphinx's original footman seemed as insubstantial as a reed before a sickle. Still, he bravely squared his stooped shoulders as he joyfully proclaimed, "Good morning, unexpected guests. Miss Adelia invites you to bog off!"

Marat raised his sword and, with a casual swat, struck Mr. Ekes's head from his thin neck. The footman's headless trunk toppled and clattered like a broomstick upon the floor.

Mr. Grudge stepped forward, and because the shoveling armadillo was reversing into his path, he hiked up his leg, set it to the engine's rear quarter, and shoved the tractor out of its rutted track. When the steam shovel marched forward again, it missed the column and proceeded to a back corner of the gallery. Satisfied with the space he'd cleared, Gedge again cracked his gauntlet back, exposing the six dead eyes of his infernal gun.

Edith shouted, "Scatter!" and they broke apart even as a renewed frenzy of bullets scorched the air about them.

Since the willowy legs of the mortar bug afforded little cover, Senlin doubled over and dashed for the pilothouse of the crane they'd recently cleared. Taking refuge behind the crane's chain track, he was surprised to find Voleta had followed close on his heels. He looked about for signs of the others. The side of Iren's face was just visible from behind a column on one side of the hall; on the other, Edith and Reddleman appeared to be pinned down behind one of the vacant platforms. Exposing only her gun, Edith emptied her pistol in a series of blind shots, an effort that only earned her Gedge's undivided attention. He focused his fire upon her stage, cratering its expanse and striking up a storm of splinters. Thornton took advantage of Gedge's bulk to screen himself as he rattled off shots at Iren's column.

Senlin had to speak loudly and near Voleta's ear to overcome the din of gunfire when he said, "Don't let Mr. Gedge's armor fool you. He's clumsy and slow. If we can get him on his back, he won't be quick to get up." He looked up at the turning arm of the crane and the four-fingered claw it swung in an endless lazy circle. They had to duck to keep from being struck by the corner of the turning cabin and the narrow walkway that encompassed it. Though the crane's arm moved slowly, Senlin was sure the weight of its anchor would compensate for the sloth of its stroke. "If we can entice him toward us, I think we can knock him over with the crane's claw. We just need some sort of lure to—"

He was interrupted by a sharp twang, followed by a crash and a tumbling of metal as one of Gedge's errant rounds severed the steel cable that held the crane's grab. The heavy claw clattered and bounced along the stone floor.

"So much for that idea," Senlin said.

"It's still a good plan, Mr. Senlin," Voleta said. "You get him close enough, and I'll ring his bell." Not waiting for an answer that would've initiated a debate, Voleta scrambled up the side of the cabin and onto the crane's arm where she was scarcely protected by shadows and the skeletal lattice that crisscrossed the boom. Realizing that if she were noticed, she would be an easy target, Senlin gathered his courage, gripped the lip of the passing walkway, and pulled himself onto the skirt of the spinning cabin.

He ran along the narrow catwalk in sympathy with the crane's rotation. He imagined that when he popped out into the open, he must've looked like a tin duck in a shooting gallery. His appearance was so unexpected that it took Mr. Gedge and Thornton a moment to swing their barrels in his direction. By the time they had, he had completed his half circuit and was safely behind the cabin again. It was only then that it dawned upon him that the upper half of the unoccupied wheelhouse was composed almost entirely of windows, a revelation that was almost immediately followed by a sleet of broken glass.

He ducked under the partition and hunched his back against the shards that pelted him. The steel of the cabin walls pimpled with the arrival of Gedge's salvo, an intrusion that was so frightening, Senlin forgot for a moment that the crane was still spinning until he drifted back around into the line of fire. Knowing there'd be no time to run around the maypole again, Senlin threw himself over the front fender of the crane, rolled through an unpaned window, and fell into the empty cabin just ahead of a surge of bullets. He crouched low and panted among the broken glass as Mr. Grudge punished every side of the house.

Taking off his white jacket, he waited for a pause in the gunfire to wave it overhead, then he stood, with hands raised and shoulders shrugged up to his ears. "Truce! Truce. I've obviously picked the wrong side of this little kerfuffle. I would like to surrender."

Creaking like an old gate, Mr. Gedge twisted at the waist and turned his head to consult with the zealot. In answer to the unspoken question, Marat gave a brief, small frown. The black knight faced forward again, dropping his still-smoking cannon as he did.

"I accept your surrender, Hodder Tom. Here is my dove of peace!" Mr. Grudge lumbered forward, raising his ghastly halberd like a javelin. When the pole left his hand, Senlin hadn't time to duck or fall backward. All he could do was turn his shoulder. The twin prongs of the flat blade slid by quick as a spark from a flint. One inch closer, and the halberd would've pruned his necktie; a second inch, and it would've pruned his throat. As it was, Gedge's poleaxe entered through one window and fled out another, cutting naught but a draft along the way.

Framed by the window of his fierce visor, Gedge's expression of surprise made him look like the jester in a puppet show. Senlin could not help but smirk. Then, out of the corner of his eye, he saw the swinging approach of the crane and the unusual pendant that dangled from the end of the frayed cable. Senlin shouted, "Since we're exchanging doves, here's mine."

Wheeling into view, Voleta swung her diamond bat at the black knight's head. Her club connected with the side of his helmet hard enough to turn it askew and make the golem lurch. The blow made Voleta spin like a top at the end of her line. As Thornton tried to draw a bead on her, Senlin drew his pistol and opened fire. His second shot ricocheted off Thornton's chest, forcing him to turn and shield his vulnerable face behind his bent back. Mr. Grudge collapsed in an awkward heap, making no effort to raise his hands to catch himself. Senlin doubted that the man inside was still conscious, a suspicion that was confirmed when the wood louse, returning from its corner, trampled over Mr. Grudge's splayed form, crushing and twisting his limbs.

Tangled between the engine's stout legs, the limp knight looked like a dead man being rolled up and down a beach by the surf.

Stepping out from behind the pillar, Iren once again summoned lightning to her hands. She had no doubt about her target. Now that the chattering cannon of the walking turret had been toppled, the greatest threat to their survival was perfectly clear in her mind.

The first bolt from her barrel shattered upon Delyth's glass egg, blowing her from her pointed feet. The second bolt caught the spider's cart mid-tumble. Sparks crazed over her chassis as the electricity followed the mazes of her plumbing. Delyth rolled onto her side, her legs curling over her smoking undercarriage like the fingers of a fist.

Iren was preparing to deliver a third shock to the mangled nightmare when she felt a sudden jerk at her back. The ribbons of light that fluted her wand flickered and died. She turned to find she was standing face-to-face with a hairless doll. The head swung on a neck that stretched into the shadows. The only other part of the machine that Iren could see was the scythe-like arm that staved the battery on her back.

As if lifted from a yardarm, Iren was carried from her feet by the straps of her pack. She felt for the buckle at her chest, undid it, and prepared herself for the fall to the floor. Then the monstrous engine flicked its mighty arm. She flew from her straps. The room began to somersault, turning into a carousel full of beaming lights and frightening beasts. Gravity seemed to have abandoned her, and she wondered for a moment if she would ever reach the peak of her flight or if she would just bump along the ceiling forever.

The arrival of the floor came as a terrible shock. Each organ and limb seemed to cry out in pain all at once as her forehead bounced twice upon the marble. She put her hands down to push herself up but found herself falling into darkness instead.

From Voleta's perspective, it looked as if Iren had been attacked by a compacted shadow. When she saw her friend flung through the air, she released the crane's cable and landed in a crouch nearly halfway to the pillar that Iren had lately been torn from. A pale elliptical face hung high in the darkness like a gibbous moon.

The engine that Edith had called Penelope ambled into the light, her massive front legs cocked up about her chin. The red lips and taw-like eyes of her face made the pose seem nearly demure, an impression that was quickly dispelled by the grisly serrations that ran down the length of her forelimbs. Iren's battery pack, still skewered upon the engine's talon, crackled and spat like water sprinkled on a hot pan.

Penelope twisted her vacant face down toward Voleta, cocking it this way and that. Recoiling from the inspection, Voleta said, "There, there, Penelope. You'll find no enemies here. No enemies at all, only fr—"

The towering mantis struck much as a tightrope snaps: quick and without warning.

After seeing Delyth humbled by lightning and his heavy artillery knocked unconscious by a young woman with a glass bat, Marat seemed prepared at last to enter the fray.

At a word, Thornton stopped trading potshots with Senlin and jogged after Cael, who was already making a beeline for Edith and Reddleman's position. Senlin thought to rally to their side, but as he climbed down from the cover of the pilothouse, he discovered that he was the target of the zealot's ire, and as such, would be of no use to anyone, least of all himself.

Marat steamed at him like a train rolling into a valley, and Senlin felt as one tied to the tracks.

Raising his sidearm, Senlin lined it up with Marat's chin and squeezed the trigger. The resulting impotent click seemed to reverberate with the same vigor of a gunshot. Senlin glowered at the traitorous instrument. It was an inconvenient time to realize he had no notion of how to reload the unfamiliar sidearm. Attempting to breach the pistol, he discovered it had no hinge along the top. He lost his hold on the now sweat-slicked pommel. The weapon leapt from his hand and clattered to the floor.

Marat drove his heel against the pistol as if it were a roach, and the firearm gave an equally small crunch of protest. "Oh, Tom," Marat sighed, and Senlin fumed at his all too familiar condescending lilt. "If you wish to turn around, I promise to make it quick."

Senlin composed a lighthearted smile. "Oh, I'm in no hurry."

"All the better." Marat hiked his leg and kicked Tom as if he were a stubborn door.

Senlin's lungs ejected every trace of air even as he found himself soaring through it. He bounced painfully upon the unforgiving teeth of the crane's chain tread, a collision that bleached his vision with splotches of white. Falling to his hands and knees, he crawled alongside the tracked wheels, breathless, thoughtless, and whipped along by the animal desire to escape the cause of his suffering.

The moment he cleared the crane's treads, Marat battered his ribs with a gilded instep. Though the kick seemed to toll every nerve in his body, Senlin knew the zealot must've held something back; otherwise, the blow would've caved in his chest. Luc was toying with him, taking his comeuppance in the crude currency of pain.

Even allayed, the force of the kick still sent Senlin rolling a dozen feet, a journey that emptied the cartridges from his pockets and strewed them across the floor. He came to a stop against a stanchion. In his agony, he found some small relief in stillness, and yet he knew he would be killed if he didn't get to his feet.

Using the brass post as a crutch to pull himself up, he rose to face his fate.

It was then, with pitted vision and empty lungs, that he suffered a moment of clarity. He was not defenseless. No, he was armed with the knowledge of Marat's flaws. Senlin understood that the trouble with insisting upon one's own perfection was that it prevented one from either addressing a flaw or effectively concealing it. As an egotist, Marat flaunted his own weaknesses—his farsightedness, his inability to turn about quickly, the slippery quality of the soles of his feet—and they, rather than his strengths, had become his defining characteristics.

Spying one of his cartridges rolling not far from the line of Marat's approach, Senlin steered the zealot toward it by scooting to one side. Marat corrected his path to track him, unsheathing his falchion as he did. Raising his blade over his shoulder, Marat prepared a high, off-balanced, overconfident stroke. Senlin bided his time until he knew he had passed into the fog of Marat's farsightedness. The zealot's foot shuffled against the unseen casing. Senlin lunged.

He did not spring at Marat, but rather to one side of him. Attempting to follow with the stroke of his sword, the zealot took a small, mincing step directly onto the brass jacket. His foot slipped backward, throwing him forward. The zealot staggered past Senlin into a velvet rope, which further hampered his attempts to stop his fall. Marat toppled to his hands and knees, his machete skittering away from him over the polished marble.

Senlin snatched up the stanchion and swung the weighted base at Marat's back, knocking him flat. Senlin then stamped the lead-footed pillar upon the filigree of Marat's spine, denting the armor and eliciting from Marat an insensible grunt. Like an irate clerk, Senlin again raised his brutal stamp over Marat's bare, unguarded nape, meaning to cancel the tyrant once and for all.

A tentacle wrapped about the stanchion in Senlin's hands and tore it from his grip.

He followed the unexpected seizure of his weapon as it flew over the crest of Delyth's crystal dome.

Behind the glass, Delyth's eyes blazed like a lit fuse. An unholy light seeped from the slits in her gauzy wrapper. Senlin had thought Iren's lightning had killed her. In fact, it had done the opposite. The sparking wand had been as a bellows to her coals; it had blown upon the fire in her veins.

Clawing at the wall of her terrarium, she came at him with no quarter, and he fled without hope.

Reddleman was somewhat surprised to discover that he was the only one having a wonderful time. Iren appeared to be semi-lucid and crawling about on the floor like a skink; Voleta was screaming and scurrying about to avoid the chopping arms of the two-story-tall mantis; and Edith was trading obscenities with the steel-plated sot. Meanwhile, Reddleman found that his cheeks had grown sore for smiling.

His glee was not born out of dispassion for his friends, or indifference to his own well-being, or ignorance of all those who depended upon their success. Rather, he felt, as he increasingly rarely did, abuzz with mortality and absolutely fixed to the present moment, with all its uncertainty, velocity, and pungency. The present seemed an intemperance far superior to the muffling warmth of wine or the Sphinx's medium. Though his natural wont was to study the cause of any phenomenon, he could not help but shun inquiry and revel in the moment instead.

He hadn't minded in the slightest when the titan had snatched away his field gun and pulled the barrels apart as easily as one might shuck an ear of corn. Nor had Reddleman flinched when his foe had snapped his rapier at the hilt with a hand that brought to mind the knuckle coupler of a train car. Even reduced to his last resort, Reddleman continued to radiate pleasure. He liked the simplicity of the leather awl: the bulb grip, the barb of steel, its sharp but not needlelike point. It was a perfect tool for probing a skull and severing the threads of that silvery web where the conscious mind hunkered like a house spider.

Leaping onto Cael's back, Reddleman bounded from one potbellied shoulder to the other, evading the titan's ponderous swats as he did. Reddleman tried to attack his rival's orifices, but each time he angled his awl toward the canal of Cael's ear or the corner of his rolling eye or a terror-flared nostril, he was forced to abandon his assault at the last moment to avoid having his bones reduced to jelly by the grip of an iron mitt.

Finally, Cael seemed to tire of the game. He brought both hands up at once, the pistons of his forearms grinding against his plated biceps. Reddleman slipped onto the Wakeman's broad back and pulled at the collar of his sleeveless shirt like the reins of a runaway horse. Protesting the sudden pressure on his throat, Cael staggered backward. Seeing the column that the titan reeled toward, Reddleman relinquished his hold, balled himself up, bounced upon the floor, and rolled between Cael's churning legs. Reddleman popped up again as Cael careened into the column.

Hacking for breath, his hands tugging at the collar that had raised a red welt across his throat, Cael fixed Reddleman with a murderous glare. In reply, Reddleman gave him a clipped round of applause like an audience admiring the work of a soloist amid a longer composition.

Then the medium flooded out from his spinal reservoir, summoned to his veins by the sudden activity. His senses fled one by one: auditory, olfactory, visual, until he was a disembodied thought diving into unfathomed time. It was a hasty plummet. The hall streaked with the traffic of ghosts from the past, then the columns shrank into the ground and the talcum of construction puffed all about him. The interior walls blew off and the sun beamed in as the ceiling opened. Then the floor fell away. Looking down, he observed the Tower's recession, leaving him stranded on the empty air. While day and night vacillated into an endless twilight, Reddleman watched the Tower deconstruct to its foundation. As it shriveled, the surrounding desert began to color with grass and scrub. Muddy streams fattened into glistening rivers that flowed toward a central blue lake. Treetops rolled down from the foothills: a green avalanche spreading to fill the valley.

Reddleman held up his hand as if to stroke the ancient forest, or fork the wind, or catch a single ray of the sun-moonlight. But the vibrancy of the view imparted him with no life, afforded no opportunity to influence even an atom of what he beheld. As a visitor to the past, everything was alive except himself.

Then, as he watched, his hand shriveled against the dusky quilt of pale stars. His bones shattered; blood seeped from the compacted mass of flesh. A distant pressure summoned him back to the present in a dizzying rush, and there, within the rebuilt museum, he saw Cael, holding him off his feet by his crushed hand and cocking back a fist to club him.

Reddleman felt the warmth of his own life run down his arm and could not suppress the smile that bunched his cheeks.

Edith knew better than to present Thornton with another sword to crack in half, and since neither of them had given the other a chance to reload their sidearms, they were left with no other option than to grapple out their grief. Her engine arm was stronger than either of his, but having only one, she was forced to expend it on her own defense. This left her flesh and blood hand free to attack, though with the relatively small, soft, and loathsome target of his head. Still, she managed to once again bloody the nose she had recently broken. He quickly repaid her with a haymaker punch. The blow only glanced her chin, but still succeeded in snapping her head around.

Taking advantage of her daze, Thornton lowered his shoulder to her hips, grasped her behind her knees, and flipped her onto her back. He scrambled on top of her, barred one forearm across her throat, and raised his fist, presumably to flatten her nose before he proceeded to iron out the rest of her. Wrapping her legs around his waist, she used that grip as leverage to knock his pinning arm away with her neck. Having shifted his weight, she hunched her back and spun in place, hooking one leg up behind his head. Pulling him into an armlock, she punished his ear with her free fist while he struggled to get his knees under him. When she could hold him no longer, she shoved him away and bid a scuttling retreat.

As she regained her feet, she saw from the corner of her eye Senlin rush past, head back and arms chugging. Delyth, who was very much alive, pursued him, her whiplike stinger slashing as his coattails. The fiend chased him through Penelope's writhing shadow. The mantis stabbed the ground with the scimitars of her forelegs while Voleta hopped about like a frog on a hot stone. Iren, meanwhile, was still dragging herself about and trying to recover from the rough landing of her brief flight. Everywhere Edith looked, she saw her crew in a state of desperation. A fact that made her present engagement with a fuming drunk all the more tiresome.

Thornton massaged his bloody ear and worked his jaw as if to retune his hearing. "Wasn't that your beau who just ran past? Delyth's been trying to get him in a corner for days. Looks like she'll finally get herself a taste of ol' Tom."

"I'm sure it was a nice change for her, having a man around."

Thornton squared his shoulders and twisted his toe upon the ground like a man squelching a cigarette. He lunged at her with murder in his eyes.

Falling backward, Edith brought up one foot, catching his chest. She grasped his wrists to direct him and let the energy of his assault carry him as she rocked onto her back. Hurled through the air, Thornton came down, bouncing and rolling like a tumbleweed along the heart of the colonnade. Barreling through a velvet rope stretched out like a finish line, he finally squealed to a stop, facedown and splayed out like a starfish.

He shook his head dazedly as he pushed himself up from the floor. His hand seemed to find the staff of Mr. Gedge's halberd the same instant Edith saw it. The discovery of the grim weapon appeared to reinvigorate him, and he sprang to his feet, wearing a gory, near-toothless grin. He presented the poleaxe as if he meant to joust with her, and said, "Let's try that again, you old drab."

Sighing at his apparent allergy to death, Edith drew her rapier. Rocking her weight onto her back leg with blade extended, she stood ready to receive him.

The flash of steel was so quick it seemed a silent streak of lightning, a phenomenon so brief, Edith at first doubted that it had even transpired.

Thornton's head rolled back over his shoulders, bowled down his spine, and cracked wetly upon the tile. His steel physique stood frozen in place, placid as a statue, and just as lifeless.

Crawling out from the shadows, Penelope dipped her vacant face to inspect her work. She probed the bare shoulders and spurting stump of the upright corpse with the point of one foreleg.

Edith found the vision so horrible and fascinating she did not notice that Voleta had stolen up beside her until the young woman whispered, "Come on, Captain. While Miss Penny is distracted, we should..."

As if harkening to her name, Penelope's neck curled in their direction, her bottomless glass eyes peering through them.

Gripping the sleeve of Edith's greatcoat, Voleta hissed, "Run!"

Chapter Fifteen

The ground is full of self-righteous bones, but we would do well to remember it is the cause, not the loss, that ennobles sacrifice.

—*Homage, Vol. II* by Jumet

Much like the lizard who, when gripped by the beak or claw of a predator, elects to leave its tail behind, Reddleman chose to shed his hand in deference of his life.

It had taken little more than a twist, a tug, and the will to do it. Then his wrist joint popped like a cork from a bottle, and he dropped onto his heels. The battering ram of Cael's fist roiled the air above him, and Reddleman watched the dark piston course past like a train on a trestle.

The lack of any resistance to his blow threw Cael off balance, and he stumbled forward even as Reddleman retreated. Jogging backward on the balls of his feet, holding the rough stump of his surrendered hand overhead, Reddleman shouted, "Come and get the other one, young man! Don't leave me with an orphaned pair."

His face curdled with unvarnished disgust, Cael lumbered after him.

Reddleman did not wish to risk another inopportune fugue while locked in combat, so he chose instead to lead his assailant on a foot chase, hoping that the burden of the titan's arms would sooner or later tire the beggar out. To keep Cael in pursuit, Reddleman risked an occasional close call. He let Cael nearly catch him by the toe when he vaulted the head of a clockwork hippopotamus, which resembled the gleeking fountains of the Baths; he narrowly ducked the thunderclap of Cael's paws as he slid under the carriage of a mechanical elephant with a shovel-like trunk; and when Cael dove low to relieve him of his knees, Reddleman sprang onto the square frame that boxed the drum of a steamroller.

Reddleman only discovered that the roller was active when the frame lurched beneath him. Reddleman looked up to find he had clambered onto the carriage of the ox-headed dynamo named Horace. The machine's spiked cylinder crunched across the polished floor, shattering it as readily as the shell of a hardboiled egg.

Cael snatched at his ankles, chasing Reddleman along the narrow lip of the frame. Reddleman had little choice but to cross the beam that barred the front of the engine. He teetered between the teeth of the drum on one side and the path of the crusher on the other. Horace's erratic path further complicated Reddleman's highwire act as the roller lurched from forward to reverse without warning or apparent provocation. The first time that the engine changed directions, Reddleman had to throw out one leg and thrash his arms to keep from falling under the ruthless wheel.

Still, Cael pursued him. The titan chugged after the drum when it retreated, and shuffled away when it advanced, chasing Reddleman back and forth along the girder with all the tenacity of a tomcat. As the mouse, Reddleman quickly soured on the game, and began to look for some means of escape. But the undercarriage of the bull that straddled the drum hung out of reach, and Reddleman had no doubt that if he tried to leap onto Cael's shoulders again, he would be caught and compacted into blood pudding.

Even as Reddleman hunted for some workable stratagem, his fate was decided by the capricious jury of coincidence.

Cael reached for Reddleman, forcing him to hop into the air. In the same instant, Horace's roller changed course and began churning forward, bringing Cael's fingers over the cleats of the drum. The titan might've snatched the hand back in time had not Reddleman landed on his knuckles. The pressure was enough to drive Cael's fingertips down between roller and frame. And as went his fingers, so followed his hand, his forearm, and his elbow in shrieking succession as Horace continued his advance. Not wishing to feed his bones to the wicked mill, Reddleman flung himself down Cael's back and landed ingloriously on the floor upon his rump.

Not for the first time, Reddleman marveled at how predisposed the species was to compounding misfortune with instinct. It was perfectly natural for the victim of a riptide to drown those who swam to their rescue, natural for the immolated soul to fan their own flames by attempting to outrun them. It was as if, having whetted oblivion's appetite, the human animal could not help but feed the abyss.

So it was with unthinking desperation that Cael braced his free hand against the drum to stop its progress. But rather than redeem his lost limb, he only succeeded in ensnaring his remaining arm. Chewing through iron bones and oily blood, it wasn't long until the gnashing wheel snapped at Cael's bare chin.

For a moment, it looked as if the Wakeman would be pulled through the vicious wringer, head to toe, but when the grinder reached the cauldron of Cael's shoulder, the engine stalled and ground to a shuddering halt.

Like a man held in a pillory, there was little Cael could do but hang his head and wait to be freed.

Tearing a long strip from the silk lining of his jacket, Reddleman tied a tourniquet around the wrist of his absent hand, stanching the flow of medium. Even as he tightened the knot with his teeth, he saw that the captain and Voleta, either through accident or intention, had succeeded in capturing the undivided attention of the colossal praying mantis. Her thorax, big as a longboat, swung back and forth as she pursued her quarry with singular determination.

"Excuse me." The melodious voice seemed to come from just behind Reddleman's ear, and the pilot turned in time to sheathe Marat's sword between his ribs. The zealot rammed his battered breastplate against the hilt of his falchion, until the handguard stapled Reddleman's lapel to his chest and the thick blade protruded from his back.

Hand reaching into his pocket, Reddleman grasped after the wooden bulb of the leather awl. But he wasn't given the chance to draw it out before Marat rammed him off his sword and swept his legs out from under him. Landing hard on his back, Reddleman soon felt the full weight of the zealot's feet as they cracked his sternum and split his skull.

The zealot forded his body as if it were a shallow brook.

As they scattered before the doll-headed behemoth, Edith became aware that she and Voleta were being herded, slowly but inexorably, into the corner of the museum, a place flush with shadow but short of cover. If Penelope pinned them there, the only egress left to them would be through an open grave.

Already, the mantis had corralled them between one bank of columns and the wall. Whenever either of them attempted to break out onto the museum's central avenue, Penelope sprang forward to cut them off with savage speed.

The moment one of the mantis's forelegs became briefly lodged in the fat trunk of a pillar, Edith pounced upon the exposed limb that was still encumbered with Iren's lanced and oozing battery pack. Edith got in three solid strokes on the captive elbow with the ham of her engine before Penelope wrenched her limb free of the pillar. The only evidence Edith saw of her attack was a dishearteningly small dent on the head of the hinge pin.

The distance that remained between them and the chamber's corner quickly evaporated. Edith was surprised when they passed the Sphinx's animal-headed footmen, posed in a solemn receiving line, near the wide mouth of the elevator lobby. Voleta yelled at her to duck, and Edith stooped just ahead of Penelope's passing scythe. The three footmen were not so nimble. The spider-eaters' shepherdess cut them down above the waist, and they came apart with a great complaint of rending steel, tearing fabric, and shattering bones.

Penelope's stroke cleared the line of sight, and Edith saw the Sphinx's corpse, slumped like a beggar, hands bowled in her lap.

If Edith had the chance to reconsider her hasty decision to defer Voleta's question about the Sphinx's fate, she would've told her the truth, would've better prepared the young woman for the shock she now faced without premonition, warning, or the consolation of a farewell.

The cry of heartbroken denial that leapt from Voleta's throat turned the hairs on Edith's arm stiff as quills. Even while caught in the shadow of the looming reaper, Voleta took a moment to scowl at her less than forthright captain.

All at once, Edith saw how covetous she had been of her bereavement. She had spared Voleta the terrible revelation of the Sphinx's death not only out of pity or expediency but also from the desire to be alone in her suffering, as if the mere act of sharing that loss could in some way rob her of the distinguishing burden. And hadn't that been the cause of the Sphinx's ruin—the conceited belief that she alone could bear the consequence of her choices, the weight of her secrets?

Suddenly, Edith felt overcharged with vying currents of emotions, passions that she had spent months adding to and tamping down, overfilling a heart that now leaked like an old wineskin. Shame and sorrow and longing and ire all swelled inside her. She felt as unsettled as the lightning sea. All it would take was one more drop of disappointment, just a single errant spark of self-doubt, and the lightning sea inside of her would...

Explode.

That was what happened when the medium was overcharged. It exploded.

Edith threw herself at the Sphinx even as Penelope's forelegs speared the remains of her fallen footmen. Scrambling after the Sphinx's lap, Edith saw the twin prongs of the tuning fork lying across her open hands as if in offering. She snatched up the wand with her engine, rolled onto her back, and pointed it as the monstrous Penelope reared on her hind legs, her face eclipsed by the spotlight behind her, the sabers of her hands pressed together, not in prayer, but in bloody contemplation. Edith willed the lightning to spill forth. The bolt jinked from the wand: a crackling, ragged cord of light. The thunderbolt broke upon the lightning caster's battery that braceleted Penelope's sickle.

An orb of molten color swelled out from the pack, expanding in spasms of wavering force. The air hissed with electricity, coating Edith's bare skin with a static charge that felt like warm oil.

Then the spectral bubble collapsed.

Falling upon a central point, the implosion bounced outward again with the incipient brilliance of a new star. The blast flattened Edith onto her back where she could only watch as the roiling light turned Penelope's upper body into a shadowy blob, a retinal stain.

Blinking the afterglow from her vision, Edith saw the top half of the Sphinx's shepherdess had been reduced to soot that now drifted down upon her like volcanic snow.

She sat up, leaning upon the elbow of her engine, and regarded the Sphinx's wand with a mixture of awe and sadness.

Voleta yelped the start of a warning that she did not get to finish before a golden toe swooped into Edith's view and kicked the instrument from her grasp. The Sphinx's wand flew, end over end, to be swallowed by the thick shadows beyond the final exhibits.

Luc Marat raised his heel over Edith's head, elbows out, teeth bared in a frenzied leer.

A chain hooped over his head and cinched about his neck.

Pressing her back against his for leverage, Iren bent forward, heaving the zealot from his feet. The great burden of his mechanical legs made the veins in her neck stand out as she wrenched the two ends of her chains.

From under his dangling legs, Edith saw what Iren could not; Marat's breastplate included a reinforcing band of armor at his throat. He was not as helpless as the amazon believed. Swinging his heel into the back of her knee, he caught her off guard. Iren tipped sideways, losing her grip on her chain as she fell to one knee. Marat came down on his feet again with a resounding clang.

Though Iren's attack had failed, she had succeeded at least in giving Edith enough time to scurry out from under Marat's shadow, though her relief was short-lived. Edith saw that she would not be able to rise to Iren's defense in time as the zealot brandished his barbarous knife over her where she knelt, propped up on one hand.

Voleta launched herself at Marat's back with a two-footed kick. The zealot staggered past Iren, narrowly avoiding joining her on the floor.

When he gathered himself and turned around, he was confronted by the three women who faced him as a wedge, Edith at the fore, rapier in hand.

Sheathing his sword, Marat rolled his visor from his head into the crook of one arm. He swiped the sweat from his shorn scalp and said, "Come now, Edith."

"Captain," Iren said.

Marat laughed. "All right. *Captain*. Haven't we sparred enough? Look at the mess we've made! Why are we ruining our own inheritance?"

"I'd be happy to accept your surrender on the Sphinx's behalf," Edith said.

"The Sphinx! Where *is* he hiding? Why won't he come out?"

"He only greets his guests. The miscreants he leaves to me."

"And what, exactly, is my offense?"

Voleta folded her arms. "We could do them alphabetically, or save time and just list the crimes you haven't committed."

The gold-shod varlet did not grace her with his attention. Instead, he spoke to Edith as if they were alone. "Are you not sick of living with so many questions? Are they not like ghosts? Do they not haunt your thoughts, night and day? How long can one be satisfied with riddles instead of answers, parables instead of plans? Aren't you tired of begging for meaning and purpose and—*perish* the thought—autonomy? Why do you serve a man who is happy to withhold the very thing that sustains you the moment you question him? We shouldn't have to subsist on crumbs. The answers are attainable. The prize is out in the open! There is no mystery! The convolution is the lie. I opened the Bridge of Babel and what was revealed? Another false door. Another charade. Another waste of time. I should have known better. We both should've."

As he bloviated, Edith straightened the yoke of her coat, flattened her collar, brushed her tails. Seeing it was her turn to speak, she said, "You talk about purpose and independence, but what you really mean is dominion over others. You don't wish to understand the Tower, you want to rule it."

"I only suggest that we claim the power that is within us. Why not enjoy our gifts? *Oh, but think of your responsibilities!* the Sphinx would say, *Think of the future!* Bah! The future is not so frail, nor is the Tower so fragile. The world is overripe! It would spoil in the hands of a timid sovereign. The Tower cries out for a confident king." A speculative simper pulled at the corners of his lips. "Or, if you like, a confident king *and* queen."

Edith rolled her eyes. "You wouldn't share a seesaw much less a throne." She advanced a step, and Marat retreated the same distance.

He bristled, his neck lengthening with the indignity of her refusal. "You would turn down half a kingdom out of, what, pettiness? Umbrage? Devotion to a dead icon and his aged disciples? Are you really so foolish?"

Voleta and Iren close at her back, Edith did not slow her approach. She pressed the zealot, and he continued to retreat. "You wish to be adored, attended to, and feared because you lack the courage to love, to serve, to protect. You aren't mighty. You are a trembling waif. You are a mewling child. And despite every opportunity, you have failed to grow, to develop empathy, to recognize the sacrifices others have made to help you. You have taken every gift that has ever been given to you as repayment for some imaginary debt. You think you could rule the Tower with your shortsightedness, your vanity, your cowardice? If I did not stand in service of the ringdoms, I would give you what you seek just to watch the Tower break your will and drain your life. The throne you reach for would be your gallows because you are not an emperor; you are a pretender."

As she berated him, they passed beneath the closer, brighter lights of the elevator lobby. Their footfalls became muffled as they crossed from stone onto carpet. The broad doors of the lift stood sealed at Marat's back, their polished surface enlarging his closing reflection.

A dull clatter and feverish scratching commandeered their attention. Looking to the end of the lobby, they saw the narrow entry to the changing room was under attack. The leper of the Silk Reef drove her carriage against the doorframe, again and again, searching for an angle that would grant her entry. The spearheads of her feet shredded the carpet about the door while her knife-tipped tentacle slashed at the space beyond. They heard a familiar yelp, a voice pitched somewhere between exasperation and horror. Delyth had cornered the headmaster in the changing room and was now so entirely absorbed by her effort to dislodge him that she was unaware of the notice she had attracted.

Though Edith had only glanced away, when she returned her attention to Marat, she found he had opened the doors and entered the lift. The zealot lurked at the back of the spacious car, wearing a grin like a growling hound. "You know, you sound like the Sphinx." Marat rolled his helmet back onto his head. "Let's see if you run and hide like him as well."

Edith reached out to hold the lift doors before speaking over her shoulder. "Help Tom. I'll handle this."

"Are you sure, Captain?" Iren asked.

"Utterly." Edith stepped onto the lift and let the doors close at her back.

Voleta watched as Iren's concern for the captain hardened into determination, a surety so intense that it manifested as calm. Her broad shoulders were low and loose as she stretched her neck and fanned out her fingers, all while observing the jarred wretch scramble wildly against the doorframe.

Iren took a single heavy step toward the unpleasant chore when Voleta reached out and grasped her arm. "Wait. What if we leveled the playing field a bit?"

"What'd you have in mind?"

Putting on a pinched, impish expression, Voleta hiked one thumb over her shoulder.

When Iren saw what Voleta was pointing at, she gave a terse laugh. "You can't be serious," she said, knowing full well that Voleta could be and most certainly was.

* * *

Senlin regretted allowing himself to be cornered by Delyth in what appeared to be a changing room for harbor seals. Dark rubber suits hung along one wall across from a row of slender lockers. Neither supplied him with any cover. A long bench split the room, providing ample opportunity to trip as he leapt back and forth to evade Delyth's vicious flail.

Delyth's efforts to wedge her carriage into the changing room left her an easy target, a fact that was sadly wasted upon an unarmed man. Already, he had hurled at her impenetrable bubble five rubber boots, seven gauntlets, and a pair of trousers. He'd thrown one of the brass helmets, as well, but after she batted it back and crowned him with his own missile, Senlin elected to stick to softer discouragements.

Not that he had an abundance of time to lob anything at the fiend amid her relentless picking. Her stiletto pursued him to the corners, slashed under his feet when he pulled himself up the visor shelf, and pierced his coat as he rolled under the bench. He flung open a locker door to fend her off and was disappointed when her blade cut through the steel panel as if it were crepe paper. He would've been skewered then and there had the knife's slightly wider base not knocked against the narrow gash.

While Delyth struggled to dislodge her stinger, Senlin scanned the contents of the locker. Its shelves were crowded with curious instruments that boasted crystal dials, copper antennae, the colorful facets of unlit lights, and every manner of knob and trigger. Each was a delicate marvel of engineering and machine tooling, and still he would happily have traded every last one of them for a club.

Delyth crashed against the doorframe with renewed vigor, shattering the plaster above the lintel and splitting the wood of one jamb nearly in half. Senlin felt a shock of despair as he watched his only defense begin to crumble, but then he beheld what was behind the latest ramming, or rather who was behind it.

Iren and Voleta sat piled together inside a crystal sphere carried along by eight gilded legs. Their clockwork arachnid held Delyth pinned against the open door, where her legs churned and scraped in protest.

Twisting at the waist but unable to bring her carriage about, Delyth threaded her tentacle between her legs. She attacked the forelimbs of the gilded spider, hacking one off at the knee in a matter of seconds to the obvious horror of the engine's occupants. Iren, sitting with knees drawn to her chin, fought Voleta for control of the steering throttle. The young woman slapped her hands away and hunched her shoulders to defend her territory. Their squabbling brought Delyth's attention to their vehicle's entry hatch, and she turned the point of her knife to the base that they both sat upon. Her blade pierced the steel between Iren's feet, and the startled amazon pressed up the side of the bubble in retreat, clutching Voleta to her ribs and leaving the controls unmanned.

Staring over her shoulder, Delyth had for the moment forgotten Senlin, and he seized the opportunity to ransack the rest of the lockers for some useful weapon. He found the fire axe hanging in the third cabinet he searched. Taking it, he twisted the handle as if to wind the cog of his courage. He charged the black rind of Delyth's armature, axe raised above his head, eyes locked upon his target: the root of the infernal tentacle. He swung with all his might. The brash knell of metal stung his ears as the wooden haft in his hands shuddered so violently it felt as if he'd been electrified.

Inside her glass bell, Delyth's head snapped about. Her narrowed eyes all but vanished amid the thatch of yellowed bandages.

Senlin looked down to find the head of his axe embedded in the frame beside the tentacle's base. He had missed the mark.

He rocked the handle to free the axe even as Delyth yawned about a voiceless scream and beat her fists upon the glass. Senlin heard the flinty rasp of her blade as it dragged through the blown-out carpets, across the exposed steel floor. It rolled out from under her carriage in a wave that whizzed past his ear. The knife point snapped the air behind him. Senlin swung the axe once more.

The tentacle fell lifeless, slapping the bench and flopping onto the floor as oil bled from the stump beneath the axe-head. Delyth spat upon her glass and drew a familiar anatomical figure.

Rather than feel insulted, her vulgarity only made Senlin feel depleted. His conscience ached with a sense of injustice, and he felt as he sometimes did upon meeting the parents of a classroom terror and discovering in the father or mother the forge of the child's anger, resentment, and violence. Bullies were cultivated, not born.

He touched the glass where her saliva ran, and said, "I don't want to do this. But I know you're not going to let me out of here. I'm sorry, Delyth. You deserved better. But there's somewhere I have to be; someone I have to meet."

Teeth gritted with resolve, Senlin raised the axe over the first of Delyth's legs and with a cry brought the hatchet down.

Blushing plasma licked down Edith's rapier as she drove its point into Marat's armpit, a spot that had been left exposed by another ambitious over-the-head stroke. Her sword found a nerve, and the zealot shouted in outrage and agony as his hand spasmed. The unlidded eye that embellished his breastplate seemed to stare in surprise rather than foreboding. His falchion clattered to the floor of the lift, having drawn from Edith not a single drop of blood.

At first, Edith had been nervous about fencing in such close quarters with the zealot, but both the size of the lift and its unsteady ascent worked in her favor. Marat's powerful hips were slow to turn, and his balance was readily unsettled by the car's lurching. She found it easy to get on his weak side, or even behind him. When she forced him into a corner, the reach of her rapier, being superior to his machete, gave her a welcome advantage. She probed the seams between the plates of his armor while he swatted behind each of her strikes. Becoming incensed, Marat's attacks had grown frenzied, obvious, qualities that only widened the windows for her ripostes. Before he dropped his sword, she had cut him twice more: once in the side, once upon the chin. And there was blood on his teeth from where she'd cracked his mouth with the crosspiece of her sword.

If they had remained in the car of the elevator among the feathery sprites of pink light, if she had only pressed him a little harder, pushed through his ribs in search of his lungs and heart, she might've won the fight.

Instead, she caught her breath and let him catch his.

The doors opened behind her upon the short spoke of a catwalk that connected the lift to the barren widow's walk. A shuttering violent flash in her periphery enticed her to look out over the depleted sea. She saw the naked pitted iron walls bowling up about them. A dark high-water line showed just how much of the medium had already drained away. What remained of the reservoir now coursed in a fiery halo around the lighthouse. Arcing bolts of energy leapt from the torrent like spawning fish.

Her distraction, though brief, proved more than sufficient. The sole of Marat's foot struck her flat on the chest, hurling her to the outer rail of the encircling walkway. The bars caught her roughly, unevenly, and her rapier flew from her grip and fell twirling into the lurid maelstrom below. When it touched the surface of the rough sea, it evaporated with a flare of light.

Edith was still trying to bring her head up when she heard Marat's pounding approach. The grated floor plates leapt and clapped beneath him. She rolled along the iron balustrade to one side just as his heel cratered the handrail, bending it nearly to the breaking point and loosening the welds that held the surrounding bars in place. Marat swung his arm out at her, his vambrace catching her on the jaw, the ear, filling her head with noise and searing pain. She reeled away from him, her legs failing to keep pace with her top half. Falling, she grasped the inner rail and pulled herself blindly along—forward, onward, away—realizing just how much of the advantage she had lost by exiting the lift. There was no getting behind him now, no skirting his attacks. He had her in an alley, and the range of his feet was far greater than the reach of her arm.

He stamped upon the edge of the grate she half crawled across. The floor plate bucked, cracking her on the chin and ending her tenuous upright progress. On her stomach now, she could only pull herself along, tears filling her eyes, turning the sparks that leapt from the drain at the foot of the lighthouse into bleary amoebas. She expected to be trampled, but she wished to face her end, to remind Marat of what he could not destroy: the will to resist.

Rolling onto her back, she found him looming over her. Sucking the blood and slaver from his cheeks, he tilted his head forward and spat a lavish glob upon her face. She did not flinch. He raised his heel over her head, and she met it with her engine, grasping the arch of his foot. The pressure she felt was inexorable, uncontestable. She tried to twist his foot away, to divert what she could not stop, but bracing himself on either handrail, Marat hunched over her and forced the iron knuckles of her hand down upon her face. Seeing he meant to cave in her head by her own hand, Edith clenched her jaw to keep from crying out. She felt as she had long ago riding her horse at a thundering clip through an impenetrable fog: the wild exhilaration, the utter terror, the unwillingness to ever stop until some lance jousted her from her saddle. What had life been for if not to charge upon the darkness, to show the unknown she was unafraid?

His weight abated all at once. Marat seemed to stumble off of her. He snorted strangely, like a man who'd swallowed a fly and was attempting to evict it from his throat. Edith listened to his arhythmic, uneven retreat as she swatted the tears from her eyes and beheld at last what encumbered him.

Reddleman sat on Marat's shoulders with his legs crossed under his chin. Her pilot's head was jacketed in blood, its shape elongated like an egg. One of his eyes bulged from its socket; the hand he held against the side of Marat's gilded visor was a gory stump. As mangled as his body was, his grin was as immaculate as ever. His teeth, each big and round as a fingernail, evoked a lunar sort of delight.

He held the bulb of his leather awl pressed against the corner of Marat's eye. A long tear of blood streamed down his cheek. The zealot stared vacantly upward as if marveling at heavens only he could see.

Reddleman whispered, "There, there. All quiet now, all calm. That's it. You're free, Luc. Gently, now. Gently."

Seized by some morbid spasm, Marat jerked backward. His thigh struck the guardrail, and it dipped under his weight. Realizing what was happening, Reddleman tried to abandon his doomed mount. He leapt from Marat's shoulder, even as the zealot toppled over the brink. Edith dove after him. Out of instinct Reddleman reached for her with his absent hand. He fell after Marat, the pair of them sharing a tumbling orbit.

When their bodies struck the frenzied, sunken sea, they shattered like lightning into ten thousand tangling sparks.

Lying on her stomach, arm still stretched out in offering to the void, Edith stared after her atomized pilot, disbelieving that he was gone.

She did not know how long she reached hopelessly after him, nor how long she watched the mesmerizing currents thin into bands, then ribbons, then threads as they shrank to a coronal ring that slipped into the lapping grates at the lighthouse's base. The darkness that descended upon the drained reservoir was only broken by the wan glow of the guide lights that haloed the beacon's peak.

When her crew found her, she was completing an inspection of her bones. She found many bruised, but none broken. She embraced each of her friends in turn, feeling at once numb and overly tender. Iren presented her with the sword they'd found abandoned in the elevator: the zealot's falchion. Paradoxically, it seemed smaller in her hand than it had in his.

Edith offered a brief and halting account of both the end of Marat's ambitions and Reddleman's noble death, news which seemed to pain Voleta more than the others. Edith consoled her, saying, "He saved my life, just as he saved yours. It's up to us now to make sure his sacrifice was worthwhile."

When Iren piloted the windscow back to the Fundament and Edith unlocked the heavy hatch with her arm, they surprised a young man wearing the uniform of the lumenguard. Leaning against one of the bare walls in the company of a lantern and a penny whistle, he swallowed his song with a startled trill of notes and quickly pocketed his instrument.

He'd been dispatched to wait for their return and guide them through the maze of halls and lifts back to the surface. Though none of them was particularly keen for such a long walk, they did what they could to lessen each other's burdens. Voleta wore Iren's chain belt like a sash to spare the bruises the first mate had accumulated on her hips and back. Though Edith could walk on her own, her collision with the handrail had stung a nerve in one of her legs, and so she found it agreeable to accept the offer when Senlin presented himself as a crutch.

Much like two people sharing an umbrella, their proximity necessitated conversation. While there seemed so much that needed to be said, Senlin knew this was not the time for gravity, so he opted for sincerity. "I haven't said thank you for the rescue. So, thank you."

She surprised him by laughing. It seemed an expression of exhaustion and relief rather than the belief he had said something funny. "Oh, this wasn't a rescue. You're my prisoner."

"Am I?" He adjusted his grip on her arm before they mounted a short flight of stairs.

"Naturally there'll be an interrogation."

"Naturally. But why don't we start with you?"

"Did you really think I was going to let you get away without listening to every excruciating detail of my recent adventures? No, no, Headmaster. I'm going to bore you until you beg for the plank. But first, we have to introduce you to your cellmates: your beautiful daughter and a long-suffering wife," she said, and Senlin smiled, feeling an upwelling of gratitude and joy he could not quite articulate. She continued, "Then, after all the tears and kisses have dried, I'll tell you about the time I kept the Tower from falling on its ear."

With exaggerated awe, he gasped and said, "Incredible! How'd you do it? What was your secret? Was it my hat?"

Edith chuckled. "The hat helped. But, to be honest, here's the trick: Whenever the Tower starts to lean one way or another, you have to go right to the source of the problem and straighten up the earth."

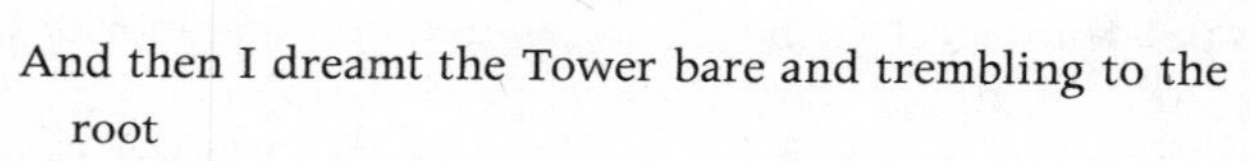

Chapter Sixteen

And then I dreamt the Tower bare and trembling to the root
As fall to winter's table bore a most peculiar fruit.
—*Music for Falling Down Stairs* by Jumet

They emerged from the cavernous underground to a city in turmoil. People ran through the streets, shouting in panic and gawping up as if in anticipation of a missile. The crystal bell that had for generations been quilted in an impenetrable fog was now unveiled. Naked blue sky blazed over the blades and braids of golden spires. Birds flocked about the limit of their sky, searching for escape but finding none. The ground continued to rumble like a train on rough track. Leaves shivered on ancient trees; fruit fell from loaded vines.

Senlin might've been rooted to the glistering street by his awe had not Edith been there to pull him on by the hand. Voleta announced that she was going to retrieve Adam, and Edith told her to hurry. They'd have to seal the western windstile soon. Voleta saluted, winked at Iren, and fled toward the pyramid that held aloft a beaming pyramidion.

They jogged in a pack, Senlin bouncing back and forth between Iren's and Edith's shoulders as they passed thriving gardens and stately trees. Children in fancy dress darted and scattered, chased by adults who bore expressions of grave concern and scarcely contained panic.

"Should we evacuate them? Bring aboard whoever we can fit?" Iren asked, between chugging breaths.

"No," Edith said. "We have to believe the Sphinx. She said we'd be in more danger out there on the verge than in here."

"What's happening?" Tom asked.

"I don't know. But I think the Brick Layer is finally getting his wish," Edith said.

They found the western windstile unguarded but shut. Even from some distance, they could see a figure was waving her arms and beating upon the glass beside the steel gatehouse, trying to get the attention of someone, anyone.

"Ann!" Iren shouted, and quickened her painful stride. Still several steps behind, Edith raised her engine arm, willing the hatch open. The doors of the vault swung wide. A coursing wind made the portal whistle. Ann rushed around to meet them at the end of the golden path. Dropping to one knee, Iren caught her and squeezed a little of the breath from her beloved's lungs even as she recovered her own. Iren kissed her like the waters of an oasis; kissed her as if no one could see.

Hands on his hips, Senlin gave Edith a look of happy surprise. He had so many questions but knew they would have to wait.

With apparent reluctance, Ann pulled herself back and, speaking over Iren's shoulder, said, "I came to fetch Marya. She took little Olivet for a walk about three hours—"

"She *what*?" Edith said, her face loosening with undisguised exasperation. "Who let her take a—No, never mind. Iren, escort Ann back to the ship, go to the bridge, get to the wheel. I expect we'll have to shove off in a hurry."

"But where's Voleta? Where's Reddleman?" Ann asked.

"Go!" Edith said sharply enough to discourage any further discussion. The two women fled through the short tunnel of the windstile. The skirts of Ann's dress whipped in the wind as they crossed the silver verge toward the ship, where it crouched upon a rug of red light.

Senlin turned and shouted Marya's name into the trembling city. He ran several paces down the road to where it forked and shouted once more in either direction. Turning, he was a little surprised to see that Edith still lingered on the threshold of the western gate. She was looking outward rather than inward. Senlin returned to her side and, believing he had discerned the cause of her hesitation, said, "Yes, of course, you're right. She'll come back this way, surely. Unless she's lost or... *but* if I go looking for her, and she returns, then we'll be no closer to getting everyone out." His voice shook with unexpected anxious laughter. "What we need, I suppose, is a good rope. You could hold one end of it, and I the other. You could give it a strong tug if Marya—"

"Tom. The mountains."

Looking past her, Senlin saw the peaks of the surrounding mountain range. They seemed to serrate the edge of the world like a knife.

Still gaping, he was about to ask what it was that she meant for him to observe, but then he saw: the mountains were shrinking.

No, the Tower was growing.

Senlin began to speak but found his breath knocked from his chest by the heel of her hand. He stumbled backward, tripped over the lintel of the hatch, and fell to his rump as the hatch swung shut with her on the other side of it.

He clambered to his feet, and in a state of utter confusion pressed his face to the bulging glass porthole in the center of the vault. When he saw Edith's expression—her tightened lips, the resolute line of her dark brows, the activity in her eyes—he understood her intent.

She raised her engine, made a fist, and rapped upon the steel three times. The gatehouse tolled with the familiar tattoo: hard, soft, hard. Senlin put his knuckles to the window and replayed the signal that spoke what could not be said, acknowledged what could not be expressed, forgave what could not be forgotten.

Then Edith turned and stepped into the strengthening gale with her hand on her hat and her engine on the zealot's sword.

Senlin grasped the arm of a man jogging the other way down the golden lane. Though Tom could not discern his rank, he marked him by his white-and-yellow uniform as someone in authority. Breathlessly, he said, "I need to find someone, a recent arrival. Can you help me, please?" Only then did Senlin take in the man's wide-eyed fear and relative youth, aspects that made his ability to recover some composure and answer Senlin's request all the more impressive.

"Yes, sir. There's a registry of immigrants posted outside the Cavaedium."

"The what?"

"Go that way. It's the only wooden structure; you can't miss it."

And indeed, the young soldier was correct. The Cavaedium's facade of unmilled logs looked as out of place among the spires of precious metal as a tree stump in a tearoom. All about the gloomy entrance, papers had been haphazardly posted with thumbtacks. The lined sheets held dozens of names in a variety of hands, most of which grew rougher and more slanted the farther down they went. Ignoring the unending tremble that made his knees grate and his teeth rattle, Senlin's gaze plunged down one page, then another, and another. He scoured the hurriedly assembled inventory with a growing sense of dread. What if she had slipped outside the crystal dome unseen? What if she was wandering along the brink of the ringdom, battered by a hurricane, clutching Olivet—lost and locked out?

The feeling of desperation that flooded his ears with blood, turning his heartbeat into a broadcast, reminded Senlin of when he'd first fawned at the foot of the Tower, combing the Lost and Found for a message, a hint, a hope where there was none to be had.

Then, there she was.

Her name rested upon his fingertip, lighter than an eyelash and heavier than the earth: Marya.

But Marya Senlin no longer. She had reverted to her maiden name of Berks.

Two names followed hers that he did not recognize, Kapal and Nia, and a street address, 4908 Peony Drive. This, he committed to memory before turning again to the meandering street. He was surprised to find it deserted. As Tom looked up, the color of the sky seemed to be darkening like the water under a boat as it leaves the sandy shelf of the harbor.

Hurrying to the nearest crossroads, he looked down each path, and seeing neither signpost nor person, he fled to the next intersection. There, rounding the corner of a yard, onto a street lined with domed dwellings, he saw a keg-chested man jogging at an exhausted, shuffling pace. Senlin chased after him, calling for him to stop. The man obliged, though perhaps only to catch his breath. The front of his uniform was undone, showing the sweat-thinned undershirt beneath. He had scant hair and an undershot jaw, but a kind light in his eyes.

"Ah, another immigrant, I presume. I'm Captain Dyre, and I would advise you to get indoors, sir. At least until this blows over. Whatever *this* is. If you haven't been assigned an abode, you can weather the storm in mine."

"I'm looking for someone," he said, and seeing that the captain would argue, hastened to add, "It's my wife and child. I have an address. Please, if this is to be the end, I'd like to spend it with them."

Apparently moved by Senlin's entreaty, the captain asked for the address, and Senlin quickly shared it. Scowling at the destination, which apparently lay some blocks away, Captain Dyre said they would need to find a bandy, whatever that was. The captain began scouting down the alleys between homes. It wasn't long before he spotted an abandoned horseless chariot idling in a garden alley. Ushering Senlin aboard, Dyre recommended that his passenger avail himself of the handrail before engaging the bandy's throttle and backing them roughly over the curb and onto the street. The spoked wheels chirped upon the golden cobble as they raced deeper into the curving streets of the shuddering neighborhood.

The restless ground made their journey feel longer than it was. The chariot rocked upon its struts and skidded about corners, and even so, the time it took them to reach 4908 Peony Drive seemed entirely insufficient for Senlin to compose his thoughts. He'd made such a bungle of their last reunion, but apparently had learned nothing because now he couldn't imagine a single fitting phrase. He wasn't even sure whether a physical greeting of any sort would be appropriate or indeed welcome.

And so, when he found himself approaching the doorstep of a strange home with Captain Dyre's bandy already retreating down the street behind him and the world rumbling toward destruction beneath him, Senlin concluded that no plan, nor script, nor rehearsal of this moment would be sufficient. He would have to speak from what he had spent so long arraigning: his bloody heart.

Even as he knocked, he heard a commotion of voices inside: a woman, children, a crying infant. The door flew open with a crescendo of complaints, and her face turned away as she said over a pair of protesting tots, "Shh-shh-shh, it's all right. It's all right. Just stay under the table. Kapal, hold your sister's hand, please!"

Her unpinned hair was as colorful as autumn. A small fist held a lock of it. The infant's face that perched upon her shoulder was pink from bawling, though her cries broke the instant she saw him, or whatever shape he cast in her still-forming vision. Senlin was not vain enough to think she knew him as her father. To her, he was just a shadow, indistinct and novel.

Marya turned and blinked. The fright that had seemed to possess her expression and voice a moment before was replaced now by wonder, or perhaps only uncertainty.

"She's beautiful," Senlin said.

Marya cast her free arm over his shoulder, hooked him, and pulled him in. With Olivet held between them like a shared heart, she pressed her cheek to his cheek, and he warmed her temple with his tears.

In a voice made hoarse by emotion, he said, "I wandered so far from you. I've been so lost. I thought I'd never find my way back again."

While Olivet burbled between them, Marya whispered beside his ear, "I told you, Tom. I told you this is where we'd rendezvous—top of it all, end of the world."

Aboard the *State of Art*, Edith had just put her foot onto a crowded bridge when the floor pitched toward the bow and her ship's hull rang, first with the boom of a collision and then the scraping of metal as the prow continued to drag upon the crowning ringdom's wide brim.

At the pilot's yoke, Iren's shoulders were fairly balled about her ears with the effort of righting the ship. A pair of alarms rang with competing songs. Finn Goll, who was strapped in beside Iren and looking rather iffy, asked what all the racket was, and Byron, who was belted in beside him, answered for the preoccupied amazon. "They're proximity and collision alarms."

"Bit like ringing the doorbell on your way out, isn't it?"

Stalking with a wide stance toward her captain's chair, Edith was about to ask why they were bumping the bottom when John Tarrou from the gunner's station shouted, "Tree! Tree!" as he pointed at the trunk of a silver antenna that loomed larger in the forward magnovisor frame.

"I see it!" Iren barked back, turning sharply to avoid the post. The maneuver brought the aft down, and it dug into the ground. Like a carriage fishtailing on a patch of ice, they yawed into the post, flattening it with their starboard side, a blow that sent Edith stumbling back the way she'd come and nearly out the hatchway again.

"The ground's rising!" Edith shouted.

Iren gritted her teeth as she wrestled with the horns of the ship. "I know! I'm trying to get her nose up."

"Don't! It's climbing too quickly. We can't outpace it. We're a fly riding a swatter. Keep her level. Full speed ahead, Mister Iren." Edith stamped back to her chair. "How long until we're clear?"

"One hundred and twenty feet and closing, Captain," Byron said.

Edith scanned the magnovisors. The mountains had been entirely eclipsed by the limn of the rising disc, which now seemed just a silver horizon shelving an indigo sky.

The squeal of metal on metal returned as the keel of the ship contacted the ground, not at one point or another, but along its entire length. They rasped across the surface like a blade on a whetstone. Edith could feel their momentum dwindling even as the sky about them continued to darken. If the ship ran aground here, she wondered if there'd be any chance of rescue or if they would languish there forever, a barnacle on the hull of the Brick Layer's launch.

They were too close to the edge to even see the brink when the ship at last ground to a halt. They were pinned. Nebos's ascent was too quick for their engines.

Iren unstrapped herself from her pilot's seat and bounded to the gunner's station where Tarrou sat gripping his harness and looking rather cadaverous. "Trade with me," she said, and the two quickly swapped seats. Iren began plying the bank of switches even as she explained her intention. "Permission to fire the rear cannons with the sled locks on, Captain. It'll ruin the guns, but the recoil should give us a little push."

"Do it," Edith said.

The boom of the four aft guns made the ship ring as if it had received rather than launched the barrage. Though the ship seemed to shift a little, the only change to their view was the addition of stars, which had begun to appear in the sky's darkening bowl.

Iren said, "Reloading. Aft cannons two and three not responding. Firing." The second volley was fainter than the first, but again the ship shook. Outside, a grinning moon came into view. "Reloading. Cannons two, three, and four not responding. Firing." The final blast seemed a scant echo of the first. A thin shiver passed through the bulkhead. Outside, the stars blinked like the lights of a city out of reach. An entombing silence gripped them.

Then metal groaned and the ship pitched forward, levering upon the ringdom's stark edge. The mountain peaks rose again within the magnovisor screens. The foothills followed, then the desert and the bazaar as the ship slipped from its fulcrum and began to plummet to the earth below.

Iren, who'd not finished clasping her harness, was nearly flung from her station. She caught herself by one strap. Even as she struggled to re-secure herself, she said, "John, pull the horns. Pull!"

As Tarrou hauled the yoke back, what was a tumble became a slope that soon leveled into a coast.

From the navigator's seat, Ann pointed at the frame that showed the view behind them. An object loomed over the Tower. "My god, what is it?"

Edith summoned her periscope and, wrenching it around, found Nebos, unmoored and floating in the sky. Its shape was reminiscent of the stopper of a decanter—round at the top and tapering to a point—and indeed, the Tower appeared to have been uncorked. The hull of the craft was far from smooth. The sinews of arcane ducts and dark plumbing swaddled the underside of the vessel, a bleakly coiling mass that was broken here and there by blue nodes of light and interrupted centrally by the presence of a great ring of red that was bright as molten iron poured into a mold. The city's crystal dome was no longer visible, but the silver rind of the ringdom seemed to beam down upon them like the coronet of a solar eclipse.

Without looking away from the hood of her scope, Edith said, "Mister Iren, take the helm. I mean to follow them, if we can."

"Aye, sir."

Then it was as if the Tower became a trumpet and the earth its trumpeter who blew a note from its murky core, a terrestrial fanfare that made them all grasp their ears and cinch their eyes and shrink in expectation of the inescapable fire to come.

But when the roar rumbled away, and the flames did not crash upon them, they opened their eyes to find that the floating head of the Tower had vanished, leaving nothing behind but a brief, inexplicable rain.

Still trembling on Marya's doorstep, Senlin feared that her phrase "end of the world" would prove eulogistic. And indeed, if this were the end, for the first time in a long time, he did not feel out of place.

Then all at once the quaking stopped and the character of the light changed entirely. Their embrace broke, and they wandered onto the lawn. Glancing either way down the lane, Senlin discovered they were not alone in their dazed exit or their shared relief that the ground had recovered its familiar fixedness. Though it was the sky that held everyone's attention: The heavens were utterly changed.

What had been clouds, then blue sky, then moon and stars had become a churning field of vibrant galaxies that seemed to gather, stretch, and traverse the dome like rain down a windowpane. Above them, stars scattered, gaseous tendrils reached and withdrew, whole worlds flew past like gnats.

And as they stood watching the ethereal kaleidoscope, a stronger light began to pale the darkness outside. The pyramidion dazzled more intently, its light glaring upon the dome to make a gauzy sort of sky. The passing stars outside turned ghostly in the artificial daylight, and so surrendered a little of their mesmerizing effect.

"What's happened?" Marya asked.

"I don't know. I think we just set sail."

"For where? And why us, why now?"

"I don't know. But look around us: homes, gardens, an artificial sun, everything we'd ever need for a long trip. I suspect we'll have time to puzzle out our questions while we're underway."

Olivet began to fuss at Marya's breast. "More time is good." Nia and Kapal had gathered in the kitchen behind them, their expressions wide and uncertain. Marya touched Senlin's rough cheek and smiled when she said, "Will you call on me tomorrow, or maybe in a few tomorrows? We need to talk, Tom. There are some things we need to say. But first, I need to think."

Smiling to hide his heartbreak, he said, "Yes, of course. Whatever you need. Yes, I... I shall call again later."

She closed the door on him softly, and still it felt sharp as the bang of a storm-blown shutter.

Senlin turned to face the street. A mechanical tortoise hummed along the edge of the lawn, clipping the grass with blades encased inside its shell. Something resembling a dragonfly, but large as a gull and scaled in chrome, passed overhead. The smell of ripening peaches struck him like an epiphany. How long had it been since he'd eaten a peach? He glanced around for the source. A horseless chariot rolled past, then a second. A chime like wedding bells rang through the city. He had the strangest sense that he had fallen into a nightmare that had softened into a dream.

On the stoop of the gilded igloo across the street, a white-haired woman in an evening dress with an ostrich feather boa around her thin neck gave him a tentative wave. Before her, a pair of young girls tumbled across the lawn, crawling through each other's legs and screeching with delight. The woman's dazed expression seemed to mirror his own.

Waving back, he said, "Hello. I don't suppose you happen to know the way to the nearest hotel?"

Chapter Seventeen

If mankind ever attempts to colonize the islands of the stars, we should crew the ships with children and put the youngest at the wheel.

—The *Stone Cloud*'s Logbook, Captain Tom Mudd

While the Tower still trembled, and the blue sky cleared, and his sister and the captain lingered underground, Adam had elected, against his own common sense and Runa's good counsel, to do a little reconnoitering.

The unlocked chamber set high in the side of the pyramid was possessed by an ambient purr like the drone of a conch shell pressed to the ear. It was the hum of blood that filled the air—the thrum of bottled life.

At first, Adam thought the cavity unlit, but when his eyes adjusted to the gloom, he saw the contours of four walls, rising to a common peak. Directly before him were the backs of a pair of unusual chairs, the shape of which reminded him of the trumpeting bloom of a calla lily. These floral seats attended a sloped panel whose surface was bathed in shadow. But it was what dominated the wall above this station, and indeed the entire room, that held Adam's eye the most. The enormous rose window, rayed with minutely leaded panes of inky glass, made him feel as if he were standing behind the grand dial of a clock tower.

Then he realized the room was not entirely without light. The floor, a seamless polished sheet of some unfamiliar material, shone dimly as tarnished silver.

Adam had expected to be greeted with the sour odor that usually accompanied a long shut-up room, but the air smelled as if it had been recently stirred by the passage of lightning and scrubbed by the ferns of a forest. It seemed not stale, but very new.

All of this, he observed from the threshold of the short corridor that connected the murky chamber to the floating stairs outside where his nerve had apparently abandoned him. He'd felt so eager to explore just a moment ago. Now, he was thinking of turning back.

He had asked Runa to wait for him at the foot of the steps. That way, if he failed to return in a reasonable amount of time, she could go for help. She had not liked the idea and had suggested instead that they wait for a moment of less frenzy, a time when others could go with him and some safety measures could be arranged. But Adam had felt compelled to take a look. What if the means for ending the ongoing earthquake lay inside this open tomb? What if they had unsealed their salvation just in time? Surely they could not ignore such an opportune invitation.

So he had surmounted the steps alone, had turned the corner on the face of the pyramid and climbed on while the city bucked and the birds flocked. He climbed without rail to lean on or ledge to grip, climbed until he was level with the neighboring spires and the entrance to the crypt was at last in reach.

And there, his courage had faltered.

Caught in the vestibule, his pride pressed him to enter, but what remained of his reason held him back. What if it was a trap? What if he stepped inside, and the vault gobbled him up? What if the Brick Layer's golden shrine craved some human sacrifice?

A voice, near as the hairs on his neck, said, "Adam?"

With a yawp of surprise, he turned to find his sister silhouetted by the light of the pyramidion outside. "Voleta! What are you—"

She banded her arms about his chest and buried her head into his neck. He stood, elbows raised like a man wading through high water, utterly surprised by her embrace and the insistence of the hold. She hadn't hugged him like that in years.

Softening his posture, he squeezed her tight and said, "Are you all right?"

"No, I'm not. I'm all wrong! The Sphinx is dead. Reddleman, too."

Adam sighed and rocked her. Though he had not really known either the Sphinx or Reddleman, they were obviously important to his sister, and so he consoled her. "I'm sorry they're gone. It's awful to lose people, and terrible we've had so much practice at it."

"I missed you."

"I missed you, too. It hasn't been the same withou—" he began, but she interrupted him again.

"I'm sick of running off and being on my own. I'm tired of giving you every reason to think I don't care. Because I do care. I care loads, cartloads, trainloads. I love you."

"I know you do. And I love you, too. Always. Even when you smell like a wet shoe." He rubbed the shag of her hair playfully until she ducked away.

It was only then that she seemed to see the chamber beyond. "What's all this?"

"I don't know. It opened up when we laid the capstone."

"Then the Brick Layer must've wanted us to find it. The beacon certainly is bright enough. No wonder he called it the Wick of the Sun. But that looks like some sort of control station or—" She moved to enter the room, but he gripped her arm. "What is it?"

"It might be a trap."

She gave an incredulous smirk. "It's a little elaborate for a trap, isn't it?"

"Said the tourist who'd never been to the Tower before."

Voleta rounded her eyes. "Fair point. Well, I say we go in together or not at all. I'll leave it up to you which it is. It's your turn to choose."

He frowned, his suspicions roused by her deference. She gave a little bow and flourished her arm as if to say *after you*. He surveyed the chamber again, reconsidered its static murmur and the imposing window that seemed to look out upon a moonless night. Somehow it was less baleful with Voleta at his side.

"I suppose it would be a rather *extravagant* trap," he said, and she looked at him inquiringly. He offered her his hand. She accepted it, and together they stepped into the vault.

They passed through a static curtain, similar to the ones that protected the Warren from curious insects. The prickling sensation abated as quickly as it came. All at once, the argentine glow of the floor brightened until it seemed they were traipsing upon solid light. Undaunted, they continued to advance until they stood behind the bloom-like translucent chairs set close to a bank of knobs, throttles, and buttons, each as intricately carved as a cameo, and all a uniform shade of ivory.

A ribbon of white ran up the darkened rose window like fire devouring a page. When it reached the peak of the circle, another illuminated band chased it, then a third. Crossing streams of color began to flow horizontally across the glass loom, adding weft to the warp of light until the circle blazed with a brash and evolving tartan.

Entranced, Adam had to blink to pull his gaze away. Turning his head, he found Voleta, mouth lolling and eyes locked upon the spectacle, slowly lowering herself into the petaled bowl of one chair. Seeing her comfortable slouching inspired him to join her, and he slid into the remaining seat. The glass was cool to the touch, the armrests comfortably sculpted. Settling in, he returned his attention to the kindled stained glass.

They were so enthralled, they scarcely noticed when the quake that had plagued the ringdom for hours came to an abrupt and placid end.

Gradually, the scramble of light resolved into a shape. At first, Adam thought it resembled the head of a pawn, then shoulders appeared beneath the neck, and he recognized the bust of a man. The vague figure appeared to lurk like a nervous father over a crib.

The myriad discrete scales of the rose window, which seemed capable only of projecting a single color at a time, fractured the figure's appearance like the ripples of a lake carve a reflection. And still, Adam recognized the pronounced ears, the smile-creased cheeks, and the enveloping gaze.

"The Brick Layer," he whispered almost with the same breath that Voleta spoke the words. They looked to each other to share their surprise and confusion. They would've conferred more had the Brick Layer's voice not arrested them. It possessed the air like the midnight gong of a grandfather clock.

"Welcome to the bridge of the *Nebos* of Port Babel. This is a Tussock Class vessel with a gross tonnage of three point five million and a maximum capacity of sixty-four thousand souls. The *Nebos*'s Nautilus drive has an operational lifespan of nine hundred and forty years and a flank speed of 13,470 leagues per second on the surface and 538,000 leagues per second submersed." The Brick Layer's features moved in sympathy with his speech, and yet the dreamy character of the stained glass made the two seem slightly out of sync. "You are presently submersed and cruising at standard. Your current position can be seen via the bridge's observation panes."

The darkened walls around them began to swarm with globs and pinwheels of light. Stars streaked all about them like embers blown from a fire. The riotous display, which was itself a marvel, was compounded by the revelation that this was not some pretty artifice; this was their present environment. They were sitting in the pilothouse of a ship that had shoved off from the shores of the earth into the unexplored depths of night.

Adam looked to Voleta and found her staring straight ahead though she held her fingers outstretched toward him. Her face streaked with the reflected glow of fleeting stars. He grasped her hand, feeling much as he had the day their train car rolled into the valley of the Tower. His heart thundered with wonder and unease. *The stars,* he thought, *we're sailing into the stars!*

"How is this possible?" he murmured.

Voleta took a breath as if to answer him, but then the Brick Layer's voice bled once again from the sieve beneath the rose window. "Your dominion over the operations of the *Nebos* will be limited during the voyage except in matters pertaining to the administration of passengers and crew, the management of resources, the monitoring of cargo, the maintenance of engines, and, if occasion requires, a response to emergencies, including but not limited to environmental collapse, collisions, and hostile encounters."

"Excuse me, sir." Adam's interruption passed unacknowledged, as the Brick Layer continued his somber oration that increasingly sounded like the reading of a will.

"These duties shall be carried out by the pilot and the navigator, here present and elected, offices which may only be vacated and transferred hereafter at the injunction of the Conservator. For reasons of security, only the pilot and the navigator shall be permitted access to the bridge and licensed to unlock certain sublevels. Decisions of the first order, such as emergency deviations from the determined course, shall require the presence of both officers to enact."

The heavy clap of metal brought their heads around. The shaft of light that connected them to the outside world had vanished. The tomb of the bridge had been sealed.

"Not a trap, she says," Adam murmured, squirming in his seat.

The Brick Layer continued: "Before we proceed further, the officers must be bonded to their stations." The stars that coursed about them disappeared at a stroke as the walls took on the subtle blush of a cloudless twilit sky. "Will the present and elected pilot and navigator please remove any gloves, socks, and shoes."

Adam leapt up from the glass lily and looked to Voleta, expecting her to follow. Instead, he found her pulling at the heel of one boot.

"What are you doing?" he asked with evident dismay.

"Oh, I'm baking a nice Bundt cake for the—what does it look like I'm doing? I'm taking off my shoes!" Voleta hurled the first boot to the floor before attacking the second.

"We can't do this! We can't accept whatever this is."

"I think it's very clear what this is. We're being promoted." Voleta pulled her socks off by the toe, a process that required an inordinate amount of tugging.

"Please remove any gloves, socks, and shoes."

The inflection of the phrase was the same as before, and yet it somehow sounded more impatient. "But we weren't elected! We just wandered in here."

"All right! But you heard him: We can fix that later. Have the Conservationist—"

"The *Conservator*."

"The *whatever*-tor sort it all out."

"Please remove any gloves, socks, and shoes."

Leaning back in her glass throne, Voleta stuck out her legs and wiggled her bare toes. "Besides, I don't think he's going to let us leave until we follow through."

Unhappy with the state of things, and yet seeing no alternative, Adam sat down again and quickly hauled off his shoes and rolled his socks down his feet. The moment his naked feet were on the floor, the Brick Layer's head turned in his direction. Adam recoiled a little under the gaze. "Will the pilot please place his hands flat on the armrests and set his feet upon the floor?" Frowning with suspicion, Adam did as he was told. "Prepare for bonding."

It felt as if he had placed his hands and the soles of his feet on a red-hot flat iron. Though the searing sensation was brief, it was still sufficient to elicit a yowl from him as he threw out his limbs like a dog resisting a bath. Seeing Voleta's horrified look, Adam feigned a quick recovery. "Only joking," he said. "Nothing to it."

The Brick Layer looked to Voleta, the elected navigator, and requested she make the same preparation. When the floor and the arms of her chair, presumably, gave her the same searing treatment, Adam was perplexed when she showed no reaction.

"Didn't that burn?" he asked.

Reflecting upon the question, Voleta shrugged. "I suppose it did."

Adam would've liked to have delved a little further into her newfound apathy toward pain, but the Brick Layer was not quite finished with them.

"Directions for using the bridge's controls are housed in the Delectus. You are advised to avail yourself of those resources before making any adjustments to the interface. In parting, I will say that the *Nebos* is designed to sail with minimal intervention. When in doubt, do nothing. Here is your present course and estimated duration of travel."

The Brick Layer's face vanished, replaced by a colorless void, though quickly specks of red, yellow, and pale blue began to populate the darkness. There were other formations, too; small clusters of pink and pale green. Yet all were sparsely laid within the dominant black. Adam marked its resemblance to a night sky at once, and also recognized the track of a charted course. A line of glowing white bowed from one side of the astral model to the other. At one end, a node upon the line shone a brighter shade of white; at the other end, a yellow spot beamed like the eye of a cat.

Pointing at the white dot, Voleta said, "Do you suppose that's us? And that yellow point, that's where we're going?"

Before Adam could reply, a string of craggy numbers appeared near the bottom of the display: 02:01:19:23:07:35.

The final number changed regularly, ticking off the passing seconds. Working his way back through the string of minutes, hours, days, months, and finally years, Adam sighed at the only conclusion he could come to. "We're more than two years out."

"Two years out from what? Where are we going?" Voleta asked, then stood and waved at the supernal map as if to attract the attention of whoever stood behind it. "Excuse me, Mr. Brick Layer! Excuse me. You didn't say where we're off to. What's our destination, sir? To where are we bound? Hello?" When no reply came and the view of their fantastic window did not change, Voleta began to scan the row of keys before her, each button like the pale back of a scallop half buried in white sand.

Reading her thoughts, Adam quickly intervened. "No, no, no. You heard him. We don't fiddle with anything until we've consulted the Delectus, and even then, we only intervene when we have to."

"But don't we *have* to know where we're going?"

Adam coughed out a hollow laugh. "I've never known where I was going. I can hardly expect that to change now." Collecting his socks and shoes, Adam stood and padded barefoot toward the sealed door. He was vaguely aware that the lucent floor changed under his bare feet as it had not when his boots were still on. The white light broke like snow under his heels and toes, leaving gray footprints that gradually vanished with his passing. But this dim novelty was overwhelmed by his relief when the gold-plated slab rose before him. They were not trapped after all. "Come on. Runa will be worried."

He turned to find Voleta with arms folded still studying the map and the slowly draining numbers of the clock. "You go on. I'll catch up in a few minutes."

"Promise you won't touch anything."

"I'm an officer now, little brother. Can't be running off half-cocked anymore."

"You're an officer *for* now," Adam said, and stepped onto the top step of the unguarded stairs. The face of the pyramid closed behind him as snugly as a dovetail joint.

Gazing out over the familiar city washed in an unfamiliar light, he regarded the half-disguised galaxies behind the glare-frosted dome. He drew a breath and held it.

Two years.

Two years without leaky orlops, drafty hammocks, stone pudding, stale water, or sleeping with a pistol in his hand. Two years without pursuing warships or outstanding warrants or inconsiderate winds. There'd be no treasure to hunt and no treasure maps to haunt him.

Two years. It seemed a long time when he considered it.

And somehow not long enough.

The moment her brother was out of the room, Voleta untucked her shirt, unbuckled her belt, and pulled down her trousers. Finding the padded wallet still strapped to the inside of her thigh, she undid the ties that held it and sat back down. She unzipped the wallet, and the crimson light of six fully charged batteries illuminated her chin, her jaw, the tip of her nose. Her primary reserve had been in her coat in a pocket that had not survived the battle of the attic. But she had learned from recent outings that packing a spare to the backup was only prudent. Her life depended on it, after all.

Congratulating herself on her forethought, Voleta ejected the first of the six all-but-spent vials from her cuff. She tucked the dead battery between her hip and the armrest and replaced it with a fresh cell.

As she turned her wrist to extract the second depleted battery, she began to mutter to herself. "Play coy with me, will you? Oh, I am done with the riddles and half answers, old man. No more tottering off the minute I have a question for you. I'm going to find you and make you tell me where we're off to, even if I have to drag you out of your muddy cradle. We're going to have this out, once and for all!"

"Hello?"

The last of the exhausted vials leapt from her fingers, tumbled through the air, and shattered upon the floor. She stood in a state of shock, wrenching her trousers up, snapping her head around in search of who had spoken. Not bothering to buckle her belt, she pulled her knife and shouted, "Who's there?"

The room was so open, it required hardly a glance to see that she shared it with no one. The door was still sealed, and the rose window's map was unchanged but for the slowly draining clock.

"Oh! Oh good! You can hear me! Hello, hello!" the voice came again. She realized that it had initially seemed remote, faint, a shout from a sewer grate. Now, the voice seemed nearer and more distinct.

The fact that the speaker was closing upon her and still invisible only heightened Voleta's anxiety. She swung her dagger toward each wall in turn, searching for air vents, but discovering none. "Who are you?" she barked at the empty peak of the chamber.

"Is that... is that *you*, Voleta?" The voice now seemed to be right in front of her, and with that proximity came the revelation of familiarity.

"Reddleman?" she gasped.

"At your service."

"Where are you?"

"I don't know. I think I'm in the ship. Sort of rattling around the plumbing."

"But you died. You fell into the reservoir. Captain said you... sort of exploded."

"Oh, I'm quite dead. There's no question about that. I felt my body pop like a soap bubble. I'm gone, but apparently not entirely forgotten. At least, I still remember myself." As he spoke, Voleta searched for the source of his voice. It seemed to emerge from the same perforated plate beneath the rose window that had delivered the Brick Layer's address. Reddleman prattled on as she stared into the rows and rows of minute holes, marveling at how he could possibly fit in there. "This medium is a funny thing. It keeps trying to tease me apart, and I keep pulling myself back together. Luckily, I've had a lot of practice at that."

Tucking in her shirt, Voleta said, "Can you see me?"

"No. I can't see anything. I don't have any eyes. I'm not sure how I can hear you, to be honest. Your voice is the first thing I've heard. Well, that and what sounded like breaking glass. What was that?"

"Nothing," Voleta said quickly. Collecting the spent vials from her seat, she tried to keep the glass from clinking together but did not entirely succeed.

"It sounded like one of our empty batteries. I've broken a few of those in my time. You're replacing your cells, then?"

"Yes."

"And lying about it. Interesting. What were you planning to do?"

Zipping up the wallet again, she saw no reason to continue the deception. After all, what could he do to stop her? "I'm going to take a little stroll through time so I can ask the Brick Layer a question or two."

"An interrogation? Right now? Do you think that's wise?"

Tightening the locks on her revivified cuff, Voleta said, "I think it's ingenious, actually."

"You realize the captain's gone, don't you? The ship, too. They couldn't make this journey." Hardly were those words out before Voleta rushed to the sealed door. The slab rose too slowly for her liking, and she gave it a wallop with the heel of her hand and ducked under it. Toeing the treacherous golden tread high above the city, she looked to the west, through a pair of braided high rises, over the green gardens and golden knuckles of the igloo homes, to the gate in the crystal barrier. Sharpening her eyes to peer through the glare, she saw the spot on the silvery verge where the *State of Art* had been moored. It stood empty.

They were gone.

It had not crossed her mind that the silly little wink she gave Iren when they'd parted hardly an hour ago would be the last thing that passed between them for years to come... if not forever.

She slunk back across the bright floor of the bridge in a daze, her thoughts swinging from self-recrimination to cold comfort to utter sorrow. How could she have forgotten the captain's warning, forgotten Iren, Ann, and Byron? They had just tumbled from her thoughts the moment she saw the stairs leading up the face of the pyramid. She had lost them. No, she had surrendered them.

Iren! Her only real friend in the whole world, the only one who didn't have to love her, but did, the only one who ever made her wish to change, to be better, to be more. Gone. Ann would take care of her, of course. And they would be happy together. Ridiculously so, Voleta hoped. Ann would love and treasure her as she deserved to be, as she had seldom been, and Iren would never again have to worry about Voleta slinking off in her nightgown in the middle of the night or making a mess with Squit... *Squit!* Voleta had forgotten her as well.

Why was she suddenly forgetting the people that she loved? What was happening to her? Had she always been so horribly conceited, or had she gotten suddenly worse?

"They're gone," she said feebly as she dropped into the navigator's chair once more.

"I'm sorry," Reddleman said. It seemed a perfunctory commiseration. "But what else was on the ship? *Think* for a moment. What else have you lost?"

"The vials."

"Yes, yes! Do you really believe it's wise to plunge through the last of your supply, and the only thing keeping you alive, before you find another source?"

"I suppose not," she whispered, arms drooped over the leaves of the armrests. She wished she could melt into the floor. Perhaps it wasn't so bad to lose one's body. Surely there were benefits to becoming a nobody.

Reddleman went on: "More to the point, do you really think that the Brick Layer, after all the opportunities he's had, would suddenly divulge his secrets to you, an unexpected temporal apparition? No, if he was going to tell you the truth, he would've told you by now."

"All right, all right! You've made your point." Voleta slumped further into her shapely throne. Hoping to end the scolding, she sought to change the subject. "Do you miss it? Miss being alive? Do you miss your body?"

"Well, I certainly don't miss clothes."

"I never understood why you were always pulling at your uniform."

He expressed his amusement with laughter that sounded like a thumbnail raked down the teeth of a comb. "I found that once I became aware of my clothes, I could hardly think of anything else. Every time I found myself enthralled by some lofty thought or tantalizing epiphany, my attention would be wrenched back by a rough collar or a tight button or a bunched-up sock. There's none of that now! It's quite *frictionless* in here. Though there are still plenty of distractions. For one thing, I have to mind where I wander. It seems all roads lead back to the Nautilus, and I'm sure there'd be no pulling myself back together if the Allonomia ever tore me apart."

Voleta grimaced at the image, then sat up straight as another thought occurred to her. "So, now that you're inside the ship, does that mean you know everything there is to know about Nebos, about the Tower, about the Brick Layer?"

"Far from it! It's more as if I'm winding through a maze in a fog. This is a byzantine dark. There are—I don't know quite what to called them—*soft spots* here and there. If I press upon them, I can access parts of the ship's records and instruments, if only briefly. It's all very tenuous right now. I'm not entirely sure how I ended up here on the bridge, to be honest." His voice betrayed the marveling quality of a lost tourist who was still too awestruck to be afraid.

"These soft spots, have they revealed anything interesting?"

"Yes, they have, in fact. I found several artifacts in here that suggest that there is more than one Tower."

Voleta swatted the air. "Oh, I knew that. The Brick Layer told me. What he didn't say was *why* there were more, or how many, or where they are, or anything else, really."

"Well, from what I've been able to ascertain, there were or are or will be eight other Towers, each similar, at least functionally, to our own. But I'm not sure whether those Towers are contemporaneous or aspirational. We could be on our way to a reunion of sorts. Wouldn't that be a sight to see: eight other arks like our own! Or perhaps we were the first Tower to successfully enter the diploid phase of life, as it were, and shed our spore upon the universe."

Voleta squeezed her forehead. "Wait, wait. You're going too quickly. What's an ark?"

"A preservative ship—a lifeboat meant to carry all the provisions, persons, plants, and beasts needed to begin again in a new world or an old, ravaged one."

"I only jogged through Nebos, but other than birds and flies, I didn't see many beasts. Doesn't seem like much of an ark."

"That's because most of the beasts are hibernating in the Warren. They are being held in a suspended state of nascency. There are embryos of chimney cats, elephant eels, spider-eaters, bull snails, pepper bees, asper bats . . . all frozen and waiting to be born."

"No regular old house cats or horses?"

"I don't believe so. We seem to be carrying only fauna that was native to the Tower. And I don't think it's a coincidence that each of these animals contributed some biological ingredient to the creation of the Sphinx's medium. Perhaps it's not so much an ark as a pantry."

"All right. Let's say it's an ark. We land upon another world; we construct another Tower, we build another Nebos; and we fill another reservoir with boiling medium. Then what?"

The sieve that bled Reddleman's voice buzzed again with laughter. "We couldn't do any of that without the Brick Layer."

Voleta raised her hands to accept the fact. "Pretend we could. What would be the *point* of it, ultimately? To make infinite arks? Maybe. Perhaps someone just wanted to create little repositories of their favorite creatures throughout the universe. But perhaps it's *not* an ark, or rather, perhaps that's not its final purpose."

"What other use could a ship like this have?" Reddleman asked.

"The ship is protected by an impenetrable dome and outfitted with titanic cannons. What does that sound like to you?"

"A warship."

"Exactly." Voleta began to pace, her bare feet slapping the illuminated floor, leaving ghostly prints like wet feet on dry stone. "What if the Tower was just an elaborate shipyard? It required centuries of labor, energy, and resources to build a ship of this magnitude. Just think about the amount of gold present in Nebos alone! Think about how much metal had to be pulled from the earth to build all of this! That has to pose quite a burden to a world, doesn't it?"

"An interesting point. You'd not be the first to call the Tower a leech."

As she paced, Voleta swung her arms as if she were seeding a field. "So, there are other arks, other ships like this, and they were used to plant other Towers, other shipyards. Then the question becomes, where do all the arks go? If this is an armada, where is the battlefield, and who is the general? Who is the enemy?"

"And why are we at war?"

Feeling a sudden upwelling of revulsion at the whole prospect, Voleta gripped her hands behind her head. "Or maybe we have it all wrong. We're conjuring a novel out of tea leaves here. I knew the Sphinx, and she was good. She cared about the preservation of the ringdoms, she despised suffering. I can't believe she would make her life's work to serve as a recruiter for some foreign war."

Reddleman made an equivocating noise that sounded a bit like a door buzzer. "Perhaps she didn't know herself. She was just doing what she was told to do. The only thing we know for a fact is that the Brick Layer is stingy with his truths."

"Which leaves us to be generous with our guesses." Voleta rubbed her face, feeling unprepared to entertain any further abstractions. "We'll have to see what the others make of all of this."

"Do we? There's a lot more sailing to be done. Perhaps you and I can learn a little more about what lies ahead before we bring our findings to the other passengers. No reason to cause a panic with unanswered questions and wild speculation."

"You don't think they'll speculate all on their own?"

"Of course they will, but you could be a voice of reassurance, of measured calm. Tell them that the Brick Layer has a destination in mind for us. Remind them that the gifts of these parks and gardens and magnificent homes would seem to promise an even more lavish port of call, and at the very least a benevolent host."

"And that could very well be the case." Privately, Voleta was not convinced that she and Reddleman would be able to make any real progress on their own. They were fumbling through, as he had called it, a byzantine dark. At the very least, she would tell Adam. He was already more familiar with the city than either of them. "What about you? Do you want to stay a secret?"

"For now. You need time to find a new supply of medium, and I need time to explore. I'd like to poke around a bit."

"Well, don't poke *too* hard."

"Of course! Gently, gently. Now, if you'll excuse me, there's something, something just out of reach...I can almost get my mind around it. Oh, I see...fascinating, fascinating..." he said, his voice draining into the distance as his presence flowed into other corners of the ship.

Listening to him go, Voleta's thoughts turned to the animals sleeping below. She imagined them tucked in little doll beds and curled up like kittens in baskets. The image brought to mind Squit nestled inside her sleeve and bounding between her shoulders. She pictured the fat-cheeked squirrel scrambling up Byron's curtains and charging through his table settings as if it were a steeplechase. Voleta saw Squit trembling at the bottom of the port master's gilded cage.

Voleta wondered if that wasn't what Nebos was underneath it all: another pretty jail.

Sometimes, it was difficult to tell the difference between independence and imprisonment. The two could look an awful lot alike. Were they refugees on an ark or conscripts aboard a warship?

Of course, the only reliable means she knew for discerning freedom from captivity was to try the door. And to think, she'd nearly believed all her great escapes were behind her.

Chapter Eighteen

Like a drowning soul floundering at sea, the hand of history reaches for objects of convenience rather than perfection. And so are heroes gripped.

—*Homage, Vol. III* by Jumet

It had been three days since Edith had carried the Sphinx's body to its sepulchral stage amid her gallery of engines, three days since she'd rapped upon the hatch of a sealed windstile and watched Senlin's expression writhe with recognition that their reunion was doomed to christen yet another parting, three days since she'd witnessed the Tower's crown shed its woolly veil, rise from the great trunk of stone, blood, and mortar, and vanish with a volcanic roar.

She sat at the Sphinx's desk, her back to the matrix of shelves that held the curios, talismans, and trophies of another's existence, a life far more spectacular than she could ever dream of living. Feeling both small and fraudulent, she consciously kept her spine straight and her shoulders level as she read and wrote and worried.

Byron had thoughtfully packed away the Sphinx's tools and the objects of her tinkering to make room for Edith's labor. The work surface still bore the grease stains and gouges of its former use, but those ghosts of the Sphinx's genius were rapidly disappearing beneath stacks of correspondence, newspapers, billets, bulletins, and reports, all of which represented a looming crisis of one variety or another.

Queen Hortensia, the derelict regent of the soiled vineyard, had sent the Sphinx a declaration of her intention to ally herself with two cousin kings who would join her in removing the fugitive hods who'd illegally taken possession of her palace. King Leonid of Pelphia, who'd originally been amenable to hosting the scores of spark-smiths who descended upon the ringdom to help repair the devastated electrical system, had announced his desire to renegotiate the terms of his ringdom's compensation, citing a sum that was nothing short of exorbitant. The daily dispatches from the newly installed head of the Monitorius included an abundance of concerning news, from the state of the Tower's aquifers to the alarming progress of a novel fever in the middle ringdoms of Paphos and Simbersae. Though Marat was no more, his acolytes were still pursuing sabotage on several fronts, a fact that complicated Edith's ambitious plan for disencumbering the hods of their debts and converting the Old Vein to a public thoroughfare that would be accessible to all. To make matters worse, *The Acorn* had begun to publish a series of exposés on the abrupt disappearance of the terminal ringdom, an event that *The Acorn* attributed to the Sphinx himself, who—having now demonstrated the power to carve up the Tower and swallow it, slice by slice—was no longer an innocuous novelty that the ringdoms could afford to abide. According to *The Acorn,* the Sphinx *was* the apocalypse. The message had found a ready audience. People were frightened.

Edith could scarcely blame them.

Sometimes, upon remembering the Sphinx's interrupted benediction, her destroyed last words, Edith felt a pang of anguish at the irretrievable loss. She tried to imagine what great secret or arcane wisdom the Sphinx wished to impart to her. And Edith found that her inability to imagine even the gist of that invaluable advice only made her feel more incompetent.

The world had changed, and she was unready.

Edith did not believe that Nebos had been destroyed, or rather she could not *bear* to believe that Tom, Marya, Voleta, Adam, and all the young refugees had ascended like a firework only to suffer the same end. Surely the Brick Layer would never have contrived such an elaborate flowering just to vaporize the seed. No, Nebos had survived its launch and was riding upon the empyreal swells. The dome and the lightning mortars would protect the voyagers, and the gardens would sustain them, and the transposed sea of medium would power their city for years and generations to come.

Though Edith could not guess the purpose of the weightless island, nor the Brick Layer's reason for creating it, she had every confidence that the expedition had a destination. Nebos was bound for some foreign shore where an implausible port waited to receive them. The island city would arrive there safely, and hopefully, one day, she would return.

The fate of Nebos and her friends was a topic she had scarcely broached with Byron.

It was not the only neglected subject. Neither of them had remarked upon Reddleman's death, nor the ambivalence the loss inspired. On one hand, Edith was saddened to lose a faithful crewman who had, in his final moments, once again proved that his loyalty was not an act. His courage and sacrifice were undeniable, laudable, and indeed the very font of her survival. And yet, his occasional amorality, his interest in experimenting upon the living, and his metaphysical musings had always made her uneasy. She would miss his insights and his geniality, but she would sleep a little better, too. It was with a muddle of guilt and relief that she mourned her pilot's passing.

And then there was the Sphinx.

The Sphinx's footman had absorbed the news of his master's death with incredible poise. In fact, his aplomb had been so great, Edith took it as a careful performance, one intended to spare her the indignity of his grief. She believed he wept in private and saved his composure for her. It was a gift, a charity that she appreciated amid the tumult of her abrupt inauguration as the Tower's steward. But it was a strain she knew could not continue indefinitely. Soon enough, they would have to reckon with the loss. They needed to carve the splinter out before the scar closed over it.

But there was just so much to do.

She couldn't afford to let the Sphinx's presence depart from the public eye, and so the *State of Art* remained at sky under Iren's command, assisted by a skeleton crew composed of Ann Gaucher, Finn Goll, and John Tarrou. Edith had promised both men a generous salary for a month's labor, which would give her time to interview and hire a crew. (Already, she had an inkling that Tane of the Cistern would make both a dependable officer and a good resource for recruiting airmen.) But it was no longer enough for the long-absent Sphinx to be merely visible; she had to speak as well. And so, Edith had spent much of the past three days listening, reading, and preparing to address the Tower.

Jotting down notes for her rebuttal of the most recent edition of *The*

Acorn, Edith heard the slow and grinding arrival of the elevating corridor and so was not surprised when Byron entered, carrying a tray before him.

"Care for a cup of tea? It's nice and tepid now that I've spent ten minutes puttering up from the kitchen. We really must do something about the corridor."

Shifting papers to make room for the saucer Byron presented, Edith said, "We're lucky it runs at all." Since they had returned to the Sphinx's abode and found Mr. Gedge's dynamo spliced to the house's electrical system, they'd been using it as a generator, refueling it via a sink in the rear of Marat's stranded excavator. "Did you refill the reservoir this morning?"

"I did indeed, though we can't keep it up forever. We're running through gallons of medium a day. And when the cistern runs dry . . . well, that will be that." Byron smiled, a thin veil to conceal the anxiety of their situation. With the reserves in the attic gone, and the means for making more of the obscure brew uncertain, the house, the *State of Art,* the brick nymphs, the Wakemen, and the Sphinx's footman all depended upon the medium stored in the cistern and in the racks of collected vials. It had only recently dawned upon Edith why the Sphinx had been so assiduously stockpiling and replenishing those batteries when last she had seen her: The Sphinx must've known the contents of her attic reservoir was destined for other work.

"And how are the houseguests?" Edith asked, sipping her lukewarm tea.

"Cael finally stopped sobbing, which is a relief. He still has to be spoonfed, of course, and his other . . . necessities attended to. For some of those, Mr. Gedge has volunteered his assistance; others not. Delyth is communicating again and is as obscene as ever. That woman could make marble blush."

"And Gedge, what did he think of my proposal?"

"Frankly, I don't know what *I* think of your proposal. Giving him tools, letting him repair the damage to his friends. It seems awfully trusting. He's both very clever and deeply resentful. Keeping him around is like using a loaded gun to clean your ears. Surely the risks outweigh any reward."

"Perhaps. But as I see it, practically, we have three options. We can keep him here and give him work, which admittedly would be fraught. We could imprison him elsewhere where he might escape or be conscripted to another's cause, which would be alarming. Or we could kill him, which would be deplorable. Besides, it would be a cruelty to both you and Cael to continue the current arrangement forever. Has Gedge had a chance to review the agreement?"

"Never thought I'd see the day when Edith Winters started doling out contracts."

Edith bobbed her head from side to side, an equivocating nod. "Well, we certainly can't do this on our own, and as far as Gedge and the others know, the Sphinx is still alive. I don't think it hurts to continue that impression."

"Just so." He had been cradling the tea tray under one arm, but now he removed it and set it upon one of the side tables. "Edith, could we adjourn to the conservatory for a moment? There's something I'd like to show you."

The adjoining music room was noticeably cheerier than it had been when Edith had discovered the Sphinx's body. Byron had swept up the leaves and given the Brick Layer's ash tree a much-needed soak. Already, its canopy seemed a little restored. Byron had also shoveled out the ashes from the fireplace and dusted the mantel clock and filled the enclaves with cut flowers and green garlands. A small fire warmed the room and made the shadows of the chair legs dance across the checkered tiles like fingers across a keyboard. The air smelled as if it had been sweetened with incense, and yet it wasn't until Edith saw the black sashes bracing the backs of the armchairs that she recognized the cause of the effort: Byron had decorated for a wake that had not happened and a loss that stood unmourned.

"It's lovely, Byron. She would've appreciated this."

He sniffed, the long edge of his mouth tightening. Edith couldn't tell if he was repressing laughter or tears. "She would've called me a gloomy old mope. But I didn't do it only for her." He presented one of the chairs, nodding in invitation. She sat down, feeling momentarily self-conscious of the fact that she was sitting in the Sphinx's chair. But then the cushion softened her posture, and with that softening came fatigue. The fire hissed like a bleeding radiator. She stared into it, allowing her mind to empty.

When after a moment she looked back around to Byron, he was holding the silver dish of the Sphinx's mask. He seemed to admire it as if it were a portrait. Observing his tender expression, Edith thought that this would be the moment that he would speak of his loss, his sorrow. She was ready to listen.

Then he surprised her by turning it around and offering it to her with two hands and his head bowed.

The gesture was unmistakable.

She stood, scooting the chair back, making the legs squeal upon the tile. He looked up in surprise and seemed confused to find her posed in palm-out refusal. "Byron, I can't wear that. I couldn't begin to pretend to have half the genius, half the will she had. I would just be deceiving the world *and* myself. I can try to keep the ship afloat, but I... can't replace her."

"Did you know the Sph..." He stopped, smiled to himself, and began again. "Did you know Adelia was herself a substitution? Oh, yes. There have been quite a few Sphinxes throughout the centuries, or so I was told. The first Sphinx, the one who designed the beer-me-go-rounds in the Basement, was the Brick Layer himself. He found that the introduction of certain technologies made his followers uneasy, suspicious, resentful. So, he created an alter ego, a counterpart who could shoulder the misgiving and dread that accompanies innovation. His workers would ask him where he got such and such a marvel, and he would blame the Sphinx. Eventually, people wanted to meet the Sphinx, so he conceived of a disguise, one that he, or an actor, or an understudy could wear.

"Like those who came before her, Adelia understood that myths are not without solace or strength or, indeed, plasticity. Not all of the Sphinxes were wizards of engineering. No, some were diplomats, others were strategists, managers, historians, astronomers, and poets. The Sphinx has long been an omnibus of talent, an authority without apparent nation. An outsider. A peacekeeper who advocates for the continued aspirations of the race."

Edith dropped her hands, her refusal softening as her inner turmoil grew. She suddenly felt a kindship with the girl with the paper boat who stood in the shallows of her fate, gobsmacked by the enormity of her misfortune. Or perhaps, when Adelia had toed that verge between the shore and the uncertain depths, she had accepted her own abandonment as an invitation to take responsibility for others, to shun bitterness, diffidence, and self-pity, to choose a life of service and self-effacement because she recognized a great need in the world and her potential to alleviate it.

Seeming to perceive her protestations were eroding, Byron said, "Before we left, the last time I saw my master, do you know what she said to me?

She said, 'I picked Edith because she's the sort of person who doesn't let a hat shape her head.' Adelia didn't want you to conform to the mask, to let the robes mold who you are. No, she knew you would possess them, crease them, make them your own. That's why she chose you."

Edith felt a thrill of relief at the thought—no, the *conviction*—that these words comprised the blessing that had been lost to time. The Sphinx's confidence in her refreshed her faith in herself.

She accepted the mask and, with Byron's assistance, adjusted the interior's forehead and chin brace and the harness that would hold it in place. Feeling a little foolish and a little daring, she slipped the mirror on. She could feel her disheveled hair standing out through the straps, and imagined her locks framing the looking glass like dark snakes slithering about a reflecting pool. "How do I look?"

Pinching the fur at his throat thoughtfully, Byron turned his head one way, then another. "You look a bit like a teaspoon." He smiled when she put her hands on her hips to show indignance at the joke. "The real question is, how does the world look to you?"

Edith observed the cheerful fire, the mantel clock, the mending tree. The mask made her voice sound more resonant in her own ears, as if she were speaking into her hand and projecting from a stage at the same time. She said, "The same. Everything looks the same."

Chapter Nineteen

Do not race your postcards home. Dally long enough for word of your adventures to arrive before you. Let them announce you and lay the foundation for your legend.

—*Everyman's Guide to the Tower of Babel*, I. I

"Are you sure you want to do this?" Runa asked, not for the first time that morning. She looked to Adam to see whether he was coming around to her point of view. There was no reason to rush into things. So much had been upended in recent days. Why not let a mystery rest for a day or two?

Runa had been there when the twins had gone to Captain Dyre to confess their unintentional promotion, which left the ship's inscrutable bridge accessible to no one but themselves. Dyre had listened to their account of the Brick Layer's recorded message with wide-eyed concern. Voleta shared her theories as to the *Nebos*'s ultimate purpose as celestial ark or perhaps deployed warship, notions that only troubled Dyre more.

When Adam had suggested they call an accord to select a more suitable pilot and navigator, Dyre shook his head, saying, "Let's not overwhelm everyone with questions just now, especially while we don't have all the facts. We have our hands full with the children at the moment."

Voleta had then suggested an expedition to the ship's lower decks. "The Brick Layer said that the pilot and navigator have the authority to open up more of the sublevels. Why not have a look around? We could gather information, come back, confer with you, and decide when to present our findings to everyone."

Dyre had agreed, which was how they came to stand before a bulwark of a door deep within the Warren. The hatch was as pitted as pumice and dark as basalt. It did not ring when Adam rapped it with the base of his dianastra. It seemed a thing forged for the purpose of discouragement; a blockade that said *go away*. Its only ornamentation was a smooth handprint set at eyelevel that interrupted the otherwise uniform roughness of the slab.

Voleta answered Runa's question at last. "This is our home now, our ship, and our charter. It's our solemn duty to..." She squinted in search of the right words. "Have a snoop about, isn't it? I think so. Yes, I'm pretty sure."

Runa couldn't help but smile at the vacillations of Voleta's confidence. "Everyone's had a go, you know. Come down here to set their hand on that hand. It seems to call out for it. It's been a rite of passage, a popular dare, an excuse to bring a date down here. Not that the reasons matter. The door's locked. Always has been."

"And the Tower always had a cloudy head right until it didn't. I think we've seen the end of always." Voleta held her hand out over the sunken palm that was several sizes too large. Adam trained his weapon on the dismal door as she slid her fingers upon the ancient hand.

The door cracked along a central hidden seam, parting with a squeal of unseizing hinges and a scrape of metal. After a moment, the wings of the gate clanged against the walls of the corridor beyond. The light of their lamps seemed little more than a puddle about their feet. The great darkness that loomed before them groaned with the distant sounds of churning machines, or perhaps the lowing of alien cattle.

The point of Adam's dianastra quivered in sympathy with his nerves. Runa huddled closer to his side to reassure him and herself.

Voleta looked back at them. Her eyes appeared to glow a little brighter for the darkness that framed her. She gave them an encouraging smile. "Come on."

"There could be anything in there," Adam said, staring down the sight of his weapon.

"Which is why we have to look." Voleta huffed a small laugh as she returned to them, forcing her brother to lower his sidearm. When he did, she took his empty hand, then reached for Runa's. Runa offered it in return and felt as if she were touching the buzzing strings of a harp. Voleta radiated such a strange energy. "We want to know truth, don't we? The truth about this ship, and the Brick Layer, and where we're going, and what they expect from us when we get there. I mean, aren't you tired of waiting for the secrets to come dribbling out? I certainly am. If the Tower taught us anything it's that if you wait around for someone to tell you what everything means, you'll live and die with nothing but questions, mysteries, and lies. I'm through waiting for answers to come to me. It's past time we went and found them ourselves."

The headmaster's new blackboard was somewhat smaller than he would've liked. The legs sank into the grass unevenly and stubbornly resisted every attempt to level them. The board was reversible, a nice feature in theory, but since the hinge lock was missing, Senlin was forced to grip the frame whenever he wrote upon the board to keep it from dumping all his precious scraps of chalk into the clover.

But these were petty quibbles. The fact that he had a blackboard at all was a minor miracle. There certainly had been stiff competition for classroom equipment and supplies.

As deep as Ossian's trove was, the hoarder was not prepared to outfit dozens of classrooms at once, so the citizenry was called upon to help fill in the gaps. Local artists donated easels to the effort. The city's potters fired unglazed tiles that could be used as slates. Woodworkers converted cabinet doors to lap desks. Clutches and purses were loaded with pencils and rulers; leather belts were reemployed to grip and carry books.

Grumbles over these sacrifices were rare—the result, no doubt, of the accord that was held soon after the city's unexpected ascension. That accord had resulted in two important decisions. First, there were no hods in Nebos; there were only Nebosans. Second, the accord dictated that after the questions of shelter, sustenance, and guardianship were settled, the city's next priority had to be the education of their newest citizens. To this end, hundreds of the more seasoned Nebosans, Senlin among them, had volunteered to assist in the classroom as teachers, tutors, and proctors.

The children were broken up according to their ages in an effort to accommodate their facility for taking instruction, or in the case of the youngest, their inability to sit still. Senlin had been assigned a dozen thirteen-year-olds—a difficult age, some would say, though Senlin preferred to think that all stages of human development came with both difficulty and opportunity. There was no benefit to stigmatizing one phase of growth over another.

Even so, there were *challenges*.

Bickering, whispering, and teasing were popular additions to his lessons. Gossip traversed his open classroom quickly and inspired many conflicts that were made worse by the age's aptitude for perceiving and exposing one another's insecurities. Having long ago been introduced to the insensitivities and sensitivities of adolescence, Senlin knew to address these disruptions with a combination of mediation, modeling, and distraction.

Though distractions were hardly in short supply.

His lessons had to compete not only with puberty, but also with their lavish and baffling surroundings. Whenever a student's mind wandered from his instruction to marvel at the majesty of a willow, or the fragrance of a hyacinth, or the flocks of mechanical butlers that buzzed from house to house, or the city's sculptural spires, or the sun-like pyramidion whose sustaining light only partly obscured the galactic swirls of stars that streamed outside their diamond globe... well, Senlin could almost understand how the object of a preposition could be mistaken for tedious.

Then there were the quirks of individuality to contend with. Despite the unfathomable grimness of their former lives on the black trail, the personalities of his new students were not uniform. If anything, the variety and manner of their temperaments reminded him of the students he had taught in Isaugh. Some were quick to mock, and quick to take offense. Some would lash out when corrected; others would wilt when praised. Some carried an underlying desire to please him; others held authority of any sort in utter contempt.

Yet, his newly assembled class could be kind, clever, and curious... when they were not rolling their eyes at him.

Though he could hardly blame them when they did.

The first day of class, he had felt entirely incapable of imparting anything noble or useful to another living soul. He did not feel fit to instruct a dog to sit, much less spark the intellectual curiosity of a youthful mind. He stood before their uncertain stares and felt entirely exposed: He was a fraud, a thug, a barbarian dressed in civil drag. Still, a captain was not relieved of duty by hardship, nor a teacher by their self-doubt. Senlin scoured the corners of his character and swept together a few slivers of his shattered confidence.

They began with the alphabet and how to hold their pencils and how to make a line, a curve, a circle, a dot. Though it was not the purpose of the lessons, the process proved therapeutic for Senlin. By returning to the foundations of learning, he was forced to revisit his own slow growth as a student—the frustration that had followed every small failure and the elation that had come with each trifling success. The more he taught, the more his confidence grew. And with it came the marveling excitement that he thought had been destroyed forever by the Tower. He'd long ago despaired that he would be given another chance to share the accrued knowledge of the species with a new generation of dreamers and thinkers. And yet here he was: addressing the men and women of the future who would contribute their own inquiries, insights, and corrections to the expansion of human understanding!

"And now, we turn to the diphthong!" Senlin beamed at his students, who sat with wilting interest in the sprawling shade of a live oak. "The diphthong complicates matters a little. It is sometimes called a 'gliding vowel,' and we all remember what a vowel is? Yes? Very good. It's called a 'gliding vowel' because it—"

"Who cares?" The lad sitting cross-legged near Senlin's foot dropped his hands into the grass to demonstrate his exasperation. His name was Milo, and Senlin had recently moved him to the front row in the hopes that he might better hold his attention there. Apparently, he'd just succeeded on focusing his boredom. Milo continued his complaint: "Why do any of us need to know what a diphthong is, or a vowel, or how to read, or any of it? There's a button in my kitchen that brings me pudding when I push it! What else do I need to know?"

"Ah, Milo! What an excellent question. It makes me think of other questions—questions like, how does that button work? What lies behind it? Who makes the pudding? What is the recipe? What would you do if the button broke?"

Milo crossed his arms and hunched where he sat, apparently displeased by the headmaster's answer. "Does *everything* have to be complicated? Can't I just enjoy a pudding?"

"Of course you can! We don't have to know everything about everything to enjoy the world. I don't have to know all about stamens and ovules to enjoy the fragrance of a flower, or how to build a house to appreciate a roof over my head. But understanding *nothing*, or very little of the world, and having no desire to understand more than you already do, well, that invites entitlement. What was a privilege becomes a right. And that, I think, is dangerous."

"Are you saying I don't deserve pudding?" Milo's scowling question sparked a little sympathetic grumbling from his peers.

Senlin hastened to reassure them. "Goodness, no! I can't think of anyone who should enjoy a pudding more than you. But my hope is that you don't go on to make the same mistake that the ringdoms of the Tower once made, including our new friends and neighbors here in Nebos."

"What mistake was that?"

"To conflate *want* with *need*. To believe that the resources required of either are infinite, or to think that our understanding of these marvels is innate. It would be a terrible error to believe that the fragile things our ancestors built and gave to us are inexhaustible and eternal."

He saw at once that, in his zeal, he had spoken over their heads. He steepled his fingers and pressed them to his lips as he reviewed an alternate explanation. "Have any of you ever heard the fable of the Inheritance Chest? No? Well, it goes something like this...

"There once was a modest merchant. His life was not extravagant, his business was rather middling, but he was comfortable enough and respected. He had a loving wife who gave him a son, and the modest merchant's fortunes were sufficient to provide for all their needs.

"Then one day, the modest merchant took ill. What at first seemed a slump turned into a steep decline, and it wasn't long before the doctors said he would not recover. Lying upon his deathbed, the merchant called his son, who was scarcely a man, to his bedside to receive his inheritance. The son was very excited to think of his coming fortune, and so was rather surprised to find that his inheritance was an old, ugly, and empty trunk that sat at the foot of his father's bed. Its hinges were rusty, and the key in its latch turned and turned without catching. The son couldn't help but feel offended by the humble gift.

"But the modest merchant quickly explained that it was not an ordinary trunk. No, it was a magic trunk, one which would provide the son with whatever he needed. All he had to do was close the chest, speak his need out loud, and turn the key three times. When he opened the trunk, whatever he had asked for would be there.

"After his father's funeral, the modest merchant's son, feeling understandably doubtful, decided to test the magic trunk. He took a moment to think about what he wanted most in the world. He certainly didn't want to be modest. He wanted to be rich. So, he closed the lid and said aloud, 'I need a thousand gold coins.' He turned the key three times in the broken lock and opened the trunk again. He fell to his knees when he saw the glistening treasure held within. He counted it all out on the bed: one thousand golden coins.

"Time passed. The rich merchant spent his gold upon his home. He took a loving wife who gave him a son, and all was gladness and goodness until the rich merchant thought of something else he wanted. He wanted somewhere to walk in the mornings and something to drink in the evenings. He wanted land; he wanted an apple orchard. He bought land with his gold, but the ground was hard and the soil bad. So, he returned to his magic trunk and said, 'I need a river to water my orchard.' He turned the key three times and opened the trunk. Out rushed a river. It poured from his bedroom window, ran down the street, and snaked a path out to his arid land. Soon, his orchard began to bloom, and the apples swelled. The rich merchant named the cider he pressed after himself.

"Time passed, and now the rich cider merchant thought of something else he wanted. He wanted a reliable wind to fill the sails of his fleet to carry his cider to ports far and wide. He wanted his name to be known in every corner of the world, wanted to be toasted in every pub and parlor. He addressed his magic trunk once more, saying 'I need a wind to move my ships.' Three times he turned the key, then opened the trunk. Out leapt a strong and steady gust that flew from his bedroom window and coursed down the street and out to the port where it filled the sails of his growing navy.

"So, it went for many years. The rich and famous cider merchant would think of something he wanted—a racehorse, a villa, an island—then he'd ask the trunk, and turn the key, and out his wish would fly.

"Many years later, on his deathbed, the rich and famous cider merchant called his own son to his side to give him his inheritance. His son, who had left home long ago to make a fortune of his own, was heartbroken that his father's life was waning, but overjoyed to hear of his inheritance. 'You have to understand, Father,' the son said, 'my life has been very hard. I put money in the bank, but it vanished. I dug a well to water my fields, but it ran dry. I built a mill to grind my flour, but there's never any wind.'

"Distraught to hear of his son's misfortunes, the rich and famous cider merchant rallied his strength and rose from his deathbed. He said, 'I don't want to die and leave you to suffer alone.' Then addressing his magic trunk, the merchant said, 'I need forty more years of life.' Turning the key three times, he opened the trunk, and his son fell dead to the floor."

"That's a horrible story," Milo said.

Senlin nodded. "It certainly is heartbreaking! But tell me, why is it horrible? What happened?"

"Whatever the merchant asked the trunk for was taken from his son."

"Exactly. And did he *need* all of those things he asked for—the gold, the river, the wind—or did he *want* them?"

"He just wanted them," Milo admitted.

"The reason we study and learn, the reason we take only what we need, is because we have all been given a great gift—the gift of civilization, the gift of understanding, the gift of mastery over our environment—and if we misuse these, if we take these things for granted, the ones who will suffer most are our sons and daughters. There is nothing wrong with enjoying the fruits of our ancestors' labor. We should relish the pudding. But that privilege does not relieve us of our responsibility to be faithful custodians of the world we leave for our children."

Senlin had called upon Marya every afternoon since their first reunion. She had greeted him cordially, allowed him to hold Olivet, though naturally under close supervision. Their visits took place on her stoop or her lawn or occasionally in the garden behind her house, but never inside. He did not care where they spoke; he only wished to hear her voice, to glimpse her life, to have some small window into the landscapes of her thoughts.

They chatted about his lodgings and joked about his misguided assumption that a ringdom without tourists would have any need of hotels. They indulged in the popular pastime of idle speculation, swapping theories about the harborage they were bound for and who might greet them there. Senlin believed they were being summoned to meet the genius race who'd conceived of the Tower and bred her remarkable bestiaries. Marya wondered if they were not just riding in a grandiose lift that was bound for the true top of the Tower, which would likely prove to be full of the most insufferable and spoiled people the universe had ever produced.

On the occasion when such ruminations began to spark too much dread, they'd switch to the lighter topic of their recently enlarged families. Senlin had been given a dwelling not unlike hers and charge over two adolescent boys who called him their warden, though he thought of himself more as the ringleader of an unsafe circus. Marya would ask about his classes and whether he was eating and if he'd found anything else to wear besides his white linen suit and pink shirt. He'd answer that his students were good, his appetite was average, and that his chances of securing a new ensemble anytime soon were poor.

Likewise, he would ask after Olivet, and Marya's newly adopted children. How was she managing all of it? Marya would confess the challenges of her new responsibilities, which she likened to playing three different instruments at once with two hands and one foot. She was sleeping in snatches, eating in spates, and missing someone named Ann terribly. In addition to caring for Olivet's increasingly active interest in the world, she was having to devise ways to entertain young Nia during the daytime hours since she was too young for school. In short, she was busy and tired, but not unhappy. He made every offer of help; she acknowledged each without acceptance.

Whenever Senlin attempted to broach the tender subject of the past, she would bring the visit to a civil conclusion either by excuse or by explicit declaration that she needed more time. He never pressed her and always exited with gracious haste.

So it went for days and weeks, until at last, when Senlin arrived at her door early in the evening, having stayed late to help young Master Milo with his letters, Marya opened the door with Olivet on her hip, and forgoing the usual niceties said, "I don't know if I'm ready to talk, but I'm willing to listen. A little."

"All right. Wonderful. Thank you," he said, and though he'd spent the days preparing, he felt a little flummoxed. He took a deep breath to settle himself and said, "I worry that I ensnared you in a marriage that was a great luxury to me and a poor bargain for you. It took the Tower to make me see what a small man I was. And every day that my estimation of myself shrank, my esteem for you grew. I burdened you with my mediocrity. You are capable of—you *deserve* much more than me or what I could give you. Your success in Pelphia proves as much. I know that stage was built on another man's lies, his avarice and lust, but the genius, the talent, was yours, not his. The applause was not misplaced. I could scald my hands clapping them together every hour of every day for the rest of my life, and it wouldn't be sufficient to demonstrate how much I admire you, your strength, your gifts, your—"

She frowned with such concerted force his words stumbled to a stop and he nearly faltered from the stoop.

She said, "Do you really think me so shallow? Do you think I wanted applause from you, wished to marry my audience? Tom, I wanted to share a life with you! To grow together like two vines; to tangle, and thicken, and… and *bear fruit*. Even now, after everything, I can't believe you continue to doubt my affection—"

"I only doubt that I merited it."

"I wish you had as much respect for my judgment as you have for your own."

Senlin wore the sudden pained look of a man who'd bitten his tongue, but he saw at once she was right. "Yes, of course. I'm sorry. You're absolutely right. How horribly condescending of me. I just want you to understand that I would give anything to—"

But Marya wasn't finished with her point. "It isn't fair to say you weren't good enough for me when *I* wasn't the one to abandon our life. I didn't reject you. I didn't take another man. I was kidnapped! Our child was a hostage! On the Merry Loop, I sent you away to protect Olivet, yes, but to protect *you* as well. I gave up even the dream of our life together to give you a chance for happiness with E—"

Senlin interrupted her with an anguished wag of his head. "That was a shameful mistake."

Marya answered with a small shrug of a smile. "So men have said since the first vows were broken. But it is only a mistake in retrospect. At the time, it was a choice made out of desire."

"That was me at my very worst, my most cynical and despairing."

Marya scoffed dryly. "Oh, I met her, Tom. I don't think you were *that* despairing."

Senlin accepted the unpleasant but not inaccurate judgment with a nod. "I have lived so long with my own thoughts that I have once again pretended to know yours. I am sorry, Marya. I am sorry for my excuses, sorry for my self-pity, sorry for my faithlessness. I am sorry I brought you to the Tower, and most of all, I'm sorry that my arrogance was the cause of so much of your suffering. Can you ever forgive me?"

Marya sighed as if she were blowing out a candle. "I may say that I do; I can even wish to, but forgiveness is a feeling much as love is. It is mysterious and difficult to conjure on command. All I'm willing to promise is that we shall at least be cordial to one another, because I still like you, Tom, and I want you to be a father to Olivet—"

"As do I!"

"But forgiveness..." She shook her head. "That will take time. Perhaps a little; perhaps more than we have."

"Then in the meantime I shall be a loving father to Olivet and a grateful friend to you. If you ever wish to talk about what you endured, what you felt and thought, I promise to only listen and be enlightened. And if forgiveness ever blooms in your heart, I will count myself doubly blessed."

"Thank you," she said at a whisper with a brief, civil smile.

Believing he had been dismissed, Senlin turned to go.

"Tom, wait." When he turned, he found her expression had softened again. "Perhaps you could take Olivet for a walk. I need to scrub behind the ears of two very unwilling children. At first, they regarded bath time as a curious ritual, but the novelty has long since worn off. There have been protests." As she spoke, she prepared Olivet by tucking up her swaddle and daubing the spittle from her chin.

"Yes, of course. It would be my pleasure." Senlin accepted Olivet with an awkward but awe-filled tenderness. He pressed her to his chest, resting her chin upon his shoulder. Marya appeared satisfied with his hold on her.

"She likes looking at the lights outside. Since it's getting dark, you might take her to the edge of our little fishbowl." Senlin said he would, and she surprised him by then adding, "Have you had dinner?"

He swayed with his daughter with all the thrilling nonconfidence of a boy embarking upon his first dance. "I have not."

"I eat after the children are in bed. I'd like to talk a little more then. If you're willing to listen."

Senlin nodded because he was afraid to speak and spoil the moment. She turned her head, and he hung upon the retreating flash of her nose, cheek, ear, hair as it swept across her shoulders. He saw again the brim of a scarlet helmet enveloped by a crowd. Then the doorlatch clicked. Olivet inhaled, and they shared a contented sigh.

Strolling down the lane, he observed the nightly dimming of the pyramidion and the growing presence of the cosmic spree beyond the clearing glass. They wound around gardens, out through a park, past a little castle cloaked in ivy, and on toward the darkling sea that swam with galactic fish. He spoke to Olivet in a voice full of reassurance and happiness, saying, "You and I are pioneers. Indeed we are. We are explorers aboard a spectacular ship, voyaging to shores unknown on worlds unseen. Just think of all the curious, marvelous wonders that await us! We're well out of the classroom, now, Olivet. I'm just as new as you to all of this."

He turned her around in the crook of his arm so he could see her face, and she could observe their advance upon the crystal barrier. When he touched her cheek, she gripped his thumb with fingernails bright as pearls.

And so it was with callow hand around calloused knuckle that they walked up to the stars.

The End

Acknowledgments

I began writing *The Fall of Babel* shortly after the birth of our first child, a blessed event that came with equal measures of disaster and delight (neither of which could be deferred), and I finished the draft in quarantine some twenty-eight months later. Penning a fantasy novel during this moment of upheaval and frozen frenzy often felt a bit absurd, if not at times impossible.

I doubt I would've finished this undertaking had it not been for the support and assistance of a handful of people, all of whom deserve recognition and praise in far greater measure than I can offer here.

I'm very thankful to the consummate professionals who helped bring this rickety cart to market. My publisher, Orbit, was quite gracious with my repeated requests for deadline extensions. My editors—Bradley Englert and Emily Byron—once again played an integral part in the cutting of the rough gem that I delivered to them in a brown paper sack. My agent, Ian Drury, and all of the estimable members of Sheil Land Associates supplied great counsel and support. My copyeditor, Kelley Frodel, saved me from being outed as both a harrier of the language and a bungler of hyphens. During such a turbulent passage of life, I could not have wished for more sympathetic and accomplished company.

Even as the universe of the Tower expanded to fill this final volume, the spheres of my personal life contracted. Had it not been for Ian Leino, who never failed to call with insights, camaraderie, and levity, I'm sure I would've grown a wizard's beard and absconded to a seaside cave. I cannot imagine those phone calls were pleasant occasions for him as he always found me in a state of either laconic depression or manic frustration. And yet, he persisted, leaving me with little choice but to follow his lead.

My parents, Josiah and Barbara Bancroft, who share this book's dedication with my daughter, were an inexhaustible source of cheer and ready assistance amid the Dawn of Maddie. They are responsible for provoking my love of literature, my fascination with language and antiquity, and my belief that there is a higher calling in life than the enlargement of one's own ego and capital. Robert and Carol Bricker, my in-laws, eagerly supplied good humor, serenity, childcare, and homecooked meals at a time when all were in short supply. I count myself doubly blessed to be a part of two loving families whose great character and wisdom has fortified my own.

Additionally, I'm deeply grateful to Jesse, my sister, for her honesty, conviviality, and perceptiveness. Remarkable and accomplished, she is a font of goodness in a wayward world, and I hope she knows it. The Batstones—Jeffrey, Liam, Charlie, and Gabriella—are a rare clan brimming with talent and high spirits, and I've delighted in watching them explore themselves and their world, carving new paths through old pastures.

It's impossible to overstate the role that my wife, Sharon, played in this long and laborious conjuring. If I'd not met her, if she had not adopted me into her heart, I'm certain I would've spent my life lurking in corners, fidgeting with coasters, and complaining about things I could've changed had I only a modicum of confidence and persistence. The bricks of the Tower were fired in the kiln of her patience and assembled by the light of her love.

A Catalog of Ringdoms

from the Library of

Joram Brahe, Capt. of *The Natchez King*

Lower Ringdoms

Middle Ringdoms

No.	Ringdom	Common Names, Personal Notes, & Exports
1	The Basement	Free beer, mud, luggage
2	The Parlor	Maniacs and frauds. Exports: Eyeballs
3	The Baths	Loafers & easy marks. Exports: Hods
4	New Babel	"The Bedroom." Bats and hydrogen gas
5	Pelphia	"The Closet." Insufferable fashionists
6	The Silk Gardens	"The Silk Reef." Shipwrecks and spiders
7	Algez	Not to be trifled with. Exports: Cannonballs
8	Morick	Minor shipyard. Exports: barges, gundalows
9	Euphydia	Home. Exports: Musical instruments, dreamers
10	Oyodin	Nudist gambling house. Exports: Horcum
11	Jinst	Unfriendly. Exports: Certainly not charity
12	Harrakesh	Cheap anchorage. Exports: Rud Tobacco
13	Valadi	Growers of gray berries. Exports: Inedibles
14	The Cistern	Flies a plague flag. Exports: Plague, presumably
15	Nineveh	Well-off. Rumored hod enclave: "Mola Ambit"
16	Luden	Prudish tanners. Exports: Slippers, daughters
17	Boskopeia	Aggressively unremarkable. Exports: Yawns
18	Paphos	Glassmakers. Exports: Bottles, mirrors
19	Simbersae	Bourgeois idlers and retirees.

Middle Ringdoms

Upper Ringdoms

20	Tuwin	Salvagers, lens grinders, and pickpockets
21	Barua	(Toy & doll makers) Exports: Basic automatons
22	Keskin	(Chemists) Exports: Poisons and cures
23	Rasanadra	(Houses of ill repute) Exports: Syphilis
24	Ogun	(Smiths) Exports: Swords, hinges, and hooks
25	Elodonia	(Philosophers and pranksters)
26	Japhet	(Royals, guards, & gold) Exports: Hanged men
27	Barakat	(University of great renown and little use)
28	Asteria	(Solicitors and Notaries) Exports: Legal fees
29	The Bole	"Mid-Bole" (Central market) Exports: All
30	Cuvella	(Engineers & Machinists) Exports: Stolen tech
31	Lathyras	(Coopers) Exports: Barrels, butts, etc.
32	Banner-Wick	(Libraries and archives) Exports: Pulp, Fees
33	The Atrium	(Wealthy tourist trap) Exports: Mysticism
34	Dugaray	(Head-butters, professional players of Swattle)
35	Vinegard	(Order of delusional 'knights.' Avoid at all cost)
36	Pin's Folly	(Unfinished ruin overrun w/ thieves, festivities)
37	Brim	(Physicians, surgeons, butchers, and last resorts)
38	Zweibel	(A taxidermy nature preserve of nightmares)
39	Merris Tet	(A maze of stinks posing as a perfumery)
40	Tarsus	(Investment houses and banks) Exports: Debt
41	Fell Quiesce	(Mortuary & morgue) Exports: Used clothes
42	Whitlaurel	(Cheesemakers) Exports: Soft cheese, hard gas
43	Moink Wallow	(Cowsow breeders) Exports: Moink, questions

Upper Ringdoms

44	Issero	(A curious excess of cats) Exports: Dyes, yarn
45	Andura Sur	(Artist colony) Exports: Unlovely art, art critics
46	Andura Nur	(Stoics and bobbies) Exports: Fines
47	Mundy Crete	(Candy makers & dentists) Exports: Gums
48	Dove Cove	(Pigeon racing) Exports: Pigeon pies
49	Thane	(Makers of Firearms, Artillery) Exports: Blood
50	Norwid	"The Shipyard" Exports: Overpriced sloops
51	Martello	(Silk production) Exports: Envelopes, bolts
52	Gorse'reath	(Aeronaut and military academy; best avoided)
53	Ulcrest	(Falcon fanatics) Exports: Smugness and giblets
54	Fal	(Hub of Ur tourism for elites wishing to escape)
55	Chaffsward	(Fez-wearing farmers) Exports: Pinchwheat
55A	The Monitorium	"Misanthropolis" (Repository of the unwed)
56	Kanene	(Avian conservatory) Exports: Eggs
57	Sol Ternion	(Astronomers) Exports: Charts, instruments
58	Yalwort	(Paper-winged pirate angels; give a wide berth)
59	Foundling's Bight	(Creche and bastardage for the rich)
60	Cairopolis	(City of Kings) Imports: Toadies
61	Glave's Beacon	(Unfinished tomb turned hippodrome)
62	Arcana Grus	(Unvisited. Off-putting amount of artillery)
63	Cilicia	(A posh bohemia) Exports: Inkberry wine
64	The Sphinx's Lair	(Uncharted and unsafe)
	Collar of Heaven	Exports: Thunder bolts and orphans

extras

meet the author

Photo Credit: Kim Bricker

JOSIAH BANCROFT started writing novels when he was twelve, and by the time he finished his first, he was an addict. Eventually, the writing of *Senlin Ascends* began, a fantasy adventure not so unlike the stories that got him addicted to words in the first place. He wanted to do for others what his favorite writers had done for him: namely, to pick them up and to carry them to a wonderful and perilous world that is spinning very fast. If he's done that with this book, then he's happy.

Josiah lives in Philadelphia with his wife, Sharon, their daughter, Maddie, and their two rabbits, Mabel and Chaplin.

Find out more about Josiah Bancroft and other Orbit authors by registering for the free monthly newsletter at orbitbooks.net.

if you enjoyed
THE FALL OF BABEL
look out for
THE JASMINE THRONE
Book One of The Burning Kingdoms
by
TASHA SURI

Tasha Suri's* The Jasmine Throne *begins the powerful Burning Kingdoms trilogy, in which two women—a long-imprisoned princess and a maidservant in possession of forbidden magic—come together to rewrite the fate of an empire.

Exiled by her despotic brother when he claimed their father's kingdom, Malini spends her days trapped in the

Hirana: an ancient cliffside temple that was once the source of the magical deathless waters, but is now little more than a decaying ruin.

A servant in the regent's household, Priya makes the treacherous climb to the top of the Hirana every night to clean Malini's chambers. She is happy to play the role of a drudge so long as it keeps anyone from discovering her ties to the temple and the dark secret of her past.

One is a vengeful princess seeking to steal a throne. The other is a powerful priestess seeking to save her family. Their destinies will become irrevocably tangled.

And together, they will set an empire ablaze.

PROLOGUE

In the court of the imperial mahal, the pyre was being built.

The fragrance of the gardens drifted in through the high windows—sweet roses, and even sweeter imperial needle-flower, pale and fragile, growing in such thick profusion that it poured in through the lattice, its white petals unfurled against the sandstone walls. The priests flung petals on the pyre, murmuring prayers as the servants carried in wood and arranged it carefully, applying camphor and ghee, scattering drops of perfumed oil.

On his throne, Emperor Chandra murmured along with his priests. In his hands, he held a string of prayer stones, each an acorn seeded with the name of a mother of flame: Divyanshi, Ahamara, Nanvishi, Suhana, Meenakshi. As he recited, his courtiers—the kings of Parijatdvipa's city-states, their princely sons, their bravest warriors—recited along with him. Only the king of Alor and his brood of nameless sons were notably, pointedly, silent.

Emperor Chandra's sister was brought into the court.

Her ladies-in-waiting stood on either side of her. To her left, a nameless princess of Alor, commonly referred to only as Alori; to her right, a high-blooded lady, Narina, daughter of a notable mathematician from Srugna and a highborn Parijati mother. The ladies-in-waiting wore red, bloody and bridal. In their hair, they wore crowns of kindling, bound with thread to mimic stars. As they entered the room, the watching men bowed, pressing their faces to the floor, their palms flat on the marble. The women had been dressed with reverence, marked with blessed water, prayed over for a day and a night until dawn had touched the sky. They were as holy as women could be.

Chandra did not bow his head. He watched his sister.

She wore no crown. Her hair was loose—tangled, trailing across her shoulders. He had sent maids to prepare her, but she had denied them all, gnashing her teeth and weeping. He had sent her a sari of crimson, embroidered in the finest Dwarali gold, scented with needle-flower and perfume. She had refused it, choosing instead to wear palest mourning white. He had ordered the cooks to lace her food with opium, but she had refused to eat. She had not been blessed. She stood in the court, her head unadorned and her hair wild, like a living curse.

His sister was a fool and a petulant child. They would not be here, he reminded himself, if she had not proven herself thoroughly unwomanly. If she had not tried to ruin it all.

The head priest kissed the nameless princess upon the

forehead. He did the same to Lady Narina. When he reached for Chandra's sister, she flinched, turning her cheek.

The priest stepped back. His gaze—and his voice—were tranquil.

"You may rise," he said. "Rise, and become mothers of flame."

His sister took her ladies' hands. She clasped them tight. They stood, the three of them, for a long moment, simply holding one another. Then his sister released them.

The ladies walked to the pyre and rose to its zenith. They kneeled.

His sister remained where she was. She stood with her head raised. A breeze blew needle-flower into her hair—white upon deepest black.

"Princess Malini," said the head priest. "You may rise."

She shook her head wordlessly.

Rise, Chandra thought. *I have been more merciful than you deserve, and we both know it.*

Rise, sister.

"It is your choice," the priest said. "We will not compel you. Will you forsake immortality, or will you rise?"

The offer was a straightforward one. But she did not move. She shook her head once more. She was weeping, silently, her face otherwise devoid of feeling.

The priest nodded.

"Then we begin," he said.

Chandra stood. The prayer stones clinked as he released them.

Of course it had come to this.

He stepped down from his throne. He crossed the court, before a sea of bowing men. He took his sister by the shoulders, ever so gentle.

"Do not be afraid," he told her. "You are proving your purity. You are saving your name. Your honor. Now. *Rise.*"

One of the priests had lit a torch. The scent of burning and camphor filled the court. The priests began to sing, a low song that filled the air, swelled within it. They would not wait for his sister.

But there was still time. The pyre had not yet been lit.

As his sister shook her head once more, he grasped her by the skull, raising her face up.

He did not hold her tight. He did not harm her. He was not a monster.

"Remember," he said, voice low, nearly drowned out by the sonorous song, "that you have brought this upon yourself. Remember that you have betrayed your family and denied your name. If you do not rise . . . sister, remember that you have chosen to ruin yourself, and I have done all in my power to help you. Remember that."

The priest touched his torch to the pyre. The wood, slowly, began to burn.

Firelight reflected in her eyes. She looked at him with a face like a mirror: blank of feeling, reflecting nothing back at him but their shared dark eyes and serious brows. Their shared blood and shared bone.

"My brother," she said. "I will not forget."

1

PRIYA

Someone important must have been killed in the night.

Priya was sure of it the minute she heard the thud of hooves on the road behind her. She stepped to the roadside as a group of guards clad in Parijati white and gold raced past her on their horses, their sabers clinking against their embossed belts. She drew her pallu over her face—partly because they would expect such a gesture of respect from a common woman, and partly to avoid the risk that one of them would recognize her—and watched them through the gap between her fingers and the cloth.

When they were out of sight, she didn't run. But she did start walking very, very fast. The sky was already transforming from milky gray to the pearly blue of dawn, and she still had a long way to go.

The Old Bazaar was on the outskirts of the city. It was far enough from the regent's mahal that Priya had a vague hope it wouldn't have been shut yet. And today, she was lucky. As she arrived, breathless, sweat dampening the back of her blouse, she could see that the streets were still seething with people: parents tugging along small children; traders carrying large sacks of flour or rice on their heads; gaunt beggars skirting the edges of the market with their alms bowls in hand; and women like Priya, plain ordinary women in even plainer saris, stubbornly shoving their way through the crowd in search of stalls with fresh vegetables and reasonable prices.

If anything, there seemed to be even *more* people at the bazaar than usual—and there was a distinct sour note of panic in the air. News of the patrols had clearly passed from household to household with its usual speed.

People were afraid.

Three months ago, an important Parijati merchant had been murdered in his bed, his throat slit, his body dumped in front of the temple of the mothers of flame just before the dawn prayers. For an entire two weeks after that, the regent's men had patrolled the streets on foot and on horseback, beating or arresting Ahiranyi suspected of rebellious activity and destroying any market stalls that had tried to remain open in defiance of the regent's strict orders.

The Parijatdvipan merchants had refused to supply Hiranaprastha with rice and grain in the weeks that followed. Ahiranyi had starved.

Now it looked as though it was happening again. It was natural for people to remember and fear; remember, and scramble to buy what supplies they could before the markets were forcibly closed once more.

Priya wondered who had been murdered this time, listening for any names as she dove into the mass of people, toward the green banner on staves in the distance that marked the apothecary's stall. She passed tables groaning under stacks of vegetables and sweet fruit, bolts of silky cloth and gracefully carved idols of the yaksa for family shrines, vats of golden oil and ghee. Even in the faint early-morning light, the market was vibrant with color and noise.

The press of people grew more painful.

She was nearly to the stall, caught in a sea of heaving,

sweating bodies, when a man behind her cursed and pushed her out of the way. He shoved her hard with his full body weight, his palm heavy on her arm, unbalancing her entirely. Three people around her were knocked back. In the sudden release of pressure, she tumbled down onto the ground, feet skidding in the wet soil.

The bazaar was open to the air, and the dirt had been churned into a froth by feet and carts and the night's monsoon rainfall. She felt the wetness seep in through her sari, from hem to thigh, soaking through draped cotton to the petticoat underneath. The man who had shoved her stumbled into her; if she hadn't snatched her calf swiftly back, the pressure of his boot on her leg would have been agonizing. He glanced down at her—blank, dismissive, a faint sneer to his mouth—and looked away again.

Her mind went quiet.

In the silence, a single voice whispered, *You could make him regret that.*

There were gaps in Priya's childhood memories, spaces big enough to stick a fist through. But whenever pain was inflicted on her—the humiliation of a blow, a man's careless shove, a fellow servant's cruel laughter—she felt the knowledge of how to cause equal suffering unfurl in her mind. Ghostly whispers, in her brother's patient voice.

This is how you pinch a nerve hard enough to break a handhold. This is how you snap a bone. This is how you gouge an eye. Watch carefully, Priya. Just like this.

This is how you stab someone through the heart.

She carried a knife at her waist. It was a very good knife, practical, with a plain sheath and hilt, and she kept its edge finely honed for kitchen work. With nothing but her little knife and a careful slide of her finger and thumb, she could leave the insides of anything—vegetables, unskinned meat, fruits newly harvested from the regent's orchard—swiftly bared, the outer rind a smooth, coiled husk in her palm.

She looked back up at the man and carefully let the thought of her knife drift away. She unclenched her trembling fingers.

You're lucky, she thought, *that I am not what I was raised to be.*

The crowd behind her and in front of her was growing thicker. Priya couldn't even see the green banner of the apothecary's stall any longer. She rocked back on the balls of her feet, then rose swiftly. Without looking at the man again, she angled herself and slipped between two strangers in front of her, putting her small stature to good use and shoving her way to the front of the throng. A judicious application of her elbows and knees and some wriggling finally brought her near enough to the stall to see the apothecary's face, puckered with sweat and irritation.

The stall was a mess, vials turned on their sides, clay pots upended. The apothecary was packing away his wares as fast as he could. Behind her, around her, she could hear the rumbling noise of the crowd grow more tense.

"Please," she said loudly. "Uncle, *please*. If you've got any beads of sacred wood to spare, I'll buy them from you."

A stranger to her left snorted audibly. "You think he's got any left? Brother, if you do, I'll pay double whatever she offers."

"My grandmother's sick," a girl shouted, three people deep behind them. "So if you could help me out, uncle—"

Priya felt the wood of the stall begin to peel beneath the hard pressure of her nails.

"Please," she said, her voice pitched low to cut across the din.

But the apothecary's attention was raised toward the back of the crowd. Priya didn't have to turn her own head to know he'd caught sight of the white-and-gold uniforms of the regent's men, finally here to close the bazaar.

"I'm closed up," he shouted out. "There's nothing more for any of you. Get lost!" He slammed his hand down, then shoved the last of his wares away with a shake of his head.

The crowd began to disperse slowly. A few people stayed, still pleading for the apothecary's aid, but Priya didn't join them. She knew she would get nothing here.

She turned and threaded her way back out of the crowd, stopping only to buy a small bag of kachoris from a tired-eyed vendor. Her sodden petticoat stuck heavily to her legs. She plucked the cloth, pulling it from her thighs, and strode in the opposite direction of the soldiers.

orbit